W9-CKJ-199

Do with me
what you will

for Patricia Hill Burnett

PART ONE
Twenty-six Days

PART TWO
Miscellaneous Evidence

PART THREE
Crime

THE SUMMING-UP

PART ONE
Twenty-eight Years, Two Months, Twenty-six Days 1

PART TWO
Miscellaneous Facts, Events, Fantasies, Evidence Admissible and Inadmissible 165

PART THREE
Crime 309

THE SUMMING UP 469

PART ONE

Twenty-eight Years, Two Months, Twenty-six Days

I

Premeditated crime: the longer the meditation, the dreaming, the more triumphant the execution!

He was looking again at the school, memorizing the building. But he had already memorized it. Yes, he had already learned everything about it, and now he was sitting in his car, parked, and looking at it. He was very calm. It was ten o'clock in the morning.

Emmet Stone Elementary School. It was set back in a cramped yard, not far from the boulevard and its thunderous trucks, a building of three stories—heavy and protective and exciting as a prison, made of dark-streaked brick, with basement windows of opaque mud-splashed glass and iron bars that belled slightly outward, also splashed with mud. He had never seen the inside of the school, but dreamily he imagined its bleak, echoing corridors, shoulder high in a kind of dark wood, and shoulder to ceiling in another color, maybe faded green. He could loose himself to wander weightlessly along the corridors, glancing into the classrooms, into the cloakrooms and the lavatories, seeing the bleak, correct rows of washbowls, the footprints of dried mud that were the size of children's feet, no larger.

The front yard was wide but not very deep, so that the noise of the trucks must be distracting in those front classrooms; he could imagine the rumbling, the vibrations. He could imagine someone at one of the windows, glancing out to see him, his car, parked here—but he had a new, handsome, gleaming car and would not attract any attention. There were hundreds of such cars in this city.

A wide concrete walk led from the street to the front doors of the school, dividing the yard exactly in two. Trees had grown in the yard at one time, but now only three stumps remained. Children had scrawled words on them, not decipherable from where he sat; he had memorized the appearance of those words, but had never read them. They were shapes, signs, like hieroglyphics, with a secret meaning. To the left of the building was a narrow side street and on its right was an asphalt playground that ran the length of the school building, back to a rear street that was also narrow. A six-foot fence protected the playground from the street, an ordinary chain-link fence that had begun to rust and come loose in places. In fact, in eleven places. Scraps of newspaper and children's lunchbags and wax paper and other harmless debris had been caught in the fence, soaked with rain and then baked dry, shredded. The asphalt of the playground was cracked everywhere and weeds grew up through the cracks, highest along the fence. Some of the weeds had begun to flower in small yellow buds, more each day, a handful more each day. . . . He thought the flowers very beautiful, though they were only weeds. And yet it was the prim, drab fence and the building that excited him.

Emmet Stone Elementary School. The universe condensed to a few acres of city real estate. With high, dirty windows, at which a stray face sometimes appeared, a face floating inside, mysterious, unknowable, above the ridge of blackened brick that formed the window ledges. Fugitive faces, half imagined, children or adults?—it dizzied him to wait for them, and then not to really see them, to not quite see them. They were ghostly, but the building itself was inert, totally visible, a small fortress. The cornerstone was marked with the faint numbers 1923.

It was May 4, 1950.

He checked his watch: still ten o'clock. He adjusted his glasses, which fitted his face poorly, and sat behind the wheel of his new car, fighting back a smile of excitement. That was the one thing you should never do if you are alone—you should never smile. His eye roamed freely over the barren front yard and its small hills and holes and tree stumps, and rested for a moment at the basement window that had been broken and mended with what looked like a square of cardboard, and then to the arched doorway, to the words *Emmet Stone Elementary School* chiseled above the doorway, then over to the playground and the fence. He reached around to the back seat and picked up a hat and put it on his head; he had to adjust it with care on his thick, high, curly hair.

He got out and closed the door gently behind him, so gently that it did not even catch. No matter. He checked his watch again and saw with pleasure that two minutes had passed, very quickly. Over at the fence he paused, as if by accident, to light a cigarette. He fumbled for a while in the pockets of his coat, absentmindedly, letting his eye move swiftly around the playground. He checked off all the familiar sights: the asphalt's swollen little hills and slopes, its cracks, the two sets of swings, very still, motionless, so that it was difficult to imagine children swinging in them, the teeter-totter, the slide near the rear doors of the school, not a very high slide. It was polished smooth at its hump, but tarnished elsewhere. Near the back of the playground was a mass of metal tubing, pipes, for children to climb on; he had forgotten the name of it.

He thought: *Without the mind of man, without rational calculation and preparation, what pleasure would exist in the universe?—what art?*

Though it was May, he wore a dark overcoat that was too long for him, and too warm; his hat was made of stiff gray felt, with a brim that was quite wide and stylish; his face seemed framed by it. Patches of hair stuck out beneath the hat, thick shiny brown curls with a synthetic gloss. The skin of his face was pale as if with abstraction, intense thought; the metal frames of his glasses, made of thin, pale gold, were a little higher on the right side of his face than on the left. He was in his early forties, a slight man of about five feet seven or eight, now lighting another cigarette in a methodical, self-conscious way.

He thought: *Twenty-five more minutes.*

Now the playground was deserted and bleak, but at ten-thirty morning recess began and the children would stampede out through those side doors. And at noon, also, on good days, some children would come out to eat their lunch; otherwise they ate inside, with the children who did not bring their lunches, and then they all stampeded out into the playground at about twelve-twenty, even in bad weather. From the sidewalk, you could hear the buzzers sounding; everything was regimented and predictable.

He strolled along the sidewalk, along the fence. No hurry. There were small puddles from last night's rain beneath the swings and in the shallow places beneath the teeter-totter. So empty, so scarcely imagined, the playground reminded him at such times of a newspaper photograph, all grays, its texture nothing but a surface, its shapes really nothing more than microscopic dots. If an event took place here, the playground might be photographed for the newspapers and transformed into a real picture of itself; otherwise, no one would ever notice it except him.

Running his fingers lightly along the fence . . . sometimes allowing a finger to hook into one of the loops, tugging at it as if playfully. . . . No hurry. The fence was loose in some sections; parts had been allowed to rust through and could be broken easily. At the bottom it looked as if animals or maybe even small children had already been scrambling back and forth, squeezing themselves through. But he could not be certain. He did not want to stoop to investigate.

Was anyone watching? Behind him, no, nothing, just the boulevard and its usual traffic, trucks bound for the inner part of the city. He would attract no attention. He smiled that pleasant, tight little smile; it was a smile the width of a hair.

At the edge of the school property he began to walk faster. He headed around the block. Now he was in an ordinary neighborhood of small frame houses, a few old apartment buildings. The street behind the school, Floyd Street, was narrow; cars were parked on both sides, so that it would be difficult to maneuver along here. And what if you met an oncoming car? No, it was obviously necessary to park out front. He approached the playground and the fence again, from the rear, and now the maze of metal pipes and the slide were near him, and he could see the scratches on their surface, the dull spots, the highly polished spots. All familiar, like a secret language. From the back the mud puddles looked larger. Wetter. A small pile of papers had gathered beneath the slide; weeds pushed up through the cracked asphalt. He caressed the fence, reaching up as if to measure it, then letting his hand drag down along the links until it was level with his thigh, then his knee. The fence wobbled on this side. If he wanted, he could lift it; but at its bottom it was jagged and if a child crawled through the child might be injured.

Behind him, an apartment building, blank blind windows, five floors. Was anyone watching? There were too many windows, too much to think about. Calculation became useless at such times; the hell with it. He walked away, around the block and back to his car on the boulevard. He got in again to wait, lighting another cigarette, gazing at the windows of the school again, half-imagining wisps of faces there, a certain face, a single, definite face, *one face* out of all the universe. Greedily, he could almost see it. It was a miracle, yet terrible: that face. It did exist. Because it existed, the universe was not at peace, would never be at peace; but it was beautiful, miraculous. . . . It was a face to be dreamed over, cherished. It was a child's face and had that bright alert blindness of children, who see everything and yet who don't understand what they see, don't really see it. You would have to snap your fingers, shout, shake something to make a commotion before those eyes would come into focus. . . . Yes, adults were cursed with the necessity of seeing everything, of calculating, making plans endlessly; especially they were cursed with the necessity of seeing other adult faces. Try to make your vision go out of focus, try to escape! It wasn't possible.

The playground doors were being opened. Ten-thirty! He checked his watch and saw in amazement that it was past ten-thirty!—and now some older children appeared—boys of about eleven, with armbands, who patrolled the playground—and now a line of children, marching out. There they came. Yes, they marched out, and as soon as they were in the playground they broke out of line and ran in all directions.

He thought he saw her—a flash of blond hair. He adjusted his glasses.

In the doorway stood a woman, a teacher; she wore a dark blue dress, with a sweater over her shoulders. She was smoking a cigarette. It would happen that the patrol boys would gather at one end of the playground, and the smaller children would play by themselves. This was the pattern he had observed. And the teacher who supervised the playground would disappear after five or ten minutes.

He waited. The bigger boys were drawn to something happening by the swings. They were standing with their hands in their pockets, laughing at someone. At the doorway the woman turned to go. It was all regimented, predictable. He waited, and then he carefully got out of the car, smoothing down his coat as if presenting himself for inspection. He walked over to the fence without hesitating and his eye moved swiftly through the groups of children, the running and yelping, through all the mazes of faces and legs, to the child with the blond hair—yes, there she was, unmistakable, standing near another child who was squatting and arranging something on the ground, pieces of things he could not make out. They were not far away.

The child was small, about seven years old; she wore a light or faded blue dress and a white sweater, which he had noticed a few times before. Her hair was striking: very light, almost white, it seemed to glow about her head, like a cap of small, frizzy curls. Out of the confused crowd of children that child's hair glowed, drawing the eye to it, relentlessly. There was nowhere else to look.

He hooked his fingers into the fence. His hands were small and boyish and bony. He tugged at the fence and in that instant a current of strength, an almost painful current, ran through his arms and shoulders from some powerful center in his chest, deeper than his chest. His muscles tightened. How easy this was now, how easy! And what triumph in it! He began lifting the fence without moving, his feet planted solidly, not budging in spite of the terrific strain. From the back, his body gave no indication of the strength coursing through it; even his face would have shown nothing except a pale tightening around his mouth and eyes.

He was very strong. A slight man, but very strong. It was not often that his strength was required, but when it was, he was always surprised, pleased. He seemed to give way to it, to his muscles' slow shrewd power. He believed he could lift this fence up entirely from the ground, he could tear the posts out of the asphalt and throw everything aside. He needed only to stand here, his feet apart, balanced, his weight perfectly balanced, his mind concentrated on the task before him—giving calm, slow directions to his arms and hands—he could do anything, he could dislodge the entire pavement of the playground, the entire universe. The sun came out and seemed to spurt about him, transforming part of the playground—and a child-sized patch of intense sunlight moved across the side of the school building dreamily.

Yes, this is why we live.

The girl was looking toward him.

"Come here," he called.

She looked at him. He moved one hand in a cautious, restrained greeting. He was trembling, but at this distance she could not notice. He said again, louder: "Come here. You, little girl, you there—you—come over here for a minute."

Her hair was so beautiful a color that it would have been impossible for him to look anywhere else. It was heartbreaking, that color and that face. He stared greedily at her and had to twitch his face in order to adjust his glasses, which were sliding down his nose; he was perspiring. "Come here, please. You. Elena. I know your name—Elena. Come here for a minute."

Were other children watching? Was anyone watching? He could not see.

She approached the fence slowly. It was maddening, how slowly she walked. Another child ran past her, shrieking. But she did not notice. She was staring at him.

"Your leg—when did you hurt your leg?" he cried.

He saw a small Band-Aid on her left knee.

She did not answer. She had stopped a few feet away, smiling shyly at him. His eyes were suddenly warm, stinging; he wanted to tear the fence out of the earth and throw it aside. But he said softly, "Elena, I know your name, don't I? Isn't that a surprise?"

Her face was a small, perfect oval. Her eyes were very blue. He believed he had never seen so beautiful a child and had not imagined her this beautiful.

He could feel his insides trembling.

"Elena, do you know how I know your name? Do you? No? Because your mother sent me to bring you home from school. Your mother. She wants me to bring you home, dear." The little girl stared, half smiling. Her gaze was vague and diffused. He didn't think he could look into it much longer. —And not too far away something happened, boys shouting and piling in a heap —he glanced at them and back again, swiftly, to the girl. "Elena?" he said softly. "Is that your name? Little Elena? Is it?"

She nodded.

"Well, your mother sent me to get you. We'd better hurry or she'll get mad. Can you crawl under the fence, dear, if I lift it?"

She was at the fence now. He stared down at her, his eyes hot with tears. A kind of heart was beating in his face—between his eyes—a powerful, terrible heartbeat he had never felt before. It thudded in his face.

"Elena. Elena. Come to me, dear, crawl under the fence, dear, can you do it? Can you, sweetheart? Don't be afraid." He pulled upward at the fence, almost staggering under the strain, but then his feet settled more firmly and the muscles in his shoulders and arms swelled, rocklike, joyous. A pain shot through the lower part of his abdomen but he ignored it. Like this, like this! There were so many surprises in life! His jaws tightened, his eyes narrowed almost to slits, but he was able to say gently: "Now. Crawl under, Elena. Hurry. Now."

She hesitated.

"I said, crawl under. Now. Now, dear. Right now. Now. It won't catch in your dress—I won't let it fall back—" He gasped and almost staggered again, but caught himself. He muttered: "Obey me, Elena. Obey me. Yes, like that, yes, don't be afraid—crawl under—crawl under—"

And the child crawled under the fence.

2

"Don't cry," he said. "That's the only danger."

They were parked on a gravel drive behind a warehouse. It was the right place to be, but he could not exactly remember having driven here. His head was still pounding. A sign caught his eye: NO PARKING THIS SIDE.

He shifted the gear into neutral and did not turn off the ignition. Smiling at the girl, he snatched off his hat and tossed it into the back seat, on top of the suitcases. "Surprise, Elena, a birthday surprise—a few months late, I know—but anyway—" He ran his hand through the bushy brown wig and snatched that off too, smiling. The child stared at him. He paused to examine himself in the rear-view mirror: his own hair was blond, graying, thinning, but still neat. Without the wig and the hat, his forehead seemed to push forward, outward, a bony serious forehead.

"What do you say, Elena? Are you surprised? Is it a nice surprise?"

The child stared. "Daddy . . . ?"

He leaned down to hug her. "Of course, *Daddy*—your own daddy—who else? You're a little sweetheart, aren't you? Not to cry, not to make any fuss. You're my little birthday girl, aren't you? Excuse me, honey," he said, as he opened the glove compartment. He took his own pair of glasses out, a pair with pinkish-transparent plastic frames, and extricated the others from his face. The wire earpieces had made his ears sore. "Now you recognize me, don't you? No mistake about it?"

The child must have been too astonished to smile or to show any sign of recognition.

"Elena, dear . . . ? You'll hurt your daddy's feelings if . . ."

He grabbed her and pressed his face against the side of her head, breathing in that filmy hair. For a few minutes he seemed to go blank, the pounding in his head seemed to be accelerating. Then he leaned away, panting.

"Did she tell you I was dead, Elena?"

The eyes in that small face looked enlarged, distorted. He

peered at her: eyes of a water-color blue, like eyes on the cover of a magazine placed in prominent view on a newsstand, not quite real. And yet real. The eyelids were fringed with very pale blond lashes, which were short but very thick, like small paint-brushes. These lashes began to move, the eyelids began to blink rapidly, the black dots in the center of the eyes seemed to move into sharper focus, focusing upon him.

"She told you I was dead . . . ? Yes, she almost believed it, she believed she had the power to annihilate me, I know, I know," he murmured. He kissed his daughter's forehead. "But you remember me, Elena, don't you? Even though I'm supposed to be dead?"

After a moment of hesitating she said faintly, "Yes. . . ."

He kissed her again happily. Tears came into his eyes but he didn't want to cry in front of her; that might get her started. "No fuss," he said harshly, merrily.

Now he could relax a little. He climbed out of the car and unbuttoned the overcoat in one, two, three, four grand gestures, forcing the cheap black buttons through the buttonholes as the child watched; and he threw the coat off, expelling his breath with exaggerated relief. He allowed the heavy weight of the coat to fall from him. "Much too hot for this lovely day," he said. For emphasis he kicked the coat a few feet from the car, but a pain like a snapped rubber band shot across his abdomen.

He stiffened, drawing his breath in slowly. No pain. He was in control. Somewhere a nerve was still pounding in his head, but he was able to thrust it out of himself by an effort of will, as if with an opened hand, thrusting everything from him that was a distraction. When he opened his eyes he saw Elena staring out at him. She was still blinking, though more slowly now. Her lips were parted and damp.

"Mommy said . . . Mommy. . . ."

He cupped his ear but she did not continue. So he laughed and clapped his hands and said, "The hell with Mommy! In fact, I declare Mommy dead; yes, right now, right this minute, let me check the absolute time. . . . Yes, Elena, on ten forty-seven A.M., May 4, 1950, your mother died and your father came to take you away. Remember that. Do you promise to remember that?"

She gaped.

He looked around and saw no one, nothing. Only the old abandoned warehouse, an abandoned house with a sign from the Department of Health forbidding entry; a field of weeds; an unused stretch of railroad track. The sun had transformed the sky into something quivering with blue and filmy streams of cloud . . . but he thought: *I can't be distracted by beauty. Not right now.*

He was wearing a fine new cloth suit of checks, very small black and white checks. It was not an outfit he would have chosen for himself ordinarily; it was a little too stylish. But now he was pleased he had bought it. He was still warm from the overcoat, almost panting with discomfort, so he loosened his tie and unbuttoned the collar button of his starched white shirt, which was also new, taken right out of the package that morning. Very starched, stiffer than he would have wanted. The nerve in his head still pounded, a strange sensation between his eyes, as if a third eye were struggling to emerge. His daughter remained motionless in the car, watchful, obedient. He tried to smile at her but his smile did not quite connect with her. She was gazing at him blankly, her small face empty, peculiar, her lips very wet. He wondered if he should wipe her mouth. But she was seven years old, not a baby.

He got back into the car and closed the door. Elena flinched. "Yes, sweetheart, your mommy died and was taken away, and your daddy came to get you at school. That's easy to remember. And you recognized me at once, didn't you? I won't forget that," he cried. "Never! And the way you obeyed me!—I'll always love my good little girl, my sweet beautiful daughter— Your mommy told you a lie, didn't she, when she said I was dead? Didn't she?"

Elena seemed about to speak, to say yes. He urged her, nodding, nodding eagerly; but she did not exactly speak. She nodded a little. Her head seemed to rock forward, nodding a little, as if in imitation of his nodding. "That's right!" he cried, patting her head. "And the two of us are bound together forever now, by magic, dear, and not even your mother can destroy it. Not the lawyers, not the judge, not any court orders or injunctions—what has the law to do with love?—you and I transcend such declarations, don't we? That's my blood in your veins, you know. My blood."

Solemnly he put his hand beside hers and traced with his forefinger the bulging blue veins, and then the tiny, almost invisible veins in the back of her hand. So small, so delicate! He seized her hand and kissed it. "Wouldn't she be surprised to see us!" he gloated. "After all her maneuvering. . . ."

Elena withdrew her hand from his, slowly. "Are we going home?" she asked.

"Home, yes. Yes. I'm glad you asked that question because we should be on our way," he said, coming to himself. "The two of us should be starting out, we have a trip ahead of us, thousands of miles. . . ."

"Does Mommy know I'm coming home? From school like that . . . ?—coming home early?"

"Your mommy is dead. And she doesn't know a goddam thing."

Seeing the bewilderment in her face, he leaned over to embrace her. Gently, gently. He must be careful. But for some reason she drew back. It was gentle, her drawing back, but it maddened him that she should ease herself so carefully away . . . she had never done that in the past, never. She had been a loving, obedient daughter; she had loved him very much. It had been her mother she'd drawn away from, frightened by Ardis's shrill voice and the roughness of her embrace. So he hugged her closer, pressing his jaw against the top of her head. He felt with surprise and affection her skull, her thin child's skull. He remembered the softness of that skull when she had been an infant. . . .

She gasped as if about to cry.

"No, don't cry, that's your father's only command," he said.

She did not fight him. It was amazing how small she was—her shoulders so frail, her chest so slight. It did not seem possible to him that this child would grow into a woman, an adult woman like her mother. . . . He almost recoiled from the thought, it was so shocking, ugly. It was a really ugly thought. The heartbeat in the center of his face accelerated.

He drew away from her and said in a new, lighter voice, "Well, I missed your birthday, didn't I? Your poor daddy! But look, honey, here are your presents—here—I bought them on January sixteenth and I've had them ready for you all along. You know, your mother got them to forbid me to visit you—she threatened to have me arrested—and on your birthday I was a hundred miles away, sick, taken sick with influenza, but I got out of bed and went out to a lovely toy store, just to keep from going mad—and

I bought you some things, Elena, chatting away with the saleswoman as if I really had a daughter who would open these presents—and that did me good, honey, I think it saved me. Here. Look." He had taken a box out of a paper bag, and inside the box was a gift-wrapped box, wrapped in very bright yellow paper that said "Happy Birthday" all over it. Elena did not seem to know what to do with it, so he undid the bow himself and unwrapped it. "See? See? Do you like it, sweetheart?" he said eagerly. He took out a doll made of flesh-colored rubber, with a hula skirt and inflamed cheeks and eyes bulging with excitement and happiness. "Your little dolly isn't crying, is she? She looks happy. Good girls don't cry when they're with their fathers, do they?—on their birthdays? You mustn't cry, dear," he said gently.

His daughter took the doll from him and seemed to be staring at it. He pulled a clean white handkerchief from his pocket and wiped her nose and mouth; she didn't resist, but did not seem to notice.

"And I have other presents for you if you're good. Nicer presents than your mother thought up, I'm sure! What does your mother know about little girls? She was never a child herself, not that woman!"

Elena looked at him. She said carefully, "Is Mommy at home?"

"Is Mommy at home!" he laughed. "Didn't I explain to you what happened? No more mommy! You might as well erase that word from your vocabulary. Anyway, you and I are going on a long trip, to another home in California. You've heard about California, haven't you?"

"But Mommy—"

"No. No mommy. No. Gone. Vanished," he said with a patient smile. "I don't want to hear the word, Elena. That's enough. And no crying, please. You don't want to attract attention to us."

She handed the doll back to him woodenly. She seemed very distracted. This was the kind of odd, vague behavior that had angered Ardis, but he would never shake Elena the way his wife had. He would never hurt his daughter, even to discipline her. That had been one of the causes of his wife's fury. So he said gently, "You shouldn't hand it back to me, dear, it's a present. That's rude. What do you say when someone gives you a present, Elena?"

She wiped her nose on the back of her hand.

"Thank you," she said.

"Thank you, Daddy."

"Thank you, Daddy."

"That's right. Say it again, now . . . don't make me angry. . . ."

"Thank you, Daddy."

"Yes, good. And where are we going now, dear? You and me?"

She was staring down at the doll. A tear fell onto the doll's cute, tense, rounded little stomach.

"Where are we going, you and your daddy? Where did I just say we were going?"

"Home. . . ."

"Home where?"

"California," she said blankly.

"Yes, do you know where that is?"

"California. . . ." She repeated the word, the sound of it. She might have memorized just the sound of it.

"Do you know where the Pacific Ocean is?"

She shook her head slowly.

"Look at me, Elena. Why are you frightened? You know your own daddy, don't you?"

She looked up at him, squinting. He was struck again by the frail, perfect oval of her face—was this his child, his own child? He could see nothing of himself in her, not really. His blood ran through her, he had given her life, but he could not really make a claim on her; who would believe it? She resembled her mother slightly, around the eyes, the short, pert upper lip, and her hair was the same color as Ardis's. . . . "You know your own daddy, don't you?" he said urgently. He held her face in both hands and with his thumbs he stretched the skin of her cheeks, as if to force her eyes open, to force her gaze onto his. She panicked and tried to scramble backward.

"Don't fight me! Don't make me angry!"

She was breathing in short, frightened gasps. He felt her heartbeat inside her small body, or was it his own heartbeat, a new heartbeat in his thumbs? A kind of mist passed over his brain. He loved her so much, loved her helplessly. . . . "Your daddy looks skinny and weak because he's been sick, and all his life he's been thin and weak-looking," he said quickly, "but your daddy is very strong, Elena, men are very strong, much stronger than women, and your daddy is going to protect you. Your mother told lies about me, dear, in fact she told lies under oath, in a court of law—her and her lying character witnesses, and that bastard of a lawyer—and my own lawyer, it turned out, *my own lawyer* was on her side, collaborating with her lawyer to defraud me of my daughter. I didn't catch on until it was too late. When you're older you will understand, Elena, that I didn't die and I didn't go away and leave you, that your mother told you lies and poisoned you against me—don't cry, honey—now we have a lifetime ahead of us, and I'm going to try to make things right. Your mother is dead, gone. Your father is here. You know you must be very good, very quiet, don't you? So that no one notices us? You understand why we have to be cautious, don't you?"

She was quieter now. He kissed her, pleased. Ah, how he loved her! She was his own Elena again, his own doll.

As he drove toward the highway north of the city he was careful to observe all traffic lights and signs. He did this automatically; he had always been courteous on the road. But he was a little nervous and it irritated him that Elena seemed to be staring out the window, away from him. "Elena, dear, what are you looking at? You should look at *me*. You haven't seen your father for so many months, you should look at *me*. I wish I had thought to bring a scarf along, to cover up that hair of yours . . . it's bound to attract attention. . . ." She turned obediently to him and he squeezed her hand. It was such a small, cool hand! so soft it did not seem like a human hand at all. "It's quite natural that a father and his little girl should be driving along like this, within the speed limit, with a few suitcases in the back seat . . . why not? It's true that school is in session at the moment, but special arrangements are sometimes made. For a funeral, certainly, special arrangements would be made. When your mother wanted to take you out of school she certainly did it. But then, she was always violating order, breaking rules, with her evil energies. . . . How is your mother these days, dear?"

Elena nodded vaguely. He repeated his question.

"She's working. . . ."

"Ah, working! Is she? Is that what she calls it? Don't forget I know every corner of her mind, every pothole—so she's working, is she? What color is her hair now?"

The child thought a moment. Then she touched her own hair. "Like yours again? She bleached it back to that color? Well, that's the prettiest color . . . I always preferred her hair natural. . . . What kind of work does she do, Elena?"

"I don't know."

"Do people call her on the telephone?"

"Yes."

"A lot?"

"I don't know. . . ."

"Do men call her?"

"I don't know. . . ."

"When does she work, daytime or nighttime?"

"Night."

He laughed angrily. "So her hair is blond again, eh?"

Something happened: a car was braking to a stop just before him, its red taillights on. He had been so excited about this news of his wife that he hadn't noticed how close he was. . . . "Jesus!" he cried. He pressed down on his brakes at once and his car skidded, he heard a sickening squeal from somewhere beneath him . . . he reached out to keep Elena from pitching forward. . . . "Hold on, honey!" he cried.

His car left the road and skidded out onto the shoulder of the highway, skidded to a stop. Quiet. Silence. He was safe.

Someone had made a sudden turn off the road, into a driveway; but nothing had happened, no accident, he was safe. He checked Elena and saw that she had not hurt herself. "My God, what a close call," he whistled. He felt a little sick from the near-accident but he made his voice sound cheerful; he knew he must never show any weakness in front of his daughter.

"Just don't cry," he cautioned her, wagging a finger.

Once out on the highway his shakiness receded and he began to drive faster. He hadn't really been close to hitting that car, not really. He had been in control. He had always driven well. And now it was good, marvelous, to be out of the city and on his way at last. He intended to drive several hundred miles before night; he would put an immense distance between himself and *her*. "At the playground the police will be asking questions and your little playmates will tell them about a man in a black coat, a man with a hat, with brown curly hair. . . . That is, if they even noticed me," he said cheerfully. "But when they call your mother she'll say at once, she'll scream, *her father!* I wish I could hear that, I wish I could see her face at that moment. And then she'll say, *Leo Ross. Leo Ross.* And she'll describe me perfectly, and she'll have a photograph ready for them, the same one she used in the past . . . she always pretended to be afraid of me, afraid I would kill her."

Elena did not seem to be listening. He wondered if she had fallen asleep.

During the months of the divorce proceedings he had hinted he might . . . he had almost hinted he might . . . might *do something* to his wife if she kept on. But he had made no threats, no open threats. He was too clever for that. No words. Only once had he drawn his finger across his own throat—only once—at a meeting with the lawyers, when both lawyers had been reading something, peering at a document on his lawyer's desk. Ardis had been staring at him and he couldn't resist drawing his forefinger across his throat, swiftly. She had stared. And then she had begun to smile, smirking. Mocking. She must have thought it was a joke, that Leo Ross thought he could kill *her*.

"Go right ahead," she said out loud. "The police will be waiting for that. It wouldn't surprise anyone."

The lawyers had looked up, startled. Leo was very embarrassed.

"Is something wrong, Mrs. Ross?" Ardis's lawyer had asked sternly.

"Not a thing," Ardis had replied.

Not a thing. And at this moment they might be examining the fence he had lifted and one policeman would be saying to another, *Whoever he was, he must have been very strong. . . .* Leo's foot pressed down on the accelerator, gradually increasing pressure. Now he was driving about five miles over the speed limit, which was not like him, but he knew he could handle the situation. The highway was dry and there wasn't much traffic. He kept imagining his wife, seeing her in that office, the way she'd smiled so cleverly at him, he kept hearing her voice, *Not a thing;* he saw her suddenly wakened out of sleep by a telephone ringing, stumbling to the phone, naked, sour, picking up the receiver to be told the news about her daughter. . . . *Whoever he was, he must have been very strong,* they would tell her.

Leo laughed. A quick, sharp flash of pain ran from his abdomen down into his groin. But he said cheerfully, "Elena, tell me: does your mother get up to make breakfast for you? Or does she still sleep past noon?"

His daughter did not reply. She might have been sleeping.

"Elena, wake up," he said, touching her. "Tell me, honey, does your mother make breakfast for you? Does she bother to help you dress in the morning? Or—?"

Elena looked at him, moving her head slowly. Slowly she said, "I don't know."

"What? Don't know? Does she make breakfast for you or not?"

"No."

"What do you eat then, honey? I mean, what did you eat?"

"I don't know . . . some cereal . . . I can make it myself, some Sugarstix and . . ."

"Just cold cereal, then? Nothing hot?"

Elena did not reply.

"Are you happy to be going on a trip with your father? To a new home?" Leo asked delightedly. He glanced at his daughter and saw that she was half-smiling in his direction, though her blue, watery gaze seemed transfixed on something invisible. His old amazement stirred, the amazement of his *being a father*, being so hopelessly bound to this child, hopeless in his love. . . . And he had loved her mother too, he had loved her hopelessly, miserably. "You love your father, don't you, Elena?" he asked.

She must have been awakened by something in his voice. She said, "Yes," at once.

"And not your mother? No more? Never again, not your mother, no love for her—?"

"No," Elena said vaguely.

With that word and the joy it released in him he rushed them westward, west into Ohio. The highway was excellent, an excellent invention. His car, which he had bought the week before, was powerful and would not disappoint him. He knew automobiles well, he admired them, had faith in them. Automobiles and highways and maps, the means of motion, no deceit in them, no possibility of error: they were the inventions of men. And guns also were the inventions of men, for the use of men. Leo was afraid of guns but he had bought one to use only if necessary; it was in an ordinary paper bag on the floor of the car, near his feet, where he could reach it easily. But he did not want to use it. Only if necessary, he cautioned himself.

Back in Pittsburgh, years ago, Ardis had emptied a purse of hers on a table. Things fell out for inspection: a pink plastic billfold, a golden compact, a golden tube of lipstick, a comb, keys, coins, and a small black pistol, a revolver.

Leo had exclaimed: "What is *that*?"

"For protection," Ardis had said.

"How long have you had that?—carried that around with you?"

She laughed at his nervousness and picked up the gun, which fitted her slender hand perfectly. She weighed it in her hand, making two slight downward motions, dropping her hand only an inch or so; Leo had always remembered that gesture.

"Since I was fifteen," she said.

"Have you ever used it?"

"Are you the police, that you're questioning me?" she had laughed.

For every question anyone had ever asked her, Ardis had an answer: that was Ardis.

Just over the Indiana border he stopped for gas. Elena was asleep. He got out of the car to stretch his legs, instructed the station attendant to fill up the tank, and joked a little with him. In the midst of his joking the pain flashed through his groin again. He must have flinched; the man said, "Something wrong . . . ?" but Leo shook his head emphatically, no, no. Blood rushed into his face. He walked away restlessly, and noticed across the highway a small store—*Cappy's Beer & Liquor*. He called back to the attendant, "I'm going across the road for a minute—watch the little girl, will you?—she's my daughter."

He ducked across the highway, impatient with the traffic. The driver of an enormous trailer truck, piled high with crates of live hogs, yelled out his window at Leo. Leo ignored him. He bought a quart of gin and, on the front porch of the little store, he opened the bottle and took a sip. That did him good. The pain in the pit of his belly was reduced to a dull throbbing ache, which he believed he could control.

When he returned to his car, the attendant said: "Hey, mister, your little girl is crying or something. . . ."

"She isn't crying," Leo said at once.

He leaned in to check and saw that she had drawn her knees up to her chest and was pressing her face against the tops of her knees. She looked very small. "Elena, dear—?" he called. When she turned to look at him he saw with relief that she wasn't crying, though her eyes were pinkened and there seemed to be a bruise on her forehead, an odd orangish-purple mark. He couldn't understand where that had come from.

"She wasn't crying," Leo told the attendant. He paid the man and said cheerfully, leaning back into the car, "Elena, honey, you weren't crying, were you? Just a little tired from driving. Elena, honey, would you like to use the bathroom while we're here? Because. . . ." She seemed not to understand. "The ladies' room, honey, as long as we're stopped. You'd better, honey."

"I'm afraid," she said.

"What? You'd better use it now, dear, we might not stop for a while. And I'll bet you're hungry too—I should get us both something to eat."

The gas station attendant was now wiping the windshield of Leo's car, moving his dirty rag in swift, tight circles, and this rapid motion seemed to distract Elena. She narrowed her eyes, squinted. Leo had the idea that she hadn't understood him. "Crawl over this way, Elena, because your door doesn't work . . . see, honey, the handle has been removed . . . so it can't open accidentally. Yes, honey, this way, you'd better use the ladies' room while you can. I insist, dear." She slid across the seat and he helped her out, slipping his hands beneath her arms gently; for a moment he believed she was a much younger child, hardly more than a baby. But she did not resist. He walked her over to the door that said LADIES. The attendant smiled at them and said, "You got a cute little girl, mister. She's real cute."

"She's beautiful," Leo said. "She's worth dying for."

It was my father, saying something to me. Smiling down at me from a doorway, leaning forward, smiling. Love rimmed the sockets of his eyes but there was no color in them, because the daylight was behind him and I was in a room, a little dark room, a room somewhere, I don't remember.

Come out, honey, you aren't crying are you, honey?

He had pushed the door back with his foot. I saw a white collar, something stiff and white, very white. The room was dark and smelled bad. I wasn't crying. He put out his hand to me and said, Come out, honey, we have a long way to drive before dark. . . . His hand approached my face, floating, floating like a fish. It was narrow and pale and the fingers reached out to touch me, the right side of my face. That side went stiff. He stroked my face and like magic my face went stiff.

. . . wash your hands? . . . ready to come out?

I couldn't hear him exactly. But I wanted to hear him. I wanted to hear what they were saying, the other people too, and my mother too, but they shouted so loud I couldn't hear.

He was calling to wake up the bad side of my face, he was angry, no, he wasn't angry because he was smiling. He said, That's a good girl, now we're all set. California-bound.

He walked me back to the car. I had to get in on his side because the other door didn't work. The handles were gone. Over the broken-off parts were patches of tape, so that I wouldn't scratch myself. He said, Bought you something, and gave me a candy bar. It was a Mars bar. He said, Now we're all set. He had a Baby Ruth bar for himself and something to drink.

I wasn't hiding in the bathroom.

He came to get me and walked me back to the car but I had to get in on his side, because the other door was locked. It didn't open. I wasn't crying. He smiled at me because I wasn't crying and gave me a candy bar, but I wasn't hungry. The gas-station attendant waved good-by to us. The West is going to be like this, my father said, friendly people, good-hearted people, no tricks to them. We're starting a new phase of existence. Are you happy, Elena?

I was smiling like a mirror, with his smile. I was happy.

I said yes.

"Yes, you're worth dying for," Leo said.

3

Dear Ex-Mrs. Ross:

Postmarked Iowa but maybe I'm not in Iowa? Maybe I'm a lot farther ahead of you? In fact maybe back across the street from you, watching you, holed up with plenty of provisions and patience . . . maybe in that apartment building across the street from yours, with the shades pulled almost down to the window sill, a telescopic sight on my rifle so that I can watch you and follow you from room to room, you were always careless about the windows, walking around half dressed and someday you're going to pay for it. . . .

Call your bastard of a lawyer now. Get right on the telephone. Call the judge, he obviously liked you, and believed your stories. Call the police, the F.B.I., call the Iowa state police for all I give a damn, you won't catch up with me. You're never going to see her again.

Did I say "her"? Who's that?

Sincerely yours,
Leo Ross

Dear Ex-Mrs. Ross:

I bet you are wondering what I will do. I bet you are thinking about me all the time. Did you send the police to check across the street? Did you? And did they find anyone? Maybe one of your admirers, some innocent stranger peeking out the window and across the street into your window, where you walk around half naked and don't give a damn who sees you?

Did you show them my first letter and did you explain to them who "her" is? Do you really think you are a maternal woman who deserves a daughter?

I bet you are wondering if I am dangerous. You never thought I was dangerous, but I believe I am in a dangerous phase of my existence, like a phase of malaria, a fever I caught from you and almost died from. You can be very proud of yourself.

I want to make up to our daughter for the blight of you, what you did to our marriage, how you made the love between us rot so that it stank and any child could smell it. I want to make up to her for the ugliness of the world, through my love. This letter might be postmarked Kansas but I will be nowhere near Kansas by the time you read it, so don't bother calling the police.

I wish I could see your face right now.

Sincerely yours,
Leo Ross

Dear Ex-Mrs. Ross:

You & I never got this far west, did we? I had dreams of camping out, the mountains, trout-fishing, I wanted to go to Yellowstone back in '47 but you changed your mind, and now the hell with you, little Elena and I are here by ourselves and never think about you.

We won't be here by the time you read this.

If you could see this part of the world, how beautiful it is! It is like the edge of the world here, the clean mountains and rocks and the sky, the air, not like Pittsburgh. If sick people like you could come here you might be cured. But can you be cured or do you want to be cured? What was going to be love in you got changed to sour pus and I think you prefer it that way.

It's May but today it is snowing and I bundled E. up very well because the cabin is not well-heated & she has a cold. She never complains. She never talks about you. Every morning I ask her, "Do you miss your mother?" and she says, "No," and I ask her, "Who do you love?" and she says, "I love my father." So you see she is already beyond you & it's pointless for you to get her back into custody.

We don't mix with the other campers much. Both in good health, except for E.'s little cold. Went exploring yesterday & came across some bears, a mother and two cute cubs. Some people were feeding them and a man took pictures, real families having a good time on their vacation. E. & I joined right in. I petted one of the cubs, big as a full-grown dog, and tame. The mother bear sat back on her hind legs and watched us, tame as a dog. The man with the camera was very excited so I put Elena on the big bear's shoulders and held her and he took pictures, said E. could be a child movie star, she is so pretty. But I don't mingle much with the other campers. You taught me a lesson about people: get close to them & they will destroy you.

Sincerely yours,
Leo Ross

Dear Ex-Mrs. Ross:

The police you send after me are very easy to spot! It's a joke, the stupid bastards, they'd better wise up. Came prowling around the camp but I eluded them. Came into a tavern out here & I hid in the men's room, I'm always a step ahead of you. E. isn't always with me so I can't be identified. Maybe she looks different? Maybe all your pictures of her are out of date?

Why did you marry me, Ardis?

You think I am in Wyoming & no threat to you, because of this postmark. But maybe not. Maybe I have doubled back on my trail and am across the street from you again, sighting you through a scope right now, preparing to pull the trigger. I am friends with Joe Collier who manages the camp here, I am his friend "Robert Maxwell," & maybe he does me the favor of mailing my letters from here, to put you off the trail. Maybe I am watching you read this letter.

E. kept in a safe place. There are lots of cabins for rent out here, early in the season. Nobody sees E. Nobody knows about her.

Sincerely yours,
Leo Ross

Leo stayed at the "Flying Y" camp, just south of Yellowstone National Park, for only three days. Too nervous to stay in the cabin, jumpy, hearing things outside the windows . . . he went out for walks alone, in the cold rain. Elena had a cold and he was worried about pneumonia. He dressed her in two of his sweaters, but her legs were bare except for her short white socks. It was very cold for May. He wished he had kept that overcoat, instead of throwing it away; he argued with himself and got mad, walking out in the woods with a bottle of gin to keep him warm, then gradually he forgot about the problem.

On the last day he heard a noise outside the cabin and opened the door, and there was a wolf—or maybe a fox or a coyote. It was dragging a long snake. The animal only glanced at Leo and his daughter and then whipped the snake up into the air, cracking it. Then it began to eat the snake. "Hey! Get the hell out of here!" Leo yelled.

Elena backed away from the door.

"Damn dirty pig!" Leo yelled.

The doglike animal ignored them and ate the rest of the snake. Then it walked away. Leo was outraged. "I didn't know they were such cannibals," he said. He closed the door and looked at Elena, who was terrified. He hoped this wouldn't poison her against Yellowstone Park. He said, "This trip of ours is an educational adventure. You can learn things."

Elena didn't seem to understand.

"This famous park isn't just for fun," he said sternly. "It's also to learn about nature."

Some of the black dye he had used on her hair was on her face and neck; it was very hard to scrub off, even with strong soap. But he could always try Twenty Mule-Team soap, when he got to a store that sold it. "Anyway, we're pushing west in the morning," he told her. "We've got to keep a lot of distance between us and our past."

Elena was never hungry and he began to forget about feeding her.

Northern Nevada. Leo followed their progress on an Esso map. He brought it into a tavern with him and spread it out on the bar to ask advice about roads, which were dangerous and which were safe but not too well-traveled; he had wrapped Elena up in a blanket and left her out in the car. It was late afternoon and the tavern was dark. It smelled pleasantly of beer and mud from everyone's boots. A hillbilly love song was on the juke box and Leo wished that Elena could hear it, it was like a lullaby.

"That song is about love but nobody is listening. Nobody takes it seriously," Leo said to the bartender suddenly. "Look, I didn't either. I mean, how can you?—before you know about it? Look, thanks for your advice," he said, trying to fold the map again, "but do you believe in the existence of evil? I'm just asking."

"What?"

"Do you believe in evil?"

A man beside Leo asked, "Is this a religious controversy? I'm a stranger here."

"I'm a stranger too," Leo said eagerly.

The men in the tavern wore canvas jackets lined with thick bulky fake wool, like sheep's wool, and cowboy hats of dingy felt, and boots of various sizes. Leo was the only man without boots. His feet were wet. He leaned forward and said seriously, "I haven't had a decent conversation in weeks. Look: if a man is driven to extreme acts, he isn't necessarily guilty. The laws don't cover everything. Can they cover things that haven't happened yet?—if a man has seen a certain vision in the world, a vision of evil, and has to cleanse himself? I'm not claiming anything. I'm not religious myself."

"I'm not religious either," the bartender said. He was a lean, spare man, exactly Leo's size. But he seemed to be avoiding Leo's eye.

"The Law is very complicated," Leo said, "but it can't foresee the future. Men's minds can't be legislated. I have respect for the Law, because I am essentially a law-abiding citizen," he said, folding the map carefully, "but look: I became involved in a certain litigation a while ago and I did a lot of reading; I mean, you have to become an expert fast, or you go down in defeat. Not that I am an expert. I'm not claiming anything," he said quickly.

The man beside him nodded. He had a tanned, permanently reddened face, a friendly face. Leo turned to him. "I don't know much either," the man said.

"No, I don't either, I don't make claims," Leo said. "But look: what is the relationship between the Law and evil?"

The man shook his head slowly. Leo was encouraged by his somber, creased face. It was common out West for millionaire ranchers to dress like this, in old dirty clothes, and maybe this man was one of those ranchers; Leo had read about such things. He was eager to assume intelligence in his fellow man. He said, "The Law exists only in our heads. We all agree on that point. Lawyers are the first to agree on that point. It's an *agreement*, the Law." The bartender had walked away and was in a back room somewhere, but the man with the red face was listening closely and another man, a younger man who held his beer bottle up to his mouth and kept clicking it against his teeth, had begun to listen. Leo said, "The Law only comes into existence when somebody hates somebody else. Did you know that? And wants to destroy him."

The two men frowned and nodded. The man with the red face said, "I'm not any friend of any lawyers myself."

"I'm not either," Leo said at once. "But look: police and prisons come a lot later, after the Law gets set up. They're only instruments of the Law. The Law rises out of hate. Excuse me, but do you think he's calling the police back there?"

Both men stared at Leo.

"What?"

"Excuse me, *him*, I don't know his name—the bartender—you might know his name," Leo laughed nervously. "You might know if he'd call the police or anything."

"Why should he call the police?" the man with the beer bottle asked.

Leo laughed. He finished his drink and set his glass down on the bar slowly. "You know, I'm not a rebel and never was. I don't believe in it. I accept my responsibilities and that's why I always paid my taxes and I paid all the costs, the court costs, the lawyers' fees and all that. . . . I don't mean to sound like a crank," he said hastily, "but I did have a certain vision of evil. Lying down with evil, in the body of a woman . . . if you do that you get tainted. You have to act afterward. Have to cleanse yourself. Now, don't misunderstand me, I'm not an agitator for change. I have a sound background. I had a Ford dealership in Pittsburgh and just the used-car lot alone made me a good living. I'm happy with America as she is. Of course, all my money went, it all went . . . *she* got it. . . . And her lawyer, because I had to pay him. And my own lawyer. Fees and court costs and fines and alimony and child-support and settlement money and expenses, even her taxi-cab fares, she had everything itemized and ready. She was planning the whole strategy months ahead of time. My ex-wife is like that: you can't predict her, and even if you could, you can't guess how fast she can move."

"You had some trouble with your wife, huh?" the man beside Leo asked.

"Ex-wife," Leo said curtly. "It wasn't just the thousands of dollars and my life wrecked. . . . I had to look at her smile when she left court, the lipstick was bright scarlet and her hair was bouncing all over her head, all curls like what's-her-name—one of those Hollywood actresses—I can't think of her name at the moment— What the hell is her name, so that you can get the picture," Leo mumbled. He rubbed his fist against his eyes. Was his mind going? "Jesus, her name is right on the tip of my tongue! Well, her and my ex-wife could be twins right now, but when I married her, Ardis was like another one of them, the one with long red hair, Rita Hayworth, yes, she was made up to look like Rita Hayworth. . . ."

The record had stopped and Leo found that he was speaking too loudly, in an odd, sharpened silence.

"I don't get into the movies much," a man said slowly.

"Reno," the man with the bottle said. "In Reno there's a lot of movie houses. In fact Rita Hayworth is in a movie there right now."

He spoke in a boyish, enthusiastic drawl, stretching his vowels.

The bartender returned. Leo ordered another drink, to show that he wasn't suspicious. "Hey, what are the police called out here?—mounties or rangers or something?" He grinned. But the bartender only looked at him. Leo let his fist fall playfully onto the bar and said in his normal voice, "I bet women are different out here, out in this healthy part of the world. I bet they don't dye their hair all colors. If any of you are married, I bet your wife isn't planning any strategy against you, huh? Look: it was so bad I swear I could go to bed at night with a blonde and wake up with a redhead in the morning, it was almost that bad, I swear. How's that?"

All the men laughed at this. Leo said delightedly, "She came back with a poodle cut once—all little curls, almost like a nigger's hair, but ash-blond. Jesus! Even her face could get rearranged. Sometimes she had double eyelashes on, sometimes a big red mouth, sometimes a pink or an orange mouth, sometimes her eyebrows were just pencil lines drawn on her face. . . . The skin could be rosy or white or tan, but like glass, without any pores. She had three fur coats, presents from yours truly, and a 1950 black Lincoln with all the extras, even an FM radio and fake leopard-skin seat covers, just for herself, and when I met her she was working in a nightclub—and sometimes she did modeling —you know what 'modeling' is?—I mean for men, for photographers? Ha-ha," he laughed harshly, "yours truly fell for it all. Look: the world strikes me as a thing with holes in it—a what-d'ya-call-it, a thing you strain spaghetti in—a thing in the kitchen for the water to run through—"

"A sieve," the man beside him said.

"Right. A sieve. The world is a sieve, a lot of little holes that things fall through, flow through like water, like blood . . . like blood bleeding out of your arteries while you stand there and watch," Leo said. He was breathing now with difficulty. Something had begun to ache inside him but he was too excited to locate it. The men at the bar were looking at him with sympathy, he thought; he didn't want to appear weak in front of them. "But my little girl . . . my little girl came out of it all, I mean the mess, the hatred . . . children can survive anything. . . . She never complains, she never cries. I never intended for her to grow up in any city like Pittsburgh. A child needs open spaces and sunshine and good, kind, healthy people, not sick people. Isn't that the truth?"

The men around Leo said nothing. At the far end of the bar someone Leo hadn't noticed before, a puffy-faced man in a windbreaker, called out: "You left your wife, huh?—did you? Walked out the door, did you?"

"Not exactly," Leo said slowly. His face flushed. This was a serious moment and he felt that everyone was listening closely to him. His instinct was to tell the truth, always to tell the truth; he didn't have to be put under oath to tell the truth. It was natural in him. "She informed me one day to get out. So I did. And she had the locks on the doors changed. Did you know that is within the Law? Her lawyer got a court order against me and I had to move out of town, I mean outside the city limits to satisfy them. . . . The world is just filled with holes that surprise you every morning," he said. The sorrow in his voice sank downward, down into his stomach and bowels. He felt suddenly tired, stricken. Almost sick. He tried to speak enthusiastically. "Let me order a round of drinks here . . . !"

The men did not respond. One of them shook his head slowly, as if embarrassed. The man in the windbreaker called out, "Hey, you're from somewhere back East, aren't you? Whereabouts back East?" but Leo did not quite understand him. A sharp pain came and went in his body somewhere.

"I was advised to try for bankruptcy," Leo said. "But it was just more papers, more lawyers. . . . In the same courtroom with me there was a man, a man, he went crazy and they put one of those things on him—a straitjacket with leather straps—but I wasn't that man— No, that wasn't me," he said quickly. He finished his drink. He had no taste for it but he believed he should finish it; as he was putting the glass down something came up to meet him, the solid wood of the bar seemed to spread and go soft.

Someone spoke in surprise. Leo felt the bottom of his jaw

strike something, and then he felt someone's hands on him. He pushed feebly away. "No thank you, I can manage on my own," he said.

"Give him a hand—"

"No thank you," Leo said.

A sudden thumping, a sharp pounding near me. The car door was opened and rain got in. He pulled at the blanket and said, Honey, are you asleep, he was crying, sobbing. Another man's voice was behind him. But I couldn't hear the other voice. I tried to wake up. My head came loose on my shoulders, my scalp went hot with itching, prickles like burrs, as soon as I woke up. The wind blew everything awake in me, the red-hot bites on my head and the dryness in my mouth. He was saying, Get the hell away—I'm not sick—I couldn't hear the other voice.

She isn't sick and I'm not sick, he cried.

Get the hell away from us or I'll kill you, he cried.

4

"Like this, honey. Hold it like this."

He held her hand in his and her fingers seemed to close around the crayon. But when he released her the crayon fell.

"Such a nice coloring book and crayons, and you don't take any interest," he said with a patient smile. He was sitting across from her at the table, having a drink while he watched her color. But she kept dropping the crayon. He had brought the coloring book and a large, trilevel box of expensive crayons all the way from Pittsburgh, one of Elena's birthday presents; but she did not seem to know what to do with them. "Pick it up, dear. Keep on coloring. You know I love to see you playing. . . ."

Elena reached for the crayon but now it rolled off the table onto the floor. She squinted and moved slowly. The dye had left a gray shadow on her forehead and neck. Her hair was a very deep, slick black, but the sight of it no longer alarmed him so much.

"Be a good girl," he begged.

He poured an inch or two more gin into the glass. Now that they were safe in San Francisco, he'd sold the car and was ready to settle down permanently in this sunny rented room; he was very satisfied with life and yet subject to periods of sorrow. He didn't know why. Yes, he was satisfied, in fact he was very happy —he had Elena to himself now, with his own Safety-Guard lock on the door—and yet he sometimes felt melancholy, almost depressed. "Elena, you should try to be a better girl," he said.

Sometimes he felt so nervous, so boxed in by the small room and noises from other tenants and the constant presence of his daughter, the constant thought of her, that he had to get out. So he stuck the pistol in his pocket and walked down to the waterfront. His clothes were like anyone else's, yet people often glanced curiously at him. He stared back, showing that he wasn't intimidated; sometimes he even shot them small half-mocking half-inquisitive smiles. But more and more he found himself gravitating down to the wharf, where old men peddled seafood. They were so humble, so shifty-eyed, they were no threat to him; they never looked at him or at anyone. In spite of the stench, Leo sometimes bought steamed clams or crabs and tried to eat them, believing that this would prove he had a strong stomach and a good, healthy, normal appetite.

Then he climbed the long hill to the rooming house and he felt how exposed he was, on the street like this, and what if he should be sick suddenly?—and call attention to himself? Going down to the waterfront was all right, but returning to the rooming house frightened him. His entire body seemed to heat; he felt an odd jumpy radiance about it and wondered if anyone could notice. . . . He began to hate the bright baked sunlight of San Francisco, the blocks of uniform unattractive buildings, building after building, attached to one another with no alleys between, no place to run in case he was being followed. The streets were treeless and the constant sunlight made his eyes ache.

On his way home he would stop to buy Elena something—another doll, a comic book, pink cotton candy on sticks, which he would carry triumphantly up to the room but end up eating himself, feigning pleasure in order to entice Elena to eat. She never ate more than a few mouthfuls of anything and if he forced her to eat she sometimes vomited it up again. In desperation he had tried everything: hamburgers, French fries, even steamed crabs, Chinese food, candy bars, oranges of the brightest, most enticing orange colors, but the only thing she liked was milk, which he brought back to the room in pint-sized waxed containers. He began putting a teaspoon or more of gin into the milk so that she would sleep easily and not be awakened by nightmares.

He never let her out of the room.

The woman who had rented him the room, on a weekly basis, did not know that Elena was with him; therefore it was very important that Elena be quiet. "When I'm out don't walk around if you can help it," he cautioned. "And if you're having a bad dream try to wake up before it scares you. . . . This is very serious, honey. You know it is." But one day he noticed a louse on her neck and realized that he must wash her, must wash that head of snarled, matted black hair—and that did cause trouble, because soap ran into her eyes and she began to scream with pain. "Be quiet, Elena! My God, be quiet!" He panicked at the thought of the landlady calling the police. "Try to be quiet, Elena! You're going to make me lose my temper—"

Her cries dropped to sobs. He dabbed at her eyes with a washcloth, murmuring to her, comforting her. "I won't do it again, honey. I won't wash your hair again. It's all right, honey. It's all right."

So he gave up washing her hair. He gave up washing her; she didn't really get dirty. After he used up the last bar of soap he forgot to buy more. He didn't get very dirty himself and he needed the money for milk and liquor, because his savings were running out.

He gazed at his daughter and thought—

He thought—

One morning he finished a pint of gin sooner than he had expected, so he decided to go out. It had rained and now the sun was shining and everything was sharp, sleek, brilliant. He shivered. It was well into summer and still he felt cold. Going into a tavern near Fisherman's Wharf, he stumbled but didn't fall. He liked the dark inside the tavern. On the street he felt too exposed. He couldn't be sure if he was being followed or not, because the police sent after him would probably be plainclothesmen. He ordered a glass of draught beer and drank it down thirstily. Beside him was an elderly man who smelled of sweat and another odor, maybe fish. The man had a massive, bleary face that was turned toward Leo.

Leo shivered. He knew he was approaching an important event. But he didn't yet know what it was.

Elena had been sleeping when he left. Lying in the cot at the foot of his bed, in those rumpled soiled sheets, with her matted hair black on the pillow, her head looking heavy, too heavy to move. . . . He shivered again and patted his coat pocket, where he carried the gun. He was never without it now. He tried to think of Elena and what he had to do, but he couldn't concentrate. He ordered another beer.

The man beside him hissed a few words.

". . . What?" Leo asked politely, nervously.

"Mind your own business," the man said.

Leo stared at him. The man was not very old, but his face was a mass of veins, a ruin. He was grinning maliciously at Leo.

"I am minding my own business," Leo said.

The man muttered something about the police, about police informers. He stared accusingly at Leo. Leo finished his beer and walked out, steeling himself against the sunshine. But now it was raining; he wondered if he had been in the tavern very long. His watch no longer worked. He stood in the doorway and rubbed his face, up and down, looking from one side to the other and trying to think . . . trying to think. . . .

What would hurt his wife the most? What would come close to destroying her?

After a few minutes he walked out into the rain and headed slowly back to the rooming house. He carried his right arm close to his body, so that with his elbow he could keep checking the gun. The beer had cleared his head somewhat but still he felt dizzy, strange. He couldn't concentrate. He knew he was going to do something but he hadn't yet imagined it, envisioned it. So much planning had gone into his rescue of Elena and the trip out West that now, now, now . . . there didn't seem to be enough of his imagination left. . . . Now he was older, more weary. He knew he was still strong and that his muscles could still perform, if he needed them, but he felt strangely tired. And his soiled, wrinkled clothing depressed him. The dirt beneath his fingernails depressed him.

Then, at the corner of his street, he saw a sight that froze him. A police car was parked at the curb. Its red light was flashing but there was no siren, no noise. No police were around. Leo halted, frozen, while other people passed by him and seemed to melt into the rain, going invisible. He stared at the car and down the street to the high, narrow, ugly house in which he lived.

He could force his way in—up the stairs and into the room —he could barricade himself and Elena in there—he had six bullets—

He could fight them to the finish—

But not today. Not this morning. He was approaching his forty-fifth birthday. His body sank with sorrow, with weariness. He thought: *If I— If—*

He fled.

In a dime store he bought some notebook paper and a single business envelope and, now that the sun was out again, he went to a park nearby. *To Whom It May Concern,* he wrote. Then he ripped the page out and started again. *To The Police Dept., San Francisco (& Pittsburgh).* He dated it June 27, 1950. Then he tried to think, tried to think. . . . He found that he was sitting on a park bench, gazing out at a pond. Ducks and swans were swimming there. On an island were many more ducks, large white ducks. Waddling and quacking. Very noisy. Two ducks lunged at each other, a third nipped at them, a single white feather drifted free. . . . His head swam.

Another drink: he would get another drink.

But no, first he had to write a letter. He had to collect his thoughts and write a letter.

The noise of the birds in our public parks is enough to drive a person insane, he wrote angrily.

No. He skipped a few lines and began again. The ballpoint pen he was using was almost out of ink. *Ross Auto Sales,* it said. He had always liked the rather fine, delicate point of the pen; it made his handwriting look elegant.

Suicide is a violation of the Law. The Law is very wise, though men don't understand at first. The Law is like a wall. Throw yourself against it but it stands, it stands. A year ago I contemplated self-destruction but did not give in, and gradually I recovered from my sickness and I now consider myself a free and healthy man. But I find I must put order into my life.

My name is Leo Ross and you are searching for me. I have been here in San Francisco for some time, living in secret at . . .

He paused. What was the name of his street? He couldn't remember. No, he couldn't remember! He believed that the number of the rooming house was 1844, but even that wasn't clear. . . . His head whirled. A taste of beer rose into the back of his mouth. Names of cities, names of states . . . the numbers of highways . . . the code of maps . . . A strange befuddlement overtook him. He read what he had written but still could not think of the name of his street.

A few yards away, an elderly black woman was feeding the ducks bits of bread from a shopping bag. But the ducks were ignoring her. "Here y'are," she coaxed. A boy of about six and his father were tossing out things for them, prepared snacks from a box, and the ducks showed more interest in these, but not much more. Much honking. Quacking. It was hard for Leo to concentrate. The little boy snatched the box from his father and threw it out onto the water angrily; this drew several enormous white ducks, slapping their wings on the water. But they seemed to lose momentum before reaching the box, slowing down stupidly, their heads turning from side to side. It flashed through Leo's mind that he would like to shoot those ducks dead.

He forced himself to reread his letter. Then he began again, painfully, leaving the name of the street blank; he would check and fill it in later.

I do hereby confess of my own free will that I transported my daughter, Elena Ross, from Pittsburgh, Pa., to San Francisco, Calif., with the express intention of hiding her from the local authorities and from the authorities of Pittsburgh, Pa., in violation of a court judgment handed down against me on the 15th July, 1949, Pittsburgh District Court, the Hon. Judge Norman Lucas presiding. I do hereby put my signature to this unsolicited confession in full cognizance of the legal rights I am surrendering and the implications of my statement. I do this, however, only upon the condition that my daughter be cared for in the proper manner and that she not be extradited back to Pittsburgh, to reside with her mother, the ex-Mrs. Leo Ross. The rest of this letter will explore in detail why the abovementioned Mrs. Ross is an inadequate mother and must not be awarded custody again of . . .

Now his mind flooded again: Ardis's face, Ardis's cheerful smile, her throaty sugary voice, her habit of humming as she strode everywhere. . . . She seemed to be striding into his head, swinging a door open and stepping inside. *You poor silly bastard!* she laughed. He almost heard her, her voice. It was terrible. She opened a door and pushed it carelessly back and strode through the doorway, Ardis in her high-heeled shoes, Ardis with her contemptuous laugh. . . .

Why didn't she die?

He tried to imagine her dead. But no, no. She wouldn't lie still in a coffin. No. She was too energetic, too beautiful. Her legs were too long, like swords. Oh, like swords, trim and swift. Oh, he loved her, he felt a tinge of sudden desire for her, mixing with the pain in his belly.

Why didn't she die?

But she would never die.

Easier to think of Elena dead. A small white coffin, a child's coffin of the kind he had seen once, frightened to see it so polished and handsome and ready to use: with gold trim along the edge of the lid. Elena would be perfect in death. More beautiful than her mother, perfect, an angel, her skin like the petals of flowers that you must never touch. Only look at, never touch. He had touched her and now her skin was bruised, blotched, scabby. She had scratched at the reddened bites on her face and body and they had bled, the wounds had half-healed and started to itch again and she'd scratched the scabs off, and more blood, more blood. . . . It did no good to scold her. To threaten her with tying her hands. No good. It did no good to search for the bugs . . . wood lice or chiggers or ticks or fleas. . . . They bit him too but he was able to ignore them, he had more control of himself, more contempt for the body. . . . If Elena died, the bites would go away and she would become a perfect child again, her hair light-blond again, almost white, the color of an angel's hair. Her swollen eye would become normal again. Normal again her fingers, which were also puffy, swollen. . . .

Someone walked by the door but kept on walking. It wasn't my father—not his footsteps.

My head was very tired. I didn't move. He said not to walk across the floor but I didn't move, I was too tired; when he came back he would ask me, Did you make any noise, and I would say

No. I didn't know if it was morning now or the next day. I waited.

He said not to answer if anybody knocked, but nobody knocked.

The delicate bluish eyelids closed, the eyes closed permanently. Not seeing him. Not staring at him. Closed permanently?

Suddenly Leo got to his feet. He needed a drink, he was desperate for a drink. He needed it now. The letter was finished, he couldn't force himself to write any more, it was finished; he folded it without bothering to reread it, stuck it in the envelope, and addressed it to *San Francisco Police Dept.* Now he needed a stamp. Just a single stamp. That was all that was between him and a drink.

It got dark one day. I didn't know if he went out that morning or some other morning. Everything in my head was mixed together. I didn't move. If I lay still on the cot time ran together, it was all the same time, it didn't frighten me. What I was afraid of were loud noises: thumps from upstairs, people walking across the room upstairs. They were strangers. I thought they might break through the ceiling. Then he would take out the gun and shoot up at them and their feet and legs would crash through the ceiling—.

It was loud upstairs but then it got quiet. The thumps always went away. Noises went away.

Everything went away if you were careful.

Leo bought a stamp at a stamp machine and put it on the envelope and mailed the letter at a corner mailbox. There, that was done. That was done. His life was completed. For a while he stood there, leaning against the mailbox. Bewildered, tender, shaky as a lover. What had he done? Was his life coming to an end?

He thought about going for a drink but suddenly his legs were very weak. His whole body was weak. He had come to the end of himself, his life was at an end. The gun was still in his pocket and he could feel it weighing down that side of his body, putting him off balance.

If he came back with something to eat I would smell the food and start to gag, I would say I'm not hungry and he would say, You are a bad girl not to eat. So I didn't move. On the stairs there were people going up and down but not his footsteps. I didn't sleep. But I woke up and I was too tired to move. The bites were tiny red prickles on the surface of my skin, but now far away, melting away. I was too tired to scratch them. Then he wouldn't be angry if they didn't bleed.

Sometimes there was a thunderstorm. I saw the lightning. But I couldn't think about the lightning. I wasn't afraid. Then it was light again, light coming under the shade. I could smell the spoiled milk. But I couldn't get up to find it. I thought, If he has cotton candy I can eat that, you put your tongue on it and it melts, little dots of sugar, that's all, it is easy to eat, you don't have to swallow anything and then you don't get sick.

But he didn't come back.

I tried to tell him how the eating was bad, how it hurt me, but he would get angry. Once he held me in his arms and cried, like a little girl would cry. That frightened me. I tried to tell him how the eating was bad. . . .

"The eating was. . . . The eating was. . . . The eating was. . . ."

No, that was later. At the Children's Shelter. I tried to tell the nurse how the eating was bad and hurt me inside.

But the words went around and around in my head and didn't come out right, out of my mouth. I couldn't get them right. There were two streams of words: one in the head, where you can feel them like stones, hard little things, getting ready to be said out loud, and one in the throat and up into the back of the mouth and the mouth itself, on the tongue, and there the words are in the shape of air. Bubbles. The two streams of words come together at the back of your mouth, where you swallow, but sometimes they don't. Then people stare at you. Then they laugh.

The nurse said, "What? What are you trying to tell me?"

The girl in the bed next to mine laughed.

"They going to put you in the nut-house," she laughed.

Words in the head like little stones, but you can't touch them or get them out. Hard. They don't dissolve. They hurt. Passing through the parts of the head they hurt, they swell up and get big. Words in the throat like crying, swallows of air. You swallow them by mistake. People laugh. My father didn't laugh but he got mad. He said, "You can talk right if you want to—," but then he would hold me and kiss me.

I hid my face but couldn't cry. The girl in the next bed laughed. I took my hands away from my face and laughed the way she did, like a mirror. Then she liked me. When I laughed like her she liked me. She said she would be my friend.

But that was later, at the Children's Shelter. That was after the police and the woman came to get me. They knocked on the door but I didn't say anything. I was under the covers. They broke in and took the cot downstairs, holding onto me. They held me so I couldn't fall off. I wanted to cry because my father would come back and I would be gone. He would be very angry. He wouldn't know where to find me. "I didn't know, I'm not responsible . . . ," a woman was shouting. The first policeman got the door open. I knew it wasn't my father. I was under the covers. My eye was shut but I could see them come in, it wasn't my father.

A man came over to me and looked down. "My God . . . ," he said.

They were policemen. A woman was with them, in a policeman's uniform with a skirt. I could see through one eye how she stared at me. They were all staring.

"My God . . . ," one of them said again.

5

"Say hello! Say something!"

A woman was standing over Elena. On the other side of the bed the ward nurse was propping up Elena's pillow, helping her to sit up. Elena cringed and tried to close her eyes, but the woman kept talking to her, pleading with her. She had bright-red hair that seemed to grow outward around her head, in spiky curls. Something swung from her ears and was so strange, so glittering, that Elena tried to push herself backward, away from the danger of it, but the ward nurse gripped her shoulders and held her still.

The woman's mouth was red, very surprised and very agitated.

"Elena—" she was calling.

Elena, from a long distance; from up close, too close. The distance had stretched and snapped and now it was collapsed to nothing, everything was close up, face to face; very loud.

The red-haired woman leaned onto the bed, one knee onto the bed, making the mattress sink on that side. She was saying something but when Elena did not answer she lurched forward to embrace her, seizing her. *Elena, Elena,* came that weeping angry voice. Elena's mouth was pressed against the woman's shoulder, her skin hurt, all this agitation hurt her inside and out. But she did not fight. She did not cry. And then, as if to reward her, the woman leaned back and turned into Elena's mother.

Elena's face felt as if it were being stretched open.

"Look, she recognizes me! She knows who I am!" the woman exclaimed. "Oh, Elena, darling—Elena—it's me, your mother, you know me, don't you? She does know me! Oh, she recognizes me! I told you she would recognize me—"

Elena noticed the dark-haired man who came in and out of the ward, a doctor, and the ward nurse, and another nurse. But her mother was in the center of everything she saw. Her mother leaned forward again and sat on the bed, near Elena, and took hold of Elena's hands. She was very excited. She moved her face so that the bright flash of tears in her eyes was agitated; a tear jerked out and ran quickly down her cheek. "My God, this is so terrible . . . what is that rash on your face, Elena, and what about your hair? Jesus, oh Jesus. . . . What did he do to you? What. . . . Why didn't you tell me what she looked like?" she said to the doctor. He moved forward, summoned forward, quick and dark, his face shadowy. His voice was too soft for Elena to hear. In the middle of it Elena's mother embraced her again, weeping. Her dress was made of some rough, scratchy material, but at her throat a blouse showed through, a large lacy white bow. Earrings swung from her ears, large white stones like snowdrops. One of them was pressed against Elena's forehead and she was grateful for its cold, hard, steady shape.

"Why didn't you inform me of her condition? Why did this take so long? Do you people realize that this child has been missing for sixty-one days, sixty-one days without her mother, no, please, don't interrupt, and I waited for forty-five minutes just to get in here? Who is in charge here? Why isn't she in a private room?"

The doctor tried to answer Elena's mother.

"What *usual procedure?* What? This isn't a charity case, I don't happen to be a pauper, I happen to be this child's mother and I'm shocked at everything I've seen in this place, especially this ward, I'm shocked at the condition my daughter is in—no, please don't interrupt—I arrived in San Francisco two hours ago and it's taken me all this time to get to my daughter, and to see her like this—her hair—her face—"

"She's much better now, Mrs. Ross—"

"Why isn't she talking? Elena, honey, say hello. Say hello. Say hello to your mother."

"She hasn't been talking, but we think—"

"She's looking right at me, she knows me, look—she's smiling at me—that is a smile— Sweetheart, you're going to be all right now. I'll take you out of this place today. You'll be all right, you'll be safe back home. Nothing will ever happen to you again. Do you understand?"

Elena nodded.

"Ah, yes! Yes! You see, she understands everything perfectly," Elena's mother cried. Her eyes were bright and fierce with tears. She smiled at Elena, into Elena, her smile widening and stretching itself right into Elena, opening up Elena's insides. She felt how her face was beginning to heat, to take on some of her mother's heat, the glow of her love. "But what a shock, to walk in here like this . . . to see her. . . . She was always able to talk, Doctor, she was always a normal child. I can't understand why. . . . And why did the police take so long to find them? And why did they let *him* escape?"

"How the police have handled it, that is not anything I know about," the doctor said slowly. He was staring at Elena's mother. His voice had changed; it was not the way he spoke to the nurses, or called out orders, or asked questions in the ward. The nurse was also staring. "But the little girl is much improved, thankfully, you will be pleased to know how she has gained weight steadily, Mrs. Ross, it is all very good. Very good. And so there is no cause for your fear, Mrs. Ross—"

Elena's mother reached out to touch Elena's face. Her fingers were cool and soft, very soft.

"Say hello to your mother, Elena, say hello . . . ?"

When Elena did not answer, her mother's smile saddened. She got to her feet and brushed off her dress, slowly, thoughtfully. She turned to the doctor without quite looking at him. "Well, the police at least located her, that's an accomplishment. It only took sixty-one days. And if she's really so much better, as you say, then by God I'm grateful to you . . . I don't care how wretched this place is. . . . Are you a doctor, or . . . ? I mean are you a doctor with a medical degree?"

He laughed apologetically. "Yes, of course I have a medical degree, I am a doctor, I received my degree in Hawaii, but what you mean . . . I think . . . what you mean is if I have passed my exams for practicing in this state. . . . I will take this exam soon, soon, and at present I am an intern. . . ."

"Well, you're in charge here?"

"I am not the Director, no, of course, but I am in charge here today. . . . I am in charge, yes, Mrs. Ross, and will help you as much as I can."

"You're very polite, you're very human," Elena's mother said. "You can imagine what I've gone through, all the telephone calls and the red tape and the police . . . and even getting an early flight out here. . . . Doctor, do you have pictures of Elena when she was first brought in?"

"Pictures—?"

"Any kind of evidence. For when my ex-husband is apprehended."

"I am afraid we have no photographic evidence, but of course our reports are thorough—they are daily reports—"

"And eye-witness accounts," Elena's mother said. "This isn't a civil case now, I know, this is a criminal case, and it isn't up to me to gather evidence—but—we'll see— My attorney instructed me to never, never under any circumstances let other people take the lead if I could do it myself—sometimes evidence gets lost—it's a mystery how important evidence can get lost— And how on earth did they let that man escape? That madman?"

"Mrs. Ross, I do not know, but—"

"She was a beautiful little girl, really beautiful—you wouldn't believe it! I knew she was sick, suffering from malnutrition, but nobody bothered to tell me about her hair—imagine, dyeing a child's hair black! *Black!* A child with that light a complexion, obviously a blonde, it shows the extent to which his mind was deranged—anyone with sense would have dyed it brown, or even red—but *black!*— It breaks my heart to look at her—but you say she is much improved, Doctor? You seem to be hopeful?"

"Oh, yes, certainly," he said at once. "Certainly, Mrs. Ross. We were able to treat her before there was any permanent damage to the liver, and you can see that her color is good, very good—please do not be upset by the swellings and the bruises and the bites, those are temporary, the infections are well under control and the poison is out, that is not the serious thing, that was never the serious thing—what was dangerous was the dehydration, which we were able to treat at once— And she was always a very good patient, a very good little girl—sometimes in these cases when the child suffers from malnutrition or has been beaten there is apathy and inertia, but your little girl has always cooperated with the nurses, she has never resisted any treatment—"

"Oh, was she good? Was she a good girl here?" Elena's mother asked. She smiled at Elena proudly. "Do you hear that, Elena, the doctor says you were very good! Was she good?" she asked the nurse.

"Oh, yes, wonderful, just wonderful," the nurse said.

"And she did try to talk, she tries to talk sometimes," the doctor said. "We are all certain, Mrs. Ross, that the use of speech will return to her naturally. . . ."

"You're very good, very encouraging to me," Elena's mother said. "It's been such a shock. . . . Except one thing: my name isn't Mrs. Ross. My name is Ardis Carter, my legal name, my maiden name again. But my professional name is Bonita. Just Bonita. Just call me Bonita."

"Bonita . . . ?"

"Yes, Bonita. No last name. . . . Elena, sweetheart, are you listening? The bad times are over now, the nightmare is over. I'm taking you home and you'll be under the best possible medical care, you're going to be well as soon as possible, and happy, and going to school again, and playing again. . . . Isn't that wonderful? And you'll be safe with your mother again, and nothing will ever happen to you again, do you understand? Why don't you say something, Elena?"

Elena stared up at her mother. It was fascinating, it was like going into another kind of sleep, to see her mother's bright beautiful face again, to watch her red lips parting over her white teeth into a smile. Elena's own lips parted, her mouth opened. But it was very dry. At the back of her mouth there was a dry circle, like a bubble gone dry.

"Your teacher misses you so, honey—she was as worried as I was, all these weeks—you can imagine how worried they were at school," Elena's mother said, half turning to the doctor, "especially that woman who allowed the kidnaping to take place— You know, all this could have been prevented, my daughter could be in perfect health at this moment, if only that woman had been doing her duty and watching the playground— Believe me, her troubles are just beginning. And my husband, if he's ever caught— How could the police have let him escape? The wire services have had his photograph for two months! But I wouldn't be surprised if he was right in the city here, maybe spying on this place. He isn't crazy, but he pretends to be—he has the shrewdness of a crazy man—can you imagine what it was like for my daughter to be kidnaped by him? It's no wonder she can't talk. But they told me that kidnaping charges can't be laid against him, not the federal kidnaping charges . . . the kind that were passed after that poor Lindbergh baby was kidnaped. . . ."

"You mean with the death sentence . . . ?" the doctor asked.

"Yes. They told me it probably couldn't be brought against him, an indictment like that," Elena's mother said, "because he was her father and didn't demand ransom or anything like that. . . . But he did cross state lines, I told them. But they said. . . . Oh, hell, the law is too much for a woman to figure out. . . . Elena, honey, you're so thin! It's going to take a lot of love to make you well again, isn't it? Give your mother a nice kiss."

She leaned down again, presented the side of her face; Elena kissed her cheek.

"My sweet little girl," Elena's mother murmured, "you're going to be pretty again and safe. . . . Can you say hello to me? I bet you can. I bet you can if you try."

"If she was not hurried . . . ," the doctor began.

"Elena, what do you say? Hello to your mother?"

Elena felt the gap at the back of her mouth swell to the point of pain. It was like a stone swelling. The dry parched muscles tried to work, to move, to give shape to something. Elena's mother was staring, smiling, eyes into eyes, bluish-gray eyes into Elena's eyes, which had begun to strain now with her effort to speak.

"I'll think you don't want me here," Elena's mother said with a little downward twist of her mouth. "I'll think I made the trip just for nothing . . . that you want me to go back home by myself and leave you here. . . ."

Elena clutched at her mother's arm.

"Yes, honey, what do you say?" her mother begged. "Do you love your mother? My beautiful little girl! Do you love your mother?"

"I–" Elena began.

"Yes, yes, do you? Do you?"

Elena felt the air at the back of her mouth almost gagging her.

"I– I love you–" Elena gasped.

Her mother stared at her. For a moment no one spoke. Then, very quietly, almost in a whisper, Elena's mother said: "Tell us again, honey . . . ? Can you . . . ?"

"I love you," Elena said.

And the world became perfect again.

6

I said, I'm ashamed of the basement. She stared at me. A dot seemed to get smaller in her eyes; she held me there with her eyes, staring. I said the wrong words. I stammered and said again, I'm ashamed of the basement, and started to cry and they laughed at me. . . .

When I came home, I told her. Why did they laugh at you, she asked.

Because I talked wrong.

How did you talk wrong, she asked.

I said ashamed and Miss Frye stopped me and said, what do you mean, Elena?–do you mean afraid? Then you should say afraid. But they were all laughing at me.

Why couldn't you say afraid, my mother asked.

I don't know.

I don't want those little sons of bitches laughing at you, my mother said. I'm not going to stand for that.

"Why are you afraid of the locker room, Elena?" Miss Frye asked.

"The dark. . . ."

"What do you mean, the dark? It isn't dark down there on gym days, is it?"

"No, but. . . ."

"The lights are on when the girls go down, aren't they? Of course they are. There's nothing to be afraid of."

Elena agreed.

"When the lights are off you don't have to go down into the basement or even look down there," Miss Frye said with a perplexed smile. "So there's no reason to be afraid, is there? The other girls aren't afraid. Just march downstairs and keep your place in line and nothing will happen. . . . You're not going to be afraid again tomorrow, are you?"

Elena agreed. Then she realized she had said the wrong thing. She said quickly, "No."

What is it you see in the dark, she asked me.

I couldn't answer. I didn't know.

They lived only three blocks from the John P. Salisbury School, in Cleveland, Ohio, so that Elena could come home to lunch every day. She could even walk in a small group with other girls who lived in the neighborhood. By twelve-fifteen Ardis was always awake and out of bed, though not always dressed. She would open the door for Elena and greet her happily: she would be wearing one of her bright silk robes, or a pair of lounging slacks with Oriental designs on them, her hair often swinging free from having just been shampooed, her face clean of make-up and shining, almost glaring. She often said, "Look who's dropping in for lunch!"

She was very cheerful in the kitchen, teaching Elena how to make little meals—lunch for Elena, breakfast for Ardis—of scrambled eggs with grated cheese and paprika, or vegetable soup with fresh mushrooms sliced into it, or strong cheddar cheese melted on very thin pieces of whole wheat bread. She taught Elena to make tossed salads, holding Elena's hands as she held the large wooden spoon and fork. In the evenings, she instructed Elena in the preparation of thick, elaborate stews, the braising of fish or meat seasoned with onion and paprika; she had bought a Hungarian cookbook and gradually shifted the task of learning the recipes onto Elena, who was very eager to help.

"Mr. Kármán's wife couldn't do better than this, I bet," Ardis would laugh, leaning over to smell what Elena was cooking.

Mr. Kármán came to the apartment every day, bringing food: not just meat and vegetables but sour cream, goose fat, caviar, noodles in strange shapes, whole fishes, red cabbage, sweet red peppers. . . . Sometimes he helped Elena with her homework while Ardis went out on brief shopping trips to the drugstore or stopped by at a friend's house to pick something up. He didn't know about Elena's troubles at school and was always pleased when she showed him her test papers with their high grades.

"You are such a sweet little girl, and smart also, like your mother," he said. Elena could feel him searching for and testing words, as if afraid of drawing out the wrong words, afraid of being laughed at.

Elena was nine years old. She was in the fourth grade at the Salisbury school, and she and her mother lived in one of the apartment buildings owned by Mr. Kármán; that was how they had met Mr. Kármán—Ardis had had trouble with something, Elena didn't know what it was, and one day Mr. Kármán had stopped by to talk to her. He was a large, kindly man, with a perpetual doggish smile. He was always smiling at Ardis. It gave him pleasure to call her both Ardis and Bonita, switching from name to name as if he were in charge of a secret, an intimate code.

"Are you happy here?" Mr. Kármán asked her.

"This apartment is beautiful and of course we're happy, we're very grateful," Ardis said.

"You are happy here too?" he asked Elena.

Yes, Elena said.

They had moved up to the top floor, to what was called the penthouse. The apartment was large, wide, sunny, with old-fashioned velvet drapes and heavily ornamental furniture and a marble-and-brass fireplace that was not real. Ardis had put her own things up on the walls—photographs of herself, glossy shots that showed her face from every angle framed with every kind of hair-do. A few were of Elena. Sometimes Ardis would stride through the rooms and cry out happily, "Who are those people? Those faces? Who's so lucky?"

She was usually in a good mood, in spite of the trouble Elena sometimes had at school. Her red hair had been softened, lightened, to a pale and almost iridescent orange, a tawny orange that changed hues in different lights. She and Elena both had several white outfits: coats and hats and matching dresses. She had a lime-green suede outfit, a vest and jodhpurs. She and Elena both had fur coats, not mink but muskrat, but very fine skins, so that people stared at them on the street and could not think of any appropriate expression into which to shift their faces. At such times Ardis smiled coolly and looked away. If anyone approached her or spoke to her—any man—she sometimes stared at him with her cold bluish-gray eyes and her mocking smile and said softly, "Who the hell are *you* looking at?"

And the man would gape at her, wordless.

Elena was very happy there, very happy. On schooldays she woke at eight o'clock, when the alarm clock made a little clicking noise—it was set for that time but the alarm mechanism wasn't pulled, because Ardis didn't want to be awakened so early. In the bathroom she washed and fixed her hair, quietly, very quietly, standing on her toes to peer over the bottles and jars on the ledge that ran along the bottom of the mirror, then she dressed herself, except for her shoes, and went out into the kitchen to have a bowl of cereal or a sugar doughnut or an apple. It was important always to eat breakfast, her mother told her. And Mr. Kármán, concerned for her health, insisting that both she and her mother were too thin, would always question her about breakfast.

"And you had eggs and sausage? And buttered rolls?" he would ask.

Yes, Elena would say.

When they were alone Ardis said, "He doesn't understand America, we don't want to confuse him," and she laughed and said, "If I don't get ten hours of sleep I couldn't last through one of those conversations with him, honey, and then what? The most important thing in life is sleep," she said meditatively, stroking her face. "Absolute unconsciousness."

So in the mornings Elena would eat alone and then gather up her books and shoes and go out into the corridor, which was thickly carpeted. The railings were always polished; doorknobs and hinges were polished; the entire door of the little closet-sized elevator gleamed. But Elena took the stairs five flights down, because the elevator frightened her. And from the front steps she had only a five-minute walk to school, in daylight, so there was nothing to be afraid of, nothing. "Just think of me upstairs, watching you over the ledge, if you get afraid," Ardis said. "And think of all the other little girls walking to school who aren't afraid."

She was very happy when she came home at noon and could hear the radio already on. That meant her mother was up and in a good mood. They would make their meal and eat in the dining room, which looked out and down onto a courtyard below. If it was a lucky day the telephone wouldn't ring. But on most days it began to ring around twelve-thirty, and Ardis would eat her breakfast with the telephone receiver stuck under her chin, murmuring, "Yes. Fine. When? Sure. I'll check and call you back. . . . Oh, sure. Great. Whose car? Long or short hair? No, not him. Not *him.* I don't mean *him,* but the other one, yes, *him,* count me out if. . . . What about Elena? What about Saturday? Great."

Elena ate her lunch slowly, sadly. It did no good that her mother winked at her and seemed to be making fun of the tiny voice over the telephone, half here, half there, half with Elena and half with someone on the other side of town.

If she said, *What about Elena?* there was a terrible pause, a terrible wait. And then, if she said Great, Elena's heart sank. She blinked to keep tears out of her eyes and tried to keep up with her mother's chatter, the buoyancy of her mood, she tried to look happy when Ardis said in triumph, "Got you a little work, honey, for that private bank account of yours!—you're really on your way!"

But sometimes she couldn't look happy enough. And her mother would hesitate and say, "Elena, what's wrong . . . ? Are you sick?"

No.

"Well, what are you looking so gloomy about then? What are you thinking?"

Nothing.

"Yes, you are, honey, you're certainly thinking something—is it a secret, is it something I should know? Is it something selfish?"

No. . . .

"Is it something you shouldn't be thinking, Elena? Confess."

Nothing. . . .

"You have a closed-up little face sometimes, like one of those flowers, a narcissus, a very selfish flower," Ardis said thoughtfully. "You'd better tell me what's wrong before you go back to school. I can't let you walk out of here with that look on your face."

Elena would stare at the food on her plate.

"You must understand how valuable work is, work of the kind we do," Ardis said. "Thousands of women . . . thousands, millions of little girls are envious of us. Do you know that? What are you thinking?"

She would lean forward to peer at Elena, as if looking into her head. Half joking, but also serious, she would raise her eyebrows with the effort of staring right into Elena's head. "I can read your thoughts, I can hear everything you're thinking," she said. "So you'd better change your tune. You'd better wise up. There won't always be a mother to pay for your food and take care of you—what do you think this world is? It isn't a nursery!"

Arranged around the living room, on the walls and propped up on the fake mantel and on the tables, stuck in odd corners, were photographs of Ardis modeling: long and elegant, with a head that appeared tiny or fluffed out, a boy's head, or the head of a woman with waist-length curls; Ardis stretching to reach a flower almost beyond her grasp, tantalizingly; Ardis comically sharing a long piece of straw with a horse; Ardis seated at a wrought-iron table, demure, ladylike, prim in an organdy dress and medium-heeled white shoes, holding an enormous wide-brimmed white hat. But the photograph on the mantel was the most important one, the one that had brought her the most money and a great deal of local attention—Ardis and Elena both, Ardis smiling for the camera with her teeth and hair miraculously glossy, her eyes shimmering with mischievous health, stooping to embrace her child, Elena, a small perfect child who stared right into the camera with slightly surprised eyes and a tentative shy smile. They wore mother-and-daughter outfits, polka-dot dresses and white gloves, their hair exactly the same shade of blond—Ardis had worn a wig for the sitting, a wig of the same hue as her natural hair—and the skin identical. The advertisement was for skin cream; the caption said in accusing black letters, COULD *you* HOPE TO COMPETE WITH YOUR DAUGHTER'S SKIN?

That was the photograph Mr. Kármán cherished. The first time he'd seen it, the first time he had come to the apartment, he had picked it up and stared at it and brought it over to a window to stare, to murmur softly, "Lovely. . . . Lovely. . . ."

Ardis had admitted, "Yes, I'm pleased with that one myself."

"The mother—the daughter. Yes. Perfect. It is so obvious you are mother and daughter, truly, and not just models, not just strangers posing for a camera," he said. He looked at the photograph for a while. His profile was severe and reverential. "It is amazing, a miracle," he said oddly, "how the flesh can be arranged on the bones . . . . certain angles and patches of skin . . . and the effect is one of such beauty . . . it is such uncanny beauty that almost one does not want to look into it."

Ardis said nothing.

"Knowledge of such matters does not help," Mr. Kármán said. "It is not powerful enough to help. . . ."

Sit still. Like that. Don't move. Don't blink. Be good, be a good girl. Yes. Perfect.

Ardis bragged to the photographers and their assistants and the other models that Elena had been born with a natural gift, that she could sit under those hot lights for half an hour, not seeing anything, not moving her face, not even sniffing, hardly breathing; she was a little doll.

"You really are a little doll," people agreed.

Men propped her up onto stools, tilted her face, shaped a smile with their fingers, left the smile, came back to it in a few minutes and reworked it, bringing their serious, frowning faces close to hers and yet not close at all. She felt them but did not really feel them. There was a distance between them; she was not threatened. Even the lights did not burn her eyes.

A little doll.

Once, after a long session that lasted until late in the day, a man took Ardis and Elena downstairs to a restaurant of some kind, a dark place, and Elena couldn't see. She stumbled into something. She kept blinking, her eyes began to water helplessly, she was very ashamed. "Is something wrong with you?" Ardis asked suddenly.

She and the man both paused to look down at Elena.

"Her eyes are watering," the man said.

"It's all right," Elena said.

They were sitting in a booth somewhere. It was very dark, soft. Around the big cave-like room lights were glowing but they were soft, watery, indistinct. "Why are you blinking like that?" Ardis asked.

"Her eyes must be sore," said the man.

Elena did not answer. She waited. In a few minutes her mother would forget, would turn away; she could rely on that. But for some reason Ardis slid her arm around Elena's shoulders, gently, and examined her eyes. It was very embarrassing because the man, a stranger, was watching. "Now, tell the truth, honey. Can you see all right?"

"I don't know."

"Do your eyes burn?"

"A little." She did not try to squirm away from her mother, though she wanted to. She wanted to tell both her mother and this man that she was all right, it didn't matter. She hated them to look at her so directly.

"Elena, you should have said something up in the studio, if the lights were shining in your eyes," Ardis said. Elena did not know how to reply. She sensed something unusual in her mother's voice, a tone Ardis wouldn't use if they were alone; she wouldn't have used it either, with Mr. Kármán; it had something to do with this man. So Elena did not know what her mother wanted her to say. "As soon as you felt your eyes begin to burn, you should have told me," Ardis said.

"I'm sorry," Elena said.

"You're a very good little girl to sit so still," Ardis said, "but if this happens again you should tell me. . . . Unless . . . unless you did it to be bad, to get out of work tomorrow. . . . Was that the reason, Elena?"

"No."

"To make your eyes water and get red and ugly, so you wouldn't have to work tomorrow . . . ? Elena, tell the truth. Was that it?"

"No," Elena said miserably.

Ardis looked at the man. She let both hands fall limply on the table. "Sometimes I can't handle her, I can't figure her out. She's very secretive for a girl her age. I think she pretends to be very stupid just to get out of work. Elena, honey, you'd better tell the truth. Could you really be that stupid, to stare into the lights for an hour and not say anything? Do you expect me to believe that?"

Elena was going to say she was sorry; but she could not form the words.

"Well?" Ardis asked.

"I—"

"Do you expect me to believe that a girl your age could let herself practically be blinded and not say anything? Do you? My God," Ardis sighed. Elena waited. Her eyeballs pounded with shame. After a while Ardis began to tell the man about her problems with Elena at school—"I don't know what will become of her"—and the difficulties she had, a divorced mother, a woman with a lifelong responsibility to a child, whose husband had deserted her and paid no alimony at all—"He's a common criminal wanted in half a dozen states, quite a handicap for even a normal child to grow up with"— Then, after a while, as the man soothed her, Ardis's voice began to grow tender; Elena sensed an important change. Ardis said, "But . . . well . . . I can't complain, can I? She really is a little doll. She's so sweet. Have you ever seen any model her age so professional? She's like a little adult, isn't she?— It's wonderful how she tries not to show her feelings or to cry, even if she's hurt. I couldn't do that myself. Sometimes I wonder if she feels pain the way other children do. . . ."

A man said to her, all you need is a gold frame around you. And she laughed, she laughed.

She said, and no way out . . . ?

And no way out, the man said.

But she laughed.

Mr. Kármán clasped his hands in front of him and said how serious it was; life was serious; everyone, especially a child, needed a stable life.

Ardis laughed.

"But I am serious with you," he protested. "I am not speaking casually. . . . You must think of your little girl, even if you do not think about yourself."

"Think of her!" Ardis exclaimed. "As if I ever think of anything else—"

Mr. Kármán sat with Elena while Ardis dressed in the other room, with the door ajar so that she could call out to him. He looked smilingly through her school workbooks, he pulled out of his pockets little surprises for her—candies wrapped in tinfoil, tiny poppyseed cakes, things Elena took to school with her and gave away the next morning. Once he gave her a mother-of-pearl ring and she gave that away, to the loud, cheerful, pony-tailed girl who sat behind her, and who was too surprised to say thank you.

"Yes, Ardis, you must try to stabilize this existence, for the sake of your child and of yourself," Mr. Kármán called out. He never looked toward the bedroom, toward the half-opened door, even when Ardis didn't reply to his remarks. "For instance, yesterday, it was yesterday I tried to telephone you and you were never home. . . ."

"Yesterday I took Elena to the doctor," Ardis called.

"What? A doctor? Why?"

"She's so frail and susceptible to colds, you know that, she may never be completely normal again. . . ."

"What? Is she sick?" Mr. Kármán asked. He looked severely at Elena. "Which doctor did you take her to?"

"Oh, I don't know," Ardis called from the other room, her voice muffled. "It was a specialist—it's always the same story, they want money, all they care about is money—"

"Did you take her to Dr. Renfrew? The doctor I told you about?"

"Oh, I don't know, they all want so much money," Ardis said.

"But Ardis, Ardis, just tell me how much—"

After a while Ardis appeared, her hair not fastened into place, her hand at her throat. She stared at Mr. Kármán. "I don't like to burden you with my private problems," she said.

He rose and took her hands, he led her forward. He said, "If you would only tell me, Ardis—please—"

They began to talk about money. Elena had heard this before, she knew how her mother would sigh, would glance nervously around the room. And Mr. Kármán would hold her hands in his, looking right into her face, smiling. "But you have your own family," Ardis said.

"My family! Grown-up children who have no need of me, and a wife—a wife—well, I will not talk of her, but she has no need of me either, not as you do."

He was a heavy-set man with enormous sloping shoulders. His

hair was scruffy and graying, his eyebrows thick, ridged, melancholy. Sometimes he stared at Ardis, bearish, perspiring, not daring to touch her, his eyes filmy, watery, golden-glowing, very tender. He said gently, "Ardis, what other happiness is there for a man? Except to raise someone higher than himself, to love and honor someone higher than himself . . . ?"

Sometimes they talked about leaving Cleveland together, with Elena. And Elena's heart leaped. But always, at once, Ardis would say: "No, I can't. You have your own family."

"Why, why do you say that? That is a torment to me!"

"I couldn't do it."

"Ardis, my wife and I are not close. No. Not for many years. As many years as you are old, Ardis, think of that. . . . Do you know what that means, to live without love for so long? Without beauty? There is no goodness, no worth to life, unless a man can raise the world into the beautiful and the immutable; you won't deny me that?"

The beautiful and the immutable.

Elena loved him.

But Ardis said, "If I broke up your family I couldn't live with myself. . . ."

He talked to her. He kept talking. He laughed, in his bewilderment, his frustration, his hope. He talked about his childhood and young manhood in Budapest; he talked about his belief in saints and angels. "We were not so poor as some, but we were poor, yes, and it was a shame to us . . . but my mother was very religious, and she taught me to believe as strongly as she did, because it was a help for her and she knew it would help me, even if I couldn't hold onto it when I got older . . . but I loved the statues, the saints and the angels, I loved how beautiful they were . . . and how still, how perfect, they never asked anything or judged harshly. . . . You are both like angels to me," he said in his slow, guttural voice, a voice of wonder. "I dream of you, Ardis, but also of your daughter . . . the two of you together . . . who must be protected, cherished. You must let me help you, Ardis, you must bring your hectic life into order."

Ardis did not reply for a while. Then she said slowly, "I know that's true. But I don't know how to do it."

"Ardis, why do you say that? You know how I am anxious to help you . . . ?"

"I'm in debt. Medical bills for Elena, even dental bills . . . and they want me to start some kind of speech therapy, the teachers at Elena's school. . . . A child is a responsibility you're never free of. I got married when I was so young, I was a mother when I was so young . . ."

"How much are you in debt, Ardis?"

She shook her head. "No. I can't take money from you. The gifts are different, the apartment here . . . no, I'm quite sincere, I will never take money from you. It's pointless to talk about it. . . . Did I tell you I took Elena downtown for x-rays? And while she was being x-rayed, right at that moment, I happened to read in the *Reader's Digest* out in the waiting room about how x-rays might contain something dangerous, maybe something radioactive, that hurt the bone . . . the marrow of the bone. . . . Isn't that terrible? I almost went into a state of panic. And Elena is already so high-strung, so sensitive, she isn't like other children who are blunt and brutal and don't feel pain. . . ."

"Ardis, we must talk more about this. We must. We must put all our lives into order."

My mother came to get me because I was in the nurse's room and couldn't talk, they had to telephone her and she was angry. I couldn't move. I felt the vibrations of her walking in the corridor and I was afraid. Her hat around her head was tight, filmy white feathers that moved and seemed to breathe by themselves. Her coat was orange with dark blue stripes. Her face was painted pink. She cut through what Miss Frye was saying and said, what is down in that basement?

It isn't a basement, it's the locker room—

Locker room, what locker room?

For the gymnasium, Mrs. Carter. On Tuesday and Thursday mornings the girls have gym, they change into their gym clothes in the locker room and for some reason your daughter is afraid and—

My mother looked at me.

Elena, you tell us, she said.

But I couldn't talk.

Her face flamed up. You, Elena, you, you tell us—she cried—you tell us—you—

They had put me down on the nurse's cot and there was a white cotton blanket up over me, a thin blanket. Miss Frye and the nurse and the principal herself carried me. They were very surprised. Sometimes a girl or a boy from my room would get a nosebleed and leave the room, sometimes someone would get sick to his stomach and come in here, but now I was in here. I wanted to get well and talk.

Damn you, my mother said, I won't put up with your tricks, she said, you have some explaining to do—

Mrs. Carter, the girls were going downstairs and I'm not sure exactly what happened—Elena must have said something, or stuttered, and the girls were laughing at her—and then she just stood there, she seemed to become paralyzed. I've never had anything like this happen before and I—

Are you the principal? You're the principal? And you allow this kind of thing, this intimidation of a child, forcing her to go down into some damn basement and harassing her?—a minor?—do you know I could bring suit against the Board of Education and against you personally, are you aware of the risks you are taking in this ignorant haphazard—ignorant—asinine—this incompetent manner you are administrating—administering your duties?

Mrs. Carter—

My daughter was perfectly normal before she enrolled in this school and now look, my mother cried, now look—

But—

She pulled the blanket off me and yanked me up. And I came awake, I felt my legs coming awake. She said, Elena—? You are perfectly all right, aren't you?

Yes.

You are perfectly normal and always have been, my mother said, but on the way home when we were walking she said, you're not normal and I won't stand for it. You're doing it to spite me. You want me to interrupt my work and run over to that goddam school and make a fool of myself in front of those ugly old bags—

I started to cry.

Oh go ahead and cry and ruin your face, my mother said, but you have some explaining to do when we get home.

I said they were going to turn the lights out, they told me they were going to turn them out—

What lights?

To scare me because they knew I was afraid—they said—they said the boys were hiding down there and—

What boys? What lights? What the hell is all this?

I was afraid of the basement and they always laughed at me and—

Then why did you pretend you were paralyzed? Do you want people to think you have polio? I could get rid of you, put an ad in the paper and get rid of you, I could give you back to your father—the two of you probably have planned all this, to drive me crazy—

I was crying. I said, Then on the step I—on the step five steps from the bottom I—I couldn't—

Oh shut up, this is driving me crazy. I don't believe any of this.

I didn't want to—

Oh shut up, she said, and put her hands over her ears, over the fluffy white feathers. Up in the apartment she picked up a picture of me, sitting in a playsuit by a Christmas tree with lots of dolls around me and she said, I'll put this in the paper and say that a bad girl is for sale, a bargain at twenty dollars! But you're too old to sell, nobody wants idiots your age—if you were just a baby yet I could put you out for adoption, but it's too late now—

She ripped the photograph in two.

She said, Wait until I tell him about this.

Ardis whipped off the hat with the white feathers and threw it down. She telephoned Mr. Kármán at his office. Her face was stern and she wouldn't look at Elena, who was still crying. "That's so kind of you, to come over right away," she said. "My life lurches from one crisis to another. . . ." When she hung up she hurried into her bedroom, still ignoring Elena. Elena sat on the edge of the sofa. In a few minutes her mother reappeared, and her hair was a pale, pale blond, cut very simply and elegantly around her face, and she was buttoning up a white satin blouse. She walked toward Elena but did not see her. She lit a cigarette. She was breathing hard, in short eager pants, holding her torso a little high, her breasts unnaturally raised. Her skirt was made of a rich black wool. Elena looked shyly at her but she did not look at Elena.

When Mr. Kármán came, Ardis took him by the arm and said, "There's no one here to eavesdrop, but let's go into the other room anyway," and he glanced guiltily at Elena, sad, stricken himself, as if he and not Elena had made a terrible mistake. Elena sniffed hesitantly, questioningly. But the door to the bedroom closed.

She waited.

When her mother and Mr. Kármán came out again, after a while, Elena didn't know how long, Ardis was crying and Mr. Kármán looked as if he too had been crying, his face somber and strained and red. He came to Elena. He said, "Elena, your mother and I have at last made some vital decisions. At last your mother will listen to me, and we will seize happiness out of this troubled time in all our lives. . . ." Elena, very anxious to understand, to hear everything, looked from Mr. Kármán over to her mother; but Ardis was looking out of the window. Mr. Kármán was saying something about a stable life, about marriage, about a single household, and Elena listened in terror and heard him say, "—but my religion forbids such normal desires—my wife—it is too complicated for a child to understand—but the tragedy is not permanent because a normal family life can be established even without the marriage bond—a normal life of routine, which you require so desperately but which circumstances have denied you—Elena—and so—"

She listened. She blinked up at him, into his flushed, heavy face, smelling his clothes and the eagerness of his love. He was telling her about a clinic in Chicago, "the finest in the country—and I have made inquiries everywhere, because no expense is too great—Elena, my dear, you and your mother will bear my name, your mother will change her name legally to mine—it will be exactly like a marriage, you will be my child— Your mother has at last agreed to this, Elena. You're going to Chicago and I will join you shortly and we will all live together, Elena, in a house—in a real house—and you will have the best medical attention that is possible—"

Ardis was watching now. She stood with her arms folded, at the window; her white satin blouse gleamed.

"You are happy with this, Elena? You are happy, at last . . . ?" Mr. Kármán asked.

Ardis came to the sofa now and knelt beside Elena and embraced her. For a moment she said nothing. Elena could feel her heartbeat. Then Ardis said, almost laughing, as if delirious with relief, "Oh, the baby! Who's a darling little baby with all her bad dreams ending? Who's going to have a real father, a real father and a real house? And the best school in the world, so you won't ever stammer again and won't be afraid of the dark, and we're going to move into a real house, Elena, and Mr. Kármán will join us in a week—"

"A week is too short," Mr. Kármán laughed, "I wish it could be a week—but—soon, very soon we will be together—"

Elena's face opened into a smile.

Ardis laughed delightedly. She tried to hug and lift Elena, but Elena was too heavy.

Elena looked from her mother to Mr. Kármán and back to her mother again and saw that everything had changed, that everything was different; now she smiled, smiled, and her mother smiled so that her face was beautiful again. Everything had changed.

"I want to change my name to yours," Ardis said to Mr. Kármán fiercely. "Yes. It isn't just a gesture. I want Elena and myself to have your name, yes. And then someday I want to be your wife, I want to belong to you."

"Thank you," he said quietly.

"I want to get free of my old life," Ardis said, moving her arm so that the entire living room was included: the photographs, cast-off items of apparel—the white feathered hat, a single red leather glove with a half-moon cut out at the knuckles, which lay on the arm of a chair as if it were a real hand, a long golden chain that was either a necklace or a belt, lying on the window sill. "I'm an adult woman, a mother; I'm responsible for another human being. When I model clothes at the department stores, at the fashion-show luncheons, I look out with such envy at the women there—so refined, so good, well-mannered, real ladies—and I think of how I want to be like them, to get free of my past life— I want to be good. I want to change my life."

"You will change your life. It will all change," Mr. Kármán said.

"Just to have a real home. . . . I know that Elena needs it, but I need it too, almost as badly. I've been deceiving myself for years. I need stability, protection, I need to feel safe from . . . from *him*. . . ."

"*Him*? But he hasn't contacted you, has he? Hasn't threatened you?"

"No. But I keep waiting for it. . . ."

"Ardis, that man would never dare come back. Never. The police—"

"They'd arrest him, yes, but he could do harm to me before that," she said slowly. "Oh, I know it's absurd, but I keep seeing him—I mean, I think I see him—on the street, the other day driving a taxi, a man who looked exactly like him—"

"You're just very sensitive, Ardis, and you're going through a difficult time. Please don't think about him. He would never come back, never—and you'll be moving soon to another city, and I'll be coming to live with you—"

"Thank God," Ardis said.

One day they went downtown to a courthouse, and Ardis and Elena had their names changed. Now they were *Ardis Kármán* and *Elena Kármán.* Elena saw the document herself.

"What's your name, honey?" Ardis asked.

"Elena Kármán."

They went out to lunch then at a restaurant. "Do you really want . . . ? To be seen in public with me . . . ?" Ardis asked shyly.

"Yes. I have had enough of secrecy," Mr. Kármán said.

Ardis was very excited. She talked about the problems of moving—all the boxes, the crates, the reservations at the Chicago hotel—she talked about how nice they had been at the courthouse—about the houses she was going to be shown in Chicago, which Mr. Kármán had arranged—"in a lovely suburb of Chicago, right on the lake!" she told Elena. And then her attention moved warmly onto Elena and she said, "Aren't you proud of your little daughter? She really is beautiful, isn't she? With her hair cut and curled like that, her face is like a buttercup, the way her hair cups it—isn't she lovely?—do you think the other men in this restaurant are jealous of you, look how they're staring!—because you own us both, after all— Some of these men know you, don't they? What do you suppose they're thinking?"

"I don't care what anyone thinks now," Mr. Kármán said.

He handed Ardis an envelope and Ardis smiled at him as if in a trance, her eyes fixed upon his face. "Thank you . . . ," she said. She groped for her purse, not looking down, brought her purse into her lap and opened it and put the envelope inside.

"Thank you," she said.

She glanced at Elena. Elena said, "Thank you."

*

"Telephone as soon as you get to the hotel," Mr. Kármán said. "And drive carefully, Ardis. Very carefully."

"I'm a perfect driver," Ardis said. She held out her hands to show how steady they were.

"It's so late in the afternoon, I almost wish you would wait until tomorrow—"

"Oh no, no! I couldn't wait, I couldn't bear to wait another day!" Ardis said. "I'll drive very carefully. . . . Do you love us? Both of us?"

Mr. Kármán was leaning in the car window. He looked both haggard and happy. "Of course I love you and . . . and I will miss you, even for this short while . . . but I will fly up next weekend just to visit, and look at houses with you, and . . . and. . . . Elena, you will help your mother with the map? You will help your mother?"

Driving out of town, Ardis switched on the radio and began humming along with a song. That morning she had shampooed her pale orange hair and it was very fresh, very shiny. Like Elena, she wore clothes for traveling—wool slacks and a pullover sweater. Elena was so excited she stammered when she talked about the map, and Ardis laughed gently and patted her hand. Mr. Kármán had given Elena a book of maps for the entire United States, and he and she had plotted out the simple route Ardis would take to Chicago.

"Just for fun," Ardis said, "look up the map of New York State."

"New York?" Elena leafed through the book, to the N's. "Here it is."

"Do you know anything about New York City?" Ardis asked.

"No."

"Well, you will."

Elena looked at her mother. "What? Why . . . ?"

"Because that's where we're going."

"What?"

"We're going to New York."

"New York . . . ?"

"New York, yes. I've changed my mind; I don't want to go to Chicago."

"You don't want . . . ?"

"No, not Chicago. I've changed my mind. We happen to be heading the other way, sweetheart, which you would have noticed if you knew anything about the location of the sun in the sky—don't they teach you anything at school, those sad-faced bitches? We happen to be heading east."

"East?"

Elena stared out at the bright, clear winter sky and saw nothing. Her vision went in and out of focus.

"Yes, we've been heading east for the last twenty minutes," Ardis laughed. She reached over to pinch Elena's cheek. "Who's a cute little girl, eh? Who's a darling? But you don't know your directions of east and west yet, do you, or your way around the world? What's your name, eh? Is it Elena Kármán? Do you like that name? Do you know what that name is worth?"

Elena had difficulty following this. She said, "What—what are—"

"Guess," Ardis said.

"I don't—"

"Your name and my name, guess how much they're worth—our lovely last names— Guess how much."

"I—"

"Guess, honey. Choose a number and put a dollar sign in front of it."

Elena blinked out at the rushing buildings, the other cars.

"But what about Mr. Kármán . . . ?" she asked.

"I said choose a number, honey. And don't be stingy either."

"Aren't you going to c-call him tonight?"

"Just choose a number."

Elena tried to think. "A million," she said quickly.

"Too high."

Elena's mind raced. She tried to think of numbers, numbers written on a blackboard. . . .

"Try again, honey."

"A thousand . . . ?"

"Jesus, no!" Ardis laughed. "I hope I can do better than that. Can you multiply that by seventy-five, though?"

"Seventy-five times a thousand . . . ? Seventy-five thousand?"

"Seventy-five thousand *what?*" Ardis asked.

"Dollars . . . ?" Elena asked blankly.

"Not *forints,*" Ardis said.

7

They lived for four years in New York City, from 1956 until 1960.

They began in an apartment of six rooms that overlooked Central Park, on the eighth floor of an old, enormous, expensive building with plaster ceilings and antiquated molding and an elevator that reminded Elena of Mr. Kármán's apartment building; then, eighteen months later, they moved to a smaller apartment on a street that led into the park; when that lease ran out, Ardis sullenly moved herself and Elena and their things to a still smaller apartment on Third Avenue. Alarmed and angry at the way their money was dwindling, she finally sublet that apartment and moved again to a very modern high-rise apartment building on 80th Street, with thin walls and a balcony about three feet long and half a foot wide. Their two and a half rooms were classified as "luxury" and yet on the first day Elena discovered cockroaches in the kitchen.

"Kill them and shut up about it," Ardis commanded. She stood at the window and stared out at the layers of sky.

She didn't speak again until that evening, when she said, "If you could just catch on as a model . . . if you could just catch someone's eye. . . ."

From the window I could see all the people, the cars—so many separate lives passing down there, all the traffic in its parts and hunks, surging and stopping. . . . I could lean out the window and slowly fall, slowly, my balance tilting out and down and slowly I could fall, down there, into all those people.

I never fell.

When I was awake I had to think about them, so many people, it was unmanageable, I had to walk to get a bus, I went to one school and then another school and then another school, I had to memorize the combinations for the locks on my lockers, I had to memorize street names, I had to sit very still when she fixed my face or the tweezers might slide into my eye. Do you want your eye poked out, she said.

Who had time to record all the births and deaths? Who cared? Who noticed when someone fell, who was down on the street waiting with the clean-up brooms and hoses? Pictures in the newspapers could be of anyone, old pictures used again and again.

When I walked out there I never made a misstep. I numbered my steps and I walked in a rhythm from left to right, left to right, along with the sound of my heart, which I could hear perfectly. It was timed by my mother's heart. The same rhythm. When she wiped everything off my face with a strong white cream and wiped that off with a sharp, prickling, acidlike green liquid and covered that with a layer of white paste that turned to powder and contracted, I kept time with her heartbeat, I could hear it perfectly. She was saying, Our future depends on how you do tomorrow, but underneath that I could hear her heart beating, beating, which meant that I was safe.

A man approached Elena, frowning, staring, from outside the circle of lights. She could tell that he was coming to her and not to one of the other girls. He said in exasperation, "She just looks too young." He rubbed her breasts hard; he straightened up and tapped his front teeth; he said finally, "Oh, fix her up, make her bigger on top—but hurry up—come on—" and he walked away again and Elena thought *Thank God.*

Those happy accidents didn't occur every day.

She said, If you could just catch on as a model. . . .

She said, There are just too goddam many beautiful women in this city.

Her eyebrows rose and arched thinly, regally. The important bone beneath them was accentuated by a smear of white. Elena stared at herself; it looked as if the bone were showing through.

Edgy, glancing sideways at people, she noticed how they walked in the street, slowing or quickening their paces, girls her own age, with bad posture or bad skin or hems that were not even, their shoe-boots stained with salt from the sidewalk, people who picked openly at their ears and talked loudly to one another, ugly people, all of them ugly and real. For awhile she glanced at them, frightened of them. Then she stopped looking. She wasn't afraid of the city, the horns and crowds and trip-hammers; she stopped noticing it, she had memorized the route to and from school, to and from the grocery store, the drugstore, the subway.

Noise in the other apartments didn't bother her when she did her homework or watched television; sometimes Ardis pounded viciously on the ceiling with a mop handle, or went next door to yell, but Elena was not really bothered. She was happiest at home, she liked television: the screen was just the right size, all the tumult scaled down and not nightmarish, and if it swayed suddenly and exploded into dots or zigzagging lines she could just switch it off.

On Sundays Ardis was always in an excitable state: she leafed through the *New York Times Magazine,* assessing the models, figuring out their probable ages, sometimes holding the magazine up next to Elena's face and shaking her head slowly, doubtfully. She might begin the day irritated and depressed but end it optimistically, and the next morning she would drag Elena around to the modeling agencies again, with a portfolio of photographs, forcing herself to be patient and sit and wait, wait. She complained to the receptionists that back in Cleveland both she and her daughter had had a lot of work, more than they could handle. Sometimes the receptionists were bored, sometimes sympathetic, but they were all beautiful themselves, they did not look like the receptionists back in Cleveland. Ardis knew she herself was a very beautiful woman, and that a certain power resided in her face and in her body, but for some reason this power had dimmed. . . . What was wrong, what was breaking down? "Why do we stay in this damn city?" she asked the receptionists.

They didn't know.

She was given a few assignments, and Elena a few more, but in the spring and summer of 1959 they had only one high-paying session, another advertisement for skin cream. It turned out so well that Ardis was certain it was really the beginning of a new career. The advertisement was run in several of the high-circulation women's magazines and it did look good: a full-color, two-page spread in which mother and daughter held out their perfect hands and smiled their perfect smiles, both blond, with ten-inch page-boy cuts, very American and very sanitary, and a teen-aged boy, an apparent suitor, staring in awe at them both as if he could not decide between them. *Could you choose between these beauties?* A paragraph beneath the picture explained that this was indeed a mother-and-daughter, a real mother-and-daughter, but could you tell who was the mother and who was the daughter? Could you? If you looked very closely, maybe. But could you be certain?

Elena sat and gazed at the advertisement, first gazed at herself on the left—the sixteen-year-old who looked eighteen but who was really only fourteen—that is, Elena herself was fourteen—and then on the right, the thirty-nine-year-old woman who looked eighteen but who really was thirty-six, Ardis's true age. Sometimes she believed she was on the left, sometimes on the right. But no, that was her mother on the right—just the hint of a thickening beneath the eyes, but not really—you had to imagine it there—and when she glanced back at the other model, on the left, she saw the same hint of age, of an imperfection. The boy model was twenty-one but he too was sixteen years old in the picture. He looked a little older, maybe seventeen. Elena thought that his expression—of bewilderment, wonder, pleasant surprise—was overdone, but he was handsome, handsome enough. But not too handsome.

"I think your trouble is that you're too beautiful," Ardis said. "Ugly girls are coming into style. People identify with them—who gives a damn about a beautiful girl? I don't myself. Do you? Does anyone?"

"I don't know," Elena said nervously.

"Little ugly black girls are coming into style," Ardis said in disgust. She kept waiting for new assignments, after the Lily's Skin Cream success, but for some reason nothing happened. Nothing happened. She rummaged through one of the packing crates they hadn't bothered to unpack since the last move and pulled out Elena's old muskrat coat, which she had outgrown. She brushed the fur reverently. "I can sell this and my old ranch mink," she said. Elena knew her mother blamed her for their troubles, for the fact that what Ardis called the "Cleveland savings" were running out; she saw the unopened envelopes lying around—bills, letters from the bank—but if she asked her mother about money Ardis always said coldly, "Our financial state isn't your concern."

She went to five furriers and got five insulting offers for the coats. She said, "What! These skins are beautiful!" Elena stood in misery while her mother argued, then became sarcastic, tossed Elena's little muskrat coat onto the counter and said, "Take it for nothing, then, make a muff out of it!—make mittens out of it!" Finally she accepted a few hundred dollars and walked out.

"I hate this city," she said.

They walked home slowly. No, she could not manage New York. She could not accomplish anything here: couldn't get the right modeling assignments for either herself or Elena, couldn't hope to find anyone as understanding as Mr. Kármán. And she hated all the noise, the streets always under repair, buildings being demolished and sites razed and new foundations poured, air hammers, the clanking of cranes, horns always being honked. Yet she didn't want to leave. Where else could she go? Back in Pittsburgh she had a few relatives, "relatives of yours, too, Elena, but they're worse off than I am—so that's out." She knew Cleveland, had contacts there and could probably get good jobs—but Cleveland was out.

"You could try a regular job . . . an ordinary job," Elena said uncertainly.

"Sometimes I almost wish I'd gone to Chicago," Ardis said. They stood waiting quite a while for the elevator; finally they gave up and walked the six flights to their apartment. "But the thought of him mauling me was repulsive. . . . If it's one thing I can't stand," she said, "it's men mauling me. It's very annoying, it's boring. You won't like it either. You try to think about something else but you can't. Men are like machines, they're like automatic washers that must go through certain cycles, one after the other, it's all so predictable and boring . . . for women who have no imagination, who can't think of anything better to do with their lives, maybe it's all right for them, but not for someone like me."

Elena, embarrassed, did not reply.

Back in the apartment she said again, shyly, "One of the girls I know at school . . . her mother has a job. . . . She. . . ."

"Make some coffee for us, honey," Ardis said.

She sat at the formica-topped table, in an alcove that opened off the living room; she tapped her long silver fingernails impatiently. "Damn it," she said, "I should have bought a house when I had the money. Thirty, forty thousand would have gotten us a decent place somewhere, in some stupid one-horse town in Ohio or Pennsylvania, damn it; goddamn it, why did I want to come to

New York? I had such inflated plans. . . . But why didn't they work?"

She picked up a woman's fashion magazine, leafed listlessly through it, and tossed it down again.

When Elena sat across from her she said suddenly, "What are you thinking about, Elena? You have such a strange expression on your face."

"Nothing," Elena said.

"Yes, you were thinking of something. What was it? Something you don't want me to know about?"

"No. I don't remember. Nothing."

"What I said about men . . . ? Was that it?"

Elena started guiltily.

"No."

"Yes," said Ardis. "I can read your mind."

"Mother, you can't read my mind," Elena said.

"I can't?"

"Mother, that isn't possible," Elena said with a nervous laugh.

"Yes, you were thinking about men . . . and about Mr. Kármán. You liked him, didn't you? He was a good person, I liked him too . . . he was very good to us both. Men like him exist, Elena; it's a challenge to locate them. . . . Elena, do you believe in God? Do they teach you about God in school?"

"No."

"Well, do you believe in God?"

Elena hesitated. "I don't know. . . . Do you believe in God?"

"If I said I did, what then?"

Elena laughed. "Then I might believe too."

"Well, relax. I don't happen to believe in God or in anything." She raised her coffee cup slowly, thoughtfully, staring at Elena. "I believe in luck. Good and bad luck. That's a way of saying I don't believe in anything, isn't it?"

"Maybe," Elena said cautiously.

"I believe life is experimental," Ardis said. "Each person experimenting to see how far he can get. What do you think about that?"

Elena nodded. She thought she might as well agree.

"But if I told you to believe in God, the Bible and all that, you would believe, wouldn't you?" Ardis asked.

"I don't know."

"Wouldn't you? If I proved it to you?"

Elena's head swam. "Yes. If you proved it. . . ."

"Well, I could if I wanted to."

Elena nodded. She felt dizzy.

"You're very sweet, Elena," Ardis said. "Don't feel bad about the modeling—I don't think it was your fault, I think it's just this city—there are too many people here. You tried. And you're not finished yet. My philosophy is: you're not a failure until you die. And after that, who cares? We're our own ideas, we make ourselves up; some women let men make them up, invent them, fall in love with them, they're helpless to invent themselves . . . but not me, I'm nobody's idea but my own. I know who I am. I know who you are too. We'll both do well, don't worry," she said cheerfully. As Elena watched, Ardis seemed to become younger, her lips twitching up into a smile that was a surprise of a smile. Elena stared in amazement. "So, honey, I'll take your sensible advice and get a job. As you say, a regular job. An ordinary job."

"A job . . . ?"

"Yes. What's so surprising about that?"

"I . . . I didn't think you heard me."

"I hear everything," Ardis said.

The next day Elena came home from school at a quarter to four and found a note on the table: *Might be late, might have a surprise for you.* She smiled. The apartment was very peaceful, very empty. She sat down at once and did her homework, grateful not to be interrupted. Then she shampooed her hair. She noticed the time: only six. She would make her own dinner, would eat by herself; wouldn't have to listen to Ardis teasing her, picking at her, questioning her. *What are you thinking? What are you always thinking? What is that on your forehead—not a pimple?*

The apartment was quiet, peaceful. Elena wandered out to the front room, looked out the window. The telephone rang but it was a wrong number: a woman who sounded rushed, angry. Elena considered telephoning one of the girls in her class, but could not decide which one. She did not have any best friend, any close friends. She believed that other girls liked her, but they were not really friends of hers. . . .

She hadn't much appetite to eat alone, but she found something in the refrigerator—a container of yogurt, some potato salad she'd made for dinner the night before. Eating, she noticed how quiet the apartment was, how her fork clicked against the plate. A television set was on somewhere, very loud. It must have been right over her head.

After a while she brushed out her hair, brushing it slowly and methodically. She half turned, imagining her mother in the doorway—*Clean that hairbrush when you're through,* her mother would say.

She spent the evening watching television, waiting. Small jabs of panic: What if her mother didn't come back? On the eleven-o'clock news there was a picture of a young woman murdered that afternoon, in her apartment on West 58th Street. Assaulted and then strangled. *Assaulted. Strangled.* The woman was twenty-nine years old and very beautiful.

Nervously, Elena listened and heard someone yelling: an argument somewhere. A man's voice. She got up and turned the television volume louder to drown it out. Her mind skittered helplessly and came to rest on something that had happened to her a few days before—nothing important, she had not told Ardis and had hardly thought about it at the time; but now she remembered it clearly. A hefty young man in a denim jacket had bumped into her on the sidewalk, knocking her textbooks out of her arms, and he'd stood there grinning while she picked them up. She had had to bend over to pick up the books. The young man said certain words to her. He was joking, happy, in a strangely exuberant mood, as if a little drunk. But he hadn't followed her and she had walked away, not fast, and had forgotten it.

He had walked right into her.

She got up nervously and went into the bathroom. She cleaned the hairbrush in the sink and rinsed it several times to get the disinfectant out.

She went back to watch television. But she had trouble concentrating. Was it a documentary?—something about a jungle, men in a long canoe? She switched to another channel and recognized the face of James Stewart. Then a door opened and Joan Crawford came in, walking briskly, her expression stern; so Elena left that on. She sat on the sofa and watched the movie, not bothering to look away when the commercials came on. She stared at the blue-gray screen, all the bustling figures and moving mouths, until that movie came to an end and another movie began. She stared as if hypnotized, holding herself stiffly.

Finally Ardis came home: a rattle at the door, Ardis's surprised voice.

"Elena, are you still awake? It's four in the morning. Why didn't you put the safety catch on the door?"

Elena jumped up.

A man was with her mother, a stranger. He was tall, thin, morose-looking.

"This is Mr. Sadoff," Ardis said. "Mr. Sadoff, my daughter Elena."

Elena stared at him. He shook hands with her and smiled. "Very pleased," he said. There were slight dark pouches beneath his eyes.

"Elena, turn off that television, it's all buzzing and crazy lines," Ardis said. "Mr. Sadoff is my new boss. I have a job starting tomorrow night."

Mr. Sadoff nodded.

"Don't you even want to know what my job is?" Ardis asked.

Elena looked at her blankly. She was elaborate, lovely, with a headful of dark auburn curls she hadn't worn for years cascading like a mane onto her bare shoulders. She wore a cocktail dress of black satin, the neckline low, scooped out. Elena wondered for a moment if this was really her mother; this woman was mixed up with the movie she had been watching some hours ago. But of course it was her mother.

"Elena, you look like a zombie, and don't you have school tomorrow? Children just love television. I don't think it's healthy for them," Ardis said, making a *tsking* noise. "Go to bed, honey. Mr. Sadoff and I are just going to have a little nightcap. . . ."

Elena stood looking at her mother and this man, confused. Ardis pinched her cheek. "Now, off to bed! She is a lovely kid, even if I say so myself, isn't she, Mr. Sadoff?"

"Call me Robie," he said.

8

Sadoff managed a nightclub in Manhattan, not far from Times Square. He was a dog-faced man in his forties or early fifties, oddly handsome, with a dark-jowled, thin, nervous face, tall—over six feet three or four inches—always gulping with laughter and then going silent, as if life were a barrage of comic routines that had to be acknowledged and then dismissed, acknowledged because they were paid for, then dismissed because they weren't really funny.

Ardis worked as a cocktail waitress at the club—the Black Flamingo—and then as hostess, in a series of costumes of black chiffon, some with transparent skirts and transparent bodices dotted with black sequins in the shapes of flamingos, some of her own invention, because she liked to invent things for special people, she told Sadoff, and he and his club were special. She designed her own costume when she became "hostess"; she thought the club needed an atmosphere of elegance. Sadoff agreed. He was married to a girl twenty years younger than he, but he was very fond of Ardis. She explained politely to him that she was interested only in working at his club, in learning about his club. She wanted to learn about it from the inside. She was retiring from modeling—she waved away his protests—yes, she was retiring from that, and she was retiring from men as well; that was the truth, she wanted only to work seriously and she believed she could do a good job working for him. And it was true, she was an excellent waitress. He was so pleased with her that he fired the young woman who was "hostess" after Ardis had been at the club only a few weeks. He told the woman the club was entering a new phase and that she didn't contribute to it.

Ardis carried herself regally. Sadoff was proud of her.

"She's very ladylike," he told people enthusiastically in Ardis's hearing. "There's no fooling around with Ardis."

Sometimes he gave her presents—an inexpensive stole of rabbit fur, dyed an odd red-orange, some necklaces of cultured pearls, things Ardis accepted gratefully and then passed along to Elena, pointing out that they were secondhand, she was sure—maybe things stolen from Sadoff's wife's possessions? Because the Sadoffs were not happily married. Sometimes Sadoff gave Ardis a gift specifically for Elena, a charm bracelet that appeared new, in a box with "Cartier" on it, a leather shoulder bag he thought Elena could use to put her books and pencils in. "How old is Elena now? She's only about fourteen or fifteen, isn't she?" he would ask. Elena left the charm bracelet on a cafeteria table at school, where she had been sitting with some girls from her homeroom; she returned in five minutes, experimentally, and noticed that the charm bracelet was gone. The stitching on the bag came apart in a few days and she threw it out.

In 1960, Sadoff's wife began divorce proceedings against him and Sadoff decided to leave New York; he had an opportunity of buying into a nightclub in Detroit. He wanted Ardis to come along with him. He said he needed her. He was doggish, with cruel slitted eyes that moved about Ardis's body continually, always ready to burst into laughter if Ardis said something funny—around Sadoff, she soon learned to be funny—and then falling back into a kind of surprised, bewildered gloom. But he had a genuine laugh, an appreciative laugh. Sometimes Ardis's jokes made him screw up his face in a paroxysm of laughter and he had to wipe his eyes. She watched him at such times, her own face merry and animated and cautious. If he let his hand fall casually upon her bare shoulder or thigh, she moved away. No. Not her. Sadoff had been involved with most of the waitresses and the woman who had been hostess before Ardis, carrying yard-high menus with gold tassels, a lovely effortless job, and Ardis knew enough to draw away from him.

She was a businesswoman, she explained. Nothing else. She was like a man: he could trust her.

So in the end he agreed; one day he said in surprise: "You really are like a man—I can trust you."

He had become dependent upon her and he begged her to come with him to Detroit. "It won't be a dump like this," he said. "It will be a place to take pride in."

"I don't know," Ardis said slowly. "I hate to uproot my daughter. . . ."

"How old is your daughter now? Fourteen, fifteen? It might be good for her to get out of this city. The Midwest is a better environment for a child."

"Elena has friends here and she's doing so well at school," Ardis said doubtfully. In a way she thought of Elena still as fourteen; it was discouraging to remember her real age, and to be forced to automatically add twenty-two years onto that age. Ardis didn't believe in "ages" anyway, but she could not explain that to Sadoff. "She's so sensitive. . . ."

"Then let me take her out of New York. It's no place for a girl like her."

Ardis hesitated.

"Come with me. It's a new adventure," he begged.

"But my home is here. . . ."

"Home, hell! This place is nobody's home!" Sadoff fell silent, troubled. Perhaps he was thinking about his wife. Then he said eagerly, "You can help me more with the books, you know, sort of ease into that; maybe I can talk my partner into giving you a little percentage, you know . . . on top of the regular salary and the tips, you know . . . I mean. . . . Look, Ardis, we'll both make money. That's where home is."

Ardis hesitated.

I was the girl photographed in the wreckage of the plane, body intact except for the smile, which was missing. No, I was the girl photographed for my high-school graduation, with a smile, but the newspaper was using the photograph to illustrate a front-page story about a girl who had been decapitated "by an angry suitor." The decapitation took place six years after the high-school graduation but newspapers aren't allowed to publish pictures of heads without bodies. . . . But I wasn't either of these girls. No. It didn't happen. And I wasn't the woman who "plunged to her death" off a bridge but landed on a concrete abutment, which in the newspaper's front-page photograph looked ordinary and blank except for the X someone had drawn. They use the same X for all these photographs. It is the same X if you are a woman or a man, any kind of victim. It marks the spot where photography begins.

I wasn't on the front page.

I was the girl stepping out into the sunshine with two rented borzoi dogs on two leashes, the dogs' heads high and elegant, my head high and elegant, framed by twenty-inch straight blond hair in the style of the day. I came out of the club's ornate doors five or six times, smiling spontaneously for the photographers and the readers of the Amusement Section. The caption said, "Exotic guests at opening of new Pyramid Club."

The "Pyramid Club" was near the General Motors headquarters in Detroit, set back from the Boulevard, in a gigantic asphalt parking lot equipped to handle hundreds of cars. Its exterior was decorated with mosaics in the shapes of triangles and the profiles of Egyptian heads; after a disappointing initial six-month period, it began to do well, though Sadoff always complained and worried. He went over the books with Ardis, kept no secrets from her; he was a good friend, sometimes depressed but then easily cheered up; it made him happy to do favors for Ardis, so she allowed him to make the down-payment on a house so that she and her daughter could live like normal people again. It was her dream, she said, to "live like normal people." She wanted Elena to finish high school like a normal girl, not like a model or a child who had been kidnaped by her own father, a madman. "A girl who looks like Elena also has to be protected against things," Ardis said. Sadoff agreed. "At least we got her out of New York," he said.

To Elena, Ardis was always saying: "Invite girls home for dinner, why don't you. Or to stay overnight. Do kids still have slumber parties . . . ? Robie would be delighted to send over all the Coke and pretzels and things for it, anything you ask. Go ahead."

Elena always hesitated.

"You should be proud of our house," Ardis would say vaguely, zipping up the back of her tight, sparkling dress as she prepared to go to work. It was in a good section of Highland Park—"still white," as the realtor pointed out—a three-bedroom brick home on a fairly large lot. Elena liked the house very much. But she always said falteringly, "I don't know anyone yet. . . ." Then, as the months passed, she said, "I don't know anyone well enough yet. . . . I don't like anyone well enough."

"You should be proud of our house," Ardis said often.

When Elena got off the bus she always looked hungrily, eagerly, down the block to the house—yes, there it was—the house. She lived there. It was six houses from the corner and almost identical with the others, except its shutters were painted a bright cheerful yellow and Ardis's new car was always parked in the driveway, near the sidewalk, while the other driveways were always empty at this time of day. As she walked to the house Elena would say to herself silently, *White, black. White, black.* She would stare at the house and its drawn blinds and keep pace with her heartbeat, saying to herself, *White, black. White, black.* If she turned up the walk to the house on the word *white,* that meant it was indeed her house, she did live here, it wasn't a mistake.

If she turned up on the word *black,* there might be a stranger inside waiting for her.

Once when they were out shopping at a supermarket, Ardis said sharply to Elena: "Are you talking to yourself?"

"No," Elena said at once.

She was very embarrassed.

"I thought I saw your lips move. What were you saying?"

"Nothing."

"Not praying, were you?" Ardis teased.

Elena stiffened and would not answer.

"If you were praying, who were you praying to?" Ardis laughed.

Elena carried herself with her chin slightly raised, as Ardis had taught her, the skin of her throat bared regally. To prevent premature wrinkles. *You'd better take care of that face, carry it like crystal,* Ardis had said. And now Elena thought impulsively, angrily, *What a joke.*

And yet it was true.

Something could be a joke and yet true.

If she waited long enough and did not annoy her mother by defending herself, Ardis would change the topic. And in a few minutes she said, enthusiastically, "Elena, Robie wants to take us both out Saturday night. He says he's been neglecting us both, he doesn't see enough of you and wonders how you are. It would be a real treat for him, he said."

Elena recalled Sadoff's hound-dog jowls, his cool, sad, appraising stare that moved slowly around her body and came to rest in the area around her face.

"I don't want to," Elena said.

"What?"

"I don't want to," Elena said faintly.

"Unless you happen to be busy on Saturday night."

"You know I'm not busy on Saturday night."

"With all those friends of yours, all the friends you seem to have made here in Detroit," Ardis said mockingly.

"You know I'm not busy on Saturday night."

They were at the end of an aisle. But Elena, who was pushing the cart—it was wobbly, veering to the left unless she pushed hard to the right—could not think for an instant what to do. She forgot where she was. Her mind swam: should she be busy on Saturday night? Did her mother want her to be busy then? Or . . . ? Her mother wanted her to have girl friends, friends who were girls, but never any boys, never boys. No boys. No friends. But, Elena thought swiftly, shrewdly, Ardis might really be pleased she wasn't busy on Saturday night, so that Mr. Sadoff could take them out. That might be.

She couldn't decide.

"I'm going to let you decide," Ardis said, exasperated.

"Decide what?"

"Which way to turn. Which aisle."

Elena looked around. Cereal boxes, cans of soup with red and white labels. . . . She could not remember which aisle they had already gone down.

"I don't know," she said blankly.

"You're not observant. You never pay attention to your surroundings," Ardis said. "I don't think you're normal."

Elena looked from one side to the other. She was seventeen years old. She could not move. But a stranger, a woman with a small sexless child perched in her grocery cart, was right in front of her, waiting to turn into this aisle, to move between the cereal boxes and the soup cans, and it was necessary for Elena to get out of the way.

One way or the other?

It did not seem an important decision, but it was somehow important.

I thought, Am I supposed to be busy on Saturday night? My mother was smiling ironically. Disappointed. Always a little disappointed, but proud too. I was not beautiful enough; I was too beautiful. I wasn't beautiful at all. I was only pretty.

Who gives a damn about a beautiful . . .

You don't and neither does anyone else because you are not beautiful and don't run the risk.

If you saw the photograph of a dead woman in the paper, and if the face was a beautiful face you would think swiftly: Got you! But then you would reconsider and think: Tough luck! And then the third time, before your eye moved to another column, you would think: what a sad thing. . . .

You would read the rest of the paper in a good mood.

If she had friends she would have been busy on Saturday night, and safe. But she did not have friends. The other girls seemed to like her, but they were not friends. The boys could not be friends. They looked at her. Her teachers praised her because she memorized everything, she memorized what they said—sometimes even before they said it—she knew the style, the intonation. Except one day in biology class Mr. Hollander was irritated by her bright, blank face. He had asked her a question and she knew the answer. But as she sat at her desk she had been invisibly pressing each of her fingers down, her fingertips pressing into the wool of her pleated skirt; she had been counting to herself in a perfect rhythm: ONE. TWO. THREE. FOUR. FIVE. SIX. SEVEN. EIGHT. NINE. TEN. She could not answer Mr. Hollander's question until she came to the end of this, she could not even hear it. First she must finish counting, she must complete the series of numbers, in that strict rhythm, not speeding up; then she was able to hear his question, to replay it to herself. But it was almost too late; it *was* too late. He was already asking the question again of another student and Elena had to interrupt him, and so he had been irritated. Puzzled. He had stared at her.

Ardis grabbed hold of her and gave her a push. "Jesus, you're blocking the way! Can't you see she wants to get by?" With a rude swing of her head indicating the other woman, Ardis shoved Elena to the right. "I swear, you're not normal. You're going to grow up just like your father, it must be a degeneration of genes. . . . Why can't you remember anything from one minute to the next? We always go the same way in this damn store."

"I'm sorry," Elena said.

Ardis snatched a can of something off a shelf and threw it into the cart. It clattered. Then, slowly, another can came loose and rolled and fell, and another. They fell into the aisle and rolled. "Oh Jesus Christ!" Ardis cried. She jumped back innocently, out of the way.

"I'll pick them up," Elena said.

She bent and picked them up. Five cans had fallen altogether.

Canned asparagus tips. Elena carefully put them back on the shelf while her mother watched. Elena knew that her mother would forget about being angry in a few minutes. She pushed the cart along and at the end of the next aisle she remembered which way to turn.

Ardis was saying, ". . . told him you were getting excellent grades, that you didn't waste time like other girls your age. Not running around with boys, and not gawky and giggling like other girls. I hate teen-aged girls. The ones you see on the street. I hate their bad complexions and the way they use lipstick—they don't know how to use it—and the way they hang around in bunches, white or black. You're smart to stay to yourself, Elena, to keep aloof."

Elena nodded slowly.

"When I was your age I was totally independent. Of other people, of other people's ideas of me. I didn't give a damn for anybody. I didn't have any friends and I didn't want any. I never told you, but I moved out when I was thirteen, I got my first job at the age of thirteen, and paid for my own room and board . . . to get out from under my parents. . . . They were all right, I liked them, but I wanted to be independent. Turn to the right, honey, we've already been down that aisle . . . do we need coffee, instant coffee? It's this way."

"Yes," Elena said.

She hoped her mother would talk about herself now. Sometimes Ardis alluded to her own childhood, her girlhood, her marriage. But she always mentioned these topics incidentally, as illustrations of something else; and if Elena seemed too interested she would abruptly change the subject.

"Oh, low-calorie bread too," Ardis said, snapping her fingers. She was always on a diet. Elena went back to get the bread and by the time she returned Ardis had pushed the cart along, humming to herself, and turned to Elena with an appraising smile: "But you, honey, you should gain a little weight. The general public doesn't appreciate thinness . . . men don't."

Elena nodded.

"After all, you're not a model any longer; you have to make certain compromises with life."

On the way home she said suddenly, "Let's buy you a new dress, for Saturday." She drove down to Saks, humming. Elena was relieved that she was in such a good mood. Elena tried on several dresses, and Ardis chose one with a smooth fitted jersey top, blue and white stripes, and a flaring skirt; Elena had no other outfit quite like this. The material was very fine, very rich. The dress was oddly feminine, even a little showy, and it did not seem like anything Ardis might have chosen for her in the past.

Ardis stood behind her as Elena stood in front of the three-way mirror and pulled her long hair back, trying to arrange it on top of her head; stood analyzing her appearance for so long that Elena was embarrassed. She was aware of the saleswoman watching them.

"Is something wrong, Mother?" Elena asked nervously.

Her heartbeat was slow, steady. No fear. No danger. She watched her mother's calculating eyes in the mirror, saying to herself: *White, black. White, black. White.*

Ardis ignored her. After a while she released her hair and put her hands on Elena's shoulders, her gleaming fingernails on the shoulders of the striped dress, bringing her face next to Elena's. Elena saw that she was passing judgment on her, but not personally. She was not personally in danger.

"Okay," Ardis said.

On Saturday evening Sadoff drove them to the club in his new Cadillac, which he had picked up only the day before; he was very pleased with it, in an excellent mood; he smiled often and his gums looked pink, rejuvenated. He said to Elena, "Your mother says you're doing well in school, going to graduate in a few months! Time flies!"

Yes, Elena said. She was sitting between Sadoff and her mother.

"How do you like Detroit? How do the schools here compare with New York?" Sadoff asked. Elena noticed the rings he wore, one on the third finger of each hand—a large signet ring and a bulky gold ring with a raised design. "Is integration far along here?"

"Yes," Elena said.

"Well, I'm optimistic about this city myself," Sadoff said cheerfully. "I believe in integration, in the principle of it. It fits in with democracy. Are there many Negro kids in your school? You don't mind that, do you?"

"No," Elena said.

"Bet you can't wait to graduate, eh? Or—?"

Elena said nothing. Ardis laughed and said, "Elena likes school, she does very well at it. I think her vanity is flattered a little, isn't it, honey? I don't blame her. And it's an easy life, being a student . . . but that kind of life can't go on forever; the world isn't a nursery."

Sadoff chuckled. Then he sobered. "But she's just a baby, you know. She can't go out on her own."

"I suppose not," Ardis said thoughtfully.

"It's hard for a young girl," Sadoff said. "I know. My wife had a hell of a time in New York before she met me . . . the better-looking the girl, the worse a time she has. It isn't just show business but life itself. It should be the other way around but it isn't. Of course, my wife, I mean my ex-wife, is a famous bitch," Sadoff said viciously; then his tone altered, eased back to its original conversational note, and he was saying something about the night air and the economic boom the city was enjoying. He smiled at Elena, who was leaning to the right in order to have a few inches between herself and Sadoff. "You're so quiet and thoughtful," he said. "What are you thinking about?"

At the club they were seated at a table in a corner, Sadoff's favorite table, he said, because he could see everything from here. Elena had not been inside the club since she had helped with publicity for the opening, and now she did not recognize it, did not try to make sense of the noise and complications. A band was playing very loudly. There was a female singer and then a male comic, interruptions of applause and laughter, and half-shouted conversations between Sadoff and Ardis and other people who came to the table from time to time, most of them men. They carried their drinks along with them. Elena was disturbed at first to realize that her mother knew so many people, so many people. . . . Sadoff invited everyone to sit down and help him celebrate. He was celebrating the completion of the first phase of his divorce case, back in New York.

But it was going to be a complicated case and it was going to cost Sadoff many thousands of dollars. His wife was divorcing him and he had filed a countersuit. New York State law recognized only adultery as grounds for divorce; both Sadoff and his wife wanted to claim adultery charges, but Sadoff's attorney had explained to him why this was impossible. If the court believed that both Sadoff and his wife were guilty of adultery, no divorce would be granted and they would remain married. In the meantime Sadoff's wife's detectives claimed to have a taped telephone conversation between Sadoff and a woman that would be very damaging to Sadoff, but Sadoff and his attorneys believed the tape did not exist. On the other hand, Sadoff's detectives had genuine tapes of his wife's conversations with several men, though of course he could not use them if he himself wanted the divorce to go through . . . though maybe he would use them, maybe he would, to block her demands for alimony and an extravagant settlement. . . . And on and on. Elena gauged when it was time to smile or to appear sympathetic by her mother's reactions, which were a little more emphatic than usual, as if Ardis were aware of Elena's observation. Elena could see herself faintly, or someone who looked like her, in a frosted mirror not far away: the head held high, stiffly, the head of blond hair like a wire cloud around her head. She checked the image every few minutes to make sure it was still there.

Near the end of the evening two men came to their table. Sadoff jumped to his feet. He had been drinking for hours and he nearly fell forward onto the table, but he recovered himself and was alert and sociable; he said excitedly, "Hello, John! And Marvin Howe—isn't it? We've never met but I know you from your pictures— Very pleased to meet you, sit down, please sit down!"

The men shook hands with Ardis and Elena, stooping over them.

"Very honored. Honored," Howe said.

He was a large, broad-shouldered, handsome man perhaps in his forties, stylishly dressed. The other man, whose name was Potter, was balding, impish, one of Sadoff's Detroit attorneys; the talk was immediately about a court case. Elena listened to the conversation but could not see the connection among these men. Howe was from St. Louis; no, he had just flown back from St. Louis. Evidently he was a lawyer too. He had just won a case that afternoon.

"Congratulations," Sadoff said. "We can help you celebrate. Is it something we should know about?"

"It didn't get much publicity up here," Howe said.

"Sure it did," Potter said. "It got carried in last Sunday's paper, a feature article. Don't you remember?—the one where the man was found on the street, twelve stories down, and they tried to blame the wife and her boy friend. But it turned out they had no case. Carl Goldsmith, the man who owned the cereal business."

"Goldsmith, yes, I did read about that," Sadoff said excitedly. "So you won it, Mr. Howe? They were acquitted?"

"Mrs. Goldsmith was my client and *she* was acquitted," Howe said. "Her friend was found guilty of second-degree murder."

"Goldsmith was found dead on the street, yes, I read about that," Sadoff said. "The coroner said he had been drunk, he was all battered up, yeah, it must have been messy. But you won it for the wife, eh? And she collects? What was it, a million-dollar policy?—she collects the insurance, eh?"

"That's the usual arrangement when a woman's husband dies and has left an insurance policy naming her as his beneficiary, isn't it?" Howe asked.

"How much of the insurance money will she get to keep?" Sadoff asked gaily. "I read it was a million-dollar policy!"

Howe ignored this question. He gave his order to a waiter and ignored Sadoff, who was still leaning forward, as if poised over an abyss, trembling, swaying. Elena saw in the mirror how he wiped at his nose, how his face darkened into an instant melancholy. The other attorney, Potter, changed the subject skillfully and they began to talk about some local murders, a chain-reaction series of murders set off by a dope trader's encroachment into someone else's territory, thirteen murders so far, "and it's just gaining momentum, it's going to spread out like a Malthusian tumor," Potter said with zest. Elena stopped listening, but her head rang with all the voices. She tried to isolate her own heartbeat, to check it.

After a while Sadoff recovered from being snubbed and was laughing again, more loudly than anyone else. He was leaning against Elena. At one point, as if absent-mindedly, he slid his arm around behind her on the black leather rim of their seat. Ardis talked with the men, asking questions, shaking ashes from her cigarette into the ashtray—it was a genuine camel's hoof, scooped out and sanitized and made functional. It was quite large.

Then the conversation seemed to shift, to soften. Elena looked up and saw that Marvin Howe was smiling broadly at something Ardis was saying. It must have been an anecdote about Elena herself, because, bringing the story to a close, Ardis squeezed Elena's hand and brought her face close to hers, as if the two of them were on television. "—but we decided against it, in spite of the money. I don't think that California is a healthy place, I mean for a girl like my daughter. Things disintegrate there."

The men agreed. They were looking frankly, curiously, at Elena. But they stared impersonally, as if she weren't even present; it was not rude.

"Women who make films acquire a certain hardness," Howe said thoughtfully. "I mean physically, a hardness in the face, around the eyes. A calculating expression. I think it's because everything in their lives is accelerated, like film: they run through too many lives, too many people. It would be unfortunate if your daughter got like that."

"Yes, it would, Elena is so sweet," Ardis said. "Competition would destroy her. She just isn't competitive. She has led a very sheltered life. . . ."

Elena smiled vaguely. Really, it did not concern her. She was not embarrassed. In her head she began to go through all the rooms she had slept in, moving across the rooms slowly, to the beds, lying down on the beds and staring at the ceilings, the perpetual ceilings. . . . She worked backward from the room she lived in now: backward, slowly backward. She was in no hurry. But another room pushed into her consciousness, and she had to accept it; she accepted it fondly, impersonally, it was just another room. With another ceiling. Then suddenly she was lying beneath three ceilings at once. This would have frightened her if she had been alone, but with so many people around her, talking and grinning, she could not show any alarm and maintained the same three-inch smile. She was in no danger.

Now the subject was the St. Louis case again: a prosecution witness who had turned out to be a police witness, paid to testify. But hard for Howe to crack, because the man was from out of state; he had been boyish and popular with the jury until Howe had managed to break him down. . . . They all congratulated Howe again. Then Sadoff began to joke about his own troubles. People laughed. It seemed that Mme. Trottier, the wife of the French consul, had walked through the plate-glass door of the club some months ago, though the door was clearly marked with gold leaf—"Should I have painted a sign on it, DOOR, BEWARE OF DOOR?" Sadoff cried—and cut herself so badly that it took twenty-five stitches to sew her up. She was suing the Pyramid Club, Sadoff and his partner, for forty thousand dollars. "The scar is an improvement; she should pay us," Sadoff said. Then, he said, only a week later two customers had tried to drive out of the parking lot at the same time, very early in the morning, and had smashed each other's cars. The club was being sued by both drivers, because one of the parking-lot floodlights had burned out at the rear of the lot. But Sadoff and his partner were themselves initiating a lawsuit, through Mr. Potter, against a construction firm that had never adequately completed one wing of the club, and now a countersuit had been started against them by the president of that firm for alleged slander. Last year a complicated legal action had been started by the club against a famous nightclub comedian who had walked out on the second evening of a week's run, claiming that the Detroit audience was too drunk to appreciate his routine and that he would not perform; the club's owner, Mr. Sadoff's partner, had sued for breach of contract, but was being in turn sued by the comedian and his agent for failure to live up to all the terms of the comedian's contract, which specified a dressing room of a certain size—which the builders had never finished. "They say he's rotting away in a so-called health farm out in California and I don't give a damn," Sadoff said bluntly. "He never made me laugh much. I hope he's insured."

Howe laughed as if surprised, startled. He finished his drink. Elena noticed that he drank quickly, as if wanting to get each glass emptied.

Sadoff said, "It's an honor to meet you in person, Mr. Howe. I've never met a genius before. Everyone I know says you're a genius, but I don't want to embarrass you. I like people to relax and be themselves, you know, be incognito in my place at any time. But when I murder my wife I hope you'll defend me," he said, barking with laughter.

"Don't talk like that," Howe said.

"Oh, it's just a joke, I like to make jokes," Sadoff said. His face sagged again. "I didn't mean it," he said.

"Do you take on a lot of cases at once?" Ardis asked Howe, as if embarrassed for Sadoff. She was energetic and very pretty. "I've read about your work and I've often wondered."

"I have a number of associates in different parts of the country," Howe said. "They do much of the work for me, research work. . . . I show up for the pretrial motions and maybe a few times during the preparation, then when the trial begins. I'll probably have to start slowing down with age," he said, smiling at Ardis. He smiled also at Elena, his glance sliding from Ardis's face to Elena's.

"No, you won't, a man like you will never slow down," Ardis said. It was a spontaneous, conversational remark—half shouted because of the din—and yet it was strange, surprising. Ardis said, "But your family—it must be difficult for them—you're always traveling, and the publicity— How has your wife adjusted to your work?"

"I'm divorced," Howe said. "I haven't seen my wife for fifteen years."

"I'm sorry," Ardis said at once.

Howe shrugged his shoulders.

"Can I ask you one thing?—or maybe it's too personal?" Ardis asked. "What is your fee?"

"That isn't personal at all, that's professional," Howe said. "But I can't answer you. I charge anything from zero to over a million—whatever I can get. Whatever the market will bear, and anything in between."

"Over a million . . . ?" Sadoff said. "Is that often? Do you collect?"

"Eventually."

"Oh, eventually—? Then not right away? Then there's sometimes disagreement, a fight over the fee?" Sadoff asked. "What do you do in that case?"

"We collect eventually."

Elena was listening to him, though close against her eyes was a vision of something oppressive, incomplete, not quite imagined, a ceiling pressing low, easing down upon her—she could not help but listen to Howe's words, his voice breaking through the words. She began to look at him. The ceiling faded. It gave way to him, to his face. He seemed to be watching her through the ceiling and then the ceiling faded.

His suit was almost white, cream-colored, cut in a youthful

style. His shirt was Chinese-red silk and his tie was made of a rich satin material, so shiny that it had no color at all. It was held in place by a diamond stickpin. The diamond gleamed. Like his face, it gleamed, it was public, meant to be looked at. As he talked he moved his shoulders restlessly inside the suit coat; he kept shifting his weight, as if crossing and uncrossing his legs under the table.

His skin seemed blotched, as if papered or pasted over. He kept laughing, creases came and went in that face. There was a tension in him, but it seemed to be under control. His eyes were heavy lidded, he had Sadoff's look of cunning, but it was a warm, quick cunning, not reptilian and perplexed like Sadoff's.

"You won't say then whether she was innocent or guilty . . . ?" Ardis asked.

"Innocent."

"Yes, I know, she was found innocent by the jury, but. . . ."

Howe laughed irritably. "If she was acquitted of the charges by the jury, then she was acquitted of the charges. She is innocent."

"But did she *do* it?"

Potter interrupted with a laugh, "Ardis, there is no point to that question. That isn't even a question."

"Why not?" Ardis said.

"The law has nothing to do with history, it doesn't replay history and make it permanent, it doesn't provide us with scientific sensory proof of anything," Howe said. "It finds for the defendant or for the prosecution."

"But you defend guilty people."

"No. Never."

"You never defend murderers, never—?" Ardis asked in exasperation.

"There are no guilty people. The law establishes their guilt, it establishes whether they have violated a law, the decision becomes a matter of public record and you can look it up. As for murderers—who are murderers? What do you mean by murderers?"

Ardis laughed, but her laughter was not really convincing. Elena felt the odd, nervous tension in her mother; she did not understand why Ardis was talking like this. "You don't understand," she said. "I'm asking you whether you would knowingly defend a—"

"*You* don't understand," Howe said. "There are no guilty people under American law, not until someone finds them guilty."

"I don't believe that," Ardis said hotly. "I reject that. Men are guilty of all kinds of things—crimes—I know they are—I *know*. People commit crimes and they are guilty whether anyone catches them or not, whether they stand trial or not. We all know this. The murderers should be punished. They should all be punished."

Howe shook his head.

"No? What do you mean?" Ardis asked. "That there are no murders, no crimes?—nothing?"

"I'm not a judge. I don't judge. I defend; I'm an officer of the court and my work is to defend accused people. I don't make judgments, I don't prosecute, I don't execute. Would you like to do that?—execute? Would you like that part of the law?"

Ardis stared at him. Then she seemed to come back to herself, to remember where she was.

"We all have different roles in . . . in life," Potter said hesitantly. "Is that what you mean, Marvin? I think that's what he means."

"You'd like the executing role," Howe said to Ardis, but sociably, smiling at her. Elena saw in a flash how handsome he was, smiling at her mother like that. "Why don't you answer? You can tell the truth."

Ardis laughed and put out her cigarette in the ashtray. The hollowed-out hoof skidded a few inches across the table; Ardis caught it and steadied it.

"I will tell the truth, I always tell the truth," Ardis said. "I believe crime should be punished, that criminals should be punished. I don't think we have to wait for decrees, to know what crime is. . . . As for executing people, no, why should I execute anyone? There are executioners. There are paid executioners."

". . . there are paid executioners."

"Yes, that's true," Howe said slowly. "Some of us had hoped they might be out of work in a few years . . . since capital punishment is illegal, after all. . . ."

Ardis laughed angrily. "Illegal! That's ridiculous!"

". . . it's contrary to the Constitution," Howe said.

"Is that true? Is it?" Sadoff asked. His face showed a quick, sorrowful excitement, as if he were not really interested in this question but only in re-establishing himself in the conversation. ". . . if he says so, it must be true; he's a genius; he's one of our few Detroit geniuses. . . . As I said before, if I ever murder my—" He broke off with another bark of laughter, confused and embarrassed.

"Illegal, is it? Capital punishment?" Ardis asked ironically. "I thought you said nothing could be illegal, Mr. Howe? How could the executioners be guilty of anything, if all they did was kill people?—or the judges, or anyone else—in fact, *everyone* else in the country—how could they be guilty, please tell us, if they are never brought to trial—?"

"You're right, you're right," Howe laughed. He glanced at Ardis with a shrewd, half-hostile, half-admiring look. "Yes, you're right, there will always be paid executioners, of the kind you mean. Always. Constitutional or unconstitutional, the executions will continue. . . . You're quite right, you speak with the voice of absolute authority, the spirit of the folk, the instincts behind all the words, the books, the law."

For a while Ardis did not reply. Elena felt how tense she was, how keenly excited—as if she might at any moment do anything, say anything. It was dizzying, this freedom. Ardis's eyes moved around the edge of the table, as if measuring it. And then everything softened in her face, seemed to become blurred and chastised.

She shook her head as if she hadn't understood, as if it were too complicated for her.

"Women don't understand the law," she said.

"Don't you?" Howe asked. "A person commits a certain act, at a certain point in time, and that time remains fixed while he evolves. That time is lost. It can't be recovered. We have only consequences to go by, a multiplication of possibilities; we can't experience the past. Even the man who is found guilty of murder and is therefore a murderer under the law, is not the same man who committed the act that was judged to be an act of murder. The murderer evolves. The act is the same, it's fixed in time, but the murderer is no longer the same person. His soul may be altered by the simple contemplation of what he did, which is part of what he is; he is a consequence of his own action. But he wouldn't experience this contemplation if it weren't for the law."

Everyone sat in silence. From another part of the club came a wave of applause.

Ardis said softly, "And you have your place in it?—you have a certain place in it, which you believe in, don't you?—it isn't just for money, is it?"

"We all have our places in it, we aren't free of it at any time," Howe said bluntly. "Even if we claim not to understand it."

"Yes, ignorance of the law is no excuse!" Sadoff said. He cleared his throat. He said, "Sounds as if you get very involved with your work, your clients, Mr. Howe. Sounds as if they really get their money's worth. Oh, no offense," he said nervously, waving his hands. "I've had a little to drink tonight . . . celebrating. . . . Glad to help you celebrate your very good luck on the Goldsmith case. . . . Everyone is proud of you back in Detroit. . . ."

"It wasn't good luck," Howe said.

"Oh no, not good luck, I mean your good work . . . however it turned out."

"Thank you," Howe said.

"What are you going to do next?" Sadoff asked. Almost against his will he kept talking, dreading Howe and yet unable to stop. Elena sensed this, watching Howe. She studied his face while he spoke, his overlarge, perspiring face: it seemed almost too large a face to be understood. He was telling them about a case in collaboration with a Chicago attorney, a case that did not excite him; then about a challenging case, a twenty-two-year-old soldier charged with shooting a young girl in the Philippines, near his Army base. He and another soldier had forced the girl to stand with empty beer cans on her head for target practice; the young man had shot the girl through the left eye.

"The Army is putting up twenty-five dollars a day for his defense," Howe said.

"I don't want to hear about that," Ardis said.

"It's just an event that became visible," Howe said, shrugging his big shoulders. "It didn't bother you when it was invisible."

"What do you mean?"

"Things move from invisibility to visibility," he said slowly. "There are tremendous forces, like hurricanes or floods, that people have inside them. Sometimes there is a break and the force rushes out. It can't be stopped. . . . But then there's calm again. It's as if there were terrible ghosts inside us that were always prodding and testing our skins, looking for weaknesses. Then one day they rush out into the world, outside us. And so a 'crime' is committed. And yet everyone is innocent until the crime he has committed is given a name. Until then he's innocent."

Elena said suddenly, "Everyone is innocent . . . ?"

He looked at her in surprise.

"Everyone is the same. Everyone is innocent . . . ?" Elena asked.

"Under the law, yes. Yes. As long as we stay invisible."

He spoke courteously to her, but he did not smile. His lips tensed.

"Not just the bad people, but the people they do it to . . . the crimes to . . . ?" Elena said slowly, falteringly. She stared at Howe intensely; it was the first time she had spoken and she was aware of everyone looking at her in surprise. Howe himself seemed embarrassed. ". . . those people . . . they are innocent too? Even though they never get put on trial . . . ? I mean the victims. . . . They're innocent too . . . ?"

Howe looked at her. He did not answer, as if he hadn't understood or even heard her question. Over his shoulder the mirror was blurred, smoky, empty: it did not show any image of Elena.

Ardis tapped her long fingernails against the table.

"Come with me, Elena. Excuse us please," she said, getting to her feet.

Elena rose slowly, uncertainly. But she had to follow Ardis.

The restroom was decorated in black and gold wallpaper, with large clay urns and electric lights in the shape of flaming torches; it smelled of incense. Ardis waited until two women, talking loudly, left and then she said to Elena: "What are you doing?"

Elena half smiled, frightened.

"No, don't play innocent: What are you doing? Why did you talk like that?"

"I wanted to know—"

"Wanted to know what? What? Are you crazy, talking like that? Well, maybe they'll just think you're drunk. My God! You are so strange, so unreliable. . . ."

Ardis approached her, frowning.

Elena watched her guiltily.

"What are you thinking, Elena?"

"Thinking? About what?"

"Don't play innocent, please. You're not a child. I asked you: What are you thinking?"

"Nothing."

"No. Don't lie. What have you been thinking about tonight at the table? Since those two men joined us?"

"What–? I don't know– I don't know," Elena said helplessly.

"Don't lie to me, please. It's an insult to me. I know what you haven't been thinking about: Mr. Sadoff. You haven't been thinking about him, have you?"

Elena stared blankly.

"You haven't been thinking about the future, have you?–about when you graduate from school? Are you so self-centered you assume I will support you forever, a grown-up healthy girl like yourself? Seventy-eight dollars for that dress–there you stand wearing it, a lovely dress like that, and you simply absorb it, you absorb the gift of it, without thinking of where it came from. You know nothing, you're aware of nothing! Do you think life is a continual party, with all the presents going to you?"

"I–"

"You're selfish to think of no one but yourself. You shut other people out–you've shut Mr. Sadoff out completely– You wouldn't even remember to thank him for tonight, would you, if I didn't tell you?"

Elena felt tears gather sharply in her eyes. But no. No. She would not cry. No. She said, "Mother, I–"

"Shut up. I know what you're going to say–*you're sorry*–you're always sorry–"

"No, Mother–"

"*Mother, Mother!* It's so insulting to me, that you should try to manipulate me! What are you trying to do?"

"The other one, not Sadoff–"

"What?"

"If I have to–if you–if you want me to– If I–"

"What? What are you trying to tell me?"

"The other one–Marvin Howe–Howe– He– I could–"

Then, suddenly, Ardis was everywhere in the black and gold room, in the dense perfume; her laughter was part of the music piped in overhead, the mechanical clashing of cymbals. She took hold of Elena by the shoulders and shook her once, twice, in a kind of final exasperation. "Marvin Howe!" she exclaimed. Rudely, bluntly, she laughed. Her face was very close to Elena's. "Marvin Howe, is it? Howe? So famous he's written up in magazines—a millionaire—he has warehouses with things stashed away—furniture and fur coats and cars and television sets—loot from his clients—he has his own plane, did you know that?—did you sense that? Marvin Howe! You say his name as if you knew him, you're like one of his evil clients crying out his name to be saved—he's an evil man himself, and I—I—"

She pushed Elena away. Angrily she took a cigarette out of her purse, she lit it, she wiped at her nose in a gesture that reminded Elena of Sadoff. . . . Then she looked across the smoky little room at Elena, who stood waiting.

"You have too much of an imagination," Ardis said. "It's too much for you. You'd need help. You could never keep up with your own imagination, you'd need help, wouldn't you? Wouldn't you?"

Elena did not know how to answer.

9

She laughed and said, You have such an imagination! And I would have to smile against my will, because she teased me into smiling—the two of us brought up close together, walking by each other in the corridor of the house, meeting in the kitchen. When the telephone rang she went to it. She put her hand over the receiver and said, Elena, go into the other room—

Then she would say afterward, With all your secrets you might not know that other people can have secrets too, and I scanned her face to see— What did it mean? What did it mean? When would it happen?

I didn't ask.

One night he took my hand because the finger had been hurt—the car door had happened to close on it—he stared at the blood around the edge of the nail. My face was bright and hot. He asked me something, I couldn't hear, my face was so strange—he asked me about the finger, the pain—and I was ashamed, I couldn't answer, I wanted him to forget about it. I didn't feel any pain, I couldn't concentrate on pain. I didn't feel anything except the way he held my hand, another person's skin against mine. It must hurt, he said, why don't you cry if it hurts—

I didn't cry.

They met Marvin Howe at the end of April. By the following Monday Elena had stopped thinking about him. She did not think of him at all. She came across the name "Martin Howe" somewhere and for a moment she believed that was the man she had met: then she remembered that he had had a different name. She forgot his face but remembered the shape of it, its presence. When she closed her eyes she saw or felt a hazy, powerful oval that might have been the fading glare of the sun on the inside of the eye, fading even while she tried to recover it; if she tried to bring it back, she could not.

In the back of her mind, in other rooms, she knew her life was being prepared. She knew it the way she knew the rhythm of her heart: it kept going, kept going, it did not betray her. The way her mother might suddenly say, "Come on, let's wash your hair," a sudden tender strange statement—when Ardis was dressed to go out, had only a few minutes—the way Ardis would talk, idly, cheerfully, about the need for a change in her life: "I can't do any more over there with the club, it doesn't inspire me. And this house: It's ugly. It's worse during the day." Ardis began to talk about television work; she had a friend who directed a television station. "We all need new adventures," she said.

Elena did all the housework. When she came home from school she needed to put school out of her mind, so she worked. Often Ardis was not home. So she vacuumed the rooms, slowly and methodically, she washed the dishes, grateful for the quiet mindless hypnotic ritual of washing dishes in miniature white bubbles, rinsing them dry, reaching in her pink rubber gloves for dishes beneath the surface of the water and guessing, knowing, exactly which dish it would be, rarely making a mistake. . . . To predict the exact dish was a kind of magic. She knew them all, had memorized them; when there were only two people in the house, the same ten or twelve dishes were used constantly. It was a kind of magic, knowing these things. So she was disturbed when occasionally she picked up a dish and brought it out of the water and saw it was something she had not predicted.

She didn't want to think about the high school, the halls and stairs and high-ceilinged rooms, the girls' lavatory, the locker room, the antiquated gymnasium, the other students. *Just ignore them,* Ardis told her. Once Ardis saw her standing alone, in a kind of trance, and her face must have shown her sorrow because Ardis had come to her and touched her, waking her. And she had not teased her, had not said anything about Elena's secrecy. She had guessed it was school. *Just ignore them,* she said.

Elena knew she was safe, that her life was being prepared, arranged, and yet she was frightened by the complex noises of the school, the complex faces, relationships, the pounding of feet on the old stairs, the accidental touch of other people. They were her own age, but somehow older. Two things happened to her but she told Ardis about only one of them.

She was putting her things away in her gym locker one morning, after gym class, when her billfold somehow fell out of her purse and a number of coins rolled on the floor. Three other girls were nearby, two white girls and one black girl. One of the white girls bent over with a grunt and picked up a coin that had rolled near her and tossed it back to Elena. The black girl, a small, trim, very dark girl who was always joking, put her foot down over some of the coins and stared expressionlessly at Elena. Elena tried to smile, automatically. "Whatcha gonna do?" the girl asked. The other girls laughed.

Elena didn't know what to do.

"You want your money, whatcha gonna do about it?" the girl said.

Elena tried to smile again. But she couldn't smile. She began to speak and heard herself say faintly, "You can have it . . . it's all right."

The girl blinked in amazement.

She turned away and Elena said, "No, you . . . you can have it . . . it's all right . . . I. . . . Please take the money. . . ."

The girl slammed her locker shut, so hard it bounced open again. Elena looked down at the coins: two pennies and a quarter. "Go fuck yourself, you big-deal high-class bitch," the girl said. She walked away and the two white girls giggled wildly, not looking at Elena, who remained standing there for a while, even after the other girls left and the locker room was empty.

She was late to her next class.

Ardis said of this: "Don't mix with niggers, and that kind of damn degrading thing won't happen to you."

One day a boy grabbed her in the hall and rubbed himself against her; he reached out and yanked her over to him and grappled with her while the other boys laughed—Elena smelled whiskey—she was too confused to know what to do—she tried to push him away but she was too weak, frightened. A few girls who were standing nearby hurried away. Someone caught her from behind, sliding his forearm beneath her chin, almost choking her. She struggled, she tried to get free, clawing at his arm. The boys were close around her, laughing. She heard the excitement in their laughter and she seemed to go dead, all sensation flowed out of her, her brain went dead, black—

The boys ran away. A man was talking to her, down into her face, and Elena's hand fumbled against the front of her blouse, which had been ripped. But she held it closed. She stood very calmly, very quietly, she said, "No, I'm all right, it's all right." The man was a teacher in the vocational arts program, a tall burly man. He was trying to comfort her but Elena said politely, "I'm all right."

She didn't remember if the boys were white or black.

Early in May, Elena walked into the house and her mother was waiting for her. She was sitting on the sofa, waiting. Elena's heart began to pound. "I was talking to someone today, just this afternoon," Ardis said. "You remember Marvin Howe. . . ." *I knew what it was but I wasn't going to do it.* "Actually, he has been calling quite often but I didn't let him talk to you," Ardis said. "It's a very awkward situation for me . . . because of course I'm responsible for you, and he's so much older. . . . And Robie, who knows more than I do, has said certain things . . . about Mr. Howe's background . . . and . . . and of course it's always an awkward thing for a mother to. . . . I told him how sheltered your life has been, I told him I couldn't let him see you, it wouldn't be right. He has telephoned several times but I didn't want to alarm you. . . ." Elena stared at her mother's face but it was not readable. It was not yet readable.

Ardis laughed suddenly. "Do you ever notice anyone following you, Elena?"

"What? Following me?"

"Yes, on the street or on the bus—do you?"

"I don't know. No."

"But you're not very aware of other people, you probably wouldn't notice. . . . You walk around in such a dream, sometimes I wonder what you really see," Ardis said, with a half-pitying, tender smile.

"Who would be following me?" Elena asked in amazement. "My father—?"

"Your father!" Ardis laughed.

"But—"

In the past Ardis had often spoken of the danger of Elena's father returning, of how he would want revenge: she believed she had seen him, or someone who looked like him, once in a department store, and once in a newspaper photograph of some anonymous men in a tavern who were congratulating an Irish Sweepstakes winner. Whenever this happened Ardis was quite shaken. But now she dismissed the idea scornfully.

"And the telephone tapped? Would your father be doing that?"

"Is the telephone tapped . . . ? I don't understand," Elena said dizzily.

Ardis came to her and held her face, her cool, soft hands framing Elena's face. Elena held her breath: but she was safe.

"You are so sweet, so innocent," Ardis laughed.

Now her face was readable.

10

I started to laugh but not so she could hear. We were facing the mirror. She put a towel over my shoulders and wiped my face clean, wiped everything off, hard. Then my face was like the opening of a dream: when everything is experimental.

She took a comb and parted my hair down the middle, the

center of my skull. Long hair, long blond hair. I wanted to laugh because I thought of how it might look dyed black. If she left me alone for half an hour I would dye it black. But that wouldn't happen.

She stood behind me and I saw her two hands framing my head, my face, I felt her fingers beneath my jaws, firm. She was talking to me, instructing me. I could feel the love, the strength, flowing out of her and into me.

You are so beautiful, she said, you're at the center of the world. She stared and said, Elena, you are at the center of all the adventures, you are what men think about . . . women dream about you . . . about you. Think of the statues, the famous statues made of stone, Elena, think of how perfect they are, the peace in them. . . . They aren't like the rest of the world, where people are fighting one another. I'm in that world, I know it, I belong to that world; but you're at the center, the center where everything is at peace. Remember this.

I looked down upon my own body and saw that it had gone into stone, and the folds of my dress had become the creased folds of a gown. Such a body does not even need a head. I could see my own arms, what my arms had become, absolutely at rest. My mother stood behind me, holding me in her arms, which had gone into stone also. We had no weight, we were floating, we were half lying in space. We were gazing out into the distance or into time, into the future, we were both at the center of time and nothing could disturb us. People staring at us could not disturb us. . . . I was happy because I could feel her joy, the joy of her arms holding me. And I lay back lightly against her. There was no danger.

Afterward he said, Do you miss her? do you resent me for keeping her from you? and I told him no. I didn't miss her because she was still with me.

When they turned into the drive a large shape darted toward the car—a dog, not barking, but running silently alongside the car, its tongue lolling. The silence of the dog, its large, intelligent head, its stiffened ears, seemed to Elena something terrible. But Marvin Howe said to them: "That's a beautiful animal, isn't it? Absolutely infallible."

Five or six German shepherds ran up to the car, leaping and whining for attention. Howe told them to keep back and they backed away, panting, sniffing, while Elena and Ardis got out of the car. The dogs were shuddering with excitement.

"Because they see you're with me, they accept you at once," Howe explained. "They would never hurt you. They're infallible."

The house was like a fortress, illuminated by floodlights, its ground-floor windows protected by thin curved iron bars. A cool wind blew toward them from the lake. The dogs had begun to bark in short eager yips, following them up the walk to the house. Ardis was asking Marvin Howe something about the dogs, but Elena could hear a certain strained, almost timorous quality in her mother's voice. *The dogs wouldn't kill?—wouldn't injure anyone?* she asked. *They're trained not to kill,* Howe had answered carefully.

Elena looked up to see the darkened second and third floors of the house: darkened windows. Ivy grew in thick, wild patches on the stone sides of the house, even over a few of the windows. Someone took Elena's arm—it was Marvin Howe—and pointed out a coat of arms above the doorway, an antique piece of heraldry brought from England. A unicorn and a bear, several men, a single man on a large white horse. He was explaining the symbols and Elena stared up, obediently, very conscious of his touching her. "I came out of nowhere myself," Howe was saying, "and that's why I respect tradition so much. History—a long unbroken recorded history—English history and English law—I can't explain what such things mean to me."

They passed between thick stone columns, into the house and along a passageway. The dogs rushed in behind them and then around them, panting, whimpering with delight, leading the way. Marvin Howe was still talking, in a grave, almost reverent voice, explaining to Elena and her mother how he had yearned for this house—this particular house—for many years, how he had coveted it, almost violently, and how, at last, he had been able to buy it at auction—at the age of thirty, the exact age he had set for himself to "step up into his real life." Elena did not understand, but she said nothing; Ardis said nothing either.

He came between us and frightened her: I think that was why I began to love him.

They spent the evening in a room that confused and dazzled Elena: though she looked slowly at the things in it, though she tried to make sense of the various arrangements and objects, there was so much in it unfamiliar to her that she kept losing her way, she felt childlike and intimidated. But this was a kind of protection; she could sit in silence, knowing exactly what she looked like on the outside, in utter control of her face and even the vision of herself that would be stimulated in anyone's brain, womanly and childlike at once, paying only vague attention to what Marvin Howe and her mother were saying.

A few yards away one of the dogs lay chewing at a large, bare bone, slobbering onto the carpet between its forelegs, whining with pleasure.

The room was not very large but its ceiling was distant, oval shaped, and from its center hung a chandelier. The crystal pieces were motionless and yet seemed to Elena always about to move, to twist; she watched them. The walls were high, paneled in a kind of dark smooth wood, shadowy in part, gleaming in part, as if there were reflections of people or perhaps even people themselves, strangers, inside the wood, beneath the perfect surface of the wood, watching. Howe had told them, in triumph, of his outbidding everyone for this house: outbidding even the man who should have inherited it. The house and many of its ornamental features had been brought over from England at the very end of the nineteenth century, reassembled here, put together by carpenters and craftsmen also brought from England.

"For a boy from Oklahoma. . . ." Howe laughed.

The room was filled with furniture and mirrors and pictures inside carved wooden frames. There was so much that Elena's eye kept moving helplessly from object to object, sliding along a table to the corner of a painting, drawn to the painting itself: dark oils, a stormy sky, a ship shooting up the crest of a wave as if with the force of a rocket—was this beautiful or ugly?—was it expensive? On the marble mantelpiece was a bust, a woman's head, on a kind of pedestal, a very plain, smooth face with blank smooth eyes.

"I'll be frank with you," Howe was saying. "If you've felt any curiosity about me—and I wouldn't blame you—" he laughed, "you will already know about as much as you need to know. If you've done any research, I mean." Ardis laughed nervously. Yes, she had done research: she had spent a day at the Detroit library, looking up information on "Marvin Howe." She had brought home a stack of Xeroxed pages, gloating, incredulous;

she had forced Elena to read through them before even allowing her to take off her coat. "Then you know I was born in 1919 in the country outside Tulsa—by 'outside' I mean about a hundred miles west—and my family was dirt poor, and they're all dead; I treated them well while they were alive, so I feel no guilt about them. You have to treat human beings with that in mind. You know that, don't you?" he asked. Ardis agreed at once. Elena agreed. "All my life I knew by instinct how the dead reach out for the living, how you must be careful to prepare for the deaths of those near you. Of those who love you. Your own death—that's inconsequential; it's these other deaths you must anticipate. Otherwise you will suffer terrible remorse. I knew this by instinct, the way I know most things, but in my work—dealing with people who have suffered the deaths of others, usually close to them, and usually not accidental or natural deaths—I came to know just how true this is."

Ardis was sitting in a gilt-framed chair, not quite relaxed, leaning forward to listen. Though Howe spoke slowly and clearly, as if conscious of the value of his words, there was this odd pressure in everyone—even Elena—to push a little forward, to concentrate on his words and on his face. Yet Elena found herself thinking suddenly of dyeing her hair black: she could almost see, superimposed on Howe's face, the white tile walls of the bathroom at home, and then the sink, the black dye she would get from a drugstore, the warm water in the bowl, the noise the faucets would make, the dye spreading in the warm water, the rubber gloves she must remember to wear. . . . She would feel slightly dizzy, leaning forward to sink her hair into the black water, into the odor, the final dead odor of black that would stain every hair, every single thin miraculous blond hair, every part of her scalp, her soul. . . .

"I had no real education, I taught myself everything I know, mainly history and a little science," Howe was saying. "Then, in the Air Force, I assisted a legal officer and I became acquainted with the workings of the law inside the military courtroom . . . then after that I financed myself through law school—not a particularly good law school, but it served my purposes because I wasn't going to need any connections or anyone doing favors for me. I knew what I was going to do, and I did it. I set myself the goal of making and keeping, unencumbered in the bank, at least one million dollars by the age of thirty; but I got there four months ahead of time. In interviews that always sounds rather blunt, especially if the interviewer is biased against me and wants to retaliate, in his writing, for any feelings of inferiority he might have suffered during the interview—but it happens to be the truth, and I worship the truth when it can be told. Because not much of it can be told," he said seriously.

"Yes," Ardis said. "Yes. That's true."

"Now, in at least one of our conversations, I told you that my family life—my immediate family—would never be of any concern to you or to Elena," Howe said. He smiled at Elena. Behind him was a wall of books, many of them aged, water-stained, the bindings loose and faded; others were new, smart, in uniform bindings with gilt letters on their spines; here and there magazines had been stuck in, between books, partly ripped, bunched up. Elena smiled shyly in return. "My wife and I are divorced; I haven't seen her for fifteen years and never intend to see her again, and of my children I won't speak right now—in fact I probably never will. I have three children, two boys and a girl, and those facts are public enough, they're a matter of public record, but beyond that—nothing. They have nothing to do with us, with the present. I'll only say that I feel no guilt in relationship to them or to my wife; that's the most important thing I can tell you. Do you understand?"

He was looking at Elena. She nodded.

"When it's a matter of remarriage . . ." Howe said slowly, ". . . a matter of beginning again, the only important thing is: has the old relationship absolutely ended? And in my case it has."

"That's true . . . that's true in my case, our case also," Ardis said. "I mean, with Elena's father. . . ."

"Yes, I understand that's so, the relationship is ended," Howe said, nodding. "But this Leo Ross, this ex-husband of yours and Elena's father, has never been located, has he?"

"No, but—"

"If I thought it was a matter of real importance, I could possibly locate him," Howe said. "But. . . . In a kind of superficial, routine way," he said lightly, with a half-embarrassed smile, "I did try to trace him . . . I didn't go to any trouble, really, it was just a perfunctory matter. But it all ends in San Francisco, as if he'd died there. Maybe he did die."

"Die . . . ?" Ardis asked strangely. "Oh, no. No. I don't think so. A few times I think I've seen him . . . but of course it was a mistake, I was jumpy and mistook someone else . . . but . . . but I don't think he's dead, really. . . ."

"We can assume he won't come back; he wouldn't know who you are, he wouldn't know where you are," Howe said. "Certainly he wouldn't know where Elena was. Let's assume he died in San Francisco."

Howe glanced at Elena, who faced him still with that small, lovely smile; his gaze seemed to become entangled with hers, to turn vague and loose for a moment. Then he laughed self-consciously and rubbed his hands together.

"Now," he said, "there are various rumors about me . . . some facts and a lot of lies . . . I don't advise you to bother trying to sort them out, they're irrelevant. All that part of my life, my outside life—let's say my professional life and my private life outside this house—is going to be irrelevant to you. I'll be frank with you: since my marriage I've had to struggle with a real dislike for women, a distrust of them, almost a terror of them. But I've never been free of them and I won't lie about it." He got to his feet and began to stroll around the room; he paused at the corner where the dog lay and rubbed the dog's large, shrewd head with the heel of his foot—the heel of his gleaming shoe just slightly raised; he thrust his hands in the pockets of his sports jacket and turned back to Elena and her mother, frowning, passing along a wall that was all draperies and tapestries. "They always fought me in the end. They began by loving me and then they fought me and I had to get rid of them, the way you have to tear off clothes that are too tight or suddenly disgust you. But I never married after the first time. There have been so many people in my life," he said almost helplessly, looking over at Elena.

"I think we understand," Ardis said slowly.

One evening they were alone, Elena and Marvin Howe, and he discovered she had hurt herself—a trivial accident, her right forefinger bruised when a car door swung in upon it. He seized her hand, inspected the finger, where a few drops of blood had oozed out from under the nail. "Elena, why didn't you say something? Elena, this must hurt very much—"

Embarrassed, Elena tried to pull her hand away. "No, it's all right, it's nothing," she laughed.

"But—it must hurt— Doesn't it hurt?"

"I don't know, I don't feel it, it's nothing," Elena said.

He kissed her finger. He pressed her hand against his cheek, seemed for a moment almost about to weep; then he smiled at her. "You're so sweet, so good," he said. "Whatever you hear about me, Elena—about the past, or about women now, women who try to make claims—because I can't organize that part of my life very coherently—you wouldn't understand, Elena—whatever you hear, don't give it much value. It doesn't have anything to do with you. I've explained this more thoroughly to your mother and she understands. Do you promise, Elena?"

"Yes."

"And your finger—it doesn't hurt, really? Or should I take you to a doctor?"

Elena laughed. "It's nothing. But it looks ugly, so don't look at it."

She drew it away from him. She felt a slight tinge of shame, an almost pleasurable sensation. Deep in the pit of her belly, an ache . . . and she found herself thinking of the boys in the hall of her high school, the crowd of boys, the way one of them had grabbed her and pressed himself against her. From time to time, involuntarily, she thought of that. And the same half-pleasurable, guilty sensation would begin in her, but it was always too faint to hold onto, to strengthen. And now, with Marvin Howe, the sensation was too faint; it faded.

I said to myself what a joke this is, the telephone calls and the visits and the talking, the talking. I said to myself I didn't want it, but then I remembered that I did want it, I wanted something. I wanted to take my face off with a Kleenex and throw it down on the floor and say, There it is! Down there on the floor!

Then one day Ardis was saying angrily: "It's an insult and I'm not going to put up with it!"

Howe wanted to keep the marriage secret.

He left Detroit and Ardis waited, and during those three days she raged, not bothering to fix herself up, even to get dressed. She lit cigarettes and stubbed them out angrily. She kept saying to Elena, "Why? What did you do wrong? He must be embarrassed by you!"

"I don't know what I did wrong," Elena said indifferently.

"He's been so disillusioned with women . . . I can understand that, and the business about not wanting children, yes, I can understand that," Ardis said in a rushed, incredulous voice, "but a secret marriage— No. You won't do it. No. Absolutely not."

A dozen times a day she read through the document—the marriage contract Howe had given her—and threw it down again, baffled.

This contract contained forty-five clauses.

Ardis had taken it immediately to an acquaintance of hers, an attorney whose office was in the Fisher Building, near the Pyramid Club, and the attorney had told her that forty-five clauses were not much; that the document was not extraordinary; that it could probably be broken, in part, if it were ever contested strenuously. He explained to her that a marriage does not take place between two people, but between two people and the law, and that the state is a third party to any marriage contract, carefully worded or not. No, the document wasn't extraordinary. Certain parts could probably be broken, but in general it would hold. For Howe to marry without this legal caution would have been absurd, the attorney said, and Ardis had had to agree. Still, she was curious why divorce wasn't mentioned—wasn't that the main idea? To protect his estate against a divorce settlement and alimony?

"Public policy forbids any mention of that, of the dissolution of marriage," the attorney said.

So she came back to Elena and said, "It's airtight. It means you're waiving interest in his estate, it adds up to that, and the other clauses aren't important. . . . They're important, yes, but they don't have anything to do with money. But still, you're not going to sign this thing yet."

When Marvin came back to town he telephoned Ardis, and the two of them met for lunch. Ardis returned, flushed, very excited, and told Elena he not only refused to withdraw that clause, but had added another: that Elena not be subject to any outside influences, "meaning me, meaning your mother! Meaning me!" she cried.

She opened her purse and threw down a vial of pills.

Elena looked at them.

"What's that?" she asked.

"Sleeping pills! Barbiturates!"

Elena walked into her bedroom. Her mother followed and turned on the light. "I told him you were very upset—very emotional— I told him I wouldn't be responsible for what might happen to you—if you felt he had rejected you, that he was ashamed of you—"

Elena shuddered.

The next morning the telephone rang and Ardis answered it on the sixth ring. She hadn't bothered to wipe her make-up off from the day before, she was so disgusted and wrought up. Her face glowed. Her eyes glittered. She listened for a while and then she interrupted: "All right, fine, good, you do your traveling and she isn't going to mind—she has agreed to that—so far as she can understand it, yes, of course—she's led a very sheltered life and— And look: I don't particularly care to have a son-in-law your age, born in 1919, so I have no designs on forcing family life on you—forcing a mother-in-law on you at your age and at my age!— Fine, good! I happen to have plans for a life of my own, believe it or not! You are not the only person who thinks about the future! She will agree about the traveling, the time you'll spend away from home, yes, yes, and everything under that heading, but she won't agree to the last clause and—and I won't be responsible for anything that happens to her either—you can imagine how a young girl would feel, a girl like Elena who is—who happens to be— What? What? One year? One year, and then—? No. Absolutely not. That's the same thing. No. I realize you aren't an ordinary man," Ardis said mockingly, "I realize from all the things I've read about you that you're a little eccentric, but that's all right, you're also a genius or so they say—but—my daughter isn't going to masquerade as— No, it doesn't matter where you live, it wouldn't change anything if you lived somewhere else. What? No. I said no. She does love you and I am willing to admit that you love her, yes, and respect her, or you'd never go to all this trouble—but you don't respect her enough—not quite enough— And— What?"

She listened, staring at the floor. Elena was watching. She had never seen her mother so excited, so beautiful. Really, she was beautiful—even with the day-old make-up, and her hair only partly combed, and her dressing gown falling open. *I called out to myself from a distance, Elena! Can your life be a joke and yet serious? Can you swallow a handful of pills as a joke, die as a joke, but die dead?*

Ardis put down the receiver. She looked at Elena and reached, groping, for her crumpled package of cigarettes, in which only a single cigarette remained. Her eyes looked enlarged, unnatural. But she flashed Elena a smile and Elena knew they had won.

"You're set for life," she said.

He kissed me and said he had never been afraid of being a fool. Never afraid of taking risks, or of people laughing at him. He said, My secret is that I don't have any limits. I take a chance on anything.

I said it would take all my life to understand him.

He said, No, you won't understand me, Elena, but he was gentle because he loved me.

I loved him. I did love him. I was his wife and I loved him.

II

—A ten-foot piece of furniture, with hard carved edges, a mirror that gave back a slightly distorted, discolored view of Elena and her husband; the doors inlaid with gold and ebony, an odor of dust and aged furniture polish. "Eighteenth-century, a German cabinet," Marvin said. He was reading the yellow tag attached to one of the drawers. "It's beautiful, Elena, isn't it?"

Elena believed it was beautiful, yes. Her face floated, ghost-like, in the mirror. Her long hair was fixed in thick braids and wound around her head, so that she looked like an eighteenth-century woman herself, peering shyly out at them, trapped somehow inside this stern, fussy piece of furniture. She saw her husband's face beside hers, not floating but solid, heavy, fixed to his shoulders. "Yes, it's very beautiful," she said. Her fingers came away from the cabinet dusty.

—A small train: too large to be a child's model train but too small for anything else, too small for anyone to sit inside it, a handsome locomotive, several boxcars, passenger cars, even a *wagon-lit,* even a caboose. Marvin stooped over to peer inside the windows. "Little tables set up for dinner," he laughed. "Little people sitting at them . . . white tablecloths and bottles of champagne. . . . This strange thing is worth five thousand dollars. That's what it brought at an auction: five thousand dollars. Do you like it?"

Elena smiled, not knowing what to say.

"It came from the Croxley estate, all the way from New Jersey," Marvin said. "I didn't want it, but what the hell. . . . It came along with three vanloads of excellent things."

—A life-sized portrait of a woman with a low forehead and wispy, curly bangs, skin that was too flesh-toned to be natural; a high, tight bodice of lace, slightly padded shoulders, long dark velvet sleeves that came out to the middle of the woman's small pink hands. Like Elena, she was wearing a dress that covered her all up, the chest and shoulders and arms. She was chaste but dowdy, and a thick film of dust covered her and the heavy gilt frame surrounding her. "She looks like an American housewife dressed up as the mistress of an English country house," Marvin said. He bent to look at the tag. "Yes. That's what she is. Caryl Swift's wife—Swift, the yachting-accident man—yes, I remember him, though it was a very short trial. I don't know why he gave me this damn thing; it obviously has no value to me. People's portraits have no value. . . ."

"She looks very unhappy," Elena said.

"No, she doesn't look unhappy, you're reading that into her face," Marvin said bluntly. As if to soften his remark, he put his arm around Elena's shoulders and continued to study the woman in the portrait. "I see there a self-satisfied, ignorant, semiliterate, semiattractive millionaire's wife, one of thousands. You can read the contempt the artist felt for her in the color of the skin; no sane painter would make skin that color. Unless he was joking."

"What happened to her?" Elena asked reluctantly.

"They disappeared. They fell out the bottom."

"Was her husband guilty?"

"We won. But they had to sign everything over to me."

—A dining room table opened to its full length, piled high with tarnished silverware, goblets, mismatched plates, fruit bowls, candlestick holders, matchboxes, cigarette boxes made of delicate carved wood, a velvet-lined jewelry box heaped high with jewelry, carelessly folded draperies and tapestries woven with designs of flowers, birds, fantastic animals in wool and silk, even a few dusty bottles of wine tipped over into jumbled heaps of golden doorknobs and curtain rods and door hinges. Marvin pulled a necklace out of this mess and put it around Elena's neck; it was made of what appeared to be gold, and was quite heavy. "That looks perfect," Marvin said with satisfaction. He pawed through the debris and came across a rope of pearls, but when he tried to pull it free the string snapped and the pearls fell loose. He grunted with amused irritation as the pearls bounced around his feet and rolled away into the dust. Then he found another pearl necklace. He came to Elena and put this around her neck; she bent her head submissively.

"It's perfect," Marvin said.

He stared at her. Close up, he was not a handsome man. But his face was powerful, as if it were all muscle, tensed and cunning muscle. His skin appeared almost to be multilayered, of different thicknesses. He was solid, heavy, deep, while Elena felt the skin of her own face to be so delicate that a pencil mark might injure it. Marvin smiled with satisfaction, judging her, exposing his large, slightly crooked, rather discolored teeth. He was staring at Elena but did not seem to be aware of her. "These things were waiting for you for decades," he said. "In fact, for centuries. Beautiful things like this are just in the temporary keeping of ugly people, of ordinary people—they are really destined for someone like you, for someone like me to give to you." He looped another necklace around her neck, a long light golden chain studded with stones of some kind. Elena felt his warm, meaty, intimate breath; it seemed to her she had been feeling it all her life. They had been married now for nearly a year. But the year had stretched out, it seemed to be stretching out farther and farther into the past, obliterating Elena's past, making it uncomplicated and orderly and safe.

"Thank you, they're very beautiful," Elena said.

"I want to give you everything," Marvin said.

On the side of his throat was a wrinkle lined with dirt. His jaw and cheeks had been shaved that morning, as always, but unevenly, and already his beard had begun to push itself out again, so that another face seemed directly beneath the bumpy surface of this face, shadowy and shrewd. The heavy lids of Marvin's eyes were always moving, his gaze always centering upon something and then recentering, refocusing, so that the mechanism of his thought, his thinking, was visible. Elena could see him thinking. At night he sometimes pressed himself against Elena, asleep, unconscious, groping for her and finding her. Not able to sleep herself, Elena would see how his face was mysterious, dark, unfathomable, any man's face, but her husband's face, *her husband's*. She loved him. She would hold him in her arms and feel the ceaseless alert movement of his eyes, though he was asleep. He was still looking, still thinking. His eyes were still focusing upon something though he was asleep. . . . This would have frightened Elena except he was her husband, he was not set in opposition to her, he was not dangerous to her. He protected her. His strength had to do with the words that flooded his head, the ceaseless mechanism of his brain. She was grateful to be lying beside him, his wife, holding him in her arms while he slept his restless sleep; as his head filled with words, Elena's drained dry.

As the machinery of his brain worked, a deep holy silent peace spread through Elena's brain like ink.

"Why do you look so thoughtful? What are you thinking about?" Marvin asked.

". . . thinking of all the beautiful things here . . . the things that are lost. . . ."

"They're not lost," Marvin said, correcting her. "We have them."

"But we don't know what they are. . . ."

"But we have them, we own them."

He found a ring inside a ceramic dish and slid it on Elena's finger, but it was too large. He laughed and slid it on his own finger: it was a man's ring, carved of what appeared to be a kind of tusk. "Yes, we own everything," he said cheerfully, "whether we bother to make an inventory of it, or seal it up and forget about it forever, let it rot or burn down or be devoured by moths. . . . Nobody else owns it. Nobody else can get to it." He was in an excellent mood. He took Elena by the shoulders and kissed her. "Do you love me? Was this a nice surprise for you?"

"Oh yes, I love you," she said in a whisper.

—A ravaged chest of drawers, scraped and scratched, a sideboard piled with filthy lace curtains and yellowed brocade, a television set with a very small screen, "one of the first sets manufactured anywhere," Marvin declared; but without much interest. Cut-glass vases filled with more jewelry and small tarnished ornamental things, doves, elephants, horses, parts of broken figures, human and animal, all mixed together like the pieces of a jigsaw puzzle, hopelessly confused. This would have made Elena dizzy except for Marvin's hand closed lightly about her arm. In another mirror—propped up against some stained velvet cushions—she came across her own face, the surprise of her white-blond hair and the impeccable chastity of her cheekbones and lips, and she thought with surprised pleasure that her face continued its existence, independent of her, of her thinking or her emotions, that it was a constant, as predictable and stable as anything in the universe. Marvin's ruddy face appeared beside hers, but he was looking at something else and did not notice her watching him. "This antique," he said, reading a tag, "is evidently a copy of Queen Victoria's writing desk. Look at all the gold . . . the handles, the knobs . . . and mother-of-pearl on every drawer. . . . It's like a torture machine, a nightmare someone threw together. Or do you like it, Elena?"

"It wouldn't fit in our house," she said.

He noticed the mirror she was looking into, and lowered his head beside hers, self-consciously, almost shyly, as if he feared looking at himself so openly. His hair was thick and tufted, sandy-colored in part, in part a deeper brown-red, and around his temples gray, even gray threaded with white. He seemed a different kind of human being, or a creature who belonged to a species other than Elena's. His skin was remarkably coarse beside hers. But he smiled at her. "Monsters have too much personality, like some of the antiques here," he said. "Like me. . . . They don't fit into anyone's house, really." Most of the time he seemed to forget himself, though he always dressed well, or began the day looking well; but sometimes he made joking, derisive comments about himself, brushing dandruff off his shoulders, feeling his face for pimples or bumps, pacing restlessly around the house and rubbing his hand across the wide front of his stomach and lower chest, complaining of being heavy, middle-aged, slowed-down before his time. . . . He worked all the time, maybe sixteen hours a day. Then he stopped work suddenly and went somewhere: to the north of Michigan, to hunt with men Elena never met, to go canoeing, white-water canoeing, which was dangerous but good for him, as he said, "good for his heart." Or, on one of his business trips, he stayed over for a few days to hunt or fish or hike in the mountains; not long ago he and three other men were deep-sea fishing off the Florida coast and were caught in squalls for twenty hours. When he returned from these feats he was always in an excellent mood, a few pounds lighter, but he went back immediately to his long crammed days of work. "Do you think I am a monster, Elena? A freak?"

"Why do you ask that?" Elena asked, surprised.

But he laughed self-consciously, flushing. He did not explain. Instead he opened one of the little doors in the writing desk and came across a clock, decorated with gold leaf. He tapped at it, as if to get it running again; but it was very delicate, or maybe it had been already cracked, because the glass face broke.

"All this junk," he said slowly.

—Rolled-up carpets, sofas draped with sad-looking white covers, chairs stacked upon one another; a corner of the warehouse jammed with refrigerators, their doors open, very white and silent and aggrieved; a large, beautiful rocking horse with a glazed palomino hide and a shredded mane and bulging, astonished eyes; a Victorian doll's house with a gabled roof and many rooms, even a ballroom, now stuffed with items, with bits and fragments of things. Paintings were stacked together, most of them in heavy frames. Elena lifted up one of them to look at it: the portrait of a middle-aged man. "*He* looks civilized, but he was a maniac," Marvin said. "Tried to fire me after seven months of work. He was a maniac . . . that saved him in the end. . . . Jesus, look at all these portraits! All these people! This place is like that part of the ocean where all the debris winds up, whether it's expensive debris or just seaweed. . . . And I own it all. . . . I don't even know who these people are, these faces. Imagine them sitting for an artist, sitting patiently and paying so much money—such vanity!—only to wind up stacked together here, for me to look at, the first time in five years I've bothered to drop in here. I should get rid of it all, but. . . . I have a sentimental feeling about these things, possessions, especially things other people have owned or cherished, expensive things. Money is so abstract; in a way it doesn't exist; but things are very real. . . . A great crowd of people with money and time spent their lives accumulating these things, and in a way I assimilate them, their lives, simply by owning their possessions, whether I bother to look at them or not." He spoke cheerfully and simply, looking through the portraits. Elena thought the people in the portraits shared the same expression: vague stupefied alarm, bewilderment, terror. Even those who smiled were smiling out of fear, staring up into Marvin Howe's face. "I don't recognize most of these people. Who the hell are they . . . ? Even my clients fade out of my mind . . . everyone fades . . . it's too much of an effort to remember people once you're finished with them. . . . This man looks familiar, but I don't remember his name. I don't remember what he was charged with . . . probably murder. . . . You know, Elena, at one time in my life I must have known this man thoroughly, better than he knew himself, much better. I knew who his parents were, I knew his friends, his business associates, his enemies, his employees, I had conversations with the man who sold him newspapers at a newsstand near his office, one of my assistants might have become friendly with one of his girl friends, or his wife, I had long tearful conversations with his children, his mother-in-law. . . . And then, as soon as the case was finished, I wiped everything out of my mind: I cleansed myself of him completely. . . . Oh yes, *this* man . . . this is Miles Stock. I haven't forgotten him. Did you ever hear of the Stock case, in Chicago?"

Elena stared at the thin-faced man in the portrait, who reminded her of her father: he had that same tense, birdlike expectancy about his head and shoulders, a look of somehow leaning out of the canvas. But he was fairly young, perhaps around thirty, with sleek dark hair parted neatly on the left side of his head.

"Miles Stock. He was convicted of first-degree murder, in Cook County, and his family hired me for the appeal. I got him a retrial and finally an acquittal, and the bastard disappeared. He left the country. His mother came to my office and handed me the key to her house in Chicago, just handed me the key and walked out again. This happened only a few years ago and I think of Stock from time to time, I'm almost waiting for him to return, to show up someday in my office to kill me."

Elena turned sharply to him. "What? Kill you?"

"I mean try to kill me, *try* to . . . because nobody is going to kill me, never. That won't happen. I'm going to be around for a very long time yet. This man, Stock, thought I had insulted him, and he was very hateful to me. I told him I couldn't represent him if he lied to me, but he persisted in lying for days, days on end, and then finally he broke down and told me the truth—which of course I already knew—and he wept in my arms, and I pushed him away. I didn't think, I was just repulsed by him, I shoved him away. He said, 'You're rejecting me physically,' and after that he hated me. He had killed someone in Chicago but I got him acquitted because of . . . because of. . . . Actually, he was very strong," Marvin said, half-admiringly. "He looked thin but he was very wiry and strong, like men of that physical type. They're like weasels or rats; they surprise you."

"How did you get him acquitted?" Elena asked.

Marvin laughed and rapped his fingers against the man's face, an irritated contemptuous gesture and yet halfway affectionate. "I don't want to talk about it," he said.

Elena was startled.

Marvin said vaguely, "I don't want to contaminate you with my work . . . not even the work I've successfully completed. . . . If you ask me about these people, I'm inclined to answer just to please you, but I would rather not have you ask. In the Stock case, the prosecution's case was all circumstantial evidence, Stock and his boy seen here, seen there, at nine-fifteen, at ten-thirty, bits of hair and blood in the back seat of a car. . . . The usual thing, a series of absolutely damning facts that mean nothing. The second time around Stock had an intelligent defense and he went free."

"It's terrible to know a guilty man is thinking of you somewhere," Elena said apologetically, knowing she should not speak and yet somehow unable to stop. "That he might come back. . . ."

"He won't come back. Forget I said that. Forget everything I said," Marvin said. "But here's my advice: Don't allow anyone to cry in your arms. If a man cries in your arms, you're stuck with him for life. If you try to push him away or escape him, he'll want you to die."

—Terrace furniture, chipped lawn furniture, bird baths, parts of dismantled fountains, a harpsichord piled high with toy soldiers holding bayonets like toothpicks, but sharp-looking and deadly, dolls in evening gowns and wedding dresses and ballet outfits, Royal Doulton figurines, broken and whole, old piano sheet music and *Cuddeback's Second Year at the Piano,* an orange, wrinkled book; and a narrow bed with a canopy of scalloped brocade, velvet-covered pillows in a tumble on the satin bedspread, a thick brass curtain rod lying across it as if thrown there in anger. Marvin took hold of one of the bed's posts and gave the bed a shake. It creaked. He pushed the brass rod off onto the floor, making a clattering, hollow noise; the bedspread kept the rod's indentation. The headboard was cushioned, quilted, a design in faded greens of women and animals and filmy trees.

"Three hundred years old, an Italian piece," Marvin said. "Obviously put together with love. It's beautiful, isn't it? I remember it from the last time I was here. I must have walked back out this way, because I remember this bed. . . . I can imagine someone sleeping here, can't you, Elena? Maybe a queen? An Italian princess? A young woman lying on this satin spread, a beautiful young woman. . . . Like you, Elena. I can imagine the face, the skin like porcelain, the hair loose like yours when you take it down, I can imagine a body lying there, a young girl in her own bed, an unmarried girl. . . . Imagine her there, looking out at us in the year 1961, two Americans who have inherited everything! We've inherited her bed, her elegant brocaded canopy, her carved posts, her spirit. . . . Lie down there for a moment, Elena. Lie down, dear. Please."

Elena hesitated.

"Just lie down for a moment, dear."

Marvin's voice had tightened and was no longer playful. She heard the sudden tension in it. So she obeyed, and when the heavy necklaces swung forward, she felt herself being drawn down as if someone had grabbed hold of them. But she only laughed and tried to adjust them. She lay back on the uncomfortable pillows, smoothing her dress down around her legs.

Marvin stood staring at her.

"Yes, like that. Like that."

He stood at the foot of the bed, his hands closed about the two posts, watching her. She seemed to see him receding, and then coming closer, framed by the posts and the top of the bed; she felt as if she were floating, drifting, in a kind of suspension that might have been her husband's vision of her, weightless and holy.

I am Elena Howe, she thought. Behind her husband the warehouse was a confusion of angles and shapes, and she did not see it. So many possessions, so many objects created out of love and bought and sold and sold again, expensive and beautiful and lost!—but she did not see them now. She saw her husband, a tall bulky man who carried himself well, his face partly shadowed, made stern now with love, almost stricken with love. He stared at her and she almost saw herself, his wife Elena. *Elena Howe.* On the first night of their marriage, when he had knelt above her and slowly, cautiously, and then in a kind of angry frenzy made love to her, helpless to control himself, she had lain like this and suddenly she felt herself inside his head, contained by the hard powerful skull, embraced totally, totally. If she cried out in pain or surprise she did not hear herself. She did not feel pain or surprise. And when he made love to her in the months afterward, she felt no pain, no alarm; she felt nothing, but drifted like this, absolutely still, gentle, opened to him and empty, her soul flawless as the undersides of her eyelids seeing nothing.

"Do you know how I love you, Elena?"

He seemed to be calling out to her across a great distance. Yet he was right at the foot of the bed, tense and watchful. Very close. His mouth moved into a kind of smile. Stricken, staring. Elena smiled at him, her own face lying very lightly on the flesh of her skull.

"Elena? Do you . . . ?"

She realized that she was expected to answer him. And so she whispered, "Yes," and wondered if it was the right word, the magical word he wanted. *Yes.* Then she wondered, seeing his face, if he would hold himself back from her for a minute, two minutes, if he would finally come to her and bury himself in a sudden half-angry convulsive movement in her, inside her. . . . And she waited to accept him, she waited. She would go perfectly still inside his embrace, opening to him, his terrible, frantic, helpless energy.

This either did or did not happen.

12

I'll be frank with you.

Sometimes it's as powerful as an explosion, but slowed down and dreamlike, strangely dreamlike, the sudden awareness of what is going to happen. When the future is suddenly clear. . . . Sometimes it's as if I were high above the earth, alone in an airplane, able to see for myself the magical curve of the earth, which no one else has ever really seen. And I see it all—I see everything—with my body, my insides, the sensitive skin on the back of my neck—I see everything and I understand it, the terrible excitement of the truth.

Then I know what will happen: exactly how the future will turn out. The present divides itself routinely and tamely into days, court sessions, recesses and breaks and weekends, testimonies, newspaper accounts, a few hours' sleep every night, the surface commotion of real life. But a point has been passed. Other people may sense this turning, this pivoting point . . . but I understand it; in a way, I have contrived to bring it about, and my reward is the absolute certainty of what has been passed. So I can see into the future. I have sailed over that point like a man in an airplane, while everyone else is plodding along on the ground. I have felt it, taken it in with my guts, the subtlety of it, the feathery steel of its certainty. And I am never wrong. After that point I know not only that I have won but how well I have won, how deeply I have pushed myself into the imaginations of other people, how powerfully I have guided their wills. It only remains for enough days to pass in order for the fact of my victory to be realized—in what is called "real life."

Do I feel I may explode, containing such energy? Yes.

He turned heavily. I could hear him breathing, I could feel him sweating. It was about two o'clock. No, later. He sighed, his breath was raspy and impatient. Dreaming. He twitched violently, his leg jerked against me. In surprise my heart pounded. Was he running somewhere? Struggling with invisible enemies?

He sighed and the sigh became a groan. Then he jerked his entire body again: then he was awake.

I lay in silence, not asleep.

I heard his eyelashes parting, the stiff dry separation of the lashes. Awake. The mechanism of his brain had worked so violently that it had pushed itself out of sleep into consciousness. He was breathing thoughtfully, quietly, the breath of a man who is awake, making plans. I breathed softly, almost inaudibly, the breath of a woman who was asleep. But it's good. The tension, the terrible power in me—I accept it, it's a fact of my life, it must be good. I never sleep more than a few hours a night, any night, because I have too much to figure out. Some of it I do in my dreams—in fact I get my best hunches in my dreams—but the rest I have to do at my desk—I need to get a pencil in my hand, I need to pick up a pencil in my fingers. So I can't waste time in bed, I have to get up. It seems to be getting more obvious as I grow older—the pattern of sleep and waking, of dreaming about work and then waking, suddenly, when the dream has fulfilled its function and I need now to think logically, cunningly. . . . What am I afraid of . . . ? Growing older? No, absolutely not. No. In fact I am more certain of myself each year, more confident of my powers. When I was a young man the energy inside me, the insomnia, the sweating, the nervous stomach, the misery if I couldn't work, work for many hours a day—these things frightened me—but now I accept them all, I recognize them as a part of my personality, my *self.* I can count on that energy to give me a victory another man would not quite achieve, he'd maybe come close to it but lose it, it would elude him because after all he would be only human, and I. . . . I'm a little different.

No, I don't fear old age or death, so I don't fear any aspect of mortality. . . . Because . . . I think it's because I've already lived so many lives, I've competed and fought and struggled and triumphed in so many lives, saving men from death, from long prison sentences, bringing them back to life again when everyone else wanted them destroyed. But I refused to let that happen, I refused, I fought to save them and I won. *I won.* And so in a sense I have lived a multitude of lives, burrowed more deeply into certain people than they did into their own souls, more in control of their destinies than they were themselves. . . . Once you know what that feeling is, once you taste it, you know that somehow you are immortal; even if you die. You have been immortal.

I felt the shifting of his weight in bed, the careful movement away from me. He didn't want me to wake up. In a minute, very carefully, he would ease himself out of bed and go away, away somewhere, another part of the house. . . .

. . . like a mural meant to represent all of creation, an ancient mural, a great multitude of people drawn with meticulous detail, loving detail . . . a frieze around a temple showing processions that seem to go on for years, for centuries, vast crowds of people strung out in single file, all headed for the same destination. . . . I'm all those people, one after another. My work is human beings. My religion is human beings. That means I have to love them . . . in order to save them, I have to love them.

He got up. I heard him at the bureau, pulling out one of the drawers—he would be taking out another pair of pajamas. He sweated so, always hot, restless, a big man with a gleaming restless body, a brain that would not stop. I loved him and yet I lay very still, as if hiding. On my side of the bed, hiding. I loved him but I dreaded the damp warm mattress where he had lain.

I'll be frank: no, I don't want to change the world. I don't want to reform the country. I don't believe the courts are in existence for that purpose. I'm not a reformer, I'm not out to make our society into a paradise, I approach my clients one by one, as individuals. Now, there are certain cases, yes, obviously there are cases that must be dealt with as social events, when men violate the law because of economic or racial pressures that you and I can't comprehend, and I need to explain this to a jury. I will explain it to a jury every time . . . unless I think that by explaining it I will be making a tactical error. I explain only as much of the truth as is necessary for a victory. Too much truth . . . is a tactical error. I don't hit juries on the head with someone else's misery, just to make them feel guilty, to displace the guilt, unless I need to for a victory. Everything is determined by that: what will assure me a victory. The rest is idealism, it's selfish, it violates the right of my client to be represented only as himself, not as a member of a group. My clients are not ciphers, they don't represent anyone except themselves. If I didn't see them that way I couldn't love them. And if I couldn't love them I couldn't get as deeply into them as I do, and I couldn't save them. *He left the bedroom; I felt the vibrations of his weight everywhere in the house, his footsteps, his pacing, his thinking. I thought: now I can sleep.*

From the time I was a child I felt the world wasn't large enough for me. Even those vast spaces, the scrubland of Oklahoma! No, I wanted somehow to make it expand into other dimensions, to *force* it into expansion. All my life I was made excited and miserable by my need to work, to work hard, harder than anyone else, to compete, to fight, to win—and only when I became a lawyer, a trial lawyer, did I really use that energy the way it was meant to be used. Just before a case opens I feel that my head isn't big enough for everything I've put in it. I'm a crowd! I feel I'm growing taller, I'm shooting up toward the ceiling, I feel a heartbeat in my eyeballs that will drive me mad if it doesn't get out. I feel so strong, so very strong. . . . Does it embarrass you to hear a man confess his happiness in his work? I think it does. Most men confess only their failures, their miseries; they're ashamed of their few moments of joy. Or maybe they don't have any . . . ? Well, I do. I have many moments of joy, moments of almost unbearable happiness.

Without him the bed was immense. Lonely. Cold. I reached over to feel that side of the mattress—yes, very damp, cold. The place where he had lain. I turned on the light and saw that it was after three o'clock. I pulled back the cover to look at the bed: a large damp stain where his body had been.

No, I'm not afraid to take risks. I've taken many risks in the past, following my instincts, my dreams. Why not? I don't fear making mistakes. Being laughed at. Being ridiculed. I want to stretch the boundaries a little, push the world out into another dimension, distort it, change it; I'm like anyone who takes chances and isn't afraid: let's say like great conquerors, religious leaders, madmen. They told the great explorers of the oceans their ships would sail off the edge of the world—and the explorers replied, Why stay home because of that? Why not sail off the edge of the world?

I thought: now I can sleep.

But when I turned out the light I lay awake, my eyes open. I could hear him going downstairs . . . I could hear him down in his study. . . . But if I called him he would come back. He was still here with me; in a way, he never left me, I was never alone. I had been married to him now for years and I was never alone, married to him, his wife.

And, somewhere beyond him, on the other side of him, there were people who would come to me if I called them. . . . My mother: my mother would come if I called. I never saw her now, I hadn't seen her for a very long time, but if I called her in this darkness she would come, approaching the bed, saying, Elena? Do you want me? There was a concentration of shadow that could have been my mother. And I could summon my father. . . . I could call him to me, to the side of the bed, I could draw him forward to me, I could look into that face of his again, into that expression of pure pitiless love. . . .

You call it the Establishment—all right, I call it tradition. I happen to believe in the status quo. I'm a maverick, but I respect the tradition I operate in. The tradition makes me possible, it makes my victories possible. . . . I don't want the laws changed because I know them, I operate in them, I. . . . And now you part company with me, don't you? I can see it in your expression! But I granted you this interview because I respect the magazine you work for, though I don't respect its political bias, and I won't stop telling the truth just because. . . . Yes, I know what you're thinking: there isn't any need for you to protest. I know exactly what you're thinking. But I'm asking you to listen to my point of view, because it's a point of view that gets very little publicity these days. These days, every kid out of school who goes into criminal law thinks he can reform the country, turn things upside down, by using his clients as wedges, levers. . . . Men like that have no real respect for the law. They jeopardize the law, its sanctity, and that is a terrible thing. We need the law because the law is what's left of divinity.

The same people who want to crucify Christ in every generation want to crucify the law now, now that Christ is dead and buried—no, never mind about my personal religious beliefs, that isn't the issue here. The churches are being destroyed, all right, maybe God Himself is destroying them, no matter. I'm not a theologian. I'm not a religious man. But the courts are not going to be destroyed. No. They'll stand. They are what's left of divinity and not even a murderer would want to destroy divinity—not the last of it—even a murderer would draw back in reverence.

We need what's holy. The law is holy. It will never be destroyed because there is no salvation outside it. *I lay awake, not sleeping; I thought of him downstairs . . . a homely handsome man, perspiring, excited, his face gleaming. . . . Pawing through papers, transcripts, notes, photostated copies of documents, the unstoppable flow of words, words he had mastered. . . . I could not understand him. I never tried, now, to understand him. He was a man so alive, alive. . . . Alive, living. . . . I had felt a thousand times the terrible leap of his life in me, deep in my body.*

I move on.

The men who are my opponents one day are my friends the next day. I don't hate. I don't have time to hate. Enemies of mine exist all over the country, yes, certainly, but I don't remember who they are . . . I don't have time for them. I don't hate anyone and I don't hate myself. You look surprised . . . but hating oneself is very popular today. Hating this country. Hating history. It's a complex way of hating oneself. But I accept myself: *this* is my personality. My fate. I accept myself thoroughly, in fact I admire myself . . . I love myself. Maybe I'm embarrassing you, but I insist upon telling the truth. I love hearing my own voice—I love the way people are forced to look at me, sometimes against their will, not just juries but ordinary spectators in a courtroom, spectators anywhere. . . . I love those people when they look at me, when they listen. There is a great joy, a miraculous joy, in the power of words as they flow among people . . . the emotions, the currents and waves that hook human beings together . . . like molecules bouncing off one another and colliding with others, a ceaseless, eternal motion, a divinity. . . . Yes, this must be what it is to be divine.

This must be what it is to be divine.

13

"Suppose someone wanted to destroy you, would that be easy?"

Elena indicated that she did not know.

"People think it would be easy, very easy, but it wouldn't be—that's where I come in! In fact, destroying a human being, as distinct from just killing a human being, is very challenging." The man smiled into Elena's face, a smile flashing of excitement and confidence. Very quick, deft, alert. He moved closer to her, stooping from his height, trying to make himself heard over the noise of other conversations. "That's where I come in, my profession is based upon how well murderers meet that challenge, and they don't do well at all—they're very clumsy, they don't have much imagination. How would you destroy a body?"

Elena laughed in amazement. Then she said, seeing his seriousness, "I don't know."

"But think, think! What is the first thing that comes into your mind?—burning, fire? A fire that would seem accidental?"

"I don't know," Elena said.

Someone passed close behind her and Elena had to step forward, and the man pressed nervously toward her, still staring at her with a look of pinched, strange seriousness; then he smiled again, a happy boyish smile that illuminated his face. "Let's say someone wanted to destroy you, Mrs. Howe, and strangled you, and set the house on fire—then what? Then what?"

It was the spring of 1965. A reception somewhere in Detroit: thousands of squares of highly polished parquet, a floor that gleamed cruelly, beautifully, each square reflecting light in a way distinct from the others. Different angles of light. Different tones of light. Jarring, warring, yet set down in harmony, beneath the feet of these hundreds of people who did not glance down. Elena could see their faint shadowy reflections there, in the floor. While she smiled she felt her gaze drift downward, to her own reflection—*there, there in the floor*—beneath her feet, another person, waiting and listening and perhaps not smiling.

"Ha!" the man said cheerfully. "You think fire would work, do you? Well, it wouldn't. Your strangler would fail to destroy you, no matter how violent the fire was—burned, charred to a crisp, just a blackened mass, a few ounces of ashes—still you'd remain Mrs. Howe, and I could sift through whatever was left and come out with the evidence for an absolute identification. Once the identity of the victim is known, it's almost always easy to find the murderer. An anonymous corpse is a terrible problem. But who can remain anonymous? There's a young man working for me, a specialist in forensic odontology, who is so brilliant—so painstaking—he could identify someone if all you handed him were a few teeth, or part of a bridgework, or an old gold filling! Just hand it to him, put it in the palm of his hand, and come back in a few days—it's astonishing!"

Another man was trying to join their conversation, approaching Elena from the right. She sensed him coming, turned with a vague encouraging smile to him, smiled, and the three of them waited for the subtle, almost imperceptible rhythmic break in a conversation that allows another person to enter. The man who was talking so eagerly to Elena hesitated; he said, with a forced smile, "Hello, Judge Couteau—how are you? This is very crowded, isn't it? I was just telling Mrs. Howe some professional secrets—"

Elena glanced around and saw her husband in another group: she fixed him there, in that place. He would usually remain in one place for most of the duration of a reception like this—other people drifted to him, around him, finally past him, but he would remain on a few square feet of floor. He was talking vehemently with two men, one of whom Elena recognized—an assistant for the tax attorney Marvin had hired a few months ago to represent him in Tax Court; the Treasury Department was making certain claims on Marvin's income, a complicated case Elena did not understand and had made no attempt to understand. Marvin had told her it was not important.

Her face shifted into its easiest expression, a half-formal, half-girlish smile. She was somewhere in Detroit, in a large hall-like room, with a polished floor and banks of flowers and waiters in white suits making rounds with trays of drinks, black waiters in white suits. Someone was talking to her. Toward her. At her. No, about her: she must listen.

"Yes, I was telling Mrs. Howe that nobody could really destroy her, every inch of her," the man was saying. "Unless he was a real professional, of course. . . . Take another example: simple burial, in a lonely place, with the hope of decomposition. This was much more popular in the past! But now we have so much land dug up, you know, new housing developments and shopping plazas and— It's very hard to find a good lonely grave, just six feet or so that won't be bulldozed up in a few months —Isn't that right, Judge Couteau?"

"Call me Carl, please!—we're not in court!" Couteau said graciously. He winked at Elena. A handsome graying man, in a suit with stylishly narrow lapels, a shirt of peppermint stripes; Elena noticed pearl cuff links.

"Just to remove all traces of a body's sex, for instance—is not easy. If you trust decomposition, the so-called natural process of decay, it won't work—and if you put lime on the body, like people in novels and movies, it will in fact help to preserve the body. Did you know that?"

"Yes," Couteau said.

"I meant Mrs. Howe," the man said coldly.

"I didn't know that," Elena said.

"Yes. And you'd remain a female for quite a while, after you were dead and even partly decomposed, did you know that? Let's say your murderer was very industrious and cut you up into chunks and buried the chunks all over—and let's say the police call me in, and what do I do? I simply examine the bones, to begin with, and I can tell the police immediately what your sex is. Not to mention the womb—"

"The what?" Couteau asked, sipping at his drink.

"The womb. In female bodies that have almost totally decomposed—I mean that seriously, almost *totally decomposed*—you can often find the womb, the womb remains when all the other organs have disappeared."

Elena smiled. No, she didn't smile. In a sudden helpless panic, she stared at the man who was speaking but did not hear his words. Then she did smile, to show her interest and surprise and. . . .

Judge Couteau was now talking. A waiter passed behind him and he had to step forward; he glanced around irritably, holding his glass close to his chest so that he would not brush it against Elena. A crowd of people, not countable. But yes: countable. If

Elena had time she could certainly count them. She could count the squares of parquet if she had time. If she had time she could count the lights in the ceiling, the pairs of eyes, the fillings in all the teeth.

She had begun to shiver.

But Couteau was talking to her, leaning over her. By a steady almost imperceptible movement of his right elbow he was excluding the other man, almost unconsciously, slowly, half-inch by half-inch, moving that arm and that elbow and finally that shoulder around, subtly, gently, perhaps not consciously, while the other man sipped nervously at his drink and drew in his breath to speak, but found no opening. Elena gazed past Couteau's slim gray arm and noticed the man's odd curved incisors, which seemed a slightly different color—not so white—from the rest of his teeth.

That was the day I learned about my body: they said the womb wouldn't rot.

Then how could you get rid of it?

They didn't say it would shrivel up without any child in there to keep it moist and elastic. They said it would not rot, would not burn, would not go away, would remain like a shoe buckle or part of someone's bridgework or one of those small fossil fish you can buy for a few dollars to set up on a rack in your husband's study, on display like a cup and saucer.

I was very cold but I didn't shiver.

Now this was 1965.

The ceiling of the large elegant room was made of a white substance, something that appeared to be very light, like hardened foam, a mysterious synthetic substance like a hardened cloud; nothing Elena recognized. She was thinking about her moist elastic womb located somewhere deep inside her body, but where—? Judge Couteau was talking to her, with his graceful agreeable smile; she was grateful for him, for his talking, because it would not be necessary for her to reply; he would not really expect her to reply, only to listen. She must listen.

Another man joined them, pushing in. Graying red hair, sad-merry pouched eyes, his large fingers closed about his glass. Judge Couteau made way for him. Now there were several men, and Elena knew she would be safe: no need to talk. She allowed her gaze to shift upward, up to the ceiling, which was not as complicated as the floor. No shadows there, no reflections, no shapes like human beings. . . . But there were many lights, fluorescent lights buried in the ceiling, almost concealed, hidden. All corners of the big room were illuminated equally. Perhaps there was a quiet, omnipotent hum from the fluorescent lighting, but Elena could not hear it. Somewhere a giant air-conditioning unit was humming, vibrating, but Elena could not hear it. People moved slowly about this room, drifting from one area of parquet squares to another, smiling, talking, recognizing one another, safe with one another, moving from one part of the floor to another. Everything was countable. There was no need to feel panic.

"The poor bastard!—he wrote up his own petition for habeas corpus that was two thousand pages long! Two thousand pages! His life story, a pile of papers that began with the date of his birth, sometime in the twenties—the whole thing written by hand, bad spelling, bad grammar, sentences that began nowhere and ended two or three pages later, all mixed up and messy, things scratched out, notes in the margins and unnumbered pages of what he called an 'appendix' at the end— Now doesn't that make you wonder, really, how the prisons are being run? A man with so much free time, evidently years of free time, not to mention the supplies and someone's obvious encouragement—to write a two-thousand-page book nobody is going to read—! Jesus! Who's in charge, just who's in charge? That's the question I would like to ask and there'll be some pretty red faces around this state if I get around to asking it—"

"Aren't you going to Washington?"

"Yes, I am going to Washington, but I am not abandoning Michigan; I am never going to abandon Michigan."

The conversation jumped to a new topic: a Detroit man who had campaigned for the Democratic nomination for governor of the state, who had spent all his money and his wife's money, but no one knew how much, not even within ten thousand dollars, who had lost badly and was not at this cocktail reception, though his son-in-law was here. The son-in-law was drunk.

Mrs. Couteau joined them, sliding her arm through her husband's. She was small, compact, with a smooth powdered face that showed no wrinkles, no expression but mild pleasure. She was pleased. She was agreeable. She interrupted the conversation to say something—as she spoke, Elena noticed that she began to appear rather hard-eyed, so Elena allowed her gaze to shift away again—something about a newly elected criminal court judge, not here because he had not been invited, whose name was Patrick O'Gorman, and who had presented himself for election—he had been an ordinary lawyer—on the basis of his name, the popular appeal of his name. And he had won.

"Are you serious?" the man with the pouched eyes cried.

Yes, serious.

O'Gorman and his wife and friends believed that his name on a ballot would look good, just the look of it; he had even explained this to the bar association, sincerely and earnestly, even modestly; he had no background in public work, he really knew nothing, but he thought he would stand for an election. . . . The bar had not endorsed him. But he had run for office and had won by a large majority.

The conversation drifted back to the man who had tried for the Democratic nomination for governor, who . . .

Elena drew her breath in slowly, as if testing herself. Yes, she felt better now. She was safe now. She glanced over to where her husband stood—and he was still there, still arguing with the same two men. The young tax lawyer looked heated, distressed. Marvin's complexion was ruddy. Around them were slow-drifting groups of people, the women with air-blown hair, shining and perfect, their arms bared, a few of them with their shoulders bared, smooth and flesh-toned as women in expensive portraits. Primed, heated, quick to laugh, to agree to laugh. Practiced in smiles. Teeth were shown without hesitation, in delight, because they were perfect teeth. Most of the women were beautiful; impeccable. Perhaps not beautiful but handsome, agreeable, with their perfect spontaneous smiles and their stiff lacquered hair. Their lips appeared to be lacquered also, moving ceaselessly to shape words and smiles. Elena noticed a very striking young woman in a long floor-length dress of green velvet, the front slashed to the waist and fastened together by silver spikes.

"What does Marvin think of him, Elena?"

"I'm not sure . . . I don't know. . . ."

Mrs. Couteau lit a cigarette and blew smoke energetically around her.

"I know what *I* think," she said.

A black man in a freshly laundered white outfit was on the perimeter of Elena's group, asking them something in an earnest voice. More drinks? Yes, said Couteau. Yes, said the sad-eyed man, with a grin. Don't think I'd better, said Couteau's wife. Elena still held her drink, the ice cubes melted into a tepid brown-beige liquid, no thank you, nothing. Elena's gaze met the black man's by accident and both were opaque, unseeing, not an exchange of looks but a collision of blind stares, coming together in the space between them and then going motionless, dead.

Certain people cannot see each other; they cancel each other out.

Around her neck she wore one of the antique gold necklaces Marvin had given her; a heavy, ponderous gold, very beautiful. It was a weight she had to combat. It pulled one way and she pulled another way. Mrs. Couteau was admiring it. Someone else admired it, a man, but he knew enough not to come too close. Mrs. Couteau could touch it with one perfect polished nail; but not the man. . . . Though he almost touched it with his forefinger. He said:

Elena thanked them both.

That day I learned from them about the immortality of the womb: you can't kill it. There were other things to learn but I couldn't concentrate. I was very cold. I was eager to be taken home, to go home with my husband, to be safe at home . . . but then I thought, what if I can't sleep, what if I feel it inside me, the little uncurled-out sac inside me. . . .

My mother once said, You don't want children, you don't have the figure for it. Your pelvis is too small. Don't ruin yourself.

More guests pushed into the room, the air was noisy and smoky and very happy, and Elena felt a sudden rush of happiness herself, a knowledge that she was privileged to be here, to be standing here, and that she would be privileged in a short while to be taken home. She wanted to go home, she was almost greedy now for that house, for her husband and that house. . . . So many cheerful people! It would take a lifetime to know them all. Elena was very safe among them, standing on a few squares of the parquet floor, one of the younger women, with her blond hair in a thick gleaming coil and her neck in a comfortable tension, pulling against the weight of that necklace. She had not moved very far all evening. Other people moved slowly from group to group, always changing the composition of the room, but the room itself was ultimately finite and the people crowded in it were finite. A game might be in session, involving parquet squares like squares on a chess board, people like players who had come bravely out onto the board to risk themselves, in person, but Elena didn't know its rules and did not think about them.

She was grateful for the finite safety of the world, its countable parts.

"I see Marvin hit the newspapers the other night," someone said. "Were you frightened? Lucky he was home!"

"Oh yes," said Mrs. Couteau, "what happened? Someone broke into your house?"

A man had climbed over the wall a few evenings before, and the dogs had attacked him. Elena had heard the barking, the snarling, a man's screams. When she ran out the front door she saw a man on his knees on the sidewalk, begging her to call off the dogs—then Marvin ran out behind her—

The man hadn't been hurt badly, a few small bleeding wounds.

He began to cry while they waited for the police; he told Marvin that he was desperate, that he had wanted to talk to him, to Marvin Howe, but hadn't been able to get an appointment; he was desperate because he had been arrested by two vice squad detectives for "homosexual activities," but he was innocent, he would swear he was innocent. . . . He'd been picked up in a bar when a man standing beside him asked him a question he had not heard exactly, and he had replied, "I think so. . . ." The man turned out to be a plain-clothes detective and he and another plainclothesman had arrested the man right there, and he was innocent and desperate for someone to help him. . . .

"A familiar story," Couteau said contemptuously.

"Is Marvin going to press charges?"

"No," Elena said, surprised. She hesitated. She had thought this story would evoke other responses; now she saw she had been mistaken. She said slowly, "No, he went to see him in the hospital . . . he gave him the name of someone in Legal Aid. . . ."

"Marvin should press charges," a man said flatly. "That's the kind of attitude I don't like. I hate to criticize your husband, but he isn't being responsible and he knows it. And isn't breaking and entering more serious after dark?"

"That law was just changed," Couteau said.

"Well, it is more serious after dark, the law shouldn't have been changed. That law was based on something quite profound. I'm surprised at Marvin Howe."

"When was the law changed?"

"It wasn't being enforced anyway."

"That doesn't make any difference—"

A woman in a black dress came over to Elena and claimed her. She was middle-aged, kindly; she said, "Elena Howe! I haven't seen you for a long time, dear, how are you? I was just talking to Marvin and telling him there is someone I must introduce you to—"

Elena disengaged herself from the group she was in and allowed herself to be led somewhere. People made way for her and the woman, whose name she did not recall; people glanced at *Elena Howe* and stepped aside, smiling, even the mayor of the city in a dark outfit, with a dark turtleneck sweater instead of a shirt, smiling at them. The woman was chattering about something but Elena couldn't hear her because of the din in the room. She felt the fierce flamelike leap of attention from people, and then the recoiling from this attention, the men tilting the ice cubes in their glasses and then going polite again, tame, no threat to her or to anyone, not on the square feet of this floor.

"This woman is fascinating, and I know she'd love to meet you," the woman in black was saying over her shoulder. "I've been trying to get you together—you'd be perfect for her interview show—"

The woman led Elena to a couple, a man and a woman she didn't recognize; evidently they were joining the very end of a conversation. The man was saying, "Rape can't be a very serious crime, it happens every twenty minutes or so around here. . . ."

Elena was introduced: to a woman named Marya Sharp, to a man named Homer Tate. She gathered that they were not here together, they were not really a couple. The woman, Marya, was about Elena's height, quite slender for a woman of her age—she must have been in her forties—and very pretty, with her chestnut hair fluffed up and out, the colors of her face pink and a light, even tan. She smiled at Elena and said, "I'm very pleased to meet you, Mrs. Howe."

Elena stared: there was something familiar about this woman. "I'm very pleased to meet you . . ." she said.

The woman in black was saying enthusiastically, "Wouldn't she be perfect for your show, Marya? People are so curious about Marvin! There's so much local interest in him, so much local pride, just think of all the people who would turn on your show just because of the subject–"

"The women I interview are career women, not the wives of men," Marya Sharp said.

"Yes, but there is such an interest in this, I mean, the problems of being married to– I mean, the excitement of it and even the danger–" the woman said falteringly.

Elena looked at Marya Sharp's face and saw it shift slowly into the face of someone she knew.

Ardis?

She stepped back in surprise. The woman in black glanced at her but did not stop talking. "–such a shame, Marya, to rule out a wonderful interview like this–are you sure? I mean, are you positive? Because–"

Marya smiled ironically at Elena. Sternly. She made a slight nodding motion with her head, very slight: *Yes. Yes. Don't stare at me.*

"Well, there might be a possibility," Marya said slowly. "It goes against the principles of my program, but. . . . Let's talk, Mrs. Howe." She took Elena's arm in a quick proprietary gesture and turned her away. "Excuse us," she said to the woman and the man she had been talking with, who both stared. "Stupid damn bores," she muttered to Elena.

Elena walked blindly.

She had not seen her mother for a long time.

"Elena, my God, do you have to gape at me like an idiot?" Marya whispered. "You certainly knew who I was, didn't you? My television name?"

"No–I mean, she didn't say who–I didn't–"

"You knew I was getting a television show at last, didn't you?"

"The last time we talked you didn't know yet–"

"Well, it came through finally. Don't you follow anything up on your own? You must have seen the notices in the paper—don't you even read the television page?"

"Yes, sometimes, but—"

They were near one of the walls, beside a table that had been cleared off, its soiled white cover folded in two. A vase containing pink and red roses was tilted a little, half on the tablecloth and half on the table. Elena felt the impulse to right it.

"Elena, you are so disappointing!" Marya sighed.

Elena's face burned.

"Anyway, the show materialized just as I had hoped it would, right down to the name I've taken on—Marya Sharp—and the format I wanted, everything. I'm being sponsored by Lovecore, the cosmetics, and the first two shows went perfectly—you mean you didn't even watch?"

"I didn't know about it," Elena said. "I'm so sorry—Marvin has been very busy and—"

"You just don't pay attention to your environment," Marya said. "I would have thought you'd be proud of me. But anyway, now that you're not so shocked, you look very well—I'm pleased you still wear your hair that way, it really is very becoming on you —a woman needs a perfect face for that kind of hairdo— I've been watching you off and on here, and I've liked what I've seen," Marya said critically. "But that color, that pink, isn't right for you. Did Marvin pick out that dress? I hate pink; you should avoid it. How are you? I'm sorry I didn't call you back. I almost called you when I saw that item in the paper, about somebody robbing your house, but anyway, how are you? Happy?"

Elena said dizzily, "Yes, yes . . . I'm very busy. . . . I'm taking a course in art appreciation . . . an adult-education course at the Rackham Building. . . . And I'm going through my old French textbooks again, you know I had two years in high school and I'd like to be able to read and translate . . . there are essays in French Marvin sometimes needs to know about. . . ."

"You're busy. Good," Marya said, pleased. "But aren't you going to congratulate me? Everyone tells me my show is going well."

"Oh, yes," Elena said, risking a smile now that her mother was not so critical, in fact smiling happily, "yes, that's wonderful. Marvin will be very pleased too. I don't think he knows about it either —I mean, I didn't know what your name was going to be, I don't think you mentioned it, so even if I had read about the show—

even if I– If I happened to see the show I might not have– You look so different, I–"

"Well, Robie made me a present of two weeks in Dallas, in this lovely mansion down there, before my show began. They did a nice job," Marya said, patting her face and running one finger back behind her ear thoughtfully. "The operation on the second day, and then rest and recovery and exercise—they fly clients out to a ranch by helicopter, for horseback riding, and I met some fascinating people there. Even a man, a ninety-two-year-old Texan, he said it was his third time, he had everything done including the buttocks," Marya said. "What a crazy world! As for my hair, it looks like hell yet."

"I think it looks very nice," Elena said.

"No. It's all my own hair, and much too thin. They were bleaching it back in degrees, you know, because I had black hair for a while, and one morning when I brushed it it started coming out. It was horrible. . . . I thought it might be the end of me. It came out in handfuls, it was horrible. . . . So now I have to be very careful."

Elena stared at Marya. It crossed her mind that this woman was not her mother after all. Her mother's voice had not been so soft, so carefully modulated.

"Wasn't that a joke, that terrible woman bringing you over to meet me!" Marya laughed. "She's been telling me for weeks she'd like to introduce me to a young friend of hers, Marvin Howe's wife—and I tried to stop her, I made excuses—but she has to have her own way, constantly; the wives of all these millionaires make me sick!—they think they're everyone's mother, they *must* do favors for people and coerce them into things. She tried to introduce me to some bachelor, too, some cousin of hers, but I managed to avoid that. By the way, Elena, you know Robie isn't too well."

"You said something on the telephone—an operation—"

"Two operations in two months, for ulcers. The poor bastard, he's lost a lot of weight, you know he asks me about you and wonders why Marvin doesn't bring you to the Club. Marvin drops in himself, you know, once in a while—or doesn't he mention that to you? So Robie can't figure out why he never sees you. But I tried to explain to him that your husband is very guarded with you, he wants to keep little Elena for himself, doesn't he?—but of course he's perfectly right. I'm surprised he even lets you take adult-education courses."

"He wouldn't mind if you and I saw each other now," Elena said, "I mean . . . so many years have passed. . . . I could come down to your studio and watch your show, maybe, or we could have lunch together. . . . I'd like to talk to you about something. . . ."

Marya shook her head, smiling. "I don't think so, Elena, really. Marvin doesn't want you to be influenced by me."

"But he wouldn't mind now, I could ask him," Elena said quickly. "Let's go over and talk to him right now. . . ."

"No, Elena, really. He made his feelings known when he married you. I can't go against his wishes."

"But–"

"Elena, don't be so stubborn! You're very sweet and very lovely, but you're still stubborn and you've got to grow up. You're his wife now. You're not my daughter, I mean not officially, we have two quite different names now. . . . In fact, Marvin offered me money to leave this area, but I refused, I told him absolutely that I would not interfere in your life. And I haven't."

"When was this?" Elena asked.

"Before the wedding. He took me out for drinks, to the Top of the Flame on a thundery afternoon, and he was awfully nervous, like a bridegroom. In fact he was a bridegroom–at his age. . . . He talked for a very long time and I became quite sympathetic, he told me how he dreaded your being dragged back into the past. Of course he knows about everything, your father and even that man in Cleveland, you know, the man who owned the apartment building . . . and he said, frankly, he wasn't pleased with it all, he didn't want me influencing you any longer. He was very frank. He said I should keep in contact with you, mainly by phone, and arrange to see you once in a while–because you would want that–but our meetings were to be very rare. Of course I agreed with him. It was necessary to agree."

"I didn't know about this," Elena said faintly.

"People don't say no to your husband," Marya said. "Really, by the time he finishes talking, you believe he must be right. You might start out disagreeing, but you end up agreeing . . . you just can't remember your own arguments. And he is right about this, really. I don't resent him at all."

"I'm glad you didn't leave the city," Elena said.

"No, I like Robie and my other friends here and of course this television show is very exciting for me. It's an entirely new adventure. So I don't resent Marvin; in fact, he and I are almost friends now. . . . Of course, if he doesn't bring you down to the Club, I understand why. He's quite right. Did he ever tell you how he checked us out?" Marya said, lowering her voice.

"You mean with a detective?"

"A detective! A whole agency, Elena!" Marya laughed. "He must have spent thousands of dollars. He knew every fact about you, honey, even doctors' files right up to a few weeks before the wedding—I don't know how on earth he got them, if his men broke in the offices and took pictures, or if they paid some doctor's secretary. Isn't he cautious? And he loves you very much, honey. What more could you want in a husband?"

"Nothing," Elena said slowly.

"What more could you want out of life? So please, Elena, don't endanger your own marriage by talking to him about me. When we meet I'll be Marya Sharp. You're a lovely girl," Marya said fondly, "but, frankly . . . well . . . at this point in my career I don't really want a grown-up daughter. . . . Do you understand?"

Elena was looking at the vase. But her stare did not quite take it in, she couldn't really see it.

"You shouldn't agitate for trouble," Marya said. "What more could you want, with the life you and Marvin lead?"

"Nothing," Elena said.

14 SIXTEEN UNRELATED TIME RELATIONS

1 *Hurtled across the landscape, picked up in one place and set down in another . . . at the back of his mind he carried me, he never released me. He was always in motion. I was still.*

I never thought about the faces offered to him—not just the women, but the men, the crowds of people, all those strangers. I never thought about losing him.

Elena sat alone at the dining-room table, reading a postcard from her husband. He was involved in a malpractice suit in Phoenix; the trial was in its second week. Elena read and reread the harsh hurried scrawl.

On the back of the card was a slick, brightly colored picture of desert and mountains, spiny trees that held their limbs up like arms, praying, pleading. The colors were bright blue and bright orange-red and the too-dark green of the cactus trees, which seemed stamped on the outlines of the trees, not convincing. Elena stared at the picture for a while. She touched one of the cactus trees, outlining it slowly with her finger.

When he was away from home he telephoned her twice a day: once in the morning, once in the evening. Sometimes he telephoned in the late afternoon as well.

She placed the card before her and glanced through the other mail: two small white envelopes, invitations, a large envelope from one of the Detroit organizations Marvin was associated with, a brochure explaining the 1967-68 plans for one of the companies Marvin had investments in, many advertisements, magazines, a notice from one of the charities Elena belonged to, her name and address stamped on the envelope. . . . Then a letter from Miami Beach, addressed to *Mrs. Marvin Howe,* a handwritten letter.

Elena pulled this envelope out of the pile of mail and studied the handwriting. It did not look familiar; it was ordinary, very neat. It was a woman's handwriting. Elena thought, *I can open this or not open it.* It was addressed to *Mrs. Marvin Howe* correctly. The number on Lakeshore Drive was correct.

She watched herself turn the letter in her hands several times, and then start to open it, slowly, not tearing the envelope; evidently she was going to read the letter. But she thought, suddenly: *I don't have to read this. . . .* She took the small note-sized piece of stationery out of the envelope and for a few minutes looked at it, without reading it. Then, almost against her will, she began to read:

> Ask him about Ursula down in Miami Beach. Do you dare ask him. Your husband is no stranger to this Ursula. Observe his face carefully.

Elena read this several times. Behind her the house was silent, comfortable with age, many rooms of quiet, stilled air. The walls were thick. Even the layers of wallpaper were thick, layers of tissuelike skin upon skin, to slow everything down. Elena read the note again, slowly. If she were to glance up her eye would skid effortlessly along the gleaming table to the black and gold wallpaper and to an ornate engraved clock.

She placed this note before her, next to Marvin's card. She leaned forward and looked from one to the other.

2 In the classroom at the Rackham Building she sat in the exact center of the room, the fourth desk in the center row. She had come to that desk by instinct, automatically, on the first day; the other students sat in different desks from time to time, but Elena always took the same desk. She opened her notebook to the notes she had taken on the last lecture. The next page was blank and she wrote at the top of it: February 11, 1969—Professor Brauer—"What You Should Know About Real Estate Transactions." This was her class in law, "Law for Laymen," and they were to have read a chapter on real-estate transactions that week.

Dr. Brauer was late: he told them he had to drive all the way from Ann Arbor, so he was often late. The class met each Thursday at 4:15 but it rarely began at 4:15.

The man who sat next to Elena said to her, "You know where he is? He's across the street in a bar."

Elena smiled to acknowledge this, but did not comment.

By the time Dr. Brauer hurried in it was 4:35. He was carrying a briefcase stuffed with books and papers, too full to close, and he slammed this down on the podium at the front of the room. He looked harried, impatient. He looked around the room once, twice, then quickly into the center at Elena; then he began his lecture in brief explosive sentences, while he stared out the window.

"He was over in the bar at three-thirty. This time I'm going to report him," the man beside Elena whispered angrily.

At 5:20 the instructor shoved up his sleeve and looked at his watch and announced that the class was over. But as the students put on their coats and began to leave the room he remained standing at the podium and seemed to be gazing toward Elena, with an odd neutral smile. He was not a friendly man.

He said abruptly, "Now do you know what you should know about real-estate transactions, Mrs. Howe?"

Elena said yes, she thought so.

She smiled at him.

He walked out the door with her. In the corridor he said, "Do you have a way to get home, or what?—do you need a ride anywhere?"

"No thank you," Elena said.

"Okay," he said, and walked away.

Was it sometime in February, that day? What did I look like? Was I looking toward the door, waiting for the instructor to walk in the room? Was I sitting there not looking at anything, just sitting in the center of that room . . . ?

Was I waiting for someone to see me?

What did I look like?

3 She leafed through the French grammar until she came to the chapter on the subjunctive, then she looked up the imperfect subjunctive. She had memorized all this but she didn't want to trust her memory; she was translating an article for Marvin. It was all familiar, the endings, the -sse, -sses, -ʌt, etc., yes, but she was afraid to trust her memory.

She had been working for several hours on the translation, which was a study by a French pharmacologist on the variations in tissue reactions to certain types of poison. She forced herself to go very slowly, meticulously, rereading what she had translated after each sentence, to see if it all seemed logical. It was 2:30 in the afternoon and she was alone in the house; she had hours ahead in which to work, before he came home at 7:00. If the telephone rang late in the afternoon it would probably mean he would be late, but he would be home sometime that evening and she had all the hours between 2:30 and that time for this work.

She reread part of a paragraph:

> . . . all that remained of the alleged Mlle Legère was some decomposed soft tissues hidden in lime; all the bones and head had been removed, and never located; the only useful evidence was the isolation of a poison (hyoscine), some hair, and a birthmark miraculously preserved on a three-inch piece of skin. It was this birthmark that. . . .

Elena was pleased with this, so far, though she rechecked a few words. She rechecked a verb ending. But the words seemed to flow smoothly and mechanically enough and she was satisfied that she could go on.

4 "We are trying to conserve nature . . . we feel that time is running out."

"What do you say to charges that you are operating against the interests of certain businesses?—that you're therefore endangering the jobs of workingmen?"

"We are trying to establish priorities. What matters most is the preservation of the planet and of the species as a whole, not isolated individuals and their money and their jobs. . . . We feel that time is running out."

Marya was interviewing an attractive middle-aged woman, who talked nervously and kept glancing at the camera or at something behind the camera. Marya spoke in careful sentences and she smiled often to encourage the other woman. Her hair appeared stiff as a helmet, and there was a sleek look to her shoulders and throat that made Elena think of the poise of a long-necked bird, patient and ready to strike.

Marvin was looking up from the papers on his lap. "Your mother is giving that woman a hard time, isn't she?"

"Is she? I don't know. I thought she was being very nice tonight."

"She's made the woman very nervous."

Elena had not noticed this.

"Our appeal is simply to people to use their common sense . . . to withdraw their financial support from certain products. . . ."

"An economic boycott?"

"Well, yes, an economic boycott. . . . But what is more important, the selling of fur coats or the preservation of the species of certain animals? Wild animals like the leopard and the tiger, the cheetah, and other lovely wild animals are being destroyed for their skins and are in danger of becoming extinct. . . . There are sixty endangered species today and if they are allowed to die out, no miracle of technology can bring them back. . . ."

"You are arguing more generally, though, against the wearing of furs?"

"Oh yes, yes, absolutely, the wearing of any kind of fur is unnecessary, and therefore immoral, but the wearing of these particular furs should be prohibited by law."

Marya frowned and was silent for a moment. Then she said slowly, "I'm sorry, but I can't help but disagree with you. I know my views will seem shocking to you, and probably to many of our viewers, but I can't agree with everything you've said. I want to make a very clear, controversial statement. I think that furs are lovely, worn by men and women both. I don't think there is anything lovelier than furs. It's part of human history that human beings have subjugated all the animals and have chosen to wear the furs and hides of certain animals, it's a statement about something. . . . I'm not sure what I mean but my instinct tells me that it's true. A beautiful woman, wearing the fur of an animal, is justified."

On screen, the woman stared at Elena's mother, speechless.

Marya went on thoughtfully: "The more beautiful she is, the more justified."

"Your mother is a very strange woman," Marvin said with admiration.

5 Marvin took off his overcoat and let it fall onto the leather sofa. He went to make himself a drink. Elena watched his back, the brusque motions of his arms, the rigidity of his body. Without turning toward her he asked, "What did you do today, Elena?"

"I stayed home."

"Didn't you have a luncheon to go to?"

"It was canceled."

"Oh. Was it. That's good. You're happiest at home, aren't you," he said vaguely. Elena looked at his overcoat and wondered if she should pick it up. . . . But that might annoy him. He was always telling her to let his things lay where he threw them, he didn't mind a mess, he sometimes liked a mess. He didn't want her waiting on him, he said. So she looked at the coat but didn't touch it.

"You didn't listen to the news tonight, did you?"

"The six-o'clock news?" Elena said. "No."

Marvin sat heavily on the edge of the sofa and raised his glass to his mouth. Elena waited. His face was flushed; Elena guessed he had been drinking on the way home. That day he had been in court, conducting the defense of a Detroit manufacturer, a man who had been indicted for conspiracy to defraud his investors.

Elena stared at him, waiting. She was quite certain the trial was not over yet, it hadn't been that far along, and so Marvin could not have lost. That couldn't be it. But something might have happened in court today that meant he could lose. . . . Or it might have nothing to do with his winning or losing: one day he had come home upset, like this, and Elena found out a few days later that a woman had run up to Marvin in court and attacked him, screaming at him, and had had to be dragged out. Marvin had refused to press charges or to talk to reporters. Elena had never asked him about it; she knew it had nothing to do with her. . . . Another time, a national newsmagazine had published a long interview with him, a really vicious article Elena had come across by accident in the Grosse Pointe library a month after it had come out. Beneath a photograph of Marvin and her—Marvin looking older than he really was, Elena looking younger—had been the caption, "Millionaire Lawyer Howe & Wife: Claims of Divinity?" Marvin had never said anything to Elena about the article and Elena had never said anything to him.

"Elena, come here," he said. He pressed his face against her and held her clumsily. For a while he said nothing. Then he murmured, "I left home around seven . . . and then what did you do, dear? . . . I want to know what you did so that I can imagine you here by yourself, here, just you, I don't want to think about anyone else tonight. . . . Talk to me, dear. Talk to me."

6 "If you relax it won't hurt as much," the doctor said.

Elena relaxed.

The nurse, a girl of about twenty, in a stiff white cap, smiled nervously down at Elena.

Closing her eyes, talking to herself about that part of her body, detaching herself from it, making it numb, only an idea. . . . She instructed her brain to annihilate it, inch by inch, and now the surrounding tissue, all the tissue going nerveless and relaxed, limp, asleep. She had been gripping the edge of the table; she considered her fingers one by one, loosening them, calming them so that even the damp palm of her hand went numb.

She felt a stab of pain. But no, nothing; it went blank again.

Another current of pain, high inside her.

". . . almost over," the doctor said.

Elena closed her eyes again. She felt the nurse's presence, close to her, almost an irritant; better for her to be alone without another woman in the room.

Then it was over.

The nurse was wiping blood off an instrument. Her face was strained, as if she had experienced the pain Elena had not.

There, so deep in there, no sensation but what you imagine: you must imagine everything.

Back in the doctor's office, sitting in front of his desk, Elena kept seeing the blood, the blood-soaked tissue; the doctor was talking cheerfully. "Most women get tense for even these routine examinations, and then they suffer pain that's quite real. It can be quite severe. But actually there's no need for it. Actually," he said, "that part of the female body is not sensitive at all, it's poorly supplied with end organs of touch. In fact, the internal entodermal origin of the lining of the vagina makes it similar to parts of the digestive tract—sensation must be mainly psychological—I think—it must be mainly psychological and not physical, not natural—"

You must imagine everything.

7 False facts.

The detour around the construction, the mud, the planks in the mud, Elena walking carefully on one of the planks, and one of the men yelling down at her. Cupping his hands to his mouth, yelling. Another man laughing. Another man, stocky in his work-clothes, throwing something at her that hadn't enough weight to carry itself to her—just a crumpled-up paper bag, a lunch bag.

False facts: they didn't really want to hurt her.

Didn't hate her.

Didn't want her dead.

False facts: the recitation of the weather around the country, the temperatures recorded at all the airports. You believe it must mean something but it will not.

False facts: blood on instruments, no proof of pain. Proof only of blood.

False facts were like the entrance to one of the rooms of the house: you came to the doorway, looked inside, stepped quietly inside. And then? You believed the room and its furniture had been prepared for you. It must mean something. In a film, on television, this would mean something; it would be an entrance into something. It would not be simply an extension of the room you had come from. . . . But the room and its furniture were false facts because nothing was going to happen. Therefore the room is safe to enter.

A false fact: teeth in a laboratory vial, shaken up, treated with chemicals and analyzed and rearranged. They mean nothing.

The date, September 18, 1970: another false fact.

At the head of a page that date would indicate something, something false. Better to see it in its place, on a calendar, one day out of many. Elena yawned, checking the date on the kitchen calendar. She yawned luxuriously. Her hair was loose, drying, and she let her head fall forward when she yawned so that her hair fell slowly forward, slowly onto the kitchen counter.

What did it mean, September 18, 1970?

8 "Both intelligence and patience, yes, an intelligent patience, *n'est-ce pas?*—but also the artistic sense, residing almost I think in the fingertips—"

A man in a dark suit and a white turtleneck shirt made of a thin crepy material, smiling. Wings of white hair were brushed back damply from his forehead; the rest of his hair was very black.

His bright dark eyes moved fondly around the room, lingering on one face and then another, and Elena waited tensely for him to seek her out, certainly he must seek her out, *her,* she had worked so hard. . . . Prince S. Stelp, standing with a wooden spoon raised halfway to his mouth, and his tongue still moving slowly and thoughtfully inside his mouth as he caressed his students with his soft bright eyes, passing judgment almost against his will. *Sauce bernaise.* Elena stood primly and waited, waited for him to look at her . . . waited for him . . . hardly hearing his soothing words, his hesitant gracious accent, "to achieve the perfunctory in this case is itself a success . . . but one among you has surpassed even that, she is a genius this evening as so many evenings since our class has begun, I think you anticipate it is—"

9 Elena washed her hair and dried it in a towel and let it lay loose, damp, heavy on her shoulders and past her shoulders. She wore a dancer's practice costume, black synthetic fabric, sleeves to her wrists, bare legs. As she did her exercises she whipped her hair around her, front and back, forward, backward, until she lost count of how many times she had snapped her body erect and then reached down again to press her fingertips solidly against the floor. Dizzy, staggering, she paused to stare at herself in the adjustable mirror: her blond hair like a mane about her face, tumbling past her face, her face flushed with good health, *there is Elena Howe in the mirror,* in the handsome silken bedroom.

Her heart pounded but she began to move again, into the hard relentless whiplike rhythm of the exercises, flinging her wet hair forward, backward.

10

I am not requesting any financial reparation in the slightest, because I am of comfortable background, but only an acknowledgment from him of my existence. I live alone now, and things have happened in my life I will not mention because just to list them would be self-pitying, and I know how he hates self-pity in women or in anyone else. I do not know you, Mrs. Howe, but I challenge you to truly believe that your husband was ever as close to you in your intimate moments as he was with me, and I challenge you to ask him if this was so. He could not lie if confronted with the truth! I ask you also to check back to 1969 and the end of 1968 and notice how often he made visits to Albany. If you will dare to ask. . . .

Elena reread the letter. It was so familiar, the uphill charge of the handwriting, the small pinched angry letters in dark ink. . . . And the stationery was familiar: heavy dull green with buff edges. She was certain she had received a letter from this woman before, this *Sylvia Murchinson* from Albany, New York.

Elena folded the letter back into its original folds—three crisp folds. And then she folded it again, carefully, creasing it with the edge of her hand. Then she folded it again, and once again, though it was now more difficult; the stationery was thick. When it was as small as she could get it, Elena dropped it into the wicker wastebasket she brought to the table with her every morning when she went through the mail.

The next letter was quite ordinary: a personal request from someone's campaign manager asking if Marvin might like to align himself with this candidate, who was trying for the Republican nomination for mayor of Detroit. Elena folded this as well and dropped it into the wastebasket. Marvin stayed clear of politics.

11 Shopping on Kercheval one pleasant day, on the Hill, Elena happened to see her mother striding ahead of her—a woman in a tawny wool suit with puffs of fur at her neck and wrists, bright fox-colored fur. Her mother was walking quickly and Elena hesitated, not wanting to call out—there were women shoppers all around her, and it would have been strange for anyone to shout; the other women would have stared at Elena in amazement. So she hurried after her mother, who seemed almost to be hurrying away from her. Ardis's shoulders looked strong and confident; her hair was fixed now in a French twist, so that her head appeared small, sleeker than Elena remembered. They passed a new art gallery in which tear-drop-shaped plastic objects were displayed, and an antique shop with wrought-iron dogs and geraniums in kettles guarding the door, a gourmet and health-food store that displayed kits for making yoghurt at home, and, as Elena's mother paused to look in the window of the Christian Science Reading Room, Elena breathlessly caught up with her.

"Mother—?"

Ardis turned to her, startled. Elena saw that her face had been slightly altered: she wore pale green eye shadow, her cheeks were carefully rouged, her lips quite red . . . the face designed by Fanny Price, of London, a young girl who had recently toured the United States to promote her "Raggedy Doll" line of clothes. . . .

"Or should I call you Marya?" Elena asked.

The woman smiled in recognition, happily. "Oh, you're mistaking me for Marya Sharp, aren't you? I take that as a compliment!"

Then, seeing Elena's look of confusion, she smiled sympathetically. "It's the strangest thing, but a few months ago a man mistook me for Marya, in Hudson's downtown, and he just *wouldn't* believe I was someone else. He was quite angry about one of her programs. . . . But then nothing at all happened until just yesterday, and then again it was in Hudson's, in the bridal registry, a woman this time—a saleswoman—and she thought I was just being modest, you know, pretending not to be Marya Sharp— And now again this morning, what a coincidence! But I'm afraid I'm not Marya, I'm only Olivia Larkin."

Elena stared. She had not made sense of all those words.

"Olivia Larkin?" she said. "But— Is that another name? I don't know what—"

"We know each other, dear, don't we? We've met somewhere or other—at the club downtown, the DAC, wasn't it?—you're Marvin Howe's wife? Yes, I know we've met, and I've seen your picture in the paper. But I want to thank you for the compliment! She's such an intelligent and stimulating woman, isn't she?"

"I wish you wouldn't— I mean, I— I wish—" Elena stared at her mother's smile, which had not slackened. She was frightened of that smile, which was much broader than any she could recall, and the bright spots of rouge were a mistake, a sign of bad judgment even if that face was now fashionable. It wasn't like Ardis. And this woman was taller than Elena remembered, and her voice was shriller. . . .

Elena shook her head. Confused. Confusion. "I wish that— I— I—" she paused. Then she regained her own voice and said evenly, "I wish I wouldn't make such mistakes—I sometimes make mistakes like that— I—"

"Oh, we all do!" the woman cried enthusiastically. "It's so human, I do it all the time myself—and please don't apologize for making such a flattering mistake!"

Elena smiled and gazed vaguely at the window of the Reading Room and listened to the woman chatter, wondering how she could escape, how she could get back home, safely back home. It seemed to her that a maze lay behind her and ahead of her and that it would demand her greatest concentration; but she could not think at all.

12 Four couples invited. Ten persons altogether.

Sat. 7:30 Jan. 30 1970. Invitations sent out Jan. 10.

Completion of holidays: back from trips, tanned faces, eagerness for news of friends, acquaintances, problems at home, etc. Mr. & Mrs. ______. Mr. & Mrs. ______. Dr. & Mrs. ______. Mr. & Mrs. ______.

She begged him to let her make the dinner herself. At first he said:

Then he said:

And she said thank you.

The menu: ______

______

______

______

______

______

and afterward

______

Important conversation, earnest and loud, loud. Even the laughter was earnest. Elena felt so intoxicated with the evening, so heady, heavy-headed, she could not listen to anyone; triumphant and chaste, Mrs. Howe, glowing out of the house's lovely mirrors. A successful evening. People stayed late and talked loudly and earnestly. Elena felt feverish with success.

Lovely smiles, faces, nudging of old friends—someone's wife & Marvin, a little drunk, merry and comradely, telling jokes. Jokes about—? Elena couldn't quite hear. Then she lay sleepless and enchanted beside him as he slept, his head hot on the pillow, Elena's face hot and dry, feverish, as the evening replayed itself in her head and replayed itself and

13 "Mentally Handicapped Children of Wayne County Fund-Raising Luncheon." E. picked up at the house by friends, driven to Belle Isle, staring happily at the dull cold sharp March day, the usual leafless trees, the forlorn remnants of newspapers and lunch bags. Women talking: almost musical in their exclamations and laughter. A woman wearing black leather gloves was driving; E. notices rings bulging sharply beneath the leather. *Something is*

hurting me, she thinks, and pulls off her glove to examine her hand: a chunk-sized diamond, a white-gold band encrusted with diamonds, cutting into her flesh.

"What time is it"

"Which way do I turn"

"The monument is over there—we always get lost here—"

"No the monument is to the right"

"You passed the monument"

"I always get lost on Belle Isle"

"Is that the Canadian shore there or did we drive all around the island in a circle and"

"It's dirty here"

"There will never be another riot because"

"There's that other monument up ahead—that statue—"

Through the sparse woods. Icy-looking waves of the lake, nameless birds E. guesses at, their features fluffed out, cold. E. watches them rise into the sky.

At the Detroit Yacht Club, a handsome special sign: "Mentally Handicapped Children of Wayne Co. Luncheon," pointing the way into the banquet room. Warmth. Noise. Pomegranate, chopped & seasoned prawns, lobster. E. notes the cashews & berries, figures it is Marilyn Van Dusen's idea, the main course, because Marilyn Van D. was in the Prince's cuisine class; this was one of his favorites. But not a practical dish for so many people. The Prince would be alarmed. E.'s eye moving at leisure, from table to table to the long flower-laden speakers' table, happy women, almost musical in their clothes & voices & the delight each finds in all the others. Name-places on the tables, simple good taste. *Elena Howe.* Two hundred others.

Now the nervous speech: the nervous fingers of the woman who is speaking, into a microphone that may or may not be working. Someone comes by, passes out ballpoint pens, all miniature, mother-of-pearl, meant to be a souvenir?—or? E. accepts hers & puts it into her purse as the other women at her table do, smiling gratitude.

The burden of decreased federal aid, E. hears. But she half-dreads watching the speaker, a pretty five-foot-one quavering woman, mid-forties, very nervous. *The responsibility of the state ignored. County committee hands tied. So to us. We are faced with. Need vast contributions, cooperation of business & industry & all citizens. Tragedy of handicapped children. Make plight known. Pledge cards for distribution, take all you hope to. National shame.*

Cream? No, nothing. Cream here? No.

The harassed waitress, bent a little to minimize herself; embarrassed. Cream at this table? No. She comes by E. with the tray and asks, Cream here?

Coffee & raspberries *Lelaine*. E. crumples the tough crust, too tough, & arranges it on her plate with her fork. No nervousness herself. No panic. While two girls from the Home, thirteen-year-old twins, tap dance on raised platform. Glass-eyed twins. Slack smiles, mouths, round noses. "Aren't they cute," someone whispers. "You wouldn't guess"

Wouldn't you?

E. doesn't want to look up. Not the eyes, the glazed slack smiles. No. Behind them a glass wall showing the river. A piano: "Tiptoe Through the Tulips," smart sharp clicking of tap dancing, memorized dance, *very professional* someone at E.'s table whispers.

E. opens her purse & pretends to look inside. Where? What? Pulls out the little mother-of-pearl pen. Printed on the side: "Save-the-Opera-House Fund."

Afterward in the powder room, opens the purse again; handful of pledge cards; will ask Marvin what to do with them. E. checks her own face in mirror. Other women checking their faces. "Where are my car keys?" someone asks. "The attendant has them," someone says. "Those girls were so well-trained, you couldn't believe" "My sister's oldest boy is like that" "Friend of mine's brother back in high school" E. in eye-to-eye communication with self, long row of mirrors, a black attendant, fat, waiting nearby, smiling, get a quarter ready for her &.

"No, I have the car keys—but I shouldn't have them—my God, I should have left them in the ignition! If the attendant wanted to move the car he—"

A woman says, "Mrs. Howe? I'm Joan Tyler, I teach French at the Larner School." Smiling. In her thirties, attractive but not pretty. E. smiles. Quarter in her hand, getting damp. "I just wanted to say hello, isn't it crowded in here?—never met you or your husband either but have the greatest admiration for him—

excuse me–" The woman steps aside, three women are leaving, smiling apologetically, pushing through. Then another woman comes in. Then the woman who is speaking to E. squeezes over to E. Says, "Just amazing work!–I've helped him out a little but never had the privilege of meeting him, just his secretary over the phone, sends me work–translations–very technical things but fascinating– I teach Latin too. I majored in Latin and French at Middlebury. Husband's work fascinates me–love to meet him someday–but almost makes me sick sometimes! A man in Rouen cut up his brother's fiancée & so much about poisons & chemicals but fascinating to translate & wondered what use he was making of it? Preparing for a trial? Love to meet him someday–his secretary is the sweetest thing– And so nice to meet you, isn't it crowded here?–"

Nice to meet you, E. says faintly.

14 "Mentally Handicapped Children of Wayne County Fund-Raising Luncheon." Mon. Apr. 12 '71. Detroit Athletic Club. E. picked up at the house by friends. Women's entrance of DAC, special canopy, door on the side of the building; would be barred from men's front entrance. Special sign. Arrow pointing to banquet room. Warmth, odor of crab bisque & cigarette smoke.

Crab bisque. Hearts of palm. Crusty rolls, butter. Meringue shells.

Coffee, tea? Cream here? This table? How many?

"somewhat distressed over poor response to Campaign Week. Mentally Handicapped taking back seat, cancer charity overemphasizes self, selfish publicity. Certain politicians out for votes, Senior Citizen vote bloc, a discouraging start in March & then picked up end of month, somewhat encouraging but far below goal for six-week period. Do you think we need more p.r. work, television, spot announcements, think our executive committee needs to reimagine total campaign?"

E. seated beside Mrs. Couteau, Judge's wife. Mrs. C. poking meringue with spoon, bored. At the podium, the chairwoman with too-large hat, nervous. "We know Detroit & know it is a good-hearted city despite ugly national reputation, simply have to hit upon right approach, remember marvelous response Aid to Biafra–and I don't want to embarrass Carolyn Connor who's right in this room but she was the guiding genius behind that—how many millions?—got right on television & you know the rest, city shaped up behind her & dug in & went far over stated goal, poor tragic starving— Now our challenge, difficulty explaining Mentally Handicapped, our problem to compete with cancer & multiple sclerosis & muscular dystrophy & air pollution— Problem Mentally Handicapped Children *cannot* show afflictions, photographs etc., no wheel chairs & people *do not* want to think. Must explain & re-explain *not* insanity, *not.* Don't know how many times must explain to supposedly well-educated college graduates differences between Mentally Handicapped & Yet my heart goes out to some of these poor"

"What's the use of this?" Mrs. C. says suddenly.

Out loud.

E. glances at her, startled. Other women at table pretend not to hear. Mrs. C.'s too-bright eyes, eaten-off lipstick.

The speaker brings hands up before her, almost in prayer: very feminine. "funds depleted after expenses & printing bill & now new challenge ahead have asked *Detroit News* to publish week-by-week chart of contributions might be embarrassing but must take drastic action— What do you think? What do you think? Am I forcing us all out on a limb exposing us to possible embarrassment or is the kind of prodding we all really need to make us work hard harder victory?"

A moment's shocked silence, and then applause. Finally a roomful of applause, generous, enthusiastic, all the women at E.'s table applauding, even E., even Mrs. C., four or five loud hollow mocking claps.

"Oh hell, this makes me feel like puking," Mrs. C. says loudly. She gets to her feet, staggering. Swerves, her chair tipping sideways & E. manages to catch it. A black waiter, out of nowhere, puts chair back, staring, & Mrs. C. snatches both her earrings off & drops them in her purse. Says to table: "Going to the john to be sick, sick of *her* big mouth. What's the use, fixing the kids up? Retarded or crazy or what? Will it make them happier?—I don't like crab, anyway the sherry wasn't mixed in right, feel like puking."

Mrs. C. walks away. E. picks up her purse, calls out "Mrs. C." & hesitates & then gets her own purse, follows. Waiter looking at her in alarm. In the corridor Mrs. C. is vomiting on carpet. Another waiter, also black, takes half-step toward her, shocked; Mrs. C. swings around & says, "Don't you touch me." Brushes at the front of her dress, a T-shaped design in embossed fawn suede covering her bosom, flicks something off, onto the carpet, careens sideways down to powder room. E. hesitates. E. follows.

Inside, Mrs. C. is being thinly sick in a gold-rimmed marble sink. E. waits, holding both purses. Embarrassed. Can think of nothing to say. Mrs. C. is muttering about the crab, her own peckish stomach, the old-fashioned heating system in this building, the boring speech she had to sit through. Reaches around, groping. E. is quick enough to take a small face towel from the startled matron and hands it to Mrs. C. Mrs. C. yanks it from her, wipes her face. Spits once more into the sink. E. turns on one of the heavy brass faucets and cleans the sink.

Mrs. C. is muttering: "Now I offended them and my ride home will be frigid, a carful of silent offended women all the way back to Grosse Pointe. Jesus. As if they didn't all drink themselves. Who are you?" She peers at E. "Oh. Yes. You have your hair done just before me, don't you, at the Pavilion, with Pierre, you're Marvin Howe's wife." E. doesn't have her hair done anywhere, but she is M.H.'s wife. She agrees.

"I hate that phony French accent of his, but he's the only one who can make me look decent," Mrs. C. says. "My hair is coarse like a horse's mane, believe it or not. . . . Pierre is so sweet, isn't he? I don't know why my husband has this hatred of people like Pierre, men like that, I tell him that men like that can be very sweet. Can you reach me another towel, dear? And take this awful one away. But we had this conversation once about our son Matt—have you ever met him?—at Harvard?—when he was just a baby, and we asked each other what could be the worst fate for him, the most dreadful thing, and we both decided independently of each other, Carl and I, to be a *homosexual.*"

E. hands her another towel.

"I don't hate them the way Carl does," Mrs. C. says in a more restrained voice. "But I would rather see Matt dead, it's such an ugly thing. My husband is a judge and he sees everything, oh believe me, it's enough to make you sick—the underside of our society. Of course Carl is *always* armed when he sits in court; he doesn't trust just the police guards. . . . All this talk about love, drugs and love and mysticism, Carl thinks it's just a secret homosexual code or religion or something—it's *their* way of communicating with one another, and we can't understand. We've had such discussions! The Communists are either using homosexuality to weaken American youth for their revolution, or the homosexuals are using Communism to advance *their* cause. Carl and I discuss it all the time but he can't convince me that anyone as sweet and pathetic as Pierre. . . . Oh, I feel much better now," Mrs. C. says. "I really feel much better. . . ."

E. waits while Mrs. C. dabs make-up on her face. What to do? Return to the luncheon? A boy was going to give a recitation of the Bill of Rights. E. thinks: No. Can't sit through it. She feels a little dizzy suddenly, now that Mrs. C. seems steadier. Mrs. C. is putting lipstick on her mouth, carefully, leaning over the sink so that her face is brought up close to the mirror.

Mrs. C. is saying something to her: perhaps thanking her.

". . . . ."

E. half hears it, loses it. She smiles, acknowledges the remark. Yes. Music is being piped into the room from somewhere. That is why she can't quite hear Mrs. C.

Was today's date another false fact?

Was today itself a false fact?

". . . . ."

15 Mon. Apr. 12 '71 1:45 PM

Which she notes on her way down, the carpeted stairway, a carpeted corridor, splendid draperies and wall hangings and chandeliers, settings for important dramas that happen somewhere else. E. looks at her watch, a bracelet of jewels, small blue and white jewels. Engraved. Quite light. Her watch seems to have stopped at 1:45, she knows it must be later than that. Should wash hands again: a slight odor of vomit. Odor of his clothes, his shoes; pajamas, flung over the back of a chair to dry. His breath. A halo of his love around her. *You don't want to have any children. You don't have the figure for it.*

She almost hears the voice—her mother's voice—she almost hears it, those words, those exact words. She pauses, struck by the words and the strange nearness of her mother's voice.

Suddenly she wants to talk to her mother.

Suddenly, almost greedily, she wants to talk to her mother. She goes into a phone booth and calls the television station, asks for Marya Sharp. Please. Is she in? Yes, she will wait.

Marya isn't in.

"It's very important," E. says. "This is her daughter and it's very important—"

"Her what?"

A baffled silence. In the background someone laughing, a girl. E. thinks with sudden sad certainty that it is lunchtime, of course, and so her mother will be out. She stands with the receiver in her hand, listening to noise in the background, another telephone ringing and answered promptly. Calls come in, some are accepted. A switchboard directing calls, plugs in holes. Good luck and bad luck.

"Hello? Who is this?"

It is her mother on the telephone. E. cries: "Mother? It's—"

"Louder, please, there's a tower of Babel going on in this place," her mother says. "Who is this?"

"This is Elena—am I bothering you?—can you talk? I—"

"Elena? What do you want?"

"I think I want to come home for a while," E. says quickly.

"Honey, I can barely hear you, what's wrong there? Are you home? Is he out of town, or what?"

"I thought—I was thinking—if I could come stay with you for a while and—"

"Elena, I just can't hear you, I'm going to take this call in my office—I'll put it through and you just wait, honey—"

So she waits. Clicking noises from the telephone: another dime needed. Yes, she has another dime, good luck. Good. Her fingernails scrape crazily for the dime, she can hear typing in the background now, someone talking, one half of a successful conversation on another line. It is an ordinary office there and calls go through, are accepted.

E. waits.

Outside at the coat check an elderly man is gazing her way. She cannot tell if he really sees her or is just looking in this direction, vaguely. Dreaming with his eyes open. Did he see her go into the telephone booth and is he waiting for her to come out again? Is—

Another false fact, E. thinks. People staring.

Glances again at her watch, which is stuck at a quarter to two, on a day she can't remember from the beginning. A day that steadily silently decomposes, until nothing remains except an organ the size of her hand, her hand made into a fist, pulsing with heat and terror. Where is her mother? Why that clicking, typing, laughing in the distance? Why so far in the distance?

The minute hand on her watch doesn't move but there is need for another dime. Minutes have passed. Are passing. E. closes her eyes, listening to the phone, the dead line. A dead receiver gives back a strange immediate vacuum, as if you are pressing your ear up against your own ear, head against head, hoping for a message.

She hangs up.

16 1:45 PM

In her white coat and out into the steely light of an April day in Detroit, remembering to use the correct doors going out, blinking into the light like someone released from prison with a shove: E. knows she justifies the deaths of great valleys and caverns of animals, mountain ranges of animals, unresisting bodies piled high, blue-gray minks or silver foxes or rabbits dyed any color, all the animals of creation, yet somehow she feels a little sick, dizzy, she keeps seeing and hearing and smelling Mrs. C. and smelling the crab bisque with its slight cooling surface scum. . . . And she must draw on her gloves, she must pull them tight across her knuckles, feeling almost with satisfaction the pressure of the rings into her flesh.

Lovely fingers, Marvin says, kissing them one by one. Then her arm, the unresisting inside of her arm. Her breasts. Her stomach, the flat curve of her stomach. She obeys and is very still, unresisting. Kissing loving worshiping her: lie still. Go into stone, into peace.

Don't people love in this way?

In the parts of themselves too deep and too still to have names, safe there, unresisting?

She is walking, walking at an ordinary pace, thinking for some reason of a girl: in a movie she must have seen, or in a photograph of some kind, a girl mauled by a gang of boys, grabbed and pushed around and loved, laughed at, not resisting but still laughed at but still loved, one arm hooked under her chin, the threat of suffocation, the threat of her neck being snapped. . . .

E. feels a sudden uneasiness, restlessness, deep in the pit of her stomach, a surge of desire at the memory of this girl. . . . But it is undefined, too faint to comprehend. She sees that she is walking along Madison Avenue, at a normal pace, approaching a park she has never noticed before. Going to the club, coming from the club, she has always been in a car; no one walks around here, really. Now she crosses over to the park, being very careful of traffic. Watching the traffic lights isn't safe enough, *not the way people drive around here.* Who said that? It seems to E. that someone has just said it, she could hear a voice right in her head, not her own. She glances at her watch nervously—but no need to be nervous, she should try to relax—no need to think about the luncheon, the odor of food and perfume and cigarette smoke, her slightly estranged body. She will not be sick like Mrs. C.; she is never sick to her stomach and will not be sick now. She will simply walk down to her husband's office, which is a few blocks away. She will go to his office and talk to him.

She relaxes and tries to read the inscription on the base of the Alger Memorial. A damp darkness to the April air. Mysterious currents in the air, like the trails of many breaths. Marvin doesn't mind the air of cities: each city has its own smell, he says. You put up with it and in the end you become fond of it, he said. E. smiles, hearing him. She can almost hear him. Yes, she can hear his voice inside her head.

She looks around the drab little park. Aged men in overcoats sit on the few benches, each by himself as if scornful of the others. Their mouths appear toothless, moving in perpetual dim arguments that are not quite audible. One old man is asleep, his head tipped sideways at a severe, almost unnatural angle, as if his neck has snapped. Nothing to be afraid of, E. thinks. A public park. These old, sickly, disheveled men are not dangerous, not even the one who is eying her so intently. Not dangerous. She is not afraid. She even attempts a smile at him, a very brief smile; his face tightens at once, but he does not smile back. No smile for E. You cannot charm everyone. The man does not smile but stares at her, almost angrily, a small red-eyed runny-nosed man in his sixties with thin gray dirty hair, a dirty unbuttoned overcoat. His fingers twitch on his knees.

A trim white truck pulls up, coming between E. and the old man. White with blue letters on its side: *Detroit Rodent Control.*

She crosses the street quickly and walks out to Woodward Avenue. Walking more quickly now, why? She passes shops that are boarded up, appear to be barricaded as if against attack; then there is a record shop squeezed in between two vacant shops, a record is blaring, someone's scream right inside her head. It is either a man's high-pitched scream or a woman's high-pitched scream. E. glances at her watch: 1:45. She feels a little better now, on her way to Marvin's office. She is not going to be sick. She notices people shuffling around her, in no hurry, not shoppers, but people who appear just to be walking around here, idly, pausing, turning back, stopping to gaze abstractedly across the street—as if they lived here, on the sidewalk, and had no interest in walking anywhere else. A few white men, most black men; a few black women. They glance at her, dazed and curious. A black man in a fluorescent pink ski jacket makes a mocking little bow to her, or is she mistaken?—and she brushes past with her coat buttoned up firmly. No danger here. *I love this city, Detroit is home to me, with all its smells and troubles*, Marvin has said. E. would agree. She isn't afraid now and feels much better. . . . Passing a shoe store with a brilliant red and yellow sign, *Cancellation Shoes,* two bins of heaped-up shoes on the sidewalk, people pawing routinely through them . . . something about the jumbled shoes and the shoppers makes E. realize that this is good, this world is good, there is no danger to it. A teen-aged girl with a bluish-purple face glances up at E., her lips parted upon two enormous protruding teeth—a half-smile like E.'s normal smile. No danger. Then someone collides with her—she believes it is a white man—and says earnestly, *Excuse me lady I'm sorry* and E. says something in reply, quickly, not pausing, but not afraid either.

She feels that this is all good, good. And she herself, walking through it, must be good; completed. Her life is completed. She is in no hurry, no hurry to force time to move toward her as she walks in one direction and the sidewalk moves in the other. She looks dreamily at the confusion of traffic—DSR buses, taxis, cars—and the crowds of pedestrians on corners, waiting patiently for lights to change; yes, she can see why Marvin likes this city. *Pure energy. This city is pure energy.* The world is pure energy and must be respected. E. agrees with that. And what else? That today's date 1971 is a false fact. Yes. And therefore no threat, because nothing will happen. But she cannot tell Marvin that, she

must keep such stray thoughts to herself. As long as you keep quiet. Innocent. Invisible.

Instead: she will tell him about the luncheon, the disappointing financial report, the plans for a new campaign . . . tell him about the judge's wife, drunk & sick & the strange things she said. . . . He will be entertained by all that.

. . . The end of Woodward Avenue, the tip of Detroit: handsome new buildings, semitransparent, powerful, noble. She crosses to the City-County Building. The sky is thick but there is an odd, almost spirited vitality to the air, thin streams of sunshine around the clouds, penetrating the clouds. E. notices a fountain, jets of water. Beauty. She does not feel so shaky now. Recalls & dismisses Mrs. C. The vomiting, the sink, etc. Will forget. She feels well now and looks around deliberately, the only person on the sidewalk who is not hurrying. The people who push through the revolving doors of the building are well-dressed, most of them, only a few shabby shuffling people. Only one stray aimless man, elderly, propped up against a concrete wall. No need to look at him. Marvin's office is not far away, she will be up and safe in his office in five minutes, less than five minutes; no danger. But why should there be danger?

She glances mechanically at her watch—1:45—and just at that instant remembers that her watch has stopped. But no matter. She feels well. She is drawn to the statue in front of the City-County Building, which everyone else passes without seeing. It is a large, heavy statue. Green. Steaked with gray, like salt-tears or the rivulets made by tears. The figure of a man—immense, godly. The statue is called "The Spirit of Detroit." People hurry past, not bothering to glance at it; E. draws nearer. She reads the inscription. Looks again at the statue, the enormous thighs, really gigantic thighs, pure muscles. But his waist is strangely narrow, almost pinched. Narrower than a woman's waist would be. The figure's hands and fingers are gigantic. Everything is oversized and it is almost disturbing to E. to look at it . . . the strange disproportionate thighs and arms and torso . . . the small waist. . . . In his left hand the figure holds an object meant to be the sun, with stiff spike-like rays of gold emanating out from it; in his right hand the figure holds a small couple, a man and a woman, the woman holding an infant, and all these small figures are raising their hands to the sky. . . . What does it mean?

E. studies them, sees the small clear human faces, the hands raised above their heads . . . appeal, prayer? . . . yet they do not look terrified. They look peaceful, even blank. E. comes closer so that she can read the inscription. II Corinthians 3:17: "Now the Lord is that spirit and where the spirit of the Lord is, there is liberty." The inscription continues, explaining: *God, through the Spirit of Man, is manifested in the family, the noblest human relationship.*

E. contemplates the greenish-gray substance, the muscles gone into metal, hard, remorseless, the rivulets made by tears. She sees the man and the woman and the infant, this time clearly, a family being held in someone's hand; *yes, I understand what is being said.*

Yes.

The time is 1:45.

The time is 1:45.

She does not move, staring at the statue. Her eyes move slowly, very slowly, to one end of the figure's great arms, to the little man and woman in his hand, and very slowly back, back, to the spiky sun and its hard gold rays, and slowly back again, coming to rest in the center; *yes, I understand.*

It is 1:45.

She stands without moving.

Straight, poised, the posture unbreakable; backbone like steel.

A skin marked by tears, turning slowly greenish-gray. Gone into perfect hardness. Yes. She feels very well now, very happy. Yes, yes, everything has come to rest, in perfection it comes to rest, permanent.

1:45.

Stopped.

Permanent.

1:45.

Stuck. She does not move.

"Mrs. Howe?" someone might say. A stranger's voice, and a stranger's hesitant hand on her arm, "Mrs. Howe . . . ?" But if she hears she will not reply, will not even glance at him. She is beyond anyone's touch.

"... I am a lawyer. So I can never get away from evil."
—FRANZ KAFKA

PART TWO

Miscellaneous Facts, Events, Fantasies, Evidence Admissible and Inadmissible

I

January 18, 1953. At exactly seven o'clock in the morning, in a northwestern residential area of Detroit, a man named Neal Stehlin woke from sleep, then got out of bed in order to shower and shave and dress, neatly, preparing himself for his death, which was to occur at seven forty-five. As if he knew he must hurry, he was impatient and couldn't force himself to wait for the steam to evaporate from the bathroom mirror—he wiped it away with the flat of his hand, though this left a smudge.

At the same time a man named Joseph Morrissey was or was not asleep in his car, which had been parked since four in the morning in a supermarket parking lot on Livernois. Morrissey had no clear memory of sleeping and so he could not know if he woke or not, or what time it was; he did not shower or shave, did not even adjust his disheveled clothes; the only gesture he made toward cleaning himself up for the event ahead was a few seconds' nervous picking at his shirt front with his fingernails—dried stains, stiff stains that looked like vomit, but he didn't remember having been sick. When? It was a mystery never cleared up. His watch was not on his wrist or anywhere else, it must have been stolen. He judged it was early morning. He checked his wallet and it was still there, which was a pleasant surprise. The gun was on the seat beside him, hidden beneath his rolled-up overcoat.

Stehlin, a building contractor, *an amateur cellist, active in the Northwest Detroit Community Planning League, the eldest son of the philanthropist Max Stehlin, aged forty-eight, survived by his wife and his sons Mark and Robert,* hurried downstairs with his suit coat over his shoulder, his graying hair damp, his appetite good, downstairs to the handsome oval foyer of his house, which had just been redone with a floor of Dupont marble. Stehlin had time that morning only to glance around, absorbing with pleasure the beauty of his house, which he had bought a few years before in a bad real estate market, for less than $70,000; now, in 1953, he judged it might be worth $120,000. But he had no interest in selling. He was re-imagining the entire house and had plans for knocking out walls, making the living room two stories high, adding a second terrace and a swimming pool.

This was the old Quant house at 778 Fairway Drive, overlooking the golf course of the Detroit Golf Club. Stehlin's neighbors on the right were the E. J. Travens; on the left, the T. R. Windnagles. His own father, Max Stehlin, now dead, had lived in an enormous Georgian house at the other end of Fairway Drive, near Seven Mile Road. Stehlin had grown up in this neighborhood and said that he would never leave, would never panic and move out, would spend the rest of his life in Detroit, a city he loved. According to his wife, *Stehlin seemed absolutely normal that morning, unworried, only a little impatient to get to his office . . . he had not spoken of Joseph Morrissey for quite a while, for weeks;* at seven twenty-five he was already on the telephone, and Mrs. Stehlin, in a dressing gown, was in the kitchen opening the refrigerator—"*I was just reaching for the orange juice, Neal had orange juice every morning of his life*"—

Joseph Morrissey had tried to start his car but the battery must have gone dead. He wrenched at the steering wheel angrily but silently, holding it firmly with both hands and yanking at it as if to tear it out. Then he leaned sideways and with one tight, hard kick smashed the windshield on the right side; this must have hurt him but he did not remember any pain. The partly smashed windshield and the fine radiating cracks were to be photographed later.

Morrissey stuck the gun in his pocket and trudged up Livernois Avenue, that dismal street, his head bowed against the cold and his unbuckled overshoes flopping around his feet, and by the time he got to Six Mile Road he had forgotten about his car, his fury over that car; he was beginning to get warm. *I warmed up fast on that walk.* He turned east on Six Mile and trudged several blocks into the wind again; the wind seemed to have shifted, and now fine grains of snow and ice were being blown right into his face, *but didn't slow me down in the least; nothing could have slowed me down.* Early-morning traffic passed him, moving in spurts. Ice creaked underfoot. The University of Detroit was deserted at this time of day, the parking lots empty, only a few lights on in the residence hall. Buses pulled up beside Morrissey, other people got on, hurrying, as if to lure him into boarding the bus and allowing it to take him away, anywhere, to distract him from his purpose; but he paid no attention and walked faster. *Listen: it's going to take a million bolts of electricity to slow me down. Have the doctors examine my heart and they'll tell you.*

When he crossed Oak Drive he was almost struck by a car—but wasn't hurt—turned to stare at the driver but saw no one—rushed on by and forgot about the incident. This driver was an internist named Maguire, on his way to his downtown office: "*A man who appeared to be drunk or drugged or in an extreme emotional state walked right in front of my car; I slammed on the brakes, he didn't seem to know how close he had come to being hit . . . he walked away in a kind of fast swaying shamble, holding his arms very stiffly at his sides. . . .*"

Morrissey approached the Stehlin house from the rear, walking through someone else's lawn, swinging his legs over someone else's low stone wall. The golf course was a white haze, a near-blizzard of fine stinging particles of snow. But he knew the way. *My footprints were already there in the snow, ahead of me. Nobody else could see them. But I could see them and they led right up to Neal Stehlin's house. And then when I saw it . . . my mind just blacked out. It went black. All the snow got in it and my mind went black with so much swirling snow. . . .*

The maid cried out and when Mrs. Stehlin hurried to see what the boy sat rigidly, tightly, his arms stiff and his dark, intelligent face blank.

"You want to save your father, don't you?"

The boy sat blankly, staring at the underside of Howe's shoe.

Howe said: "Your husband loved his son Ronald—Ronnie—very much?"

The woman began to cry.

"Mrs. Morrissey, your husband loved Ronnie very much? Ronnie's death was the event that changed him permanently?—seemed to drive him crazy?—crazy with despair—?"

An anemic narrow face, no longer pretty, with bluish veins that appeared to grow darker as Howe stared: veins on the left temple, a large vein on the left side of the throat. The woman wrung her hands ceaselessly, narrow anemic hands with blue veins that seemed to tremble; she wrung her hands without knowing what she did, like a patient in a mental hospital or an actress without any lines, any words, just sitting there and wringing her hands.

"He blamed Neal Stehlin for the death, of course, and he became obsessed with Stehlin? He talked about him constantly at home?"

The woman glanced at him timidly.

". . . don't know how to answer . . . ," she whispered.

"What? Speak louder, Mrs. Morrissey, please. . . ."

She began to cry again. Howe waited a few minutes, patiently; he noticed his coffee cup amid the pile of papers on his desk, picked it up, took a swallow of the cold coffee. Very bitter.

". . . I didn't go to school much," Mrs. Morrissey said. "I had to quit oh around fourth grade . . . I . . . I don't know how to talk so well . . . in the courtroom . . . I. . . . I'm afraid. . . ."

"You just have to tell me about your husband," Howe said. "Just tell me. Now. Don't think about anything else. About your husband . . . ?"

"I'm afraid of the judge . . . the courtroom . . . ," she said slowly. Her small bloodshot eyes never exactly met his. He watched her, he watched her in despair, and realized that she was not thinking about her husband at all, she had forgotten her husband, she was just sitting there in a kind of near-paralyzed dumb terror, a moronic terror.

After a while he went out and called the daughter in. Her name was Alice; she was sixteen years old, extremely shy. Howe said: "Your mother is a little upset today. Maybe tomorrow we can talk . . . ?"

The girl nodded abruptly.

"And you and I also . . . ? Can you help me?"

She was breathing rapidly and shallowly.

"You're not afraid of me, are you?" Howe asked. He tried to smile, to laugh. *All these people are guilty,* he thought. *Guilty and terrified.* "Alice, you and I can talk tomorrow . . . ? And you can help me, help your father?"

She seemed to be shaking her head, shyly.

"Alice?" Howe asked, not believing this. "Alice? You will be able to help me, won't you?"

She said, "Jack will."

"Yes. Jack will help too. I plan to talk to Jack again, of course . . . but your brother is rather reticent and. . . ."

"Jack will have to do it," the girl said.

"Do it? Do what?"

She stood for a moment in a kind of mental stasis, not struggling to speak, but blank; and then, after a painful wait, she managed to say in a voice Howe could barely hear: ". . . say the things . . . the right things. . . ."

Howe thought with a sudden anxiety, so deep it was almost exciting, of that boy: that stubborn little bastard.

3

1953. A day in January. Another day in January. Always a day in January, which had begun at the earliest minute of the year but which would not end; Jack thought wildly that he was stuck in it, stuck in it with other people, the frozen streets and the snow that seemed to fall already soiled and the questions he had to answer, the words he had to draw out of his head and arrange.

Again and again: January 17.

Relive it, remember it, get back there inside it. Talk.

The lawyer was taking notes. Frowning, snuffling, his chair creaking violently under him, smiling at Jack with his half-faked half-genuine smile, saying *And then what? Then—?*

Jack held himself tight, always. He was fifteen years old and not shy. He was quiet, silent, stubborn . . . but he knew he wasn't shy, he hated the possibility of being shy. He was five feet eight now and not so anxious any longer about his height; for years he'd been one of the shortest boys, but now. . . .

January 17 had been the day before the murder; January 18 had been the day of the murder; but it was another day in January, later in the month, when Jack realized wildly that he was stuck in January with these people—said to be his father, his mother, his sister—and that he would never get free.

In a near-panic, almost sobbing, he interrupted the lawyer's question about something he hadn't heard, and asked: "Help me out of this—can you help me?— Can you—"

Howe stared at him. Then he smiled. He smiled broadly, as if startled, pleased, excited; he even let both feet fall heavily to the floor so that he could sit up straight. Behind him the cream-colored wallpaper of his office kept a shadowy outline that Jack realized, in the following days, was really a smudge, a vague greasy stain, from the back of Howe's head.

"Absolutely," Howe said.

February 1953. Jack fingered the bumps on his face, dreading and half-admiring their hardness, the firm stubborn slopes and valleys that seemed to his fingertips enormous, terrible. So it was always a surprise to catch sight of his reflection in a mirror and see he was not disfigured; no one could know, seeing him, what he really looked like.

What was most striking in his face were his eyes and his dark stubborn eyebrows: people saw them. *Jack Morrissey's public face,* he thought. It looked strong. He had to stop smiling that half-twisted frozen defensive little smile, which was exactly like his sister's smile; he had to stop that.

He stopped.

"Let's go over January seventeenth again," Howe said.

Jack drew in his breath. He had picked up the habit from someone—an older boy at school, or Howe himself—of crossing and uncrossing his legs, causing his body to jerk carelessly, as if he were not really aware of his body, while retaining his stare into someone's face. He knew it was a sign of shyness, of weakness, to be afraid to look at people. So he forced himself to look, he forced himself not to flinch. He had begun to recognize and to despise weakness, timidity, silence . . . the halting, groping lapse into silence of his mother, his sister, his father in the days before he had changed. . . . His sister went everywhere with her pinched meager face turned downward, she seemed afraid to look up from the sidewalk, she looked furtive, guilty; a kind of madness flared up in Jack when he saw her outside the house, walking like that, and he wanted to run over to her and yell into her face–

His mother didn't go out at all.

"January seventeenth," Howe said.

"I can't remember anything more," Jack said irritably.

Don't you want to help your father?–save your father? Jack felt that Howe was asking him this. Folding his hands across his powerful stomach, staring at Jack, assessing him, waiting. But he didn't ask the question. He had only asked it once, during the first week. Jack noticed that. He dreaded the question and yet waited for it; but Howe never asked it again.

"It's getting to be like a dream," Jack said. "Things that happened in a dream that wasn't mine . . . the order is all mixed up. . . . I know the way things happened, one and then the other, but it's because I memorized it, I don't really remember."

Howe said nothing. Jack scanned his face nervously and saw there sympathy, patience. But almost impatience.

"Sometimes I think my mind is going . . . going over the edge of something," Jack said. "I'm losing track of my own mind."

"I have to help you remember," Howe said. "That's why we're going over these facts."

"But I'm losing track. . . ."

"No."

Jack rubbed his eyes and then his forehead, slowly, and beneath his sensitive fingertips there were wide, shallow bumps, hollows, mysterious patterns that Marvin Howe could not see. Howe said: "When you testify you'll remember everything perfectly. Jack? Are you listening? You'll remember it all because you're not going to rely upon your natural memory but the memory you and I discover. Which you will memorize."

Jack listened to these words and replayed them, sorting them out in his head. Howe said: "Your own memory isn't any good, nobody's is . . . nobody's mind is any good by itself, naturally, don't you know that? You can make your mind about anything you want it to be, but you've got to know how to do it. You understand this, don't you?"

"Yes," Jack said.

February already and he had outlived January, survived every day and every night of that endless month, which really began on January 17. But when Jack considered the months ahead, the two months until his father's trial, the twenty-four-hour spaces of time that would have to be endured, he felt a blankness that was not even worry or despair but something empty, inert. It wasn't the nauseous terror of those first few days—the sudden attacks of vomiting—but something worse, a vague emptiness, an unpopulated space he knew must be *Jack Morrissey.* But he did not feel strong enough to populate it with anyone.

How do you live, how do you exist?

But when he was with Howe he felt how quickly, how powerfully, he was populated with something: with a soul, with a voice. And he could not even remember his vague terror, the vacuum of his sleepless nights. . . . Yes, he could remember it but he could not understand it. It seemed to belong to another person, a boy he would despise.

He asked Howe one morning: "Is craziness catching?"

Howe ignored his ironic frightened smile, didn't smile himself; he said thoughtfully: "In a way, yes. Yes."

Jack's smile faded.

"The law makes distinctions between sanity and insanity that have no meaning," Howe said, his voice becoming almost abstract, as if he were repeating something he had read or had already spoken, and now he was especially patient, kindly. "There is no reality in the mind that can be measured . . . everything is states of consciousness . . . whatever you think, whatever you imagine . . . much of it against your will. The world of mental things can't be measured or examined. But it's there. I respect it as a human being . . . but as a lawyer, as the man who is representing your father, I'm going to believe that it can be measured and I'm going to handle it. *As a lawyer I'm not afraid of it.* As a man . . . well . . . that's different and has nothing to do with. . . . Now, Dr. Hill is going to testify that your father was insane during the forty-eight-hour period of January sixteenth and January seventeenth, and that happens to be true. The prosecution's doctor is going to testify that your father was sane. That isn't the truth, that's an error. The jury will listen to both men and decide whether Dr. Hill is correct, or whether the other man is correct . . . and the jury will then decide whether your father was sane or insane back in January. They are going to come up with the real diagnosis."

Jack swallowed nervously. "But . . . but I mean. . . . If he was insane. . . ."

"You don't understand," Howe said. "Sanity doesn't exist. Its opposite doesn't exist. Those words are legal terms."

"What . . . ?"

"They are words, *legal terms.*"

"But I mean . . . if he was. . . . What happened to him. . . ."

"You can't go crazy, you can't go insane or even sane, unless someone diagnoses you and records his decision," Howe said patiently. "You have to be put on trial first."

Jack stared at him. He did not understand.

"Your testimony will be one of two intelligent, coherent testimonies; the other is Dr. Hill's. And that man who almost ran your father over—Maguire—he'll make a good minor witness, and he happens to be a doctor. You'll do well. You won't be confused, you won't be upset. You'll come through."

Jack said slowly, "I mean . . . whatever happened to my father, whatever it was called . . . or will be called. . . . Could that happen to me, is it catching?"

"Do you want it to happen to you?"

"No."

"Then it won't. But what did happen to him?"

"I don't know."

"His personality altered, he became very emotional . . . ? And what about your mother, isn't she different now, since the arrest, isn't she extremely emotional too?"

"Well, she was always emotional. . . ."

"This emotional?"

mind, not responsible for your acts," Howe said. "Don't worry."

Morrissey grinned.

". . . his house, I knew his house inside and out," he said excitedly. "He had me over lots of times . . . I was a good friend of his but you won't get the truth from his wife or that nigger maid. . . . All that screaming made me nervous. I almost lost my way. I had an important mission, God knew what I was doing and didn't say anything, didn't put any obstacles in my way. He stood back in the beginning, when Ronnie died, and He stood back at the end. . . . They used to invite me over, one time I knocked on the side door and they let me in, Mr. Stehlin talked with me in the kitchen, there was some leftover things like little sandwiches with toothpicks in them, sandwiches made out of very tiny round pieces of bread . . . from some party they had; the nigger maid brought them for me. . . . The next time they said he wasn't in but I caught up with him downtown on the street, I called out his name, and he tried to turn his back on me. I said we had to unite with each other, we had to be brothers, something awful would happen if he denied me . . . but it was by his warehouse, he was getting in a car with some men, and he laughed at me and made them laugh at me. He said he'd call the police to beat me up. I just stood there. The men tried to spit on me—"

"Joseph, what? They tried to spit on you?"

"Yes. Spit. Yes, they did," Morrissey said simply. "My mind went down into a tiny hole, like water going down a drain, and I couldn't see. It was Christmastime. Christmas was on my mind. I was thinking about how Ronnie loved Christmas, the Christmas tree, the word Christmas, Christmas—"

"Those men didn't try to spit on you, Joseph, did they?"

"Christmas. Christmas," Morrissey murmured. He frowned. "That is a careful word. It falls into two equal parts."

"Your mind was on Christmas and on your son, yes, and—?"

"He drowned in six inches of water."

"The incident at the warehouse, Joseph, that took place on December twenty-second, didn't it? Did you threaten Stehlin at that time? If you said anything at all about hurting him, if you threatened him at all, it will be brought up at the trial. What did you say?"

"If it could have been Jack instead. . . ." Morrissey said

slowly. "I loved Ronnie best, he was so sweet and never picked a fight with me, but Jack is . . . Jack is. . . . Ronnie couldn't talk, you know, that kind make a fuss and scream and try to hurt themselves, but they don't talk, they don't hate you, they need you for everything—like being fed, being bathed and loved. They're beloved best of God. The priest told us. . . . If they don't talk they never turn against you. Then he crawled under the fence and drowned in some water."

"Why do you say your son drowned, Joseph?"

"That was why, when the insurance thing went against me, when the law let me down, I thought . . . I thought I didn't want to do something bad . . . I would try to love Mr. Stehlin like a brother, like it was the son of both of us. Because he did feel sorry. And his wife too. They were real sorry. Then they got over it and changed back into people I didn't know and it worked on my mind, it was like drowning . . . and then I knew what I had to do. . . ."

"After the police took a confession from you, after that, what happened?"

Morrissey shook his head.

"You say your mind was blacked out. When did you regain consciousness?"

"I never did."

"You never did?"

"Never."

5

Jack sat close beside his mother and she gripped his arm. They were facing his father through the wire screen, only a few yards from him; his father's eyes were alert, bright, restless. Jack's mother was asking him if he was well, if he slept well, and she kept digging her fingers into Jack's arm.

"Mr. Howe is so wonderful . . . he says to convince the jury, that's all he has to do . . . to explain to them. . . . How you weren't in control, you weren't feeling right. . . ."

She glanced at Jack and he had to look at her, had to see the pinched lines at the corners of her eyes. Jesus, Jack thought, don't you start crying. No. Please. Not here.

"It's all right, keep talking," Jack whispered.

"He won't answer. . . ."

"Yes, he will, he'll answer," Jack said miserably.

His mother looked timidly over at his father again. "Joseph? Can you hear me? Do they let you sleep long enough? Are you in good health?"

There was a dull, dead smell to the air down here in this stifling room; it was stale and yet overcharged, alert, excitable. Jack's father was sitting stiffly, attentively, but he seemed to be hearing these questions inside his head, as if they were coming from another source or as if he were remembering them.

"She's asking if you can sleep all right . . . ," Jack said.

He wanted to grab hold of the wire partition and shake it, tear it loose. He wanted to grab hold of his father.

When his father didn't answer, Jack glanced over to the young policeman in the corner—a face rosy and abstracted, as if he were trying not to listen. Jack felt a tinge of shame, that the guard should be standing there, so close.

He noticed the pistol on the policeman's hip.

"Mr. Howe says . . . he says. . . ." Jack's mother cleared her throat, cleared it again, as if her voice were disappearing. "Joseph, he says it will be over soon. . . . I know he's right. He said the newspapers printed so much bad about you to hurt you, but that he would make up for that. He would get very honest jurors who would listen to our side. How did it go, Jack, what did he say . . . ? He said . . . ?"

"Unprejudiced jurors," Jack said. His father's face tensed, as if he were now hearing Jack's voice. "One of his assistants is going through the county records, looking up jurors . . . to see if people who've served before are prejudiced . . . if they want to punish people. . . . He said he would try to know about them all so if. . . . If any of them are called. . . ."

"Yes," Jack's mother said quickly. "Yes. He says the only thing is to explain it to the jury, how you lost control, and they would understand. Jack is going to talk for you, about the night before . . . and other times . . . and I'm going to talk if I'm strong enough. . . . But I get so afraid and so nervous. . . . They published that awful picture of you in both newspapers, when the police carried you out to the car . . . and all our names and ages, the address of the house, even where Jack and Alice go to school, oh it was awful, even where you work . . . and a long write-up about Mr. Stehlin, the work he did for the city, and his father, all the donations his father made. . . . To stir up hatred against you. . . . A doctor said in the newspaper that you were in your right mind, a police doctor, and. . . ."

She fell silent, confused. Jack's father had begun to nod slowly, shrewdly. Yet he did not seem to be truly aware of her.

Over in the corner the policeman stood. Not listening. Jack's eye darted again to the gun, the holster, the polished leather belt. . . . The gun was larger than Jack would have imagined a pistol. Yet it was a handweapon. To fit into the hand, easily into a man's hand, to be raised and aimed. . . .

"Oh . . . yes . . . yes, Joseph, I almost forgot," Jack's mother said, her voice rising with faint enthusiasm, ". . . Mr. Howe went back to the old neighborhood, you know, and talked with so many people . . . the Dempseys, and the Kovaks, and Pete Koenigberger in the grocery store, he still remembers how nice you were when his wife was sick. . . . And at work, so many men at work, they all know how you were under a strain and. . . . He told me all the character witnesses! I started to cry, I was so . . . I thank God there are such good people in the world. . . ."

Nervously Jack waited, waited. In a few minutes he would get her out of here, on the bus and back home. Safely home. His father seemed to be listening, nodding slowly, his lips pursed and his cheeks going slightly hollow, as if he were sucking them in, concentrating.

Jack's mother was crying now. Murmuring something about how they all missed him, missed him, loved him and. . . . Jack squirmed with desire, a sudden flash that was almost sexual; if he didn't get his mother out of here, if he didn't get them both out, he might grab the gun away from the guard and start shooting. . . .

During those months he had trouble sleeping; he was going to have trouble sleeping for the rest of his life. But when the misery of his insomnia was at its worst, when he felt that his life, his being, were somehow in danger of extinction, he thought of Howe and Howe's voice, his rough, ruddy complexion, his physical presence—which was so easy, so easily achieved, that Jack believed he would survive.

He loved/hated Howe; he was too close to him, as if standing with his own face up to a mirror, so that he could not see. Did he love himself or hate himself? Did he know that much about himself? He thought it wisest not to wonder, he began to adopt Howe's swift, skillful deflation of unanswerable questions: *Don't worry, don't think about it,* he told his mother.

As a boy he had believed in God, nervously, and he had carried the presence of God around with him everywhere, a vaporous substance, not exactly friendly. But he hadn't believed in God for a few years. Now he carried around with him the fact of his father's lawyer, the man who kept saying he was confident of this, confident of that, *he did not think about that,* and he began to believe Howe knew when he, Jack, was not telling the truth.

"Why does he insist that your brother drowned, when he really died in another way?"

"I don't know."

"Your brother died when some debris fell on him, he died of internal injuries, didn't he?"

"Yes. Sure."

"Why do you think your father says he drowned?"

"Well, he didn't always say that. Before he got bad . . . before he got so strange. . . . He just started saying it, I don't know when, I. . . . It's because he's crazy. . . ."

"Yes, Jack," Howe said.

Jack thought: *I almost drowned once.*

Howe waited. "You don't have any other idea? Any other explanation?"

Jack felt a strange tension in his body, almost an exhilaration, though he could not understand it. His heartbeat increased slightly, he felt almost a change in the taste of his saliva, the taste of himself: suddenly brighter, fiercer.

"I said I don't know."

He looked at Howe without flinching. How he liked that face! How he liked the physical bulk of the man, the expensive, stylish outfits he wore—today a suit of blue and sea green, the colors mixed together coarsely. But Howe kept jamming a ball-point pen into the pocket and already it had begun to tear at the edges. He was looking thoughtfully at Jack.

Jack wiped his nose with the edge of his hand. It was a sudden gesture, weak and childish, shameful. All his life he would remember it: wiping his nose like a child while Howe watched him.

"You're the only intelligent one," Howe said slowly. "I can't put your father on the stand . . . even if he becomes more rational. . . . He wouldn't talk to you and your mother, would he? Well. . . . Tell me about your relationship with him, please. Tell the truth."

Jack swallowed. He smiled as if challenged. He said, "We didn't get along very well . . . because . . . he was always after my mother, I mean . . . in a quiet way, not out loud . . . he blamed her for the way Ronnie was born, maybe. I don't mean he said that. It was a strain for them, the way Ronnie turned out . . . it was awful for all of us, my brother never learned how to use the toilet, even, he was always a baby, an infant. That went on for ten years . . . he was ten when he died. He'd get very angry, furious, he'd go wild and one of us would have to hold him down and then at the end he was getting very strong. . . . One day he sat on the kitchen floor bending a piece of metal around, playing with it, cutting his fingers on the edges, and when I took it away from him I discovered it was something off the back of the refrigerator, that he'd torn it off, and. . . . And. . . ." Jack realized he was talking quickly, guiltily. "My father loved Ronnie, he said he loved Ronnie. But he wasn't around him the way my mother was. My mother was always with him, constantly for years, she'd go shopping or something and my sister or I would stay with my brother, but outside of that she was stuck with him. For years. I mean for ten years. She's very religious so maybe that helped. . . ."

Jack hesitated. He had not been talking about his father.

"My father always worked hard, even though he hated his job," Jack said, "and he used to drink a little . . . but it got worse after Ronnie had the accident, and after the business with Stehlin fell through, the lawsuit, when the judge decided that Stehlin wasn't at fault. . . . Because it wasn't his fault, how the hell could it have been his fault? My brother was so. . . . He got out of the house and wandered away and burrowed under a wire fence, like an animal, and. . . ."

Howe waited. Again his patience, his contemplative silence. Yet Jack felt he was not really patient at all.

"I can't remember . . . I can't remember what you asked me," Jack said.

"I asked you about your father, your relationship with him."

"I've told you everything," Jack said irritably. "I've gone over all this so many times . . . I'm sick of it, I feel like being sick to my stomach, all this misery over *him*. He used to go around the house with just his pants on, maybe a dirty old undershirt on top, go around drunk and half-crying and feeling sorry for himself— Feeling sorry for himself because my brother was dead! 'I loved Ronnie,' he would say, stumbling into things and crying, *I loved Ronnie—*"

"All last year, then, he was like that," Howe said. "All right. He was undergoing a change in character, he was heading for a breakdown. Your testimony will establish that, how he was obsessed with Stehlin, how he began to get violent at home—shoved your mother around, smashed the lamp—all right, fine—he went *temporarily insane*, didn't he? And now he's improving steadily, he'll be well again, won't he? He's no longer violent, and though he doesn't talk to you and your mother, he does talk to other people. He's beginning to make sense. That's fine, I have no questions about that. I'm just asking you today, this afternoon, why you don't believe he really went out of control that morning, why you really don't believe the defense I'm presenting—"

Jack got to his feet. He laughed nervously.

"Oh, he's guilty, the bastard," Jack laughed.

Howe slammed his fist down on his desk. "He is not guilty!"

"He is guilty, he's guilty, he wanted to kill that man—that— He wanted to kill Stehlin, he wanted to kill him," Jack said wildly, "I know he did— He's pretending to be crazy, he was pretending, or he made himself go crazy—he talked himself into it—all that crap about God, about hearing Ronnie talk to him after the accident—*Ronnie talking!*—as if my brother could talk, as if he ever talked—just gurgling and screaming, enough to make you sick— What good luck my brother died! What damn wonderful good luck! Crawling up a garbage pile, a dump, whatever it was—scrap metal, concrete, junk—crawling up on his hands and knees like an animal and bringing it all down on him— Wonderful good luck, it was good luck and my father says he loved him, loved him, he says he's the only one who loved him—"

"Your father isn't guilty. He *isn't guilty.*"

"Yes, he's guilty, he did it on purpose," Jack said. "He made himself break down, he drank until he was sick . . . he'd be sick in the bathroom. . . . He hung around Stehlin and borrowed money from him, all that's going to come out, Stehlin paid for the funeral expenses and other things and gave my father money, I know he did, money nobody else knows about, I know he gave my father money and my father kept it quiet . . . except he hinted about it when he was drunk, he hinted about his friendship with Stehlin . . . about how life arranges itself and is so surprising. . . . And then the next day, the bastard would be whining about Ronnie and how nobody loved Ronnie except him. He drove me wild! He said—he said—he told my mother right to her face at supper one night—right there—he told my mother that she was glad Ronnie was dead, glad to be rid of him—"

"But he isn't guilty."

Jack felt the surprising, fierce pulsation of his heart: so central in his body, so certain of itself. He kicked his chair aside, back against a filing cabinet.

"Sit down. Stop. He isn't guilty."

"I went over there the other day, the construction site. There are signs all over, KEEP OUT, DANGER, NO TRESPASSING. He burrowed under the fence like a weasel, like a pig . . . he was like a pig himself, he couldn't eat by himself but had to be fed, he. . . . My father said. . . . He said. . . ."

Jack edged past him to the window so that he could lean out, feeling suddenly very strong, fierce, feeling Howe's eyes on him; he would be all right now, safe now, and nervously, shakily, he turned and paced back again to the chair but wouldn't sit down; stared at it without seeing it.

"What did he say? He wished you had died instead of Ronnie?"

Jack nodded.

Howe sighed and sat again heavily. He rubbed his face with both hands. Then, after a few seconds, he said in the same voice: "So what?"

Jack glanced at him, half smiling. But the smile did not hold.

"So what?" Howe asked. "Do you care, do you give a damn? Why do you care? What has it got to do with you?"

Jack did not understand. He began again: "He told us Ronnie was giving him instructions!—he told you that too, didn't he?—first to be a brother to Stehlin, to love him, and then to kill him if he didn't—if they didn't—*He made it all up! Inside his head!*"

"Sit down, Jack. Please."

Jack sat down. "Yes, he is guilty, I know that, I know it," Jack said. "He let his mind go to pieces. He let it go ragged. It came apart while we had to live with him, listening to him—right after Ronnie died—then he began falling to pieces; he loved it, the bastard loved it, talking to himself and arguing and puking and whining about the rest of us not loving Ronnie or him or— He loved us, all right, yes, he did love us. I know he loved us. He wasn't always crazy. He was all right. But I'm not going to lie about him. I'm not going to lie. I can't lie. I won't do it. He's guilty because he made himself go crazy—he did research into going crazy—"

"What? He what?"

"Yes, did research. Newspaper columns—those advice columns—he'd tear them out, I *saw* him tearing them out. Those damn advice columns or doctors' columns, questions and answers, in the newspaper," Jack said excitedly. "About insanity—mental illness— He'd talk about losing his mind. Sit at the kitchen table sucking beer and talk about it. He wanted to scare my mother. I don't know what the hell he wanted. He would say, *You think I'm going crazy, don't you? You're afraid of me, aren't you? Do you know the five danger signals?* He was watching himself go crazy, he loved it, he calculated it step by step, the bastard, the liar, he grinned and told us how it felt: his mind going out of his head like water draining away. But then sometimes he'd be afraid, it scared him. But he couldn't stop what was happening. He missed work—he stayed away overnight— The union is damn nice to put up this money for him, the bastard, that's how it is with people like him who make messes and then the rest of us have to live with them; he couldn't stop it once it started, like somebody poking around on a mountain to see if he can loosen a few stones, and then the stones do get loose, and rocks come loose, and the side of the mountain goes down and people are hurt—just watching it or knowing about it, you would be hurt, you would be—you would be damaged just to— Look," Jack said, "look, he said he was learning meanness. He said that. My mother and sister won't tell you, but he said that—he was learning meanness, learning murder. He bragged about it. Said he was going to catch up with the rest of the world. One week he went to Mass every morning, very religious and superstitious, then the next week he laughed at it, laughed at my mother, said that God could communicate with him directly, the hell with the priests, and the next week he'd be afraid of what was happening and try church again, or telephone Stehlin and beg and whine about how they had to be brothers, about how Ronnie wanted him to forgive Stehlin and love him and he had to obey—and then the next week he'd swing back again, he'd talk about what was happening in his head, he'd show us pictures in the newspaper of the war or plane crashes and he'd laugh, he said he could lose himself in all that, what difference did it make?—killing Stehlin or not?—he could get away with it—"

"He said that?"

"Yes. Sure. Sure he said it," Jack said flatly.

"He said that?"

"He said everything! He had his dreams out loud!" Jack said. "Rubbed our faces in it, all of us living together—listening to him—we had to live together— He took over from Ronnie, the yelling and the messes, like a baby!"

"About learning meanness, learning murder," Howe said carefully, "what about that? What exactly did he say?"

"My mother got scared as hell and went into Alice's bedroom—she was always hiding in there—and I told her we'd better call a doctor or the police or at least Stehlin, but she wouldn't listen; she just wouldn't listen. She wouldn't hear me," Jack said bitterly. "If he got better for a few days she thought he was cured. We all wanted to think that. He could go to work, put in eight hours a day and even work on Saturday overtime, and he could act normal except if you listened to the things he said, like dreams out loud—and maybe he was normal in a way; he was hitting Stehlin for loans on the side, I know of at least one loan of a hundred dollars, he bragged about it to me, so he was sane enough for that. And to memorize things out of the newspaper and some magazines he brought home—*she* won't tell you about that, the reading he did. The memorization. It was all on purpose, it was sane. Then the other half of him was like a man stuck on something, I mean stuck, just stuck, he couldn't get his mind to go forward, he had to keep thinking about Ronnie, about the accident, about the court judgment, about Stehlin, always Stehlin, a complete stranger he was infatuated with—just obsessed with—and this went on for months, him swinging back and forth, so much of it we didn't take it seriously because we heard it all the time— He didn't know if he was afraid of what he might do or proud of it. He didn't know. He told me once that it was terrible, to go crazy. I walked out of the room. He told me another time—this was just after Christmas—he told me that he could lapse on and out of the *manic-depressive state*, a term he had gotten from an article or a book and he was proud of it, he was very proud of it. He said he could flex his mind like a muscle. Right after New Year's he was on the phone trying to talk to Stehlin, but Stehlin wouldn't talk to him. That drove him wild. He said he was being forced into an experimental stage in his life, that he had to obey, he had to listen to instructions and obey them. He wanted to kill Stehlin. He's guilty. I won't lie about him. I'm not going to lie."

"Your father wasn't in control of his actions that morning," Howe said. "He wasn't responsible. He didn't know the consequences of his act. He is not guilty because no one has found him guilty, and no one is going to; he will be found not guilty because he was not in control of his actions and under the law he can't be guilty. Do you understand?"

". . . their bedroom at the back of the house . . . it's like an attack inside me, if I look in there. . . . I used to play in there when I was a child, hide in the closet at the other house. . . . I could smell them, him. I could smell *him*. We all look alike in the face, the eyes. My eyes are like his. You can see how we all come together, even Ronnie was like us, he looked like me, there's no way out of it. . . . And the plates stacked in the kitchen, stacked up to be rinsed, when you can't tell who's been eating from them, which plate is which . . . all the food mixed together . . . and the towels in the bathroom, the hand towel, we all use to dry our hands, you come in there and it's wet, it's still wet. . . . My father would leave smears of dirt on it, and he'd leave it wet. The marks of his wet hands were almost there, you could feel them.

You could see them. I don't hate him," Jack said. "I love him, I don't want him to die; I mean, I know there isn't execution in this state, I mean I don't want him to be put away . . . I. . . . He didn't know what he was doing. But he didn't want to know. He. . . . It's their room at the back of the house, it used to scare me. How I had to keep getting born in there. I mean in the two of them. . . . I mean I have to look for myself in them, in the two of them. No matter how old I get. No matter what I do. I can't get free of them. . . . But I love them, I loved him before he went crazy. I loved them both. It's like all the plates stacked together, or the dirty clothes in the laundry basket . . . we're wound around each other. . . . Sometimes it's like an attack, I know I have to get free of them. But then at other times I feel something else, almost love . . . I feel safe with them. . . . And nothing else seems important, except all of us being together. Even if he did commit murder."

"He didn't commit murder."

"I won't lie about it. Not even to bring him back home," Jack said. "I won't lie."

"You won't have to lie."

"I won't do it."

"He isn't guilty. You won't have to lie."

"He is guilty, but I won't lie to save him."

"Even if he did say he wished you had died instead of your brother, even if he said that, he still isn't guilty," Howe said. "Obviously he was emotionally unstable. A father wouldn't say such a thing to his son. He was emotionally unstable when he said that, wasn't he?"

"I—"

"He thinks you're going to betray him, he told me that," Howe said. "But why should you betray him? Why should you? Do you care about what he might have said, do you care?—why do you care, Jack? What reason is there?"

Jack shook his head dizzily, as if to clear it. He could not understand Howe's words. And yet he did understand, in a way; he did not want to allow himself to understand.

"He wasn't guilty of first-degree murder that morning," Howe said carefully. "He wasn't in control of his actions. You don't have to lie to protect him."

"He made himself go crazy—"

"But that's what people do," Howe said, raising his hands in a gesture of surprise. "And he isn't on trial for that. He's innocent of the crime he's charged with. I believe he's innocent, I'm completely convinced of it. I'm going to win the case for him. I am going to win, I don't have any doubt about it. Because he really is innocent and you're going to explain why he's innocent, you're going to tell the court what happened and you'll remember everything perfectly. And you're not going to lie because you will only answer the questions I ask you and I won't make any mistakes. I don't make mistakes," Howe said.

6

Conscience Speaks the Truth.

The plaque at the front of the courtroom, high on the wall, was permanent and yet its words were new each time Jack read them, read them half against his will, his eyes moving restlessly forward and up to them while testimony droned on: *Conscience Speaks the Truth.*

An agony of slow suspended waiting, not a precise agony, but generalized and in danger of becoming trivial. . . . Jack sat between his mother and his sister in this suspension of waiting, feeling he was helping them just by sitting here, he was fulfilling part of his duty. *The head of the household now,* someone told him, another woman in the neighborhood, and this had angered him because his father was still alive.

There he was, still alive: the defendant himself, sitting at an ordinary table near the front of the courtroom.

The defendant, Joseph Morrissey.

But Jack could not concentrate on him. The activity of the courtroom, the movement of the starts and stops of testimony, did not seem to have anything to do with that particular man. Other human beings were more important and naturally, aggressively, drew attention, like superior animals. . . . In this big drafty room you glanced nervously around to locate yourself:

one of a fair-sized crowd of spectators. And then you located the defendant who sat with his back to you: not a very important back, an inexpensive suit. But then you fastened your attention on the defendant's attorney and on the prosecution's attorney and on the judge, you only glanced at the jurors in their pewlike box, and after that you forgot about everyone else except those three men. Like superior animals, thrown up out of a chaos of squirming mute animals, bred out of their own instincts for a certain dangerous environment, they were alertly at ease and gave the impression of being physically larger than anyone else. Even their faces seemed larger, stronger, deeply and intelligently conscious. . . . That was it, Jack thought: they were conscious while everyone else dreamed, woke in jerks, starts of consciousness that were like flashes of dreams but could not be held.

When these men spoke, their voices were fearful because you could hear the words, interpret the words, and yet not really know what had been said.

Jack's head filled up. Witnesses, testimonies . . . small speeches ascending upward, building to dramatic pitches . . . but then reduced to zero again, interrupted, dismissed. The longest testimony so far had been a perfunctory, unemotional description of the *insult done to a human brain* by a bullet of a certain type. . . . This testimony should have been an angry one, but it wasn't. The doctor who testified had no anger, he presented his material quietly and dutifully and he smiled in response to a remark that indicated he had done his job well. What about the brain, the other organs of that body . . . ? Jack grew dizzy when he remembered and had to remember and felt the rest of the spectators in the courtroom remembering. A man had been shot. He was not here today, you had to remember him.

The dead man was a name now, two words. But shortened to one word: *Stehlin.* You had to believe he had once existed and did not now exist, and that this had something to do with the activity of the court. It had something to do with one man especially, a man reduced to a name—*Morrissey*—who was here in the courtroom, there at the table beside his attorney. The man on the left, in the cheap blue suit bought off the rack at Federal's, charged with *deliberate and premeditated murder.*

But it was hard for Jack to believe in the existence of "Morrissey." And "Morrissey" did not seem to believe in his own existence, did not look up when his name was uttered, sat meagerly and meekly and dumbly, never looking around. There was a "Joseph Morrissey" so important that this entire court, those clever, highly charged, highly conscious men talked of him, uttered his name: now coldly, now warmly. Contemptuously, as you would speak of an error. But then sympathetically, as you would speak of yourself. This "Morrissey," the word *Morrissey*, was very important. But the other Morrissey, a middle-aged man sitting below the judge's large raised bench, his shoulders rounded with sorrow or indifference and the back of his head shaved too high by a prison barber . . . he was not very important.

Who gave a damn about that man?

But "Joseph Morrissey" was a man you must respect: either because he was a *cold-blooded and ruthless murderer* or because he was *a man with an insurmountable, tragic grief*. . . .

Jack's numb, nervous daydreaming was always being interrupted. Howe was always getting to his feet, as if climbing up into the air, defining himself, declaring himself. He was very conscious, very real. His voice was an important voice. And his face, so familiar to Jack, the face of Jack's soothing dreams, was familiar to everyone in the courtroom now: had become familiar at once. First there was the shape of him, his size. He was a large man but he carried himself lightly, energetically. He seemed always to be raising his shoulders and growing taller, by magic. Then, after the shock of his body, there was his face—his high-colored complexion, his eyes and strong straight nose. And then his voice. His voice was loud and penetrated every corner of the room, but it was without apparent effort, no effort at all, a voice as conversational and logical as the voice everyone carries inside his own head, the voice of a good friend who won't betray you, your only good friend. . . . A voice that sounded everywhere, the most manly voice Jack had ever heard. It woke you up. It forced you to focus your gaze upon Howe, it forced everyone to wake up, to look. Jack felt the shift of attention when Howe got to his feet, he felt the sudden intensification of interest. And when Howe declined to ask any more questions, or when he withdrew to sit down again, something seemed to soften in the air, to grow shapeless and confused.

So it must be put right: must be argued back into shape. And

Howe's opponent, a man named Fromme, used his sharp, rather high-pitched voice to force it back into shape. Fromme was in his fifties, nearly as tall as Howe, not so stylishly dressed but very neat, fastidious, with a tidy fringe of gray hair and a morose, sensible, sane face. Everything he said was convincing because it was sane; it had to do with dates, times of day, people's names and professions and addresses, inevitable inescapable facts no one could contest. When he argued that "Joseph Morrissey" was guilty of first-degree murder, it was because "Joseph Morrissey" had demonstrated certain acts that required premeditation. Buying a gun? Buying a gun illegally, an unregistered gun? Carrying it around with him for two days, two days . . . ?

Obviously, this established premeditation.

And five shots had been fired. But not in rapid succession. *Not in rapid succession.* This was important, very important, because it established the fact that the defendant had paused after the first shot, as if to consider whether he would shoot again and, though he could see the effect of his first shot, though he had several seconds in which to view the terrible physical effects of that first shot, he chose to shoot again. And then again, three more times.

And "Joseph Morrissey" had no history of mental illness.

The Morrissey who sat beside Howe, up at that table, might or might not be mentally ill; might be ill in an ordinary trivial way; he had lost about twenty pounds since his arrest back in January, maybe more. But that did not seem important: he was bleached-out and unemphatic, a very ordinary citizen, like one of the jurors.

What was important was the mental state of the other Joseph Morrissey.

Jack's gaze was drawn to the plaque, to the mock-gold of the words *Conscience Speaks the Truth.* The movement of the courtroom, the abrupt questions and objections and interruptions, the droning testimonies, the sudden brisk dismissals, seemed to take place on a kind of lesser stage, while the judge, with his shrewd regal face and the plaque above him, belonged to another dimension, more permanent and deadly. Jack wanted to believe the judge was an ordinary man, but he could not. The judge did not look ordinary. His face was not so strong, so near-handsome as Howe's, but it was distinctive; it was regal. *This is our punishment for what happened,* Jack thought: to have to see, to experience, to be judged by superior men. To have to realize there are superior men.

Only his father's crime had alerted these men. Only a crime, a "premeditated murder," had made Jack and his family aware of the fact that these men existed.

But now it was begun, it was well begun, now it could not be stopped. Too late. After the first shot, the hesitation . . . but already too late, too late. Jack stared at the judge's face and saw how he nearly nodded, very nearly agreed, as Fromme explained a point. Or had Jack imagined it? The judge hardly glanced out at the rows of spectators, did not seem to be aware of them; he had no interest in the jurors or in Jack's father, he paid attention only to the two attorneys. Sometimes he nodded abruptly, impatiently, to speed one of them up. Sometimes he interrupted. Sometimes he called both men to his desk, so that the three of them could confer in whispers, but when they stepped down again his face showed nothing, no hint of the meaning, the terrible meaning, Jack dreaded in it.

And then dismissal, adjournment; and then, the next day, the judge's impeccable polite face again beneath the plaque, as everything began again.

It was new each morning, changed, abruptly changed, and yet somehow the courtroom was the same: permanent, completed. Time changed, shifted anxiously forward. It was now early summer. It was no longer January. The date leaped from Friday to Monday, pushing time forward, and again "Joseph Morrissey," in the disguise of a man of about forty-five, was ushered in through a door at the front of the room, brought back to sit at that table beneath the judge's raised bench. And again, at the close of the day's session, he was ushered out again; and the rest of the people left, yawned and left, freely. When they returned again, time had moved ahead and everything was changed a little, except the judge in his dark robe and the plaque above him, those words Jack hated: *Conscience Speaks the Truth.*

Jack's mother wouldn't do the shopping any longer. Wouldn't go out except for the trial downtown, back and forth on the bus. She wept and told Jack that people stared at her. Women stared at her. Someone walked up to her and said, "You're the wife of that man, aren't you?" This had happened in Kroger's and she wouldn't go back.

"If I had been with you . . ." Jack murmured.

He was angry all the time, jumpy and sleepless and angry; his anger rose in sharp peaks that caused him physical pain and he wanted very much to give way to it.

His sister angered him: her long periods of silence and then her sudden chattering, almost a giddy, childish chattering. She laughed thinly and talked about girls she knew, someone almost stepping backward off the raised platform when the chorus sang for assembly, a joking bus driver all the girls liked, and Jack wanted to tell her to shut up, he wanted to strike her into silence. But he found himself trying to listen the way his mother did, even trying to smile. The trial was in its first week at this time and the prosecution was presenting its case: *the People* v. *Joseph Morrissey.*

It looked bad, very bad.

So he didn't tell Alice to be quiet, he didn't tell his mother she was imagining everything, nobody knew who she was, nobody gave a damn about her. . . .

He was so restless, he had to get out of the house. He liked to run in the park, run along the paths back into the woods, running until his body throbbed. Until his head rang. If he saw anyone he knew, any boys he thought he knew, he always turned away, ran away. Once he ran past two small black boys who laughed at him, and he felt an urge to stop and— But he didn't. He kept on running until he was exhausted, sobbing with exhaustion.

What did it mean, guilty or not guilty? Sane or insane?

Walking back along Livernois, where a stretch of old buildings was being razed and bulldozed, Jack felt his head throb with the precariousness of existence. If he ran through the woods . . . if he walked fast, like this, along the sidewalk. . . . If he rushed to smash the heads of two black children together, or if he just kept on running past them, ignoring them. . . . What did these actions mean? Were they really very different from one another? If his father had fired one shot and then stopped. If. If he had fired five shots, fast, through the window. If he had not fired at all. If he had not bought a gun. If he had waited, sanely, sensibly, cleverly, if he had waited for night and if, if he had crouched in the bushes outside the house, if he had shot from the darkness into a lighted house, those five shots into the body of Neal Stehlin. . . .

Jack could have wept for the stupidity of it, the craziness.

He was so restless that he liked doing the grocery shopping for his mother, he liked having a reason to escape from the house. It was so easy to please her now! So easy to be kind! He crossed over to the A & P, a few blocks out of his way, and pushed the grocery cart rapidly along the aisles, his eye snapping from one shelf to another, one bin to another, rapid and shrewd. He was good at math and enjoyed figuring out prices, dividing, subtracting, adding figures in his head. It gave him a kind of pleasure as he rushed past the forlorn bewildered housewives, black and white, who struggled with their heaped-up carts and their small fretting children, trying to make sense of all the signs and prices, the exclamations, the bargains advertised inside gaudy red stars. In this women's slowed-down world he went very fast. He noted the shoppers' glassy eyes, their slack, half-pleased faces: were so many people only partly awake, partly conscious? Before the trial he had never really looked at people, assessed them. Now he could glance at them and pass judgment swiftly, cruelly, almost against his will. For the world was surely divided into a great horde of ordinary people—half hypnotized, startled if they were wakened, if a fifteen-year-old boy reached over impatiently to snatch a box of soap from a shelf beside them—and a very small number of superior people, all of them men, very manly men. Jack knew this now. He knew it and wondered why he had not known it all his life. It was so obvious, an ugly obvious truth.

Once you were aware of these superior men, you could not forget them. Even in the noisy supermarket, even in the check-out line, this world in which no superior men ever appeared, even there you could not forget them. Even in bed, in the safety of bed. In the dark, all lights out except the helpless frightening lights of the brain: you could not forget.

And this shame, the shame of this knowledge, was always with Jack. His mother and sister wept, worried, tried to cheer each other up, went to Mass, wept again, washed and dried dishes and set the table and cleared it, and they seemed to avoid Jack, as if sensing he knew something they did not know. A deeper, more complex truth, a truth that would make everything worse. A new crime.

He squirmed with shame. *This is the punishment for what he did,* Jack thought. *But he's safe in jail and I'm out here, living.*

Then back to the Hall of Records, the criminal court. Back to the immense, grimy, dignified old building with the broad front steps and so many people hanging around, always hanging around. Immobile, watchful. Bums. Ordinary citizens. Well-dressed men with brief cases, climbing the steps quickly. On the first day of the trial Jack and his mother and sister had been astonished to see so many other people . . . and, inside the building, so many corridors, rooms, courtrooms . . . as if this crime were not important after all, as if Jack's father might have been tried in any of the courtrooms, for any crime. How could it matter, in this crowd? Who would notice, who would care? And the neighborhood around the Hall of Records was decrepit: pawnshops, taverns, shops that advertised bail bonds, liquor stores with windows protected by grilles.

They made their way to 106, their courtroom. In the corridors there were small groups of men, white and colored, one long line that snaked out of sight, some men sitting, some standing, and in one area men crowded together on benches in a kind of pen, waiting. Seeing this for the first time, Jack tasted panic. They were caged, penned in. And outside the pen other men stood around, smoking and talking and laughing ordinarily. It did not seem to matter: the division of men into two groups, those inside and those outside. The men themselves did not seem to care. The atmosphere of the old building was lively, unserious. All the earnest conversations—*Can you get me a deal? I want to know can you get me a deal?*—swelled to one confusion, a din of voices, all men's voices, that fitted together very well. It wasn't music, but it was musical.

As the trial went on, Jack dreaded going down the corridor to the courtroom, *their courtroom;* he almost lingered, wanted to linger, to listen to these other men: they were so alive! He hated the dreary melancholy mess of his father's trial, the building-up of facts, inescapable facts, while out here people were wonderfully alive and bargaining for small chunks of their lives, the lawyers easy to recognize, not so well-dressed or so loud as Marvin Howe, but unmistakable, and the arrested men made ordinary by being in a crowd, no danger in their faces or bodies. Their behavior was never dangerous: none of the men out here were murderers.

But they had to make their way through the crowd, back to 106. It was a large courtroom, with the slightly stale, sorrowful odor of a schoolroom, and the same dull polished wooden seats and benches. Even the American flag was dusty. It was a place to come back to, to be forced back into, a room Jack would suffer in his dreams for the rest of his life.

. . . as if an ordinary man were seized by a whirlwind, picked up and flung a great distance, and then left, shaken, without even the memory of what happened to him. . . .

Howe began his presentation. Now it was his turn. And everything shifted, changed in front of Jack's eyes: now he saw the reversal of each event, each unassailable fact, as if the hard brutal bricks of his father's walled-up fate were now picked up by hand, displayed to the audience to show how harmless, how magically light they were.

"Joseph Morrissey" were only two words, but no longer the same two words. The prosecution's long careful presentation had dealt with the murderer "Morrissey." But now everyone realized that "Joseph Morrissey" could mean someone else. And this man who, according to witnesses, kept firing into the body of a defenseless, dying man, and then threw the gun at the man; this "Morrissey" who had smashed his way through a window, who had fired in front of those witnesses, who had not tried to kill or harm those witnesses, as if not being aware of them; this "Morrissey" was a victim himself, innocent himself, driven temporarily insane so that all the acts he performed were the acts of a man not responsible for what he did. . . . And the proof of his madness was what he did, exactly what he did, for only a madman would have done what Morrissey did.

"As if an ordinary man were seized by a whirlwind, picked up and flung a great distance, and then left, shaken, without even the memory of what happened to him . . . ," Howe said, speaking to the jurors. He spoke quietly. Jack could see that he was moved, emotionally moved; he stood before the jury box and spoke simply, clearly, to the jurors. They listened. They were very still, silent as always but now stilled. One of the women stared at Howe, blinking rapidly, a middle-aged woman who reminded

Jack of his own mother. . . . And Jack felt, absurdly, that he would begin to cry himself if that woman juror cried.

There were nine men and three women on the jury, all white. All plain-faced, brothers and sisters of Jack's father in his cheap new suit and his cheap brutal haircut, as meek, meager, neutral as the real Morrissey. To Jack's nervous eye they had the appearance of being middle-aged, even the two or three younger men seemed middle-aged, uncertain about the mouth, very self-conscious because of their position in the jury box. They were being looked at and they were not people anyone looked at in real life. In real life no one noticed them. And they accepted this, they were grateful for it, because they must know there was no reason for anyone to look at them: any more than there was a reason to look at the real Morrissey.

The three women had had their hair done professionally for the trial. Waved, set tightly, sprayed into hatlike shapes, the three heads were alike and interchangeable. And the men's suits were from the same store, a better store than Federal's, but not much better. They wore interchangeable neckties and white shirts. From day to day the women wore earrings that looked alike—on this particular day, the start of the defense's argument, two were wearing small white button earrings and the third, the woman who seemed so moved by Howe's words, was wearing small clip-on gold earrings.

Howe's suit was made of camel's hair, very fine and neat in spite of his large frame; his silk shirt was a pale aqua; his tie was wide and embossed with designs Jack could not make out. What mysteries, what elegant unreadable mysteries! In real life a man like Howe would not speak so dramatically and so confidentially to these twelve people, and in real life they would shy away from him, knowing themselves unworthy of his attention or distrusting it, fearing it. In real life they would stare in amazement and scorn at his clothes. *What kind of a necktie is that?* But in the jury box they were penned in, self-conscious, grateful for his attention, his serious powerful attention, his humanity.

How human he was! Jack felt that himself.

And now everything became simple. It was like a television play; it was not difficult if you understood the plot. Howe was explaining the plot. It was not difficult if you understood the main character, "Morrissey," whom Howe was explaining.

"If you understand what this man had to endure, the months of torment, grief, and the accumulated insults of Neal Stehlin—who believed he could buy off Joseph Morrissey by handing him sums of money—if you understand what Joseph Morrissey *resisted* before he finally collapsed, you will see why he did the things he is charged with doing," Howe said quietly. And it was true, true. If you understood one thing you would understand the next, and the next; the entire plot then made sense.

The other plot, the plot the prosecution had explained, was no longer believable. It was not very interesting.

Howe moved for dismissal of the indictment. "This is obviously not a case of first-degree murder, not murder executed with premeditation . . . not murder as required by the statute defining first-degree murder." But no. The judge denied this motion. Then Howe asked for the reduction of the charges to second-degree murder, and it seemed to Jack and to the people around him that this might be done. . . . But no, again no. The second motion was denied.

Howe showed no disappointment.

And now new witnesses appeared. Now the newspaper photographer explained how Morrissey had been dragged out to the police car, how he had screamed "like a madman" and had obviously been out of his mind. And, yes, he had been bleeding from the mouth—he'd been knocked around by the police—and when the photographer tried to take his picture one of the police had threatened him.

But anyway he'd taken the picture, which had been published in the evening paper for everyone to see.

Howe displayed a blown-up photograph of a man's face, what seemed to be a man's face. It was Joseph Morrissey screaming. His eyes were shut and his mouth opened very wide. There was something queer, twisted, terrifying about the face, as if it were a demonstration of what could be done to a human face.

Several of the jurors looked away.

Jack's mother drew in her breath sharply and Jack put his hand on her arm. *Don't. Not here. Don't.*

Then Howe asked the photographer, an earnest, nicely dressed young man, if he believed that the photograph resembled the accused man as he had looked that morning.

Yes.

And this man seemed to you obviously abnormal in his behavior?

Yes.

Was he saying anything?

Screaming. Sobbing.

Where was he when you took the photograph?

Almost at the squad car . . . he was writhing, twisting. . . .

And for ten minutes Howe asked the young man about "Morrissey," the other "Morrissey." Everyone stared at the photograph. Jack's father looked over himself. His profile showed a sane enough face. Jack looked from the photograph to his father and back again and could see no resemblance, not now.

And so his father had not committed that murder . . . ?

Jack's head swam. He could not concentrate, could not make himself think: what had the man in the photograph, the murderer, to do with the man at the defense counsel's table? And what had that man to do with Jack himself? He tried to listen to Howe's earnest, convincing, believable voice, he tried to separate the words so he could comprehend. . . . But there was no comprehending, you must simply listen, listen, you must go into a kind of half-sleep, as the jurors did, listening to Howe and nodding in sympathy with his voice, the slow effortless rhythmic dips and rises of his voice.

Then the prosecuting attorney examined the photographer.

He spoke sharply, his voice was high-pitched and unpleasant. He was out of phase with the sympathy Howe had evoked, he jarred it, went against it. He did not believe. He asked scornfully whether it was true that the process of taking a photograph, not to mention enlarging it so greatly, wouldn't distort a man's features?

Yes, it was possible.

But the photographer's expression showed that he did not really believe this.

The attorney then asked whether Morrissey had really looked like this on that morning—exactly like this?

Yes.

Exactly?

Yes.

You mean there's no possibility of your being mistaken? You remember exactly yourself?

Yes.

Couldn't you be influenced by the photograph itself, especially since you took it?

No.

And where is the blood on Morrissey's face?—do you see blood there?

No.

But you still think this photograph—which is obviously a very alarming and effective and melodramatic picture of a man who gives the superficial appearance of being insane—you think this resembles Morrissey exactly?

Exactly . . . ?

Yes, exactly?

Well, then, I would have to say. . . .

Jack shut his eyes and shut his mind suddenly. *No. Don't say it.*

But the photographer paused and then said, stubbornly, with a small stubborn young-man's frown: *Exactly.*

Jack's heart leaped. It was obvious now that his father had been insane.

Therefore innocent.

When the trial was not in session Jack thought only of what had taken place at the last session; he was always faithful to the testimony, the questions, the feel of the court. He was faithful, his mind could not attach itself to anything else. In a daze he walked with his mother and sister to get a bus, he listened to their excited talk or to their complaints, their bewildered attempts to compare with each other what had happened or what they thought had happened. . . . They talked endlessly about the jurors. They repeated again and again what Howe had assured them: he'd hand-picked the jury, he knew those people's souls, he had asked them all the right questions and they had given him the right answers, *he knew them.* And then Jack's mother would timidly ask him if he thought that was true . . . ?

Yes, of course he thought it was true.

Of course.

In the back of their heads the trial was really not adjourned for the evening or for the weekend. It was still in session, back there, back in 106, with its crude warped floors and its American flag. And that man in his blue suit, day after day the same suit—he was still there, surely, always there at the defense table.

And Howe was always asking someone a question: sometimes bullying, sometimes gentle. It depended upon who you were. They repeated again and again, in astonished delight, the sharp question he'd put to the prosecution's psychiatrist, who had testified that Jack's father was sane—"But you always say that, don't you? That the accused is sane? Aren't you a prosecution doctor, haven't you testified a dozen times for the prosecution in the past few years?"

And how guiltily the man had replied!

So they gloated over it, amazed at their own capacity for joy. Then they fell silent, fearful; because they had no right to be happy. And then Jack's sister might say something that maddened him, because it was so bizarre, so crazy, but exactly what they were all thinking—*Oh, why did he have to kill that man!*

"Joseph Morrissey": brought into court, walking with a young policeman. But not young himself, not now. Thin-faced, pale, humble. He had only the briefest of perplexed, strained smiles to flash at Jack's mother, then he subsided back into his look of blank glassy peace.

It must have been strange for him, Jack thought, to be told the story of what he himself had done on that morning in January. To hear it dramatized, explained. To hear himself explained, as a character in a plot that seemed complicated—overloaded with facts and statistics and doctors' opinions about "blacking out" and befuddlement and madness—but was really very simple. You had only to look at Marvin Howe, to listen closely to what he said.

You had only to believe.

Jack thought: *I believe*. He thought: *You can't listen to this and not believe*.

But he noticed the judge's cynical head-shaking, his inquisitive glances at Howe. *What does this line of questioning mean?* But before that question could be asked Howe would stop, change his tone, begin again. . . . The judge did not like Howe. He did not much like the prosecution's attorney either. But Jack had the idea that he really disliked Howe.

And behind the man, over his head, was the plaque Jack's eyes were drawn to unresistingly. But he had stopped reading it. The words had broken apart, they did not communicate any meaning. Even the letters were separate and unrelated, they did not come together to form words, they did not make any sense. Each letter was whole in itself, and sterile. Jack no longer dreaded looking up there.

. . . the appearance of an emotionally disturbed man?

Yes, I would say so. He almost walked into my car . . . he was swaying, staggering . . . he held his arms stiffly . . . he. . . .

Characteristics of the insane . . . ?

The appearance of being in a trance, of not seeing and hearing clearly . . . exaggerated facial expressions. . . .

Sudden alterations of mood?

Yes, sudden alterations of mood. . . .

You have had professional experience with people in this state?

Yes.

Yes.

When Maguire was cross-examined, his mood did not change. He was helpful, genial. He admitted it was not his practice, of course, to make diagnoses at a distance of twelve or more feet. Obviously not. However—

Gradations of sanity/insanity?

. . . of course difficult to measure, but. . . .

But difficult to measure?

Difficult.

Impossible?

Maguire hesitated. He smiled at Fromme but Fromme did not smile back.

Impossible?

Maguire said coolly: Nothing is impossible.

Jack stared at the man, astonished. How good, how much in control! When he, Jack, had to take the stand, had to testify, he hoped he could do that well.

But he was becoming increasingly nervous.

He had started to notice in himself, when he spoke to his mother or sister or even to strangers, people in stores, an odd jovial buoyancy to his voice. It wasn't Jack, not Jack. It was the sound of someone he didn't recognize.

Then, trying to cheer his mother up one morning at breakfast, he had noticed he was rubbing his hands together, as if about to present her with something, a trick, a magical feat. And he had paused, bewildered: this really wasn't Jack. It was someone worried, nervous, guilty.

His mother had said at once, misunderstanding: "Don't worry about me, Jack, I'll do as well as I can. . . ."

When Howe called her, she walked to the witness chair as if walking to communion, devout and timid but not too slowly. This was a public place. She looked suddenly thinner, an aging woman Jack saw with alarm. Her hair had been set into narrow neat waves, like the hair of the women jurors, and she wore a very plain blue suit, darkest blue, as if she were in mourning.

She and Jack's father did glance at each other, as Jack thought they would, that briefest of glances—two strangers checking on each other.

Now Howe spoke gently. Courteously. Jack's mother sat with her hands clasped together. How obvious it was that she told the truth, that she could not have imagined any lies. . . . Yes, yes, she confirmed earlier testimony about her son, Ronald. The repetition of those facts: born 1943, first indication of abnormal development 1945, examined by Dr. ______ at the ______ Clinic; by the ______ Medical Center; examined again . . . again. . . .

But nothing ever changed?

Nothing.

And now Jack's mother began to speak faintly, weakly. Jack stared at her as if willing her to keep in control. She must keep in control. . . . But when Howe asked about Ronald breaking out of the house and wandering away and crawling under the wire fence, she hesitated as if stricken with shame: it had been her son, her son!

Howe said gently that he regretted this line of questioning, but. . . .

But. . . .

If she would only speak better, Jack thought. He felt her shame, *yes,* he had been feeling this shame for months now, but she must speak better, she must not look so guilty! He wanted almost to shout at her. Nothing mattered but that she talk well, that she make everyone believe her; the ten years of Ronald, the misery and the tedium and the shock of his death, what did it matter, any of it?—what did it matter except as a small speech now that must be delivered correctly?

. . . died in the hospital . . . Detroit Receiving . . . it . . . he . . . some things fell on him . . . concrete blocks and. . . .

And then?

And then?

. . . then afterward he was not himself . . . my husband . . . he went into a decline . . . he. . . . I would cry, I was so afraid. . . . Just after Christmas he stayed away from home and. . . .

He had never done that before?

No.

Had never come home drunk before? Abusive to you?

No. No.

How did he abuse you?

. . . tried to scare me, asked me if I believed in mind-reading . . . voices . . . people telling you what to do. . . . Said that God was giving him instructions.

Instructions?

. . . about Ronnie, about Mr. Stehlin. . . . That Mr. Stehlin was betraying Ronnie now, that. . . .

And she spoke in her faint timid voice, ashamed, about the Stehlins and her husband's telephone calls and the shame of it, the shame of it, how she asked him to stop and her husband slapped her and then her son asked him to stop and he struck her son. . . . And how Stehlin had insulted him.

How?

She hesitated.

Mrs. Morrissey, how did Neal Stehlin insult your husband?

. . . he said . . . said. . . .

You heard this over the telephone yourself?

Yes, I could hear him, the voice, I could hear Mr. Stehlin shouting . . . he said my husband was crazy, he was crazy and. . . .

Mr. Stehlin said your husband was crazy?

Yes.

He said that, that word?

Yes. Crazy.

And you were very frightened . . . ?

She opened her mouth to speak and hesitated and then spoke, staring at Howe, afraid to look anywhere else. Jack didn't know if she was telling the truth any longer because he could not remember it, the "truth" of the evening of January seventeenth, but he believed his mother was not telling it as if it were true. Her replies were faltering. The courtroom seemed to awaken, relieved, when Howe introduced as evidence several enlarged photographs of the damage Jack's father had done in the house that evening. Smashed crockery, a smashed lamp, jagged fragments like pieces of a jigsaw puzzle. Jack looked anxiously at the jurors' faces and wondered if they could see there, in those black-and-white pictures, the story they were being asked to see.

. . . a man in a rage?

. . . not himself, not my husband. Not Joseph. It. . . .

Not your husband?

Not Joseph. Not Joseph. A stranger.

When the other attorney rose to question Jack's mother, he was as gentle as Howe had been. But he asked her only two perfunctory questions and then dismissed her politely, as if he had known the answers anyway and they didn't matter. And she didn't matter.

Now it was Jack's turn.

Now he came forward, feeling the shift of attention, the eyes moving from his mother and onto him. Even the judge's eyes: but they were unreadable. Jack had rehearsed this for weeks, months, but he had not known how dreamlike it would be, this walking forward into a suspension, a silence, carrying his fear with him. His knees were numb and yet they were functioning as they did in real life. His hands were trembling and yet the trembling seemed internal, invisible to everyone else.

Now he had turned, now he was seated. In front of everyone. Now, seated, he faced the courtroom—it was a shock to see it from this chair. Everyone was looking at him, individual people staring at him with interest. Even his father stared, his dull mute gaze taking in the place Jack sat, as if not quite seeing Jack, not recognizing his son in that important place.

Faintness rose in him, up into his brain. But he would not faint. He forced himself to breathe slowly, deeply; as he had rehearsed; as he had instructed himself. *No panic. No. None.*

He was staring at Howe's face.

He heard Howe ask him: Could he describe his father's behavior on the evening of January seventeenth, 1953?

Jack paused and tried to remember. He knew what to say, exactly how to begin, but his heart was pounding so fast that it distracted him. . . .

He . . . I. . . . My father. . . .

Speak more clearly, Howe instructed. He smiled.

Jack drew in his breath and thought. Then he began to speak. His voice was stronger this time, it seemed to take hold. Jack's hands tightened on the arms of the chair and his voice seemed to tighten as well, to establish itself in the room.

. . . January seventeenth, 1953 . . . ?

He explained how his father had come home, agitated, how his father had been drinking, had struck his mother . . . how he had broken things in the kitchen and the living room. . . . How. . . .

Jack refocused his attention. He looked over to the side, to the jurors. Timidly at first, and then, seeing their sympathy, with more assurance: he explained how his father had sobbed, how he had begged Jack's mother to forgive him . . . and then he had left the house and. . . .

"We were all terrified of him," Jack said. He had begun to speak quite clearly now. "Every day he was getting worse but this was terrible. . . . My mother didn't want to call a doctor, not until that night. My sister and I kept begging her but . . . but she was afraid . . . until that night she said yes, yes, we would have to get professional help . . . the next morning. . . . She said, yes, the next morning she would let me telephone someone. But then it was too late."

"In your opinion, Jack, what brought your father to such a state of desperation?"

"The way Mr. Stehlin insulted him . . . and Ronnie's death. . . . And, and the two together, in his mind, the two things," Jack said, speaking slowly, earnestly, "that he thought Mr. Stehlin was insulting Ronnie . . . that he was laughing at Ronnie. . . ."

"Did Mr. Stehlin realize he was upsetting your father so much?"

"I don't know . . . I think . . . I think he was trying to antagonize him . . . I remember thinking . . . that . . . that he must be doing it on purpose, or . . . or why would he do it? Because he could see how terrible it was for my father. . . ."

Jack felt a certainty now, an absolute certainty. All this was true. And it was true really, though he had never expressed it in this way before. He had planned certain small speeches, certain replies to questions Howe would ask; but now his replies were different, and yet correct. Gently, Howe led him on: once again the background of his brother, once again the several facts, the dates, the date of death, once again the funeral, and then the months of his father's deterioration—information everyone had heard before, but never from Jack, never from his point of view. And he felt how sharply they listened to him, because *he* was speaking, because the person who sat in this chair now was speaking so clearly, so truthfully, that all the jumbled and conflicting and puzzling questions of the trial were being answered. The story was not complicated, it was very simple. Once you knew the main character, once you knew why the plot went the way it had, it was all very simple.

Howe led him through three hours of testimony.

Cross-examined, Jack looked at the other attorney politely and replied *No sir . . . yes sir. . . .* Very respectfully, like a boy of fifteen. And yet like an adult. He felt a thrill of excitement, tired as he was, as he sensed the antagonism of the man—the wall he represented—yes, he liked walls, good hard walls he could throw himself against! He did respect this man, this Fromme. He was a little afraid of him, not knowing what he might ask; but he respected him and in a way he hoped the questioning would not end. *Now ask me about revenge,* Jack thought, *revenge*—!

He had rehearsed several answers to this question.

And then, miraculously: "Of course it never occurred to you that your father simply wanted revenge?" Fromme asked.

How blunt, and how good the question was!

Jack said, "Yes, but . . . but then he would have done it secretly. . . . He had met with Mr. Stehlin several times, alone, and he could have killed him at any one of those times . . . or at night, through the window, at night. . . . But he didn't do that. He went right to the house, I think to talk to Mr. Stehlin again, right in the morning . . . when other people were there . . . when there would have been witnesses . . . and . . . and . . . and this proves it wasn't revenge."

The man stared at Jack. But he did not show any sign of surprise or concern; he said instead, flippantly, "All right."

Was it over?

Any further questions?

"Yes, one more question: you never thought your father might have exaggerated his grief?"

"What? Why would he do that?"

"Answer my question."

"No."

"You never thought he might have exaggerated his mental condition?"

"Why would he do that . . . ? No. No," Jack said, alarmed. "Of course not."

No, of course not.

No further questions.

So you lied?

So that was the day you fell in love with your own voice?

After this, the closing sessions. It took seven hours for Howe to sum up. Again, again, the old facts: the tragedy of Ronald's retardation, the ten years of misery, the accidental death, the unguarded construction site, the funeral, the court decision that Stehlin and his partners had not been negligent . . . and the photographs set up again on easels, that screaming face. How familiar this story was now, how inevitably it moved toward a certain morning in January. . . . You could feel it moving in that direction, you could not resist. You could feel "Joseph Morrissey" being drawn along helplessly toward that morning, that absolute unchangeable date.

No one could have avoided January 18, 1953.

". . . and so we suggest that Neal Stehlin, by his repeated demonstrations of indifference to Joseph Morrissey's personal tragedy . . . by his mistaken idea that money could compensate for the death of a child . . . and by his refusal to treat Mr. Morrissey civilly, as a human being, did drive the defendant into such a frenzy that he entirely lost control of his normal personality. . . . And we suggest that Mr. Stehlin, as if deliberately, almost as if he dared this act to be committed . . . did bring about his own death on that morning."

So *that was it*, Jack thought.

*

And, after these long strained hours, after Howe's ragged, emotional voice, the prosecution's summation was a surprise. It was jarring, blunt. It believed nothing about the defense's "Joseph Morrissey" and could repeat only its old, tired, angry accusations. . . . Jack did not want to listen, he felt so exhausted himself, so fearful. No one should listen, they *must* not listen to this. And then the judge's charge, which took only an hour: quickly, perfunctorily, spoken as if by a man who had just walked into this, detached and a little impatient.

The various verdicts, explained: First-degree murder. Second-degree murder. Manslaughter. Acquittal.

But something did not sound right.

Jack's heart began to pound again. The judge's voice was not right, not quite right. The judge did not glance at Howe, who watched him respectfully, and he did not glance over at Jack's father, who sat with his head bowed. Instead he looked only at the notes in front of him, lifting his head occasionally to glance at the jurors, as if he wanted to emphasize certain points and half doubted the jurors' ability to understand.

If you believe the defense's presentation, that the crime was committed when the accused was temporarily insane . . . then acquit him.

His face had stiffened with contempt and now Jack knew what was wrong. The judge's expression almost turned into a smile of derision. *If you believe . . . then acquit,* he said flatly.

7

Waiting, Jack wandered out along the streets, seeing all the people who were not on trial. After dark he could see into ground-floor windows, the ill-lit kitchens and bedrooms of the poor. He felt safe in spite of the neighborhood. He felt safe because it was night and he could run a block or so, whenever he wanted, and then pause to get his breath back, enjoying that brief moment of exhaustion when his mind was totally blank and waiting only to recover itself.

He circled the Hall of Records in a big distended loop, keeping it in the center so he wouldn't get lost or lose it in his mind. He had to be faithful. *Now I am walking seven blocks to the north,* he thought. They had told him to go home, it might be all night; Howe had said in his ruined, ragged voice it wasn't going to be any easy victory, *so go home.* After that day's session, after seven hours of uninterrupted talk, Howe looked like a wreck and his face frightened Jack. *Go home,* he had said bluntly, as if wanting to get Jack out of his sight.

Now I am walking . . . now I am running . . . four blocks east of it, Jack told himself. He overtook strolling men, strolling couples, who stared at him in amazement: a white boy running out here! At street corners he slowed down, panting. It was midsummer now, deep into summer. He could not remember the end of winter, the final days of winter, and he could not really remember spring or the early part of the summer. All time was the same, blended together terribly. It was still January 18 and it would perhaps always be January 18, a peak of a day, a small dangerous mountain. His father's ordinary unplotted life ran up to that day—a date on the calendar—and then declined from it.

Jack made his way through small clots of men who stood around in front of taverns, arguing and laughing loudly. Someone tossed a beer bottle out into the street. Jack didn't look around. He was afraid he would display a terrified face, eyes filling with tears—he was envious of these men and boys who were not on trial and not waiting.

He recognized this street—he had already walked this way. He noticed for the second time a pawnshop with a window that was partly boarded up. Inside, a multitude of things crammed together: even a grandfather clock, even a pair of men's hip-length fishing boots. For some reason, seeing these unrelated, innocent objects, he felt a slight leap of hope. But it was not very strong. Then his stomach seemed to sink, sag inside his lean body, for he knew he had no right to hope for anything. *I'm still fifteen years old,* he thought bitterly. It did not seem believable. *I'm too old for fifteen,* he thought. Though he had already walked down this street he walked along it again. He half knew that most of the night lay ahead of him; he should be at home with his mother, his sister . . . but he could not bear the thought of that house, that waiting, the two women so close to him and yet fearing him, dreading to look into his face as if they were terrified to see some secret, some knowledge he had withheld from them.

Again, on the corner of this street, an all-night laundromat Jack had noticed before. This time he crossed over so he could look inside. It was a brightly lit place, empty except for two customers. There were several rows of washing machines with their lids flung back and one row, against the back wall, of large driers. A white couple, a man and a girl, maybe in their twenties—at the rear, taking their laundry out of one of the driers—unaware of Jack watching, unaware of anything. Both wore jeans and shirts that looked soiled. The girl's hair was fixed loosely at the back of her head, tied with a piece of red yarn or string. Jack drew nearer, watching. He could see they were talking earnestly; he wondered what they were talking about. The man's face was gaunt, his jaws were bony. His chest quite thin. From the Ozarks, probably, up in Detroit to work in one of the automobile factories. . . .

The girl was taking their laundry out of the drier, item by item, moving slowly and methodically and with great care, as if what she was doing was very important. Jack had noticed that slowness, that almost reverent slowness, in some of the women shoppers he'd overtaken impatiently in the grocery store. While the young man watched, his arms folded, she took the things out and folded them and put them into a shopping bag at her feet. Then she had a little trouble with a sheet—a long, twisted white sheet—that she pulled out of the coil of clothes hand over hand, very carefully. It must not touch the dirty floor. The man helped her, taking hold of one end. Then he stepped back and they pulled the sheet taut between them, stretching their arms out wide, and then folding the sheet in the middle; then the man stepped in toward the girl again, so that he could take the sheet from her; they stepped together as if in a dance, a performance they had done many times, their faces peaceful with concentration.

They went through exactly the same maneuvers with the next sheet, which was also white. A few steps away from each other, the sheet stretched out, shaken a little, the folding of the sheet and the several small steps inward, together again, so that their faces were brought up close. But this time the girl raised herself on her toes to kiss the man's mouth. He grinned.

Jack was staring in at them.

He wanted–

He wanted to–

He walked quickly away. He didn't know why the scene had moved him so. The man, whose face he had hardly been able to see, the girl with her straggly dull-brown hair . . . clean wrinkled hot sheets drawn out hand over hand, lovingly. . . . There was love in the world, Jack thought, but you had to be not on trial. . . . It was a blunt, surprising thought, like an elbow in the ribs.

8

The woman stirred beside him in a shudder of dread, shame, perhaps excitement. He himself was excited. But he didn't want to look at her, not yet. He was staring at a corner of this room, this unfamiliar room, where two walls came together and formed a corner of hot stale shadow.

Finally she said, "I . . . I'm sure they didn't find him guilty. I mean. . . . They didn't, did they?"

His heart tripped with irritation at her question. She seemed to be intruding into the misery of that night, into Jack's hateful loving memory of it. With difficulty, reluctantly, he forced himself to come back: now it was eleven years later, he was not a fifteen-year-old boy, now he was an adult himself and safe. The motel room they were in seemed to him oddly small, like a scaled-down model of a room. It was not the right setting for what he felt.

"I'm sure . . ." the woman said.

Her name was Rachel, "Rachel from Long Beach." She had spoken flippantly and he had asked where Long Beach was, he'd implied he really didn't care, just the name of the city seemed to him trivial: beaches, water, people with money. She had told him it was nowhere. Her voice was scornful, a little abrasive, and he had laughed with surprise—how easily she had put it behind her, dismissed just by a gesture of her hand.

He had liked her, had been drawn to her, in spite of her eager, earnest voice and her frequent laughter, which seemed to him a little forced. But he didn't blame her or the other girls for being like that, almost hysterical. . . .

Now it was six, seven hours later. Jack and the woman half lay, half sat against the headboard of this bed, which was not very solid. The headboard was made of some odd synthetic material, not wood but not paper either, stiffer than cardboard, but like pulp—with fake wood grains stamped on it. The walls and ceiling of the little room were covered with cheap paneling, fake pine wood with simulated knotholes. Jack had hoped it might be real pine, though he should have known better; he'd been disappointed, rubbing his hand against it. Then he could see how obvious it was that the wall covering was just paper pulp.

"Well, I know a little about Marvin Howe's career," the woman said thoughtfully. "So I'm sure he didn't lose, he didn't lose a client to charges of first-degree murder."

"You're sure?" Jack said.

"No, I'm not absolutely sure," she said.

She shifted her weight to untwist something beneath her—a sheet—it was crumpled and damp, very thin from having been laundered and bleached too often. Jack wondered how it was possible to really clean sheets and towels in places like this—what hope was there of bleaching them white and pure again?—of even killing the germs from last night's clients? On the floor by the bathroom was the single hand towel that had come with the room, now smeared with Rachel's lipstick when Jack had wiped his face. That had annoyed him, that she had worn lipstick; he hated women who wore lipstick, who did things to their faces. Rachel was not really one of those women.

"Aren't you going to tell me what happened?" she asked.

"Guess."

He liked the intimate, companionable look of their bare feet, his and Rachel's. Her toes were long and thin, his were thicker, larger, and his two large toes had thickened, slightly bluish, bruised-looking nails. That was from a pair of cheap shoes he'd bought in Detroit, but he still wore them. He was too stubborn to throw them away.

"It was second-degree murder at the most. The very most," she said hesitantly. She lit another cigarette and sucked in the smoke, as if strengthening herself—he'd noticed that at the party last night, how very much she was like him, sucking in smoke as if it were something wonderful, invigorating; a kind of charge, a charge of energy. She was like Jack himself, arrogant and confident and yet nervous, restless. He didn't know her, not even her last name. But he did know her, really.

"Or manslaughter," she said.

"At the most? You think so?"

She was silent. He felt how keyed-up she was, ready to argue. The last forty-eight hours must have been exhausting to her, and the last several hours, with Jack, had brought her to peaks of near hysteria, but still she wanted to talk like this, to draw out Jack's story, even to argue with him. As if, in arguing, she could somehow change what he knew to be true! He liked that, her perversity. He rarely came across it in a woman, only in men like himself.

"He made you lie, didn't he," she said almost fondly.

"No. I didn't lie."

"No?"

"No. I don't lie," Jack said with an irritated laugh.

"Did he hypnotize you? He supposedly has that power . . . doesn't he?" Rachel said scornfully.

"I hypnotized myself," Jack said.

"You did very well, then."

"Yes, I did very well."

"Fell in love with your own voice. . . . But it's worth it, your voice," she said. When he looked at her, surprised, he saw that her eyes were dark, bright, a little shadowed with exhaustion but still clear, like his own. "So, did it work? Did you bring your father through?"

Jack noticed that his fingers were trembling—even now, after eleven years! But he was certain Rachel could not notice. He said, "Yes."

"Oh—? You mean it was acquittal?"

"Not Guilty," Jack said.

And still his fingers trembled, still his knees were weak.

"Not guilty," she repeated. "Well. My God, what good luck! I mean—yes, God yes— He got your father off completely? A complete acquittal?"

"Not guilty by reason of temporary insanity," Jack said. He felt a little lightheaded, but very pleased; as if he had just relived the moment when the foreman of the jury had announced the verdict. Yes, it had been Not Guilty. That meant: Not guilty.

"Why, that clever son of a bitch," she said slowly, admiringly. "So he got away with it!—I mean Howe, Howe himself! He got away with it—he put the dead man on trial and found him guilty and got away with it!"

Jack laughed.

"But how lucky you all were . . . back then, back then they must have been bringing in heavy verdicts all the time."

"They still are," Jack said. "But not that day. The jury was out seventeen hours, *seventeen hours* . . . and when they came back we were all wrecks, the women jurors were half dead, and Howe himself was ready to collapse. But the foreman made his announcement—he was a nice-looking old guy who had two suits, a gray one and a brown one, which he alternated during the trial; I knew all their outfits by heart. He was wearing the gray one that day and it really needed dry cleaning. He used his bravest, best voice to let us know the good news: Not Guilty. And so that was it."

But he remembered still the terror, the beating of hearts, minds, the pressure of blood in his own body, too much to endure. Human beings should not have to live through such moments. Guilty or not guilty, murderers or their victims, their children, their prosecutors, their attorneys—how raw it had been, how hellish!

"What happened to your father afterward?" Rachel asked sympathetically.

"Psychiatric care, off and on, but he wasn't crazy and he was never hospitalized," Jack said. "The trouble was, he'd made all the headlines and was a minor celebrity—the case caused a sensation in Detroit, which I really didn't know about at the time—because of Stehlin, Stehlin was so well-known and had so many friends. But none of his friends were on the jury. So my parents had to get out of the neighborhood. It took them a long time to sell the house because people turned up for Sunday open house just to gawk. Finally they sold it to a real estate con man for about fifteen hundred dollars, and moved across town where they imagined people wouldn't know them. Not that my father ever left the house anyway. And my mother stayed in most of the time too. . . . They were old, finished, they never recovered. My father became very religious and he was always agreeable, he didn't drink, he'd just sit out in the sun in the back yard and read the paper, that was what he did for a long time. He died when I was in my first year of law school—his first heart attack, and it killed him."

She touched his arm. "That's unusual," she said awkwardly. "The first attack . . . I mean . . . being fatal."

"So they said."

"But, my God, how lucky you all were. . . . Just to get Howe, to get him to take you on. That was the early fifties . . . he was just getting started then, wasn't he?"

"He was on his way, yes, and that acquittal didn't hurt," Jack said. "It wasn't just acquittal but it was temporary insanity—and not insanity—it was a perfect acquittal, exactly right. Because other men at the same time were going to mental hospitals for the rest of their lives—they still are—but my father just walked out of court free, as well as he could walk. And of course he was innocent and free, even if he never went out of the house except to sit in the back yard. . . . Jesus," Jack said, laughing bitterly, "the way that judge looked at the jury! The old bastard, Judge Wheeler, ah, he was so damn disgusted, I could see arteries swelling in his face I never knew he had there before! He was so disgusted! He didn't thank the jury, just dismissed them and walked out. . . ."

Jack paused. Now he could laugh, now he could speak flippantly—but there was really nothing funny. And the story did not have an ending. He could tell it and retell it, but it would never come to any conclusion. Before this he had told it to only three people—two men, friends of his, and another woman, a girl he'd almost married but had decided against, his last year of law school—and each time it had not ended, not really. Because he still did not know: he did not know.

Guilty or not guilty?

Howe had told him: *You'll never know.*

"As for Howe," Jack said, trying to keep the same light, amused tone, "I never saw him again. One day I was his star, his prize, almost his son, and the next day he was gone. One day he'd known more about my father and the rest of us, the pathetic Morrisseys, than we knew about ourselves, he had absorbed us completely, as if he'd created us—like a novelist writing a big crowded novel, with lots of room to keep going and no patience to look back—and no need to look back—and the next day he was gone, he was onto something else. Someone else. His next murderer was the old man who owned Baum Brothers, a higher-class client than Joseph Morrissey. He was on his way."

The woman, Rachel, laughed sharply. She scratched at her knee as if to give herself time to think. It was not a girlish knee, not modest. But sturdy. Jack liked it.

"You loved him," she said.

Jack laughed. "Sure," he said.

When they woke up it was around eight o'clock. They had managed to sleep a few hours. Lying in bed, Jack noticed something shoved beneath the door. He went over to examine it, touching it with his big toe.

"What's wrong?" she asked.

He showed it to her—a piece of ordinary brown cardboard with a shiny razor blade taped to it, inside a heart drawn with red ink. Red block letters. *Do-It-Yourself-Throat-Cut.*

Jack and the woman laughed together, at first nervously. Then they laughed with pleasure.

"It's a new razor blade," Jack said. "I can use it."

He detached it carefully from the cardboard.

They were in Java, Mississippi, the county seat of Lime County; it was the summer of 1964.

9

His head cleared fast when he got to the office, to his borrowed desk where he had set up shop. It cleared up when the telephone rang its first ring, a loud jangling noise that he liked, and he felt the grogginess, the extravagant complex emotions of the night before, simplify themselves and vanish.

This was real life: Jack at a big battered desk with many drawers and a sliding top that no longer slid into place, a desk other men had used, stuffing it with papers and notes and things no one had time to sort out. Real life: the telephone. Outside, a pot-holed street, rust-specked cars parked at the curb, black people on the sidewalks, lots of people. Jack liked this very much. It was the first time he'd been in the South. He had worked on committees, assisting ACLU lawyers on civil rights cases in the North, and as far south as Carbondale, Illinois, but this was his first time in the South; it was his first time as a consultant, without anyone telling him what to do. He had always hated being told what to do, even when it was what he wanted to do anyway.

He glanced out the window and down at the street, the humid sweet sunshine that was like nothing he knew up North, and he thought it was a good idea that this office was on the second floor above a diner—it might be safer on the second floor.

People were filing in to talk to him, crowded back out on the landing.

The day heated up.

He took notes while the black lawyer, a man from Jackson, fidgeted and perspired. The desk was such a mess, Jack had to keep pawing for the right papers—he knocked some Xeroxed documents on the floor—the black stooped to pick them up. "The man you will have to contact for this is not me, but Bob Efron, that's a minister out in—"

"I know that but he won't talk to me," Jack said. "When I call him somebody else answers and supposedly takes a message, but he doesn't call back. I've got one of the girls calling his house right now but it's obvious he doesn't want to cooperate."

"Not not cooperating," the man said slowly. "Not that, exactly. But he went through an action like this, similar to the one you're interested in, a year ago, and—"

"I know that," Jack said.

"And he is still feeling the after-effects; in fact so is everybody else," the man said. "You got to understand that."

"I understand it," Jack said. "You can't help me with him, huh?

All right. I appreciate your information. What about your own work, what's happening? You're out on bail?"

"Five hundred, they set it at," the man said sourly. Jack looked at him for the first time: he saw with a small shock that the black man was about thirty, a young man. He hadn't caught his name. So, while the man began to explain his own complicated situation, Jack ran his eye down along the list of names on the mimeographed sheet before him. X, *beaten about the head, arrested "obstructing sidewalk," "resisting arrest," Lime C. jail. . . . X, "reckless driving," bond from UCS funds, due for arraignment 7/15, whereabouts unknown. . . . X, NAACP, Jackson Miss., arrested "unlawful practice":* that was it. The name looked like Porter, Potter. The printing was smudged and Jack wondered if he could risk trying a name—*Porter, Potter?*

"Since we began the boycott the arrests been piling up," the man said, half whining, half pleased. "Some of them are likely to be cleared up fast, but how about me? What they want is to take my whole profession away from me, it's not some simple hit-and-run, now they're kind of urging me to leave—I mean the police—I mean, for instance, Mr. Morrissey, just when the sheriff's man came to hand me the summons, he had a shotgun with him, I mean he was carrying it ready to use, you know, Mr. Morrissey? He walked right in the office like that and said, 'Hey, don't make me shoot you in front of witnesses, huh?' like it was a very funny joke. Anything like that ever happen to you?"

"Well, not yet," Jack said irritably. "I've heard of worse things."

"So have I. But I have this degree I worked for, you know, and I passed the bar exams for certain privileges they are anxious to take away from me. . . . Also I don't want to get shot, but I don't want to jump bond either . . . but look, you're going to discover one thing fast: they don't take any special dislike to the people they knock around and frisk and put in the jails, I mean just regular people, you know, who are helping out with the boycott, but they *really* got it in for people like me and you. . . ."

Jack looked at his watch: almost noon. The morning had rushed past him and he had half a dozen things to do, calls to make, to return, people out on the landing waiting patiently to talk to him. . . . While the lawyer continued, as if thinking out loud, vexed, slow, quickening in his anger, Jack tried to take notes and tried not to show his impatience. "All right, I understand, I've got to think about it and I'll let you know," he said finally.

He went out to see if the call had gone through. But the girl—a very young-looking girl from New York—told him no, no luck.

The day heated up. Jack took off his suit coat but didn't loosen his tie or collar. He disliked the outfits some of the volunteer workers were wearing, especially the girls; he believed the seriousness of their work demanded formality. Himself, he wanted to look like any American citizen, someone's promising, most promising, son.

A girl came to talk with him, leaning forward as she sat in the hard-backed chair, facing him, her knees tense and white. From her accent he guessed she was an Easterner, perhaps from New England. She had been in Java from the beginning, early in the summer; she told him about the meetings back in the countryside, the fear, the defiance, cars forced off roads, the car she was driving—with a Massachusetts license plate—searched for weapons and explosives and then "impounded" for some reason Jack didn't catch. She had a plain, almost pretty, sunburned face. As she spoke Jack began to hear horns somewhere outside.

He interrupted her: "What the hell is that?—those horns?"

"Oh it's just kids, white kids," she said. "Driving around to scare people—it's nothing."

She laughed thinly.

Even here there was flirtation—the quick desperate possibility of flirtation, as if on a battlefield, between attacks.

Someone leaned in the door to toss them a newspaper. It was the *New York Times;* Jack and the girl looked through it together. They scanned the columns and saw nothing new, no new troubles, then paged through the paper to catch up on the news of a few days ago, a week, follow-up reports on a bombing in Alabama and the shooting of a civil rights worker in Mississippi, but again nothing new. Jack skimmed the editorial page and caught only certain significant words—*laudatory nonviolent methods . . . but . . . run risk . . . inflaming deeply held Southern prejudices. . . .* "Take the newspaper, I'm through with it," he said.

The girl looked with distaste at the back pages. "Christ, somebody's been swatting bugs with this."

After she left Jack took a break, went downstairs, half-wondered if Rachel was around; but he didn't want to look for her. He didn't want to ask about her. He walked out into the wall of heat, almost shivering with it, his suit coat under his arm. A walk, maybe? A short walk? He'd been in Java two days now but hadn't had time to look around. The boycott was in its twenty-third day, which meant that people were jumpy, and the white merchants were not going to be friendly to him, but he didn't take that too seriously.

This was real life: the pressure people exerted on one another, as tangible as the heat everyone had to walk through. You had to accept it, to breathe it into your lungs, or you couldn't live.

Jack felt very good in spite of the heat.

He walked the five or six short blocks over to the white part of town, the surprisingly wide Main Street with its perpendicular parking and its modern Bank of America, big plate-glass windows tinted green. But everything else, the buildings on both sides of the street, was old, homely, primly drab, like those small towns in Michigan and Illinois Jack had sometimes stared at in passing, trying to adjust his mind to them: what would it be like to live here? But he could not imagine himself living here, he couldn't imagine himself, Jack Morrissey, even living in one of those small Northern towns.

No blacks on the street over here, no black shoppers today. Jack strolled along with his coat now on, one button buttoned, neat and curious and friendly, as well as he could appear to be friendly when no one smiled at him. No one really looked at him: just a fast glance as they approached him on the sidewalk, and then eyes turned carefully aside. Only a few children stared, but without any meaning; they couldn't have known who he was.

He passed the usual stores: Woolworth's, a shoe store for men and women, a restaurant that looked empty, its front window grease-stained and cluttered with ads for Pepsi-Cola and Camels. Next door was a Rexall's, so he went in, anticipating some relief from the heat—but he wasn't in Detroit, he couldn't expect an air-conditioned drugstore—and once inside he paused, sorry he'd come in. At the rear of the store, by the pharmacist's counter, a tight-faced woman was watching him. Jack scanned the titles of the paperback books on the rack: Robert Ruark, Mickey Spillane, *The Book of Simple Investments, Victory at Sea.* The place was deserted. He turned the rack idly, but saw nothing that interested him. *Quiet in here, isn't it? Is it always so quiet? Are you losing money?*

Next door was a woman's clothing store that looked closed, at least for the day. And across the street a movie house, also closed. Its marquee advertised New & Used Cars at a nearby lot, and its posters were for very old movies—one of them, "Bambi"—so Jack supposed it had been shut down before the boycott began. Still, it pleased him to see it abandoned.

Are you all losing money? How does it feel?

There wasn't much traffic even on the central street, a few slow-moving cars, a pickup truck with several children and a panting collie in back, a Greyhound bus headed for Nuffield. That was over in Panola County, Jack's next stop after Java; things were supposed to be worse there, though no real offensives had been tried—nothing like a boycott—only routine sessions in churches or private homes, instructions in voter registration, the meaning of the Supreme Court decision concerning public school integration, legal advice. . . . But a young woman, a friend of Rachel's, had been dragged out in a field a few weeks ago, near Nuffield, and knocked around by some white boys so badly she was still in the hospital.

A big AAA-approved hotel, the Cap'n Asa Mercer, the town's only good restaurant but unfortunately off limits to Jack and the others. . . . It didn't appeal to Jack anyway, the newly painted white clapboards, the green shutters, the fake-antique look of the sign that hung from a hook: Cap'n Asa Mercer himself, evidently a Civil War hero, with a white beard. Jack went up the front steps to peer inside—cavernous, dark, probably musty, probably as cockroach-ridden as every other place in town. But it was air-conditioned and Jack regretted having to boycott it.

Now he was approaching the railroad tracks and the town seemed to come to an end: only small frame houses, residential streets. So he turned back and circled a building made of cinder blocks that turned out to be, in front, the County Courthouse. He felt a slight flash of pleasure—he wondered if he might be in there sometime, arguing the Hurley case, maybe?—if he could get through to that Efron, that Reverend Efron who never returned his calls. He went inside. Very hot, very quiet. Deathly. He passed the County Clerk's office—just two women, girls, and slow-turning ceiling fans that could hardly have stirred the air. And back to the courtroom, which was empty, though larger than Jack would have imagined. How quiet this place was, how different from Detroit! He leaned inside, looking around. A little excited, absurdly excited, as he imagined himself in here—at the front—he noticed a small raised platform and a podium near the jurors' box, some distance from the witness chair, and supposed that lawyers used that, that he would use that, standing up there and asking his questions carefully, one after another. . . .

He walked down a side corridor past the Tax Clerk's office, which was closed, and out a door that took him through an unpaved parking lot. Across the street was a newer building—though not really new, just newer than the others—that turned out to be the police station and the public library combined, the police station upstairs, the library in the basement. Jack thought that was a good combination. He glanced at his watch and saw he had a few more minutes, so he went over to the building, taking his time, wondering if anyone was watching him—a bored sheriff's deputy who had nothing to do but gaze out the window? Jack went down the steps to the library feeling pleasantly warm, heated. He was not in danger but he felt his heartbeat quicken, as if preparing his body for a fight; it was a good feeling.

But the library was a disappointment—a small room, bare concrete-block walls, a bulletin board someone had tried to decorate with a tacked-up display of photographs beneath the words *Susan Anne McKay—Miss. Authoress.* No one was in the room except the librarian, who was typing at a small metal stand and who stopped to stare at Jack. Friend? He smiled at her, tentatively. She stared without expression. Her glasses swerved up at the corners. Jack saw that she wasn't a friend, no. He pretended to be looking at the New Fiction Offerings for Summer. Very quiet in here. The librarian didn't resume her typing. Jack wandered over to the magazine shelf: old dog-eared issues of *Time, Ladies' Home Journal, Reader's Digest.* In an issue of *Time* a few weeks ago there had been a lengthy, very sympathetic story about the civil rights workers in the South, with photographs of some of the college kids, including the one who was later shot and killed, and the Director of the Hillier Foundation, which was sponsoring Jack's trip, but Jack couldn't find the issue. Maybe it had been thrown out. His name had been mentioned, *Jack Morrissey,* but no, he couldn't find it.

He leafed through an oversized, handsome magazine called *Southern Gardens.* Photographs of flowers—he could recognize roses, at least, and things that looked like lilacs—but what stunned him were the photographs of houses, homes the size of fortresses, old plantation homes. In a way he had thought they'd all been razed, destroyed. Burned down. He skimmed through an article about the Esau Cables of Atlanta, Georgia, who owned an immense home with acres of gardens and avenues, trees with moss hanging from them, bushes laden with unearthly, immense blossoms, all things that to Jack's eye looked totally foreign—was he in a foreign country, maybe?—another planet? He glanced up and saw again the name on the bulletin board, spelled out in neat red cardboard letters like something in a kindergarten class, *Susan Anne McKay,* a name he realized he'd never heard of. *Southern Gardens* featured a center section of glossy pictures showing very happy wives displaying their rhododendrons—a word and a flower new to Jack also—all of them smiling, smiling, their lips fixed up with clear red lipstick, all the women wearing the same shade. Jack stared at a picture of someone's country lane lined with big round rocks, set lovingly in place over a century ago by slaves. That had been activity to keep them busy and warm in the winter, maybe, Jack thought. A continuation of the article about Esau Cable quoted him as saying: ". . . in the present century our struggle is to preserve our way of life against outsiders bent on destruction. Our children will inherit. . . ." Yes, Jack thought, smiling, yes, he could picture Mr. Cable fighting off niggers, an army of big black ungovernable men undoing the labor of years, centuries, climbing over garden walls and stamping through the roses and rhododendrons, tearing the round rocks loose, rolling them downhill. Yes, Jack grinned, that was going to happen. Yes. The big houses were going to be razed this time, burned to the ground.

The librarian was approaching him hesitantly; he noticed her out of the corner of his eye. He put the magazine back. He knew she wasn't an attractive woman—she was even too old for him—yet he felt a stirring of desire, not for her, but for the fact of her, the situation, Jack and a woman alone together, a woman who was so obviously afraid of him. The night before, those three or four hours with Rachel, whom he hardly knew, had somehow keyed him up more, made him more aware of his body and what it could do, even when he was exhausted. . . . And this pleased him, excited him, the fact of his healthy, stubborn body and what it could do.

The librarian said in a sudden hoarse voice: "Mister, do you have a card for this library?"

Jack turned politely. He saw the narrow, frightened eyes.

"No. I'm afraid not."

"If you would like to apply for a—"

"Don't have time."

"Are you a resident of Lime County?"

"No."

"Then I'm afraid, I'm afraid, if you don't have a card, you can't use this—"

Jesus, Jack thought in amazement, she's terrified of me. He could almost smell her fear.

"I can't? Why not? Is that Mississippi law?"

He was not a tall man—and it pleased him when women were as short as this one. It allowed him to be gallant if he wanted to be. And at the same time he could frighten them, just a little, playfully.

"I—I'm afraid—I'm afraid you will have to leave," she said.

Jack obeyed; he always respected terror.

He walked back to the main street, past the closed-down movie house and the Cap'n Asa Mercer and the drugstore and Woolworth's, stepped inside the Bank of America, which turned out to be air-conditioned, very pleasant, all but one of its tellers' windows closed; and so back to the decrepit black side of town, where the NAACP-ACLU legal aid office had been set up in a two-story frame building that looked like a large chicken coop.

Nothing had happened to him.

10

That afternoon Jack got through to the Reverend Efron and tried to talk him into agreeing to discuss a certain case: the killing of a black boy of eighteen by a white state trooper that had occurred a few months before. The boy's name was Hurley and the event had caused a great deal of talk, but nothing had ever come of it; the state trooper's superior had not even disciplined him, had declined to make any public comment on the shooting at all. Jack had before him, on the cluttered desk, a number of newsclippings and notes about the incident, but every time he tried to bring the subject around to the killing, the voice at the other end of the line went vague or interrupted him.

"Mr. Morrissey," the voice said in a whimsical, lyrical whine, "the last time I organized something like this, helped prepare it and got courage up and all, the jury was out six minutes. You know why they took so long to hand down a verdict of Not Guilty? You know why?"

"I know about the verdict in that case, but—"

"Because two of the men wanted to be foreman of the jury. They argued over it. It was twelve white men, and two of them wanted to be foreman. They spent six minutes figuring out how to handle that. Finally they did it with matchsticks—somebody held them behind his back and asked the two men how many, you know, and awarded the foreman title to the one who got closest. That took six minutes. After the trial got over it was lively around here—after dark you couldn't go walking out on the road, so many cars rushing around and white boys target-practicing. The house where the boy lived—if you want to call it a house—was burned down right that day; he hardly walked out of the courthouse but they had the fire going. All his family had to move out of here. But you know what?"

"What?" Jack said reluctantly.

"It was good luck he didn't win the case."

Jack was staring at the photograph of a very young-looking black boy, a poor reproduction from an Atlanta newspaper. He tapped at the clipping impatiently. "Mr. Efron, I appreciate all that," he said. "But we have to begin somewhere. That was the beginning and now we have another case, a much more solid case, here an actual murder—a shooting before witnesses—an unarmed, defenseless victim—"

"Well, they don't allow he was unarmed."

"I need to talk with you, can I drive out? We have a rented car here I can use. I can be out in an hour—"

"No. Can't help you."

"What? Wait. The boycott is in its twenty-third day now and nobody's been hurt—only a few skirmishes, right?—and people were so pessimistic, weren't they? I don't think this is a hopeless county. I don't think a conviction for that state trooper, any kind of conviction, is an unreasonable hope, do you? I've got a car here and I'll be out as soon as possible."

"They'll follow you," the voice said thinly.

"What? Follow me? Who?" Jack laughed. "I walk all over, I walk out to the motel and back, nobody gives a damn. This town doesn't seem as bad as I had expected."

"You don't know anything about this town."

"If you tell me how to get to your house—"

"No, can't. Can't do it. This is not the right time. This is a very bad time."

Jack hesitated. Then he said, "All right, then, I'll go talk to the parents instead—I can talk to them directly—I would rather go through you, but I can contact them directly."

"Now, Mr. Morrissey, I do not recommend—"

"We've got to begin somewhere. The Hurley case—"

"You let those people alone, now. You—now, you know—you have the experience, Mr. Morrissey, I credit you with that, you know that the family is not going to pull out like you will—you have the knowledge, if not the personal experience, I believe, that the family of the deceased in such a case has to remain where they are? That they cannot take a plane back North and escape?"

"Then can I come out to talk with you?" Jack asked. "I think if we sat down and discussed this, if I outlined to you how I would proceed—"

"I been through this before," the voice said faintly. It was not guarded but subdued. It was vaporous, insubstantial. Jack's senses quickened: he felt that the Reverend Efron was about to give in.

"I know what you've done for people around here, I know a great deal about you," Jack said warmly, "and if we could only discuss it—if I could explain to you—"

"If I could explain to *you*—"

"Yes, but in person—not over the telephone—"

The voice seemed to withdraw. Jack waited tensely. He somehow knew he would win; his life was a series of small sharp victories.

"Mr. Morrissey," the Reverend Efron said, as if getting a new grip on the telephone, his voice closer to Jack's ear, "I am asking you to consider the Hurley family for a minute. Not only they lost their son that way, and all the publicity, but they are fully cognizant of the fact that they are being watched. Even the road leading by their house. You understand what I'm saying?"

"Yes," Jack said, "but—"

"The last time we went through this in Lime County things got stirred up for six months and they are not settled down yet. And now the boycott is in session and I applaud it, I applaud all the work and planning that went into it, and I support it spiritually, but I'm out here with my congregation and staying clear just this once—which it is my turn to do, I think. Let me tell you about that case last year: it was assault, two white men shoving around a boy named Glover on a bridge out this way, and they pushed him off and he fell pretty far onto some rocks and got hurt. Now, this was a Sunday afternoon and people were out for rides along the river, so five witnesses happened along that had stopped their cars to watch the fun. They were all white. But now, listen, now in one of the cars there was an old lady, a white lady, somebody's grandmother, and she got very angry at the white men that pushed Glover off, and declared she would tell the whole world what happened, she was so disgusted. So she did. So at the examination she put the blame where it was due, and she didn't lie. And after that somebody came down here, from the Lawyers Defense Committee, and talked it up with all of us, and we got very excited about the possibilities here. Because the white lady was going to testify and—"

"I know about that trial," Jack said.

"Now you hear me through, Mr. Morrissey. You count up the original witnesses, which make four on their side, plus the doctor that the sheriff called, who turned out on their side too—said the boy wasn't hurt from falling, but from trying to crawl off the rocks. Said he slipped on the rocks once he got down there, it appeared, because the rocks were wet; so that makes five on their side. And on our side there is the old white lady and of course the boy, who is out of the hospital now on crutches and patched up. So the trial is set. So the whole state is tuned in on this, and the old lady is being interviewed in the papers and on the radio, and she is extremely stubborn, she is *not* going to withdraw her testimony. Then, you know, you know this, then on the Friday before the Monday, the old lady is taken out to the rest home north of Oxide, and put in, and the papers all signed, and she's up there right now. . . . So that leaves one witness, the boy. Did you read the transcript? He was fourteen years old and so scared he could hardly talk. The witnesses all swore he had started the fight and then jumped off the bridge by himself—and then of course the doctor pointed out how he wasn't hurt anyway from the fall, but from slipping around on them big rocks. The jury was out six minutes arguing about who should be foreman."

"That was the first case and it wasn't handled right," Jack said. "I mean, obviously a great deal of preparation went into it, but you were vulnerable because you had only one witness—and she was—"

"The boy's family, they all had to get out, and the house was burned down, yes, they were vulnerable on some points. . . . Not to mention some of us that chose not to leave."

"Did anything happen to you?"

"Never mind about me, I don't talk about me, I'm not the subject of this conversation. Did you read the transcript?"

"No, I didn't read it, but I know about it," Jack said. Having to make this admission angered him. But he tried to keep calm. "Mr. Efron, look, we need to talk face to face on this. We're both on the same side. It's urgent I talk to you, otherwise I will have to try the parents directly—"

"If there is a favor I ask you, it's to leave them alone. Mr. Morrissey? Look, just wait around Java a while, with the feeling high like it is—look, with your friends strolling up and down the main street, I'm not saying you are one of them because I don't know you personally, but friends of yours, or co-workers on this project, the little white girl with the black boy friend?—that's from New York or somewhere? They stroll around Java much more, like they been doing, and you'll have a good case to litigate. You keep lots of witnesses on hand for when the Java boys target-practice on those two. *That* will be a case you can all put your hearts behind."

"I'm not responsible for those kids," Jack said angrily. "Look, I'm not a college kid, I'm a lawyer, I'm an adult and my work here is purely legal, I'm not helping to bring food in from Jackson, or giving spiritual advice; I just arrived in town to give legal advice and—"

"Are you asking them to stay off the streets?"

"That isn't my job. They wouldn't listen anyway. They have nothing to do with my end of this—I'm accumulating information, I'm trying to get through to people—like you, or the Hurley family, or—"

"Last time, that New York lawyer that worked so hard, I believe he was pretty well relieved to lose his case. I believe he was, yes. I believe that even those six minutes aged him a bit. . . . There was two or three hundred people milling around the courthouse that morning. Out on the street too. Across in the police station and on the steps and hanging around the police garage, just waiting for the verdict, and I believe that lawyer had never thought so far ahead, to figure out what he would do with a victory. How he would get out of Java, would he be air-lifted? Because he didn't arrange for it ahead of time. He was just lucky he lost and they all laughed at him and tossed a few things, no real nastiness, just jokes. Now I'm going to hang up, Mr. Morrissey."

"I've got to see you. I insist. I'm not leaving until I see you," Jack said. "I can be out there in—"

"All right, come tomorrow night, come for supper at six," the voice said flatly.

Jack blinked in amazement. He smiled. He said evenly, in an unsurprised voice, "It really was necessary for us to agree on this."

"Your arm is bruised," Jack said in surprise. He drew the sleeve of her blouse back. He uncovered a wide, yellowish bruise on her upper arm; his senses quickened at the sight of it, as if she had surrendered to him again for the first time. "What happened?"

Rachel laughed in embarrassment.

"It's nothing, it doesn't hurt," she said.

"Did someone bump into you?—on the street?" Jack asked. He'd heard one of the girls talking excitedly, in a corner of the office, about some men bumping into them on the street. But Rachel pulled the sleeve back down and said wearily, "I got so damn sunburned today, I must look like hell. My face is burned in patches. But we did a lot, I think we accomplished a lot—we're all very enthusiastic about it. Once they see we're on their side, we're not going to report them or check on them for welfare requirements or anything, they really open up. They're very . . . they're very good, good people," she said slowly. "It's hard to explain. They're very religious and for most of us religion is finished . . . but these people are truly religious, and their religion is so simple, so direct . . . they're just *good* people, with conventional imaginations. . . ."

"Ordinarily we would never be meeting with them," Jack said. He caressed her arm and shoulder gently, in a gesture of affection that was not really characteristic of him—but he was trying, with this woman, to overcome both his usual bluntness and her apparent nervous indifference to affection. "We wouldn't be talking with them like this, except history is forcing us together. . . . There are such surprising meetings, such unexpected encounters when a society begins to break down. It's very exciting. It's making us all intimate with one another."

He half-closed his eyes and thought of high walls caving in, falling slowly . . . rocks rolled loose . . . fists smashing windows, pounding on doors and breaking down doors . . . feet raised so that the full strength of the foot, the hard, reinforced heel, could strike. . . . It was a new intimacy, a very exciting intimacy.

"Yes. That's true," Rachel said.

Jack felt so good after the telephone conversation with Efron that he wondered if he might love this woman: with her sisterly, uncoy, unvain manner, her serious face. She was about his own age, a few years older than the other girls. The years between them seemed to add up to a generation, oddly; Jack could have been attracted to any of the younger girls, but he could not take them very seriously. They admired him too quickly, too shallowly. But this woman, Rachel, the only woman in the Java group of her age, seemed always to be withholding her agreement, thinking, calculating the way a man would, and then pronouncing judgment: therefore it was flattering when she did agree with him. "That's true. The intimacy. Yes, that's true," she said, nodding vehemently. The first evening he had met her, he'd noticed immediately her harsh, strident voice, her vigorous disagreements and agreements with the others. Her approval was not easily won. At first she had looked across the room at him suspiciously, as if disliking his clothes—everyone else wore sports clothes and sandals—and then, after they had begun to talk, she had said suddenly that he was right, he was right to dress like that, because he represented something very formal and very real, very deadly. It was honest of him not to disguise himself.

"The whole country is going to change," Jack said excitedly. "An avalanche is on the way . . . breaking up things, walls, houses, people . . . making us all very close, like lovers, intimate as lovers or people who've bled onto one another. Even the government is going to become very personal. I'm sure of it. All the spying, the photographing, the films, the tapes, the fingerprinting, the computers and their information—this is all very intimate, very close to us—but now we'll be able to see what's going on, to look back through the keyhole at them. Like a trick two-way mirror suddenly turning into plate glass: so we can look right at them and see who they are."

"You sound very optimistic," she said.

"I am optimistic," said Jack.

"There's a lot of agony to get through first," she said slowly. "I've been down here longer than you have . . . I'm optimistic too, of course, but it isn't so easy. . . . Just us coming down here, just the news of us coming, has hurt many people. ADC mothers cut off welfare lists, just like *that,* just cut off the lists by some county clerk drawing a line through their names. . . . The excuse is that the tax reservoir has suddenly sunk. What the hell? These women and their children have to eat. It's really a foreign country here. . . . I know the North is bad, I know the North is no paradise . . . but they really do things differently in the South. It's like the smell around here, these little baking towns, and all the insects . . . giant-sized cockroaches they don't grow up in New York. God. It's like an island, and the connections are down with the mainland. Sometimes it's hard to believe in the mainland. Like the newspaper here. . . ." She picked up the *New York Times,* which was two days old, soiled from having been passed around to so many people. "You almost think it's a fake, printed up specially in Mississippi. It's possible to get very paranoid down here."

Jack laughed; he felt very good. He was stretched out on the bed and Rachel was sitting beside him, casual as old friends. On the marred bedside table were several cans of beer, wadded tissue, an ash tray heaped with ashes and matches and other debris.

"Don't you like pressure like this?" Jack said.

"I like pressure, yes. . . . But this situation is dangerous."

"I like it."

"Well, Jack, someone might get hurt, someone might get killed. . . . The city isn't giving in and the boycott is hurting them like hell, and tomorrow is the twenty-fourth day. That's almost a month. Jesus. The first few days, we were really scared, we thought something was going to happen from one hour to the next . . . now we're getting a little more relaxed, but maybe we should be getting more and more tense. It's hard to know. You can lose perspective, being so close to just one group of people."

"Yes, it's dangerous, but you don't get anything accomplished without danger," Jack said. "Without pushing, prodding, getting in there where it hurts someone . . . and of course he'll react, he'll try to defend himself. But the pressure is good, it's like good fresh oxygen. It's forcing us all forward into the future."

Rachel turned to look at him. Her face was almost attractive in this light; in the daylight her skin was rather grainy. Now she smiled down at him. And Jack felt, between them, a pressure, a tension—an almost combative joy, that a woman should look at him so intimately and yet so coolly.

"And if someone gets hurt . . . ?" she said.

"Then we made it happen. *We* made it happen," Jack said. "That's the important thing, that we forced something into existence. There's a difference between a boy of fourteen thrown off a bridge just for fun, for Sunday-afternoon fun, and another boy shot down dead because he and some other people are blocking a mayor's office. One thing just happened, it would have happened anyway. The other was forced into existence. It wasn't just fun, it wasn't to break up a boring Sunday afternoon—it was an act of self-defense, of terror. It's a change. It means we're moving forward, into the future. Even if I get hurt myself . . . and after this I go to Nuffield, where things are supposedly worse . . . I wouldn't change what I've just said. I mean it. In my own life, Rachel, I've had a lot of good luck, good breaks. I made the right connections between things. That summer when my father was on trial, I did a lot of thinking, I was transformed . . . and when I went back to school I was ready for it, I was ready to use everything I could get, and everyone I could get. I had good luck with people; I've always had good luck because I insist on it. I just keep on asking questions. I keep pushing. I have good luck because I *want* something more than my opponents want it, every time. And even if somebody gets to me someday, breaks me down or drags me out in a field—what the hell—it's a risk I want to take. Do you understand?"

"Yes. I understand."

"You're the same way yourself—? Maybe—?"

"Maybe," she said.

II

A lush, fragrant, shadowy planet: the dark side of a sphere. Why else all these trees and moss, the splatting of insects against the windshield, the abrupt changes between sunlight and dark humid shadow? The country road was flat in places, open and obvious. Then it banked steeply into small forests, like spurts of shadow, so that it was difficult for Jack to see well. Nearly six o'clock, yet the sun was still high in the sky. It seemed early afternoon yet.

He had to keep slowing down because of the sharp turns. But there was an odd pressure in him to increase his speed, as if to show Rachel and himself he was not intimidated.

They were driving out into the country, twelve miles to the Efrons' house.

The car was tight and new, a rented car with a full tank of gas, and it handled perfectly. Jack liked to drive. And he liked driving with this woman beside him, who sat back with one foot on the dashboard, so casually, so intimately, it was a compliment to him. She wore sandals with heavy leather straps and her feet and legs were bare, unevenly tanned.

They were passing small houses, cabins set up on blocks that might have been made of concrete or wood, in plots of grassless clayey soil. In the damp heat the edges of these houses were very sharp. Jack could sometimes see right through them—right out the back. Black children peered at the car, looking up startled. Jack and Rachel, seeing them, said nothing to each other.

When they arrived at the Efrons' house, Jack was stunned: the house wasn't much better than the cabins they had been passing. A minister's house?

But Rachel showed no surprise so Jack said nothing. When he turned in the driveway some children appeared at the corner of the house, to stare. A tall, thin black man in a suit like Jack's, with a white shirt like Jack's, opened the screen door and came out, stepping carefully on the front steps.

So they met, shook hands, introduced themselves—Jack with a too-broad smile, *Jack Morrissey,* and the black man with a restrained smile and a formal title, *Reverend Efron.*

Inside the house Jack kept on smiling, saying hello to the people he was meeting—Mrs. Efron, another woman named Mrs. Myron or Byron—Jack couldn't quite catch it—several other black men, even children. It seemed to him strange, so many children here. And the odor of food and something unpleasant—kerosene?—was strange. All the while he was staring everywhere, trying to absorb, to figure out—the house had maybe two rooms, two large rooms. People seemed close to one another in here, crowded close; and why so many children? Who had invited them? A television set was on but no one was watching.

They sat down to eat almost at once. That was strange also, and Jack was too excited to think about food, wondering when he should bring up the subject of the Hurley boy—or would Efron bring it up?— He watched Efron, a little unsettled by him. First of all, the Reverend Efron was younger than Jack had imagined. He wasn't much older than Jack himself, no more than thirty; Jack had the impression from his telephone conversation that Efron was older, wiser. That politeness, that almost vaporous courtesy—Jack sensed it wasn't natural, it was a kind of withdrawal. An insult? He wondered if he should be insulted. And another thing that annoyed him: Efron spoke so quietly that Jack had to hunch forward to hear him, he had to keep saying, "What? I didn't hear all of that—" and this threw him off. For the first half hour they talked about the boycott and people they knew in common, the boycott leaders, the workers from the North, nothing that interested Jack, and he had to keep smiling, agreeing, while the commotion in the room made him so nervous and angry, he could hardly concentrate on what was being said. Why was the television on?—if it was on, why didn't the children sit still and watch it? Damn these people, Jack thought helplessly, are they trying to drive me out of here?

He couldn't eat much, though he accepted more food and allowed someone, one of the women, to heap it on his plate. Big mounds of mashed potatoes, slowly hardening before him, taking on a kind of crust . . . a dark green vegetable he didn't recognize, like spinach but not spinach, overcooked, which lay cooling on his plate, uneaten, because he had absent-mindedly sprinkled too much salt on it . . . thick chops with borders of fat, pan-fried and greasy and crisp as hard-crusted rolls, with a square inch or so of edible meat inside them, but, hell, it was too much trouble to maneuver that tiny block of meat out, and anyway he wasn't hungry, and anyway he had to keep leaning forward to ask Efron what he was saying. . . . Jack looked around the table at the faces, skipping over Rachel's face: they were all telling him *no.* Even before the reason for his visit was brought up, they were telling him *no.*

It was only quarter to seven and dinner seemed to be over: the plates were taken away, one of the children carried them into the other room, a giggling girl of about ten who dropped something just as she passed behind Jack's chair. More noise, commotion, laughter—the girl's mother scolded her and jumped up to straighten things out—some of the children by the television set ran over to join in the laughter. It put Jack in mind, suddenly, helplessly, of the years back in Detroit, himself and his parents and his sister enduring the screams and messes of that brother of his. . . .

He glanced at Rachel but couldn't read her expression: she was listening to the plump, pretty black woman who sat beside her, nodding vigorously. Jack felt a little jealousy, an envy of Rachel's ease with these people.

Supper had gone fast, and now dessert was being served. Large pieces of pie were being set in front of everyone, even in front of Jack, though he didn't want any, he hadn't the chance to explain, the giggling girl ran back and forth from the kitchen serving them. . . . So Jack picked up a fork and penetrated the crust, four prong marks in one direction and then four in another, and then in another, until he judged that a momentary pause in the conversation was going to be long enough for him to start talking.

He laid his fork down carefully and told them why he was here.

He heard his voice explaining, explaining. He knew he spoke well, and the logic of his argument was not assailable. And they all smiled at him, as if encouraging him; even Efron smiled, a small smile; but it was a way of telling him no, *no.* He pretended not to know this. He ignored even the first frowns, the hesitant expressions. Efron's wife stared at him with a peculiar vacant interest, almost a look of affection, though it seemed she had stopped listening to him.

". . . and it wouldn't be done at long-distance, either," Jack said, "I'd be right here all the time, no matter how long it took to prepare the case . . . and I'd work with anyone you want, your first choice, anyone, and he wouldn't have to do it for nothing either. I'm ready to. . . ."

They seemed embarrassed as he fell silent. The woman beside Rachel had an odd habit of picking at her face, even her hair, absent-mindedly, and now she ran her forefinger slowly and contemplatively around the inside rim of her ear, not looking at Jack. She was staring a few inches to his left, as if staring at someone else. Jack had the peculiar feeling that he was saying words they had already heard.

The woman said, sighing, "Well, Mr. Morrissey, yes, I am really happy to hear this . . . it's a privilege to listen to you, and an honor, for you to be so interested in my brother . . . he was my brother, Bobbie Hurley . . . only my name is different from his. . . . Yes, it is certainly an honor," she said gloomily.

"I didn't know he was your brother," Jack said.

"Oh yes, but I can discuss it without swaying to one side or the other," she said slowly. "Bobbie was a lot younger than me and I didn't know him too well, but anyway, anyway it's not that, it's my parents we got to explain to you about. . . ."

"Yes, all right," Jack said miserably, knowing exactly what she was going to say and yet doomed to sit and listen to it, to *listen to it,* to be polite and listen and not interrupt. . . . So he sat hunched forward, in an attitude of concentration, a pretense of serious sympathetic concentration, while an invisible nerve beneath his right eye started to vibrate. *Oh these people, these people . . . these fine, good, suffering people, these victims. . . .* He liked this woman, he liked everyone here. Even the Reverend Efron, who didn't show much interest in Jack, didn't seem to admire him the way other people did . . . even him, all right, it didn't matter; Jack liked him too. Jack wanted to help him. But he was trapped in this hot, airless, noisy place, at this table, and he *had to listen* to them talk: in their own language, their own slow words that were sometimes surprising to him, in a way toylike, words he wouldn't have thought of using himself, somehow *toylike* words. He liked this too. It was another language, this was a foreign country. But he was becoming impatient. He had to listen to a woman describing her mother and father, *first of all they are decent hard-working people,* and he had to resist the desire to nod, nod, to speed her up. He was like a judge handling a very stupid lawyer, trying to speed him up, pitying him, wanting to help him with his case and yet knowing that was forbidden. But to sit and listen!

And his own arguments, in reply to hers, were all familiar: yes, there were sometimes reprisals; yes, of course, no one was discounting that, but . . . but this was the white South's strategy, wasn't it?

It seemed to Jack that everything was said and resaid, again and again, even the same arrangement of words. Now the Reverend Efron repeated something Jack himself had said, as if taking it seriously, and then he gave his answer to it, which was a repetition of something the sister of the dead boy had just said. . . . Then another of the men joined in, sadly, shaking his head. It was like a ceremony; it was going to take a long time to get through it, to argue his way through it, and he had the terrible anticipation of being told, after all of this, *no.* The *no* was part of the ceremony too, but it came at the very end.

Rachel tried to help him. She pointed out that Jack sympathized with their fears, as everyone did. That he knew about the other case, the aftermath, the threats . . . the pressure on the Hurley family and on everyone else to forget about Bobbie Hurley and whether or not he was murdered or shot by a state trooper "in self-defense" . . . and. . . .

Jack took up the argument from her eagerly. He was excited and frustrated and caught himself doing something he was trying to break himself of doing, half-grabbing at his hair, a habit he had picked up from someone, somewhere, and despised. How it must look, for Jack to be seen grabbing at his own head! But he was so frustrated. He told them that he certainly sympathized with them, *but I don't sympathize with you because you're*—yes he sympathized, he understood, but when was it all going to end? How many murders, lynchings, assaults, how much inhumanity? The line was being drawn now, this summer, the summer of 1964, and nothing would ever be the same again. They must know that. Didn't they? He tapped on the table, he leaned forward so that his wobbly chair was balanced on two legs, he talked, he talked, very rapidly he ran through the details of the shooting again, though he realized everyone knew them: these absolutely incontestable facts, the testimony of thirteen witnesses at the examination who had sworn the state trooper had no provocation. . . . And yes, of course the other side had witnesses too: three white men. Three. And the state trooper, which made four. But the coroner's report stated that the angle of the bullet was downward through the upper part of the chest and into the heart, very sharply downward, so it was obvious the boy had been shot while sitting down, at close range. . . . And no broken bottle had been found either. The state trooper had sworn that Bobbie Hurley was threatening him with a broken bottle and that he had fired at him in self-defense. But—

"There's a Coke bottle," Efron said quietly.

"A Coke bottle?" Jack said. He looked around the table at the quizzical faces. "Yes, I know about a Coke bottle they're making claims for, but it doesn't have the boy's fingerprints on it. It's all smeared. That Coke bottle is an obvious fabrication, just something somebody grabbed hold of to bring along as evidence. . . . They were probably swilling Coke, the police, and brought a bottle along. Any jury would recognize that as an obvious fabrication. . . ."

Efron was shaking his head slowly.

Another of the men began to speak. He explained he was a schoolteacher and a friend of someone—someone Jack was evidently supposed to know, probably one of the black boycott leaders—and that he was on Jack's side; ultimately, he agreed with every word Jack had said, but—

Anyway, the dead boy's sister said, anyway, a lawyer from the NAACP had been out talking to everyone and had taken plenty of notes and *he* thought. . . . Another lawyer had told her personally that the case was a risky one because of the Coke bottle and because. . . .

"A Coke bottle!" Jack cried in amazement. "Look—a *Coke bot-*

tle? Is it a capital offense to pick up a Coke bottle? Is it punishable by death, on the spot, a bullet right in the heart? Is it? Is that the law in Mississippi?"

"Mr. Morrissey, the fact of whether or not Bobbie ever touched any bottle is—"

"You don't shy away from a case of this magnitude, you don't back away terrified because of a *Coke bottle,*" Jack said. In frustration he pulled at his hair, as if trying to yank it off his head. "And I don't give a damn what some other people have advised you, because *I think*—"

"Jack. . . ." Rachel said, cautioning him.

"*I think* this is the right time, right now, with the boycott and the publicity, and I think the case could be a famous one, it could make Lime County a famous little place; I don't give a damn if other people are afraid of taking it on, and I don't give a damn about a Coke bottle some friend of that murderer's picked up off the sidewalk—" He noticed them watching him with the same patient expressions, Efron's wife now glassy-eyed, Efron himself distant and polite, and he couldn't help it, he let the fleshy part of his hand fall heavily, impatiently, on the table before him. *Damn it. Damn you, listen.* "You could start a flood of cases, right here. You people. If you would just talk the parents into agreeing. . . . From here, right here tonight, this table here, you could start the whole South . . . you could begin . . . you. . . . Look, do you know how changes take place? In history? The only way they take place? How you must push people, get them angry, terrified, make them reckless?—the way people are when they know they're at the end of their lives?"

Rachel tried to interrupt, but Jack kept on talking: "Look, I know how history freezes and needs cracking up, I know you can't wait for it to thaw, there isn't going to be any lovely spring melting—big glaciers melting and turning into little streams you can wade in and fish in, for Christ's sake!—I know—look, I *know* that the system down here, the system is doomed, it's only a matter of which one of us gets in there first to break it up, to start the cracks going in all directions—right?—it's a matter of taking a chance, of hoping for good luck— The system is doomed, you must know that, don't you? You want it to break down, don't you? Because it isn't yours, you don't own any of it, *any of it,* you have nothing to lose, do you?—when you own nothing, you have nothing to lose, do you?" he said wildly. "How low can you exist, how low can you still find oxygen to breathe?—is this human life?—is—"

Rachel got to her feet. "Jack," she said sharply.

"What? What?" he said.

He knew he had been speaking shrilly and angrily, but he could not help it; even now, conscious of having said something terrible, he could not force himself to apologize.

"I feel very strongly about this," he said.

They seemed to understand. One of the men nodded. The boy's sister was picking nervously at her jaw with the fingernail of one long dark forefinger; the nail was moon-shaped, flesh-colored. She nodded also, but her expression was not readable.

"You feel very strongly about Bobbie, we know that," the Reverend Efron said. His voice was soft, light, and didn't really sound ironic; but Jack knew exactly what he had said. He felt stung. The sarcasm went right into him, through him, and he got to his feet in a daze.

"I— I'm—"

And now, slowly, everyone stood and the supper was at an end. The room was stifling. The television set was still on—applause and laughter, laughter punctuated by applause. Jack stared down at the table, saw at his place something he had been poking at with his fork, shredding it unconsciously, and though the insides of it were now visible—a plum-colored substance—he didn't know what it was and remembered only with difficulty that it was food, something given to him to eat.

He heard himself say he was sorry, he'd been too emotional, and someone else said no, no, that was all right; and Rachel said, feelings are very high among all of us; and another woman, either the Hurley boy's sister or Efron's wife, said. . . . Efron himself said quietly that they were honored to talk with him like this, and Jack, his face burning, didn't know if this was sincere or not, he didn't know whether to smile and shake hands or to show he'd been insulted, he was not going to forgive them so easily. . . .

He tried to smile. Tried to calm down. He kept saying he was sorry.

Sorry.

But. . . .

But still. . . .

They all walked out to the car with Jack and Rachel; even the children came out and played in the driveway; and while Jack tried to brush mosquitoes away from his face he heard himself saying the routine ritual words of good-by. Must shake hands again. Again. Must not forget anyone. Must not allow the Reverend Efron to sense his agitation. Must back away with a smile. . . .

They knew how to contact him?

Oh yes.

A few more minutes and then it was all right for Jack and Rachel to get in the car. Jack managed to back the car out of the deep-rutted driveway, feeling very self-conscious because they were watching him, the children were watching him, *damn these people,* and then he was safe on the road.

Rachel struck the dashboard with her fist.

"You bastard," she said.

Jack turned to look at her in amazement.

"You damn bullying bastard," she said.

She was too angry to sob, her voice was thick, almost guttural. He could feel the muscular struggle in her to speak.

"What? I didn't—"

Jack felt sweat breaking out all over his body, breaking through the coating of old stale sweat his body stank with— He stared at the woman beside him, at her angry, distorted face. "You—you come out to their house—you sit there— You use your mouth the way other men use their fists or knives or— You bastard! Bastard! I know what it's like to lie down flat on my back and to have a bastard like you stick himself in me, like it was a knife or a gun or—prodding, stabbing, sticking— And a bastard like you, because he's on top, he gives all the commands—*lie still, turn over, get on your knees, put your face down in the dirt*—and the niggers and anybody else on the bottom had better move fast—" She was so angry she could hardly speak, she began to scream at him: "I'd like to take a broom handle and stick it right up you, right up inside you, you bastard, so you know what it's like to be fucked for once in your life—"

Jack braked the car to a stop. He jumped out to get away from her.

She was still screaming at him. This was a night without real darkness—marshy, humid, the wrong air for Jack's lungs—he felt he might suffocate—he wanted to press his hands over his ears to stop that voice of hers, that screaming—he wanted—he wanted only to be quiet now himself, to be held in a woman's gentle arms, forgiven, loved; he wanted the frenzy of his heartbeat to be calmed, he wanted all the voices shouting at him to be answered: no, no, a mistake! It was a mistake! He wanted them instead to cry *it isn't you, you are not to blame, you aren't guilty, you didn't drag anyone out into a field, didn't shoot anyone in the face—you are innocent—always innocent—*

12

Three years later, back in Detroit, Jack leafed through a copy of the *Nation* in someone's office at the Legal Aid center . . . and he saw the name *Hurley,* a name that sprang out at him. He picked up the magazine and scanned the article: *Spring Offensive Planned in Three Dixie Strongholds.*

He walked out of the office, dodging people on the stairs without looking at them, trying to read the article as he went along . . . but it was difficult to hold the magazine up and to keep the pages from flapping and to carry his briefcase as well. The handle had broken again and he had to carry it under one arm. Finally, out on the icy sidewalk, he stopped, read the article through swiftly—five cases were going to be reopened, one of them the shooting of the Hurley boy, and a lawyer from New York named Arnold Levey was going to be in charge. The litigation was being sponsored by the New Democrats Defense Committee.

Jack was angry. No, ashamed. They had turned him down three years ago, and now they had agreed to this. . . . He had never heard of Levey.

Bastards, Jack thought.

He noticed that it was cold; he had forgotten to close his jacket, to put on his gloves. Too late. He had the briefcase under his arm, a damn clumsy bulky thing and very heavy; and he held the magazine in his right hand, staring at the print while his face burned. He didn't know if he should be angry, really, after so long. He had tried to rush them; they hadn't been ready yet. Now, three years later, they had a much better chance of winning their case. . . . But that wasn't the point, Jack thought, the point hadn't been to win but to instigate change, to open the way for other cases. They had refused to understand.

Jack half-closed his eyes and remembered the hot, stifling evening at the Efrons'—the heaped-up plates of food, the smells, the noise of the children, Rachel screaming at him— His soul seemed to shrivel in shame. He had tried not to think about that evening since leaving the South.

He shut the magazine impatiently and rolled it into a cylinder.

Crossing a street somewhere, a wide, icy street, he must have been staring at the pavement blindly, thinking about the magazine article, when he felt a weight shoved at him from the side—striking his right shoulder and hip—a terrible blow that made him lose his balance. He fell heavily onto the ice. *Jesus,* he thought, looking up to see that a small truck had hit him. It was a U.S. mail truck and the driver, a young black man, jumped out the door. He looked very surprised.

"Hey, you all right? What'ja do, walk right in front of me?" the man cried. He tried to haul Jack to his feet. Jack wanted to tell him to go to hell, he wasn't hurt, but he allowed the man to help him up. His legs were a little shaky, but strong enough to hold him. He was all right. The man was protesting that Jack had walked right in front of him, stepped right off the curb, and lucky he'd only been driving about five miles an hour—

"All right," Jack said. "I'm not bleeding."

He walked away while the man was still talking. The pavement was bumpy, ridged with sharp furrows of ice; the soles of his shoes were thin and he had to be careful or he'd slip. He was always reminding himself to be careful out here. He was always reminding himself to watch where he was walking, not to stare down at the pavement while his mind raced.

Anyway, he hadn't been hurt. He didn't think he was bleeding.

Awkwardly, he tried to brush off the seat of his pants and the sleeves of his jacket. It was a thick woollen jacket, olive-green, with wooden buttons and loops for buttonholes, made of cord; his trousers were wrinkled anyway, he'd been wearing them for a week straight. No loss. It angered him that he was always doing such awkward things, carrying a broken briefcase, trying to read a magazine article. . . .

He couldn't resist glancing at it again as he walked: the news was good, the tone of the article optimistic; the words "spring offensive" seemed to him good words. That particular committee, the New Democrats, was being funded by an excellent foundation; Jack wondered how much they had. He'd lost contact with civil rights actions in the past two years, since quitting the Hillier Foundation. Everything had gone so slowly, bogged down in a kind of legal dreamworld. . . . The Director had accused Jack of being impatient, but Christ, how he had squirmed in the presence of that slow, grave, grim man! So many middle-aged civil rights lawyers had that reverential, maddening grimness about their work, as if it were sacred and could not be enjoyed. As if it had to be discussed and rediscussed, every possible fact and condition analyzed, every impulse toward action analyzed. . . . Caution had been urged onto Jack and some of the other assistants so often that they had made a joke out of it. Then, when the Foundation decided to restrict itself to cases in which there were violations of the Constitution, Jack had written an angry letter of resignation.

Now he half-regretted it. He wondered impulsively if he could contact Levey, if he could go down and assist him . . . ? If there were some stray funds he could latch onto—he didn't need much; in fact, he wouldn't mind volunteering . . . he had been very interested in the case, almost obsessed with it at one time. It would be difficult for him to let another man handle it, but. . . . He wondered if he could afford to volunteer. . . .

By habit he had walked to the bus stop, and he was standing there when the bus came. So he got on, noticing that it was the correct bus, which would take him up Third Avenue and so to Virginia Park, where he and his wife lived; once in a while he got on the wrong bus, absent-mindedly, his head filled with the countless snarls and sorrows of the Legal Aid center. But today he got on the right bus. It was only a fifteen-minute ride so he didn't mind having to stand. Most of the other passengers were blacks, and Jack looked at them thoughtfully, remembering again the evening at the Efrons' house. Jesus! And Rachel screaming at him, screaming at him. . . .

He had been in the South for several weeks afterward, in a dozen towns, but that evening had been the worst one. He had not experienced anything so disturbing since.

He got off half a block from the house, a small shabby mansion divided into apartments and rooms, where he and his wife were able to rent a furnished apartment for only seventy-five dollars a month. At first Jack had disliked it—the house was Victorian, elaborate in small trivial ways, with high gables and peaks and soot-blackened chimneys, a vestibule with stained-glass windows, an odor about everything of dust, aging woodwork, ancient foods, confusions. After the first several months he had grown to like it well enough; he didn't demand much. It pleased him that his rent was only seventy-five a month and that their friends were always telling them they had a bargain.

The first floor had been partitioned off into three small apartments, and in the front apartment lived a black woman with several children, her blinds always pulled, the children's broken tricycle and other smashed or shredded or wheelless toys lying on the sidewalk or inside the vestibule. Jack had learned to step carefully over them. On the second floor, one of the apartments had been vacant for quite a while, an uncarpeted, bare, drafty place, but now a group of people were living there—full-time tenants or not, Jack didn't know. Three or four young men appeared on the stairs from time to time, but never the same men; occasionally a girl appeared; but Jack couldn't keep the faces all straight. He didn't mind, as he told his wife, except there was a danger the police might raid that apartment for drugs and, knowing the police, they might also break into the Morrisseys'. "In that case," she had said vehemently, "we'll sue for false arrest." Jack had recently helped defend a young instructor at Wayne State University who had been arrested by police in a "drug raid"—the police had broken into one apartment, arrested the people there, and had charged down the hall to another apartment, where the instructor and his wife lived, and though neither of them used drugs, both had been hauled down to the police station. The instructor had been fired from his job. After eighteen months of litigation, of suits and countersuits, he had given up and left Detroit.

So Jack thought probably he and his wife should get out of

here before it was too late; it could ruin his career to be arrested, even falsely.

When Jack walked into his apartment he was disappointed to hear voices—Rachel was arguing with someone in a loud, exasperated voice. It was a young man Jack half-recognized, who turned nervously at Jack's entrance. Jack nodded abruptly, not bothering to smile.

"You know Tony, don't you, Jack?" Rachel said. "He just walked in here out of nowhere."

The young man seemed very nervous, agitated. He had ratty, frizzy hair and his heavy black sweater was very soiled. It had started to unravel at the cuffs. Jack didn't reply but let his briefcase fall onto a sofa. He took off his jacket and let it fall there too.

"Somebody called, I took a message," Rachel said. Jack was irritated that someone was with her; he had wanted to show her the article in the *Nation.* "Did they get through to you at the Center? I told them to try you there. I just got home myself."

"Who was it?"

"Someone named Emmet, I think. I don't know what he wants."

"There's too much going on," Jack muttered. "I can't keep things straight." He went through his pockets and pulled out a scrap of paper—a telephone number, but without a name. He couldn't remember whose it was. On the back of the paper he'd scrawled "Wed. 10am" but he couldn't remember what that meant either. In another pocket he found a very small slip of paper with "Emmet 6pm" written on it. "Oh yes, Jesus," he said, "this man is coming here at six . . . to the house here. I don't know who he is. It's for his son, the son is up in Toronto and won't come back to be drafted. I told him to come by and see me tonight, because tomorrow I'm so damn busy. . . ."

"That was nice of you, Jack," Rachel said. "He can stay for dinner then. Good. And Tony, what about you? Would you like to stay?"

"Hell, that's too much trouble—"

Jack waited patiently, trying to keep the irritation out of his face. He had wanted to have a quiet evening tonight. He was very tired. And he felt a little groggy, maybe from being hit by that damned mail truck. There was too much going on.

"Look, Tony," Rachel said with a mock-angry affection, "did you eat today? When did you eat last?"

"Oh hell I don't know—I don't get too hungry—"

"You can't even take care of yourself, can you? You'd better stay. Frankly, you look like hell. You look so strung-out, the police will jump you as soon as they see you."

Jack had had enough of Tony, so he said something about doing a little work before Emmet came. He went into his study, a small room that faced the street, and closed the door behind him. He saw with shock that it was already twenty-five to six. . . . Where had the day gone? He was working with so many people now, so many near-hopeless cases, trying to shake them out of their stupor and into consciousness, trying to bully landlords and finance companies and social workers and the welfare administration. . . . He liked this work, but it was sometimes exhausting. Every evening he came home and emptied his pockets of half a dozen slips of paper, names and telephone numbers and memos, arranging them on the old kitchen table that served as his desk. Then he would sit down and look at them and try to straighten out his thoughts.

Then, when he was feeling competent enough, he dumped out his briefcase and really got to work.

This afternoon he sat down and tossed the *Nation* onto a pile of other magazines and rubbed his face in exasperation. He could hear Rachel talking out in the living room. Her voice carried shrilly, but Tony's voice was only a murmur. Jack did not dislike Tony, did not wish him ill, but it angered him that Tony was out there; if not Tony, then someone else. It was always someone. His wife was involved with the Detroit-based "Committee to End the Vietnam War" and she was always down at the committee's storefront office, or back here with someone who needed help. Now she opened the door and leaned inside and said, "Jack, can we lend Tony ten dollars?"

"No," he said. He paused. "If you want to, go ahead. It's all right."

"You don't mind?"

"No. I said it was all right."

Rachel left.

Jack leaned forward, his elbows on the table, so he could look out the window and down into the street. He liked this room very much. He felt good here, very much in control. He and Rachel had hauled this old table up from the basement of the house, and now it was piled with papers and magazines and books. It was much wider than his desk down at the Center. He liked the view here too: he could see right down into the street, the numerous parked cars, still that same old Ford jalopy at the corner —obviously an abandoned car. One of these days he should get around to calling the police about it. Jack could see some black children playing out at the curb, slamming a small object against the pavement.

For most of his adult life—since he'd been seventeen—he had lived in single rooms, in odd unheated corners, in attic rooms with sloped ceilings and exposed beams and ill-fitting window frames, in basement rooms with walls that oozed, in furnished rooms everywhere, all over hell, and he had never really paid much attention. Really, he hadn't cared about his surroundings. So now it was a surprise to him, this small, quiet, private room; he felt almost guilty for possessing it. On principle, he was against owning property, he was against owning almost anything, he hated the idea of buying a car and put it off from year to year. . . . He hated, almost, his own selfish pleasure in a place like this, where he could be alone and concentrate.

Rachel returned, this time knocking before she opened the door. "Tony decided to leave. I'm sorry he was here when you came home—he just dropped in, out of nowhere. Those damn leech friends of his, you know—? That ran out on him around Christmas? They're back and want to move in with him again. The girl's pregnant."

"Is that so," Jack said flatly. He waved the subject of Tony away; he couldn't burden his mind with any more people. "Here, read this," he said, handing Rachel the magazine. He watched as she skimmed the article. She frowned at once, recognizing the name. She was wearing dark blue slacks and a heavy cable-knit beige sweater because of the draft in the apartment; her hair was pulled back from her face and fastened into a kind of loose, girlish pony tail. When she frowned like that her forehead creased just the way Jack's did.

"Hey . . . well. . . . Well, after so many years," she said slowly. "I hope they win. I hope they know how to win."

"I was wondering if I should go down," Jack said.

"What? Why? In what capacity?"

"Just as an assistant, just to hang around," Jack said vaguely. He realized as he spoke that he would never go; it was too impractical. And he wasn't free any longer. He had a job, a regular five-day-a-week job, he was advising Rachel's anti-war committee and several other committees, he even had a tricky, very promising private case.

"We can't afford it," Rachel said bitterly.

"I could get some money, maybe," Jack said.

"Where?"

He shrugged his shoulders.

"I've heard of Levey a little," Rachel said. She was still frowning. "He's supposed to be good, and very conservative. I think they need someone like that. Yes. It might work. They're not exactly pioneering any longer. They might win."

"Two men just got acquitted in Texas for shotgunning some kids on the highway. Black kids," Jack said thoughtfully. "But they might win anyway. They might have good luck."

"We could all use some good luck," Rachel said.

She sat on the edge of the table and folded her arms and sighed. "How are you, how's your cold?" she asked. She adjusted his collar; it must have been crooked. "You look a little tired."

"My cold must have gone away," Jack said. He'd forgotten about it. He smiled up at Rachel, who looked as tired and harassed and yet as oddly content as he did. It pleased him that Tony had left and that he had a few minutes—more than ten minutes—before this stranger was due, he'd forgotten the name, the man with the son in Toronto. He said, "Well, the Center was as bad as ever today, and some people showed up for appointments with me that I didn't know anything about. But I worked them in. Jesus, what a jumble! Sometimes I can't remember my name, I'm just a voice telling them what to do, what not to do, giving advice, giving instructions the way you would to a five-year-old. But it seems to be working out all right. . . . I can't complain. I suppose I like it."

"You're doing very well," Rachel said.

"The only trouble is, there are so many people who need help," Jack said. "And they all deserve it, they deserve my complete attention. . . . Nothing much matters to me except people like this, individuals, you know . . . they're all we have . . . I mean, to help them. . . . But sometimes I get so mixed up I can't remember my own name or what the hell I think I'm doing."

"You're doing all right," Rachel said.

He knew this was true, but it pleased him to hear it.

Jack followed the trial—*The State of Mississippi* v. *Storr*—and even sent Levey a letter, in which he spoke of his interest in the case, his hunches about how to handle it, his hopes for a conviction, and his hope also that Levey might contact him when the trial ended. But Levey never replied. Jack read about the last days of the trial and the verdict, his face burning as if the news concerned him personally: the jury had been out only four minutes.

"Damn dirty sons of bitches," Jack said.

That was in July of 1967. Jack read about the case in several magazines, wrote another letter to Levey beginning, "What rotten luck . . . ," and continued for half a dozen pages, in a rapid, smudged scrawl, commenting on the progress of civil rights litigation in the South and elsewhere, trying to console Levey by mentioning snags in his own work, the crackdown on drugs in the city here, the outlandish prosecutions and the welfare cutbacks, all the standard messes of the North. . . . Maybe, after all, the South hadn't been the place to begin, Jack wrote.

He mailed the letter to Levey in care of the New Democrats Defense Committee, in New York, but never got any reply.

"The bastard could at least acknowledge my existence," Jack said bitterly.

"He probably gets too much mail. Probably hundreds of letters," Rachel said. "Forget about it."

Jack more or less forgot about the Hurley case. But then, in January, 1969, when much in his life had changed and he was no longer with Legal Aid—having quarreled with the supervisor—and he and Rachel no longer lived in the house on Virginia Park, which had been raided once by the narcotics squad and was obviously a marked place, Jack ran into a young lawyer who had assisted Levey on the Hurley case. His name was Rick Brauer; he had a meager private practice out in Ann Arbor, and he drove to Detroit once a week to teach an adult education course for extra money. He was a tense, intelligent young man, somewhat like Jack himself, but much more cynical, with a hacking derisive laugh that turned into a cough and back into a laugh again. "Oh, Jesus, don't ask about the Hurley case!" he said, putting his hands up to his face.

He and Jack went to a bar to talk. Jack was still interested in the case, since it was mixed up with a part of his life now past and yet not completely past; the Hurley business had brought Rachel and him together. Since 1967 there had been a number of cases in the South, for smaller and easier rewards—charges of manslaughter or conspiracy to violate constitutional rights—and these had resulted in convictions against white Southerners in spite of the all-white juries, so times were changing gradually, the whole subject wasn't as depressing as it had once been. Jack was surprised and rather annoyed by Brauer's skepticism.

"It's fantastic you would remember my name," Brauer laughed. "I don't exactly publicize my role in that, and only a few articles mentioned me. I didn't do much, really. But I can't say I would have handled it much differently from Levey anyway. He just had bad luck. . . . Well, you know Java, do you? Not as well as I do, lucky for you, I spent seven weeks down there and it's a good thing we lost, or I might be buried down there. Bastards! The whole county—the whole northeastern part of the state—was arming itself for weeks, and everybody was acting out their parts as if it was a bad television show, state troopers flagging us down for speeding, checking our licenses and driver registration, fat slobs bumping into us on the street, even little kids calling us names! The jurors just trooped out and then trooped back again with their verdict. I don't think it even took them four minutes."

Jack nodded sympathetically.

"The most important witnesses for our side looked like *hell*," Brauer said. "I don't know what happened to them—whether they were scared or that was their usual style. I think they were doped up. On the other side, the state trooper's friends were well-mannered and well-dressed and all their stories checked out together, again like a television play. A very bad neat play, with perfect timing and polished dialogue and no hesitations. They all said the same thing—the Coke bottle, the shooting in self-defense; Jesus, they might as well have given their testimonies in unison, as a chant! After the verdict came in, the place went wild—hugging, kissing, women crying, even the murderer crying—I forget his name—Storr—it's a name I've tried to forget. The mayor of the town gave a victory party."

Jack nodded again. But he thought: *Thank God it wasn't me.*

Then, as Brauer went on to talk about other things, he thought: *I could have done better. . . .* And he imagined the miracle, that jury returning after hours of deliberation, the foreman pronouncing the miraculous word: *Guilty.* It might have happened. And the headlines of *Guilty Guilty Guilty Guilty. . . .*

Brauer drove to Detroit on Thursdays, to teach a course in real estate law for adults, and he and Jack sometimes met for a drink. Whenever Jack got together with Brauer he felt oddly exhilarated, as if by the thought of the case he hadn't taken on and hadn't lost; not Jack Morrissey. Another man had gone down, not Jack. So he felt an odd sense of relief, gratitude, and enjoyed Brauer's company when Brauer wasn't too loud or too negative. He found himself playing the role of a more affirmative Morrissey, in an attempt to cancel out Brauer's cynicism: if Brauer said, "I don't know why we give a damn," Jack always said, "That's bullshit; you know perfectly well."

One day in February, an especially wintry day, Brauer seemed more ironic than ever, standing with Jack at a crowded bar on Woodward Avenue; he was a little drunk and showed no interest in going to teach his class. Jack noticed that he was already a few minutes late. He said, "Do you know what time it is?" and Brauer shrugged his shoulders.

"Oh hell," Brauer said listlessly. "I'm going to be late anyway. I'm always late."

He finished his glass of beer. Jack hadn't bothered to finish his; he didn't really like to drink during the day. It made him nervous that Brauer should stand at the bar like this when he had a class to teach across the street.

"There's something about this class . . . that repels me but also attracts me," Brauer said. "I put off going to it and I put off thinking about it because. . . . Well, let me show you."

"What?"

"Let me show you something."

"Show me what?"

"Walk over to the Rackham with me and I'll show you."

Jack didn't want to waste any more time this afternoon. He said doubtfully, "What is it?" It might have been the smoke in the bar, but his eyes had begun to ache; he had the idea he was straining them with his work and that he might need glasses. This depressed him.

Brauer looked playful now, almost coy.

"Something interesting," he said.

Jack stooped to pick up his briefcase—still the same briefcase, with a handle of smart black plastic—and followed Brauer outside.

"I have a long night ahead," Jack said.

"Oh hell, give yourself a treat. I want you to see something. It's something to see, it's something freakish."

He laughed.

"A thing or a person?" Jack asked.

"A thing."

13

"What do you think?"

"Of who? That woman sitting there?"

"Yes, of course that woman sitting there!" Brauer said. He leaned back against the wall so that he could watch Jack's face. "What do you think?"

Jack saw a blond woman in her twenties, sitting in the center of a drab room of desks and other people; her notebook was open, she sat like any student, waiting for class to begin. He had an impression of her being very pretty but not believable. His eye would have skimmed over her ordinarily, but something in Brauer's attitude, his peculiar smile, made him pause. What was wrong? He wondered if there was something he had missed.

"She's pretty. So what? Is that what you mean? She's very pretty," Jack said, shrugging his shoulders.

Brauer's odd conspiratorial smile, his rather noisy breathing, made Jack uneasy. He really did want to get away. Brauer said, "Come on, don't be so casual. What do you really think of her?"

"Frankly, I don't think anything," Jack said.

"Oh come on, Jack, what does she make you think of?"

"What the hell? Are you in love with her or something?"

Brauer made an impatient gesture with his head. "I am not in love with her, I don't particularly like her, in fact I don't even know her," he said in his normal voice. "But there's something about her. . . . She isn't human. What she does is, she sits there at that desk every Thursday, and she's in my head for an hour and fifteen minutes . . . and . . . and sometimes she drifts back into my head during the week. . . . Do you think she's real? With a face like that?"

Jack peered through the window of the door to get a better look at her: she seemed to be in her early twenties, though dressed in a way he believed to be worldly, elegant, expensive, the kind of appearance he hated. Her face looked like a face he might have glimpsed on a magazine cover, while he stood at a newsstand buying something else. He never would have bought the magazine with *that* cover.

"You're in love with her," Jack said flatly. "How long have you been seeing her?"

"I haven't been seeing her," Brauer said. "I don't even know her, I'm happily married—you know my wife, you know how good my marriage is—that isn't quite the point. I mean. . . . What does she make you think of?"

The woman glanced toward the door, as if toward Jack. But he guessed that she could not see him. Around her, the other students were talking, one middle-aged man looked pointedly at his watch; but the blond woman simply sat, waiting. She gave the impression of being prepared to sit there permanently.

"Isn't there something about her face," Brauer said, "not just the way she looks but the way she's looking out of it—as if she's behind it—isn't there something maddening? I know I've been drinking too much, I've been talking too much, but—I have this fantasy, this humiliating fantasy, that in the middle of a lecture I knock the podium aside and crawl up the aisle to her desk and take hold of her ankles, or her feet or something, and she just looks down at me. . . . Don't you think she would do that? She would. Then it gets me madder than hell, that I'd think of such crap, and I start thinking instead of grabbing her by the back of the neck and. . . . You'd have to do that, to get her attention."

"She means more to you than she should, that's all," Jack said. "Now, I'd better be going—"

"I smile at her and she smiles back at me, but it doesn't mean anything. It doesn't catch hold. Since this damn pathetic class began a few weeks ago— Look, Jack," Brauer said, squinting at his watch, "I don't really mean any of this— Maybe it sounds a little strange to you, a little sick, but— You know my wife, you know what a good, strong marriage I have, like you and Rachel, exactly, you and I married women we can respect, didn't we? So someone like this woman is aggravating to us, isn't she? But I didn't exactly mean what I was saying, I always exaggerate. I'm not in love with her, I don't even know her. . . ."

Jack began to notice the oddity of the woman's face now, as he glanced back and forth from her to the other faces in the room. She was composed, a pleasant blankness that was almost a blur, almost nothing, except that she was so beautiful: that was the shock. The other people were real people. Most of them were men, some middle-aged, some younger, all of them ordinary—one fat man red-faced and really ugly, his face doggish, with jowls and sagging chins. There were only two other women in the class, both of them in their forties, perhaps, both quite ordinary. One looked something like Rachel, the triangularity of her features—dark eyebrows, eyes placed quite far apart, a small mouth—very much like Rachel's.

". . . also her mind, her mind doesn't seem quite human," Brauer was saying. "This class is adult ed., you know, so they get all A's and B's and the hell with them, it doesn't count; in fact I don't bother to read their papers. She's getting a B–. Her handwriting is so perfect, she can't be very intelligent—anyway it would depress the hell out of me if she was intelligent, because—I read her first paper, she had everything memorized perfectly, but I gave her a B—anyway. She seems pleased with her grade."

Jack laughed and was startled at the boyish, snickering sound of his laughter.

He was elated but he didn't exactly know why. Because Brauer had admitted to something degrading? Humiliating? Because Brauer had been the one to tell him about another man's failure in court, another man's humiliation . . . ? It might have been Jack's failure, and no failure was so public as a failure in court. A sickening defeat had lodged itself in someone else's guts, but not in Jack's; he, Jack Morrissey, was doing fairly well these days.

". . . anyway . . . she's married to Marvin Howe, how do you like that? For an additional surprise?"

"Who?"

"Marvin Howe. You know. There was this talk a few years ago, that he'd married some girl, a very young girl. . . ."

"Is that her?" Jack asked, shocked.

"That's her."

"That?"

"The bastard married her when he was over forty," Brauer said, "and she was just a girl—I mean like a child, I remember all the talk. So now she turns up as my student."

Jack stared in at the woman.

"A surprise, huh? The first day of class, I walked in, just walked in a few minutes late, and my God I looked at her and thought—*that one is in the wrong class!* Then I called out their names from the class list and she turns out to be 'Elena Howe' and I put two and two together—this is Detroit, after all—and it's her, it really is. You know, he wouldn't sign the petition for Kamensky last year; can you believe it? The selfish son of a bitch. I really hate bastards like him. I remembered that people said he was trying to educate this wife of his, this very young girl, that he was ashamed of her—she was illiterate or something— But— It isn't important, Jack, forget I brought up the subject."

"All right," Jack said flatly.

"I'd better go in, I'm later than usual," Brauer sighed. "I don't know if it's the class I hate, or if it's her— I didn't offend you, did I? I was just shooting my mouth off."

"Sure," Jack said, backing away.

"Give Rachel my love, okay? See you sometime soon again?"

"Sure," said Jack.

He walked quickly away, to the end of the corridor.

When he looked back, Brauer had gone into the room. He paused, thinking that this was all a waste of time, he'd wasted hours with Brauer, what was the point of friendship anyway?—what was the point of wasting so much time? He felt a little dizzy from drinking and this disgusted him. But still he felt that strange elation.

He went back to the door of the classroom and looked in again, now prepared for her—Mrs. Marvin Howe—and for his own sense of revulsion. That dreamlike face: but not his dream, not his invention. Someone else's. The expression absolutely open, empty, enchanted, the cheekbones high and firm beneath the skin, artificial perfect skin. She was perfect as a glossy poster, without pores. He felt he hated her, yet it was a hatred springing out of him against his will, like the hatred of deformity: the way children hate the deformed, out of their terror of deformity.

Brauer must have been lecturing because she was taking notes, writing slowly. Her face was peaceful, composed; it was obvious she wanted to be nowhere else. She was fulfilled in that moment, her head inclined slightly to one side, a head of thick blond hair arranged in coils, layers; Jack found himself staring at her and thinking. . . . But he didn't know what he was thinking. He thought: *I'll back away and see her get smaller, like a face at the wrong end of a telescope.*

He went back to his small rented office, in a new concrete-block building near the Lodge Expressway. There he made coffee for himself, instant coffee, and sat scratching irritably at his head. His hair was too long. Must get it cut sometime, sometime. It was very thick and seemed to get dirty fast. . . . At a few minutes after five one of his clients showed up, a black woman who was supposed to have seen him the day before; but Jack didn't bother asking her where she had been. It was too much trouble to sift through unskillful lies to get to a pointless truth, a truth of no value to either of them. That was too much like his professional work.

"Can you do something about him, Mr. Morrissey?" she asked.

"Yes, yes," Jack said automatically.

"Can you help me?"

"Yes," said Jack. Yes. Will try to. "I'll get you a better class of problems," he said, trying to smile. But she didn't get the joke: she gaped at him. "Don't worry, I'll get you an injunction against him," he said, and these words seemed to satisfy her.

While the woman complained to him of her husband and his threats and his blows—two teeth of hers knocked out, the kid's eye blackened—Jack found himself thinking of Howe's wife, not thinking of her, exactly, but seeing her. The black woman was talking about her son's ruined stomach: when he was two years old he'd swallowed some bathroom cleanser and now he couldn't eat right or digest food right and all the doctors said it was no use. Jack stared at her, but he wasn't seeing her. He nodded vaguely, mechanically. "And Herman, he said, he said he would have a conversation with the police about my brother, and I told him, did he want us all beat up?—did he want himself knocked out the window? Because you know, Mr. Morrissey, it ain't exactly a secret, my brother is in the big league and he don't listen to anybody like me, if they should ask him for mercy or whatever. That man is pulling in five thousand a week and a small fry like Herman, why he is just on the way out, ain't he, I told him that myself, if he tries to push me around or blackmail me or—" She was very real, very strong-faced, a woman in her thirties with massive forearms and her coat sleeves pushed up a little, strangely, as if she were too warm. Ordinarily Jack would have been curious: *five thousand a week?* Her brother must be dealing in heroin. But even so—five thousand dollars! And she was paying Jack so little. But today, this afternoon, he half-listened to her and nodded sympathetically, not seeing her. He saw the other face. He began to feel a rage that was almost a taste in the mouth, bitter as some tart potent poison, bitter as bathroom cleanser. . . .

"Herman turned my brother against all of us, trying to blackmail me," the woman was whining, "and I am scared as hell of him, Mr. Morrissey—"

"Him? Who?"

"Herman. Because he could precipitate violence if my brother gets going."

Jack listened to her, his eyes becoming glazed. *I'd like to take hold of her by the back of the neck,* he was thinking; or someone was thinking. Not this woman, but the other. Not this heavy, sad-faced, angry woman, but the other woman whose face was like something flashed on a screen. One face was very real, heavy, of a certain density and texture that might be handled, a *weight;* the other face was only an image flashed on a screen, paper-thin, only the idea of a face.

"Don't tell me any more," Jack interrupted. "Your brother's private life is his own concern, not mine. You're here to discuss your husband with me. So remember: you didn't talk about your brother to me. You started to, but then I asked you to stop. Will you remember?"

"Oh yes, Mr. Morrissey," the woman said at once.

He sat listening to her, gone inert and blank now himself. Must get more sleep tonight: he hadn't been sleeping well lately. Four, five hours a night wasn't enough. He was losing weight. His eyes sometimes smarted. While the woman talked, slowly, falteringly, then gaining strength in her anger, he tried to imagine her as a body: a physical thing, a woman he might make love to, another human being who happened to be female. But he could not believe in her, really. She was immensely real, so close to him that he could see every blemish on her face, yet he could not believe in her—he kept seeing the other face, a flash of it, like a flash of madness. A hallucination. At the same time he was bewildered, because it was all a waste of time, the conversation with Brauer, the emotions he'd felt, wasteful emotions that would help him with nothing; what the hell did he care about Marvin Howe or his wife, or about any woman? He had never been very interested in women, certainly not in pursuing them. It was all a waste of energy, a distraction from his work. Before Rachel he'd been involved with only four or five women, casually, because they had been available to him and made no demands on him; he'd liked them all well enough, he liked everyone well enough, but he didn't love anyone. No: that was wrong. He loved Rachel. He respected her, he had married her, pleased that so intelligent and uncompromising a woman had liked him. In a way she was more dedicated than Jack himself—so he respected her very much and feared her a little. He had never been unfaithful to her. He had never thought of it, being too busy. . . .

He squirmed behind his desk, waiting for the black woman to finish her business with him and get out. She was ugly and yet somehow attractive to him; he felt a discomforting desire for her, which he tried to force out of his system by concentrating on her thick, agitated hands, the discolored nails. . . . And her strident voice. Her whining voice.

How he feared women, really!

He drove home to the other side of town, to the apartment building in which he and Rachel now lived, which faced a vacant lot, everything darkened and sober and deserted, like a bombed-out section of a city. He was absurdly grateful that she was home, and alone. "You look tired," Rachel said, surprised. "Did something happen?"

"The usual," Jack said.

She followed him into the bedroom as he took off his suitcoat and tie, and then his white shirt, which always bothered him as soon as he was home: too formal, too uncomfortable. He threw his things down. He noticed the bed hadn't been made and this pleased him. "I'm glad nobody's here with you, I'm glad nobody's coming for supper," he said. "Let's lie down."

"Now?"

"Right now," Jack said.

Afterward he slept for seven hours straight, a deathly lovely sleep.

14

"Then what?"

"I got very . . . I got very excited and. . . ."

"Did she look at you?"

"Yeah. And it made me want to. . . . It made me want to go after her, you know, like grab a hold of her. . . . Because she was thinking the same thing. She was afraid of me and she was thinking. . . ."

"She kept looking back at you?"

"Oh yes, she did. Yes. Back over her shoulder. I got so excited that I just followed her, I mean I must of followed her, I don't even remember my legs going. . . . It was just her, looking back over her shoulder at me, like checking on me, and me following her, just her and me and nobody else on the street. I never saw nobody else. I just saw her ahead of me but I didn't even see her face, I was too excited."

"When did she start to run?"

"Oh my, I don't know, I . . . I guess it was by . . . uh . . . that drugstore there, what is it, some drugstore that. . . . Well, it was closed of course, because of the late hour. Uh . . . some name you see all the time. . . ."

"Cunningham's."

"Oh yes, yes. Cunningham's. But I don't know if I really saw that, Mr. Morrissey, so clear as that . . . any place at all . . . like I know the neighborhood upwards and downwards but I wasn't watching too close at the time. Because I had my eye on her, you know, to see she couldn't get away. She was like a fox would be, going fast all of a sudden, and damn scared. That makes them clever, when they're scared."

"Then she started to run? Where was this?"

". . . the other side of the drugstore . . . across a street. . . . I don't know the names but they got them written down, the police. They could tell you."

"I don't want any information from them, I want it from you. The intersection there is St. Ann and Ryan Boulevard. Is that where she started running?"

"If that's what they said. . . ."

"That's what she said. She told them. When she started to run, did you run?"

"Yeah."

"Right away?"

"Yeah, right away."

"Did you start running before she did?"

"No. I don't know."

"But only after she started running . . . ?"

"I think so."

"Did you? After she started running, but not before?"

"Yeah."

"Were there any cars waiting for the light to change at that intersection?"

"I don't know . . . I was in a frenzy. . . . You know how you get when things happen fast and you can't pay attention. . . . I . . . I saw her running and I thought to myself, *You ain't going to get away!* I was almost ready to laugh or to scream out, it was so. . . . It was so high-strung a few minutes for me. . . ."

"Did she run across the street, or out into the street?"

"She . . . uh . . . she started screaming. . . . That was when she started screaming. But it didn't scare me off. She ran out into the middle of the street . . . yeah, I can remember that now . . . out into the middle, where it was very wide. . . . I remember some cars waiting for the light to change, now. But I didn't pay much attention to them then."

"Then what happened?"

"Well, uh, she got out there and something like, like her shoe was broke, the heel was snapped . . . and she was yelling at this guy in a car that waited for the light to change but then couldn't get away because she was in front of the car. And . . . uh . . . that was a . . . a Pontiac Tempest, a nice green car. . . . And it was a man and a woman, both white. She was yelling for them to let her in. But when she ran around to the side of the car and grabbed the door handle, well, it was locked of course, and she couldn't get it open and I was just waiting by the curb to see how it would go . . . and the guy, he just pressed down that accelerator and got the hell out of there. Man, he shot off like a rocket, I had to laugh. And she looked over her shoulder at me where I was waiting, you know, and. . . ."

"Yes, then what?"

"Well, then, then I, uh, I got her. There wasn't anything to it, she was pretty tired by then, and. . . . I just grabbed her and dragged her back somewhere, you know, the way they said . . . she told them all the things that happened. . . . I can't remember it too clear myself because I was crazy-like, like laughing because I was so high, you know. I wasn't scared either. I felt like a general or somebody in a movie, where things go right, like I came to the edge of a country or a whole continent, you know, and naturally I wouldn't want the movie to end just yet. . . ."

"But you don't remember everything that happened?"

"I don't know. Maybe. But no, I guess not, I mean. . . . You know how you get in a frenzy. . . ."

"You signed a confession."

"Yeah, I s'pose so. I mean, I wanted to cooperate a little. I figured they had me anyway, and anyway I was still so high, I couldn't come in for a landing, I wasn't scared or anything and felt very good. So I signed it."

"Did they tell you you had the right to call an attorney?"

"Yeah, maybe."

"You had the right to counsel . . . ? Did the police tell you that?"

"*Right to counsel.* . . . Yeah, I heard something like that. I don't know. Maybe I was a little scared. My mouth was bleeding down my neck."

"From being struck?"

"Before they got the handcuffs on me I was trying to get away. So somebody got me in the face."

"Did it hurt?"

"No, naw. I didn't feel it. I started getting wet, then one of the policemen in the car, he wiped me off with a rag, because it was getting on him. I don't know if it hurt or not. Later on it hurt. The tooth was loose and I fooled around with it, wiggling it, in jail, and took it out myself; so I wouldn't swallow it or something at night. My whole face swoll up afterward. . . ."

"So you waived your right to counsel?"

"I don't know. I guess so. If they said that, then I did."

"Why did you waive your right to counsel?"

"I don't know."

"Were you pressured into it?"

"What? I don't know. I . . . uh . . . I was mixed up and a little high. . . ."

"Did you say, maybe, that you didn't have any money for a lawyer?"

"Uh . . . yeah. In fact I did say that, yeah. I did."

"You did?"

"I think so."

"You did say that."

"I think I said it. . . ."

"You told them you couldn't afford a lawyer."

"Yeah."

"And did they say you had the right to counsel anyway? Did they say that if you were indigent, counsel would be provided for you?"

"Indigent . . . ?"

"Yes, indigent. If you didn't have money for a lawyer, you'd be given one anyway. Didn't they explain that to you?"

"What was that . . . ? *In* . . . ?"

"Indigent. They didn't explain that to you, did they?"

"About what?"

"If you were indigent, counsel would be provided for you."

"Indigent. . . ."

"Indigent. Did they use that word? Do you remember it?"

"Well, uh. . . . Lots of words got used. . . . I. . . ."

"Did they use the word *indigent?* Did they explain your situation to you?"

"What situation? . . . I was kind of mixed up and excited and. . . ."

"And they had been banging you around, right? Your tooth was knocked out . . . your face was cut . . . your face swelled up. . . . So you signed a confession, right? After Mrs. Donner made her accusation, you agreed with her, you signed a confession for the police, in order to cooperate with them and not be beaten any more. I think that was a very natural thing to do under the circumstances. Do you know which one of the police hit you?"

"Oh, they all did, they were all scrambling around after me. . . . Damn lucky I didn't get shot. I was fearless, I didn't know shit how close I came to getting killed. Jesus. Never come in for a landing till the next day, I was so high. Pulled the tooth out by the roots and never felt it. But later on it hurt like hell. . . . I couldn't remember much."

"Were you examined by a doctor?"

"No."

"A dentist?"

"Hell no."

"Let's see your mouth. . . . What about those missing teeth on the side there? What happened to them?"

"Them, they been gone a long time."

"It looks raw there."

"Yeah, well, I don't know. . . . It looks what?"

"It looks sore."

"Well, it might be sore, I don't know. My gums is sore sometimes. They bleed sometimes by themselves."

"What happened to your mouth?"

"I got kicked there. Two, three years back."

"Your mother told me you'd had some trouble back in your neighborhood off and on, and I see you were arrested for some incidents, but what about some trouble with a girl . . . ? Did you ever get into trouble with a girl?"

"What girl?"

"Your mother says it was a girl in the neighborhood."

"Yeah."

"Yeah what?"

"Yeah, it was a girl, a girl. She never made no trouble for me. Her father was out after me, but he got in trouble himself. So I don't know, I mean, it passed on by. She was. . . . She didn't want no trouble, it was her old man tried to make a fuss. What's my mother been telling you that old news? That's damn old news, that's last year's news."

"You weren't arrested for rape, were you?"

"No. I tole you, it was only her father; then he had to leave town."

"Before this you've been arrested twice, right? And put on probation twice? And no jail sentence."

"That's a way of looking at it."

"How do you look at it?"

"I hung around a long time waiting to get out . . . waiting for the trial. . . . You know, the trial or the hearing or whatever it was. Then the judge let me go anyway."

"You waited in jail, you mean."

"Sure I waited in jail."

"Why couldn't you get bond?"

"My momma said the hell with me."

"According to the record you were arrested for theft twice. You pleaded guilty. What about the assault charges?"

". . . from roughing somebody up? Well, uh, that stuff got put aside. There was a deal made."

"So you got off on probation twice."

"Yeah, that worked out okay."

"You were arrested for the first time when you were nineteen years old, right?"

"If that's what it says."

"That isn't bad. Nineteen years old . . . that's a pretty advanced age for a first offense. . . . And no jail sentence, just probation. Now tell me, is all this accurate: your father served a five-year sentence for armed robbery, right?—then he left Detroit? Your mother has been on ADC from 1959 until the present, right? You have four brothers and two sisters, two children are still living at home with your mother, and your sister has a baby herself?—and you don't live at home, but nearby somewhere? And you give her money when you can?"

"Yeah."

"It says here you're unemployed. Were you ever employed?"

"Sure I been employed."

"It isn't down here. What kind of job did you have?"

"How come it ain't down there?"

"I don't know. What kind of job did you have?"

"Look, you write it in yourself, Mr. Morrissey, because I sure was employed. . . . I call that an insult. I was kind of a delivery boy off and on, I could get references to back me up."

"This is just a photostat copy of your file from Welfare; I can't write anything in. . . . Where did you work?"

"Some store that's closed up now."

"Whose was it?"

"I disremember the exact name."

"You're unemployed at the present time, at the age of twenty-three?"

"Well, I can't help that. I. . . . Mr. Morrissey, you going to make a deal for me?"

"I won't have to make a deal."

"Huh? Well, that woman is awful mad at me. She's out to get me."

"Don't worry about her."

"In the police station she was half crazy, she was screaming so. . . . Her clothes was all ripped. I don't remember none of that. The front of her was all blood. Jesus, I don't know, I must of gone crazy or something. . . . When they brought me in she was already there, waiting, and she took one look at me and started screaming. That was the end."

"She might reconsider, she might think all this over carefully. Don't worry about her. Let me worry about her. In fact, you have no necessary reason to believe that the woman who identified you was the woman you followed and attacked. . . . It might have been another woman. You didn't really see her face. All you know is that she was white, and probably all she knows about her attacker is that he was black. I won't have to make a deal for you. Don't worry about that."

"She's awful mad at me, she ain't going to back down. . . ."

"Let me worry about her. Tell me: how did the police happen to pick you up? Did they have a warrant for your arrest?"

"Hell no. It was a goddam ass-hole accident like a joke. . . . I, uh, I was running away from her, where I left her . . . and . . . and . . . I just run into the side of the squad car. Like that. Was running like hell and run into the side of the car, where it was parked, without no lights on. So they picked me up like that."

"Because you were running, they picked you up, right?"

"I run into the side of their goddam fucking car."

"So they got out and arrested you?"

"One of them chased me."

"Did he fire a shot?"

"Sure he fired a shot."

"So you surrendered?"

"I hid somewhere, by a cellar window. But they found me. It was just a goddam stupid accident. . . . Jesus, I don't know. I must of been flying so high, couldn't see the car where it was parked. They had it parked back from the big street, with the lights out. I saw one of them with a paper cup, some coffee that got spilled down his front, when I banged into the door. He was surprised."

"So they brought you into the station and the woman was brought in also, this Mrs. Donner, and she identified you. Is that it? She took one look at you and seemed to recognize you?"

"Started screaming like hell."

"She identified you absolutely, in spite of her hysterical state?"

"I guess so."

"And you admitted attacking her?"

"I guess so."

"Was that really the correct woman, though? This 'Mrs. Donner' who is accusing you of rape?"

"Huh?"

"Could you have identified her?"

"Me? I don't know. No. I don't know."

"Let's go back to the bar. You said there were three women there, all white women. Did they look alike to you, or what?"

"I don't know."

"Did one of them catch your attention?"

"Maybe. I don't know. One of them . . . she kind of was watching me, I thought. They was all horsing around."

"It was very crowded in the bar? And this woman, this particular woman, looked at you. Did she smile at you?"

"They was all laughing, you know, and if they looked around the place, why, it would seem they was smiling. . . . I don't know which one it was. I'm all mixed up on that."

"Would you say that this woman, let's call her 'Mrs. Donner' temporarily, this woman was behaving in a way that was provocative? She was looking at you or toward you, and at other men?"

"There was a lot of guys in there, black guys, and some white guys too. I liked the tone of that place. There was a good feeling there. I wasn't drunk, but. . . ."

"Yes, you were drunk."

"Naw, I was high on my own power, I only had a few drinks."

"You were drunk; that happens to be a fact. That's an important fact. Don't forget it."

"I was drunk . . . ?"

"Yes. You were drunk. And a white woman did smile at you, in a bar on Gratiot; let's say it was this 'Mrs. Donner' who is charging you with rape. Do you know anything about her? No. I'll tell you: she's married, separated from her husband, the husband's whereabouts are unknown, she's been on and off Welfare since 1964, she worked for a while at Leonard's Downtown, the department store, and was discharged because she evidently took some merchandise home with her . . . and she's been unemployed since September of last year, but without any visible means of support; no welfare. So she won't be able to account for her means of support since September, if that should come up in court."

"Uh. . . . You going to make a deal with them, then?"

"I don't have to make a deal. I told you to let me worry about her. She has to testify against you, and she has to convince a jury that she didn't deserve to be followed by you, that she didn't entice you, she didn't smile at you. She has to convince a jury that she didn't deserve whatever happened to her. . . . She did smile at you?"

"Well, uh, you know how it was . . . a lot of guys crowding around, shifting around. . . . I don't know which one of the women for sure looked at me, there was three of them, maybe they all did . . . or maybe just one . . . or. . . . It was confused. Some guys was buying them drinks and I couldn't get too close, I didn't know anybody there. I liked the tone of the place but I was on the outside, you know? I was having my own party in my head. Then I saw this one woman get mad and put on her coat—"

"A light-colored coat? An imitation fur coat?"

"Jesus, how do I know? Saw her put her arm in a sleeve. . . ."

"And she walked out? Alone?"

"Yeah. So I . . . I got very jumpy. . . . I thought I would follow her, you know, just see what happens. . . ."

"But you didn't follow her with the intention of committing rape."

"I. . . ."

"You wanted to talk to her, maybe? She'd smiled at you and you wanted to talk to her?"

"I don't know if. . . ."

"This white woman, whose name you didn't know, had smiled at you. She then left the bar—that is, Carson's Tavern—at about midnight, completely alone, unescorted, and she walked out along the street. Is this true?"

"Yes."

"When did she notice that you were following her?"

"Right away."

"Then what happened?"

"She started walking faster."

"Did she pause or give any sign to you? You mentioned that she kept looking over her shoulder at you—?"

"Yeah."

"Then she started to run?"

"Yeah."

"She tried to get someone to stop, to let her in his car, but he wouldn't. He drove away. She was drunk, wasn't she, and screaming at him?"

"She was screaming. . . ."

"She was drunk too. That happens to be a fact. You were both drunk, those are facts. This 'Mrs. Donner' who is accusing you of rape was drunk at the time. So. . . . The driver in the Pontiac drove away, and you approached her. Was it the same woman who had smiled at you in the tavern?"

"I think . . . uh. . . . I don't know. . . ."

"She was the woman from the tavern?"

"That got mad and put her coat on? Sure. She walked out. . . ."

"Did all three women more or less behave in the same manner? They were very loud, they'd been drinking, you really couldn't distinguish between them . . . ?"

"I don't know."

"When you caught up to the woman, what did she say to you?"

"Say? Nothing. No words."

"She was screaming?"

"Oh yeah."

"What did you say to her?"

"Nothing."

"Could you identify her?"

"I . . . uh. . . . That's where I get mixed up."

"Why?"

"I don't remember no face to her."

"Why not?"

"Must not of looked at it."

"Back in the bar, you didn't look either?"

"Well yes . . . but I. . . . It's all a smear, like. Like a blur."

"This Mrs. Donner says you threatened to kill her. Is that true?"

"If she says so. . . ."

"No, hell. Don't worry about what she says. What do *you* say?"

"I don't remember."

"*Lay still or I'll kill you.* Did you say that?"

"Is that what they have down?"

"Did you say it? *Lay still or I'll kill you?*"

"That don't sound like me."

"You didn't say anything to her, did you?"

"When? When we was fighting?"

"At any time."

"I don't remember."

"In the confusion of struggling, it isn't likely you said anything to her, is it?—anything so distinct as that? Or maybe it was another man, another black man, who attacked this 'Mrs. Donner' and she's confusing him with you. . . . ?"

"Uh. . . ."

"Did you intend to kill her?"

"No."

"What did you have in mind when you followed her out of the tavern?"

"Oh, you know . . . I was kind of high-strung. . . ."

"She had smiled at you, so you thought she might be friendly? A pretty white woman like that, only twenty-nine years old, with her hair fixed up and a fancy imitation-fur coat, who had smiled at you, a stranger in a bar. . . . ? You thought she might be friendly, wasn't that it?"

"Friendly? Jesus! I never expected no friendship, that's for sure."

"Well, put yourself back in that situation. Don't be so sure. If a white woman smiled at you, and you followed her out onto the street, it would be logical you might expect her to be friendly toward you. Keep your mind clear. You don't have to believe what other people tell you about yourself; you don't have to believe that you assaulted that woman, just because she says you did. Things aren't so simple. Did you expect her to fight you off?"

". . . don't know."

"If she hadn't fought you, there wouldn't be any crime committed, would there? She resisted you, she provoked you into a frenzy. . . . But don't think about it. I'll think about that angle. I'm the one who's going to question Mrs. Donner and then we'll see who's guilty of what. . . . But one important thing: why didn't you tell the police yourself that you really didn't recognize the woman?"

"Huh? Jesus, they'd of been mad as hell—"

"Yes, they would have been mad, they might have beaten you some more. You were terrified of a further beating. So of course you didn't protest, you didn't say anything. Because she's a white woman and you're black. Isn't that the real reason?"

"I don't know."

"There weren't any black men in the station. You were the only black man there. So you thought it would be the safest, most prudent thing, to confess to everything, because this white woman and the white police had you, they had you, and you considered yourself fair game. And already you'd been beaten, your mouth was bleeding, and you didn't know you had the right to an attorney, to any help at all. You were completely isolated. They could do anything to you they wanted. . . . Your instincts told you to go along with them, to cooperate. Nobody can blame you for that; that's how you survived. Does any of this sound familiar to you?"

"Some kind of way, yes. . . . Yes, I think so."

"And the police demonstrated their antagonism toward you, their automatic assumption of your guilt, even though the woman who accused you of rape was a probable prostitute, a woman of very doubtful reputation who led you on, who enticed you out into the street . . . and then evidently changed her mind, or became frightened when she saw how excited you were. Is that it? Why do you think she identified you so quickly, why was she so certain?"

"Must of seen my face."

"How did she see your face, if you didn't see hers?"

"I saw hers but didn't take it in, you know, I kind of blacked out . . . she was fighting me off and that drove me wild . . . it was good luck she stopped, or . . . or something else might of happened. . . . You know how frenzied you get. There was a street light there, and I thought to myself, *She ain't going to forget me.*"

"Why not?"

"Gave her a good look at my face. My face is important to me."

15

The worst cynicism: a belief in luck.

So Jack instructed himself not to believe in luck—good luck, bad luck. No, he believed instead in human control and direction, in his own control, his own powerful will. He tried to keep out of his thoughts the almost physical sensation of relief he sometimes felt when he did well, and it flashed through his mind that he had been *very lucky*.

And yet . . . in his imagination he could see a kind of control board, with small light bulbs that flashed occasionally to indicate catastrophes, accidents of annihilation that would be catalogued and assessed as history . . . in fact, made into history and immortality. One of the lights flashes: another inch of the globe gone.

Was anyone working the control board?

No.

But Jack didn't want to believe this, he loathed the slovenliness of such a belief. After all, he was an adult. He was a man with a good, workable, tireless brain, a rather astonishing brain, and a body to go with it—tireless as long as it kept in operation, quite energetic and dependable. Sometimes he said to Rachel or to their friends, *If I could locate the center of the universe you can be damn certain I'd go there and I'd have perfect leverage there to change everything.* For years he had said this, and Rachel and their friends had said it, in different words, telling one another the same truths again and again, as if they were religious truths that must be uttered often so they would not fall into disuse and be forgotten. *If I could locate the center of the universe . . . I'd change everything. . . .* Jack did believe this. He never lied, even to himself. And yet sometimes he could see, in his imagination, that control board, a complicated melodramatic control board of the kind used in movies, to register catastrophic events the script cannot handle.

Lights going on and off throughout the country, the world, the universe: flashes to indicate the newest ravines blasted into mountains, ditches lined with broken bodies and toys, collapsed houses, hillsides, towers . . . all of it surrounded by untouched ordinary zones, suburban housing developments or national parks in which people picnicked, a little bored, on their annual vacations. . . . What did it mean? Why did he think of these things? Jack despised the mind that had invented the control board, a cynical God who had to be Jack himself, since his own mind was all he really knew. Good luck, bad luck: it was evil to believe in luck, almost obscene.

The worst cynicism was a belief in luck, Jack thought, and all cynicism is death.

So he resisted believing in his own good luck, he tried to resist that flash of gleeful relief when he won a victory, even a minor victory, the delight of the successful criminal who knows that all the luck is on his side and who thinks as he walks out of court: *I got away with it.* Jack remembered the hours, the months of work that sometimes went into one of his victories, he tried to keep track of the actual number of hours he spent on any case so that, when he won, he would feel he had deserved to win and hadn't just been lucky. But still. . . . At the back of his mind was the sly conviction that no amount of work, no dedication to any cause, could guarantee a victory in the courts or in life. All of his adult life he had marveled at the men around him, slaving, killing themselves, and all for rewards Jack himself would have considered a joke—who the hell cared, who cared? Who was watching? He knew lawyers his own age who worked as hard as he did, who were emotionally involved in their work, who were good men, intelligent virtuous men, and who were defeated when they most deserved a victory: *bad luck.* But he, Jack, did very well: *good luck.*

And yet he had to resist believing this, because such a belief excluded him, his personality.

After a case, after he won, he lived through a day or two of euphoria in which most of the trial would come back to him, though not in any dramatic order, and his own voice would ring in his head, powerfully, beautifully: *I suggest that . . . I insist that . . . I demand that. . . .* He was not only the man who said these words, an actor who performed his role to perfection; he was also the man who had written those words. It was dizzying, the joy of such an accomplishment. He imagined it was close to the criminal's amazement when he realizes that all the luck is his, that he has gotten away with his crime. . . .

In January, 1970, he won an acquittal for a twenty-three-year-old black man charged with rape, and he believed he was at the peak of his life. How cleverly he had managed the case, and what good luck had gone into his winning! Rachel and their friends assured him that he had deserved to win, that the young black deserved acquittal, and Jack had agreed, yes, he had even agreed with Rachel when she said that some people had the right to steal, even to commit rape, even to commit murder. . . . Because the white totalitarian society was murdering them, wasn't it? Jack agreed with her or pretended to agree, because he respected her ferocity: she was involved now with a new inner-city program, the co-ordination of several large, famous corporations and some social welfare agencies trying to match the employable unemployed with job-training programs. "Black prisoners in our society are really political prisoners," Rachel said. "They should be released. They should be retried and found not guilty." Jack half agreed with her, though really he did not believe this; he believed in the law, and the absolute structure of the law, which allowed for his good luck to perform such feats.

The *People of the State of Michigan* v. *Hale* was a case that had received a great deal of publicity, not just in Detroit but in the entire state, and in Ohio, Illinois, and Wisconsin as well. Jack had been very pleased with winning because he had gotten Hale a verdict of Not Guilty out of a jury of middle-class whites, and seven of them were women. People had told him he'd be crucified, but he had sensed a way of managing Hale's case that was something new for him: he had analyzed and reanalyzed the chances of the jury's disapproval of the woman who had been raped, and he had litigated his defense with that in the background. Only one local newspaper had really attacked the verdict. Times were changing, a new fashion was on its way, a new ideological fad; Jack certainly did not believe in the depth of this change but he believed in his ability to exploit it. Therefore he had litigated on a main issue that would have been suicidal a few years before in Detroit: the guilt of the victim, the conscious or unconscious role of the victim in the crime. And rape was an excellent issue, because it involved not only some very subtle degrees of physical activity, but because—in a sense—it was a crime only if the victim resisted; it *became* a crime only through the strenuous activity of the victim. And what about the black-white relationship? The enticement of the black male, his being provoked into a "frenzy"? And what about the role of the jury? Jack had plunged into an account of his client's history, a case history of the usual messes, and he knew he could rely upon the shadowy, mysterious, damning half-acknowledgment of guilt on the part of the jury, who happened to be white. When he led Mrs. Donner through several hours of cross-examination, recounting with her every second of that night, remaining polite and civilized himself, but leading her into confusions and one outburst of anger against him—when she let slip one slangy expression, just one, that shot through the jurors in an instant—he could feel how beautifully he was doing, how correctly he had guessed at the mood of the courtroom of January, 1970, in Detroit.

He had guessed right, and he had won.

After the Hale case he took on a suit for false arrest, on the part of another young black man handed over to him from the state ACLU, a man charged with transporting stolen goods—the police had stopped him without a warrant and pried open the trunk of his car, in which a half-dozen fur coats with their labels ripped off had been stuffed. Jack had won that case too, he had won a suit for false arrest; and again he felt that he was at the peak of his career, of his life. And he was only thirty-two. But then a plum of a case came his way: he acted as an assistant and then as chief counsel for the folk singer Aaron Zimmern, arrested at an illegal folk-rock concert in Kensington Park in April. Zimmern had flown in to help local musicians with a mass public concert, "The Declining West's Last Love Feast," much feared and debated about and finally forbidden by the authorities, but held anyway. The concert began early on a Sunday and went well enough until late afternoon, when small fights began and miscellaneous people of all ages and sizes and types surged together helplessly, some of them in costumes, some naked, some carrying anti-war signs or banners for the Angry Brigade or the White Panthers. . . . The concert turned into a near disaster, with many arrests and many heads banged by the police, including Zimmern's. But Jack had gotten Zimmern and his codefendants off with fines and costs at a time when, in other parts of the country, people like Zimmern were receiving jail sentences.

The local papers viewed this with alarm. Jack laughed over the headline: COURTS CONDONE PUBLIC OBSCENITY?

But around him the lights flickered and flashed, and another area of the globe disappeared, reduced to zero. However well he did, other people hadn't his good luck; other people were going under. A friend of his, a lawyer his own age, was caught up in a near-hopeless case involving a young white man sentenced to fifteen years in jail for a second drug offense, a very trivial and probably unconstitutional "crime against the statute." He couldn't even get his client out on bail while they awaited a retrial. A friend of Rachel's, named Estelle, whose husband had been involved in the anti-war movement and was so harassed by the police that he left town, had killed herself—in a spectacular manner, by jumping off an expressway overpass down into traffic. She had left three small children behind.

"This country is destroying people," Rachel said sadly, angrily. "It's driving them crazy so that they destroy themselves."

"The country goes through convulsions," Jack said. "First one way, then another. We'll be all right."

"You can't possibly believe that," Rachel said scornfully.

But he didn't want to argue with her.

She brought home people Jack didn't know, strangers to him,

and they sat around the Morrisseys' for hours, sometimes most of the night, talking and arguing about the future of the country and their role in it and what must be done. . . . Jack skimmed a mimeographed pamphlet one of the men had written, not knowing if it was meant to be prose or a poem of some kind:

Consider for a Brief Second the Soul-States of 50 Human Beings
crowded into 400 square ft. Property of U.S. Government &
Taxpayers Inc. How long do they/you remain Human?
What is the People Density of the U.S. Prison?

"This is a time in our history when people are beginning to be afraid of one another," Rachel said. "I feel it myself, don't you? Jack? Are you listening?"

"Of course I'm listening," he said.

"I think you should give Zimmern's fee away," she said. "We don't need all that money, just the two of us. It's terrible to have so much money."

Zimmern's agent had handed Jack a check for twenty thousand dollars.

"We'd better keep it," Jack said. "Not spend it, just keep it. Someday we might need money fast."

"It isn't moral, to keep that money," Rachel said.

Jack dreaded her bringing the subject up in front of other people, but he couldn't keep himself from saying angrily, "Don't we need money too? Do we live on air, on ideas? Are we so pure?"

"I guess we're not," she said flatly.

She stared at him. The space between them seemed to stretch out to a long, thin minute, a space of time terrible to live through; and he thought suddenly that this woman was exactly the woman he had married, years ago, and he was exactly the man who had married her, but the marriage between them had somehow gone invisible. . . . It was like a trick shot in a film, a couple surprised when the walls around them disappear, when they realize they're on view, just two individuals.

This thought frightened him. Rachel seemed to sense it too, for she smiled nervously and tried to apologize, and Jack interrupted her with his own apology: "You're right, honey. You're my conscience. I'll give Zimmern's money up. I should have thought of it myself."

So he gave away the money to one of the national anti-war defense committees.

And he felt very good about it.

She really was his conscience; Jack had not been exaggerating. She was strong, fierce, tireless; always in and out of the house, attending meetings, teaching impromptu classes . . . she even wrote letters to certain nationally known people who were friendly to liberal causes, asking for donations or for help in the form of personal appearances or at least endorsements, not ashamed to plead with them, even to badger them on the telephone. She had completed her Master's Degree program in Social Work at Wayne, but she wasn't able to get the kind of job she wanted; it was her belief that most social workers simply pandered for the system they were meant to reform, or even to demolish; they were just civil servants, they were police agents. She despised them. She had done secretarial work for the Michigan Civil Liberties Union, but quit when the Union had decided not to defend an Ann Arbor professor arrested by the Government for having made an unauthorized trip to Hanoi—the Union would defend him only indirectly, and Rachel had been furious. Jack himself quarreled with some friends of his in the Union; he felt his wife was right. He had to admire her ferocity, her refusal to be placated. Yes, she was his conscience, his bright unsleeping conscience.

So he hid from her his moments of triumph, his raw, selfish, marvelous moments of triumph, and tried to pay attention when she and her friends complained about what was happening: the United States was turning into one vast prison system, they said. There wouldn't be any need for actual prisons, or for concentration camps; even the mental asylums, the most diabolical of all prisons, might as well be shut down. The whole country was a prison.

"This is no time in history to be happy," they said. "Private happiness should be forbidden. . . ."

While Jack brought freedom to his thieves and rapists and minor criminals, while he extended their daring with his own, he was aware at the back of his mind of the terrible control board, the flashes of good and bad luck, the universe he and other men could never control. *If I could locate the center of the universe.*

. . . He worked every day, seven days a week, from about six until one or two in the morning, trudging around to visit people, to ask questions, to do research, having coffee with colleagues and ex-colleagues, listening to their problems, advising them. Preparing affidavits and briefs and motions, he found he could work steadily, unaware of the time; but when he talked to people, even to his wife, he sometimes experienced a sense of panic, a heart-thumping realization of the time he was wasting that he would never be able to retrieve. He was in his early thirties now. He had never had enough time, not really, to prepare a case perfectly, to learn as much about anyone as he should have learned, he would not live long enough to ever do his job right. . . . And his victories in a way anesthetized him to his own imperfections.

In the sixth year of their marriage, his wife said to him one morning: "When are you going to admit it?"

"Admit what?" he asked quickly.

"About yourself. You know," she said.

"What?"

"I can't explain," she said.

"Admit what?" he asked, baffled.

But she wouldn't explain.

Admit what?

He believed in the innocence of all his people, even those who were evidently innocent in fact; he believed in the justice of his using any legal methods he could improvise to force the other side into compromise or into dismissals of charges, or to lead a jury into the verdict he wanted. Why not? He was a defense lawyer, not a judge or a juror or a policeman or a legislator or a theoretician or an anarchist or a murderer. . . .

16

But there was a poison in him.

He could not understand it, and he could not understand his wife's disapproval of him. He knew the work he did was important, that very few men could do it as well as he did—Rachel and her friends talked about changes to be made, but they really did little to change anything. They made conditions worse, he told them: their demonstrations and their picketing, their mimeographed handbills, their recklessness made everything worse. "You're the enemy the government had to invent," he said sourly.

"You don't understand," Rachel said.

It happened that a citizens' grand jury had been organized in the county to investigate the "illegal drug trade." Under Michigan law the identities of the witnesses summoned to appear before the jury were kept secret, and it was a violation of the law for any witness to reveal that he had been summoned; but Jack had the idea that people they knew were being called and that it was only a matter of time before Rachel or even Jack himself might be subpoenaed. If that happened, Jack said, they would have to appear and they would have to answer the questions put to them.

"Like hell I will," Rachel said.

The jury's publicity was frightening: it seemed to have little to do with the real drug trade, with the organized network of drug dealing, but, instead, with the influence of certain radical leaders, always called in the public press "leaders of youth." Jack saw through this at once and wrote a long letter to one of the newspapers pointing out how the grand jury was using its powers to suppress freedom of speech, not to investigate any professional criminals. *This is a crudely naïve and outrageous attempt to suppress all "radical" activity, mainly the anti-war movement in the state,* so said Jack Morrissey in print; and instead of summoning him, the jury summoned his wife.

"I'm not going to go," Rachel said.

"Goddam it," Jack cried, "you're going! You have a summons, it's the law, it's a rotten unconstitutional law but it's on the books, so you're going! Other people we know have been summoned, I'm sure of it. And they've gone. They're not in jail. Why the hell should you make a martyr of yourself and go to jail?"

"I don't care about going to jail," Rachel said. "I'm not going to inform on anyone."

"You have to answer the summons, and you have to answer their questions," Jack said. "You can't plead the First Amendment. You can't have a lawyer. Just go and answer their questions, and don't lie, and see what happens. It might be that you won't have to inform on anyone—you don't know anything about the drug trade, do you?"

"That isn't the point. That isn't the point," Rachel said bitterly.

"I know it isn't the point, but this happens to be real life and not theory," Jack said. "If you're declared in contempt and you go to jail for three months, Rachel, you'll see what real life is. Jesus, I'm sorry I got you into this . . . they really hate me around here, they obviously want to get at me but for some reason they're afraid . . . so they want to get you, and they'd be delighted if you refused to appear. What good will you do your committee if you're in jail? I advise you to—"

"I know what you advise me," Rachel interrupted. "But I'm not going to inform on anyone."

On the evening before Rachel was scheduled to appear before the jury, she and Jack went out for dinner. It was the only way they could be alone; people were always dropping in at their apartment, in fact a couple on their way to the West Coast were spending a few days there, and Jack wanted urgently to talk to Rachel, to talk very seriously to her.

They went to a cheap restaurant in Greektown, a brightly lit place with tables crowded together, small groups of Greek men eating and drinking noisily, a jammed, anonymous, rather pleasant place Jack liked. He felt that he had won a partial victory, just by getting Rachel out alone like this. And she hadn't told anyone she had been summoned, except Jack. She seemed cheerful, unnaturally cheerful, until halfway through the meal when she said suddenly, "I'm degraded by it. By what's going to happen. By tomorrow morning. . . ."

"Rachel, no. Jesus," Jack said.

"I can't . . . I can't surrender like that. . . . I might betray people we know. . . . I. . . ."

She had stopped eating. Jack stopped too and, very carefully, laid down his fork. His mind worked swiftly and cunningly to head her off. He said, "The grand jury has power to put you in jail, but it doesn't have much power, ultimately, to act on what you say. You'll see—when it's disbanded in a few months, they'll hand down only a few indictments, and of those indictments they'll get maybe one conviction, and that conviction will probably be overturned by a higher court. I can predict it. This has happened before. Don't you believe me?"

She stared at him. "But . . . just by appearing before them I'm acquiescing to their power. . . . I'm being degraded. . . . I. . . ."

Jack pushed his plate aside and lit a cigarette. He was trying to break himself of the habit of smoking—he smoked forty cigarettes a day, sometimes more—but that first inhalation of smoke was such a lovely experience, like a shot of adrenalin, that it seemed to him impossible to quit.

"Look, those bastards have power under the law, so you go and play their game with them," he said. He spoke carefully. "Otherwise they find you in contempt and you go to jail. You can't appeal it, you just go to jail—you go directly to jail, like in that kids' game. Right? No appeal, honey, and no lawyer. No counsel. You don't even have the First Amendment because they're granting you immunity. So you appear before them and answer their questions."

"I don't have to answer anyone's questions," Rachel said.

"Yes," Jack said carefully. "I realize that. I mean only this: the grand jury has a certain amount of power, and you have to recognize it. You don't have to respect it. Consider a child with a machine gun: you don't have to respect his power, but you have to recognize it."

"I don't have to recognize any power outside my own conscience," Rachel said.

Jack didn't look at her. He felt the opposition in her, her wall-like resistance to him. And it infuriated him, because he was accustomed to something quite different: even in his densest, most silent criminals, a respect that flowed into him seemed to feed him so he became more himself and therefore more able to save them. He was accustomed to desperate people, desperate needs. Almost, in them, there was a desire for him—the totality of his being, his soul, not simply his voice and the skillful grace of his intelligence.

"You really don't understand me," Rachel said stubbornly. She was waiting for him to look at her, to reply. "You think that keeping out of jail—keeping my body out of jail—is so very important to me, don't you? Everything is concrete to you, concrete blocks and sidewalks and buildings, all the types of confinement. . . . You don't really know how to talk to me any more. You did at one time. Why can't you talk to me? Is it because I'm not one of your guilty clients?"

Jack glanced at her in surprise. He felt the shock of her statement—but immediately he denied it. "It's because you have no political sense," he said.

"I don't? *I* don't? No political sense?" Rachel said.

"Politics is the manipulation of power, currents of power," Jack said coldly, in the voice he used in court to sum up and to dismiss his opposition's arguments, "and you and your friends don't know anything about it. You know how to talk. But politics is making things happen and not getting crushed in the process, or maybe *not getting caught*," he said contemptuously. "So you aren't guilty? So what? Do you think that matters?"

"Yes, it matters. It's the only thing that matters," Rachel said loudly.

"It doesn't matter at all. It's irrelevant."

"You aren't used to innocent people."

"I'm not used to self-destructive people."

"No, no," Rachel said wildly, almost happily, "no, you're used to people who are destructive of others—you can talk to them—you can understand them, can't you? You like them, don't you? You prefer them to innocent people—"

Jack pushed his plate a few inches to one side, then a few inches back. He realized it was important he keep very calm. It was true that he preferred guilty people, if the evidence against them wasn't overwhelming; they were pragmatic, they knew what might happen to them, what they deserved, and they gave themselves up to him entirely. No opposition, rarely much conversation at all. The innocent bored him. To win them an acquittal was really not much of an accomplishment—only what they deserved anyway, a turning of their dials back to zero. It was his wife's innocence he hated; he realized, smiling ironically, that he had been hating it for some time.

But when he turned to her his face showed nothing. He tried to smile at her, a husbandly smile; but her face was white with its stubborn, almost tactile opposition to him. Her dark brows looked heavy, ridged. He could see faint but apparently permanent lines in her forehead—so many years of frowning, of using her face! Only the innocent wore their faces out so quickly.

"You're upset about tomorrow morning," he said gently. "And you've been trying to do too much—you're out of the apartment about as much as I am, you don't even sleep as well as I do—and why the hell, honey, do so many people drop in? Those kids from the war committee? Don't they have anyone else to feed them except us? You're too generous, you try to do too much. . . . Right now we have people staying with us, for Christ's sake, I don't even know the Resnacks or where the hell you picked them up. . . ."

"They're both very good people, they're good friends of mine," Rachel said.

"Yes, all right," Jack said evenly. "But the fact is that you and I are forced out of our own apartment, so that we can discuss this problem of ours. Right? You try to befriend too many people, you even try to feed them—what's the point of it?"

"I want them around me, I need them, they need me and—"

"So you're exhausted most of the time?—and right now you're so emotional about this trivial grand jury, this ritual persecution the Republicans have dreamed up, you can't think straight. What's the point of it?"

"My friends mean a great deal to me," Rachel said angrily. "They're *my* friends. You don't have any. You don't give a damn about people, you're always daydreaming or planning or calculating, whatever goes on in your head, you don't even know me!"

"Rachel, look—"

"I'm sorry, Jack," she said. She drew her hands roughly and wearily across her face. "I shouldn't be saying these things when I'm so nervous. . . . I love you very much. I think I know you, from the inside, and I love you. But you don't really know me. I love you but it isn't enough for me. It's so private, it's so selfish. . . . Love . . . loving. . . . I need to be with other people, I need to work with them. We're doing a kind of work you can't understand. You can't respect it because it isn't organized, it's fragmented and haphazard and maybe futile. I need other people, I need to know there's a family of other people like myself, that the world isn't broken up into small selfish units of couples, of marriages. . . ."

"Then you don't love me," Jack said.

His voice was a surprise: almost a child's voice.

"Oh God, yes, I love you," Rachel said. "I don't think I could keep going without you . . . in spite of my work. . . . I'd go dead without you, I might not want to live. Before I met you, I . . . well, I wasn't. . . . I wasn't as self-sufficient as you might have thought, I. . . . But I. . . . But, Jack, please, I have to tell you the truth: it isn't enough for me, just our marriage. I need more. I feel . . . I feel a terrible hunger, a hunger . . . there's a part of my mind that doesn't belong to my body, to this particular body at all, but to the world of other people. And that part is always wanting things, always yearning for change, frustrated because it's so hard to change things, to remake the world. . . ."

Jack listened, dreading her words. He had been hearing these words or similar words for many years, he had been saying these things himself—of course he wanted to remake the world!—but until this moment he had never realized their meaning, not really. His wife was speaking quickly, urgently, her face pale with passion as if she were confessing a miraculous love—but it was a strange, foreign love, one he had not guessed at.

"I seem to want. . . . To want. . . . To want perpetually," she said.

He stared at her, bewildered. It seemed to him impossible to bring their conversation back to earth, back to the fact of the next day and the grand jury. . . . Part of his mind respected her, even feared her a little, but another part, Jack's usual self, had to resist a tremendous rage over her tense, pale, abstracted face. She would not listen to him, she *would not listen.* He was accustomed to clients who lied, sometimes clumsily and sometimes very cleverly, and he was accustomed to tracking them down, leading them through a maze of questions for hours, tirelessly, pursuing the truth that he knew did exist—sometimes he knew exactly what the truth was himself, before his client told him—but he was not used to this stubborn abstraction of what was a very simple issue, this insisting upon a seriousness the occasion did not justify. To his lying clients he kept saying, patiently, *I can't help you if you lie to me,* telling them this every few minutes as they stumbled and faltered and seemed to forget whole segments of their own histories. Then, when the truth was presented to him, he could reach in and pick it up and examine it, to see what kind of weapon it might make: maybe it would work, maybe not. But Rachel evaded him, seemed to defy him almost unconsciously. It had been so long—perhaps years—since they had talked like this, alone together, that Jack felt dismayed, as if he were trying to speak in a language he had nearly forgotten.

"If I didn't think we had a chance of . . . of modifying the country . . . of doing some good, some real good," Rachel said painfully, "I'd . . . I think I'd sink down, I'd just sink into death, into nothing. . . . But I know we're going to win."

"Going to win what?" Jack said with a smile. He took her hands and caressed them; they were thin, blue-veined hands, the nails filed down blunt and even. As a wedding band, Rachel wore a wide silver ring from Mexico, which was so large that it exaggerated the narrowness of her hand. It reached from her knuckle to the joint of her finger, and Jack found himself running his fingernail back and forth across it as if that hardness, that stubborn cool metal, were his wife's essential soul.

"The country," she said slowly. "The United States."

Jack nodded to show that he was sympathetic, he wasn't critical, he wasn't embarrassed at her words. But she seemed to sense his dismay. She drew her hands away from his self-consciously, and glanced up as if she'd forgotten where they were. Most of the tables were occupied now. A handsome, dark-faced man had even sat at their table with them, at a corner of their table, and he was drinking a glass of wine and pretending not to be eavesdropping on their conversation. Rachel stared at him with an odd, strained smile. Then a group of men at a long table burst into laughter and she looked around at them, almost longingly. They were all Greeks—swarthy-faced, lithe, white-shirted men whose ages Jack wouldn't have been able to gauge except to think, ironically, that they were more youthful than he and his wife.

Rachel turned back to Jack and lowered her voice. "I mean the country, the nation. It isn't Washington and it isn't any government, it isn't any men at all. It isn't artificial. It's an expanse of land . . . it's very beautiful, very open . . . it's our country and we've got to turn it around, to get going in another direction before it's too late. No one else seems to care except us . . . or maybe they can't see what is happening. . . . It's people like those men on the grand jury, they're murderous without knowing it, I mean they just don't *know*, they think people like us are the enemy, but. . . . I want to explain to them that . . . first of all . . . that we have to stop murdering. . . ."

"You won't be allowed to talk about those things," Jack said.

"I just have to answer their questions? I have to sit there, an adult human being, and answer only the questions they ask me?"

"Rachel, you're taking this much too seriously. It's only a county grand jury and—"

"It is important, it is very important," Rachel said, emphasizing each word equally. "Look at Larry's client, that kid—he's in for *fifteen years*, Jack, for some damn little drug conviction. You know that. But it's really because of his attitude toward the war—isn't it?—you know it is! That other kid, Dawe, that we met one night, the police are always harassing him, what about him? He's a really good person, almost a saint, and they're making life miserable for him, and nobody gives a damn—"

"Who's Dawe? I don't remember Dawe," Jack said.

"It isn't important, that isn't the point," Rachel said. "The point is what you explained in your letter to the newspaper—you said it all, and very well—they're just going to use the threat of drug arrests and long sentences to shut us all up, about the war or about anything—but then we shouldn't cooperate with them, it's immoral for someone like myself to acquiesce—"

"Don't use that word *acquiesce*," Jack said, with an irritated laugh, "and maybe you won't have such a tough time. It's your vocabulary that is boxing you in."

Rachel laughed also. "My poor, good husband. . . . You're more afraid of this than I am, aren't you? You're really a lawyer, a man of the law, an officer of the court. That's your first loyalty."

"The hell it is," Jack said.

"Yes."

"My first loyalty is you and me," Jack said.

"No, you believe in the law. You really do. It's like any arena where a game takes place—a football game, a baseball game—and when the game is in session you believe in all the rules, every sub-heading and footnote in the rule book. You'd never violate a rule. And outside the arena, outside the game—you don't give a damn, do you? In a court of law you believe in law. Fifty million pages of transcripts. A billion pages. To the moon and back, all the tedious crap of the law, English law, precedents, whatever you people claim to worship. . . . I think it's because you believe only in yourself, you're just an isolated person, Jack, a cynic."

"That isn't true," Jack said, startled.

"It wasn't true a few years ago," Rachel said. She spoke seriously, as if passing judgment on him; as if the judgment were being forced from her. "You weren't cynical when we first met. I think you were as enthusiastic as I was, I think in those days you would have supported me in this. . . ."

"I would not have supported you," Jack said. "I've never been naïve."

"I admired you so much, Jack . . . I still do. . . . You're still doing important work, good work, I don't mean that you're selling out . . . not for money, but . . . but. . . . You're getting a reputation now and you could have a much greater influence than you do, but. . . . These cases are so isolated, these victories of yours. . . . I think you like to fight, but just for yourself."

"Look, Rachel—"

"Don't interrupt me, please. You're always interrupting me."

"Am I?" Jack said angrily. "Am I really? Always interrupting you?"

"You're always interrupting everyone," Rachel said.

Jack made a gesture of impatience. He lit another cigarette while she continued in her slow, thoughtful, almost reluctant voice, as if these truths were being forced out of her: "I love you, Jack, and I want you to be a good person. I want you to be worth what people tend to feel about you, not just me but other people . . . they do admire you . . . and it's important for you to justify—"

"Why are we talking about *me,* why not about *you?*" Jack said. "I don't understand this."

"Don't interrupt, don't change the subject, please. We're talking about both of us. And the future. Because if people like you and me don't get ourselves in order, don't know what they're doing . . . there will be no one else. . . . I know you've done very well, Jack, everyone knows it. But you like the system as it is. You don't really want to change it. This country is a cesspool, you know how rotten it is from top to bottom. . . . Maybe at one time in history, before the government stepped up the war, maybe then people like you could help, as individuals, inside the law, but not now. . . ."

"Oh for Christ's sake—"

"The law itself is rotten. You know that. You're just a pimp for it, Jack, aren't you? You're running around down in the arena and you love it, because you know all the plays, you've memorized all the strategies, and you can run fast, and you're invisible—you love it, don't you? Isn't this the truth you won't admit to yourself?"

"Shut up," Jack said.

"Don't worry, I'll go and appear before your jury. I will."

"It isn't my jury!"

"Yes, you defend it. Really, you defend it. You would defend it, in the end, against me and . . . and against the people who really want to turn this country around. . . . Because you believe in the law, and you don't want to admit that the law is dead. It's dead. It's dessicated, rotten, dead."

"Oh, it's dead, is it? Dead? You think so?"

"I know. Its moral power is dead. A lot of machine guns and electrified fences and people filed away on microfilm—that's all—but it has no moral power, no strength. No, it's dead. The new generation—"

"The new generation," Jack said, sneering, "is a lot of shit! There isn't any *new generation!* There is never any *new generation!* It's just the same people used over and over again—there's nothing new about them!"

"You're so angry, I must be telling the truth," Rachel said slowly. "I must be really upsetting you. You don't get like this in court, do you?—you're very efficient and civilized there, aren't you, because nothing important ever gets said. You're looking at me as if you'd like to—"

"People are listening," Jack said. "Let's get out of here."

"I don't mind people listening."

"Well, I do."

"No, you like an audience, really—you like people to listen to you—if you can get the last word—"

"Look, Rachel, you're upset about the hearings, right? So—"

"Yes, I'm upset, yes, about that and about a lot of things," she said. Her face was still pale and very tense. She said carefully, deliberately, "Do you know what our friends say about us?—about you? They say that you're jealous of me."

Jack was stunned. "I'm what?"

She nodded emphatically.

"Jealous of you? Why the hell should I be jealous of you?"

"Because . . . because of my freedom . . . because of my work."

Jack wanted to laugh, he was so surprised and so angry.

"Oh, your freedom?" he said mockingly.

"Yes. You wouldn't dare do what I do."

"Wouldn't I? Do our friends say that? But you told me I didn't have any friends—they're all *yours*—and who are they, precisely, who are these people who know so much about me?"

"I wouldn't tell you because you'd hate them, you'd turn against them," Rachel said. "And they would suffer from it, because they do admire you . . . they're afraid of you. . . ."

Jack couldn't stand it any longer; he got to his feet. His body seemed to be pulsating, surging, with the wonderful elation he felt in court, after the first half-minute when his voice sometimes faltered, when he realized that he might fail . . . but that he wouldn't fail. Rachel looked up at him without flinching. She said, "I'm sorry, I shouldn't have said all these things . . . I didn't mean to hurt you. . . ."

Yet her manner was not apologetic. And this infuriated him all the more.

"Didn't mean to hurt me? *Me?* What makes you think you've hurt me?"

"I wanted to tell you certain facts, certain truths, because I love you and I want to respect you—"

"You love me? Good, fine. And so what?"

"—I want to respect you—"

"No, you want to be superior to me, you and your damn friends—sitting around bitching while I work my ass off—you like to praise one another, you're all so saintly, aren't you? And you, Rachel Morrissey, turning into a mother for them, aren't you, a tribal mother?—cooking them food, listening to them and their fantasies—and how they all love you, how they crowd around you! And the kids get younger every year, don't they? And they do praise you, at least to your face, and you can all sit around congratulating yourselves for being outside the system, for not having jobs, for going to jail, you can all say, *Jack Morrissey would never do what we're doing, he would never violate the law—*"

Rachel shook her head slowly. "You're not going to make me hate you," she said.

"Go to hell, then! Get yourself in contempt, go to jail, be a martyr, go to hell!"

Jack pushed his way around the table, conscious of people looking at him. He walked out.

On the sidewalk outside he collided with a young man who was with a girl and another couple. The young man stepped back, surprised, coming to rest heavily on his heels. "Mister, watch out—"

"Go fuck yourself," Jack said.

He walked away.

He thought: *She can't make me hate her either.*

He kept walking, not knowing where he was. He walked out of the block or two of Greek restaurants and stores, into a darkened side street. Now his head hammered! He would have liked to rip out someone's throat. He felt white-hot and sickish, as if he were waiting out those long terrible hours while a jury was deliberating, his fate out of his own control, horribly beyond his own powers. Vomiting would help, to get the pressure down; but he couldn't vomit out on the street. Sometimes, awaiting a verdict, he would force himself to vomit, emptying out his stomach. It did him good. It really did him good. But he couldn't vomit here, like this, he had to keep walking. . . . His anger passed over into frustration, and the frustration into a sexual rage. . . .

Then he was thinking of someone, a woman: a face. He was thinking of Marvin Howe's wife.

It was a face he hadn't thought of for months. Blank as the blankest wall; a face that had to be imagined, it was so unreal. He had not thought of the woman for months. One day he had leafed restlessly through the morning paper, looking for something to distract him, not knowing what he wanted, and on the Women's Page he saw her photograph: *My God,* he thought, *there she is.* And he had felt the sickness of shame, of defeat, a nameless inexplicable failure.

Elena Howe (Mrs. Marvin Howe), here photographed in her Grosse Pointe home, says her duties as the wife of a famous criminal lawyer are challenging and refreshing. Asked what it is like to live with the much-sought-after Marvin Howe, Mrs. Howe replied that each day was a wonderful adventure and that she tried to keep pace with. . . .

Jack had thrown the paper down in disgust. But he remembered all the words.

"Oh what crap, what obscene inhuman crap!" he had said.

But he remembered the words, and he remembered the face—just an oval there in the newspaper, a miracle of tiny dots printed on cheap paper pulp. He remembered. He felt sick, ashamed, his mind skittered back from this darkened street, past Rachel, back to Howe's wife, to the woman sitting in the classroom.

He remembered it all, the woman and her face, even the words in the newspaper. It disgusted him, that he should remember.

He didn't hate his wife, Rachel; he hated someone else's wife. It was not himself he hated, but another man. He had hated Marvin Howe for years. He did hate these people and it was right of him to hate them, because they were legitimate enemies. He did not wish them dead—not quite. And yet if he had seen that photograph of Elena Howe on the front page, if the caption had told of her having been raped and strangled, "the unsolved homicide of the year," he would not have been saddened, maybe. . . .

By the time he got home it was after three o'clock. Rachel was waiting for him; they embraced, wearily, sadly. They did not hate each other. Jack did not hate her. He would love her the rest of his life.

17

Several people were sentenced to jail for refusing to cooperate with the grand jury, but only one of them was anyone Jack knew—and it wasn't his wife, but a young black girl who allegedly spat into the face of the jury's foreman, a retired university president and a one-time Air Force hero. The Morrisseys attended a party for the girl, whom they didn't know well and really didn't like, and Jack noticed with pity his wife's hectic, overheated face as she talked with guests that evening—there seemed in Rachel something she must say, get said and registered, but she never really discovered it, never managed to express it.

After she had appeared before the jury, she came to Jack's office and said: "It's over. I got through. It's finished." And she smiled at him nervously, rather mockingly, putting out her hands toward him as if to show they weren't soiled—or were soiled—Jack didn't know, he was so relieved to see her.

He didn't ask her what had happened, what questions had been put to her; he knew better. And Rachel said nothing either. He believed the jurors had asked her questions she could answer by saying she didn't know, she hadn't that kind of information, and so she had been dismissed as a witness. . . . But he didn't know what had happened and he never asked.

Or maybe she had lied. But he didn't want to know about it.

You are an isolated person, a cynic. He knew that wasn't true, but he kept thinking it, hearing the words not in his wife's voice but in his own voice, trapped inside his head. He didn't want isolation. His life was a life of busyness, of other people, of shouting and plotting and worrying, and rejoicing too, in a very public way; it couldn't be true that, inside all this motion, this perpetual motion, he was really isolated. And he didn't want the dead-end economy of cynicism; he detested the several cynical men he knew, lawyers like himself, though older, their eyes yellowish as if with tobacco stains, like their fingers, their own lives of perpetual motion running them round and round inside the same spaces.

Recoiling from them, Jack tried to spend more time with Rachel's friends: he tried not to argue with them, tried to give them advice, to act out the role of the slightly more knowledgeable, more clever revolutionary. Because they were always talking about *revolution*—using that word—and while Jack thought secretly that they didn't know what the hell they were talking about—they were using this word and others like kindergarten alphabet blocks, just to touch and play around with and share with one another—he knew someone had to listen seriously to them. All the young men on the Michigan United Against the War committee had had indictments handed down to them, charged with violating the drug law, and Jack volunteered to take them on for no fee. This was partly to please Rachel; partly because Jack knew they were in for trouble and required an attorney who would not get them into more trouble. He kept advising them on which words to use when they spoke in public, *which precise words to use,* so that they would not be guilty of more violations . . . but they kept forgetting, as if to display to Jack their primitive, uncunning virtue, to display to Jack how much better they were, really, than Jack himself.

What did it matter? What the hell, Jack thought, even if they were self-righteous noisy bastards, somebody had to represent them.

But a kind of poison passed over into him—from them or from something in the air of Detroit itself. He did not understand it. He hadn't time to think of it, being too busy for theories. . . . Sometimes he could almost taste it, the air of fighting, of combative sizing-up and measuring and testing, constant testing; not just in the courts but out on the streets, people glancing at one another, men and women, whites and blacks, those long-haired slovenly kids who sat on the sidewalks around his office building, a few blocks from the University. It was a mysterious thing, this poisonous air: egos raw, cold, the friction of their coming-together a kind of monstrous caress, human contact gone wild. He tried not to think about it. He wanted to like the people he defended, he wanted to like all people, really. Otherwise the world was hell; all lives were hell, and no one could save him. He might save others, but no one could save him.

But he rarely thought about this, it was not a clear "thought" to him at all, only a mood. The harder he worked, the less he felt this mood. And that was good. That was the meaning of his life. So he rushed along, headed for the middle years of his life, a youthful, lean, dark-haired man of average height, with lines in his forehead that were beginning not to fade; dark-eyed, sometimes squinting, frowning, very animated, articulate, argumentative, very charming.

One day in April Jack was walking downtown, headed for the parking lot near the river where he had left his car, when he happened to catch sight of a woman who looked familiar.

He was feeling good, almost elated. He had just come from a hearing in which he had demanded to have the right to examine the grand jury's entire minutes—all the evidence, the photographs and documents, the statements of various witnesses, even the names and addresses of the witnesses—and while he had supposed most of his motions would be denied, now it looked to him that he had a better chance; the District Attorney's assistant, assigned to this case, had seemed rather uneasy. His name was Tyburn and Jack wasn't worried about him. He was Jack's age. The "drug offense" case that most interested Jack, the defense of Meredith Dawe, seemed to be propped up entirely on the testimony of a police agent, a young man who had befriended Dawe and who had even lived in the same house with him before "witnessing" a certain "violation of the Public Health Law". . . . Jack thought this was outrageous, this was really incredible; certainly he would argue entrapment and win an acquittal for Dawe, whom he didn't much like—Dawe was one of Rachel's young acquaintances—and it excited him to have so incredibly clumsy an opposition. The District Attorney's office would probably be forced to drop the charges against Dawe, but if they didn't it might work out even better for Jack: because this case could receive a great deal of publicity and might work to modify the drug laws. It would certainly publicize the dubious morality of police undercover work, the careful arrangement of "crimes," "criminals," and "witnesses," and Jack could make quite an issue of that, once he got going; he despised the police.

Maybe the old-fashioned Marxists and the newer, less articulate revolutionaries were right, he thought: it was to the advantage of the people, and of history itself, when the established ruling classes became so deranged and reckless, charmed by their own omnipotence, that they allowed their most primitive representatives to do outrageous things, to create almost theatrical situations that made their evil so obvious that anyone would understand. . . . Jack, who had always argued against his Marxist friends, and his pseudo-Marxist pseudo-Revolutionary friends, did believe that there was a point in history, an almost exquisitely subtle, balanced point between two directions, when a single event can tip the scales and alter everything. And how he would have loved to be there, and to recognize that moment, and to very deliberately bring his fist down on one side, the side of justice, and to alter history!—to alter the entire universe!

Such thoughts elated him so much, he felt almost intoxicated with a sense of his own privilege—he knew he was doing well in his profession, and he believed his profession ruled the world. Anything could happen. He might someday find himself standing there, the unknown Morrissey, a poorly paid, poorly connected man from Detroit, with an undistinguished law school behind him—standing there at just the right moment in history —and then—

He walked quickly along, his eyes fastened to the sidewalk while his mind raced. He hardly knew where he was. His next appointment wasn't until three o'clock—an appointment with an eye doctor on McNichols, which he had been postponing for months. But today he would go through with it. He felt lucky today; he could absorb any bad news today.

He happened to glance up and saw a woman across the street.

She was crossing toward him. Everything between her and Jack was movement, motion: an unco-ordinated stream of traffic, stops and starts, the blaring of horns. The woman walked toward him, slowly, not hurried by the impatience of the drivers around her or not aware of them; she seemed to be looking at Jack or through him at something behind him, not seeing him at all. It was Marvin Howe's wife, a woman absolutely familiar to Jack.

There she was.

His first instinct was to step back, so that she wouldn't see him. But she didn't know him, there would be no danger. So he stood by the curb, watching her, beginning to smile . . . yes, like that, like that, he thought, *come right to me.* Evidently she was coming from a drab, dirty little park, really just a square of pavement in the middle of several busy streets: a few benches there, a monument no one ever looked at. Jack wondered what she had been doing over there. In all his years of living in Detroit he had probably never walked across that square, had never bothered with it. As far as he could see there were only bums sitting on the benches, and the sidewalks were littered. Yet the woman appeared as if out of nowhere, dressed in white, that blond hair piled on top of her head, her face perfectly composed, confident, empty, almost glowing. She might have just turned aside from something or someone that had pleased her very much.

She stepped up onto the curb only a foot or so from him, not noticing him. Her coat brushed against the edge of his shabby briefcase.

Jack, feeling invisible, turned to watch her. He pivoted slowly on his heels to watch her walk into the crowd. From a record shop nearby a record was blaring, all drums and shrieks. Jack saw how the woman carried herself into that, without flinching. It was the kind of music that drove Jack wild, he hated it so, but Mrs. Howe didn't seem to notice it. A small gang of black kids swarmed around her, passing her, three on her left side and two on her right, running by on their way somewhere, but if they frightened her Jack couldn't tell . . . then he noticed a white man shuffling toward her, a bum in a frayed overcoat. This man had a plum-colored face. When he caught sight of Mrs. Howe he nearly stopped—he stared at her openmouthed. Jack, alert now, watched the two of them, the man with his eyes narrowed almost to slits, deliberately walking into the woman—ah, like that! Then he seemed to apologize, he looked very excited and shamefaced, and yet he was grinning at her. . . .

But she didn't seem to notice.

Nothing happened, she only nodded as if accepting his apologies, and passed on by. The man stared after her.

She headed down Woodward, toward the river. Jack happened to be walking in the same direction; his car was parked in one of the cheaper lots near the river. He was able to keep Mrs. Howe in sight easily, the white coat and the blond hair . . . he began to feel the tingling excitement of a spy, a hunter. The people between himself and that woman, the noise of trucks and buses and cars, all this commotion was like music, the background of something, a little distracting but somehow necessary. It was the world itself, so much noise! He felt very good.

Following her, not hurrying, not having to hurry, he felt his strange good luck. He was detached, an observer. She meant nothing to him and yet he needed to keep her in sight; she must have been headed for one of the important buildings at the foot of the avenue, and in a few minutes she would disappear, but he felt the need now, an almost superstitious need, to keep her in sight. Yet he was impersonal, detached; a stranger. He knew her but she wouldn't have known him. He felt his face to be a stranger's face, closed and cunning.

Howe was notorious for using private investigators, detectives, to do much of his work for him. Jack knew nothing about that kind of person; he had never even met a private detective himself. Now he wondered if their jobs were like this: following beautiful women, keeping them very easily in sight. It was such an overestimation of the individual, a sick, rotten exaggeration of anyone's value!—and yet Jack could imagine himself in a detective's role, in the role of an impersonal hunter, following this woman and thinking impersonal thoughts, thoughts that belonged not to any single man but to the race, the species: to men. She might be on her way to meet someone—a lover. And she would be spied upon, she would be filmed, recorded with great care, every instant in her life transformed into a kind of history, almost a work of art, simply by being so scrupulously observed. . . .

Jack thought: *She doesn't know me.*

He thought: *I'm invisible to her.*

As he kept her in sight he had to maneuver around other people, pedestrians, without taking the trouble to look at them. He didn't want to lose sight of her. He began to think about Marvin Howe and his blood quickened with hatred.

He followed her for several blocks until she stopped in front of the City-County Building. It was handsome, a high-rise building that looked out of place; just across the street was the riverfront, some old, low-lying buildings, and the lot Jack's car was parked in. Jack saw that the woman was looking at something—a statue—a thing Jack had never bothered to look at himself, though he had been in and out of this building hundreds of times. Art didn't interest him, especially art that was not verbal; he really did not see it. He didn't have time for it.

Mrs. Howe was staring at the statue—a hunk of metal that was meant to be a man, a gigantic man, holding something in his hands. Jack only glanced at it, dismissed it, and then paused to watch Mrs. Howe. He felt the odd prickling excitement of combat, of a good fight; the way he often felt in court. For some reason he felt very lean, trim, confident. How he liked himself at these times!

At these times he knew exactly who he was.

He half expected Howe's wife to turn toward him, to glance over her shoulder. And then he would look coldly away. He would walk away. But she didn't move, she didn't even seem aware of him. She was examining the statue. Puzzled, a little irritated, Jack looked at it again—just a liver-colored hunk of metal, the exaggerated figure of a man, an allegorical representation of something Jack had no interest in and couldn't force himself to study. With that woman there, that beautiful woman, how could he force himself to look at a statue . . . ?

A minute passed.

Other men walked by, most of them in a hurry. One or two glanced at Mrs. Howe but didn't pause. Jack wondered if she were waiting here for someone; for Howe himself?

He looked at his watch: 2:27.

He walked by her, very close to her. His gaze became oblique and graceful, sliding sideways as he passed, like the thinnest, finest slicing of a knife. How good he felt! His body was keen, tense, excited. As he passed Mrs. Howe he was pleased to see that she was exactly as he had imagined, the same face . . . except she looked younger than he had remembered, not quite so confident. She was a few inches shorter than Jack; good, he liked that.

She would do.

You'll do, he thought, ironically; but she didn't notice him. She didn't seem to notice anything.

Jack walked by her and didn't look back. At the next intersection he waited for the lights to change and checked his watch—almost 2:30 and he would have to fight traffic all the way up to McNichols. He would be late for his appointment with the eye doctor. For some time now his eyes had been aching, the left eye seemed to tug, it worried him and yet he didn't give a damn, he'd been breaking and postponing appointments for nearly a year. . . . Then it occurred to him that he should make sure the appointment was for three o'clock. So he set down his briefcase and searched through his pockets. He found a slip of paper, folded over many times, but it wasn't anything important; he knew he had the doctor's card somewhere, stuck in somewhere, but he couldn't find it. . . .

He happened to look back, toward Mrs. Howe. He saw with surprise that she was still standing in front of the statue.

What was wrong . . . ?

Was something wrong . . . ?

He searched through his pockets and found the doctor's appointment card—yes, it was for the 12th of April, yes, for three o'clock. But he put it absent-mindedly away again. He was staring back at Mrs. Howe, a half-block away, standing there in a kind of island inside a flow of pedestrians, immobile, peaceful, as if asleep on her feet.

He grabbed his briefcase and walked back to her.

It excited him, the way her face came into focus as he approached: yes, that face, that face exactly. But she was completely unaware of him. He could stare at her, bluntly, rudely, and she would not notice. It was the same face he had seen in the classroom, the face in the newspaper photograph, the face in his stray, bewildering flashes of memory, no mistake about it; no change in her. *There she was.* And she was waiting for him. But unaware of him. Waiting and yet unaware, asleep on her feet, just standing there on the sidewalk. . . . Her face was whiter than he remembered. It was almost ugly, the skin so drained, so white. Dead-white. Her lips, in that face, looked violet, faintly flesh-toned, like the lips of a corpse. . . . He shuddered, staring at her. He felt almost an aesthetic revulsion, seeing her, she was so extreme; she made him think abruptly of the time he had had to come to the county morgue to identify a client of his, drowned and fished out of the river and laid onto a porcelain table. . . .

He passed by her again, very close to her, only a few inches away. He wanted to touch her, just lightly, with his elbow . . .

to see if she would turn angrily. But no. He was afraid to touch her. So he walked by and then stopped. A few feet away. He was looking at the side of her face. Her expression was composed, peaceful; perfect. A vacuum protected her. An invisible bell jar protected her. Jack was bewildered: he had never seen a woman so oblivious to everything around her.

If he shouted at her . . . ? Struck her with his fist, maybe on the shoulder . . . ? He wanted most of all to grab her by the back of the neck, that lovely neck, and give her a shake. He could make her teeth rattle. He could loosen her hair, those thick exaggerated coils of hair, wrapped around her head like a crown . . . fastened with pins he couldn't see but could only guess at, an elaborate secret maze of pins that held everything inside that vacuum in place. Could shake it all loose, shake her loose. . . .

You, he wanted to say, laughing, *you, what's wrong? Are you sick? Paralyzed? Hypnotized?*

It was an insult to him, her complete isolation: she seemed protected from him by her very blankness, the neutrality of her being. He wondered if anyone was watching the two of them. He, Jack, had now come into the range of someone's scrutiny, perhaps. If Mrs. Howe was being watched. An invisible camera might be recording everything, every helpless moment. . . .

Then it occurred to Jack that there really was something wrong with her.

He saw the dead-white skin, the parted lips, the large, frozen, unreadable eyes. Startled, he saw her for the first time. He saw that she was trapped in a kind of stasis, an absolute immobility, like a statue herself. He had the right now to touch her. "Mrs. Howe . . . ?" he said. He touched her arm.

All his senses rushed, rushed together. He felt a wild beating somewhere in his face, centered about his eyes. A heartbeat in his eyes.

"Mrs. Howe . . . ?"

She didn't hear him.

His hand brushed against hers. His fingers on her arm. Gingerly, fearfully, his fingers half-closing about her arm. . . . But she stood there, staring past him, into space; looking drugged, vacuous, dead-white. She was very young. Young-looking. Her face was stricken with a peaceful, perfect sorrow, something unreadable to Jack. He had never experienced anything like that himself.

He cleared his throat. He would be normal, normal-sounding. "Mrs. Howe . . . ?"

PART THREE

Crime

I

I brought the tip of the knife against my wrist . . . just the tip . . . it was a small paring knife with a wooden handle, very light. The sensation was like that, like this, too gentle to be painful.

I watched to see what the knife would do to me. It pressed in so that my skin gave way in a little wrinkle, a little fold, and then suddenly there was a giving-way and then a drop of blood. Then another. The blood was very bright, red, very real. . . .

It fell into the sink, onto the things I had been preparing—vegetables—I think they were potatoes, smelling raw and fresh—I felt very dizzy but very happy.

There, eat that! Eat that and let me alone!

I was fourteen years old.

After a few minutes I stopped the bleeding with a cloth, and I washed the potatoes off. But I never forgot that pinprick sharp as a flash of light: freedom.

Someone was touching her, speaking to her.

She stared up at a man's tense face—a stranger who was talking to her, pronouncing that name: *Mrs. Howe.*

"Mrs. Howe . . . ?"

With his thumb and forefinger, very deliberately, definitely, he was holding her wrist and even tugging at it slightly, as if to wake her.

He was a stranger; a dark, swarthy face, a surprise to her. He was saying something in an earnest voice. Elena stared at him, not understanding. Then she felt herself rise slowly, slowly, through a kind of density, a space of thickened air that might have suffocated her, but then she was awake and breathing normally and she was able to answer him: "What do you want? What . . . what's wrong?"

Her voice was sluggish, as if she had just wakened from sleep.

But it was her voice.

"Mrs. Howe? Are you all right?"

She couldn't understand what was wrong, why this man was standing so close to her. She drew away from him. "I am Mrs. Howe," she said slowly, still in that drugged, rather hollow voice. The man was staring at her: a frowning face, showing perplexity. She began to realize that she had appeared strange to him, that something in her manner or her behavior wasn't normal, and this had drawn him to her, it had attracted the attention of a stranger. Immediately she felt embarrassed and blood rushed into her face, warming it. She tried to laugh. "I'm sorry," she said. "What . . . what was I doing . . . ? Was I . . . ? I'm all right now. I feel all right now."

The man was watching her, curiously, bluntly, as if not quite believing her or not listening to her. He was not a friend of hers. She had never seen him before.

A second wave of dizziness rose in her, almost overpowering her.

"Help me, don't let me—"

When you went under . . . ?

Nothing.

No fear?

No.

No? And what about time, time passing?

No time passed.

No time . . . ?

I went into peace and then I woke and it was later, time had gone by, people had walked by me. I had gone into stone like the statue in front of me: I had gone into peace.

You weren't terrified?

Oh no.

But when you woke . . . ?

Then I came back, I was frightened . . . I . . . I had to be myself again. The other was peace and now I had to live again, I had to come back to myself again in the world and live. . . .

Elena turned away as if to walk somewhere, carrying the dizziness with her. She didn't want the man to see her. But he said, "Mrs. Howe, wait–" He followed her. She was forcing herself to breathe slowly and deeply, the old trick to keep panic down; but it made her dizzy, such quantities of air. The air was chilly and yet stale, used-up air, the insides of a great city. The man was saying something to her. She didn't hear his words but she heard something in his voice, it was very familiar, almost bullying, she heard something that was mocking her. But people did not talk to her that way, not now. So she must be mistaken. Her mother had talked to her like that but now no one did. "Wait," he said, "you look as if you're going to faint. You must be sick . . . ? What's wrong with you?"

"No, I'm all right," she said vaguely, politely. She tried to smile at him without looking at him.

"I don't believe you," he said at once, bluntly.

Elena saw that he was carrying a briefcase. Her gaze moved slowly and reluctantly up his body, a man's ordinary anonymous body, and then seemed to dissolve as it reached his face: she didn't want to see him again, not that rude knowing familiar stare. She tried to laugh.

"You don't look right to me, you look very pale," he said. "You look like hell, frankly."

Elena's lips froze in a half-smile and she said nothing.

"I'll drive you home," the man said.

"No, I'm–"

"I'd better. Come on."

"No, I–I can– I can go to my husband's office and–"

"He wouldn't be there, not at this time of day," the man said. "Come on, I'm in a hurry myself. Come on."

"I can get home by myself," Elena said faintly. "A taxi—"

"No, come on," he said. He looked at his watch and then at her, with a gesture of impatience. Elena had the peculiar, alarming idea that she was supposed to know this man well; that there was a kind of intimacy between them, an agreement; but she couldn't understand it. It was like a trick mirror: from one side it appeared to be a mirror, from the other side it was transparent. The man was watching her through the mirror, knowing something she did not know. He had seized her wrist again, he was tugging at it. Why was he touching her? She wanted to laugh again, to laugh him away.

"I said I was in a hurry myself, I have an appointment somewhere in twenty minutes," he said. "Come on. This place is crowded, it's busy, people are going to bump into you. You still look sick to me. I'll do your husband a favor and drop you off at home. . . . Come on."

"Do you know my husband?" Elena asked doubtfully.

He gripped her arm and began walking her somewhere.

I watched to see what the knife would do. I was going to be surprised.

You didn't try for the vein . . . ?

No. The knife didn't try for the vein.

Now there's no scar. No memory.

No, it was only a scratch. I washed the blood away and wrapped something around it and held the vegetables under the faucet to clean them and then I prepared dinner and we ate, like any evening.

You were fourteen years old?

The first time. But the second time I was twenty-five . . . maybe twenty-six. . . . The vegetables weren't potatoes; I think they were mushrooms and slices of eggplant. We ate them. It was like any evening.

He walked her across the boulevard, gripping her by the arm, and she thought: He's one of Marvin's friends. But he hadn't the tone, the style, of her husband's friends; not the friends she was allowed to meet. His clothes were cheap. The briefcase was shabby, an embarrassment. Elena thought, panicked, that someone who knew her would see her with this man, this man and his briefcase. . . .

He kept talking, herding and driving her with his voice. He was explaining why his car was parked down by the river; half apologetic, half defensive. She couldn't follow everything he said because the tone of his voice, its constant nervous mockery, confused her. People did not talk like that to her. "Watch out for the sidewalk along here, it's broken up," he said. "Don't you see where we're walking? Jesus, this city is disintegrating beneath our feet! If I had known I'd be driving you home like this, I would have parked closer—but I can't foresee everything— I hope you don't mind."

He was so ironic that she said nothing. She stumbled and he held her upright, steadying her.

"Why do you wear shoes like that? You can't walk in them, can you? What is the point of it? Or are you still dizzy?"

"No, I'm—"

"There's my car," he said. He led her halfway across a muddy parking lot, between rows of parked cars; the black attendant approached them from another direction, making his way between parked cars; Elena took all this in, could not understand what she was doing here, walking in the mud. Her senses were alert now, almost raw with alertness, but baffled. The car they came to was low-slung as if weary, one fender almost touching the ground. Mud was splattered everywhere on it, but in layers, the thickest layer along the side. While the man paid the attendant, reaching in his pocket for change, then reaching in again for more change, Elena stared at the car as if this too were something she should recognize. There were several parking-lot tickets stuck beneath the windshield wipers, from other days. She knew now that this man was not a friend of her husband's.

He opened the door for her. "It opens. The door opens. It is a normal door, even a woman like yourself could open it, it won't fall off onto your feet," he said.

"I'm sorry, I—"

"Get in, please," he laughed. He seemed suddenly cheerful. "You're accustomed to people opening doors for you, right?—it's a conditioned reflex in people who are in your vicinity, I suppose."

He slammed the door after her.

He maneuvered the car out of the lot, through a narrow space between two cars, bumping along, one side of the car scraping against the ground, until he got out onto the street. "Jesus, this city," he muttered. Elena saw that he was turning in the right direction on Jefferson; as if he knew where she lived. Now that he was driving he seemed less aware of her, more concerned with the problems of getting from one lane into another. He was headed for the fast-moving left lane and it took quite a while to get there. Instead of using his rear-view mirror, he kept turning to look over his shoulder, impatiently, and she heard him muttering about the traffic or about the city, a steady half-joking series of complaints. "Look at this bastard trying to cut me out," he said. "What the hell . . . ?"

She thought she would not listen to him, she would not watch what was happening. Instead, she would relax, thinking: *I am safe, nothing is going to happen to me.* Behind her was something she could not quite remember, couldn't get into focus. A suspension, a mystery. And on the other side of that, as if in another era, in another dimension, the Detroit Athletic Club and the luncheon, the Mentally Handicapped Children's Fund, the vomiting of Judge Couteau's wife . . . all the women, the room of women, eating and talking and laughing so happily. . . .

She relaxed. She always relaxed when she was being driven somewhere; she had never learned how to drive herself, and so she paid no attention to it. It was not her concern. The openings and closings of traffic, the cars that moved so quickly and so decisively, changing lanes in order to get the best advantage, did not concern her.

Driving absorbed the man who sat beside her, drew his attention out and away from her. She could relax. Try to relax. Behind her was a gap, an opening like a chasm—she had not fallen into it, she was safe from it—and now someone was taking her home, safely home. She did not have to think about the process of getting there. She had only to sit here, in a vehicle being maneuvered skillfully in and out of lanes of traffic, in a more familiar kind of suspension that would take her home. She was headed home. *Home.*

An exciting contest was taking place, in fact dozens of contests, right outside the car—men jockeying for position, men who couldn't see one another but sensed the presence, the power, of other men; yet everything moved smoothly, a miracle of cooperation and agility, like a river gone mad and carrying debris furiously along, snatching at its banks, yet rushing forward without hesitation, with immense power and majesty. Elena still felt dizzy but she had only to close her eyes and be safe. Yet she couldn't force her eyes to close. She stared ahead at the lanes of traffic, which moved jerkily but in rhythm, not colliding in spite of their differing speeds; a current of fast-moving objects that came to abrupt stops, then started again, breaking free of one another and easing around one another, heavy and rattling with danger and yet never hitting, never colliding. There was a peculiar grace everywhere, even in the bulkiest of trucks; it must have been the grace of the driver, his clever calculating soul. You could imagine the soul of each driver, inside each car: a kind of miracle.

The man beside her sounded his horn.

A gap opened between two cars magically, and their car was allowed in. Otherwise they might have collided with something just ahead. Elena saw this without alarm, sitting relaxed, almost limp; exhausted. The man beside her muttered something—meant to be a joke—but Elena didn't understand and did not reply.

They were driving east on Jefferson, out of the city. He said suddenly: "You looked paralyzed back there. Standing there. I've never seen anyone go into a trance before—what happened? What did it feel like?"

Elena hesitated. She did not want to answer him because she feared his curiosity, his aggressive tone. And she did not want to give him access to her.

"I don't know. Nothing," she said.

He looked at her, a sideways glance. For a while he said nothing. Elena believed she could hear him speaking, though, in that same ironic, half-mocking voice, words racing through his head. She felt how busy, how noisy he was inside his silence. She thought she must say something, she must talk the way she did to people at parties or luncheons, she must break the silence that allowed for such secret conversations; especially in the presence of men, she feared this silence. But she could not think of anything to say.

When they approached Marvin's house, Elena put her hand up as if to caution him to slow down, and he said at once, "Yes, I know you live here." They were passing the wall that surrounded the house on three sides—a quarter of a mile of granite, blocking the estate from view. At the driveway, the wrought-iron gates were open. Before Elena could ask him to let her out here, he turned into the drive and she felt the shock, the dreamlike shock, of the car's tires on the gravel.

He drove up to the house, which was set far back from the road. Elena felt his strange excitement. She seemed to feel the abrupt movement of his eyes as he took in the immense house and the lawn and the expanse of lake behind it. She remembered the first time she had seen it herself; but she hadn't had this man's excitement.

He braked to a stop. He leaned over the steering wheel, looking around. Now she felt safe, safer. She would get out and leave him, she would unlock the door, enter the house, close the door; that was that.

Without looking at her, he opened his car door. He said, "I have to make a telephone call."

Elena sat for a moment, not stunned or shocked, simply in that limp, exhausted suspension; she might have been waiting for her normal self to return. She had faith in it. Then, moving very carefully, aware of herself moving carefully, unafraid, she opened the car door—it opened with difficulty—and got out. It had begun to rain. She felt the large soft drops on her face and thought them remote, strange. Why were they so far away?

She heard someone's footsteps on the gravel. He was approaching her. She couldn't tell if she was crying or perhaps standing in the rain. The tears felt very distant, chilled. It must be rain. The man was saying something to her: giving instructions, or joking? She felt the heavy weight of her hair, which she had fixed so carefully that morning. . . . But it seemed years ago, a lifetime ago. She could hardly remember.

"This is a day for trances and paralysis," the man said. "This is the kind of day things break down."

Elena looked at his feet, his shoes. They were scuffed, a nondescript pair of shoes, black leather. One of the metal tips of his shoelaces had come off. She noticed how very real, how wetly vivid, were the big chunks of expensive gravel. She had never looked at the gravel in the driveway before.

She felt the burden of this man's presence like the unnatural weight of her head.

"It's experimental," he said.

Elena didn't know what he was talking about.

She heard herself pleading with him, but not out loud.

His face looked sinister, but playful. It was a face perfectly matched with his voice. There was a kind of rhythm in him, an agility, a youthfulness that frightened her, it was so raw. But perhaps he was not young . . . ? She glanced up at him again and saw the shrewd, ironic eyes, which really had nothing young about them.

"At night this place is protected by dogs, but in the day it seems quite vulnerable," he said. "Do many men make a run for the house at night, risking the dogs?—just to get to you?"

"No," Elena said.

"Where are the dogs now, locked up?"

"Yes, they're locked up."

"I don't believe in them if I can't see them," he said.

Elena thought suddenly that he was joking with her: often she could not follow the maneuverings of a man's joking, and she was frightened for no reason. It was a language she didn't quite understand. Familiar subjects sometimes became, in the mouths of men, bizarre and unintelligible; but they were not usually important. The weekend before, she had listened, half-listened, to an earnest argument around a dining room table, between her husband and several other men on the subject of capital punishment. At first Elena had believed that the men were against capital punishment, her own husband most emphatically, but as the hour got later, as the men had more to drink, they began to compare executions they knew about or in some cases had actually witnessed—garroting in Cuba, bayoneting in Africa, by firing squad somewhere else, ordinary gassings and electrocutions in the United States—and their voices had become more and more excited, more boyish. At one point a man declared that capital punishment acted as a powerful argument against murder, and that it therefore saved lives; it was like the wrath of God embodied in the state, and it should be well-publicized, just as God used to be well-publicized. Elena had waited for Marvin to contradict this statement, but for some reason he didn't . . . or perhaps Elena hadn't understood, and the statement was not meant to be serious? She didn't know. But the entire discussion was not really important. It was dinner-table conversation.

Now there was no protection; now she didn't understand either but there was no protection, she seemed to be standing bare-headed in the rain, a few feet from a man she didn't know. He was looking at her speculatively, openly. She could hear him thinking: thinking about her. *This is the kind of day things break down,* he had said.

"If we went in the house now," he said softly, "that would be experimental. Should we go in?"

Elena shook her head slowly. That meant. . . .

"Did you ever watch yourself to see what you might do?" he asked.

"Yes. Sometimes," Elena said.

"Were you surprised?"

Elena didn't reply.

"I know your husband from years ago, when he wasn't your husband," he said thoughtfully. "But he doesn't know me. He wouldn't remember me. It's believed that anyone can commit murder," he said, speaking not ironically now, but rather urgently, his words pronounced formally, precisely, as if for an audience larger than Elena. "But that has always struck me as a fantasy, just ego-fantasizing by ordinary, impotent men, men given to intellectual theories. What do you think, Mrs. Howe? At the very moment of murder, the majority of men would back down. And they know this, they sense it; therefore they don't try. They just publicize their potentiality for murder, they make up theories about it, democratic theories . . . as if it were really available to anyone, when of course it isn't. It's a fraudulent little fantasy, a fraudulent passion. What do you think?"

Elena looked at him and said nothing.

"Do you think . . . ?" he said, his voice trailing off.

Elena felt the rain falling, she felt its peacefulness, inside anything that man might be thinking. He looked at her so openly, so contemplatively, that she could not believe. . . . Then she adjusted herself; she did believe: anything might happen. He was thinking this also.

The tension between them frightened her, but she did not want to turn away from him. Exhausted, she could not even look away, for that might give him access to her.

Then he seemed to change his mind. He said, "No. All right."

So he walked her to the front door, again gripping her upper arm, and he began to talk again in his ironic, playful voice, saying something about the rain, the fact that he was late for an appointment, he had to apologize for the condition of his car. . . . Elena didn't hear all of this, she couldn't concentrate. While she searched her purse for the key he said something further, again in that joking, mocking voice, and backed away. He was leaving. She found the key and stood staring at it in triumph, and behind her he was leaving, now on the gravel. She heard his footsteps on the gravel.

A stranger to her, a shadow-woman, might have stepped into her body. She might then have turned to watch him; she might have called out to him.

Why are you leaving . . . ?

She fitted the key into the lock and opened the door. She walked through the foyer, touching the wall lightly, checking its strength, her fingers brushing against a pillar, now the sweeping curve of the banister. . . . She was home. It was a home, a house with a door: she had the key to the door. She had taken the proper key out of her purse and she had opened the door with it; therefore she lived here.

She heard a noise at the front door. She froze.

But then nothing.

She believed it was nothing, she had imagined it. . . . Then she heard the car starting. She heard him drive away. So she knew that she was home, in a foyer with a marble floor, and nothing had happened that could be properly remembered.

But she went back to the door, her damp coat still on. She was anxious to see if. . . . Yes, he had gone. The car was gone. He had driven away and nothing had happened, though she knew she had been in terrible danger.

Mail lay on the floor, by the mailslot. The usual pile of mail. She had stepped on one of the letters by accident; it was damp and stained. She could see the name: *Marvin Howe.* Another letter, an advertisement, was addressed to *Mrs. Marvin Howe.* For some reason this pleased her. A dozen items of mail awaiting her. It meant something, all this mail. She had already opened it. Each day's batch of letters was new, a surprise, and yet she had already opened it and could not be surprised, but only pleased, deepened in her realization of what mail meant. Without bending over to pick anything up—she was afraid of becoming dizzy—she noted the envelopes, the names, the addresses. All the addresses were the same. She had opened all the envelopes already but

After the joy came the sorrow and then the leveling-off, the return to her essential self.

She thought of the way that man had maneuvered his car on the expressway. She maneuvered herself with the same skill and pride.

She never telephoned the number he had left her.

One day she ripped off the calendar page and it was May. The days were so warm now that even cloudy, gusty skies didn't discourage the sailboats; so it was spring, a time of good luck. Elena studied the calendar, tracing with her fingers the separate blocks of days until the end of May. They were countable. They were finite and easily imagined.

This calendar, from one of Marvin's banks, showed only one month at a time. And so Elena had no need to think about June or even to remember that it would follow May. She went out alone, to walk along the residential streets, with a pleased awareness of herself walking, exercising, though it was not very common for a woman in Grosse Pointe to walk; all the women drove, even one or two blocks. So Elena walked briskly, as if with an immediate destination, and she gazed at the handsome fronts of houses, and at the high, lovely walls of homes that, like her husband's, were walled off from the sidewalk, very private and silent. This part of the world was silent. No one walked, no one like herself walked; the sounds Elena heard most often were the sounds of diseased elms being cut down by tree-service crews who worked for the city and who did not belong here any more than Elena did.

Since she lived on the lake, there were only four or five directions she could walk in; she soon memorized the streets, the houses, even the landscaping around the houses. She liked to imagine the women who must live in the houses: women like herself, maybe, though probably a little older. Married to men like Marvin Howe . . . though less than Marvin Howe. But still men. Men of some kind. When she walked by the home of a woman she knew, her mind skittered onto the next house so that she could imagine the woman there. Was she unknowable, mysterious? Did she contemplate the calendar with the same peaceful, grateful calm Elena did?

May was passing.

Elena avoided a street when she noticed the city's tree-service trucks parked there, or heard the whining of a buzz saw. She did not want to see the trees cut down because that meant an alteration in her thinking . . . an abrupt change, really a brutal change. She hated the noise of the saws. And she dreaded walking by the men, because she had begun to notice men looking at her; and she did not want to look back at them.

A gigantic elm tree on Lakeshore Drive, a half block from her home, was tagged with a yellow ticket in early May by the Health Department; so every day that passed without the tree being sawed down Elena counted as good luck.

Diseased but still standing.

For a while Elena was nervous about answering the telephone, thinking it was a risk, a stupid risk like aiming a pistol at her head and pulling the trigger on an empty chamber; but she didn't dare not answer, because Marvin often called her, even when he was at his office. When he was out of town he called her regularly, three times a day, but not always at the same times . . . and she had to answer or he would be disturbed. Then, as the weeks passed, she realized that that man was not going to call her; she was safe. So she answered the telephone quite normally, in her old manner, and only once was she surprised and a little frightened—when her mother called.

Her mother's voice so suddenly, after all those weeks!

Ardis spoke in a comfortable, unhurried way, immediately telling Elena about some people, some facts and events, that Elena knew nothing about, and then she began to apologize, though not very forcefully: still comfortable, pleasant. "I hope you'll forgive me, Elena, for not returning your call . . . God, it was back in April . . . I've been incredibly busy, you wouldn't believe it! . . . and you know how I am. . . . We had a bad connection or something, I don't remember. . . . But what was it you wanted, honey? You said something about . . . ? Is everything all right out there? How's Marvin?"

Elena could not think.

"He's down in Texas, isn't he?" Ardis said.

"Yes, all week . . . I think he'll be gone all week. . . ."

"Some mess, isn't it?" Ardis laughed. "But I wouldn't mind being the beneficiary of an insurance policy like *that* . . . not to mention the oil wells . . . or are the oil wells dried up? I can't remember, it's such a crazy case." Elena let her mother talk, not knowing herself as much about this particular case as Ardis evidently did. She stood with her shoulders hunched slightly, as if in a strong wind. Her feet made shallow indentations in a thick white rug made of fur. It was Peruvian lamb. Elena followed her mother's conversation with difficulty, because Ardis had begun to speak rapidly, as if she were running through a list of topics and hadn't time now to develop any of them; also, her voice sounded a little different, deeper and more husky, like the Marya Sharp of television; and she seemed to be using certain words or phrases in a manner that was unfamiliar. But she was very cheerful.

She ran through the people she would be interviewing on her program for the month of May and the first week of June; she began to talk about her tennis club, a private downtown club she had recently joined; she seemed to be discussing, now, people Elena knew or was supposed to know, but it all went so quickly that Elena couldn't follow. But she was pleased that her mother was so happy. Then Ardis was talking about an unfortunate program she'd had, a New York magazine editor who had showed up drunk, contemptuous of Detroit and of the Midwest and, in fact, of all of America; then she switched to some alarming local news that would break in a day or two, the indictment of a certain probate judge for—and get this—his involvement with—but Ardis hesitated, no, maybe she shouldn't mention it, in case it was covered up, she'd better keep it secret; and anyway Marvin would know all about it. . . . While her mother was talking about these things Elena felt, passing near her, another person, like a shadow of herself given substance and weight, but she refused to look up. She knew she was alone.

She said she was sorry, she asked if anything was wrong . . . ?

Anything . . . ?

Far away at the end of a telescope, she was shouting, laughing. I couldn't see her.

Friday morning at ten, a date at the tennis club with the Lieutenant Governor's wife.

Exercise was very necessary.

Waving, saying good-by and hello. . . .

Elena had tried to resist remembering the day she'd called her mother, but now she was forced to remember it. She remembered the action of her dialing, the efficiency of her finger in the dial; if you can dial a number you can surely live. Staying alive is not so complicated as dialing a telephone number. Then her mind skipped to the memory of a pressure against her, a body pressing against hers. But he had not touched her. She heard the boys' laughter and wondered if she should be afraid, or perhaps join in their laughter—that might be the best thing to do under the circumstances. An article in the Sunday newspaper had explained that a woman who is attacked by a man increases her chances of *not* being murdered by five hundred per cent if she does not resist . . . that contradicted Ardis's advice of years ago, unless Elena didn't remember correctly: Ardis had always said, "Carry a knife or, better yet, a gun." But Elena did not carry a knife or a gun. What was the best advice? On a bus in New York City one day, Elena had happened to notice a man staring at her, then smiling, and then very slowly his tongue had begun to protrude, out of his smiling lips, at first slyly, then with increasing vigor and delight. Elena had watched him helplessly, not knowing what to do. Smile back? In the end she had simply lowered her gaze a few inches so that she was looking at his necktie; but she did not look away from him, for that might annoy him or insult him. . . . For a dozen blocks they rode together, facing each other, and by the time Elena got off the bus she had nearly forgotten the problem. It had just dissolved.

I wanted to interrupt her to ask: is life lived out to add up to a story, or is the story invented first so it can be lived out?

I wanted to interrupt her to

I wanted

I felt the pressure of his body though he hadn't touched me. I felt someone touching me. My mother drifted out of the end of the telescope, waving good-by. She was late for an appointment. It wasn't my mother's voice but I recognized it and answered it—

Calmly, deliberately, Elena broke the connection by replacing the telephone receiver. She waited a few minutes but her mother didn't call back.

That evening she said to Marvin, "My mother and I were talking today and the connection was broken . . . and I didn't call her back. . . . I don't know why I didn't call her back, but. . . ."

"Did she call you back?"

"No. But I . . . I don't want her to think. . . ."

Elena hesitated, confused.

"Don't worry about it," Marvin said.

In mid-May the elm near her house was still standing, though still ticketed. It was an enormous tree, tough-looking, barren; dying from the top down, but still very handsome. Elena thought it was good luck that the city hadn't cut it down.

By May 31 it was still there.

Which meant nothing.

Safely into June, well into June; and she hadn't telephoned him. She rarely thought about him now. She didn't even know where the card was, with his illegible scrawl; she hadn't thrown it away, not consciously, but she didn't know where it was.

It seemed to her that life was becoming easier to handle.

The evening of June 15 was set aside, the date on the calendar marked, because her mother was interviewing someone that night who had received a great deal of publicity in Detroit. Marvin himself had said he wanted to watch at least part of the program.

When the interview began, between Ardis and a young man named Dawe, Marvin kept saying in amazement, partly amused and partly irritated, "This is extraordinary. . . . This can't be happening."

Elena concentrated on the program: there was Marya Sharp asking questions of an earnestly ugly, straggle-haired young man of about twenty-six or twenty-seven, who had evidently been arrested not long before and was awaiting trial. Marvin knew the young man's father; he was the president of Dawe Electronics and he lived only a few houses away, also on the lake. Elena couldn't recall having met Jackson Dawe, though Marvin said she had. The son, Meredith, who called himself Mered, was evidently an artist—which was believable, he was so wild-haired, dressed in a kind of gown or sack with a sash around his waist; then, as Marya continued to question him, it was revealed that he had a degree in physics—Elena found that harder to believe, though he spoke quite well, he sounded intelligent, if you weren't distracted by his habit of squinting and roling his eyes nervously as he searched for words. It turned out he was also a philosopher of some kind; he stared past Marya and into the camera as if into the eyes of someone he feared and loved, someone who must be made to realize certain truths though they were disturbing . . . "for the sake of the race," he said.

Seeing he was so gentle, in spite of his bony, homely face, Elena feared for him; she had grown to recognize a certain sly note in Marya's voice. Dawe's voice was frank and unplanned.

Q. Mr. Dawe, or may I call you Mered—?—what were your reasons initially for establishing what you call your Retreat House?

A. To work for the obliteration of matter. To establish a sane alcove in this pestilence for people to come together and direct the future of the United States. . . .

Q. This "pestilence" . . . ?

A. The United States today. Most of the world today.

Q. Is your bitterness caused, perhaps, by your having been arrested?

A. I'm not bitter. Why should I be bitter? But I want to go on record as saying that I haven't been arrested for any drug offense, not at all; I've been arrested because certain people want to silence me.

Q. The police have arrested you because of your opinions?

A. Certainly.

Q. Does the indictment read that way . . . ?

A. What? I don't know. I don't care. I have no interest in what happens to be on any piece of paper; I'm not sure if I even read the indictment. I really scorn all that. I have nothing to do with it.

Q. But you are going to put up a defense, aren't you, Mered?

A. What? Somebody is . . . somebody hired a lawyer for me, or somebody volunteered . . . I don't keep track of things like that, I don't have time. . . . I didn't come on this program to talk about that side of my life. I scorn all lawyers and the law . . . and the judges . . . and, oh, the jurors and the whole judiciary system, because no one gets a fair trial in this country anyway and. . . .

Q. Now that bail has been granted you and you're free to give lectures again, do you intend to continue your campaign against "matter"? Or . . . ?

A. They'll have to kill me to shut me up. Nobody's going to shut me up.

Q. But the Retreat House is closed down, isn't it?

A. That isn't going to stop me. I'm giving my speeches now on the street–anywhere– The police are going to have to kill me to shut me up and I'm telling them that frankly.

Q. You contend that your father has bribed the police to harass you?

Mered Dawe moved his shoulders nervously inside his shapeless outfit. He seemed to be looking directly at Elena.

A. I . . . I . . . I have reason to suspect. . . . I know what he's capable of . . . and the police also . . . and. . . .

Q. But you did say in an interview with a *Detroit News* reporter that you're accusing certain Detroit police of accepting bribes?

A. Of course. They all do.

Q. Mered, could you explain to our viewers your reasons for working for the "obliteration of matter"–and what this means in terms of ordinary daily life?

A. To use clichés so that your viewers can understand, I'll say that I am working for the Revolution. Everyone knows that the world is undergoing a violent change, a convulsion, and I am helping it; really, it's a law of physics, and I am only helping it along and instructing people who need superior guidance. For this absolutely innocent work I have found myself persecuted by the Establishment and hounded by the police and arrested for allegedy dealing in drugs–in drugs!–as if drugs mattered!–when the United States is not only dealing in drugs, officially, but calling it by other names. The entire operation of the United States is a drug-operation.

Q. Nothing else? Nothing . . . ?

A. Absolutely nothing.

Q. You deny, do you, Mered, that you handed a marijuana cigarette to a girl of seventeen . . . ?

A. Why should I deny that?

Marvin whistled. "This is painful to hear," he said.

"He is incriminating himself, isn't he?" Elena asked cautiously.

"Shouldn't my mother be more careful, the questions she asks him?"

Q. Now, Mered, when you say the "Revolution"—you mean in economic and political terms, as in Russia and Red China?
A. Only initially. Essentially it's a reversal of everything people like you believe. And your audience. That matter is real and mind-stuff unreal. Eventually the Revolution will alter every head in the world, transform it. I think that is why old-fashioned Marxists and liberals are so violently, so viciously opposed to me; they believe in matter and not in the transcendence of matter. They believe in offal, but not in love.
Q. They believe in . . . ? What did you say . . . ?
A. Offal.

Marya looked perplexed, as if this were a word she didn't know. But she smiled again and continued in her pleasant, well-modulated voice:
Q. How do you suggest that we all reach this transcendence, Mered? You've endorsed the use of drugs, haven't you?
A. To begin with, yes. Initially. I do object to the drug trade, though, and this is another side of me that infuriates the authorities, because of course they make a fortune from the trade. And it isn't taxed, either. When I come out in my lectures for free drugs, free visions, they are incredibly hostile.
Q. Free drugs, drugs for everyone? Of what kind, Mered?
A. LSD, hash, peyote, anything you can name, aspirin, alcohol, oh, all the menu, and my reason is this: there must be no élitism, no leisure class of visions. The hallucinatory state should not be the possession of the aristocracy, as unobtainable by the masses as all the old dreams—the people must not tolerate that. They must revolt.
Q. Drugs supplied by the state, perhaps . . . ?
A. Yes. Until the state is annihilated. Ultimately we will all see that drugs are lazy habits, like rosaries. We must phase them out. I phased drugs out of my own life long ago, and this is another thing that antagonizes drug-users. They accuse me of being self-righteous, but in fact I recognize that some people need drugs and always will. We're all individuals. I don't judge.

Q. You don't judge . . . ? But you seem to have judged our society very severely, Mered, haven't you?
A. I don't judge, I love. *Who loves well, punishes well.* And I do punish, yes, but not physically—I am totally committed to nonviolence, you know—I punish through love.
Q. I don't understand.
A. Of course you don't. You're just an ordinary ignorant woman, how could you understand? I punish through love by the example of my love, my being, which puts to shame my enemies and forces them to realize the contrast between myself and them. . . .

Mered spoke easily and frankly, as if he hadn't insulted Marya; and Marya, sitting in amazement, stared for a moment at him before going on to her next question, which she read hurriedly off a card:

Q. Love . . . by love . . . by "love" do you mean, Mered, normal love, which is heterosexual in our culture and confined to the matrimonial state . . . ?
A. I mean unadulterated love. I mean heavenly, cosmic love, the basic force of the universe, which excludes no one. Women, men, children, animals, plants, rocks. Works of art. The kingdom of physical presences. Jove copulated with clouds, and I have also copulated with clouds.
Q. With clouds . . . ?
A. Yes. In the forms of people.

Marya stared. This time she could not continue.

Then, after a confused, embarrassed moment, during which Mered began talking earnestly about his concept of the "Revolution" and what this meant to everyone, Marya was able to bring the program to a close. Her last words were quite cheerful and she was even smiling, as usual, as she announced her visitor for next week's program.

Marvin switched off the set.

"Thank God," Marvin said. "That was painful to sit through!"

Elena stared at the blank screen. Finally she said, "Could you help him . . . ? I mean . . . if you. . . ."

"I wouldn't go near that madman," Marvin said.

3

One day in June, in the early afternoon, Marvin returned home suddenly and told Elena to pack her clothes—enough for a few days—and to be ready to leave for the airport in fifteen minutes—ten minutes—to hurry, please hurry, it was very important.

He went with her into their bedroom, tossed a large fawn-colored leather suitcase on the bed, and helped her pack—yanking open bureau drawers, handing things to her. Elena was astonished but didn't question him; his face was flushed, tougher than usual, and he seemed to want to avoid looking directly at her, as if she might read something in his eyes: shame, fear? His skin had coarsened with the urgency of what he was doing. Around his mouth, especially, it looked bunched-up and muscular. Elena would have been frightened except she saw, gratefully, that he was frightened in her place. So she had nothing to do but obey.

"The plane leaves in an hour," Marvin said, out of breath. He looked wildly around the room. "Do you have everything?"

"Where am I going?" Elena asked.

"California."

"Alone?"

"Yes, alone, Elena, come on, is this thing ready to be closed?—do you need anything else?—if you do you can buy it out there, you can buy anything you want out there," Marvin said. He shut the suitcase and forced the locks into place. Then he looked at her, a swift appraising glance, in which she saw everything: his love, his fear. "You're flying out alone and I'll join you in a few days. Don't worry. Don't even think about it."

He walked her hurriedly down the broad carpeted stairs, his hand closed about her arm, the large suitcase scuffing along the steps in thuds. At the front door a man was waiting, a stranger. Elena looked at him in surprise. He didn't look at her, he simply opened the door for Marvin and offered to take the suitcase from him; but Marvin in a rush, apparently thinking about something else, didn't notice and went out to the car himself and threw the suitcase into the opened trunk. "Come on, come on," he said wildly. He stretched his arm out in order to expose his watch. Elena, buttoning a coat of some lightweight material, patting her hair nervously, got into the car, and Marvin squeezed in beside her and the other man got into the driver's seat. The car's engine had been running all along.

"Get going," Marvin said.

It wasn't a voice Elena knew—short, breathless, crude, rather cruel.

On the way out to the airport Marvin kept saying, repeating, "I'll be out in a few days. What's today? Tuesday. Today's Tuesday. Give me until Saturday, no, Friday; but I'll keep in contact with you. I'll be out in a few days. Nothing is wrong. Nothing is going to happen. . . . Elena, this is Theodore, you haven't met before, but Theodore is an old friend of mine, an associate, and he's going to accompany you and take care of things. There's nothing to worry about."

Theodore was a thick-set man of about forty, balding but youthful; in a way, like Marvin himself—it must have been his very fine light woollen tweed suit and his firm, pink, healthy face. Elena glanced at him and saw that his skin looked flushed with good health or perhaps excitement.

"Can't you drive any faster?" Marvin said sharply.

They were on the expressway now, out of the city, and Theodore pressed the accelerator down. Elena felt the shock of their speed, the acceleration of it, in the pit of her stomach. The front end of the car seemed almost to be lifting. But neither Marvin nor Theodore showed any alarm. Marvin was saying, patting her arm and squeezing it fondly, almost absent-mindedly, "Nothing to worry about. It's all arranged. Harry Miner—do you remember meeting him, Elena?—a state senator out of San Francisco?—well, he's got a place all ready for you, I arranged it in fifteen minutes, he owes me a favor and he's grateful for the opportunity—though it came up rather suddenly—but—the house is on the ocean, Elena, and no one is there—no one's living there—I've never seen it myself, but— Get in the right lane, will you? Don't you see where you are?" he said across Elena, reaching over to tap on the steering wheel. "Your exit is coming up, it's the third or fourth exit, you'd better get prepared. Jesus, the way people drive along here! There are people going *forty miles an hour* along here . . . blocking traffic. . . . Good, that's good. I think we're going to make the plane."

At the terminal they left the car in a no-parking zone. Theodore carried the suitcase and Marvin propelled Elena along, in and out of small crowds, repeating that there was nothing to worry about and he'd keep in contact with her. "Now, enjoy the sun, Elena," he said at the gate, "and don't telephone anyone back home—not your mother—not anyone—not even me, because I won't be at the house or the office and you won't know my number— The thing is," he said, laughing lightly, or trying to laugh as he kissed her good-by, "that people aren't going to know where you are—do you understand? Only Harry Miner and Theodore and I. Do you understand? Now, have a good time out there and enjoy the sun—"

On the plane Elena sat next to a window. Theodore sat beside her, embarrassed. He kept scratching the back of his neck.

"Does someone want to kill me?" Elena asked shyly.

Theodore made a laughing sound, as if to show surprise.

"No. Everything is under control," he said.

Now that they were alone he seemed less confident; self-conscious, awkward, leaning his bulky torso away from her and against the arm-rest. He scratched the side of his throat.

"Why is he sending me to California?" Elena asked.

"There's no danger," he said.

"I thought maybe . . . maybe. . . ."

"Mr. Howe has everything in control and nobody is going to be killed," he said.

The Miner estate was outside San Francisco, near Monterey. It reminded Elena of the Grosse Pointe mansions, though it was Spanish in design, made of material that had the appearance of baked clay. The roofs were all twisted tile, bright orange. In the enormous, formal entrance hall there was an entire altar, evidently taken from a Mexican church: crude and quaint in design, not very large. In the dining room, one wall was decorated with a church door made of handsome carved wood. So close to the ocean, the house always smelled of water, of wind, and many of the doors were warped and would not shut properly.

"How's the sun there? Are you happy? How are you?" Marvin asked over the telephone. He called her several times a day; he always sounded exuberant and cheerful. He was always saying, "I'll be joining you in a few days, don't worry." Then he asked Elena to put Theodore on the phone, and Elena left the room . . . though she could hear Theodore saying *Yes, No, All right, Okay, Yes.* . . . This part of the conversation might last anywhere from five minutes to a quarter of an hour.

After one of Marvin's calls, Elena knew he wouldn't call for a few hours. So she was free to walk out along the ocean, from one end of the Miner property to the other—quite a distance. She stared at the waves, feeling herself hypnotized, happy, almost delirious with a happiness she could not understand. The first several times she went for this walk, Theodore followed her, hurrying along the rocky beach, slipping on the wet rocks until he caught up with her; then, embarrassed, he said he probably should stay with her . . . she might hurt herself . . . she might get lost. But after they had been at the estate for a few days, he didn't bother following her; when Elena came back, she would find him sitting on the terrace, vacuous, bored, still in his city clothes, glancing at her as if to check—was she the right person?—and then avoiding her gaze. Most of the terrace furniture had been upended: heavy chairs made of tubing, painted a stark, ghastly white, a few wicker chairs that appeared to be rotted, an old-fashioned flower cart or trolley with stained, rain-rotted cushions that had fallen onto the flagstone floor of the terrace. Theodore had placed a chair for himself and a chair for Elena in a clear, sunny spot.

He drove out once or twice a day to get food and magazines and other items; no newspapers.

In good weather they sat on the terrace, reading. Theodore leafed through his magazines, sighing; Elena had discovered an old mildewed volume of *Middlemarch*, which she was forcing herself to read. It was strange that the house had no library—only a few books lying around, best-sellers of bygone years, some of them with pages missing. A paneled room that was meant to be a library was stocked with nothing except games—children's and adults' games—and Elena investigated it, shelf after shelf, wondering if Theodore would like to play Parcheesi or Monopoly or Death Row with her. She hesitated to ask him, because he was so easily embarrassed.

In an attic room Elena came across a trunk of books on California: California law, the history of the Spanish in the Southwest, the trade routes, the explorers, even a volume that dealt with the rainfall in all parts of the state. She glanced through one of the books but had no interest in it. Then, in another trunk, she found some clothing—clothes that had evidently belonged to a teen-aged girl, sweaters, pullover jerseys, blue jeans. These things had been packed away without having been laundered. She selected a cotton jersey of red and white stripes and a pair of jeans, which weren't too dirty. She changed her clothes and went back downstairs and outside, feeling better.

Theodore glanced at her in alarm. Then he looked away.

"I'm going for a walk," she said.

"All right," he said.

The pullover jersey fitted her tightly; the blue jeans were rather small too, so that she could hardly stuff her wallet into the back pocket. She hadn't bothered to count the money Marvin had handed her at the airport, but the bills made her wallet bulkier than usual.

This was Friday morning. She walked along the beach, climbing across the boulders and huge, strangely shaped rocks. She didn't mind the wind, the chilly damp air. The ocean made so much noise she was not able to think of anything beyond it. But she felt elated, excited. She climbed up to the highway and walked along it for a while, in the good harsh sunshine, thinking that she was in California, had she been in California before? —why was she so happy?

At a Sunoco gas station in a small town she went to the single telephone booth, extricated the card from her wallet, and dialed first the code number for Detroit and then that number. She glanced at her watch and calculated swiftly that it would be two o'clock in Detroit; a good time for a call.

The telephone was answered at once.

He said abruptly, "Yeah? Who is it?"

She said, "This is Elena. . . ."

"Who? What? I can't hear you."

"This is Elena," she said.

She had begun to tremble, in spite of her elation. Her eyes were half closed now and she seemed to see him frowning, frowning into the telephone.

"*Who* . . . ? Elena . . . ?"

He was silent.

Then he said, "Well . . . Jesus. . . . Elena? You? After so long?"

"Yes," she said.

"After two months . . . ? I. . . ."

Elena could hear her own breathing. Or perhaps it was his. She put one foot up on the seat of the booth to steady herself. She began to smile.

He was saying slowly, uncertainly, "I . . . I will admit I'm glad you called, but . . . I'm surprised. . . . I'd given up waiting . . . and. . . . Why did you happen to call me today?"

She smiled, she seemed to see the quizzical set of his face.

"I thought of you today," she said.

"Today . . . ? Oh, today . . . ? But why today?" he said vaguely, almost vacantly. Then, as if not caring about that question, as if his mind had already raced onto something else, he said: "When can I see you?"

"Today?" Elena said.

"It's five after eleven . . . someone's waiting to see me . . . I. . . . It's confusing. . . . This *is* the person I think it is? This *is* her . . . ? I mean, it isn't . . . it couldn't be someone else?" he asked slowly. "Well, look, I don't have the car today; my wife has the car. But I could get a taxi. I could be out around eleven-thirty, or quarter to twelve, is that . . . is that all right . . . ?"

"I'm not at home," Elena said.

"No? Are you downtown, then? That would be better if—"

"I'm in California," Elena said.

"What? I can't hear you."

"I'm in California," Elena said. "I'm in a gas station in a small town, I think it's called—"

"What did you say? This connection is bad—"

"It has a Spanish name, the first word is *San*. . . . Maybe fifty miles south of San Francisco. I'm calling from a gas station."

There was silence at the other end.

Then he said faintly, "You're near San Francisco?"

"About fifty miles south of there. I'm in a gas station. I dialed direct," Elena said. She smiled into the telephone; she seemed to see him, puzzled, stunned, staring back at her.

"What are you . . . what are you doing there?" he asked.

"I came here to telephone you. I woke up this morning and thought I would call you today."

"Yes, but . . . I'm very happy to hear from you, but. . . . Why are you out there?"

"I don't know. I thought I could ask you . . . if anything was in the news . . . ? Is anything going on in Detroit?"

"Huh?"

"My husband sent me out here; I think something is wrong, do you know of anything that's happening . . . ?"

"Uh—God—let me think," he said.

He seemed very confused. Elena said softly, to help him, "He sent me out on Tuesday. I'm staying at a friend's house on the ocean, and no one knows where I am. Is anything wrong in Detroit?"

"Uh—let's see—yes, something is going on, a woman was killed a few days ago—yeah—the police found an address book with a lot of names in it—a man was shot on Tuesday— Yeah, his name was in that book, evidently, but I don't know what it all means."

"Is my husband's name in the book too?" Elena asked.

"I don't know. They haven't released information like that. Only the murdered man's name . . . I don't know much about it."

"Who was he?"

"The name meant nothing to me. Frankly, I don't move in those circles," he said with a laugh. "I don't move in your husband's circles."

"Do you think my husband's name is in the address book too?"

"I don't know. No, I don't know," he said. He paused. Then he said cautiously, "Elena, did you say you were in California? I heard you correctly?"

"Yes."

"You waited until today to call me?"

"I walked out along the ocean and up to the highway. It's Highway One. It's very beautiful here."

"But how can I see you? When are you coming back?"

"I don't know. He hasn't said . . . he hasn't mentioned any time for coming back. . . . Maybe next week. I don't know."

"Not until next week?"

"You could come to see me here."

"Uh. . . ."

Elena closed her eyes. She felt how simple, how sweet the composition of her soul was: all fluids, fragrant and musical. She waited.

"You don't know for certain when you're coming back?" he asked.

"No."

He paused. Then he said slowly, "Uh . . . look . . . by coincidence I am going to fly to California anyway . . . later in the summer . . . but I could move it up, I mean I could say the meeting was moved up . . . my wife knows I'm expected sometime but . . . it's to meet with some people who . . . uh . . . I'm trying to figure this out. . . ."

Elena waited.

"Look, tomorrow morning? Sometime tomorrow morning?" he said.

"All right," Elena said.

"Is it all right . . . ?"

Elena waited.

Then he said in his normal voice: "You don't know San Francisco, do you? I don't. Look, is there a telephone directory near you? Some yellow pages?" Elena found the directory. "Elena, look under *hotels,* will you, find a reasonable-sized ad—okay?—have you found anything?"

Elena came across an advertisement that showed a handsome towerlike structure; she told him the name and address. He said, "Good, that sounds good . . . I'm writing it down . . . also, Elena, give me the number of that hotel . . . so I can call you if something happens. . . . Now . . . will you be there? Will you really be there?"

"Yes," Elena said.

"You will? In that hotel, in San Francisco tomorrow morning? And this isn't a joke . . . this is a serious conversation between us . . . ? You'll be there, will you? Alone?"

"Yes," Elena said. "Alone."

4

Elena flagged down a Greyhound bus and went to San Francisco, and from the bus station she took a taxi to the hotel. It was as large and as handsome as its advertisement promised; she was grateful for the crowded lobby, the chandeliers, the well-dressed men, the efficiency of porters and other men in uniforms doing their jobs. She saw everywhere a certain kind of man and a certain kind of woman—the woman like herself, her well-dressed self. Today, in these odd clothes, she felt both freakish and invisible: if anyone stared at her, it wouldn't be Elena they were seeing.

The desk clerk did look at her, almost rudely. But she paid for her room in advance, two days' stay, and he accepted her money with an agreeable smile. "Luggage?" he said, waving a porter over; but no luggage, nothing. Elena wondered if she should be embarrassed. But the desk clerk simply handed the porter a key, and the porter led her to the elevator. He kept glancing down, toward the carpet or toward his own hands, as if self-conscious over having nothing to carry and a little disoriented. Elena, in her excitement, tipped him a dollar and felt that his startled gratitude, his smile, were good signs.

Alone, she turned off the color television he had turned on. She turned off the air-conditioning. She stood at the window and stared out, able to see the Pacific Ocean at the edge of the city, a reality that somehow made sense, that steadied the confusing, rather frightening hills of this city.

The sun was at a certain position in the sky; she would have to wait for it to move a great distance before he came to her.

To pass time, she counted the money in her wallet. She put the bills into piles, the hundred-dollar bills, the fifty-dollar bills, the twenty-dollar bills. . . . After a while she simply sorted them out without counting them, and folded them together again and returned them to her wallet. It was pleasing, how she was able to remember that man's face, the tone of his voice, even the imagined pressure of his body, in small effortless flashes, between the periods of counting and sorting bills . . . so that the counting of her money was not a waste of time, not really. Then she lay down to sleep and her sleeping was visited by memories of him, hardly more than flashes, not disturbing or very serious. She thought: *He probably won't come.* In that case, these odd little dreams, half-dreams, were fortunate—they were like memories, of a man who had not enough substance to threaten her. Then she woke. She had evidently slept, exhausted by the walk and the bus ride and the excitement. She woke, sitting up, at first baffled —then she remembered where she was. Her head felt hollow, as if she were still out along the ocean or trudging along the highway.

Things she had to do: she would be efficient and do them. She had not looked at herself for hours, hadn't even thought of herself, and that must be done. From the bathroom, she went to the telephone to call Room Service, as Marvin always did; she ordered a cheese sandwich and a cup of coffee. She was very hungry now, and the cheese sandwich would be a reward, a celebration.

But it was hard for her to concentrate on anything, even eating. There were so many hours she had to get through, an entire evening and then a night. In the morning she would be safe enough; she would simply wait until he arrived. And if he didn't arrive. . . .

What did you think of?

Not love.

In the evening, restless, she went downstairs to wander around. The hotel's arcade of shops was darkened except for a coffee shop and a drugstore. The drugstore was cheerfully lit and smelled of something fragrant, like perfume; good luck that it was still open, Elena thought, since she should buy a few items. In the glass of the cosmetics counter she could see a dim image of herself, a slight woman in jeans and a striped shirt, with her hair loose, quite long hair. A salesman seemed to be looking at her critically. But she didn't mind; she bought several dollars' worth of things, thinking how fortunate it was that the store was open, so brightly lit, smelling so pleasant. This was a paradise, with so many items for sale, so many choices! When Elena left, she glanced back and saw one of the customers watching her—a middle-aged woman in an expensive outfit—and she half-smiled, her gaze skimming the woman's face, feeling how free she was to buy these things and to walk out, an invisible woman. What did it matter if anyone saw her?—stared at her? She stuffed the wallet into her back pocket and walked away.

Rising on the escalator to the hotel's main floor, she happened to catch sight of herself in a mirror. She felt an impulse of affection for that face, for herself; what good luck—

Good luck to be a beautiful woman.

Yes, it was good luck. She realized it now. In the lobby she saw, breathlessly, how no one knew her and how free she was, being unseen. A group of businessmen were just leaving a restaurant with an entrance in the lobby, men like Marvin and his friends, with Marvin's goodhearted manner, just the right size for this large, expensive setting, and they happened to glance at Elena . . . curiously, because of her clothes but also because of her aloneness at this time of the evening. She wanted to smile at them and tell them she was someone's wife, she did belong to someone, a man they would approve of.

In the morning she woke early, looked out at the city and the sky and as much of the ocean as she could see, a little disappointed at the smog. The sunshine fell haphazardly, through broken patches of cloud. Then she went downstairs to wait for him. She sat in the center of a group of chairs, in a black leather chair, waiting, a newspaper on her lap—she'd found it on the floor at her feet—facing the revolving doors he would probably use. It was a matter of waiting now, of watching men who approached the doors, watching as they appeared outside, on foot or getting out of cabs, always strangers to her. But they were strangers who might turn into someone familiar. At first the men all looked alike, and then, as they stepped out of the slow-circling doors and walked in her direction, they became individualized in a way that was fascinating. Some became older than she had judged them, some younger, some of them—these startled her—looked like men she was acquainted with back home. Elena sat, waiting like that, from nine o'clock until eleven-fifteen, patiently, feeling the slight risk of being recognized—one of those men who looked familiar might know her—or perhaps a stranger would know her, would happen to see her and come over, surprised, and say, "Aren't you . . . ?"

As time went on she still believed, in a way, that he would come. It did not occur to her that Marvin might walk through those doors, pushing them impatiently around, or that the man he had asked to watch her, Theodore, might show up instead. Then it did occur to her, and she knew she would simply stand and put the newspaper aside and allow herself to be recognized. After that, she wouldn't have to worry.

Then, around noon, she noticed a man approaching the entrance, walking quickly, and though she couldn't see his face at this distance, she believed it was the man she awaited . . . so she stood, she put the newspaper aside, she stood and waited for him to recognize her.

But he was shorter than she remembered. He was wearing a dark suit and a white shirt and tie, and he was just taking off a pair of sunglasses, glancing quickly around the lobby, frowning, as if it were too dark in here. Something about his manner attracted her, that sharp, cautious look, even the fumbling as he tried to shove the sunglasses into his pocket. Elena almost thought: *He would do. . . .*

Then he saw her. She felt the shock of his seeing her, the recognition.

So she came toward him and he approached her, finally jamming the sunglasses in his pocket, trying to smile. But he looked so surprised, he looked so bewildered. . . . Elena smiled and hid from him her sudden alarm at his realness, his presence; she knew enough to smile, like a hostess welcoming a nervous guest, she even put her hand out toward him . . . and he took it in his, then in both of his hard, damp hands, and they smiled in amazement at this accomplishment.

"Well . . . ," he said blankly.

She remembered him now. Yet he was not the same man—very real, very close to her, and his face was probably the same face, yet something had been altered. Elena stared at him, waiting. Her head seemed to go hollow, there was almost an ache in it, a need to be filled: he must fill it. But for a long moment he only stared at her, his gaze dropping involuntarily to her body and down to her feet, to the floor, still with that expression of vague, alarmed surprise.

"You look so different . . . ," he said.

And his voice was faint, wondering. She waited for his other voice. She twisted her hand nervously in his, as if to bring out the hardness of his grip on her, to agitate him.

"I almost wouldn't know you," he said. "Would you like a drink?—a drink somewhere? Is there somewhere to get a drink here?" He looked around the lobby, confused. Elena didn't follow his gaze but stared at him; she felt her face open, exposed, like the softest petals of a flower; she waited for him to turn back to her.

Then he looked back. "No, all right, never mind," he said.

They went upstairs.

Elena walked into the room ahead of him, feeling very small, girlish in the jeans and the striped shirt, with her hair loose on her shoulders. She heard him close the door. Now a flash of something touched her—not quite panic—but she ignored it; she pushed it back into the part of her mind that had tried to recall the terrible sloping streets of this part of the world, she blotted it out, she forgot it. He was saying something to her and she must listen. He was talking about the change of temperature—the change of time—the exasperating ride from the airport—and she did not pay attention to these words, but only to the agitation beneath them, which she understood.

He was very excited, very nervous. Elena could hear his breathing. Yet he was telling her now that she was beautiful—he was forcing himself not to touch her, but to talk to her. And it was true, his words, what he said, but Elena pitied him the tension of his body; she almost feared him, holding himself back as he was. She was standing in a strip of sunlight, like a creature netted in sunlight, smiling at this man, ready to open her arms to him.

She was very happy.

Finally he came over to her and kissed her. He said tightly, "This is very serious. . . ." Elena laughed. Surprised, he almost laughed with her, but the strain of his expression was too much, he couldn't relax into laughter. It was almost as if he must keep that strain, that pale tight tension, resisting Elena's easiness. She had never felt so free, so past the need of her control of herself; but she respected his severity. So she closed her eyes to draw him nearer. He would have absolute access to her as soon as she closed her eyes.

Then she felt herself gripped by him. He was leaning over

her. They were silent now, in a kind of combat, an exertion, and when she put her hands on his arms, feeling the tight, fearful muscles there, she knew he couldn't notice anything she did. It was all private, a terrible need. She wanted to tell him how she had waited for him, gone hollow, soft, absolutely at peace, waiting for him and knowing he would come. But she did not dare speak, because she knew her voice would distract him.

So he made love to her: she felt the love being made, forced, generated out of his misery as a physical creature, grinding itself into her. His flesh seemed almost timid of her, and then violent, hard. He said something— He uttered something, a sound. And then Elena found that she was holding him, that she was lying on a bed and holding him. They seemed to have fallen here together, clumsy now and warm. Elena's eyes fluttered open and she was staring at a ceiling somewhere: squares of a beige paperish material with tiny holes.

A man without a name: a name she couldn't read.

Confused with the rocks at the edge of the ocean, the chilly salty odor.

Then he said again, as if this were an incantation, that she was beautiful, that. . . . That. . . . And in a while he clutched at her again, with almost the same desperation as before, his hands moving hard across her back, his mouth hard and combative against hers. Elena felt herself sinking back, down, in a confusion new to her; now she gave herself up entirely and did not think of him, had no clear knowledge of him at all. She felt only the sensation of him, the driving hardness, this man's need of her that was translated into inaudible cries, commands. She did not think of him as a man whose name she didn't know, a man she didn't remember and could never have imagined. She did not think of him, the mysterious strength that uncoiled in him, in his muscles, but only of the sharp penetration of her body. She did not remember it having happened before. It shocked her, frightened her—that insistent hardness, the pushing inward, inward, so that she was forced backward, her mind forced backward into a kind of darkness—

Her breath came in short, shocked gasps, like his. But he could not break through the privacy of his own struggle to get to her, and she half thought she was safe from him, from suffering whatever he was suffering, and she half thought, half feared, she must endure it. But in the end he was too unconscious of her. Her body trembled in sympathy with his, her neck went stiff as she felt the stiff, terrible strain of his neck, the cords of his neck, the weight of his head, his face, his mouth—but she escaped him, she went into a deep, self-less peace, her consciousness of her own body emptied out and no risk.

He shuddered in her arms. She held him still.

Then she breathed more easily again, as if to soothe him. Now he might imitate her, her clarity. Her sense of herself, which had been driven backward, hunted, almost squeezed out of shape, now returned to her as she felt clearly his back and the muscles of his back, the smooth skin that was somehow familiar, an ordinary man's flesh.

". . . now you . . . we. . . ."

He broke off, out of breath.

He lay beside her with his arm across his forehead.

". . . now you . . . you might love me . . . ?" he said.

Elena looked across the room, somewhere across the sun-striped air. She was conscious of the separate lengths of their bodies, though she did not look at them. What did this mean? Had she committed a crime? Adultery? Was it real? . . . Oh very real, the hum of the room's invisible fans, the expensive complicated machinery! Very real, a man's jagged breath! She loved him. What had happened was real, even if she herself were not real.

"I don't know how," she said aloud.

But he didn't hear. He was breathing quickly, shallowly. When he spoke it was in his normal voice, a voice he was forcing back to normal: "You're going back to him though . . . ? When are you going back?"

"I don't know," Elena said.

"You're not leaving him?"

Elena felt the rush of panic again, but it wasn't strong enough to envelop her. For a moment she lay beside him, wondering why he should ask that question. Then she said, "No."

He leaned over her. He was flushed, smiling. She was startled at the intimacy of his face, his dark, shrewd, intelligent eyes. His body no longer quivered with that terrible energy, that pressure that had nearly extinguished her. . . . "You were really here, waiting for me," he said, in a kind of triumph. "Now I don't need anything . . . the rest of my life I won't need anything." He kissed her again happily. She felt how his happiness excluded her, because it was so robust, and she was so soft, so empty, beneath it.

"But I almost didn't recognize you," he said.

Elena lay at peace beneath his fond, warm, intimate gaze, feeling how he was passing judgment on her, completing her. She believed it was a perfect balance, a perfect reflection as in a mirror: the Elena lying beside him, the Elena in his brain.

5

When Elena returned to the Miner estate she saw a large black car, a rented car, in the driveway. That meant Marvin was there.

She was wearing the same clothes she'd worn on Friday, and a raincoat made of thin black plastic that she had bought for $1.98 from a sidewalk vendor near the bus station. It was raining now and the temperature was in the fifties; Elena's hair fell in wet wisps onto her forehead and neck. She was exhausted. When she saw the black rented car she could not really focus any attention upon it.

Her husband came out to meet her. She was aware of him walking quickly, then running. She was aware of him shouting at her, or toward her, but she could only shake her head sleepily, groggily. *Where were you? What happened to you?* he cried. Elena was very dizzy; she had forgotten to eat for some time. Her husband took hold of her and immediately she pressed herself forward into his arms.

Are you sick . . . ? Did anything happen to you? Did anyone . . . ?

He helped her into the house. She was aware of someone else there, a man, though not Theodore, who stood back as Marvin walked with her into the house, stumbling with her. *Did anyone hurt you?*

She was able to tell him: *No one.*

Then she was lying down, on a bed. Another bed. The bedspread was complicated and rough against her face, crocheted whorls and knots rough as rope. Her face was already sore, the skin rubbed so that it felt almost raw. Elena could smell her husband's alarm, his dangerous excitement, the familiar sharp odor of his perspiration; she knew she was safe.

A doctor with a tanned, genial face was called in to examine her; he was another friend of Harry Miner's. Elena wanted only to sleep but she understood that she had to say something, it was important she say something . . . she heard herself telling them she'd gotten lost, she had walked too far and had gotten lost and was cold, tired, confused. . . . Standing over her, Marvin stared into her face and she saw at first how he believed this, and then rejected it, and then, after a long, slow, painful moment, how he believed it again. He was saying, "Elena, my God . . . I've been so worried about you . . . I . . . I didn't know what to think . . . I've been out of my mind with worry. . . ."

"I'm sorry," she said.

"Nobody hurt you? Nobody touched you?"

"Nobody," she said.

The doctor's name was Nicholson; he gave her a shot of Vitamin C, he said, for her cold. She was grateful for his presence but embarrassed that he and her husband should take her so seriously.

She slept for a while and her lover came to lie beside her, on top of the bedspread, companionably and chastely. Her body ached from him but she said nothing; this embarrassed her also. Then, when she woke again she found herself in a bedroom with high ceilings, carved wooden fixtures, strange wall lamps that were meant to be torches, held aloft by black hands that poked out of the walls. . . .

He believed you?

He loved me.

Dr. Nicholson spent a few hours with her and Marvin, complaining about a recent malpractice suit in Los Angeles, sipping a drink Marvin had made him. Marvin himself was drinking straight bourbon, a shot glass and a bottle on the bedside table, his chair pulled right up to the table. He was looking much better now and the drained, ghastly tone of his skin had vanished; he was happy, flushed with success, like a bridegroom. While he and Dr. Nicholson talked, he kept staring at Elena.

Sleepily, contented, Elena sat propped up against the enormous headboard of the bed, the water-stained copy of *Middlemarch* open in front of her, though she was not really reading. Several pages of the novel were missing in one of the early chapters. She had read right through; then the pages leaped from page 106 to 187, and she kept on reading, though with less interest. Now she looked from her husband to Dr. Nicholson and back again, following their conversation in a way. She felt much better now. It was Monday: a new week. It was still June, the very end of June, but by the time Marvin took her back to Detroit, it would probably be the first of the next month.

He had believed her, he had believed even her confusion, her faltering unconvincing account of having been lost. He had believed everything and now she half believed it herself: she had wandered along the beach, had climbed up to the highway, had gotten lost in the small hills on the far side of the highway. Yes, that might have happened. And the raincoat? He didn't think to ask about that. And the raw, reddened skin? He didn't ask.

Elena looked from one man to the other, politely, smiling politely, shyly, privileged to overhear their conversation. It was really very interesting—about medical lawsuits and the extravagant claims that were being won by plaintiffs who would not have even considered suing a few years ago. But Elena kept thinking of her lover, who had withdrawn now to the far side of the room . . . a shadowy but alert presence, overhearing everything. His judgments were rapid and cruel. He himself was not involved and so he could be hard, hard, like something you might sharpen a knife against. Elena thought of him, feeling him again, suddenly, swiftly, and a kind of spasm shot across her face as if she were in pain.

Fortunately, neither man noticed.

Dr. Nicholson, a very trim, tanned man in his fifties, still lingered on the subject of the malpractice case he'd been involved in, not personally, but as a witness for the defense. A woman had sued a prominent Los Angeles surgeon for two million dollars, claiming malpractice because her husband had died of something the newspapers called "dark depression" in their many stories on the case. One of the plaintiff's testifying physicians had even used that expression, Dr. Nicholson said in disgust . . . it really disgusted him, a medical man using such terminology. But of course the jury had been fooled. Marvin was listening attentively, nodding, but cautiously, as if he did not want to support either side. The two million dollars might have interested him.

Marvin said he hadn't known people could die of depression.

Dr. Nicholson said the patient had lost the use of both legs, following a fifteen-hour operation on his spine . . . an operation notoriously difficult, performed by an expert neurosurgeon who had not had much hope for the outcome . . . but he had chosen to take the risk anyway, and though several things had, in fact, gone wrong during the operation, three of them errors, it was not so comically disastrous an operation as the newspapers had indicated. Dr. Nicholson sipped his drink and said things looked bad, very bad. Soon everyone would be suing their doctors. No one would be safe; the only people who would profit by it would be the lawyers. . . .

Then he apologized, embarrassed at what he had said. "I only mean unscrupulous lawyers," he told Marvin.

Elena's gaze was drawn to the darkest corner of the room, where a mahogany chest blocked out part of a window. The chest had several drawers and each drawer's handle was a black hand, poking out of the wood, with a small brass stick closed in its fist. She sensed her lover there, in that corner.

If Marvin happened to notice her looking that way . . . ?

Now he and the doctor were talking about something else, an antitrust suit. Several pharmaceutical corporations had been charged with price-fixing and the trial was in its twenty-second month and still going strong. The prosecution was still presenting its side; then, after the verdict, there would probably be an appeal. And, after that, there were more than a thousand subsidiary suits waiting. Elena wondered if her lover would think this was interesting. She tried to pay attention to her husband, as if to show her lover that he was interesting, fascinating. "A half-dozen men have died so far, during the course of the trial, and it's nowhere near over," Marvin said. "One of the codefendants himself, two of the defense's attorneys, and a young assistant U.S. attorney . . . he was only thirty-two, and he died of bleeding ulcers, in fact he collapsed right in court. That cheered up one side but demoralized the other. . . ."

"Those can be nasty cases, severe ulcers," Dr. Nicholson said.

"Two other men died but I don't remember which side they were on, or maybe they were only jurors or clerks," Marvin said. "One juror was excused because he evidently had a breakdown of some kind. . . ."

"People are always having breakdowns," Dr. Nicholson said. "What they call 'breakdowns'. . . . Especially out here in California, it's an epidemic, and it really doesn't mean anything. It's all in the imagination. If you go into medicine, you have to believe in the body first and the imagination last . . . otherwise. . . . Mr. Howe, may I ask you a question? . . . I mean, it isn't a professional, uh, a piece of professional advice?"

"Of course," Marvin said happily.

"In regard to a big antitrust suit like that, or any suit brought against a private company by the Attorney General's office, what would you advise . . . ? Is there any hope?"

"Internal Revenue has been after me for a year now, but I'm fairly confident I'll win," Marvin said. "It's just a small case, anyhow. With a really big case, with the United States Government bringing suit against someone . . . well . . . if God Himself brought suit against you, what would you do? Plead *nolo contendere* and hope for a very sharp ax. That's my advice."

"*Nolo contendere* . . . ?"

"Absolutely," Marvin said, thrusting his chin upward as if to bare his throat. "'Do with me what you will.'"

Elena looked at him: he was a large, rather ugly man, a middle-aged man who now returned her gaze fondly. It was obvious that he loved her very much. He was wearing a mint-green polo shirt with the tiny figure of a golfer on its pocket, and black-and-white checked trousers, his hair tousled, looking like a wig. Though he was much older than Elena's lover, his hair was as thick as his, maybe thicker. His smile deepened as he stared at her. She saw in him the pride he felt in her, the almost surreptitious pride; there was something sacred about the way he was watching her.

He squeezed her hand happily, squeezing the rings into her fingers.

She did love him. She loved him for being her husband, for looking at her like that.

When she was better she got out of bed, left the book somewhere and forgot about it, and forgot about the corner of the room where her lover seemed to wait, watching; she believed she would never have the need to see him again.

6 13 BRIEF EPISODES

1 *What are you thinking? What are you remembering? Why were you late? Who were you with? Where are you going now? Where are you now?*

I want from you this–

And this–

I want–

I–

He said those things to her, but not out loud. She felt the small angry thrusts of words, the bitterness of his need. Then, once it was over, he would love her.

She didn't argue with him, but when she came in she looked swiftly at him to see what awaited her.

I want from you this I want this and this
But not that
I want you to do this and think this
But you must not think that
In fact I forbid you to

He was always waiting for her, in hotel rooms he rented, cheap rooms with cheap bedspreads and cheap formica-topped furnishings, worn-out carpets or very new bright carpets of bold colors and designs. He would get there early, an hour or two early, so that by the time she arrived, knocked gently on the door, it was his room, his territory, the bed sprinkled with ashes from his many cigarettes and the bedside table piled with his work: papers, books, loose notes.

As soon as she came in she looked desperately at his face to see who was there.

Against his will, often, his face hardened for a fight and he said *I loathe the fact that I'm here* but not out loud; she knew he was thinking of a woman who had just stepped into the room, the body of a woman who had come from some other set of rooms, in another house he didn't own. He was thinking of her husband, and his face hardened, his heartbeat accelerated to provide him with enough new fresh blood for a fight.

Because he was a real Detroiter, a son of Detroit: he knew who he was.

And Elena, stepping into the room, staring at her lover's face, had to wait to see who she was.

Sometimes he was not waiting by the bed, sitting on the edge of the bed; sometimes he opened the door and embraced her, and what he said was only *I love you.* Or he laughed and said *I love you and the hell with everything else.* He was unnaturally elated at such times, as if drunk or drugged; he would kiss her, rub his face against her, all the parts of her body, laughing, like a child or an animal mad for affection. Elena had not known men could be so affectionate. She watched him in amazement through her drowsy, half-closed eyes, through her eyelashes that seemed to tangle together, she would caress him even though she believed he couldn't feel her caresses, hadn't time to notice them. . . . With Jack everything was so abrupt, so highly charged, the very surface of his skin seemed so sensitive that it was beyond feeling anything; the brushing of a woman's fingertips or a hard, sudden blow from a fist would be equal, equally felt.

He loved her so much, he loved especially her fear of him, that first half minute when she entered the room and had no idea who was waiting for her. And so he could assure her, even before he made love to her:

I won't hurt you
I won't destroy you
I love you

and he would laugh at her apparent fear.

Cheerfully, tenderly, he would be the good friend who brought her good news: she wouldn't be destroyed. She had looked, the first time she came to him in Detroit, like a tourist, her hair done up in the old style and her clothes her usual clothes, expensive and protective, Elena a tourist climbing the stairs of a place said to be valuable, sacred, but believing none of the lies. And yet pretending to believe, because you must not accuse people of lying. And Jack, seeing her, had not known whether to hate her for that fear, that doubt of him, or love her because she was so afraid of him and so doubtful . . . she understood all this, just by looking at him.

Elena had said: *I can't stay.*

He had said: *I don't expect you to stay.*

So they remained in the room, Elena standing near the door, watching him, and her lover gazing abstractly around at the walls: as if at an audience. She could not think why she had come here, why she had made so many arrangements to get here, to a small dreary hotel not far from the good hotels. To say good-by to him, to say hello? It was July 9. She saw quite clearly that her lover resembled men she had been seeing often in this segment of her life: younger men at parties given by older men, the newer, younger assistants of middle-aged lawyers or judges or politicians. His face wasn't as public as theirs yet. It was still private, quite guarded and cunning; his eyes darted from point to point in space, measuring the swift jumps of thought back in his head.

Elena noticed the ugliness of the room, especially a stamped landscape over the bed, a meadow of comic-strip greens and yellows, a sky much too blue. She wondered if he had taken this particular room, in this particular hotel, just to insult her; or if he couldn't afford a better room.

She had said, trying to smile: "I told you I could only stay a minute, but . . . but . . . why should I stay? You won't even tell me your last name."

He had replied: "Why should I tell you my last name? You obviously didn't care enough to remember it, did you?"

"I. . . ."

"I wrote it down for you once and you must have thrown it away."

"I couldn't. . . ."

Look, are you staying with me or leaving?

Staying.

Even though I'm insulting you?

Staying.

Do you know why I really don't want to tell you my name . . . ?

So she stayed with him that afternoon, thinking that she had come so far, so many difficult miles; she might as well stay. But he had been almost sinister in his silence, his stubbornness. Not very loving. Not yet her good friend. She knew he was angry with her because of the telephone calls he'd had to make to her: her obvious reluctance to see him again, her obvious guilt. She had not told him of her decision not to see him again, but he had certainly guessed it. And so he must punish her a little. And in a way Elena felt a pleasure in submitting to it, to his rudeness, because it was a polite thing to do, to allow him revenge; she believed she would never see him again after that day.

So she had stayed.

And, later, he had talked to her in a soft, wondering voice. He said *I'm sorry*, over and over he said *I'm sorry*, lying with his face pressed against hers . . . making a confession to her, like a criminal. She held him. She listened to him. In amazement she realized how much she valued him, though she had come close to not seeing him again.

He said, "I shouldn't have bullied you into coming here. I'm sorry. I'm sorry I did that. And about my name, my name . . . I don't know . . . I thought. . . ." He was so close to her that she couldn't see him. The room was not dim, because he hadn't bothered to pull the shades, but his face was against hers, much too close for her to see. Yet she felt he was lying. She listened to him the way she would listen to the truth, respectfully, because you must not accuse people of lying. "I was . . . I was afraid you'd confess all this to your husband . . . and . . . I was afraid you might feel guilty, and it was so strange, out in San Francisco, it wasn't natural . . . it wasn't normal, not normal life . . . was it?"

Elena said no, to agree with him.

"I thought you'd go back to your husband, that you'd think it all over and turn against me, against it, the way women sometimes do . . . I think they do. . . . I really don't know much about women. I admit it. And so . . . and so I thought I'd better not tell you too much, because . . . your husband is a very strange man and . . . and. . . ." Elena waited. She would agree with him, to show she believed everything; and perhaps she did believe it, at least part of it. She loved him and really did not care.

"Frankly," he laughed in embarrassment, "I like life and want to hang around for a while. . . ."

Elena did not understand.

"I thought he might have me killed," Jack said.

He sat up, trying to laugh again, in embarrassment. He glanced at her to see what she thought.

Elena lay without moving. Tenderly, unhatefully, she thought: *No, you did it to humiliate me.*

"He's a strange man, a very powerful man . . . I doubt that you know him really," Jack said. "I thought you might confess everything to him and he'd . . . well . . . he would get angry. . . ."

Elena thought: *No, to humiliate me, so you could always say I stayed.* She said: "I wouldn't tell him. I won't tell him."

"Won't you? But maybe you will someday."

"I won't."

"I'm not exactly accusing him of being a murderer, please don't think that, or be offended . . . but. . . . I must sound absurd to you, like a coward, at least," he said, his face beginning to glow with that flushed, surprised glow Elena had often noticed in her husband's face after he had made love to her. Now the tension between them was over, seemed to be over; the tension of her arrival, her reluctance, the tension of his insulting her with the room and the cheap bed and his own anonymity. He was suddenly very happy. "I don't think you really know Marvin Howe, Elena, and the things he might do . . . or have done. . . . Not that I believe he's ever had anyone killed, no, absolutely not. Not yet. But I think . . . I don't think it's farfetched . . . that . . . with you. . . . You're the kind of woman men sometimes make mistakes over . . . they get deranged or something . . . I don't mean that it might happen . . . but. . . . And he might kill you too; have you thought of that?"

"No," Elena said.

"You haven't thought that? After what you did in San Francisco?"

"No."

He smiled slowly.

"You're not like other women, maybe," he said. "You don't exaggerate . . . you really don't think much, do you? . . . I mean, you don't speculate, you don't fantasize? I don't know you very well yet . . . but . . . I'm very happy that you don't exaggerate and dramatize things . . . the way I'm sure most women do. . . ."

"I won't tell him," Elena repeated.

That seemed to be what he wanted to hear.

2 But:

I want you this way and from you I want this and this and not that
And I want it now
And I forbid you to
And I loathe the thought of sharing you
Because really I loathe you
And I loathe myself in your presence
And the fact that I must be here and not somewhere else

3 "It's lovely, it's a lovely thing, how much did it cost?"

"I don't know."

He examined her watch critically.

"Are these little stones diamonds? You walk around wearing things like this . . . ? You're not afraid of someone simply stopping you, let's say on the sidewalk outside this dump of a hotel, and snatching it off your arm . . . ?"

Elena laughed.

If he wanted to know what time it was, he had a habit of picking up her watch from the bedside table, and not his own; as if Elena's watch told more perfect time; as if she were anxious to know the time.

Elena didn't care what time it was.

But he kept saying: *It's one o'clock. It's one-thirty already. It's going on two. . . .* Grimly, severely, as if she would want to know the exact time, because she had to get away from him: *It's already. . . . It's getting late, Jesus, it's already. . . .* Elena thought how pointless this was, her lover's testing of her, his stray little jabbing remarks; but she supposed he had to do it and she had to allow him to do it. It really meant nothing. If she protested very much she would feel his irritation, his bewilderment. It was like a powerful, reluctant motion in him, a current beginning again in his body.

She wanted to take the watch out of his fingers and throw it against the wall.

She wanted to say—

But she had to let him do it, because he suspected her of not loving him: that was why she had walked in here so happily, to find him waiting for her, troubled, miserable with love for her and miserable about their predicament.

"You don't seem to realize how serious this is," he told her often.

And again: "This is very serious."

Elena tried to understand him, she tried to agree. But he rejected her agreement because, after the first several times they had met, he had caught on to her exquisite politeness. He told her that he walked around in a daze, he only half-heard what people said to him, he couldn't concentrate on his work and he had very important work to do; he was often miserable, sleepless with guilt, actually twitching with guilt as he lay beside his wife; and. . . .

And he instructed himself in this, repeating to himself *This is not serious.* But it did not seem to work. He blamed her.

He pretended to blame her, joking with her; but he really did blame her. He said that he walked around in the real world with a constant numbness in him, and that probably other people had begun to notice. Certainly his wife must notice. His sentences trailed off and he wasn't always able to concentrate on the problems he set for himself . . . and . . . and he wondered if she was experiencing anything similar.

"When you're not with me, like this, what do you think about?" he asked.

It was a light, conversational question, but Elena knew better than to take it lightly. She told him she thought of him.

"You do, really . . . ? Do you?"

"Yes."

"All the time, or . . . ?"

Elena hesitated. She knew he would not believe a lie, and yet he was waiting to hear a lie. Even her hesitation excited and angered him. But she said, "Yes," and it was true, in a way: though she did not really think of him, of *Jack Morrissey,* she carried around with her the shadowy presence of her lover. He watched her from the darkest corner of any room, though the room might be populated with many people; he lay beside her and embraced her, often, with a tenderness her real lover could not always manage.

Jack laughed. "Well, I don't exactly believe that, but. . . . But it's nice of you to say so. You really are very nice."

4 One day in August they met outside somewhere, as if to experiment with a new setting. Her lover eyed her critically, nervously. Elena felt very happy. It was a day of sunshine and they were walking through a paved garden, an area of chaste concrete blocks and small, spare fountains, and ascetic slabs of aluminum and glass: here the few green things, the expensive shrubbery and carefully planted flowers, took on a value they would not have had in an ordinary public park.

Her lover didn't seem to notice any of this. He kept glancing at her, staring at her. Maybe jealous of her happiness. It was obvious that he was uneasy, meeting her in public.

He confessed that he was nervous: that she did exist for him, mainly, in rooms.

What they needed were some walls.

What he needed was—

He smiled helplessly, and took out of his pocket a pair of sunglasses that were tinted blue, a green-blue. They walked side by side for a while, as if they were friends. Elena felt that he was fascinated by her. He watched her, admired her. At such times Elena felt a flash of pure triumph, a certainty of her beauty and her immortality that was somehow selfless, existing outside her own being. She knew her beauty was not finite and mortal, but that it transported her, illuminated her, and that she was completed in it.

Her lover was a man of a certain height, with dark hair and a nerve-worn face, now partly disguised by sunglasses. He was not a happy man, not at the moment. She loved him, that he should be so unhappy, staring at her and wanting her, only a few feet from her, yet totally apart from her; he had no access to her, not out here.

She felt how he was loving her in his imagination, in one of his rented rooms. He did need walls around them to love her properly, in his style of loving. She laughed and said playfully: *You don't want me just in private, do you? Are you ashamed of me?*

Suddenly, conscious of being exposed, he seemed to realize where they were. He looked around, as if waking from a trance. They had walked through the concrete area and were near a busier quadrangle, adjacent to the art museum. Not far away people were walking, a few students from the university were strolling in casual summer clothes, some of them barefoot. Elena saw her lover stare at these people, waking from his trance. . . . He had sighted some enemies.

He said uneasily, *We'd better say good-by . . . I've got to get back. . . .*

Elena agreed. She did not ask why he was so frightened, why he wanted to escape. She did not ask *Don't you want to die?—aren't I worth it?* because that would have been too serious a question. She knew he was thinking it himself, but keeping it to himself.

A very private man.

They walked together for a few minutes longer, Elena's skirt brushing against the side of his briefcase, catching a little on one of the locks; he was careful to carry the briefcase on the side nearest her, between them.

I hate to leave you, he said.

Hate to give you up. . . .

5 Elena was sitting in the large drawing room, which had the appearance of a photograph into which people had been placed, selected people. She was listening to someone talk. The men spoke in turn, sometimes interrupting one another, but usually polite enough to wait; the hour was early, not yet nine, no one was drunk, no one wanted to argue yet. . . . Elena was the hostess for this party and she had nothing to do but watch the level of liquor and ice in her friends' glasses, her eye making the rounds of glasses regularly. Marvin would become too engrossed in the conversation to notice anything like this. As Elena sat there, in the walled-in space of a room, her mind slipped gracefully sideways through the sound of voices.

I hate to leave you, someone was saying. *Hate to give you up.*

Because she was with these people, seated on a sofa of dark brown velvet, because her legs were chastely and smoothly crossed, every visible part of her elegant, under control, beautiful, she was entirely free to slip sideways through the conversations, the smiles. Her husband and another man, white-haired, handsome, were talking about the extraordinary rise in the stock of a locally based corporation that manufactured battery-controlled burglar alarms, and Elena sensed in the distance, through the archway and out in the foyer, her lover's presence, his passing judgment on them all. How hard he was, how severe! He would not have joined this party if invited, if Elena had begged him to come in. No. Never.

But she was very happy here, seen from any point of view—from the white-haired gentleman's point of view, or from his wife's, or from Marvin's—Elena Howe sitting on a sofa, alert and smiling. Seen from a great distance, as if through the wrong end of a telescope, she was all surface, all protective surfaces.

"But the future lies in motion detectors," someone interrupted. He was a businessman, a friend of Marvin's. "Not just electric eyes, though more can be done with them, but laser beams—the most sensitive refinements of light."

They all agreed with him.

Elena's gaze moved about the room, from one glass to the next, checking the level of liquor and ice cubes. Someone was whispering to her *This is serious, this is very serious,* but she was distracted by laughter around her. Someone had made a wise, witty observation, and it was necessary to laugh.

"The future will be entirely recorded by the government and by private parties, every moment committed to microfilm," Elena's husband was saying, perhaps as a joke, though Elena couldn't really tell. "That will make everyone honest. That will take the place of God, Who used to be watching us all and remembering everything we did. . . ."

"Marvin, you're always exaggerating!" someone said.

"Marvin never exaggerates," someone else said.

Her lover came to the doorway to listen more closely. Drawn by the sound of laughter, by the conversation of old friends, by her husband's robust unreadable voice. . . .

He would never step into this room.

6 A few days later, Elena was punished for her adultery.

Marvin was away, in Texas, and the telephone rang and rang

and was still ringing when she entered the house, suddenly in a panic, hurrying to answer it.

She answered it, out of breath. It was her husband.

Across a great distance he seemed to be calling to her, out of breath himself, trying to tell her something. "Elena? Elena? Can you hear me, is this connection any good? I'm all right, Elena, I'm in one piece . . . if you should happen to hear any news. . . ."

She went rigid with panic, not knowing what was wrong. She did not know. Did not understand. She could hardly hear him except to know something had happened. He was assuring her that he was safe. She sat down on the arm of a chair or a sofa, feeling faint, sick, listening to Marvin's distant voice:

"I'm in a hospital in San Antonio but I'll be out in the morning, I'm sure . . . it's mainly for x-rays, I'm sure it won't be anything more. I wanted to call you before you heard anything and maybe worried. The pilot wasn't as lucky as I was . . . but I won't go into it now. . . . I'm fine, just a little shaken up. Elena? Dear? Where were you, that you took so long to answer the phone?"

She managed to say something.

"They're mad as hell down here, I mean the police," Marvin went on. "The hospital staff resents me too—they all know who I am—but I'll be treated well, don't worry about that. I'll be back home in a few days. The news stories will be sensational, so ignore them, sweetheart, in fact don't read any of them— The main thing is that I'm perfectly all right, just banged up a little, maybe a rib cracked—nothing important—"

Elena closed her eyes. She felt sick with guilt, dazed, sickly in her relief, in the warm ebbing dreaminess of love, her lover's love, his semen still in her body. . . . Her husband was talking to her, across a distance, assuring her he was still alive. Out of danger. She believed she was somehow responsible for this, for what had happened to him, even though she did not know what had happened and he seemed reluctant to tell her. She said, *Should I fly down . . . ?*

"God, no," Marvin said sharply. "No. They'd just make a fuss down here, gaping at you. Things are pretty wild, you know; I've kept the details of this case from you so you wouldn't worry, but the main thing is . . . I keep unearthing some amazing facts here . . . making some very powerful men a little worried. . . . Even the judge is getting uneasy and I'm going to try again for a change of venue. . . . We weren't exactly shot down, Elena, if you should happen to hear that. The bullets just damaged the tail and didn't come near me or the pilot . . . the plane crashed because the pilot panicked, not because he was hit . . . and . . . well. . . . I won't go into it now, Elena, but don't worry; I'm perfectly all right. We'll be laughing about the whole thing in a while. So don't worry, will you? And don't watch the newscasts, do you promise?—or read the papers?"

Elena promised.

7 "It was his own client who tried to shoot him down," Jack said. "I know you don't want to hear about it, and I don't want to talk about it, but I want you to know what kind of a . . . what kind of life he leads."

Elena said nothing.

Jack turned to look at her. He didn't smile. "Don't you think life is serious, Elena? Any of it?"

Elena said meekly, "Yes."

"No. No, you don't mean it. You just say what you think I want to hear," he said. "The truth is—you haven't given life any thought."

"I don't know," Elena said.

Jack laughed. He lay back and laughed. Then he began a long monologue, a gloomy joking monologue about the ways of death he risked: being run off the road, being drowned, being torn apart by Marvin's dogs. He had gone through some of these speculations in the past, and Elena wondered if she should be offended by them; what right did he have to believe she was married to a murderer?

Then he lost interest in his joking. He lay in silence, not aware of her. Elena could hear the ticking of his wristwatch.

"Oh hell," he said. "I wish I'd never flown out there, all the way to San Francisco . . . it was a risk I never needed to take. It's the only act of my life I can't account for. I'll never forgive you for it."

Elena thought: *He's worried about dying.* He seemed in another dimension from her, thinking, calculating, alert and alive, while Elena, as if she were the aftermath of his passion, his own sense of stillness, completion, lay in a kind of hazy weightlessness. Instead of arguing with him, Elena said nothing.

Jack got up and said, laughing, angry, "You must agree with me then?" He searched for his cigarettes in a pile of clothing. "Or what? Don't you care?"

"My husband isn't going to kill you," Elena said. "Please believe me. It can't happen."

"It can't? Why not?"

"These things don't happen."

"Ordinarily, no. To a man like myself, no. Never. I wouldn't be important enough. But my very good fortune has catapulted me to such heights. . . . I attract attention now, I notice people staring at me. That's because I must look so happy, so beatific. After all, I'm not an ordinary man; I'm a maniac. My wife is always asking me what's wrong, why am I so energetic, why does my side of the bed get so damp and so wrinkled, why am I always making unfunny jokes . . . ? I didn't used to make so many jokes before I met you."

"That might mean you're not serious," Elena said lightly.

"No, it doesn't mean that, it means the opposite," Jack said. "The only people who make jokes are serious people. You need intelligence, moral intelligence, to make jokes. You wouldn't understand that."

Elena closed her eyes. She heard him pacing around, going to the window, pressing his forehead against the pane—he had a habit of pressing his forehead against windows and walls and doorjambs, unconsciously—she heard him sigh impatiently. "Successful men, the kind you know, Elena, out in Grosse Pointe —they never make jokes because it isn't necessary. Normal men, sexually adjusted men, don't joke because they're happy as morons. I know that. And women like yourself don't joke and don't understand jokes; it takes both misery and intelligence for that."

"Yes," Elena said tonelessly.

"As I deteriorate in this relationship of ours I begin to notice myself getting more frantic. I'm like an entertainer. I make clumsy attempts to joke around, to entertain people I detest, who drop in at my apartment for free meals, maybe, or whatever the hell they come for. I entertain my clients. My wife. I have a routine in which I throw myself against a wall and then pick myself up and take a few steps backward, and then run at the wall again and pick myself up and wipe off the blood and keep my face carefully blank, because it spoils the fun to show any pain; you must never show pain. Would you like me to do that routine for you, Elena?"

Elena laughed.

"And another routine, for my wife's amusement: I climb on top of a woman and wait for something to happen, but nothing happens. Then I say I am very tired. Then the woman says . . . *yes, you're very tired, you work very hard.* . . . and she doesn't say what she is thinking or what anyone who might be witnessing this is thinking. So I agree with what's been said and say *I'm very tired* and I don't say *I'm in love with someone else.*"

Elena laughed nervously and did not dare look at him.

8 "You love me? You do love me?" he kept asking.

You must imagine everything.

". . . aren't pretending to love me . . . ?"

But how did women pretend? How to pretend?

Sensation must be mainly psychological and not physical, not natural. . . .

With her lover everything was extinguished except his love: his demand for her. As soon as she came to him the world ended, went blank. He loved her so much, needed her so violently, that she seemed almost to be extinguished in her own body and to enter her body again through his. Then she would feel that flash of pure, selfless triumph, the joy of her completion. . . .

In her body she did not pretend, there was nothing to pretend. She felt nothing.

9 He never said anything to her about that, but he did interrupt himself to say, over the telephone one evening: "Elena, why are you so untouched by all this?"

"I'm not untouched by it," she said.

"For instance, you never talk about your husband to me; I have to assume he's out of town or back in town; you never mention him, you must not even be thinking about him. . . . Don't you feel guilty?"

"With you? No. . . ."

"When you're with him, with *him*, don't you feel guilty?"

"I . . . I think. . . . Yes, sometimes. . . ."

"You're capable of it? Really, are you?"

"Yes."

"I don't believe it," he said. "You consider yourself such a prize, a gift to him, you don't owe him anything—isn't that it? Just your existence justifies this other side of your life and you think he's lucky to have what he has, don't you?"

"That isn't true," Elena said.

She thought: *He hates me.*

In amazement she thought: *This man hates me. . . .*

"That's isn't true," Elena said, faltering, "I . . . I don't know what you mean. . . . You don't want to marry me, you've never said anything about marriage . . . you . . . you. . . . You don't want. . . ."

Jack interrupted and said: "So you don't feel guilty with him. What about me? Do you feel guilty betraying me? What about that?"

"I. . . ."

"When you're with him, what about me then? Am I an idea to you, a memory, or what? Or do you just forget me?"

"I don't know what you mean," Elena said.

"Yes or no, Elena, tell me *yes* or *no*."

"I. . . ."

"You forget me entirely, don't you? The way you forget him, right?—and you pass from one part of your life to another, very chaste and beautiful and uncontaminated. Isn't that the truth?"

"No," Elena said, shocked.

"Yes, it is the truth. You don't have any curiosity about me, do you? You never ask me about my work, my private life, do you?—about my marriage?"

Elena was astonished.

"I didn't think you wanted to talk about . . . about those things," she said. "I thought. . . ."

"What?"

"That it was private. . . ."

"Yes, it is private, and maybe I don't want to talk about it particularly, but you and I have a marriage of our own, don't we? —an unbalanced one?—a rotten one? And you should show some normal interest in my life, or pretend to, shouldn't you?—or don't you give a damn?"

"I thought—"

"You never ask about my wife. You assume she's inferior to you, you probably think you're doing us all a favor by agreeing to meet me as often as you do," he said. He had begun to speak rapidly and very clearly. She recognized this voice of his and feared it; she could not stop it, could not prevent what he was doing to her. "Well, you're wrong. You're really wrong. My wife is a very intelligent woman, and people admire her who would be contemptuous of you. . . . Are you listening?"

She felt as if he had struck her. But she did not dare to hang up.

"I hope you're listening, because . . . because. . . ."

She listened to him but her mind seemed confused, shattered. Only the sound of his voice came through to her: such anger, such hatred! She felt sick. She looked up wildly and saw she was in her husband's study, a room that should have protected her. The distant ceiling was oval-shaped, a perfect shape that would not confuse anyone's eye, would not trap it. The paneled walls gleamed darkly, warmly, with hints of reflections somehow inside the polished surface, old reflections, old images, people who had lived and died and who were trapped inside the walls, who were at peace, watching Elena in pity. They pitied her this sudden attack. They pitied her, that she should be so suddenly vulnerable.

"No—stop—" she cried.

He did stop. For a long moment they were both silent.

Then he said, in a different voice: "Well . . . Elena. . . . Look, Elena, I . . . I didn't exactly mean all that. . . ."

She could not speak. Her eye was drawn helplessly from object to object in this room, sliding from place to place, finding nothing to stop it. On the mantelpiece was the bust of a Roman woman, the face smooth and blank and strong, as strong as rock; Elena forced herself to concentrate on it. It was a genuine Roman bust, Marvin had told her proudly: it was worth a great deal of money but Elena could never remember how much. . . .

Someone was speaking to her over the telephone, a voice that sounded suddenly frightened, as vulnerable as Elena herself, and she sat in a kind of daze listening to it because she did not dare to hang up. This voice was saying: ". . . we've been having these miserable quarrels at home . . . and . . . and she's making life hell for me . . . I don't know what to do . . . I. . . . Elena, could I see you tonight?"

She could not answer.

"Are you angry, Elena? Are you angry? Look, I . . . I didn't mean. . . . Could I see you tonight? If I could. . . ."

She heard a break in his voice, as if he were about to sob. She thought numbly: *He will cry in my arms. . . .*

"No. No," she whispered.

"Elena . . . ?"

"No."

It terrified me, that you would come to me and cry in my arms and then you would

It terrified me that you would

"Elena? Are you listening? Are you still there?"

I was that woman found dead, strangled, in a riverside luxury hotel, twenty-eight years old, auburn hair and blue eyes and

ex-model found strangled and alone

when you are strangled and dead you are always alone

when the police came they found no fingerprints "no clues" and they described themselves as "baffled" but when you read about it you thought: SHE DESERVED TO DIE. THEY ALL DESERVE TO DIE.

You might have strangled me yourself but you had no chance, but someone else did the strangling, and when you read about it in the paper you had to admit that I deserved to die.

THEY ALL DESERVE TO DIE.

10 After that he started to talk to her about his wife, whose name was Rachel. He kept repeating *I still love her*. In different ways, in different sets of words he kept repeating *I still love her.* It was a vow.

Elena listened in silence, sympathetically. But she hated to hear about this woman. She hated especially to hear the name *Rachel* and to sense the poison her lover tasted as he uttered that word, and yet insisted upon uttering it. His dislike for his wife seemed to her ugly, awful. And yet he himself did not acknowledge it but kept insisting, vowing. . . .

"We have the kind of marriage you probably wouldn't understand," he said. "I still love her, in spite of . . . the way things are going. . . ."

Elena listened, sympathetically. They met now in a room Jack had rented not far from his office, and its simple, shabby, anonymous furnishings were no distractions, like the gaudy framed prints and lampshades and Room Service advertisements of the hotels; here, nothing could distract them from themselves. Here, Jack seemed to talk more normally, more openly. But Elena was careful never to agree with him when he complained about his wife.

"Now it's the second week of September," Jack said, "and since Labor Day we've had house guests, friends of Rachel's . . . one of them is sick, he's always coughing and stumbling around, it's enough to drive me mad. . . . But she has such a need for people, she seems almost frantic to have people around her, living with her, as if she's afraid to be alone with me. She's afraid to talk to me, really. She doesn't want to know the truth. When people are around and she's busy with her work, she's fine. Then something goes wrong, someone disappoints her, and it's down, down, into a kind of void, a sour poisonous void. . . . And she wants me to be there with her, she wants to drag me down with her. She's afraid of me and yet she can't let me alone, she's always picking at me, criticizing me in front of other people. . . . She's contemptuous of me because I'm still the way I was in the beginning, when we met, and she's changed . . . she's gotten reckless, impatient, she's going from door to door campaigning for somebody I never heard of, I doubt that he has the residency requirements for Michigan, to run for public office—in fact, I wouldn't be surprised if he has a few convictions behind him—his candidacy is just a joke, but Rachel and her friends will not listen to me, they *will not listen.* I explain to them that if they simply pronounce certain words to someone who's a police informant, or a policeman in disguise, they're going to be hit with some serious federal charges—I'm talking about counseling draft dodgers, kids on their way to Toronto—but they *will not listen to me.* It drives me wild. . . . The worst thing that happened, this was around the time you and I met, but it's the kind of thing that's always going on . . . this couple stayed with us on their way to Seattle, the Resnacks, whom I don't even know, and not only did they walk off with some loose change and my typewriter, but they've been buying all kinds of things and somehow charging them to me; I keep getting these bills, Jesus Christ, it's enough to drive me crazy, but Rachel still tries to defend them . . . they're anarchists, they're politically pure, she says, and only want to live off the environment and work to revolutionize the entire world. . . . She defends them against me, she takes their side against *me*."

Elena was jealous of his passion. "But you do love her," she said neutrally.

"Oh, I suppose so," he said.

He paced restlessly around the room. It was a small, cramped room with a single window. The window frame had been painted not long ago, but the wood was warped and the paint had begun to blister; when he was upset Jack would stand by the window and pick at the paint. He was trying to give up smoking and his hands were restless.

"Sometimes I think . . . I think. . . . I'd like to walk away from it," he said strangely.

"From what?" Elena asked.

"From *it*. Everything."

"I don't know what you mean," Elena said.

"My life. My work. The world. Everything. The law, my so-called career, my so-called dedication. . . . Just give it up, walk away. Burrow very deeply into you, Elena, whoever you are, and give up the world."

Elena stared at the back of his head.

Finally she said lightly, so that he would not notice the mockery of her words: "I'm not the world, then . . . ?"

He did not notice. He said, "I'd like to get away somewhere with you, just be very still, secret, stop fighting, I'd like to tell you about myself, my life, and hear about your life . . . if we could get married and wrap our lives together. . . . I do too much fighting, too much shouting. . . . I wish I didn't like it so much, I wish I was a little different . . . you really deserve a better man. I'd like to walk away from the person I am, and the hell with it all. The hell with it."

He looked around at her. Elena shivered.

"But your work . . . ," she said.

"My work is driving me crazy," he said angrily. "My work!

Yes, it's my work, *mine,* because who would be stupid enough to do it except me? Most of the time I'm a nigger lawyer—but not the best kind because I'm not black—I get the leftover Negroes, the old civil rights believers of the sixties, all that worn-out rhetorical crap, and the young stylish blacks go to black lawyers exclusively, they wouldn't be caught dead with me—my wife explains all this to me, it's very kind of her, and I know she's right. And now, now, I'm breaking my head over this little bastard Meredith Dawe, Mered Dawe as he calls himself—it's a lyric little name, isn't it? Who else would take on such a problem except Jack Morrissey? Dawe's a saint, he's so humble and virtuous, so sweet, he can't keep his mouth shut; like all virtuous people he imagines he must speak the truth . . . even though he's out on bail and is awaiting trial. What frustrates me is that this Dawe really is saintly, just as everyone says, I mean his admirers —the others want him destroyed—he really is dedicated to changing the world, to converting people, whatever the hell mystic crap he believes in— I want to admire him, I want to like him, but— But—"

Jack came to Elena. He stooped over her. He said, "You're very sweet, Elena, to listen to me. I'm turning into a husband to you, aren't I?"

She was surprised at this. He was suddenly so tender.

"But maybe your own husband, your real husband, doesn't burden you the way I do . . . ?" he said.

"He doesn't talk to me like this. No."

This seemed to please Jack.

He sat beside her and rubbed his hands together nervously. "Now . . . today . . . there was something I wanted to talk to you about, but . . . but I don't know if it's the right time . . . and. . . ."

Elena waited. She looked away from him with a sudden apprehension.

"To return to the subject of my wife . . . ," he said awkwardly. "Now don't be troubled, please don't misunderstand, but . . . but. . . ."

"Yes?" Elena asked nervously.

"She won't discuss with me what is really our problem," he said, "but that's all right, I can understand that. I sympathize with her. But . . . but . . . last night she told me . . . she asked me if

I thought maybe we should have a child. To draw us together."

Elena waited, not knowing what to say.

"I said . . . I told her I didn't think so, I didn't think a baby would be the best idea, for her, for either of us . . . but she said she didn't mean a baby, but a child, an adopted child; it would be immoral for us to bring another life into the world at this point in history, but a child who was already born . . . who had no parents . . . who needed parents. . . . She said it would be something the two of us could do together, that wouldn't be selfish, but would be very generous. . . . So I said . . . I didn't know what to say . . . I said that maybe, maybe, it was a possibility. . . . Then Rachel got very excited. As if we'd made the decision already, she got very excited, she started telling me about a woman she knows who isn't married but who adopted a baby, a black baby, and how well it's working out for that woman . . . and. . . ."

"You're going to adopt a child . . . ?" Elena asked numbly.

"No. I don't know. I don't know."

Elena could think of nothing to say. She wanted to look at him, but it seemed too much of an effort just to turn her head. She wanted to ask him: *Would you like a baby? a baby?*

"I don't know," Jack said flatly.

11 *We were in a large store and I held your arm in public. Exposed in public. And you said: I can't buy you anything, I can't afford it. I can't afford you.*

Then the dream took us upward, like an escalator, and I laughed with the pleasure of it, you and I in public, exposed, as if we were free to be together like this.

You said: Why are you laughing? It's a serious business to be looking for this.

So I concentrated on the displays and the store got crowded, hot, from the other customers. I said to you: It's so hot, the faces are going to spoil. . . .

Because there were faces on display, fastened somehow with hooks or pins, real faces, skin and eyeballs and flesh, even teeth. I saw what they were and I was very frightened, I was sick with fear. I hung onto your arm. I could smell the flesh of those faces.

You said: I can't afford this store, I don't know why the hell you asked me to come with you—

She woke, stunned. The voice was Jack's. It was so nearly his own voice that she woke, in a panic, and wondered if he had spoken in this room. . . . But she was in her own bed, lying beside her husband.

Her heart hammered with fear, as if she believed her husband had heard that voice and was only pretending to sleep.

12 When Marvin returned from a trip to Las Vegas, in late October, he checked into Ford Hospital for a week of tests. He told Elena that nothing was wrong. He had had a slight attack of illness out there—it had been probably only indigestion, overwork, nothing to worry about—but the doctor who'd taken care of him advised him to have tests.

Elena stared at him and saw that he did look sick: older than she remembered, his skin grayish, his eyes unnaturally pink, almost red immediately around the irises. She stared at him and heard his words of consolation, his strange, almost guilty concern for her, for her; she realized how extraordinarily kind this man was. She helped him pack a small suitcase and thought: *How kind he is. . . .*

He checked in on a Monday morning. She spent the first half-day at his bedside, because the tests wouldn't begin until that afternoon; Marvin, in a hospital bed, in a white nightgown with absurd drawstrings, looked ashamed, frightened. He could not pay much attention to Elena's conversation, though he tried. He could not even pay much attention to the work he'd brought along, to glance through, or to the newspapers and magazines Elena had brought with them. . . .

"Don't tell anyone I'm here, please," he said.

She promised she would not.

"I wish I hadn't arranged for these tests, I don't think I need them . . . I hate people who worry about their health all the time. . . ."

On Tuesday Elena brought his mail, but he showed little interest in it. She wondered what kind of tests he had had to go through, but did not ask. She sat by his bedside, her hands folded in her lap, wishing he would talk to her—it was so unlike him to be silent, to be resting at this time of day—and then her mind gradually detached itself from his perfectly quiet, comfortable room, slipping sideways through a door's narrow opening, and she was in another room. A ceiling that had been papered too much, the wallpaper painted too often, beginning to peel, a single window with a window frame painted white, where her lover stood and picked nervously at the bumps and blisters of paint. . . .

Marvin said suddenly, but gently: "It means so much to me, just to have you here . . . just to sit with me. . . . But if you mind this, if you're bored . . . ?"

Elena told him, surprised, that of course she was not bored.

"I'll be through with all this, these humiliating tests, on Thursday afternoon," he said apologetically. "Then I can get back to work. . . ."

But he did not sound enthusiastic. Elena tried not to notice the weariness in his voice, she tried not to frighten herself by noticing. She agreed with him. She agreed. And then he fell silent again and she found herself again in that other room, she felt Jack's kisses on her face, her bare shoulders, she felt the exertion and strain of his love, his loving her . . . and then the triumph of his love, his perfecting of them both. . . .

Dreamily, dream-haunted, she sat for some time like this, aware of her husband but more aware of her lover, who hovered about her, kept touching her and stroking her. Two men had loved her, had made love to her, and she had never felt anything except, through them, the intoxicating love of her own self, which hadn't really a body, but was an idea. Two men had made love to her and in that way they were joined, there was nothing unique in either of them; Elena wished she could tell her husband . . . explain to him . . . how her lover's youth might flow into him, back into him, if only. . . . But he would not understand. He would give a name, a term, to what she had done: *adultery*. Like her lover, he dealt with words, terms; his power was the arrangement and rearrangement of words on pieces of paper, a power great enough to control the world; but insane.

By Wednesday, Elena took the elevator to her husband's floor, walked without looking at the room numbers to his room, as naturally as if she had done this for years. And Marvin, propped up with pillows, back from a morning of more tests—he wouldn't tell her what they were—glanced up at her and smiled and invited her in, as if all this were habitual. Evidently he was becoming accustomed to the tests because he looked less worried.

"You aren't too lonely, Elena, are you . . . ? In that big house, alone?"

She smiled at him in surprise. At first she could not guess if he was joking or not—because she was so often alone, had been alone for most of their marriage. She could not understand if he meant only now, since Monday, or since the beginning of their marriage—

"But I'll be back tomorrow afternoon," he said.

So he meant only now, since Monday. It was the only absence of his he must have understood.

Elena told him no, she wasn't lonely, she only wanted him to come home again.

The trial he had been preparing was postponed for eight weeks, but Marvin seemed anxious now to get back to work. While Elena was there he called his office and talked for half an hour. She sat, leafing through a magazine, listening to his voice and thinking with relief that he was going to be himself again, in a day or two himself again, Marvin Howe, her husband. . . .

At two o'clock she was asked to leave, so she said good-by, kissed him good-by, and went down to the ground floor, where Jack was waiting in the hospital cafeteria. He was reading a newspaper, holding it up and turning the pages clumsily, impatiently; Elena noticed how close he came to knocking over his coffee cup. He looked up and saw her and, in his public, guarded manner, nodded without smiling.

Elena laughed and sat down across from him.

He lowered the newspaper.

"We're not immune to being seen, you know," he said, "just because your husband is in the hospital."

Elena agreed. She felt very happy, almost giddy with relief; she agreed, though she did not really listen.

"You look cheerful," Jack said. "Is he better? How are the tests coming along?"

"He doesn't talk about them but they must be all right. Yes, I think he's better. He wants to go back to work."

"What does the doctor say?"

"He won't let me talk to the doctor," Elena said. "That isn't any of my business. . . . He'll be coming home tomorrow afternoon."

Jack nodded. He made a movement with his lips that was a kind of smile. He said, "Well, that's good. Good news." He folded the newspaper, tried to shove the pages back into place, and tossed it down. Elena noticed how his hand moved to his breast pocket, as if unconsciously searching for a package of cigarettes; then, finding nothing, the hand simply remained there, arrested unnaturally, the fingers stiff.

"He isn't faithful to you," Jack said bluntly.

Elena stared at him. Then she looked away, aside.

"He never has been. Everyone knows about it," Jack said. "Certainly you know about it too . . . ?"

Elena did not answer.

"Why don't you look at me, why are you avoiding me?" Jack said. But Elena, staring off to the side, where two young hospital attendants in soiled white outfits were standing, talking, seemed not to hear him. She noticed the nicotine-stained fingers of one of the attendants. Her lover was saying: "You don't claim to know nothing about it, do you, Elena?"

"I don't know," she said.

"Don't know what? Which question are you answering?"

"I don't know about his life."

"You don't?"

"Why are you asking me about this?"

"Why don't you want to talk about it?"

Fierce and hard and half-joking, always this poisonous sucking at me. You were sucking at my lips, my heart.

You were saying: Love me, only me! Love me!

You were saying: You're too beautiful. Or not beautiful enough. Or the word itself is not a serious word but a joke, spat around too often. So you are a joke yourself. Other people laugh but you cannot.

You were saying

Elena said rapidly: "It isn't any of my business, his life. It belongs to him. It's private. I've lived with him for only a small part of his life, I'm just a fraction of it. . . . I can't claim him . . . I belong to him but he doesn't belong to me. . . ." She paused, her heart pounding as if she had suddenly been forced to speak in public, before an audience, under oath; as if she'd been forced to sum up many ragged unthought thoughts into a brief, coherent speech, a testimony she had not prepared ahead of time. And its effect on the man who sat across from her was immediate: she did not want to look at him. "You asked me and so I told you," she said.

13 Marvin came home from Ford Hospital on Thursday afternoon, bringing back with him his suitcase and an armload of papers, looking rested, healthy again, anxious to get to work. When Elena asked about the tests he said, waving her away, "No trouble. Nothing. Don't ask."

Elena told him she was happy to hear that.

"Just overwork out there, too much plane-traveling, too much work crammed into a few days," he said. "The doctor said I was just exhausted. So the tests were a waste of time, three and a half days, except I managed to get some important telephone calls made this morning. So it's all over and it was nothing. In fact, I should feel very pleased: evidently I have the heart of a much younger man. But I shouldn't have wasted three and a half days just to learn that."

So he returned to work again.

Elena never learned anything further except, just before he prepared to fly back to Las Vegas, a few weeks later, she noticed that he seemed troubled once more. So she asked him if something was wrong . . . ?

"Nothing," he said flatly.

She asked if the client he was representing there was difficult, or the case looked bad . . . ?

Marvin, who never talked to her about his work, frowned and seemed unwilling to answer, as if he were resisting some harsh remark. Elena knew she should not question him like this. He said finally, "It has nothing to do with the case at all. It has nothing to do with my client. It's . . . it's the memory of what happened to me out there. . . ."

Elena waited.

". . . what happened in Las Vegas. . . . But I don't want to talk about it," he said.

"I understand," Elena said.

"No, you don't understand," he said, almost irritably, "but anyway I don't want to talk about it."

7

"He said I was worth dying for. . . ."

"My God," Jack said. "Then what?"

"Then . . . then . . . we were at a cabin somewhere, in Yellowstone Park . . . and I remember a wolf eating a snake, or a dog eating a snake. . . . I think I remember it. Or I dreamed it, it was so awful. And one day there were a lot of people around, some friendly people, some tourists in a van, and he held me up on a bear's shoulders . . . and some man took pictures of me. . . . Then we had to leave, we drove farther west. My mother told me later that we stopped in Nevada, a small town there. I remember being wrapped in a blanket, out in the car, and it was very cold, and he was trying to protect me from someone . . . he was very brave, I remember that. He was very strong. He loved me, and then I got sick, my eye was swollen shut, I don't know why . . . my mother told me I almost died . . . but. . . . But I don't think it was his fault, because he loved me and he wanted to . . . he wanted to. . . . He wanted to keep these other people from me, who would hurt me, and that was why . . . when they broke down the door . . . I . . . I was so. . . ."

Jack was holding her. He was gentle, silent, as if somehow ashamed.

Then he said finally, "How did it end? Did the police find him?"

Elena heard how cautious his voice was, how condemning and yet too cautious, too gentle, to be really condemning. Her eyes flooded with tears. "I loved him," she said.

"You loved him . . . ? After what he did?" Jack asked cautiously.

Elena's eyes stung. The tears were large and painful. She dreaded crying. She had only cried a few times in her life and she did not want to cry now, not with Jack, not in his presence. But he was so gentle, his manner so unusually gentle, that he seemed to be drawing the tears out of her, perversely—

"Yes, I loved him. I loved him," she said.

Jack said nothing but she could sense his thinking, his judging; but he said nothing at all. He spared her any words. And this was so unlike him too that she felt the terrible danger of tears, of breaking down; she tried to breathe slowly, carefully, in an effort to be still, not to agitate herself. . . . If she began to cry she would not be able to stop. She would have no control of herself, the sobs would break from her and she would not be able to stop. . . .

It was the end of November, and for most of that month the weather had been unseasonal, almost freakish, day after day of warm, overcast skies, temperatures in the sixties, rain and thunderstorms and more warm weather. Now, at the very end of the month, it had begun to snow in soft melting flakes, like tears, exactly like the tears Elena dreaded: she saw them falling, effortlessly, wetly, falling onto the windshield of Jack's car, filling up the windshield and then melting slowly, dreamily. She had been with Jack in his car for some time, yet the snowflakes had not covered the windows but kept melting, in an effortless dreamy silence. Outside, past the damp, streaked windshield, was a forest of black and white shapes, columns, siftings of snow that fell slowly and silently everywhere, as far as Elena could see. Jack had parked his car in a narrow service lane, in a woods in one of the city's parks.

She had been supposed to meet him at noon, in the room he rented for them, but on her way there Jack himself had stopped her on the street and told her that he didn't trust the situation; they'd better not go to the room. Elena glanced around at the ordinary, busy city street, and it seemed obvious to her that her lover was imagining danger, that no one cared about them, no one saw them, a man and a woman standing on a sidewalk in a broken-down part of town. . . . But she had not argued. She told him she should return home, then, if he really thought someone was watching. But Jack said that his car was nearby, he could drive around for a while, he pleaded with her to come with him. . . . "It's the situation back at the room I don't trust," he said.

So Elena was certain he was imagining everything.

She walked with him to his car, in a parking lot near the university campus, and he drove out to the expressway and down,

down into the city, and then out to the eastern part of the city, through narrow pot-holed streets, through slums that were still partly burned-out from the riots of a few years before. Elena sat beside him, at first rigid with disbelief that she was actually with him like this, in public in his car, the same car she remembered from last April—she noticed, on the floor at her feet, a filthy, ripped magazine cover that she remembered from last April. She thought it was strange, but typical of Jack, that he should worry so often about their being seen together and then, unaccountably, want to drive around with her sitting beside him.

But at least this neighborhood was safe for them—rows of slum buildings, boarded-up corner stores, vacant lots heaped with debris, everything appearing devastated, a scorched, bombed-out city that was still perversely inhabited. Many black people strolled around or were standing on the sidewalks in small groups, watching the cars go by. They paid little attention to Jack and Elena. In a side yard some children were leaping on a sofa, tearing at the stuffing as the snowflakes began to fall, and their shouts attracted Jack, but only for an instant. In this part of town he didn't need to worry.

Elena had been instructed many times not to go into this part of town. But today she wasn't worried either.

Jack was in an excellent mood. He told her about a case he was working up, a very simple case he would win without any difficulty. It would give him a good fight but he was confident of winning. His client was going to bring suit against the Welfare Department itself, and specifically against a welfare investigator who had violated a law—very obviously he had violated a law—and the man was already frightened of Jack, as he should be. But Jack, scenting fear, weakness, guilt, was not going to be stopped; the prospect of this case, after the long haggling months with the Dawe case, excited him wonderfully.

"In a few years the welfare program will be destroyed," he said. "People like myself are just going to load it up, load it up, until it collapses. . . . Then we can begin."

Elena did not understand this, but she was pleased that her lover was so confident.

He drove aimlessly, turning off one back street and onto another, and then he happened to get into a lane of traffic going down toward the river. So he drove along in that direction and then down, through an underpass, and over onto the bridge that led to Belle Isle. There were few cars heading out to the island; the morning's wet snow was now sticking and falling thickly, dissolving into the river. Jack drove slowly along the outermost road. Elena noticed a landmark—a monument—and remembered the day she had been a passenger in someone's car out here, heading for the boat club and— But she stopped thinking about that, the carload of women, the food they had to eat and the talk they had to endure and the mentally handicapped children they had to pity— And—

She stopped thinking about it. She sat close to Jack, who was driving carefully because of the wet pavement. She wanted him to park for a while by the shore so they could look out across the river toward Canada—she noticed houses there, at the water's edge, a row of homes that were very fuzzy, hardly more than blurs across the distance of falling snow. She wondered at the people who might live there, in those houses that looked so distant, so safe, in a foreign country and safe from Detroit—as if anyone could be safe from Detroit, anywhere—but Jack didn't want to stop. He kept on driving around the island, out to the farthest point, then he turned down one of the inland roads, which was deserted.

The forest opened to receive them and then closed about them in silence. And Elena began to think suddenly, sharply, of the forest someone had taken her to, long ago, in another part of her life.

She hid her agitation from him, she did not cry. She was even grateful for his own agitation, his sudden unreasonable desire for her, here in this car. At first she resisted, trying to laugh him out of it. Then she relented and tried to help him, feeling the need in him as an impersonal need, an impersonal threat, which they must both contend with. She thought: *We will be arrested.* Then she thought: *I can't stop him.* So she felt herself go limp, almost inert, her head against the bottom of the window, the cold hard window ledge. Through her half-closed eyes she saw not her lover but figures moving toward them, through the woods, running and shouting in silence and waving their arms angrily, but the figures faded, and she jerked with the sudden waking pain of her lover coming to her, abruptly, before she was really ready for him, forcing himself into her. The tears shot into her eyes again, the same tears. She helped him, her arms awkwardly around him, not wanting to see his tense face, but at the same time she felt her body tightening against him, in opposition to him. He kissed her wildly, he asked her something—she didn't hear—and again she relented, and then went tense again, feeling him so sharply and impersonally inside her—

Her mind would go under, would be annihilated by an idea too large to fit it; she felt herself twisting, squirming, to escape this idea and what was happening in her body, not a body she could control. Out of the corner of her narrowed eyes she could see, still, those figures approaching the car—she could almost hear their angry shouts—and then, because Jack paused, because he asked her if she wanted him to stop, she felt his gentleness merge with the sweet, soft inertia of her body. They were both heavy like this, they seemed very heavy, Jack helpless and apologetic in his weight. And yet, inside her, he had become light; she felt him hesitating, she felt in him almost a withholding of words, of his usual strength. At once she pressed herself toward him, up against him. She gripped him, as if listening. Her shoulders stiffened, like his, and she seemed to be listening for something in a kind of terrified alertness while he moved again in her, but gently, questioningly. Elena did not breathe. She felt a sensation like whispering in her, but her head had gone dark, she could not register it, could not think, nothing was familiar and she could see nothing now, not even visions out of the corners of her eyes, not shapes, colors, flashes that pain or discomfort or habit had always stirred when she had lain with this man, or that other man . . . her husband. . . . Yet it was gentle, much quieter than her own heartbeat, a softness that was pure movement, pure sensation. This man was so tense and yet he seemed to be protecting her, holding himself back from her, he seemed to be resisting himself; she breathed shallowly, as if fearful of disturbing the balance between them, and something drew itself up in her, suddenly, effortless and concise as the raising of a hand in an intimate gesture, a motion so graceful she experienced it in utter disbelief.

Then at its height it seemed to pause, she seemed to be forcing it there, there, holding it there, with all the strength of her straining body. And then it fell back upon her, localized and urgent, muscular, terrible. She stared past Jack's head but saw nothing. She saw nothing, as if blinded. The sensation in her had now become terrible, spasm upon spasm localized in one part of her body, which she had to fight to control—but she could not control it, it was so brutal and muscular. She could control only her resistance to it, her refusal to cry out. Jack gripped her and drove himself into her. She clutched at him, trying not to scream, and she felt how wildly, helplessly they struggled, how viciously her body grabbed at his in its agony to keep him with her, to force him again and again into her. How she needed him, how raw and crazy was her need for him, a murderous need!—she was desperate to keep him there, with her, she would have gone mad if somehow he escaped her. They struggled together like two creatures in a frenzy to come completely together, to become one thing, as if the awful burden of holding the universe together were theirs.

She felt that her face was shifting out of shape, her eyes straining in their sockets. But she did not cry out. She gripped him, she felt her nails in something—not his flesh—the thin wool of his clothing—and while she kept from screaming he groaned against her, almost a sob, and she began to think— But she thought nothing, her mind would not function. She was able to breathe now, she was able to think, her mind was becoming clear again, slowly. Yet still there was that sobbing of her body, gone fainter, a faint clutching sobbing now less violent than her heartbeat, and she tried to lift herself from it, to recover from it, to get free of it.

She lay with her arms around her lover, dense and stunned. Something was pressed too hard against the back of her head. Her hair was heavy, damp. Someone's face, too close against hers, was hot, damp, abrasive; she thought vaguely that he must not leave her, not even now, but the thought was too faint for her to hold onto. Yet her hands, as if willing themselves, coming to life, pressed down hard upon him, his back, the small of his back, the clammy, sweaty skin there. . . .

After a moment Jack lifted himself from her. Always, like this, he glanced involuntarily at her, with a stricken, questioning look—and she had always looked away to break the connection, but also to assure him she was not hurt, she was not damaged. Her husband did this also: that quick, almost furtive checking of her to see if she was damaged. But now she did not have the will to look away; she stared at him, unknowing, blank, her gaze fixed to his. They stared at each other.

She wanted him not to leave her, but she had to let him go. She shivered. Jack drew back, away; in utter silence he adjusted his clothing, self-conscious and moving slowly, like a man in a dream. Elena shivered, feeling now the air that came between them, the cold air on her exposed body; yet she could not move. She lay there, still looking at him, toward him, in a queer faint stupor, knowing she was cold, her skin gathering itself up into tiny pinpricks against the cold, and yet bathed in warmth like a protective film. She could not move.

Jack's movements were slow, almost cautious. He looked at her from his side of the car. He said nothing. Then, in a movement that seemed entirely natural, as if he had done it many times before, he slid his arms up around the steering wheel, resting there, he lay his head on his arms and looked at her.

They did not speak for a while.

Then Elena seemed to wake, to wake partly and to know she must fix herself, must change something. She sat up. She saw that it was still snowing.

Jack broke the silence by saying something, something about the time, but his voice was cautious, intimidated. Elena felt her mind clearing now. She would be able to think now. Yet no thoughts came to her, her brain seemed dark, wordless. She was touching herself, vaguely, blindly, her hand against her own chest as if searching for the heartbeat.

Jack laughed nervously. "It's all right, it didn't break," he said. He touched the pearl necklace she was wearing; he pressed his hand against her hand, his palm quick and intimate and reassuring, so that she felt the pearls there, very hard little pearls, pressing back into her skin. She had not remembered this necklace at all. She looked down at herself and saw that her coat was open, the sleeves dragged partway down her arms, her clothes crooked, disheveled. The pearl necklace was warm from where he had lain.

"You have such beautiful things," Jack said, in almost his normal voice. His eyes appeared moist, like her own. Elena straightened her clothing, each of her movements strangely slow, as if unplanned. She had become self-conscious again, because he was watching her so frankly and there was a space between them.

Elena half-closed her eyes. She wished for silence, no voices, no distance between them, no room for leverage and control. But her lover, grown uneasy, had to speak. He had to get her home. He said, "Should you get a cab from somewhere, honey, or should I drive you home myself?"

"A cab," Elena said faintly.

By the time he drove back to the city she believed she was recovered again; she was all right. She told him not to stop, not to park anywhere. She was all right. So he let her out at a busy intersection and smiled over at her, his smile gentle, almost cunning, and Elena smiled back at him. She felt a sudden impulse to return to him, to embrace him again, to press her strange, dazed body against his; she wanted at least to straighten his collar—he looked messy—but there wasn't time; the light had just changed from red to green and he had to drive on.

That was November 30, the first snow of the winter.

8

But when she woke the next morning, very early, it was still with her—her heartbeat rapid but somehow faint, weak. She found herself lying in a large canopied bed, in a room whose walls were beyond the range of her vision, everything dim, shadowy, unreal.

She sat up and brushed her hair back from her face slowly. Her hair was very long, heavy, a girl's hair, that came below her waist and sometimes woke her, startling her with the fear of suffocation. But this morning she woke as if someone had called to her, a whispering of words she couldn't quite hear. She stared out at the familiar room and at the same time felt the pulsation of her blood, the warm relentless surging of her blood, deep in her body, which was not familiar to her.

Beside her Marvin still slept, though restlessly. She turned to look at him and saw there a man as familiar as the overlarge, expensive pieces of furniture in this room, his face somehow enlarged, the mouth slightly open as he breathed heavily, laboriously; he might have been struggling in a dream, fighting, making his way through a density of people and objects, the muscles of his face twitching with the effort. Elena watched him, remembering how weak he had seemed in the hospital, how frightened she had been for him; she knew that she loved him, because he was a man who must be either loved or hated, and she could not hate him. She had been his wife for over ten years.

She thought with a sudden elation: *This is the last time I will sleep here. . . .*

The bed they lay in, which had come with the house, was enormous, canopied, with carved posts and old-fashioned silken hangings and tassels of fake gold, a bed like a boat, which Marvin joked about but which he really liked. . . . It had belonged to many other men, dozens of men, who had slept in it with dozens of women, their wives; Elena thought suddenly that she must not sleep here again. It was like a common grave.

Ten years.

Her body seemed to be experiencing the early hour, the shadowy room, the fleeting thoughts that had awakened her; she could almost feel the smallest veins and capillaries of her body, tendril-like currents of her finest, most secret blood, waking, waking slowly and terribly, pulling her up to consciousness. She felt still that strange elation, as if she were intoxicated. She could not understand it. It had something to do with her lover, who was not in this room but was somehow witnessing it, witnessing it through her, as she stared at the familiar things—the long velvet drapes, the antique writing desk no one ever used, the oversized abstract painting Marvin had been given by a client in partial payment of a fee, a painting by some famous man whose name Elena could not recall—her lover was watching, assessing, passing judgment. She wanted him here with her, closer to her. She didn't want just the idea of him, this floating, impersonal, disembodied lover of hers—

How she wanted him, how suddenly she wanted him!

She thought she must get out of bed, she must go somewhere—walk quickly somewhere—she must break out of this daze in which the minute maddening pulsation of her blood was so powerful. But she did not move. She was afraid of disturbing her husband. Because he would wake, would jerk into consciousness, would see her, would sit up abruptly, and then . . . and then he would call her by name, and she would belong to him. She looked at the row of windows, which were really doors opening out onto a balcony that ran the length of the house . . . she wanted to go to the windows, to find one that would open silently, and then she would step outside, she would stare out and down at the lake, and. . . . She wanted desperately to do this, as if her lover were urging her, as if he might be waiting for her out there. But it was hopeless, she could not move.

She lay back quietly, not wanting to wake her husband. A kind of stupor came upon her, almost a physical weight.

It didn't break. . . . She heard her lover's voice, she felt his hand brought so casually against her chest . . . she could see him, feel him, in a flurry of desire she seemed almost to be feeling him again inside her. The sensation in her body had become sharper, no longer dreamlike.

She thought bitterly of how she wanted him. . . .

But she did not want this, she rejected this. Her face tensed and closed, a brief spasm of revulsion, as she seemed to feel him entering her again, again, with that tentative gentle movement of his, which was not really Jack, not typical of Jack . . . and she believed with a sudden panic, almost a sickness of panic, that it would never happen again, she did not want it to happen again, she would close herself against it. . . .

Awake now, her eyes open and clear and lidless, she thought of how he would probably telephone her that morning. And she would answer. And they would talk. And in a few days they would meet again, in that dreary room he had been so pleased about renting—they would meet there again, yes, and he would talk, he would complain about his wife, about his work, about the complicated and degrading restrictions of the adoption agencies he and his wife were going to, and Elena would listen, and she would reply, and— And again it would be the exchange of news, of words, the swinging back and forth, Jack and Elena, her lover and herself, two very different and separate persons, sharing a few minutes of time and a few feet of space, huddling together, cringing together, Elena and her lover—

She began to cry softly. Everything in her wept: even the muscles of her abdomen tightened in anguish, and the soft, unexercised tissues of her loins.

*

Marvin woke before seven, as usual. Elena got up also and met him downstairs for breakfast; by that time he had already made a few telephone calls, half-dressed, unshaven, distracted by what was coming up that day—always a near-emergency, a surprise, good or bad or exciting news. He spooned sugar into the cup of coffee Elena handed him, drank half of it, set the cup down on his way back upstairs and asked Elena to excuse him, he'd be right back. Ten or fifteen minutes later he would hurry back downstairs, sometimes still unshaven—if he was very excited he would forget to shave—but now dressed, carrying his suit coat carelessly over his shoulder, leafing through some papers as he came back into the dining room.

Once in a while he was so distracted he refused any breakfast at all, and on rare leisurely mornings he would ask for eggs and bacon and toast and fresh fruit, but most of the time he ate the same breakfast every morning, day after day without fail: he had first eaten this breakfast on a hunting trip in Canada, many years ago, and he believed it to be the best thing for him. It was ordinary oatmeal, cooked in a saucepan for three or four minutes, a very simple breakfast he could make for himself if he got up very early and didn't want to wake Elena, if he wanted to be alone in order to glance through his work. Sometimes he ate it standing, always letting it cool before he poured milk and sugar on it, and always alternating each spoonful with a sip of bourbon, which was the way oatmeal had to be eaten. Without the bourbon, the oatmeal would have been disgusting at that time of day—so he said—and without the oatmeal, the whiskey would have been too tasty. This was his breakfast, at home or on the road, and he claimed that it was responsible for his energy and his good health.

After her husband left, a few minutes after eight, Elena remained sitting at the table. He had been especially distracted that morning and had brought the telephone to the table with him, and he hadn't even finished all of his oatmeal, which had cooled now and had begun to congeal in his bowl. Elena sat there. She had not bothered to comb her hair. She found herself staring at the congealed oatmeal, which she had served in a rather handsome cereal bowl. It was part of several sets of excellent china that had come with this house, auctioned along with everything else. She had never really examined it before. The bowl was scalloped, white and gold and not so delicate as it might appear.

It was decorated with fernlike designs that were really women, figures in long puffed-out dresses, arranged around the bowl in contrived, stiff postures, as if they were performing a dance against their will. They looked like people activated by currents of electricity or some other violent, impersonal force, giving them the appearance of energy. Elena had never noticed the design before and now she stared at it, counting the women—five of them arranged around the cereal bowl—and noting how the dried, hardening patches of oatmeal made designs of their own.

Elena smiled faintly. . . .

Her arms slid slowly from the table, her forearms sliding down, down, inch by delicate inch as she watched. She noticed how the flesh bulged out slightly; even the veins bulged under the pressure. Then, when her hands reached the edge of the table, the movement ceased. The table edge had caught the fleshy part of both hands.

Deep in her body was the memory of her lover: as if she were pregnant by him, with the sensation of him. Somehow she was pregnant with him. She carried him inside her, she would have to carry him with her as if he, the idea of him, the memory of him, were embedded in her womb. She could not reject the thought of what he had done to her. She experienced the sensation again, but faintly, like an echo. She experienced it, she could not deny it. In disbelief she knew what had happened and that she must experience it and re-experience it, not in her memory but in her body, as an echo of what had happened. If she had only invented it, she could now forget; if she had only thought of it, she could blank it out, as she blanked out so much. But she could not control the memory of it any more than she had been able to control it at the time; in a way it was not hers to control. It did not belong to her at all.

She thought suddenly that she would get to her feet, take the breakfast things out to the kitchen, wash them, dry them, put them away. And then she would find something else to do: washing of some kind, cleaning, vacuuming. A woman did come to the house to help with the cleaning, three times a week. She would not be coming today. The house was as clean as Marvin wanted it, the rooms he kept open were all clean, polished—there was really nothing to do, but she would do something. In a minute she would get to her feet and begin. . . .

She went hollow, sickened with the realization that she would never be able to forget what had happened.

Waking that morning so early, probably before six o'clock, she had been so strangely elated . . . now it was two and a half hours later and she sat as if exhausted, leaden, thinking back to that morning and to the Elena who had sat up in bed with amazement. Something in her sleep had propelled her into consciousness, and she had brought it along with her, a knowledge, a certainty, that made her very happy. But then it had faded. It was irretrievable. She had felt it fade, die, inside her. And then her husband had awakened, and she had felt the absolute extinction of her happiness, knowing she must admit this man into her consciousness, she must respond to him and listen to him and love him, and, if her lover did call, she must listen to that man's voice also, helpless to hear how his voice would profane itself, saying all the degrading ordinary things again, in his ordinary voice, rushed and slangy and confident and occasionally not so confident . . . and she would die again, everything would sink and die, the dazzling certainty of her love would die as if pounded into mute flesh again by a man's body.

. . . It was fascinating, how her hands were stopped by the hard edge of the table. They were not heavy enough to fall. And yet their very weight kept them there, motionless. She could see that her hands were quite beautiful. They were slender, delicate; perfect hands. On her left hand she wore an antique ring Marvin had given her, a single large diamond in an ornate while-gold setting, with a wedding band of white gold. She could not remember its price. It was insured. On her right hand she wore a ring Marvin had given her recently, maybe for an anniversary or some other occasion; he had designed it himself and a jeweler in New York had made it, a large emerald surrounded by smaller diamonds. This too was insured. It was a striking ring and everyone noticed it and admired it. And Jack had noticed it immediately too. He did notice things about her, he speculated and calculated and came to conclusions that somehow excluded her but implicated her: once he accused her jokingly of dressing well only when she had someone else to see in addition to him; on other days, when she came downtown just for him, she didn't bother with jewelry.

Elena had pretended to be pleased and surprised that he bothered to notice such things. He was very attentive to her. So she had explained, carefully, that when she came downtown just to see him, she felt no need to bother with her usual junk—yes, she knew it was expensive junk, seeing him wince, but wasn't it junk, really?—wasn't it absurd, so many thousands of dollars worn on her fingers, looped over her neck? When she had to see other people, to whom such things had meaning, she did wear the expensive things Marvin liked her to wear; but when she saw Jack alone, she never bothered. . . .

So in that way she had managed not just to apologize to Jack, but to flatter him at the same time. But something had flashed immediately through her mind: *He wants my husband's wife, not me. . . .*

Motionless on the edge of the table, her hands poised, helpless. She had not the energy to move. With part of her mind she heard the telephone begin to ring, just the tail end of a ring, and then the full ring, and then another. She did not move; she shut her mind against the ringing. There was no terror in answering it if she knew she need not answer it. *So beautiful . . . you're so beautiful . . . you have such beautiful things. . . .* Someone was always telling her that, thinking that. People glanced at her and then hesitated, staring. *Beautiful thing.*

Yesterday, loving her, Jack had been stricken and helpless; he had been transformed, like Elena. But she did not want to think of him now. She did not want to think of the snow falling, melting on the car's windows, the still leafless trees with their branches in complex arrangements, some tilted at angles that had not seemed natural, some obviously broken, some really dead, like the elm trees with their fatal yellow tags. . . . Right outside this house, on her husband's property, were lovely elm trees that had sickened and would not survive the winter. If she wanted, she could go to any window and see them. Gigantic elm trees, a century old, dying from the top down. . . . She didn't want to think of the dying trees, or of the trees in the park, of Jack's tenderness and the hard cold metal against the back of her head, the struggling, the awkwardness, the risk. . . . But the memory of that sensation had spread through her body, a pregnancy in her everywhere, carried everywhere by the warm, relentless veins far from the surface of her skin. If she wanted to free herself of that pregnancy she couldn't even slash herself free, couldn't slash an artery to release the dense blood; it was all too deep inside her, not even in her possession.

Sensation must be mainly psychological . . . it must be mainly psychological and not physical, not natural. . . .

The telephone rang again. It was nearly ten o'clock now. She heard the ringing as if from a distance, or in another medium—a film, a television play. It was not important. No one had to answer it. If there were any chance that her husband was calling, then she must answer—he would be upset and possibly angry if she didn't—but it was certainly not Marvin, not at this time. So she was safe. The telephone rang in its own dimension, in someone else's imagination; someone was trying to call her, someone wanted to talk with her, but she did not have to obey. The risk of Jack's voice was too much. She would never take that risk again. So she sat indifferently, hearing the telephone ring and nearly forgetting it before it really stopped ringing.

She stared at her hands, still caught by the edge of the table. She wondered when they would fall. She wondered how long she would sit like this.

When Marvin came home that evening, at seven-thirty, he asked her if anything was wrong.

"Wrong . . . ?" said Elena.

She was dressed now. Her hair was brushed and prepared in her usual way, she was perfumed, she wore several strands of pearls, she had even taken an hour to design her face, copying a face on a magazine cover. It was a "natural" face, all beiges and bronzes and fleshly golds, done with translucent make-up squeezed carefully out of a tube, the eyebrows deliberately left scanty, pale, like the eyebrows of fair-skinned children or aged Oriental men. The flesh beneath the eyebrows and behind the eyes had been colored a beige-white. But whiter at the edges, so that the eye seemed enlarged. *In such a face the focus of interest is, of course, the eyes:* her eyes were lovely as the eyes of a woman in a painting, elaborate, thickly lashed, outlined, the lids creamed-over and softened, very natural-appearing. Beneath her eyes the very delicate, temperamental flesh there—which has no pores and which is therefore precarious and must never be stretched—was pale, and then the cheekbones and the skin directly beneath the cheekbones were slightly darker, a gradual blending of shades, shadows, to emphasize the subtlety of the facial structure. And the lips. . . . Protected with a thin gloss, hardly more than a film, a translucent film, exactly the color of real lips and yet protectively artificial.

Elena knew she had never looked more beautiful. Yet, as she worked on herself, watching her face change into this face, a kind of ironic, superior, detached knowledge had ruined her pleasure in her own beauty. She glanced back and forth from her mirror to the model's face on the cover—a nameless model, thinner than Elena, with facial bones that might outlast hers—and she even came to believe that she could see, in the young woman's eyes, the same superior gloating knowledge, a terrible irony, almost a deathly irony. The woman was saying *I am not really here.*

When she was finished with herself, Elena read the italicized column in the magazine on the "natural" face and what it meant: *Designed for American women by Henri Batiste, now Director of the House of Moreau, this face is a subtle but substantial improvement, the editors believe, over the famous "nude" face of last season which was revolutionary in conception but often disappointing in execution.*

By the time Marvin came home she had glanced at herself so often, in so many miscellaneous mirrors throughout the house, that she really saw nothing unusual about herself. But Marvin said, staring at her, "Are you sure there's nothing wrong? You aren't unhappy about something?"

"I'm not unhappy," Elena said guiltily.

They were going out for the evening. One of Marvin's New York associates, who had worked with him for more than twenty years, was in Detroit on business, and they were to meet him at the Detroit Club. It was marked on Elena's calendar. They were also to meet another couple, friends of theirs, if the friends' son, who attended the University of Michigan and who had been home ill for several weeks, had improved well enough to be left alone; but it was doubtful that the Carlyles would be able to come. Their son had made frequent pirating raids on his parents' home in Bloomfield Hills, to steal carpets and antiques and other portable, negotiable bric-a-brac, in order to finance himself and his friends, who needed a great deal of money this autumn, because the price of drugs had soared for some reason. . . . And now he was home, trying to weather some kind of breakdown; Elena had heard the entire story from several people, including Mrs. Carlyle herself, who had given the most complete and the least sentimental of all the versions. Now Marvin, who enjoyed gossip and shaking his head over his friends' troubles, recounted the entire story for Elena as he changed his clothes. She sat, gazing at the complicated structure of a lamp she had really never looked at closely before—it was made of brass, with a marble base—three separate columns that were upon close examination elongated birds, or serpents with feathers, their bodies gracefully arched, so that the upper part of the lamp was balanced very thinly on the backs of their heads. The lampshade itself was made of crystal that had the appearance of fine cloth; it reared upward and must have been at least three feet tall.

"It seems to me," Marvin said with a sympathetic laugh, "though of course I didn't mention this to John, that if their son gets better—I mean if he comes to his senses—that they hadn't better leave the house. I simply don't follow John's reasoning on that point. Obviously, the sicker the kid is, the less likely he is to get in trouble. . . ."

Elena agreed.

But the Carlyles did come to the club, only half an hour late, and Mr. Carlyle had never looked better. Elena believed he was more youthful than she remembered, unless she was confusing him with another friend of her husband's. He contributed enthusiastically to the conversation, which was about the new agencies that rented guards, and the exceptional business they had done in 1971. There were over one hundred of these agencies now in Detroit alone; there were now more private police than city police. Mr. Carlyle, who was either a banker of some kind or a lawyer associated with a bank, said emphatically that the private protection agencies were going to be very important, not just a whimsical side-effect of the riots or the increase in crime, but a built-in factor, a necessary consumer item, of the future. Marvin's New York associate, Mr. Butler, said that he deplored the rental agencies—whose standards were sometimes rather shaky—but he would be forced to admit that he couldn't live in New York, in his particular apartment building, without private guards. Mrs. Carlyle, flame-haired, her husband's second wife but still a good ten years older than Elena, said she was grateful to be living in Bloomfield Hills, where there was no need for anything like that. "Not yet," her husband joked. Mrs. Carlyle glanced at him with a kind of superficial, conversational loathing.

"We should all buy into one of the agencies and work up the product," Marvin said, grinning. "I predict that in a few years we'll all have private bodyguards anyway, a plainclothes guard on either side of us, wherever we go. Walking three abreast. We'd better invest in the product right now."

They all laughed, believing he was joking.

The conversation moved onto another topic and Elena looked from face to face, feeling her triumph in sitting here, contained and normal. The dining room was large and busy, but each table was quite separate from the others, handsomely set up with a vase of fresh roses in the center and a number of functional items—cutlery, wine glasses, water goblets, an initial plate that would be taken away when their dinners arrived. At each table, as at this table, people sat leaning slightly inward, smiling happily from face to face, in each separate group, as if there were something invisible between them, the promise of a gift, a blessing, a hint of salvation, which had something to do simply with their being there, sitting there, and talking animatedly. Elena knew that the space she occupied was an important space, and if she were not present someone else must be seated there at once; a blank would be disturbing, an empty place at this round table an admission of defeat, mortality. She was not certain that it mattered who sat here, but it did matter that someone was here, and she was proud of herself for managing it so well. The roses on each table, the expensive ornamental lights, the original oil paintings on the walls of the dining room, the many beautiful young women at the various tables, were not simply objects to take up space, but were sacred in themselves, mysterious presences. . . . Elena knew there was a bright, almost glowing attentiveness in her face, a concentration that must be very flattering to the three men and the woman who were sitting at this table with her.

Yet for some reason she thought: *We're all going to die anyway.*

She had never experienced any thought like this. It stabbed

her, sank into her. Startled, alarmed at a feeling close to panic, she sat more rigidly, more attentively, trying to listen to what one of the men was saying. She tried to lean away from the sudden dark misery of her body.

As the minutes passed, she felt a little better. She strengthened herself by glancing around the dining room to see if she knew anyone, to offset the sensation of panic. Many of the members of the club did look familiar to her; she had probably met them, had been introduced and reintroduced to them for many years. Then, at a corner table across the room, she noticed a woman who resembled her mother. She was sitting alone, with a man Elena didn't recognize. But it might not be Ardis; it might be that other woman, Olivia Larkin. Elena gazed at the woman for a while, calculating the risk of a mistake. And, though she told herself she really did not care if Ardis chose to ignore her, she began to feel strangely nervous, unsettled. The peculiar edginess of the day returned to her; she found herself thinking suddenly of Jack . . . and beyond Jack, of her mother and father, the man she could see miraculously in her mind's eye as clearly as she could see Marvin, who sat right here across from her. . . . She would carry him around in her head forever, she was doomed to remember him and love him forever. And she was doomed to remember her mother also.

And now I want a child. And I want that child to carry me in his head forever, and to love me forever. . . .

Is that a sentence of life imprisonment?

A lifetime of love?

The way the world is structured?

She thought of Jack's anonymous child, a boy or a girl handed over to him and his wife; she thought with sorrow of the child she might never have, with Jack or with any other man. But her face must have expressed something peculiar, because Mrs. Carlyle was looking at her, smiling, in a rather sympathetic and uncharacteristic manner, as if Elena did not really look as beautiful as she felt. Mrs. Carlyle asked Elena something that could be easily answered and so she answered it.

But she kept glancing nervously over at that corner table. Marya Sharp? But who was she with? She knew it really didn't matter if her mother did not notice her. Maybe her mother would not recognize her anyway, with this experimental face . . . but of course she would recognize Marvin . . . and. . . . Elena tried not to anticipate the moment when the woman at the corner table would pass by this table on her way out of the dining room. She found herself twisting her wristwatch around nervously. Her head was so crowded with people! Her lover; her mother at that table across the room; her father; her husband. The man who sat across from her this evening, Marvin Howe, might be handled as one member of this group, deferentially, there was no risk at all in handling him; but the idea of her husband, that "Marvin Howe" she was contracted to, began to upset her. She was not certain she could handle him.

Then, again, the hopelessness of it swept over her; the fact that all their conversations could not help them, all their carefully selected white and red wines, their expensive plateful of food, their brandies and liqueurs and frothy desserts; that they would have to die, each in turn, and Elena in her turn, helplessly. . . .

Really frightened now, she forced herself to concentrate on the conversation. She must listen, she must get control of herself. They had drifted back onto the subject of the guard-rental agencies; now they were discussing the legal complications that were already arising. As Marvin pointed out, a private guard had the right to shoot anyone on a certain piece of property, but he did not have the right to shoot anyone—anyone at all—who was not on that property. That was incontestable. Cases had already come up of guards who had fired once, while the fleeing suspect was on the property they were authorized to protect, and, firing again, they had shot the person while he was on public property. Or the first shot had struck its victim, who then staggered off the property, and the second shot came when he was no longer on the property but, in fact, on public property—where only tax-supported law-enforcement officers had the right to shoot anyone. Mr. Butler agreed this was a seriously complex issue; court cases were failing to establish precedents that would be helpful in guiding people like himself, when clients came to him for help. "It's quite frankly up for grabs," he said.

On the other hand, Marvin pointed out, such were the times that even the police were running into trouble. He knew of a number of partly successful suits brought against the police, on charges ranging from illegal harassment to outright murder in the first degree. He had not handled any of these cases himself, but he knew of them. It was not likely that he would represent a plaintiff against the police, at least in one of the big cities, because few such victims could afford his usual fee and, of course, if the defendant was a member of a big-city police force he certainly would not be able to pay Marvin's fee. However, Marvin might very well volunteer his services if the right case appeared. He was quite sympathetic with the police, really. The law was a marvelous, complex thing, but it had to be enforced; in a sense, *some law* had to be enforced before any law could be enforced. So he was always sympathetic with the police. "When I travel around the country and visit a city that's new to me," he said seriously, "do you know what I look at first? Not the big tall buildings, not the cultural centers and the fountains and the potted evergreens, but the police—how they look on the street, what shape they're in, their height, the condition of their uniforms, their style. That's the most important part of a city. Everything else comes later."

The others seemed struck by this observation, as if they had never thought of such a thing themselves, but had to agree. Mrs. Carlyle especially agreed, in a manner that was flattering to Marvin. She kept saying, "Marvin, you're brilliant, you're always correct, I can't get over you," nodding emphatically. She had had quite a bit to drink. Mr. Carlyle said, tapping the table top to make his point, that he too was sympathetic with the police, especially because of the activity of certain left-wing agitators, who were making it very difficult for the police to enforce laws these days. These people, who had their roots in Russia and China and Cuba, and who were funded by international student committees and outfitted and in some cases trained by professional Communists, and who . . . These people, he said, were causing the breakdown of our society by encouraging lawlessness in the cities . . . and they were making it very hard for the police to apprehend fleeing suspects, claiming that the act of shooting even an obviously guilty fleeing suspect was an infringement upon constitutional rights . . . and. . . . "Well," Marvin said, joking, his face flushed and merry, "you must admit that Michigan has abolished capital punishment—even for the misdemeanors, like stealing hubcaps—" But if that was a joke, no one seemed to get it. The conversation was much too serious now even for Marvin to divert it.

"Now, I'm sensitive to all the subtleties here," Mr. Butler said, "and it pains me as much as the next man to read about those two soldiers—this happened in Philadelphia, I think—who were killed by some plainclothes men who were chasing them—I forget why—resisting arrest or something—mistaken identity or something— But look, look, we've got quite a problem in our society when a dedicated policeman, twenty-three years on the force, has to stand trial the way a client of mine did—on *first-degree charges*— a sincere, dedicated man whose work is his life, suspended from the force and brought to trial— Look," Mr. Butler said shrilly, as if someone were about to interrupt him, "this man happened to be off duty, but he had his gun with him, which is the law—and a fourteen-year-old kid, high on drugs, but you must imagine this big husky kid with wild hair, a black kid who looked at least eighteen, he looked at least twenty years old, I swear, from his pictures—this kid on a dark street or in a bar or somewhere, very confused, this kid pokes his finger at the defendant, a dedicated cop, and screams something that sounds like *I'm gonna kill you!*— and makes thrusting gestures with his finger, you know?—like he has a gun or a knife or something? I mean, well, I might be a little drunk and a little sentimental, but I mean, Jesus, if that isn't obvious self-defense, I don't know what the hell is. We rounded up four eyewitnesses who agreed. But my client came very, very close to being found guilty, and that strikes me as being a pretty sad indication of where this country is going. . . ."

Mr. Carlyle brought his fist down on the table. "You're right. You are absolutely right, Mr.—— Mr.—— I forget your name, but you're a friend of Marvin's, and you're absolutely right, every word you say is precious to me. The same goddam thing is happening here! Same thing! And we're helpless, I swear we're helpless," he said, his eyes filling with tears, "people like ourselves who hold this country together and who know how to recognize one another, we're *helpless* with the pack of Maoists and left-wing liberals and Jew-lawyers and nigger-lawyers left over from Martin Luther King— It's a sick radical coalition of dropouts from the universities and professors fired from their jobs and—and—what's-the-name of them, what's-the-name," he mumbled, turning to his wife, "that volunteer group the Kennedys started—sending kids to Africa and South America—uh—"

"Peace Corps," Mrs. Carlyle said.

"Yes! Right! Leftovers from that, and God knows what else, and social workers and teachers and even some ministers, and even some priests, and let's face it, Marvin, some loud-mouthed members of your own profession—who did *not* graduate from Harvard Law—and, to come right close to home, not to spare anyone at all, let's face it, the sons of certain prominent men who should know better—and I do mean your neighbor Jackson Dawe—"

"Jackson Dawe isn't to blame for his son," Mrs. Carlyle said, shocked. "What the hell are you talking about? You're drunk!"

"Jackson Dawe is going to stand by that maniac son of his, he's going to support him, no matter what he says," Mr. Carlyle said. He shook his finger toward Marvin. "He's *your* neighbor out on Lakeshore Drive, *you* talk sense into him! A drug addict maniac like his son Mered, running around town in a monk outfit, spouting the most subversive hysterical dangerous stuff—and defended by a Jew lawyer who has a reputation for freeing murderers and rapists—*provided* they are the right color—and I don't mean Caucasian—"

"John, not so loud, please," Mrs. Carlyle hissed.

"All right," he said, lowering his voice, "defended by a Jew lawyer who has stated publicly that he is out to tear down our society—"

Elena stared at this man. She tried to focus on what he was saying, but he was so angry, his face so dangerously red, that she felt only his rage. Then she noticed her husband, who drew his head back, almost snapping it back—and she thought in sudden terror— *He knows—*

But then Marvin said, quite calmly, "He isn't a Jew, the Dawe kid's attorney. And anyway, you don't have to lower your voice; I doubt that there are any Jews in this room."

Mr. Carlyle had lost the thread of his argument. He glanced at his wife, confused. Mrs. Carlyle put her hand on his arm and said, with a small pathetic smile, "Please excuse my husband, Marvin, but . . . you know . . . with the situation at our house . . . and this boy Mered Dawe, the kind of filth he hands out in his speeches . . . it's just like an infection, a plague, all our kids are susceptible to it. Our son is just a victim of the times. It's like bacteria floating in the air and infecting the nicest, most innocent kids . . . and then you read about the Dawe boy, getting arrested and involved with a very young girl, corrupting her, and then you read how he's going to be defended with every trick in the book . . . and committees are springing up to get money for him . . . and . . . and it just unhinges someone like my husband who loves his son so much. . . ."

After this shaky moment, the conversation became more subdued. Elena, feeling she must sit very still, fixed her gaze attentively on her husband's face and listened as he pointed out calmly that, while the so-called radical coalition of lawyers and antiwar workers and civil rights workers were achieving apparent victories in liberal courts, the real mood of the country was one of impatience and disgust, which was going to be more important ultimately. "And I know what I'm talking about," Marvin said.

Mrs. Carlyle reached over to touch Marvin's arm. "Yes, you do, I have faith in you," she said, with a fond, drunken vehemence. "You always know what you're talking about. Every word of yours is worth—it's worth—it's worth its weight in gold, I swear, everybody says so. We're all proud of you, Marvin."

"The Supreme Court," Mr. Carlyle said suddenly. He had been dabbing at his overheated face with a napkin. "The Supreme Court. Yes indeed. That's getting back to normal, indeed. Marvin, you're right."

But Marvin, who was rather sensitive about that point and had his doubts about some of the recent Supreme Court decisions as they might affect his own clients, expressed some disagreement, and Mr. Butler agreed gravely. Marvin said he was not worried about First Amendment law, no, because his clients were rarely among those who were arrested for making speeches or publishing pamphlets, his clients were usually murderers and therefore, as he said with his usual ironic, embarrassed, and yet quite serious smile, "a much higher class of people"—no, he didn't give a damn about that area of law, but he was concerned about the growing legislation to extend the police right to search and seize; cases he had handled only a year ago, which had ended with acquittals, might now be decided quite differently, and clients of his would suffer tremendously. . . . "Some are living at this moment who might be dead," Marvin said sternly.

Elena isolated this last remark, which was all she had been able to hear: *Some are living . . . who might be dead.* She stared at her husband in amazement.

He was really an extraordinary man. Everyone knew it. He looked larger than life, as if seen in a film, through a camera's lens; he was obviously a superior man, even in this dining room filled with wealthy, exceptional men. Elena stared at him. He was wearing a pin-striped suit with tapering sides and a lemon-colored silk shirt and a wide pastel necktie, handsome, a little overdone, exaggerated as if prepared for the stage, not for ordinary conversation. In recent years many men of his social class were trying to dress in this style, the way Marvin had been dressing for decades, but they hadn't his theatrical calm, his expertly controlled manners; they looked simply in costume. They looked even older than they were. Elena watched him and wondered if, in her terror, she might somehow hide in him. He had saved many people, after all; people as guilty as she. *Some are living at this moment who might be dead.* It was true. *All who are living now might be dead.*

Near midnight, the woman who appeared to be Elena's mother left the dining room with her escort, a handsome white-haired gentleman in a very English-appearing tweed suit; Elena stared at her and tried to determine . . . tried to catch her eye. . . . The woman was very pretty, in her late forties, though possibly a few years older, with her chestnut-colored hair tied back in a black velvet ribbon, which was fashionable at this time; she wore a flattering black dress that looked expensive, and some gold accessories. Just as she was about to leave the dining room she happened to see Elena. And, seeing her, she brightened, smiled broadly, and waved across the room . . . hesitated, as if about to come over to say hello . . . then thought better of it and kept going. Elena smiled uncertainly and waved back. But the woman had at least acknowledged her existence. . . .

Which proved nothing.

9

She kept herself from him, dreading even the memory of him, the threat of what he might do to her. She lived in a kind of dimness, a hypnosis of peace, blankness. If she happened to see herself in a mirror she was struck by the vivid not-thereness of her face—almost a perfection of hysteria—and she could understand why people so often stared at her. Her terror was enhanced, it made her perfect. It was kept quiet, secret, and refined into the irony of perfect beauty, a substitute for existence.

But this was external, it didn't work for her. She dreaded even the reminder of herself; every part of her flinched in revulsion from the externality of her being she saw in other people's eyes. This irony, this perpetual consciousness of her deceit, exhausted her.

When her husband was out of the house she lay in bed, on top of the bedclothes, and made no effort to raise herself into existence. She was sick, frightened, exhausted. An ordinary day, a morning followed by an afternoon followed by an evening, would have been overwhelming if she had allowed herself to consider it. She couldn't invent small durations of time to contain any infinity of time; she couldn't invent anything. *Why are you so untouched by all this?*—someone kept asking. But even to put these words together, to hear them in their logical order, would have exhausted her.

She didn't care what her husband thought, or if he worried about her, or if he suspected the truth or part of it—impossible to know him: he was too large, too generalized, for her to know. As if to damage herself, she kept thinking of Marvin's response when the subject of Jack Morrissey had been brought up, however obliquely; she kept hearing and rehearing his words, but they told her nothing. They disclosed nothing. There was no evidence in his words or in him to believe that he knew or didn't know. He was like a mirror you might approach, cautiously, because you have some reason to believe it is a trick mirror and that someone is watching you as you approach, in all your caution, and yet in your ignorance. . . . The only way out was to smash the mirror.

But Elena would never do that.

Yet she didn't care about him, she had not the strength to register his presence, except to know she was not behaving normally and that she must recover, must return to the other Elena, the normal Elena.

So, alone for much of the day, grateful for being alone, she instructed herself: *I'm not going to die . . . how could I die . . . ? I'm not going to commit suicide and what other way is there . . . ? I don't believe in death.*

But she did believe in death, she thought of nothing else. She believed she was very near to it. Everything in her strained for that, in that direction. If she thought of her lover she sickened with despair, because of him, and because of her need to die, to escape. The taste of this despair was in her mouth, a sour, deadly taste. She wondered if her husband could smell it. He knew everything, he certainly knew about the smells of dying. Yet she could not keep him from her; he owned her.

The falling snow, the tearlike flakes of snow, the damp windows of someone's car . . . the feel of a ledge behind someone's head . . . the sudden vicious struggle to hold someone inside her, always inside her . . . this sickened her, this memory sickened her. A sensation was spread out in her, everywhere in her, a kind of pregnancy of her spirit—a mute, suspended, waiting presence, almost with its own personality. It was so faceless that it didn't need a name, and the names she had called people by, her own name also, were absurd. There was *Jack Morrissey*. There was *Elena Howe*. Aware of them perhaps, but more likely indifferent to them, ignorant of them, was *Marvin Howe*. But these were only names, sounds, absurd unreal essences. She couldn't believe in them.

She had not the strength to keep herself whole. She wanted to give up, to surrender into parts, pieces, chunks of herself. Then she could rest.

But she told herself: *I'm not going to die.*

She remembered telling her lover: *These things don't happen.*

The despair always eluded her if she tried to isolate it. Sometimes concentrated in her head, so that her eyes burned; sometimes in her body, in the pit of her belly, an angry ache like an argument, the same words repeated again and again; sometimes a nausea that spread from her stomach up into her throat and the back of her mouth, staining her. She knew it would be necessary to die, to escape this. She knew if she herself did nothing to bring about her death, she wouldn't die, she wouldn't get free, and yet she was never able to invent a way of dying—that seemed too enormous a task, it was oversized as her husband's soul. She could not approach it.

It was December. But on her own calendar, a small desk-sized calendar she kept in a drawer, the month was still November; she didn't want to tear the page off. She knew other people were living in the new month, walking about ordinarily, with energy or without energy, and that they were approaching the end of the year, but she herself was not participating in that time. Her soul had no name, but was only a kind of perpetual nausea, and the time in which it lived had no name—she responded to daylight, to darkness, like a sluggish single-celled thing, and that was about all. *Elena, why don't you die?* she heard someone ask impatiently. It was an insult, to be called by that name, that degrading trivial word *Elena,* it seemed to heighten her sense of utter worthlessness. And miscellaneous parts of her body—bones, teeth, womb—would compete for survival, stubborn to give up even the worthlessness of their compositions, so that the shame of her being would outlive her.

One morning, when her husband was out of the city, Elena lay on the bedclothes and listened to a radio program, part of a lecture. . . . The telephone did not ring so often now, and she had learned to avoid making a mistake by placing a call to her husband herself, so that she would not need to wait for him to call home; so there was not much danger of the program being interrupted. She had a dread of things being interrupted, dreams or nightmares, bouts of mindlessness, even the long screeching patterns of sound of the buzz saws. She lay in bed and listened to the lecturer's voice, willing it to continue and not break or fade or be interrupted by the sudden ringing of the phone.

A man was declaring in an utterly simple, clear voice: *First we hear the theme as five notes on a clarinet. . . .*

And he played five notes on a piano.

Elena listened closely.

. . . *and then it becomes six notes on a bassoon. . . .*

Six notes, played clearly and distinctly, on a piano.

. . . and then it grows suddenly, pushing its way to life, powerfully, terribly, until it becomes this: and he played a complicated series of notes, icy cold and precise. *And the original theme has grown into this lovely complexity, a purely cerebral act of reproduction . . . as if a single-celled creature were to will itself into increasingly complicated forms of life, but retaining that single cell. . . .*

Elena lay, mindless, senseless, listening to the music. She did not really hear it, but felt its frigid, relentless vibrations; it seemed to her very beautiful. She saw patterns of microscopic life against her eyelids, flashes of light excited by the music, everything poised, perfect, relentless. But it seemed so distant from her, so inaccessible. Her fingers twitched, remembering her lover's sweaty back. As the music came to a conclusion it did not build to a climax but, cunningly, perversely, began to fade back to its original stark theme: six notes, five notes, and then silence. It did not really make a statement. It suggested a statement, a structure, which it then rejected, drawing back icily into silence as if into the void.

The lecturer's voice returned, louder than before, startling Elena. He had interrupted her solitude. He was saying something about the composer's reputation—he had been long-ignored in his native country, France, but was now beginning to be recognized in the United States—"a purely intellectual music that always excites hostility when it is first heard"—

Elena turned off the radio.

A few hours later the telephone rang again and she walked to it, closing the space between herself and the telephone in her usual small, unhurried steps. When she picked up the receiver she heard the sharp inaudible sound of surprise, and she knew it must be Jack. She said softly, "Hello . . . ?"

"Elena?"

She had prepared herself for his voice, but now that she heard it everything fell away, her heartbeat became so rapid she thought she would faint. She could hardly hear his voice. He was so faint, so distant: "Elena . . . ?"

She told him yes, yes, it was Elena.

And she felt almost wild with the desire to touch him. He was asking her something—he sounded very upset—he was demanding something, an answer, she wanted to cut through the fear in his voice and get to him, to him. But she could only reply that . . . that . . . that she had been ill, and. . . .

He hesitated. Then he said angrily: "I don't believe that. Elena? What the hell . . . ? I don't believe that, you're lying, you've deliberately cut me out. . . . Look, Elena, for the last eleven days I've been trying to get through to you . . . and I happen to know you've been home. . . . What's wrong? Why did you do this to me? I've been going through hell and frankly I . . . I don't know if I want to continue this. . . . Elena? Are you listening?"

"Don't be so angry," Elena said.

"I'm calling from Recorder's Court. I have a perfectly simple meeting coming up in ten minutes, and I feel so shaky I could vomit . . . and I haven't been able to sleep, worrying about you . . . but at the same time, goddam it, goddam you, I've known that nothing at all is wrong, that you've just decided to. . . . Elena, are you all right? Your husband hasn't done anything to you, has he? I've been calling his office too, using fictitious names, and evidently he's out of town . . . ?"

"Should I come down there?" Elena said. "To Recorder's Court?"

"God, no! You couldn't come here. We can't be seen together here," Jack said. His voice sounded closer now. "Elena, what have you been doing all these days? What are you thinking? You said you were ill . . . ?"

"You could come here," Elena said.

"I can't come there," Jack said in anguish. Behind his voice was a confusion of noises. Elena heard him say to someone *Shut up!* and then he turned back to her. "Look, Elena, I've got to hang up; I have to get to work. Are you sure you're all right now? Nothing is wrong? I won't ask you why the hell you disappeared for eleven days, but I'll never forgive you for it; you've made me feel so helpless, so frustrated . . . and so forth, and so forth; sweetheart, I'm in a rush now but, look, I'm relieved to hear your voice, and . . . and. . . . Your husband doesn't know, does he? Your husband . . . ?"

"No."

Elena listened as he spoke, a rush of eager, breathless words, and, hearing him, she seemed to lose control of her own breath; she felt very faint, very happy.

"When can I see you? When?"
"When?"

Will we always be alone? Always live alone?
Alone in our heads?—absolutely not.
But there were so many years before I met you . . . I lived alone . . . I was always alone. . . .
I was alone too, honey, but look: now we relive it all, together. That's my theory about marriage . . . a long conversation where you relive your life, remembering things, maybe inventing a few things.
Are we married, then?
In our heads, why not? . . . you don't really live alone, because after you fall in love you retell it all, it's like a book two people create together, a novel. . . . There's the need to talk, like making love. First you do one, and then you do the other.

Jack laughed, he was so pleased and so human now. With the tension out of him, discharged so violently out of him, he could be very human. Elena held him and wondered if he would fall asleep in her arms; he had never fallen asleep with her. She thought that, if he slept, the two of them would lie together in a perfect stillness, an absolute indissoluble peace.

As the year came to an end the news broadcasts reported the most recent homicide figures several times a day. Some months ago it had been established that the year 1971 would be a record year in Detroit for murders, even counting the year 1967, when the riots had occurred; and during the closing days of December it began to look as if an extraordinary 700 murders might have been committed . . . the figure hovered around 680, inched up to 683 . . . then, in a final spurt of activity, it shot up to 689 and then 690. But there it stopped. A news broadcaster declared at midnight, New Year's Eve, "In 1971 there were 690 homicides reported by the police in the city of Detroit," and it seemed a kind of disappointment; 690 and not a round 700 would go on the books.

By 12:08 the first homicide of 1972 had been reported.

"What a city! What a place!" Jack said.

Because she had come to him in a fearful, subdued mood, because she seemed so drawn, so vulnerable, Jack was in excellent spirits: it was their first time together in the new year, a Tuesday morning in 1972.

"Jesus, this city . . . ," he said, shaking his head in amazement, and yet with a kind of scornful admiration. "Someone I know said the whole country is like a prison, and that might be, but it's a prison where the inmates are having a lot of fun hacking one another up. And then, then," he laughed, "consider the obvious fact that many more than 690 murders were committed—probably more than 700, maybe 725, who knows? So some people who were rightfully murdered have been left out of the statistics. I'm sure I could put my finger on one or two myself, and I'm no friend of the police, I don't know any of their secrets. . . . But you don't think this is funny, Elena? Am I offending you?"

She tried to smile.

"You need a sense of humor to live here, it's a very delicate business," he said. He seemed about to apologize and yet Elena knew he would not. He would continue with whatever he was saying, trying to justify it, overstating it as if to coerce her into agreeing. He said, smiling sardonically: "The humor of prisons, of concentration camps . . . of battle zones. . . . That's what you need to survive here. But I shouldn't inflict my viewpoint on you, since you obviously don't understand."

"I understand," Elena said. "I think I understand."

"No, I shouldn't joke like that, it does offend you," he said. "Some things shouldn't be joked about. . . . You deserve a better man, really."

Elena smiled.

"Why are you smiling?" Jack asked.

Because she didn't want a better man. Evidently she wanted Morrissey.

Jack came to sit beside her. He was very energetic this morning. He seized her hands in his and kissed them and said, "I hope you're not going to be like everyone else—like my so-called friends—and wind up hating me. Even my wife hates me. I'm sure of it. I don't mind my opponents hating me, and people I've set out to annoy, but it disturbs me a little when people who like me also dislike me."

"That isn't true," Elena said, trying to laugh. She felt it was necessary to laugh, to smile, to match her lover's mood. But he was so vigorous that she would never catch up with him.

"What isn't true?" he asked. "That I'm disturbed about it, or that people dislike me . . . ?"

Elena shook her head, confused. ". . . that they dislike you. . . ."

"Oh hell, what about you yourself, sweetheart? Don't look so innocent. Don't you hate me a little? Don't you wish I were dead—slightly dead—don't you?"

He took her face in his hand and forced her to look at him.

Elena tried to smile but her gaze slid sideways, down and away from his. The despair of the last several days seemed to rush into her, that sour deathly taste in her mouth; the skin of her face felt dead.

Jack laughed and began to undress her. "Well, if you do, Elena, it isn't for anyone else's reasons. *Their* reasons are ordinary enough, I understand them perfectly, in fact I delight in them . . . because I know damn well, if somebody hates me, I've made some progress. The people who own everything in this country . . . they hate the rest of us just for walking on their property . . . a little wire-cutting of their fences . . . maybe some picnics on their land. . . . Why not?" he said. She felt that her body could not contain his energy and his joy, that he would destroy her. "Why not, this is a free country, isn't it?" he said. "A few picnics, maybe burn down a few houses while we're trespassing . . . why not? Tell me why not?"

Elena did not resist him. She had come back to this room, this place, dreading what would happen. She loved him, but she dreaded seeing him and the fact that he would see her, stare so frankly at her, because she didn't feel confident of herself, not today. She was nervous, very nervous. She feared she would seem less than beautiful to him and at the same time she feared she would never be any less beautiful than she was, that her lover or another lover or anyone at all, any man at all, would always be staring at her, assessing her, loving her. . . . Jack seemed not to notice her despair. He was so happy, so sure of himself, every nerve of his body was keyed-up and triumphant; it was all private, his love made no demand upon Elena at all.

So you loved me for the first time in 1972.

A nullity, an extinction. I went back into myself. I was an idea inside myself, a single cell you couldn't penetrate.

In a way Elena thought it might still be December; she couldn't grasp the idea of a new month, a new year. On December 21 she had had a kind of triumph. She had celebrated the longest night/shortest day of the year by sleeping for fifteen hours. Marvin had had to fly to the Southwest unexpectedly, and she had taken four of his sleeping pills, four quite different pills—different sizes, colors, prescribed by different doctors at different times. She had slept without waking for fifteen hours and then, when she woke, her mouth brightly sour, her eyes burning, she thought at once: *Now I will put my life in order.*

That had been December 21. She had conquered that day, but her triumph meant nothing.

Now it was January 4.

Her lover was talking conversationally; he switched easily from his usual complaints about "her"—his wife—to "them"—his clients, heaping them all up, jumbling them together. Lately he had begun to complain about the humiliating questionnaires and interviews that the adoption agencies demanded; even the so-called liberal adoption agencies expected parents to be saints, not to drink or smoke, to believe in God—"It's worse than passing my bar exam, it's a goddam obstacle course and Rachel can't keep her mouth shut, we have the most vicious arguments when we get home—"

But he was zestful, energetic even now. It was obvious to Elena that he loved to complain. He loved to talk. She was bitterly jealous of his wife, and his interest in his wife . . . but she knew better than to show this, because then he would guess how she loved him, how dependent she was upon him. And, in a way, she was not dependent upon him at all; she believed she could leave him at any time, just walk away. . . .

"Elena, are you troubled about something?" he asked.

She said hesitantly: "I should leave."

"What, why? Leave so soon?" Jack asked, surprised.

Because I can. Because I can walk away.

But she didn't want to hurt him, so she lay still, her mind beating with shouts, accusations. She hated to hear about the adoption agencies, she felt almost an unbearable jealousy at the thought of her lover and some woman, a stranger, filling out forms, conferring, exchanging glances, going home and arguing. . . . She knew how Jack argued, how he clutched at his head, how infuriated he could become. . . .

And then, coldly, she thought that she did not care, really. What did it matter? They were both going to die anyway.

A spasm of fear or revulsion crossed her face. Jack, startled, held her in his arms and said: "What's wrong? What's wrong?" and she had to tell him nothing, nothing . . . except she must leave . . . she must go back home. . . .

"You said over the phone you had all afternoon," Jack said. "What's wrong?"

She did not resist him, but allowed him to hold her; she felt too inert to struggle for anything, even freedom. Again and again the realization came to her, that she could escape all this—escape herself—only if she were able to invent a way out, a way of dying. No one else would do it for her. But she was too weak, too exhausted. To keep herself from falling into pieces, into parts, took all the strength of her soul.

After they lay for a while, in silence, Jack stroking her, she asked him about his work; what had become of the Dawe case?

"Oh, don't ask," he moaned.

He wasn't like her husband, who forbade her to ask about his work. She knew he enjoyed talking about it, and that he would be hurt if she failed to ask him; but she was rather jealous of his clients too, especially the ones he worried about most. The most hopeless cases drew all his concentration and love.

"The other side keeps postponing the trial, and all I want is to get it finished," he said. "At one point I thought everything could be finished in a few weeks. Jesus, what a heartache! I was positive I could get a dismissal. Now they keep postponing, I think their strategy is to let Dawe hang himself . . . as soon as I got him out, he went to the newspapers and television stations and got himself interviewed. It's part of his theory that communication is the salvation of the human race. If we just all speak clearly and earnestly to one another, with love, we'll discover that we are all saying *the same thing*. Have you ever heard such crap? . . . He says he has faith in communication, if not in the courts, and that his trial will be an opportunity for him to communicate with the world, maybe up to the Supreme Court eventually . . . it's his belief that his father is going to come through with money for appeals. What money? Where is it? I for one wouldn't mind seeing some of it . . . I have so many damn bills coming in, bills for things I don't even own. I can't seem to control the way money goes in our household. . . . Did I tell you that some friends of Dawe's want him to fire me? But I won't allow it."

"Fire you? Why?"

"Because I'm too conservative. I'm going to run a sane show. They resent my morals . . . my scruples . . . my *neckties.* But the hell with them."

"Maybe you should . . . you should let him go . . . ," Elena said uncertainly.

"Don't give me advice, Elena, you don't know anything about this," he said. But his voice was kindly. "About Mered Dawe I have nightmares, yes, but also sudden flashes of certainty—almost mystical feelings. I sometimes think he might be right . . . that he represents a new voice, a genuine new voice, that the country is going to listen to. . . . I wish he didn't have a talent for making enemies. He's worse than I am . . . really worse, because he doesn't seem to know he's making enemies. But, well, what the hell . . . ultimately I'm going to litigate on the issue of entrapment—the police obviously tricked him. I'll get him acquitted right here at home; any jury can see how innocent he is, essentially, and entrapment happens to be against the law. So I'm not running much of a risk in representing him."

"I'm surprised that anyone wants to talk him into dismissing you," Elena said. "I don't understand. . . ."

"They don't like me, they think I'm too legalistic. They want passion. Mered is getting fond of me, though, he's been promising me that if I stick with him I can argue before the Supreme Court justices and become famous. He despises his father, but he's very confident the old man will support him. Oh Jesus. . . . You don't want me to back out, do you?"

"I don't know anything about it," Elena said.

"The poor bastard has been a local character for three or four years," Jack said, "running a so-called Retreat House out on Davison. You've probably seen it—it's that big ramshackle house, all painted up, stripes and splotches and rainbows. The police have been raiding him off and on, and generally harassing him, and he claims they smashed a printing press he had out there—that was two years ago—and then there was trouble with two kids, I think they were from Birmingham, a thirteen-year-old boy and his girl friend, who were missing for a week and turned up at Mered's Retreat House, and that got in the newspapers. The current trouble is an indictment for possession of marijuana. This close friend of his, a guy his own age, supposedly a musician and a lute-maker, but really a police agent, came to live with Dawe and the others and after five or six weeks he somehow witnessed Dawe holding a marijuana cigarette. Dawe says it happened like this: they were sitting around, and a girl on one side of him was fooling around with this cigarette, and the police agent asked her for it, and Dawe passed it to him. . . . *The poor bastard passed it to him.* So now he's up for ten years or so in prison . . . for that half second in his life. I know Dawe and I know what prison would do to him. It would kill him. He likes to talk about love, but the first few times he gets raped up there . . . he might change his mind. So, Elena, dear, would you really like me to back out?"

"Is that . . . is that what happened?" Elena asked blankly.

"Yes. Yes, I'm sure it's true; it's too terrible not to be true."

"But I don't understand," Elena said. "He was arrested for that . . . ? For what you said . . . ?"

"Of course, Elena, don't you read the newspapers?"

"I mean . . . for handing someone a cigarette?"

Jack laughed irritably. "You must read the papers, don't you? Don't you know what's going on around here?"

"He was arrested for . . . ? But it can't be right. . . . I don't believe it . . . I. . . . All the money for the trial, and the police . . . all the time it will take. . . ."

"They can't very well send him to jail for ten years just for his beliefs; that happens to be against the constitution. So the indictment says . . . and I quote . . . my head is filled with indictments. . . . *The Defendant . . . on a certain day, in a certain place . . . unlawfully and in violation of the Public Health Law, had in his possession and under his control one quarter of an ounce of a preparation, compound, mixture and substance containing cannabis.* How's that? 'Cannabis' is marijuana, if you aren't familiar with the term."

"They must hate him so. . . . He's going to prison for a long time," Elena said.

Jack was silent. Then, sitting up, he laughed angrily and said: "I'll pretend you didn't say that."

Elena realized her mistake; then, at the same time, she realized numbly that it was really not a mistake. She turned away from him. She looked toward the wall, the painted-over wallpaper. And now if he left her, if he walked out . . . ? She lay still, listening to her lover's angry breathing.

He got dressed and walked out. He didn't slam the door, but closed it politely.

She had dreaded coming here, had dreaded being touched by him. But it had not damaged her. It had all happened so quickly, the embrace and the bout between them, a simple physical routine, like a piece of concise music known in advance, memorized, rehearsed and flawless, inside which she could go distant and blank and safe from him into a nullity she had perfected during her many years of marriage. It had happened. It was over. January 4, a kind of triumph of completion, an achievement. She had left nothing. She had eluded him, she had established a kind of triumph over him. The terror of feeling anything, of going into that frenzy of desire, of misery, was almost enough in itself to paralyze her. But Jack's abruptness, his bluntness cut her off from him, and she rejoiced in it. She had defeated him, but he had seemed not to understand or to care. That flush of good health, the glow of his skin . . . obviously he was a man at the peak of his physical existence, really separate from her, a man in love and performing flawlessly the operations of love. If he walked out, if he closed the door and walked away, it was not much different from his loving of her.

She closed her eyes.

And if he was gone, if he had walked out . . . ?

I'll pretend you didn't say that, he had said. But it was too much for him to pretend, obviously. Elena half smiled, thinking of how he must hate her, how his mind must be working against her, against her, against her! He didn't want to love her. She shut her eyes tighter and seemed to see a kind of ghostly figure, the shape of her lover and yet not Jack, not that name *Jack Morrissey;* a demonic shape straining from her . . . trying to break free of her . . . and yet not managing to get free. She half-believed he would return to the room. When he didn't, she got up and went into the bathroom.

There was no window to this small room, only a single light above the sink that had to be snapped on. Elena groped for it and turned it on. She ran hot water into the basin, grateful for privacy. Very slowly, methodically, she washed herself, glancing from time to time into the steamy mirror, thinking with a kind of stark, minimal pride of how adaptable she was, after all. She could wash herself in her husband's enormous marble bathtubs—there were three of them in that house—or in this closet-sized room, standing naked and shivering, barefoot on an uncarpeted floor. It didn't matter, really. She liked the smell of soap and the feel of soap, the sense of washing, of rubbing herself dry. Through the dreamy patches of steam she saw her pale, composed face, the overlarge eyes, the tendrils of damp blond hair. Below, almost obscured by steam, were her breasts—which seemed to her very vulnerable, not like her face. She dried herself carefully with one of the thick green towels she had brought from home. Jack had brought a few things over one day, some towels and washclothes, but they were still in the paper bag he'd brought them in from Federal's. Elena had never used those towels and apparently Jack hadn't either, not wanting to bother with removing the tags and pins, maybe, or preferring Elena's expensive thick towels. She would keep bringing them here, she thought indifferently; she wouldn't bother laundering them when they were soiled, she'd just throw them away. There was an entire closet in Marvin's house filled with towels and linen they never used—the supply was inexhaustible, Elena thought, and would surely outlast Jack and this room.

She was dressed and pinning up her hair, still in the bathroom, when he came back. Unsurprised, she turned to see him. He said hello sullenly, and Elena smiled and said hello. She slid the last pin into her hair and was ready for the daylight. What good luck that she was dressed!—that her face, and not her breasts, was exposed! "I'm sorry I said that," she murmured. "I should know better. I didn't mean it."

He was doing something out in the room, probably pacing around. She came out. He said: "That went right through me . . . it was like a knife, a knife blade. I shouldn't talk about my work with you. You're too close to me. I should know better. . . . Do you understand?"

"Yes," Elena said.

She knew he was right. She must never instruct him in that part of his life, which was sacred to him. It would make him fear and hate her, as he feared and hated his wife. He approached her and smiled again, tensely, still rather irritably. "Another thing also," he said slowly, "is your position . . . your social position. . . . Without having any interest in these things, and probably without knowing what they add up to, you're in the possession of information that might help me, bits of gossip and back-room news . . . the nervous depressions of judges, their binges and breakdowns and prejudices . . . their wives' troubles . . . and all that. You might listen, you might not. But you go to their parties and you belong to their exclusive clubs, and you absorb their views, you really know them. And I don't want to. I don't want to hear any of it, I don't want to know anything, not even information that might help me. You understand, don't you?"

"I think so. Yes."

"Because—because— Do you understand?"

"Yes," Elena said.

He kissed her and smiled down at her. Yet there was fear in him, an uncertainty that showed in his face: he half-believed she knew secrets, he wanted to know them and yet refused to know them. Elena understood. Yet she also believed he would refuse to learn anything from her, because it would be somehow beneath him.

Very well, then, she understood. If he was defeated, if he was humiliated in public—after all, it would not touch her. She was not his wife and he was not her husband. They were not linked publicly. She had nothing to do with Jack Morrissey; there was a couple known as "the Morrisseys," which consisted of Jack and a woman Elena did not know, and "the Morrisseys" were a united and powerful couple she had nothing to do with. She did not wish them ill, certainly. She had nothing to do with them at all.

"I'm sorry," Elena said.

"It's my fault for talking to you about it," Jack said awkwardly. "I . . . I take these things too seriously. . . . It's difficult for me to explain this, Elena, but . . . you must never mention anything to me, any news about *them* . . . your husband's friends . . . the people you know. I can't bear it. I'm like a man who believes in God, who can't bear anyone talking about God casually . . . doubting or questioning God. . . . I know how rotten things are, I can guess at a great deal, but there's also a great deal I don't *know* . . . because I haven't any power, any social power; I'm nobody, I'm Morrissey and I'll never be a judge, I have too many enemies. You understand? I'm very much alone in this city. All

I have is a conviction, a real faith, a conviction at the bottom of my soul that the Law is permanent and will save us. It will save us from one another. I mean that: it will save us. You understand this, Elena, don't you? *Extra ecclesia nulla salus.* Do you understand?"

She did not understand. And she did not believe it either.

IO

Judge Dan Dack, eighty-three years old, with sagging soft cheeks and a discolored face, weeping, dazed by all the attention or maybe drunk. The Judge being honored as he steps down, retiring at last, white-haired, tough in spite of the cheeks and the tears: now he rises at the flower-heaped head table, stares out across the great room of the club, at all the people gathered to honor him tonight. *I thank you . . . I thank you.* . . . Judge Harold Fox, who has given the speech and has taken everyone through Dack's long local career, glances out with a frown, indicating that they must quiet down. . . .

Judge Dack's wife stands beside him, not weeping because she has known about this evening for months, but smiling, smiling, supporting him with her arm tucked through his. Elena watches and thinks: *This is an important occasion.* Also honored this evening, along with the retiring Judge Dack, is the club's head doorman—a white-haired and unobtrusive, embarrassed man said to date back to the early years of this century; he is sitting at the head table also, though without a wife or anyone to support him, extremely nervous, red-faced, grateful not to have to give a speech like Judge Dack. Both men are wearing tuxedos.

The banquet room quiets down except for some laughter in a far corner—Judge Dack himself sends an angry glance in that direction, accustomed to people not laughing when he stands—in fact, he is accustomed to people not sitting when he stands—but he adjusts himself to this and begins his speech.

I thank you . . . thank you all . . . so many friends and col-

leagues and . . . a sudden faltering, a look both cunning and confused as he stares out at the many tables, the many faces, men with wives in a dim glittering sea of eyes and jewels . . . *you before me tonight* . . . *before me in the possession of* . . . *the most precious the highest privilege* . . . *honor* . . . a lapse of speech, some seconds passing slowly, and Elena notices one of the men at the table with Marvin and her glancing at his watch . . . *honor known to men on this earth* . . . and now his stern old voice rises as it gathers strength . . . *known to men on this earth and to God hereafter* . . . *the privilege of sitting in judgment on the fate of other human beings* . . . *highest privilege we have won* . . . *honor* . . . *terrible obligation* . . . *highest honor* . . . *our fate is to judge and pass sentence* . . . *world rests on our shoulders*. . . .

"Can't Bella Dack shut the old lush up?" someone mutters behind Elena.

Mered Dawe stood on the portable makeshift platform, leaning forward. His face was thin and eager but his gestures appeared slow, exaggerated, as if rehearsed. He was clasping his hands before him and smiling; he would wait forever, he said, until he received a sense of the audience's receptiveness.

Elena stared at him. He had evidently lost weight since the television interview with Marya Sharp, and his clothes hung loosely on him—tonight a shirt that looked like a surplice, and cheap black trousers. He waited. He smiled and his gaze moved slowly about the hall, patiently, while people shuffled in and rearranged their chairs and whispered to one another. At the back of the hall more people kept coming in, down the steps from the sidewalk, pushing in, whispering. . . .

Elena, who had come half an hour early, was sitting near the center of the hall, in about the middle of a row. She glanced over her shoulder and back to the entrance, which was filled with people, jammed solid. And yet more people kept coming, as if the hall were not being managed by anyone; there was a continuous shuffling, people pushing their way past others, through the side and center aisles. But finally Mered Dawe began to speak.

. . . *tonight we will meditate on light and heavy love*. . . .

Elena strained forward to hear him. His voice was very gentle.

Light love draws us up into the galaxy, which is ninety per cent personality-free . . . *but heavy love drags us down into the mud of self and the great mud of wars, of which all U.S. wars including the present war are merely temporal phenomena. Down in the mud we fight one another, compete from birth till death; in the galaxy we are free of that tragic struggle. . . .*

Someone cried out. Elena could not tell if it was a man or a woman. Mered Dawe stared down into the first row, his face bony, eager, yet abstracted as if he were having difficulty with his hearing. Finally he smiled and seemed to accept whatever had been said.

The way down is the way up, he said shrilly.

Elena looked to the rear of the hall again, and this time she saw him—a dark-haired man near the doorway peering over someone's shoulder, frowning, not smiling. He had not noticed her. Beside him was a woman whose face Elena could not see clearly. Her hair was dark, pulled back severely and carelessly. They seemed to be together; Jack bent to hear something she was saying.

At the front of the hall Mered was moving his arms in slow circles, leaning forward as if he wanted to come into the audience somehow, to blend into them. He was saying: . . . *simultaneity and not chronology is our salvation . . . simultaneous existence, not the old Newtonian chronological continuum: not the acquisition of material that constitutes the old Newtonian life: but the free life, the lightness of love . . . not selfish acquisition of love, people as property and property that turns into people. . . .*

Someone at the side cried out for Mered to speak louder. But a young girl in the row in front of Elena's stood on her chair and screamed for him to talk about the police and the mental hospitals and something else Elena did not catch.

Mered blinked out into the room. After a long pause he said he would not talk about the police, who were victims themselves; he would talk only about the galaxy.

"Talk about Detroit!" someone called out.

There was a commotion at the rear of the hall, but Elena did not look around. She watched Mered's earnest doomed face, trying to hear what he was saying. But she could hear only scattered phrases: . . . *material is only waves that come out of nothing . . . traveling through a nonmedium in multidimensional space . . . these waves are not reducible . . . physics answers all our questions about destiny and God if only we listen. . . .*

"Physics gave us the bomb," someone said.

Someone else protested.

Physics gives us the language for salvation, Mered continued, *it is a divine science, the queen of the sciences. . . . There is no material but only mind-stuff . . . no time and space but only mind-stuff . . . we are a cyclical scheme and not selfish wholes and we are divine because we are free of space that is finite . . . time that is finite . . . the old beliefs are just structures of pure thought we must obliterate. . . .*

More commotion at the back. Elena looked to see what was wrong, but her eye moved helplessly onto Jack's face. He appeared impassive, detached. The woman beside him was standing on her toes and then sinking back down again, trying to see, shaking her head irritably. Then, as Elena watched, she saw her lover turn to this woman and whisper something in her ear—the woman glanced at him, nodded—and the two of them started out, pushing past a row of people who stood back against the wall. Jack nudged her forward, his hand on her shoulder; they squeezed past a small crowd at the bottom of the stairs and left.

Elena turned back slowly to Mered. She could not hear his words, her brain felt so dazed, stunned, relieved—she had witnessed an intimate gesture between her lover and his wife, that pushing of her, an unconscious rude intimacy no one else noticed, not Jack or his wife or anyone else who might have seen them, except Elena. So she thought that he did love her, he loved that woman, and she had no obligation to him.

She stared at Mered and tried to listen.

What did Morrissey matter, a man named Morrissey?

You must believe this: among physicists today there is total agreement that we are a nonmechanical reality. The universe is not a monster-machine but a thought . . . a beautiful thought. . . . Physics is our way into the truths of Buddhist and Vedanta teaching, it instructs us that our souls are not accidental, not locked into our bodies, but our souls are pure thought that is infinite . . . and single . . . and. . . .

Suddenly, there was a pushing forward from the back of the hall, a burst of shouts and screams. Elena was shoved somewhere and felt pain, a sharp surprising pain, on the side of her head. Beside her a girl staggered to her feet; her face was streaming blood. Elena clawed at the back of the chair in front of her, fighting to get to her feet. She was aware of some men pushing forward, climbing over chairs—people were screaming—it was too confused to be frightening, except Elena had time to think: *My face is bleeding.* She stood, astonished, looking up at the front of the hall where Mered was being attacked by someone with a stick or a club.

Then someone took hold of her—a man's fingers closed around her wrist—and she was yanked to one side, then backward. She had no strength, she seemed to have no weight. A man right behind her slid his arm around her shoulders, tight across her chest, and half lifted her, half dragged her backward. Wildly, she struggled to get free, tearing at his arm. The girl with the bleeding face was knocked aside. Elena drew breath but couldn't cry out, she was so astonished.

Then the air turned cold: she was being hustled up the stairs. A man was walking her up to the sidewalk, fast, his hand closed around her upper arm, a hand big enough to encircle the sleeve of her fur coat. "Fast. Fast," he muttered. "Watch out." He wrenched her to one side just as someone fell backward. Another man, in an overcoat, cleared the way in front of them, swinging a club of some kind from side to side, once to the right, where it struck a long-haired boy in the back of the neck and propelled him sideways, and then to the left, and then back to the right again, like a pendulum, in a perfect impersonal rhythm.

Elena tried to pry the man's fingers loose. But he walked her along fast, in and out of the milling people, out into the street. There, a police squad car was idling. Elena stumbled but the man beside her held her up; he marched her around the front of the police car and over to the far side of the street. The pavement was icy. It was very cold.

The man with the club dropped back to walk with them. He walked on Elena's left side, a stranger, breathing hard, and the other man walked on her right side, holding her. Elena was gasping for breath. A channel of icy wind rushed down the street and into her face. She could not make sense of this; could not understand what had happened.

"What do you want? What are you going to do?" she asked.

Three abreast, they walked to the end of the block and then paused. Elena felt too weak to continue. She looked back over her shoulder at the crowd in the street. Already it seemed small. The shouting sounded distant and muffled. Elena touched her face, feeling for the wound—but no blood—no wound—it hadn't been her face that was bleeding, but someone else's.

"What are they doing there . . . ?" Elena asked faintly. She stared at the men beside her. Both were breathing very hard, great-shouldered men whose breaths were frosty and thick. They looked as if they were exhaling smoke. "Why did you bring me up here? Who are you?"

"Here," one of the men said, handing her a glove. She must have dropped a glove.

Elena put it into her pocket slowly. She was wearing a thick fur coat—a black mink coat bought two years ago, no longer her best coat. On her head was a fur hat, pulled down tight over her forehead; it had not been knocked off. In a kind of trance Elena saw a squad car approaching, without a siren. The driver's window was rolled partway down and Elena could hear the radio. She broke free from the men and ran to the car, slipping on the ice, crying, "Down there—the meeting—there are some people—Some men broke up the meeting—"

The squad car stopped. The driver, a policeman in his forties or early fifties, stared at Elena. She noted how his gaze swung up to take in her hat, and then how it dipped down to her feet. But he said in a casual voice: "What, that debate thing? It's a free country."

"Aren't you going to help them?" Elena said.

"Help who? Huh? It's a free country, lady. Anyway nobody applied for help, for police protection," the man said, turning away. He drove on. Elena nearly fell; one of the men caught her. He laughed. He said something about her shoes; didn't she know the streets were icy?

"Aren't they going to help? The police? Aren't they—" Elena said.

"Nobody pushes the police around in a free country," the man with the club said. He had stuffed it into his overcoat pocket now, and only the taped handle stuck out. Elena stared past him and down the street, where the squad car was now idling by an intersection. She was very confused. She kept touching her face, as if she expected to feel something moist and warm there.

They walked her over to a car and helped her in. Dazed, Elena did not resist. One man got behind the steering wheel and the other slid into the back seat. He leaned forward and said, "You'll be home in twenty minutes."

They drove all the way out to Grosse Pointe in silence. Only once did they speak: one asked the other if any photographers had approached him.

"I got him in time," he said.

Gradually Elena realized who these men were.

Marvin was spending two or three days in New York City, where he was conferring with one of his tax lawyers. Elena knew he would telephone in the morning, early, so she didn't go to bed, didn't want to lie sleepless in that bed; she sat up all night. The side of her head ached and there was a small swelling near her temple. She stared sightlessly at the windows, waiting for the darkness outside to change. Near dawn, she must have had a hallucination; she seemed to see a figure, a woman like herself, walking silently past her and out of the room.

She shuddered.

She thought of the sleeping pills, the barbiturates her mother had brought home and tossed down on the bed, so many years before. The plastic cap had come off and several capsules had spilled out onto the bedspread.

Her husband telephoned her at 7:30. She answered the phone at once. A sudden bright, cool, not-thereness stiffened her face. He asked her how she was, how the weather was in Detroit, and she heard herself telling him that it was very cold.

"Stay in today. Don't go out today," he told her.

"Yes," she said.

She waited. After a pause he began to talk about . . . about something else . . . and she waited, waited, and gradually her heartbeat became as cool and as impersonal as the telephone itself, something to be handled, a machine. She said: ". . . last night I . . . I went to a meeting. . . . And I. . . . Something happened and the meeting was broken up and. . . . Two men brought me home."

Marvin said nothing.

"I don't know who they were," she said. As she spoke her eyes closed; it was shocking, how seared her eyeballs felt. "I . . . I went to a meeting, a lecture, by that arrested man Mered

Dawe . . . I didn't tell you I was going because I . . . I thought you wouldn't want me to and. . . . But I did go."

"Did you," Marvin said flatly.

"I think they beat up Mered Dawe. I don't know. I was afraid to listen to the news," Elena said slowly. When her husband did not reply, she smiled, a surprise of a smile, so quick and sharp that it hurt her face. She said: "Are you angry with me?"

"Why should I be angry with you?"

He didn't know what to think, what to say, for the first time in his life. He didn't know. He listened and he didn't know.

He never knew me either.

"Why should I be angry . . . ?" asked that distant, inflectionless voice.

II

When Elena let herself in the room Jack looked up at her, staring, distracted, as if he didn't know who she was. His hair was ruffled and shabby; she saw that tendrils of hair had begun to grow down over his collar, which looked shabby too, starched and sharply ironed so that the frayed part would never really rip in two. His first gesture was to look at his watch. "What time is it . . . ? You're an hour early," he said, surprised.

Elena looked at the papers he had strewn across the bed and the bedside table; she felt like an intruder. Jack was holding a glossy photograph. He tossed it down and stood. "I'm glad to see you," he said smiling. "It just startled me, someone unlocking the door like that . . . I got here early, I was going over some work. Or did my watch stop?"

"No, I'm early," Elena said. "I came here early."

Jack tugged at the gloves she wore, pulling at the fingertips. It was a small ritual of his that he performed when he was distracted, when he wasn't quite ready for her. But he kept smiling, grinning, as if to welcome her. He said nervously, "I just didn't expect anyone to open that door for another hour. Sometimes I get here early, to go through things or just sit around thinking . . . worrying. . . . Is everything all right with you?"

"I know you're upset," Elena said. "I was there last night."

"What? Where?"

"At that talk Mered Dawe gave."

"What? You were *there?*"

"Yes, you didn't see me—I was there."

Jack stared at her, astonished. "In all that mess? My God, how did you get out? Did you get hurt?"

"I didn't get hurt, I'm all right," Elena said quickly. "But I . . . I don't want to upset you any more. . . . I. . . ."

"You mean you were *there,* last night, in that basement, in that crowd? And you didn't leave before the trouble started? Or did you?" Jack held her gloves, crushing them in his anxiety or anger; with his hair standing up around his head in tufts, and his eyes bloodshot and amazed, he seemed to Elena a man she must not come near. "I can't believe you were there," he said. "What were you wearing?"

"I saw you and your wife," Elena said. "You left just before—"

"Yes, right, we did, we walked out," Jack interrupted. "I probably just missed getting my head split open. And he wanted me to sit up front with him, he wanted me to say a few words to his disciples! What a mess people make of their lives! Did you listen to the news, do you know what happened?"

"No," Elena said.

"Mered is in the hospital, he got cracked on the head pretty badly, and something is wrong with his spine. And a girl is still unconscious. *And nobody has been arrested.* Well, yes, one bastard was arrested, but not the main one—not the one who organized it—and— Mered's going to be x-rayed and examined sometime today, and I want to see him this afternoon or tomorrow, if I can. But you, Elena, you—! I can't believe you were there."

"Why are you so angry?"

"I'm not angry. I'm— I'm not angry, but why the hell did you go to that meeting? Why didn't you tell me ahead of time? A girl who had nothing to do with Mered, just a college student at Wayne, she's very badly hurt—somebody knocked her down and trampled on her and— The police did nothing! Nothing! What was the point of it, why did you go last night? What a stupid, reckless thing to do! If your husband ever hears about that he'll be furious."

Elena looked away guiltily. She said after a moment, "He isn't going to die, is he . . . ?"

"No, he isn't going to die. No. I don't know. I don't think so. No, he's banged up but he'll live, didn't you even listen to the news? And how the hell did you get out of there? Elena, Jesus—!"

Elena tried to smile, to soften his anger. But she still could not meet his gaze. She had stayed awake an entire night, thinking, and yet not thinking, and when her husband had telephoned her in the morning she had heard herself speak to him, so gracefully, her voice had handled itself with a grace she hadn't guessed she had—but now, with her lover, she felt that any words at all would be a mistake. She was afraid of him. She could not lie to him, not even in code, as she had lied to her husband. She could not say, in her polite, sweet, neutral voice: *Two men carried me out and saved me.* She could not say: *Nobody is going to kill you, these things don't happen.*

"Please listen to me," Jack said. "You did a reckless thing, and you're lucky nothing happened to you. Why didn't you tell me you wanted to hear him? Did you want to meet him? Are you half in love with him, that saintly little mystic, like everyone else? And all those freaks packed into that basement! And you there! And all that fighting! You didn't even listen to the news, you don't know what went on?"

Elena did not reply.

"There's a group of men in a secret organization, it has a number of names, and it's patterned after—well—this wouldn't mean anything to you, not to *you*, because you're totally unaware of what is happening in the world," Jack said ironically, "but it's patterned after what they believe to be their left-wing counterparts, the kind of terrorist cells the Algerians were using. But never mind. It's like the Ku Klux Klan in other ways. There *is* a Michigan Ku Klux Klan, you know, and maybe that was it last night—I don't know—and there's also this group downriver, the 'Americammer' or whatever their name is. They got a lot of publicity a few years ago, training housewives in Dearborn to use guns. Do you remember? Oh hell. . . . It makes me sick to talk about it. More than anything, I think, it makes me sick to realize that all the negotiations of law, all the trading and dealing and arguing and grace, all the wit, these things mean nothing, they just dissolve if you're hit on the head. What good will it do Mered to sue for assault, to press charges? What good? I feel sick, I don't want to talk about it. Nothing is real but pain. But no, I don't want to talk about it and I won't," he said angrily, running both hands through his hair. "All night I've been arguing with people—including my wife—who just want to run out and beat someone up, throw a few bombs around, all that crap; I'm fed up, I don't want to talk about it now with you. But I'm asking you: why did you go without telling me? Did you tell your husband?"

"I went because I wanted to," Elena said.

"You wanted to."

"Yes, I wanted to. Why are you so angry?"

"I'm not angry! What the hell do I care what you do!" he said, smiling bitterly. He tossed her gloves onto the bed. "No, no, why should I be angry, why give a damn? What's the use?" He stood for a while looking at the floor, his face working, twitching. Elena realized she had walked into something terrible. She had unlocked the door and opened it and walked in, to this. He seemed so upset, so furious, that he was not even aware of her. She wanted to touch him, gently, to quiet him; she wanted to love him. But suddenly her own anger surfaced, she seemed to sense Jack's frustration and to claim it for her own: she would force him to look at her.

"Yes, I was there, why are you concerned about it?" she said. "I didn't care if it was dangerous. Why should I have cared?"

"Yes, why? Why should you have cared?" Jack said.

"Other people are in danger. I didn't get hurt. I didn't get cut up, but if I had—? Is that so important? Why should you care about me? Am I your wife?"

"Oh no, no, you're not, I can see that," Jack said quickly, glancing at her, "You hadn't anything to do last night—your husband is out of town—right?—that's why you're here with me now as well, a way of passing the time?—and last night, you thought last night would be educational, did you?—illuminating?—more exciting than an extension course? After all, danger is real life, you can see it on television and read about it, but it isn't exciting until you're in it, and what real life they possess, those kids and freaks! They're *so real!* You might even have been beaten up and right now you'd be in the hospital, getting x-rayed! Yes, really, why should you be afraid of anything, you're insured, you're expensive property but fully insured, and why should I mind, really?—you're not my wife."

"No, I know that."

"I don't own you, obviously, and my opinion means nothing to you—and why are you so happy this morning? Because you came to tell me this news?"

"I'm not happy," Elena said. But she knew that her face was bright, flushed as if with joy; her heart hammered with a terrible excitement. "But why shouldn't I be happy, coming to see you? I love you and I came to see you. I'm here, I came to see you, I walked into this and you—you—you want to fight me—"

"Oh no, not fight, no, never," Jack said, laughing, "why fight? I'm not fighting you. I don't want to damage you. I'm really very pleased to see you, I'm very happy. Can't you tell? I'm transformed with happiness. I'm like a pig changed into a man, seeing you, instead of the other way around—that's how lovely you are, what magic you possess! I'm obviously happy with you. I'm like Dawe, happy and transcendent wherever I am, in jail or in the hospital or in the insane asylum—after all, it's only a matter of attitude. Mind-stuff. Did you take notes on his lecture?—that part about *mind-stuff*? Then you know what I mean, my subtleties aren't lost on you, you have only to rearrange your mind-stuff and enter heaven, right here in this room. Why not be happy? Why not?"

Elena hesitated. She was becoming afraid of her lover, and yet, in a way, she wanted to provoke him further. The sharp, sweet, flame-like rush of his fury had touched her, was coursing into her. She had sat, paralyzed, most of the night—so many hours, so many years of her silence! And now, with her lover, a kind of flame-like madness teased her, rushed along through her veins and arteries. . . . But she hesitated.

When she spoke, it was in a softer voice. She said: ". . . but he isn't badly hurt? He'll be all right . . . ?"

"Oh, it's just mind-stuff," Jack said, sneering. "They can rearrange it for him and spring him good as new, better than new. Blood clots on the brain or fractures or concussions or smashed vertebrae—all in the head—all psychosomatic— Why ask if he's all right, Elena, when you obviously believe in his message?

You'd travel down into the slums of my part of the world to hear it? Why ask, Elena? What are you doing here? What do you want from me?"

"I don't know," Elena said.

"To drive me crazy?"

Elena said slowly, "But you're not angry about what happened to him. You're angry about something else. . . . About him, about your client . . . you don't really care."

"I do care about him!" Jack said sharply. "I care very much about him. I wish I didn't. I could be a very successful human being, a very successful lawyer here in this town, if I didn't care about anyone or anything—especially you; it's just a waste of time, it's unprofessional! I'm fed up. You come in here, you're all fixed up and wearing that coat somebody bought you, you always look around this room as if you hated it the first second you step inside!—you come in here, you, and drive me into a frenzy, and accuse me of not caring about my client!—and one day you predicted he would go to prison for a long time, you just casually mentioned it, you summed up my career and my prospects and my intelligence, like that— All right, believe the worst about me. All right. You live with a maniac, a monster, you should know what men are like. Believe anything you want about me—let's say I'm very pleased that my client has been banged around, this is the best thing that's happened since the indictment, he'll get some good publicity for once. In fact, I have some excellent photographs of him unconscious and bleeding. Don't think I can't use them. I can use anything."

Elena began to unbutton her coat.

"What are you doing?" Jack asked. "Are you planning to stay?"

She looked up at Jack, her face very hot, bright. She felt the glitter of her eyes and saw a tensing in her lover, almost a recoiling in him.

My eyes were sharpened to points, like diamonds.

You would shatter me if you came to me: if you forced yourself into me.

And then there would be bits and parts, hunks of bleeding flesh, blood smeared on the bedspread and the walls. . . .

"You don't care about your client," Elena repeated. "If you did you wouldn't talk about him the way you do. You abuse him, you consider yourself superior to him. . . . You don't understand what he's saying but you reject it."

"It isn't his mysticism I'm defending," Jack said. "It isn't even *him.* It's his right to spout that stuff, that crap, as much as he likes, without getting arrested and put in prison— Why should I understand it? It's just mysticism, it's irrational, I don't have time to waste on it! It has no intellectual content."

"But how do you know, if—"

Jack began to shout. "Shut up! Stop it! Do you want me to go crazy?" He grabbed her by the shoulders and began shaking her. "Is that why you're here? Why are you here?" Elena's head jerked forward and backward. She gripped him, his shoulders, to steady herself. He said viciously, "If you came here to be sweet to me, be sweet to me. Otherwise get out."

He let her go.

He backed away. His face was dark. Watching her, he tried to smile again but his smile turned into a twitch and then into a grin. His face had become a murderer's face but he seemed unaware of it; he tried again to smile, sanely. He said: "Yes, you know what I want—I want you—I want you to belong to me and you don't, do you?—that's your secret message, your code! One morning you telephoned me from California and summoned me out; maybe you were bored that morning, it was another morning you had to kill, so you called me, because you are such a prize and you knew I'd come—I could always borrow the money for a plane ticket, what the hell, not that it would occur to you that people pay cash for tickets or for anything else. But you don't get too involved, Elena, do you? If someone had clubbed you on the head last night you'd forgive him, wouldn't you—you'd hardly have noticed, right?"

Elena took off her coat.

"I came to be sweet to you," she said.

Jack laughed bitterly.

". . . because you're going to be a father," Elena said slowly, ". . . because you're moving away from me. I want to start saying good-by to you. I want to love you."

"Oh, do you? Is that—is that the idea? And nothing else?"

He stared at her, baffled.

"You are going to become a father . . . ?" Elena asked.

"I don't want to talk about it," he said. He was trying to get his face back under control. His forehead was damp. "Not today, not now. . . ."

I wanted you, I felt it like a kick inside me; the kick of an embryo.

The veins radiated outward, up into me. They were very selfish. I stood there staring at you and I could feel myself going transparent, hypnotized with wanting you.

Could nothing stop you?

No.

Not strangers, not witnesses?

No.

Not a third party? Not a thousand, a million third parties, witnesses multiplied across the earth?

No. Nothing.

What happened between them was real whether or not they were real: Elena knew that. And if anyone observed them, very well, then they were observed; then it was all the more real. It was not her imagining but a kind of history.

12

"The real heroes of our society? Not men like myself, not even men like Mered Dawe. No. Absolutely not. The drug addicts are our real heroes."

"I didn't catch that. . . . Did you say the *drug addicts?*"

Elena sat close to the television screen in the darkened room. She was watching a film clip of an interview with her lover; he had been approached in the hospital by a reporter and a cameraman. The reporter had thrust a microphone into his face and asked about Dawe, about the prospects Jack foresaw of his having a fair trial, of being acquitted; and Jack, coldly, rather nastily, had said he had no comment to make. The reporter had then said, in the same eager, apparently respectful tone: "Mr. Morrissey, would you care to comment on the existence of these secret right-wing organizations? Do you think they are a threat to our democracy, or do you think that they are signs of a fervent unrest?—I mean an authentic populist revolt against left-wing and radical gains in the United States?"

The camera had wiggled slightly as if reflecting Jack's anger. But he hesitated and seemed to be considering the reporter's question seriously. Elena saw with relief that he looked good: dressed neatly, carrying his briefcase. Televised, he did not seem as shabby as he did in real life. His hair grew down over his collar in patches, but it was not so long as the reporter's; the reporter's sideburns were bushy and very youthful.

"I think, in answer to your extremely provocative and intelligent question, which reflects the views of your broadcasting station and the newspaper that owns it, I think, I go on record as stating, that the right-wing organizations—or organization—are made up of men searching for heroes. I sympathize with them. I'm afraid of them, but I sympathize. We're all looking for heroes."

". . . heroes, looking for heroes," the reporter said, pleased. He glanced into the camera as if to encourage the home viewers. He seemed almost to want them to like Morrissey. "You mean, Mr. Morrissey, maybe you mean . . . something has vanished from American life, and it must be supplied again? And this is a dangerous time for us? And are you going to request a change of venue for your client?"

Jack smiled. "I said that I—"

"No comment, no comment? But, Mr. Morrissey, could you tell us at least if your faith has been shaken?"

"What faith?"

"Your faith in the police, or in—?"

"In—?"

"In the prospects for a fair trial?"

Jack smiled and shook his head. He looked quite calm. He was holding his briefcase under his arm. Behind him, glancing in surprise at the camera, were ordinary people—hospital visitors—a nurse who darted by, giggling. When Jack did not reply to this question, the reporter raised the microphone higher into his face and said: "Mr. Morrissey, you did actually say—you said—that you were *sympathetic* with the right-wing organizations?—but to clarify things, to clarify it for our viewers, do you mean—? what?"

"They're looking for heroes; I don't blame them, they don't have faith in God or in the country, in the people, in the masses," Jack said. "That's why they're dangerous. . . . Now, if you'll excuse me. . . ."

"But you do have faith . . . ? In what? How would you word that?"

Jack smiled and began to push away.

The reporter said quickly: "Well, then, you yourself, a man like yourself—very dedicated—and very controversial locally, I think you know—would you say a man like yourself is a hero? I mean, in your constant struggle to represent victims of our society? I mean—who are the heroes you believe in? Would you clarify that?"

Jack's smile turned into an angry grin. Elena half-closed her eyes so that she saw only the blur of his face. She was sitting very close to the television screen; she pressed her forehead against it helplessly. The volume was turned down very low. In another part of the house her husband was working. Elena had managed to catch this film clip on the six o'clock news and now she was seeing it at the tail end of the eleven-fifteen news; she was not certain she'd really heard the conclusion of it correctly. Maybe this time it would not end so abruptly and would not seem such a disaster.

". . . the real heroes of our society?" Jack said. His sarcasm was so controlled as to seem a kind of sweetness. "Not men like myself, not even men like Mered Dawe. No. Absolutely not. The drug addicts are our real heroes."

"I didn't catch that. . . . Did you say the *drug addicts*?"

"They work hardest. They deserve recognition. They're abused and neglected and criticized," Jack said. "There are so many of them in Detroit and yet they don't even organize—don't pool their strength. Unless they are secretly organized. They're the most important single group in the country . . . they're heroic."

"Mr. Morrissey, our viewers are likely to think you are impatient or angry or sarcastic with my questions, and I know you are very hard-working and—"

"Oh, sarcastic? Sarcastic? When I know how difficult it is even to communicate simple-minded little truths? Why would I be sarcastic?"

". . . obviously in your kind of work you come into contact with . . . are involved with. . . . The victims of our society, who certainly deserve legal representation like anyone else, even the rich, and you might care to comment on the plight of the drug addict?—here in one of the nation's great cities?"

"Yes, fine. They are the real heroes in a consumer society. *They* are the ideal consumers, not the housewives. They're always in motion economically. They keep the economy going. They're ideal workers, work constantly, beyond anything the Puritans imagined—twelve or fifteen hours a day, three hundred and sixty-five days a year—always hustling, no vacations or weekends. If our entire society could be transformed into a society of addicts it would run by itself, forever. Buying and selling, perpetual dealing in the streets, a market of supply and demand, very few complaints. The market would reflect economic changes very subtly, and would therefore be more consistent with the ideals of laissez-faire capitalism . . . which I think you will agree has been eroded and sold short after so many liberal administrations in Washington. . . ."

"And are these views, uh, I think these views are very interesting but maybe not serious . . . ? Are these views also those of your client, Mered Dawe?"

"He doesn't have any views. His skull has been cracked."

At this point the film clip ended. Elena stared at the screen and waited to hear something more; she had the idea that, on the six o'clock news, Jack had said a few more words. But now the program had switched back to the television studio and a boyish announcer with a wide, patterned necktie, was smiling up from a piece of paper. ". . . very serious business, when violence strikes so close to home," he said. "Now, here is Buddy Benedickt and the weather for Detroit and the surrounding area. . . ."

Elena turned off the set.

She sat with her forehead pressed against the screen. The despair of the last several weeks seemed to gather in her, she didn't know why, as if this proof that her lover existed, that he had a connection with the world that truly excluded her, was more than she could bear. But her mind could not focus on this. It kept skipping, faltering, from point to point, no more able to hold onto anything than she had been able to hold the picture on the screen, the blur that was her lover's face.

And then another part of her, speaking almost with Jack's own swift logical authority, thought quite clearly: *Does it matter?* she was confusing herself with the personality of another human being, and she was free, as all people are free of one another. She could not own him, she did not really want him. She thought: *I'm not his wife. If he loses, even if he wins, it has nothing to do with me.*

But she could not concentrate on this voice either. She sat with her forehead pressed against the screen, her eyes closed. She felt helpless and safe there, like a child.

13

Four of the 690 deaths of 1971 were caused by the fury of a Detroit father, who tracked his runaway daughter down to a tenement building not far from Jack's own neighborhood, where the fourteen-year-old girl was living with a dozen or more people. A few were sitting on the bare floor, some were standing around or entering the room or leaving it, when the father kicked the door in and began screaming at them. Later, no one was able to remember what he had screamed and he himself could remember nothing. The girl and the others stared at him and saw a man of middle age, in a windbreaker, weeping, holding a Springfield in his hands. A few seconds later three people were dead, including the daughter, and a fourth—a young man in his twenties, new to Detroit, who had wandered into the place a half-hour before, was dying, part of his face blown away. This was to make identification difficult; finally, it turned out he was from St. Paul, Minnesota.

The father, whose name was Cole, was arrested but released almost immediately on bail, a rarity in a murder case; the judge he was brought before, McIntyre, was willing to release him on the strength of the man's position in the neighborhood he lived in—obviously a good citizen, a foreman at one of the small tool companies in town, a man with no previous arrests or convictions. Local newspapers and news broadcasts showed the weeping man standing beside his wife, or with his wife and the minister of his church, Cole's face hidden by his hands. *A shattered man,* someone called him.

Marvin Howe got on the telephone at once and volunteered to defend Cole; he'd do it for no fee, absolutely nothing. If the trial took place quickly, and moved quickly, he was confident it would hardly cut into his plans for the spring. The charges against Cole were immediately dropped from first-degree murder to second degree, as soon as Howe became Cole's attorney; Cole was tried before Judge Harold Fox, in a trial that moved rapidly and lasted hardly a week, though it was highly publicized all over the state and the Midwest. Howe prepared his defense one morning while eating his breakfast, just standing in the kitchen by a counter, leafing through papers and jotting down notes, as he ate spoonsful of oatmeal and sipped at his bourbon. . . . The Cole case bore some resemblance to an "unwritten law" case he'd handled in Dallas, Texas, eight years before, where an angry husband had shot his wife and a few other people. So he hardly had to invent much. Just meeting with Cole, talking for less than an hour with him and with his wife and with Cole's other children, was more than enough: Howe knew the man completely, knew everything he needed to know.

Instructing the jury, at the conclusion of the trial, Judge Fox, himself a middle-aged man with a young daughter, pointed out that while the prosecution's argument that Cole had demonstrated (by buying and bringing along a rifle) a specific intent to commit a crime, the jurors must keep in mind certain general principles of law (most importantly, the presumption of innocence), the defendant's background, religious commitment, reputation in his community and at the tool plant, the testimony of a parade of character witnesses, and the fact that, under law, a man bereft of reason cannot be held legally responsible for his actions. Judge Fox said: "If you believe that the defendant is guilty of second-degree murder as it has been explained to you, bring in a verdict of Guilty. If you believe the defendant was not responsible for his actions, that he was temporarily so maddened by the scene before him that he could not restrain himself . . . you must bring in a verdict of Not Guilty."

Judge Fox's voice was trembling.

The jurors conferred for fifty minutes, and when they returned

Marvin Howe saw how pleased they were—how openly they looked toward the defense table—and he knew he had won.

Not Guilty.

That was the headline for the day, the excited news of the day. Marvin was photographed with his client and his client's wife, the three of them obviously very moved, tears streaming down Cole's face, his wife's face stunned; then Marvin shook hands with them and with everyone else, said good-by, and hurried to catch a plane to Sarasota, Florida, where he was fighting an insurance company for a claim of a million and a half dollars.

Jack leaned close against her, still, contemplative, pressing his jaw against the side of her face, leaning there, an almost impersonal weight. He caressed her shoulders and neck and she felt his fingers fidgeting absent-mindedly with the clasp of her necklace. He said softly: "How can you sleep with them, Elena?"

Elena stiffened.

He had followed the Cole trial closely and had attended the last day's sessions. He had said nothing to her all along, and now he spoke very gently.

Absent-minded, so depressed by the acquittal that he seemed physically ill, Jack had come a few minutes late to the room and had told Elena he couldn't stay, he had to be alone . . . he hoped she would understand. . . .

Elena said yes, she understood.

So they stood for a few minutes, their coats still on, and Jack said in a low, almost abstract, speculating voice: "I had a good idea . . . when McIntyre let him out on next to nothing . . . how it would turn out. I knew. They never let murderers out on bail in Detroit, it's happened only once or twice that I know of, under very different circumstances. But they let Cole out. You know, I had to fight like hell to get Dawe out—*thirty thousand dollars* bail—and that murderer, that devoted father, got out on one thousand."

He walked back down to the street with Elena, forgetting his usual caution. In a way, he had forgotten her.

He said: ". . . it was so moving, so heartbreaking . . . people were crying in the courtroom. . . . Your husband was nearly crying. It was all authentic, it was real life. I'm glad I was there. I didn't cry then but maybe I should have. I think it must be good people who cry, goodhearted people . . . the father, the mother, the spectators . . . it's terrible to see a father crying, so broken up, just because he has murdered four people in a fit of temper. . . ."

At the bottom of the stairs, in the small drafty foyer of the building, Jack paused. He was very distracted. "McIntyre repeated your husband's closing argument, almost the same words . . . maybe they were the same words. Yet they were somehow original with each man. Your husband . . . and the judge . . . and . . . and all the people crowded in the courtroom . . . all the people . . . all the same words, the same. . . . Only the prosecution's attorney was out of harmony; he said different words. Nobody listened to him. *There is no justifiable homicide,* he tried to argue; but the hell with him. Nobody listened."

The foyer of this old building was cluttered with wrappers and newspapers and other anonymous debris, even what appeared to be dried leaves from last autumn. Elena wondered if her lover wanted to leave with her like this, so openly, or whether she should stop him. . . . She looked shyly at the side of his face. He looked helpless, almost beggarly. She put her hand on his arm and said: "I'm sorry . . . I'm very sorry."

"Dawe's turn will be coming up in a few weeks. As soon as he's patched up. If he . . . if . . . if the Cole trial is prophetic, then I've had it . . . I'm finished . . . I'm getting out."

Elena said: "No, please. Don't talk like that."

"Why not? There's other work I can do. I'm free. The hell with this city . . . even myself, this part of myself. . . . I've been feeling off and on, this past year, that I've got to get away somewhere, Elena, maybe out of the country, anywhere. I've got to get free, to get clear of Detroit, to get the feel of it, the fighting, the love of fighting out of my system. I need to think at a distance. . . . I've lived here most of my life and I can't see it objectively. I was born here, I went to school here, one of the big schools, all thunderous stairways and kids milling around, thousands of kids, a kind of hell. . . . I've got to get free of this and maybe write about it, try to say something about it . . . that we don't have to fight, but yet we do, we must . . . simply to survive here. But it shouldn't be this way. Look: I do have hopes, everything in me isn't angry, I have an idea, a feeling, about another kind of city that isn't Detroit . . . But Detroit could be transformed into it . . . I can imagine it . . . I can imagine my own life here, back to my childhood, lived out in a parallel way, a ghostly alternative life, a different world . . . with things broken down into parts, decentralized, neighborhoods and schools that are small and human, the size of ordinary houses, a school every few blocks and very intimate, very human . . . and . . . and I can imagine Welfare shut down and all the money handed out to everyone; I can imagine people who don't have to cheat and lie and grovel and play the game . . . stabbing and making money off one another, all this pushing, fighting, all this American stage-acting and performing. . . ."

Elena, watching him, her hand still on his arm, felt with surprise his separateness from her and from the dirty little hallway they were standing in. He spoke so slowly, so sincerely . . . he hadn't any of the invulnerability he had had that day in April, taking hold of her wrist, waking her. Then, he had had the self-possession, the absolute invulnerability of a criminal; nothing could have touched him.

"Where would you go if you left?" she asked softly.

"Anywhere—out of the country—just to get free of it, to think. I don't want to go under, here— But I'd come back, because I—I would always—because I was born here, after all, and—" He paused. He looked at Elena, trying to smile. "I'm not asking you if you'd go with me, not yet. Don't say anything, don't indicate anything, please—I'm not asking you yet. That's a question I won't ask you unless I have to."

Outside, on the other side of the door, people were passing close to the frosted windowpane, shadows and shapes that kept appearing and hurrying by and appearing again. Jack glanced at these shapes but did not really seem aware of them. Elena, nervous, tried to prepare herself for the shock of the door opening suddenly; but Jack did not seem to notice.

"But it might not mean what you think . . . the trial that just ended . . . what Judge Fox said . . . ," Elena said.

Jack said: "If it had been just the judge, then maybe . . . maybe. . . . But it was everyone, the whole courtroom, the whole city. I know."

"But . . ."

"A few years ago someone gave me two novels to read, by Kafka; he thought I might like them. I only had time to skim through them . . . the writing was very strange . . . there's a man who is trying to figure something out, and he sleeps with women to help his case, but it doesn't work, in fact nothing works," Jack said. "In one or both novels he's put to death, I can't remember exactly . . . he tries to be his own lawyer, which is always a fatal mistake. But there was more to it than that. I don't like novels, I don't have time for fiction, so I just skimmed through the stories . . . but one thing stayed with me, the fact that the man kept fighting and didn't walk away . . . and I admired him for this. . . . Now I'm not so sure. Why didn't he walk away? Why not? I think I could walk away from it now myself. I could walk away from anything. . . . There are women in the novels who seem to possess secrets, who are very close to the judges, but he can't really make any use of them . . . and. . . . At least I'm not that low. And I think I could just walk away."

For a while he stood in silence. Then Elena said again, gently: "But it might not mean anything so terrible. The trial and the verdict. . . ."

"*Not Guilty,* they said. It's the greatest gift you can hand another human being. They said it, all right, *Not Guilty.* It didn't even surprise me very much."

"But maybe it doesn't mean anything," Elena said.

"Everything means something," Jack said.

Elena stood at the rear of the house, staring out at the lake, which was gray, choppy, restless; impossible to imagine sailboats there now. The wind drove the lake into waves sometimes deep, sometimes only inches high, a shifting substance that made her dizzy.

She thought of herself as a woman watching something in motion, always shifting, changing; she was, herself, not in motion; or was she in motion? It made her dizzy to think of this. Yet she kept watching, yearning. She knew the lake was only water and that water was only a shifting mass, a liquid, and that the sight of it was registered in her head: so it belonged to her and hadn't the power to terrify her. And the occasional chain saws, the remote screams and the air-rending silence that followed them, were only sounds registered in her head. They were not important.

But still she was frightened, she seemed to exist inside a condition of fear. She was in love and so she must think about her lover. *But he would die.* Earlier in her life, she had rarely thought about death, and now she found herself thinking, actively thinking, about Jack dead, Jack dying, Jack as a physical human thing, a thing that must someday die. If she stared out at the empty lake, even out there, in all that angry unhuman space, she sometimes saw a vision of him—his face, his skull. And it terrified her, because she was helpless.

Of his old fears, his suspicions that he might be killed—she did not think at all. She was certain he would not be killed. To *be killed:* what a privilege! What was terrible was the fact that he must die, in his turn, in his ordinary and unplanned turn, and that nobody would be alarmed because . . . because it would be in Jack's nature, as a physical living thing, to die. This maddened her, baffled her. At times her body seemed to dissolve in panic that was like desire, a terrible, black, impersonal wave of emotion. And she wanted to cry out for help. Then, at other times, she felt the terror as a simple fact, an uncontestable and absolute fact, and she felt almost a pull toward it, a breathless helpless desire to acknowledge it.

As if such acknowledgment might save her. . . .

But when they were together, as lovers, she kissed his mouth and felt the teeth hard beneath his flesh and her vision of his death flew up into her face, to ruin her love for him; or to sharpen it, to tease it. She felt the strangeness of him, a taste against her lips of something almost bitter to her, totally alien, separate, his mouth far on the surface of her consciousness and yet familiar to her. She had no idea of the time, the day of the week, except to know how abruptly time opened for her; she edged through it, through a dimension of terrifying freedom, and then through that doorway and into a man's arms. And he would gather her against him, loving her, she would feel the strain of his body, the start of a terrifying, alien sensation in her, which she had to resist. . . .

And she did resist it, she had grown skillful at resisting it. Stricken, she gripped this man's body, she felt at times the quivering fear in him, the fear of his own urgency, his own separateness, which would beat her back, destroy her, if he gave in to it. And he would say: *Let me love you.* . . . For a moment they would be balanced, a long straining moment, then his emotion plunged into her and could not be stopped; she rejoiced in his energy, this vicious frictional assault that had to run its course.

Into her everything flowed, everything slammed itself free to flow, and broke and did flow. She was a reservoir of darkness. With all the caution of her sanity she did want this: her acquiescing to him, her body used as a vessel to accommodate him. She did not want to match his strength, his constant risk of passion, the madness of his white-hot nerves. At times, away from him, dreaming futilely of him, she did want it; but not when she was with him. It was so much more chaste—her virginity. She could love herself only through him and could know her body only through him.

She had come close to madness with him, and she dreaded it. He had burst through the network of her veins, her intelligent calculating veins, through the structure of her nerves—that had happened only once, really, and she could resist it now, she could deny it. If she felt wounded, lacerated, physically abused—that was part of her gift to him, to a man with a specific name and a specific desire, and part of her own chastity.

One day Jack wept in her arms. It was an afternoon in February. She did not know what his tears meant—anger, relief, passion, despair? She could not interpret them. She held him, in silence; she tried to remember what it must mean, what someone had told her it meant, long ago, a man weeping in her arms.

After a while he began to talk to her about something strange: a religious ritual, Aztec Indians, the past. She knew that, with Jack as with all men, everything meant something . . . so she listened closely as he said in his half-joking, half-serious voice: ". . . these Aztec youths were evidently allowed to become gods for a short period . . . or maybe they were selected, I don't know . . . on the understanding that they would eventually have their hearts cut out at the altar in some kind of religious ceremony. They agreed to be gods, and then they agreed to have their hearts cut out. I wonder if the godliness is worth it? What comes at the end, the public ceremony . . . ?"

14

February. A confused event—a gathering of people—a man rushing up to my husband and putting out his hand as if—

You don't remember me, do you?

Reddened, not just his face but his neck, even his hands appeared reddened and thick, dense with blood. His head thrusting itself forward on his neck. I wanted to scream, to push my husband aside—people were staring in astonishment—

Don't remember? Don't remember . . . ?

*His face showed his anguish. He panted. All evening he had been circling my husband, I had seen it, had seen him. Now he rushed up to us and his full chest rose and fell, he spoke in a slightly Southern, outlandish voice, rhythms not quite suited for this northerly place—*I've changed in twenty-three years—but I would know you anywhere—I—

*Then he sank forward, down to his knees. Sank to his knees. Brought his forehead down to the floor in front of my husband's feet—sobbing—*I thank you, I thank you, I will never forget, I thank you, I owe everything to you, I—

Marvin said, embarrassed: But this isn't necessary!

"Then you don't remember," Elena said.

"No, I certainly don't remember. My mind is filled with obligations in the present, crowded with appointments and new faces and. . . . No, I don't remember, absolutely not. And I doubt that it ever happened, frankly."

Marya smiled at her daughter across her immense glass desk. Its top was comfortably cluttered and Elena could see, through the glass, that the drawers were also filled. Holding down some glossy photographs was a paperweight in the shape of a glass swan, bluish crystal, very beautiful and probably very expensive; it was the size of a pigeon.

Elena ran her finger along the swan's poised neck. "This is very pretty. . . ."

"A friend gave it to me; yes, it's very pretty," Marya said. "I'm very fond of it."

After an awkward pause Elena said again, returning to her subject: ". . . but I remember it so clearly . . . . something about sleeping pills, you'd brought them home for me . . . ? before my marriage? And the idea was, the idea was that I would take them, take an overdose, if he . . . if he didn't agree to our terms. . . . Don't you remember?"

Marya laughed. "Elena, dear, I told you I don't remember anything like that." She smiled, she seemed rather embarrassed. "Do you mean I wanted you to commit suicide?—or just pretend to? It just isn't possible, it certainly never happened in my lifetime!"

Elena shook her head mutely.

Marya said, "Elena, really . . . what if someone overheard you? I hope you never mention such outlandish, morbid fantasies to your husband. I certainly never dreamed up such a thing . . . imagine, risking my only daughter's life, and why . . . ? It isn't like me. You know that. I have both feet solidly in the real world. It's your imagination that is just as unreliable as ever . . . you're twenty-five at least, at least, aren't you . . . ? Are you ever going to grow up? Elena, really!"

"Then you don't remember. The sleeping pills. Tossing them on the bed. You don't remember," Elena said.

"There's nothing to remember, Elena. All that is distant history, isn't it? You imagined the whole episode."

"Did I . . . ?"

"I can't explain you, Elena, you baffle me. You always did. You were always thinking, plotting, having your own private thoughts."

"Yes, I had my own private thoughts," Elena said. She drew her finger along the swan's back slowly. She was silent for so long that Marya crossed and uncrossed her legs, embarrassed. Elena looked up at her mother only with great effort; Marya was very handsome, not quite beautiful any longer but striking, her skin smooth, evenly tanned from two weeks in the Caribbean, her eyes clear and intelligent and rimmed with bluish-black paint. "You know I'm always delighted to see you, Elena," Marya said with a smile, "but my days are so crowded now . . . and what an unpleasant surprise, your coming in here like this and accusing me of something so strange! . . . And I don't really like that sweater you're wearing, the way it's tucked in your belt. You've lost weight, haven't you? You've always been flat-chested and you shouldn't emphasize it, really; what does Marvin think? Your hair is all right, it's quite adequate, but aren't you tired of that style? Let it loose, let it hang down around your face. That's much more contemporary."

"Marvin likes my hair like this," Elena said.

"Oh yes, I'm sure he does! He's so conservative. . . . It was my idea for you to wear it that way, you know, and I'm very pleased he still likes it, but. . . . You're a lovely woman, Elena, and you must know one thing: you have a long life ahead of you, I mean a long life as a beautiful woman. Look at me! I don't have your bone structure, your cheekbones, and yet look!– So you must be realistic, dear, and assume a good twenty-five or even thirty years to come– What's wrong? What's wrong now?"

Elena stared at her mother. She was shocked.

"Elena . . . ? Why do you look so alarmed? I've just pointed out to you a very simple, obvious truth, which should delight you rather than have such an odd effect. . . . Is there something wrong with you, is there something you want to tell me?"

Elena felt so confused, so depressed, that for a while she could not speak. Then she said: "Yes, I wanted to . . . I came down here to. . . . I mean, I came here to ask you what I did: about the sleeping pills. . . ."

Marya laughed and waved this aside. "But honey, what morbid nonsense! Are you sure you're not ill?"

Elena smiled bitterly and said no.

"You're not in love with anyone, are you?" Marya asked.

When Elena did not reply, she went on, seriously and yet conversationally: "Did you catch my interview with Dr. Bender, that psychologist from Los Angeles? . . . the one who has done all the experiments and research about love? The interview was very controversial, of course, and very exciting. Dr. Bender says that love is destructive of the ego and therefore–therefore–destructive in some way, not healthy, I forget his exact terminology but it's entirely convincing. In fact, though I didn't dare articulate this on television, he seemed to be stating my own beliefs. . . . The program stirred up a hornet's nest. . . . Elena, I wonder if you need something like a change of scene? Get Marvin to take you to the Barbados; everyone says it's a crime, how that man works, never takes a vacation. . . . Do you get enough sleep? You aren't brooding about things, are you? . . . you were always such a brooder, a worrier, with your secret thoughts! . . . You're sure you aren't in love with anyone?"

"Yes. I'm sure."

"Because he could just kick you out, Elena, you don't have a claim to anything, really, I suspect that even the jewelry and the clothes you're wearing belong to him; it's probably written down somewhere, I wouldn't doubt it! And, of course, emotionally he might be hard to deal with, he might become rather angry. . . . I wonder if you really know him, Elena? But he's been a perfect gentleman toward me in the last few years, when we happen to meet. In fact, I had a marvelous talk with him at Topinka's on Tuesday, both of us were with other people for lunch and rather rushed for time—but he looked marvelous, dear, he's really a handsome man! He is! He was with Bennie Dack, the judge's son, and Gloriana, that strange woman—you know—the one who is casting horoscopes for the entire Ford family— What do you think of her, Elena?"

"Who? I don't know her," Elena said.

"You certainly do! You've been introduced to Gloriana, you certainly have!"

"I don't remember."

"*I don't remember.* Why, at that party where the man from Atlanta scared us all, the man who knelt down in front of Marvin and started crying—that old client of his he saved from the electric chair—why, Elena, Gloriana was there and looking a sight, with her chrome jewelry—everyone was talking about her—you certainly did meet her, don't deny it."

Elena shook her head wordlessly.

"It's terrible, how little you notice what's going on around you," Marya laughed. "You haven't changed a bit! I swear, sometimes I'm sure you don't notice *me*, your own mother, at some of these gatherings. You look right through me. It gives me the chills. There are times when I've smiled at you quite openly, and you don't seem to notice. It would be amusing if it wasn't so frightening. . . . Frankly, Elena, a few nights ago, at the Adlers', you had this daydreaming look as if you were . . . well, I don't like to say it. . . ."

"What, were you there? I didn't see you there."

"Yes, I was there, and I saw *you.* I make it a point to see everyone, it's a token of my respect for other people. . . . Now, why are you picking at the arm of the chair like that? You never used to be nervous . . . you're digging the finish off. . . . Look up at me, dear. Why are your eyes so strange?"

Elena looked up fearfully.

"You must need more sleep. I would have thought marriage might have calmed you down, you were headed for disaster . . . you were always too beautiful for your own good, and it's fortunate someone like Marvin Howe married you. You need a man like that, someone very strong and clever and. . . . Are the men bothering you, Elena? I noticed Barney Adler hanging around you the other evening, and that awful Willie Dunbar, the what-is-it, the inventor who is being sued by all those widows up in Saginaw . . . ? You can be sure Marvin notices too, he doesn't miss a thing. Don't ever seem to encourage these men by saying the wrong thing, dear, because they're very excitable and their wives are so old now. . . . My God, Elena, all this reminds me! I have some wonderful news for you and I nearly forgot to tell you. . . . I'm engaged to be married."

"What, married?—engaged to be married?"

Marya laughed at her astonishment. She turned a framed photograph around so Elena could see it: the face was thin, handsome, rather watery-eyed, a man of about sixty, with hair that was neatly parted and appeared stiff, as if dyed.

"His name is Nigel Stock. He lives in London, Elena, he's an Englishman, a marvelous man who shares many of my interests. . . . He's a shipbuilder, isn't that a surprise? Somehow I didn't think people built ships any more. But he's very successful, you'll enjoy meeting him when we can all get together. We haven't set any date for the wedding yet, but I'll let you know well in advance. Now, aren't you surprised?"

"Yes, I am, I'm very surprised," Elena said, staring at the photograph. "I hadn't any idea that. . . ."

"I suppose you think it's a little foolish, your mother falling in love at her age and getting married," Marya laughed.

"Oh no, I'm very happy for you . . . I . . . ," Elena said slowly. She was examining the photograph. Then she said, "Mother, this looks like—you know—it looks like my father. This looks just like my father."

"It looks like who?"

"My father. Your husband."

Marya took the picture from her and stared at it.

She shook her head after a moment, frowning angrily. "No, it does not. It bears no resemblance to him . . . or to anyone else. . . . It . . . Mr. Stock is an Englishman, a pure Anglo-Saxon. And anyway, Elena, you can't possibly remember what your father looked like; I don't remember him myself."

"I remember him," Elena said stubbornly.

"How could you possibly remember him?"

"I remember everything," Elena said.

"Elena, you're behaving so oddly today . . . I wonder if I even know you? It just isn't possible you would remember what your father looked like after so many years."

"I remember a picture in the newspaper," Elena said, "of someone who had won an Irish Sweepstakes ticket . . . and . . . and you were very upset, you pointed out one of the bystanders in the picture and said that it looked like my father, don't you remember? You were very upset. And the man in the paper, it was a photograph of some men in a bar, that man looked just like Mr. Stock. . . ."

Marya laughed angrily. "Your father never won any Irish Sweepstakes ticket in his life! That madman had no luck at all, and—and—this is certainly an unpleasant conversation—"

"I'm sorry," Elena said.

"You don't look sorry."

"I am sorry, I'm very sorry," Elena said.

After a tense moment, they both smiled. Marya, as if some crisis were past, laughed and clapped her hands lightly together. "Well—! Do you wish me luck, dear? And hope this marriage is more successful than my first?"

"Yes," Elena said.

Marya reached out suddenly to take hold of Elena's hand. She squeezed it. "Do you promise to come to my wedding, Elena?—you and Marvin? You won't let me down, will you?"

"Of course not," Elena said warmly.

"And you're not going to go around remembering all kinds of strange, ugly things about me, are you?"

"No," Elena said.

"Because what good does it do, to invent things, or even to remember? If you dwell upon the past, the way historians—I mean professional historians—do, evidently, you might as well alter it as best you can. Otherwise, what are you accomplishing?"

Elena could not think of any answer to this question.

That same day, later in the morning, Jack telephoned her. He said he was driving out to East Lansing on some business, and he wanted her to ride with him.

Elena was amazed.

"I don't understand," she said.

"I want to talk with you," he said. "Also, I don't want to drive alone; I feel shaky and I'm afraid of an accident."

"But Jack. . . ."

They were both silent. Elena's mind raced and she tried to think what was wrong, what he wanted.

"I'm due there for some business on an appeal and I would like you to ride with me, just to ride with me," he said. "All right?"

"But I can't. . . . I don't think I. . . ."

"Can you be ready in half an hour?"

"I can't do it," Elena said.

"Why can't you?"

"Because I . . . Jack, I can't. I can't."

"I'll remember this," Jack said.

He hung up.

The hospital was noisy and antiquated, and the only reason Dawe was alone in the room was because his roommate—an elderly man—had died the day before. The old man's bed was jacked up, the mattress curled around on itself; a screen with gauze-like curtains still protected Dawe from that side of the room. His bed was far from the window, though, and he made no effort to look in that direction.

Up close, he appeared younger than he really was. His face was all angles and clefts and slants; his eyes were enlarged, the sockets bruised-looking. Twenty-seven years old, he seemed to Elena hardly twenty, in spite of his shaved head and the stern, ascetic appearance the white bandages and bedclothes gave him. He kept smiling at Elena, blinking, as if he were having difficulty seeing her. While Jack spoke, he seemed to be paying only minimal attention to him, which began to annoy Jack.

"We'll be coming up before a man named Couteau, who's over in criminal court for a while this spring," Jack was saying; ". . . his past record in criminal court looks fairly good to me, I think we'll have a good deal. Are you listening? At least we didn't draw McIntyre or Fox. Couteau is intelligent and not too old."

Elena thought her lover's voice too loud and formal for this room, especially this corner of the room. Dawe nodded politely, as if none of this mattered much.

"So . . . if we plan tentatively on putting you up, if you'll agree to work out with me beforehand a good, coherent way for you to explain what happened, and a little about yourself, though not much . . . I think this judge will be sympathetic and I think he'll work on the jury, because he has a good record with civil rights cases . . . and a First Amendment case back in 1962 that someone I know argued in front of him. How does that sound?"

"Very good," Dawe said, blinking at Jack.

"How do you feel today?"

"Oh good, very good."

He smiled self-consciously. His hands darted up toward his head, as if to brush his hair back from his face; but he had no hair. Elena thought it strange, that this man was only a year younger than she and yet he seemed much younger, like a child. She could not think of him as a man at all.

"As soon as your vision is better and it doesn't make your head ache to read, I have some things for you to go through," Jack said. "I'll be bringing a lot of papers in later this week. Now, about one of your character witnesses . . . this art professor at U-M . . . I've checked him out and he has a 1968 conviction, arrested by the sheriff's men out in Ann Arbor on a sidewalk obstruction charge . . . so . . . it's innocent enough but I'm not sure we want to risk having that brought up . . . because, frankly, the man won't impress any jury . . . he doesn't impress me. . . ."

Dawe shook his head. "Did you hear from my father yet?"

"What? No."

Dawe's face moved nervously, in a series of twitches. Then he said, "Well, send him the bills, see what happens. Did somebody say it's a hundred dollars a day in here?"

"It's three hundred," Jack said flatly. After a moment he went on: "So I'm crossing that one off the list. Now, if you'll give me your attention . . . I think that. . . ."

"What list? Who are you crossing off?"

"This Martineau. I don't like him."

Dawe stared at Jack so long that Elena felt the danger of his silence, his peculiar groping stillness; she felt that Jack would somehow destroy it, as if reaching out with the edge of his hand and bringing it down viciously against Dawe's face. But after a few seconds Jack said uncomfortably: "Are you in pain?"

"Pain . . . ? No, the pain is out here," Dawe said. He drew a line with his hand in the air, slowly, about a foot to the side of his head. "I'm doped up. They've got me doped, so the pain is real but it doesn't belong to me. I'm in danger of turning into someone else . . . I don't believe in drugs . . . and . . . and I. . . ." He seemed confused. He made a gesture toward Jack, as if wanting to touch him. He reached for Jack's hand; but Jack, startled, drew back. "Mr. Morrissey, I know how important you think all this is, and I respect you, but I . . . I can't allow you to run away with me. I can't allow that. I have got to fight for the privilege of even feeling my own body—I have to argue with the nurses not to dope me up, but they won't listen—and with you, with you it's more important, Mr. Morrissey; I can't let you run away with me."

"What?"

"No, I can't let you think my thoughts. My thoughts constitute my soul. I can't let you tamper with my soul."

"*Tamper with* . . . ?" Jack said ironically. "That's a respectful term to use with me, isn't it?"

Dawe tried to smile. He looked at Elena as if hoping she might support him. "I don't speak in riddles or codes, I'm not sarcastic, I refuse even to translate sarcasm into my own vocabulary. I'm free of that. I respect you very much, Mr. Morrissey, though you are an enemy of mine . . . I know we could talk together if we used the same vocabulary . . . I will assume the guilt, the error; it must be my fault and not yours that we never communicate."

Jack sat for a while without speaking, tapping his ballpoint pen on something. It made a small but very precise clicking sound. Elena feared looking at him. She feared the danger they were all in, the three of them, unaware of it, helplessly brought up against it. . . . Behind Dawe's head the ugly tubing of the bed was chipped, marred, as if sharp objects had been struck against it.

A mystery, all the patterns of damage: even the walls of the room were chipped, smeared with black, as if things had been shoved against them repeatedly. Dawe was looking at her with his odd, dilated eyes, his smile that seemed no more than an arrested twitching of the lips, and she felt suddenly they were all in danger, victims of one another, not just Elena and her lover and this young man with his bruised face, but all people, everyone.

Dawe broke the silence awkwardly. "They do something to me here I never knew about before. It's a spinal injection of colored fluid . . . I think . . . and there's nothing quite like it, it's. . . . It can't be described, the pain. But look, Mr. Morrissey: I'm not going to break down. I'll survive. This will be just a part of my life, the spinal business, the pain, and the police after me . . . and the Law. . . . I'm going to get through it without losing myself, nobody is going to break me. Please, do you understand what I'm saying?"

Jack was making short sharp zigzag lines on his notebook cover. "I understand you," he said. "But you don't understand me."

"No, no, I don't, that's true, my failing with you is that I don't understand . . . I find it hard to understand you. . . ." He smiled uneasily. "Your wife was in yesterday, and she told me how you would handle all this. She told me you'd get me off, I could assume either an acquittal or maybe a suspended sentence or probation . . . she said that's what you would do for me, and that's what the goal is. I asked Rachel if she saw life like that and she said—"

"Never mind," Jack interrupted. "I'll answer you: life is not like that."

"You didn't let me finish—I meant to say—is life one goal in mind you sacrifice everything to, and mutilate yourself, or is life—"

"Life has nothing to do with *us*," Jack said.

Dawe sat back as if exhausted. He groped about his neck and head again, fingering the bandages. What Elena could see of his shaved head looked strangely mottled and ugly; it hadn't the smooth healthy gleam of the heads of bald men; it was bluish in parts, a very pale, vein-cluttered orange in others. He had suffered a concussion and had evidently been unconscious for over a week. Now he looked extremely thin, and when he inhaled deeply, as if to give himself the energy to think, his chest raised and exposed itself through the loose opening at the top of his hospital gown: a cadaverous chest that was awful to see. Elena wanted to touch him, to comfort him. She smiled at him. He stared at her, trying to smile in return, as if dazed.

Jack had introduced her as a "friend"—and he had said nothing else about her.

"I wish you could lie here beside me," Dawe said to Elena.

Elena laughed uneasily.

Jack also laughed, startled and irritated. He glanced over at Elena and she caught his look of absolute rage. But he handled himself coolly, formally, in a way Elena had not guessed was possible for Jack: as if his words were being recorded, were not private words at all, not his own. He said: ". . . visiting hours are going to be over in an hour . . . so I think . . . we should return to. . . ." He leafed through some papers. He said: "What about Warner? Have you thought that over? I have it all prepared, I have witnesses lined up, and you must certainly press charges against him. He tried to kill you."

Dawe was staring at Elena.

She looked away from him uncomfortably. Out in the corridor a few nurses were passing . . . she overheard part of their conversation, about the city buses . . . the schedules on Sunday. . . . A girl of about eighteen, with a starched white cap whose sides rose like sails or wings, a very pretty girl, glanced into Dawe's room and Elena caught her eye and, in that instant, thought: *I could have been her.*

The nurses walked by, chattering. Elena felt shaken: she knew it was true: she could have been that girl, a girl like that, in a white uniform and with a starched white cap, walking through the corridors of this cheerless old hospital. If her mother had said, *Elena, do this! Elena, do it!* And by magic, obliterating all choices and all painful deliberations, she would have been transformed into that girl. She realized now, now that it was too late, there were other lives . . . easier ways of survival.

And then I would lie beside you, she seemed to be saying to Dawe, who was still staring at her with a fondness that did not frighten her. *I would bring comfort to you. . . .*

"Let me love you, don't go away, don't let him take you out of here . . . ," Dawe said softly. He smiled. The sweetness of his smile seemed to bring into sight new, almost invisible dents and blemishes in his skin; there was a patch of tiny broken bluish veins on his left cheek. He put out his hand toward Elena, and she saw the dead-white flesh of his inner arm, bandages over the places where he had received transfusions and liquids recently, but other, older spots left uncovered, angry red marks like insect bites.

"Elena," Jack said, "you're distracting him. Why don't you go outside, maybe . . . ?"

"No, don't leave," Dawe said.

"I knew it was a mistake to bring you here," Jack said to Elena. "What is the point of this? It's just a waste of everyone's time, if he isn't rational."

"You're not rational," Dawe said to Jack.

"Elena . . . ?" Jack said.

"Don't make her leave, I'll pay attention to you," Dawe said. "What were you talking about . . . ? Oh, uh, Warner . . . ? Are you still talking about him?"

"Yes, I'm still talking about him," Jack said calmly. "But I think you should leave, Elena."

Elena did not move.

"All right, then," Jack said, putting his hand out quite deliberately and lowering it on Elena's arm, "all right, fine, then you can help me explain to Mered why he should press charges against this Mr. Warner . . . after all, you were there that evening and you witnessed it . . . right?" His fingers closed around Elena's arm, sliding down to her wrist so he could touch her bare skin. Elena saw Dawe's eyes moving along with that hand, his odd affectionate fixed gaze coming to rest at Elena's wrist. "Explain to our friend that someone wanted him to die, will you?" Jack said.

Dawe said gently to Elena: "It's just as if I were touching you like that. I can feel myself touching you. . . . Who are you, why are you here? Did you come to help me? I think you did. You could love both of us; you could love everyone. . . . No, don't let her go," he said when Jack released her. "Why did you do that? That was so nice, that was lovely, I really could feel you touching her and I could feel myself touched by you . . . because you won't do it in person, will you, Mr. Morrissey? You wouldn't touch me like that. . . . I wish, I wish . . . I wish with all my strength that. . . ."

"Keep it to yourself," Jack said, still very calmly. He tried to laugh. He reached down suddenly and scratched his ankle—the fingernails clawing at his skin. "Be very careful, keep it to yourself," Jack said, almost in a lyrical voice, a voice Elena had never heard before. He looked around at Elena and almost smiled. She felt a strange moment of freakish joy, a festivity her lover was almost acknowledging—but he did not acknowledge it. In her own body, light as music or as the most delicate vibrations of music that is not yet audible, she felt desire, affection, love. She and Dawe gazed at each other in a kind of trance.

"Elena, tell him, help me out," Jack said in his businesslike voice, as if nothing were wrong, "describe the scene, will you? You were there. At about ten minutes after nine several men pushed into the hall . . . among them Warner . . . and one of them had a sign, didn't he, and what did the sign say?"

Elena tried to remember. But she could not. "I don't think I saw a sign," she said slowly.

"You didn't? You mean you didn't see a sign, or you weren't able to read it?"

Jack looked at her patiently.

"I might have seen a sign . . . a man carrying a sign, a stick . . . but . . . but I don't remember."

"The sign said *Jail U.S. Traitors,*" Jack said, again patiently. "Then what? One of the men rushed up to Mered, didn't he, and started striking him with a weapon, didn't he . . . ? A two-by-four?"

Elena shook her head. "Everything was confused, it happened so quickly. . . ."

"But you heard this man say he'd kill Mered, didn't you?"

Elena shook her head.

"Other people heard it, heard it very clearly," Jack said. He scratched his ankle again. He laughed, a short breathy abrasive sound. "You heard him shouting, didn't you?"

"I think so, but—"

"You saw what he looked like?"

"Yes, but I don't—I don't really remember—"

"If you saw the man again, if you were asked to identify him, you'd remember. Believe me. Didn't you hear what he said to Mered?"

"No—"

Dawe shook his head slowly, still smiling. "I don't remember either . . . I couldn't swear to anything. . . . You were at my lecture that evening? Where were you sitting?"

"Whether you remember it all in detail or not, Elena, is not important, because you aren't going to be a witness," Jack said evenly. "I have witnesses. I have more than enough evidence. But you might explain to Mered, Elena, that this man, this K. R. Warner from Wyandotte, is a very dangerous man; he intended to kill that evening and almost succeeded . . . and that charges must be pressed against him in order to protect other people. . . . Can you explain that?"

"No, no, don't say anything," Dawe interrupted. "I already told him my feelings on this. I don't fight, I don't aid and abet murder even by dwelling on it."

"Look, Mered," Jack said, "the Graeson girl has suffered brain damage, and the man who attacked her is under arrest, and by God he's going to be found guilty of assault with intent to kill . . . and if she doesn't pull out of it, but dies, he's going to be found guilty of first-degree murder, that bastard, that filthy murderous son of a bitch, and you—if you— Look, if you refuse to press charges, if you hand me any more of this bullshit about love and forgiveness and—"

Dawe stared at him. "You want me to die!" he cried.

"What? What the hell are you saying?"

"Oh yes, you want me to die, like her, the girl, that girl . . . you want us both to die to make the evidence stronger. . . ."

"That is absolutely untrue," Jack said. He stood. He forced himself to behave very calmly.

"But I won't die. I'm not going to," Dawe said. He drew in deep, exaggerated breaths, as if to calm himself; he even smiled at Jack. "That's the whole point of my struggle—not to die—please listen to me, please— I would never press charges against that man, even if he thought he wanted to kill me. I can accept him, I can absorb his hatred into myself and transform it. I'm strong enough. Even with my head doped up and things so confused, I'm strong enough, Mr. Morrissey, nothing is going to break me. Oh believe me, please. I've asked him to visit me, I want to talk with him. I can help him. I'm sure he will come here, I'm confident . . . because we are both human beings, this man and myself . . . and . . . and we share a language. . . . I will insist that he didn't want to kill me; if the police arrest him I will go on record as saying that I tried to hurt him myself, and that he acted out of self-defense . . . and . . . and so. . . . And so . . . you understand, don't you?"

Jack stood very stiffly.

Mered said: ". . . a while ago, last summer . . . someone sent a bomb to my house . . . wrapped up in newspapers . . . I opened it but nothing happened . . . the police said it was some kind of device that was supposed to blow up when the victim unwrapped it, but it didn't work . . . it was supposed to blind me. . . . But it didn't. So I told them to forget about it. I told them to. . . ."

"Let somone else get blinded," Jack said nastily.

"No, no, Mr. Morrissey, no," Dawe said. "No. Don't be my enemy up so close. It isn't the territory for enemies, but only friends . . . lovers. . . . In my ordinary self I would have the strength to absorb you, Mr. Morrissey, and to convert you, but I'm weakened, I'm confused, I'm afraid of you. . . ." He closed his eyes. "I don't see you. I don't hear you any longer."

"All right. Fine. Excellent," Jack said. "I'll be back when your hearing improves."

He walked out into the corridor.

Dawe opened his eyes cautiously. He stared at Jack's empty chair.

"I dreamed him . . . ," he whispered.

Elena moved to Jack's chair, which was closer to the bedside. Dawe looked at her with his enlarged, damaged eyes. Out in the corridor Jack paused, turned back, came to the doorway and leaned in and said as if nothing were really wrong: "I'll go for a walk and I'll be back."

He walked away.

"I dreamed him," Dawe said softly.

Elena leaned over him and laid her head against his chest, and at once he embraced her, cradling her in his arms; she said, "Dream me." Dawe was very warm. Startled, she felt the coarseness of the hospital linen and the warm, somehow very sweet flesh of this man; she could hear his heartbeat; she closed her eyes as he stroked her hair and face in silence.

She calculated that she might risk no more than five minutes of this, of such peace. But it would stay with her all her life.

15

You lose yourself. And then you reappear.

Elena was staring at the photograph. Jack, maneuvering them along the expressway, spoke calmly and evenly as he drove and took no notice of Elena's silence, or seemed to take no notice. He had driven all the way out to the Southfield Expressway, exited, turned around, and was now heading back into Detroit; at about the time he exited, a light snowfall began. But the sky was partly clear. Everything had a peculiar fluorescent cast to it that distracted Elena; she kept glancing up nervously . . . then she looked back at the photograph of the child again.

The boy was smiling tensely, a rehearsed smile. Someone had commanded him one day: *Smile!* It was important to smile. So now the photograph showed him smiling, a boy of about two, with dark liquid eyes and hair that was probably the color of Jack's. Elena studied the picture. She felt the first sharp darts of panic, knowing she must say something when Jack stopped talking, when he paused in order to allow her to speak . . . but he was very kind, very cautious, he drove without speeding in the right-hand lane, as if to demonstrate his patience. She glanced up and saw with a sudden senseless relief that he was going to exit onto another expressway, going west toward Ann Arbor, and that this meant. . . .

"We're supposed to be at the agency at two tomorrow," Jack was saying. "So . . . that's at two tomorrow." When Elena did not reply he said: "He's from out-of-state, that's about all we'll know. I mean, about his origins. . . . They said he's been in two homes so far, that he's a little behind in development . . . he didn't learn how to talk at the usual time, but . . . but he's a very sweet kid, and. . . . He's had a lot of bad luck. He seems rather cautious of us. Rachel is crazy about him and. . . . So we're supposed to sign the papers tomorrow and make everything official."

"Yes," Elena said.

It had begun to snow harder. Elena saw the red tip of the speedometer drop back, beneath fifty. Outside, the sky was now a purplish black, a sudden density that was like the density of thought, of thoughts. Jack slowed down; he was being very cautious.

"What are you thinking, Elena?" he asked after a few minutes.

"I think . . ."

"Yes?"

But she stared at the boy's face and she could not think of anything.

"You knew how matters were progressing with us, I mean Rachel and me," Jack said awkwardly; "I mean . . . I always told you, but you never seemed to hear me. My life is noisy and complicated, I know, and I talk about it constantly in an attempt to get it clear . . . and . . . and all the Mered Dawe business, all that, I've been bothering you with it for months. But in the foreground, up close, there has always been this other problem, this fact, which is very real, and. . . . What are you thinking, Elena, right now?"

She looked mutely at the photograph.

"Because, Elena, look: there's this appointment at two tomorrow. Which I will cancel, and I will make another appointment instead with your husband—what do you think of that?—if you want me to."

Elena felt the back of her head darkening, the entire skull growing eerie and unfamiliar. It must have had something to do with the change of light and the confusion of snowflakes. A small angry storm. Elena glanced up from the child's face to the grimy rear of a truck just ahead of them and her eyes focused helplessly on the license plate, and, in her head, she heard snatches of voices as if she were desperately seeking the right words: *Can you, where is, who are the, when will it . . . ?*

"Honey . . . ?" Jack said.

Honey, who is, be careful of, what do you think of . . . ?

The child sinks out of sight. Layered over. And then reappears as another child. . . .

A return!

A completion!

You keep returning as a photograph in someone's hands, stared at, examined. The original frightened smile made permanent. Which smile was this? Your mind turns and turns. As if the universe could be reduced to a point, a single point, and your entire life concentrated on that point, an instant in time. A birth and a death in that instant.

I understood everything.

Jack reached over to touch her. He said softly, "Elena, honey, Elena . . . ? Can't you talk to me? Don't you love me?"

She glanced up at the truck a dozen yards in front of them and said sharply, frightened: "You're going to hit—"

Jack had been increasing his speed unconsciously. At once he slowed down. The speedometer needle dropped back. *Fifty-five. Fifty.* "I'm sorry," Jack said. ". . . will you tell me what to do about tomorrow?"

Elena closed her eyes. "I can't," she said.

"What?"

Her voice was bell-like, unfamiliar. "I can't."

"Why can't you?"

"I can't."

"You can tell me to keep the appointment at the adoption agency, or you can tell me to cancel it. And I will cancel it; I'll telephone them right now. Or . . . ?"

But Elena could not speak. *Or . . . ? if you want, how long will, is this the . . . ?* She pressed her fingers against her eyes and there, behind the lids, she somehow saw a flash of a child's face, watching her. He half-smiled. He was very frightened and no one could tell, no ordinary person could tell. . . . A child lay on a bed, one eye crusted over, under a pile of blankets waiting, watching the door, frightened also but not showing fear. *What good . . . ? Otherwise, what are you accomplishing . . . ?*

"If you're afraid of your husband, all right: I'll make the call, I'll do the talking to him, we'll move you out of there this afternoon. Before he knows. And he wouldn't . . . I don't think, once this is out in the open, I mean once it becomes a legal matter . . . I'm certain that . . . he would not behave in an illegal manner. . . . He wouldn't do anything to us. So in a way it would make us safe for the first time since last June . . . it would make us safe from him, I think, and it's the only way to get safe. You've never taken seriously my worries about him, you've always been so certain that he didn't know . . . and, well, since you live with him you must be able to judge what's going on in his head . . . but . . . still, he's not readable, he's had plenty of practice in lying, or acting, or whatever is necessary to get to what he wants. . . . So tell me what to do: cancel the appointment or go through with it?"

"I can't . . . I can't tell you," Elena said.

"Yes, you can tell me," Jack said. She felt his rising anger. "You can pronounce one of two words—*yes* or *no. Yes,* to cancel the appointment. *No,* not to cancel."

He made a sudden impatient gesture, but it was only to snap the windshield wipers onto a faster speed. Now they shot back and forth across the smeared windshield, jerkily, noisily. Elena noticed that the rubber strip on the wiper before her was partly torn and might be ripped off. . . . This made her dizzy.

"This damn car," Jack muttered.

She winced as though he had struck her.

After a few minutes he said again: "If I go down to the agency, Elena, if Rachel and I show up there . . . if we sign those papers. . . . Then what? Do you really want us to continue like this, the way we've been since last summer, or what? What? Because I can't take the confusion, the misery . . . and the risk also . . . and it's wearing you down too, you really aren't very happy with me. Are you? What do you want me to do?"

"I don't know," Elena said.

The truck had exited and now Elena found herself staring at a low-slung, rusted Cadillac with a drooping tailpipe. A black woman was driving it and her right-turn signal was on, flashing. It was maddening to see the dusty red light flash like that, again and again. Elena felt like crying out—

"Should I see your husband?" Jack said.

"I don't think so," Elena said.

"What? I can't hear you."

She wanted to speak more clearly but her throat seemed suddenly weak. Jack said, his voice breaking: "These damn windshield wipers—why is it snowing so hard?—oh Christ—" He could take the flashing red light no longer and swung out to pass the Cadillac, not bothering to put on his own turn signal. Elena closed her eyes and waited for an impact, a blow from the rear; but nothing happened. "I've been leading Rachel on," Jack said, "more or less humoring her, because she's been so unhappy lately . . . for a long time lately. Adopting Robert has been something she can focus on, something personal and not all this heartbreaking political crap; which would be bad enough for me, but I've had you. My mind just gravitates back to you, rolls down to you like a ball going down an incline, and it's been hell, but at least it's been very nice. But, Elena. . . . You're the one who has to decide about this. So . . . ? I'll do what you tell me."

They sped beneath an overpass and Elena had the idea, the sudden terrified idea, that something would be thrown down upon them, something would be blown loose and fall . . . and, in the angry whirling snow, their lives would come to an end. It terrified her and yet she could not cry out, even in her terror; she sat mute and rigid.

"Listen, Elena," Jack said, "if I bring Robert home, that's that. I can't send him back, I wouldn't want to send him back. It's final. I'm going to be his father permanently, I am not going to disappoint him the way those other people did, the way other adults have been disappointing him all his life. That would be like murdering him. And Rachel, Rachel has been—she's been waiting—at the back of her mind she knows, she knows everything, and she's been waiting for me to decide— Do you understand? If you let me go ahead and adopt him, Elena, you're not going to see me again; that's it. Do you understand?"

He was driving quite fast now, nearly seventy miles an hour.

He said: "If you—if you let this go through—if you don't stop me, you are *not* to come back to me—or to telephone me—because all this is driving me crazy and I'm sick of it, and— And I want to live a real life, a sane life again; the past year is all mixed up with this damn city, these fruitless degrading skirmishes and calculations and lies— Don't you care? Don't you? Don't you love me? What are you thinking?"

Elena closed her eyes.

"Or maybe you and I should both die," Jack said suddenly.

Elena did not reply; she sat helpless.

"I've thought of that off and on, it's an attractive idea," Jack said in that voice of false, almost sinister calm Elena had heard from him in the past. Yet it did not really frighten her; she felt helpless, numb, like a child. She felt the power in him building up and out of his control and out of her control.

You sink, and then you reappear.

If four are shot dead, four human beings . . . four more will be born around the corner. The statistics prove. The statistics bear out. Many millions of people have been born, lived, and died on a single point of the universe, in a single instant. It is not really very important.

"I could turn this wheel to the left and all our problems would be solved," Jack said. "I wouldn't even need to calculate. I could stop calculating. I'm tired. I'm sick of this. I don't even need a target to aim for, I could just drive right into the center divider. So you tell me, Elena, yes or no—should I do it?"

Outside, the air had turned into a chaos of whirling flakes. Elena stared at it. She felt the car pick up speed.

"Should I?" Jack said.

And then, almost hypnotically, lovingly, he said: " . . . pronounce a word for me, Elena, *yes* . . . or *no* . . . tell me if you want to die or live . . . tell me . . . tell me yes, tell me no . . . tell me what to do. . . ."

Inside these sounds your backbone was like a whip. The tension, the preparation. The need to hurt.

When you loved me and I stroked your back, even then I could always feel the strength of the separate bones hardening into a column, like a whip. It could be cracked in the air and its terrible point would touch, would slash so hard that it would seem only a touch, at first, because human flesh is too sensitive to register such pain. Then afterward. . . . A whip, a thinking calculating whip, with its need to discharge itself on another point of human flesh, one point in the universe. Then afterward the bleeding, the damaged flesh. . . .

The car was hurtling forward through new, fresh ruts of snow, overtaking the rear lights of other vehicles, plowing ahead, powerful and impatient. Elena stared as if hypnotized. No words. None. No words could stop it. Jack said viciously: "Say yes, then, that's what we want to hear—say yes—say it—"

But she could not speak.

And then something broke in him—she almost felt it break, the tension, the fury, as if he had been pushed to a point of madness, almost an ecstasy of madness, and then shattered, fallen free of it, softly and helplessly.

He began braking the car to a stop. It skidded in the wet snow. He released the brake and then pressed it down again, and now the car's speed was decreasing, decreasing, the car was falling back, slowing as if crippled; and someone right behind Jack began sounding his horn in anger. Jack, not hurrying, as if not aware of this noise, waited for an opening in traffic and shifted into the next lane, and then into the next, his fury now arranged in steps, one step and then the next and then the next.

The car bounced up onto the shoulder of the expressway and came to a jolting stop. Elena put out her hand to protect herself—she was thrown forward—but she was not hurt. Jack yanked on the emergency brake. The car was tilted at an angle, its left side much lower than its right.

She heard him breathing. Trying to get his breath. For a long time she did not look at him and believed he was not looking at her; perhaps he sat with his eyes closed. Then he said, finally, softly: "You . . ."

It was almost a recognition; a surprise. Elena stared at him.

"You know, you're so . . . you're so deadly, you're so virginal," Jack said. "You're really dead. You're dead. In yourself you're dead. And you want death for everyone—I can understand that—you're so dead yourself, so frigid, certainly you want the rest of the world to die, don't you? You're such a virgin, a sweet perpetual virgin! You're so perfect that you turn other people hard as ice, like you, and they want to die too—you draw them to you—you draw men to you—and then you feel nothing, nothing! Your insides are as dead as the rest of you, aren't they? You're so pure, such a gift! You are really a corpse! You almost killed us," he said in his calm, rapid, logical voice, looking right at her, "and you wanted that all along—I understand—I know—now I know *you,* now I know how holy you are, how dead and how empty you are, you thing, you dead empty thing—you *thing,* you *thing*—"

He was not shouting at her and yet Elena felt the shouts, the screams of many people, a hammering at her head, a din of voices, words, the world, the pressure of the entire world, screaming to get inside her. . . .

*

I stood before him and the dizziness drew me down, down. I couldn't see. I would be sucked away. But the floor caught me and I felt him, his astonishment, I felt the rough texture of cloth—his clothes—a man's clothes—

He was saying in astonishment: Elena. . . .

Blood rushed into my head and faded, rushed in, was sucked back, it was all the language I had ever known. I felt my face against the floor. Something solid, both the floor and the bone of my face.

Elena, what are you . . . this is . . . this isn't. . . .

I felt the surprise and then the panic in him, even him. He wanted to get away. But he did not move from me.

Elena . . . ?

Breathing with great difficulty, his eyes not closed like mine, staring. He must have been staring down at me. Having to think. To stare. His eyes not closed but open, always open; he would have to think.

My blood rushed and faded. Sucked itself to a point that was almost extinguished and then flowed back out again. . . . So helpless! And then I felt him touch me timidly . . . his fingers on my head, the back of my neck . . . like a stranger, touching me timidly . . . a lover . . . a lover who does not dare believe. . . .

Elena, *he said finally, softly, when he had recovered,* you know this isn't necessary.

That evening he took the files out of his safe. They were large legal files, tied carefully with string. While Elena watched, he placed various handsful of things into the fire, batches of photographs held together by thick rubber bands, papers clipped together, a few loose items. He had to take the tapes or rolls of film out of their metal containers, or they could not burn. He did this carefully. Then he waited as these items burned, and then gravely, carefully, he stoked the debris with a poker. Then he emptied the next folder, opening manila envelopes and shaking their contents out into the fire. . . . Elena watched. She saw the papers and the tapes and the film and the photographs ignite, each in turn, each in its turn surprised by the flame, and then surrendering to it without much resistance, blazing, flaming, then crumpling into black ashes. Marvin burned everything as if performing a sacred ritual before her; he was almost impersonal as he did it.

Yet—

Yet the next morning Elena found part of a photograph, there in the ashes. A part of something. She knew she was going to be ill, she knew there was a risk in keeping anything of her own around her, because other people might find it . . . but she found the photograph there, snatching it up out of the ashes. It showed the two of them, Jack and Elena, seen head-on, through the windshield of Jack's car. Jack's face was fairly clear because that half of the windshield was clean most of the time; Elena's own face was less clear, but it was hers. Serious, mute, listening . . . she was listening to her lover, and her gaze stopped just where the glass of the windshield began. Jack was turned toward her. His right hand was raised, as if in argument, but it looked graceful, appealing. What was he saying? Elena stared at the burned photograph and tried to remember . . . tried to remember. . . . What was he saying? What? She knew she must not keep this with her, this terrible piece of evidence. She knew she would be ill. But she had to determine, had to remember: what had he been saying? when had this photograph been taken? what was she thinking, there beside him? what was her lover asking her, what, what did he want, why was his hand raised like that? which instant of their lives had this been?

THE SUMMING UP

LEO ROSS

He thought about going for a drink but his legs were very weak suddenly. His whole body was weak. He had come to the end of himself, his life was at an end. The gun was still in his pocket and he could feel it weighing that side of his body down, putting him off balance. What would happen, what event was approaching him . . . ? There was a satisfying completeness about stamping an envelope and mailing it; that was a good feeling. Yet it meant he was somehow finished and yet . . . and yet he was still standing here, trying to clear his head.

Down the street was a package liquor store. He crossed over and walked to it, and there he bought a pint of gin; as he counted out his money he noticed that he hadn't much left. This excited him because it too suggested something . . . what do you do when your money runs out? His excitement passed over into dizziness and into a kind of dread. Though he was not drunk, or even slightly intoxicated, he stumbled at the door and the salesman asked him something . . . a few words, something . . . but Leo pretended not to hear and escaped.

He returned to the park, walking slowly. He did not really like this park, but the street dipped to it and he was gravitating in that direction anyway, and it was a good place for him to sit and figure himself out. He opened the gin bottle and sipped from it, careful to keep it hidden inside the paper bag. The bag rattled a great deal. But he had the park bench to himself and no one seemed to be glancing at him. On the pond a great crowd of ducks was swimming slowly. Some were white, some mallards—the males with handsome sleek heads, green and brown feathers, and elegant markings; the females brown and very ordinary. As Leo watched, one of the males suddenly nipped at a female; but the female darted away. The ducks made patterns in the water, slowly, and yet sometimes darting swiftly, shrewdly. Back and forth . . . around and around . . . this way and that way and around behind a scrubby island and back into sight again and. . . . And after a half hour of this, the paper bag didn't seem to rattle so much.

. . . What do you do when your money runs out? . . . your luck? . . . your manhood . . . ? Leo knew he would come to an unemotional decision, because he had no emotions left. He would not think of his daughter; or his wife. He would not allow Ardis to open that door in his head and stride inside . . . her high heels clattering. . . . No, not that. No. No longer. He was finished, tired, he had no desire to outlive himself as a man. His fatherhood was finished, his manhood finished, and. . . .

At one time in his life he had been, he knew, a successful American citizen, in an honorable American profession. He had done well and must not be ashamed of that. But it was over. Now he could contemplate that man, that Leo Ross, with an unemotional, impersonal recognition . . . just as he watched people stroll through the park, approaching the pond to toss out bits of bread for the ducks and geese: they were well-dressed, probably tourists, they appeared well-to-do and healthy, and they were all strangers to him. He felt the same way about Leo Ross who had lived in Pittsburgh and had married, in 1939, a woman named Ardis Carter. It did not matter, really. It did not matter. Just as he wished the tourists no harm, he wished that Leo Ross no harm; but he still felt emotions, emotions sprang up in him when he thought of. . . .

Don't think of her.

So he would never again think of her.

The last mouthful of gin made no impression on him, it tasted bland as water, it disappeared inside him and left him sitting there, inert, dead. He thought: *Am I already dead?* The impersonal, neutral, numb part of his soul had taken over, and now he had only to complete himself. . . . He fumbled inside his pocket and felt the gun there. Yes, good. He knew enough not to take it out—someone might be watching—but he peered inside the pocket and saw it there. It was just a Smith and Wesson .38 revolver, not good for long distances, he knew, but he wouldn't need it for any long distances.

He got to his feet unsteadily. A little sickish, but numbed, so that there was no immediate threat of vomiting. It was getting dark now; it must have been the end of the afternoon. Leo put the bottle in its wrinkled paper bag into an overstuffed refuse container, but it fell back out again, and he stooped, panting, to pick it up and force it back into the debris. In his former life he had been a neat person.

His mind clicked suddenly onto a small, quiet, private, dim room: a lavatory somewhere. Yes, good. He would find a dark private place. He left the park and descended one of the side streets . . . past some taverns, a souvenir shop, some small restaurants, drugstores, cheap movie houses. . . . At one of the movie houses he paused. The poster showed a very beautiful blond woman who was life-sized, the same as Leo himself, and she was on eye level with him and smiling directly at him. Her hair was very blond and lavish, tumbling about her shoulders and down onto her breasts. She wore an evening gown of some kind. She seemed to be leaning forward, straining forward, as if to whisper to him.

Tickets to the theater were only 50¢.

Inside, he stumbled down the aisle and located a seat, his eyes not yet adjusted to the dimness, already fixed on the screen. There a woman was speaking angrily over a telephone. Was it that woman? The one on the poster? She turned abruptly toward the camera and it was her . . . yes . . . very angry about something . . . her hair thick and long about her face. . . . Leo sat, staring. Now the scene changed and a man was leaning against a piece of furniture, something with a mirror attached to it, and then the camera drew back to show the blond woman seated at a dressing table, angrily brushing her hair. She and the man were arguing about something. Leo could make no sense of the dialogue; he stared greedily at the woman's face, her fluffy hair, the strong strokes of the hairbrush through the hair, the silky robe that seemed about to fall open. . . .

When the film came to an end, Leo sat without moving; he felt oddly exhausted. Another movie was beginning and he watched the new actors doing something behind the titles and all the lists of names, acting out some silent, complicated routine; he became interested in what they were doing. So he sat through that movie, which was in black and white, not so exciting as the main feature, and then the other movie began again and there was the woman, gazing out into the audience . . . so Leo sat through the first twenty minutes, which he had missed before. . . . It was satisfying and almost exciting, to see the events that led up to the part of the movie he had already seen. He was ahead of the actors and could tell the mistakes they were making.

. . . His favorite scene was the one near the conclusion, in which the blond actress slapped her boy friend and was then slapped by him, and back and forth they slapped each other, almost evenly matched. The other men in the audience, a dozen scattered viewers, obviously enjoyed this scene also; they laughed and one man applauded. The soundtrack whirled with music so loud that Leo felt as if he were being hypnotized. Then the woman collapsed, sobbing onto a strange curved sofa, and her low-cut dress seemed to give way, and, as the music soared, her boy friend rushed to her and embraced her. . . . Leo thought this scene was excellently done. But it did mean the movie was ending; even if you hadn't already seen it, you would get that impression. Five minutes later it had ended.

Then the house lights came on and Leo, startled, noticed where he was and that it was time to leave. The other men in the audience got to their feet slowly . . . so slowly, thoughtfully, Leo stood and made his way out.

The next day, at noon, he bought another ticket for the movie. There was something about the plot he did not understand, some small detail that had escaped him. And he yearned to see the slapping scene again . . . he couldn't quite remember how the dialogue had gone. . . . The ticket seller was the same man who had sold him a ticket the evening before, and Leo had the idea that he recognized him: he stared rather strangely at Leo. What did it mean . . . ?

Leo fingered the ticket for a while, worrying. He wondered if he should take the risk and see the movie again. If the ticket seller had been alerted by the police and had seen "Wanted" pictures of Leo, then . . . then . . . if the police came to arrest him, they would prevent his suicide . . . and he dreaded another long miserable bout in court. . . . But finally he decided he would go in, at least for part of the film; if the police came by, they would note that the movie began at 12:05 and ended at 2:06, counting cartoons and coming attractions, and then the other film began, and ended at 3:45 . . . then there was a newsreel . . . and by that time he would be gone.

A few days later the ticket seller was explaining to a police detective: "Yes, this is the man's picture all right. I noticed him the first night because he looked so strange; then the next morning he showed up and I remembered him right away. But I didn't know he was wanted then . . . Anyway, I sort of kept him in mind, I was going to notice him again when he left the movie . . . I had a hunch there was something wrong, he looked so strange . . . but I never noticed him leave. I made a point to watch everyone who left, all day long, right up until midnight, but the man never came out."

The detective said: "He must have left by another exit, then."

"No, the other exit's locked."

"He must have left the theater," the detective said.

"Sure, I know that. Sure. But I never noticed that he did."

ARDIS CARTER
(MRS. LEO ROSS)
ARDIS CARTER/KĀRMĀN/CARTER
MARYA SHARP
(MRS. NIGEL STOCK)

At the end of May, when Elena was out of the hospital and she and her husband already had been living in Maine for several weeks, they received a package forwarded to them from their Grosse Pointe address. It was a record, made of a very light, transparent, red plastic. Elena played it and heard her mother's voice:

To all my friends in Detroit and Michigan:

My deepest and sincerest regret is that I have been unable to say good-by personally to my dear friends, and that my wedding was such a private and almost selfish affair, when I promised everyone that it would be a public event. I know I am guilty of a terrible falsehood, but Nigel and I have always wanted a small, private wedding, and we both thought it best to keep everything a secret even from our closest friends. . . .

By the time you hear this, my husband and I will be settled in his townhouse on Belgrave Square, London. I have only seen photographs of it, and of the Square, but everything looks lovely, and those of you who know me will understand what this kind of life will mean to me. . . . I know that I will love London, and England, though of course I will miss the excitement of Detroit. But I have already begun studying the history of my new, adopted country, and feel that I will make a permanent home there and not just be a "transplanted" American or expatriate.

. . . For those of you who somewhat jumped the gun and sent me presents, I thank you very, very sincerely, and I cannot resist uttering special thanks to Mr. Robie Sadoff for his generous gift. It is so frustrating to be unable to personally express my love and gratitude to all my Detroit friends . . . so

I will end with a simple good-by . . . and very best wishes for the future . . . from Marya and Nigel Stock.

Elena played this record many times. As she listened to her mother's throaty, well-modulated, entirely familiar voice, she felt her eyes sting with a mysterious acrid throbbing; not exactly tears: she didn't cry. One day, when Marvin overheard her playing it, he came into the room and turned off the machine and said gently:

Elena played it a few more times, when he was out of the house. Then, one day, she realized she hadn't played it for a while—two or three weeks—so she dusted it carefully with a soft chamois cloth and slid it back into its plain wrapper and filed it with Marvin's records: between *Scheherazade* and Strauss's *Death and Transfiguration.*

MEREDITH DAWE

Number: 0187425 Michigan State Prison

August 17, 1972

Your Honor:

It has taken me many weeks to draft this document, owing to physical infirmities and a general depression of the spirit. But I have come to realize that only a direct and forthright appeal, based upon sound legal principles, will make any impression upon you and the world you represent. Am I correct? I am also sending carbon copies of this letter and its accompanying memoranda to a trusted friend on the outside, for safekeeping. I realize now that such caution is necessary in order to prevent men like yourself from misusing their authority.

Judge Couteau, I am speaking for the record not only of the State of Michigan but of the Supreme Court of the United States, which I am confident will eventually hear my appeal, and find in my favor, and also of the entire world. I am speaking for the record of your conscience, as a private, humane individual, and I hope you will give me your fullest attention.

I will outline to you the series of actions I am going to take:

My first petition is a plea for the bench to re-examine every detail of the transcript of my trial. This must be done immediately, and by an objective, just man who is not connected in any way with the Court of the State of Michigan. I request that Your Honor assign a nonpartisan observer for this purpose. This observer will surely come to the conclusion that the Assistant Prosecuting Attorney made many statements and accusations about me that were allowed to pass and to be heard by the jury, without the right for him to do so, in that his hatred of me surpassed all legal evidence and was a constant source of bewilderment and chagrin to me. Not only this: again and again the transcript notes objections made by my counsel, Mr. John Morrissey, of Detroit, Michigan, that Your Honor chose to ignore. An impartial observer must come to the conclusion that I did not receive a fair trial before you and that the entire conviction must therefore be reversed.

My second act is to give notice to you that I am filing suit against you personally, in your position as a judge, and against the Police Commissioner of the City of Detroit, for a nonpartisan referee to enforce the above-mentioned petition.

My third act is to give notice to you by this communication that I am filing suit against you in the Federal Court in Detroit for a sum no less than $1 million, in that my constitutional rights and my civil rights have been grossly violated by your action in handing down to me, Meredith Dawe, a sentence of 8 to 10 years in the penal system of the State of Michigan. This sentence, delivered by Your Honor, Judge Carl Couteau, sitting in Recorder's Court in the City of Detroit, on Monday 5 June, 1972, does restrict my freedom of speech, my freedom to move to and from any fixed point, and curtails in general the civil rights guaranteed to all citizens of the United States under our Constitution. In addition, I want to inform you that this sentence constitutes cruel and unusual punishment, since I am at present a prisoner not only in prison but in a hospital ward, and my spirit is seriously depressed by the misery all around me and by my own occasional infirmity. I note in myself flashes of fear concerning my immediate future (I am undergoing another spinal operation shortly) and the future of my adulthood, as well as the future of this sorrowful, doomed nation.

In addition, I am preparing a lengthy writ of habeas corpus to the effect that I was not truly represented by counsel during my trial and during the many weeks preceding my trial. Though this will be difficult to prove, I am undertaking the task confidently, and am only puzzled at present how to begin. I believe I will frame the writ in the shape of an autobiographical work. Your Honor will appreciate the fact (though this is not a threat against Your Honor) that such a writ, made public, will sway to my side vast segments of the American people, who will clamor for justice. At present, I am awaiting important documents concerning my family history, which are essential for any reader to comprehend the nucleus of my writ of habeas corpus, which, as I understand, must be no more than two or three pages long, must be framed by an exhaustive introduction and as many appendices and indexes as are necessary. The "Autobiography of Meredith Dawe" may perhaps be cast in the form of a novel, since no other form of communication (that is not tactile) can approach the terrifying density, the overwhelming weight, of a novel. My autobiography, properly studied, will illuminate not only a single act of savage misjustice (committed by a jury of 12 representative but tragically prejudiced citizens and compounded by Your Honor in his punitive zeal in excess of all charges) but an entire nation, a despoiled and vandalized Garden of North America, which begs us to purify it and restore it to its original innocence. How long must we await the resanctification of our gardens?

In support of this writ, and closely allied with my suit against Your Honor (for violating my rights as a citizen), I want to state for the record that Your Honor's refusal to allow me to dismiss my attorney and to act in my own defense, on the fourth day of my trial, was perhaps the most grievous single curtailment of my freedom. Considering this fact and also the fact that my attorney, Mr. John Morrissey of Detroit, Michigan, was in no way sympathetic with my basic beliefs and my personality, and approached the entire case simply as a professional challenge, any fair-minded person will see that I did not have an attorney at all. I really did not have an attorney to defend me. My own role in this confusion was a slowness to perceive what other people evidently recognized at once and tried to communicate to me, that the attorney who was defending me was not defending "me" but an abstract principle. However competent Mr. Morrissey may be as an officer of the court, he did not comprehend my state of mind at the time of the alleged crime, the time of my arrest, at any time during the weeks leading up to and including my trial, and he did not then, in fact, represent *Meredith Dawe*. Thus, the basis for my writ, which will admittedly involve many weeks of preparation. (I will state here, purely for Your Honor's information, that I am also filing suit against my ex-attorney, for a sum of $500,000, for the above-mentioned reasons, and that I will include a carbon copy of this document for your perusal.)

I give notice to Your Honor, to the Court of Appeals, and to all relevant courts, that I, Meredith Dawe, insist most bitterly that in all further litigation I will act as my own counsel. I absolutely deny the right of the court to appoint any counsel in Mr. Morrissey's place. I deny the right of anyone to speak for me and to interpret any actions or words of mine. As may be evident from this document, I have begun a study of the Law myself, using the books available in the library here. I am not going to be silenced.

In addition, Your Honor, I want to state for the record that I am bringing a civil suit against the police witness and informer Joseph Langley, in that he betrayed not only my spiritual bond with him (which I realize now cannot be proven in court) but any possibility of my exercising my constitutional and civil rights during the terms of my sentence. Your Honor was very wrong to listen so closely to him! He lied on the witness stand, as did the other Prosecution witnesses, concerning the direction in which the marijuana cigarette was traveling (it traveled *from* Shirley Klein and *to* Mr. Langley, because he requested it, and not *from* Mr. Langley and *to* Miss Klein) and also about whether the cigarette was burning or not. I maintain that it had *gone out* at the time I touched it and handed it to Mr. Langley. This renders it less dangerous and would impress any impartial observer as an important piece of evidence. . . . I am going to attach to this document several pages of analysis of the harmless effects of marijuana as a drug, reported by a federal committee, in the hope that Your Honor, not moved by such evidence at the trial, will re-examine it now quietly, away from the anger and confusion of the courtroom. This information, supplemented by many more research findings, will make up one of the indexes of my writ of habeas corpus. But I can't hope to have that document ready for many months.

In addition, I hereby give notice that I am bringing civil suits against the People of the State of Michigan and in particular Assistant District Attorney Eliot Tyburn, for violating my privacy and my right to speak freely without fear of harassment, and for the public showing of certain films of my lectures, during the trial, to upset the jurors and make them hate me. All these will be listed in a separate memorandum. At the time of my trial I publicly stated (in defiance of my attorney, I admit) that I acknowledged all these words, thoughts, and intentions, and that I would gladly stand by them, but subsequent to the jury's verdict and Your Honor's harsh sentencing I wish to advise you that I deny not the words, thoughts, and intentions of those lectures in their original form, but I do deny 1) the right of the Prosecution to show them in public and for their own advancement (I will investigate copyright law and see if a separate suit cannot be filed on this count, for I surely did not assign copyright in any formal way to the Prosecution for their use of these original lectures) and 2) the right of the Prosecution to edit them. I am at the present time preparing a petition in which I make clear how my First Amendment rights were violated by this illegal action of the Prosecution. I am also preparing a separate petition in which I argue that the public showing of these films in which I expound my personal philosophy (viciously edited and rearranged so as to seem insane) constitutes a violation of my right under the Constitution not to speak in incrimination of myself, which I believe goes back all the way to the 18th century, in English common law, and prevents the police from torturing us according to their wishes. There are many forms of torture, Your Honor.

Also, I might mention here, pursuant to the above, that I am contemplating an additional suit against my ex-attorney, Mr. Morrissey, in that he attempted to litigate the entire case for the Defense on the issue of police entrapment, and that, failing to convince the jurors of Mr. Langley's obvious treachery and his violation of a law (why has no one arrested him? why may he touch a marijuana cigarette, lit or burned-out, with such impunity?), failing to overcome the natural prejudice of the jurors *for* the police and *against* a defendant as innocent as myself (though everyone in the courtroom and in the entire world knew that entrapment obviously occurred), he nevertheless attempted (in private) to dissuade me from seizing upon my legal rights in testifying in my own defense, in order to explain to the court the intricacies of my philosophy, so as to powerfully counteract the Prosecution's claims and innuendos that I was, in fact and potentially, a public enemy (advocating the overthrow of all laws, etc.) whether or not I did, in fact, ever touch a marijuana cigarette (at which point I could not restrain myself from laughter!—which so angered

Your Honor, who surely misunderstood) lit or unlit, traveling in any direction (right to left, or left to right) past me; and having failed in this attempt to make a purely legal point supersede my own testimony, to deny my existence, as it were, Mr. Morrissey did then, when I was on the witness stand and at last able to speak directly to the world, by his very narrow questions and his strategy of interrupting me so frequently, attempt to curtail my freedom of speech, in order (as he said) that I should not offend the sensibilities of the jurors and the court, and thereby cause prejudice against my case (which he saw as *his* case). Though he was correct about this, this does not lessen his moral guilt, and I am suing him as well under a separate claim for malpractice, since his questions and interruptions and attempts to restrain me might have indicated that he lacked proper faith in his own client, which you, as an experienced judge, might have noticed. Allied with this was Mr. Morrissey's technique of repeatedly interrupting the cross-examination, and even the interruption of certain of my replies, so as to give the impression that there were things in my personal life that the Prosecution had no right to inquire about. This made everyone think I had something to hide. This obviously inspired prejudice and disgust not only in the jury, but in Your Honor. There was no moral reason why my attorney should have objected to my being questioned in open court and in any manner desired by the Prosecution, since an innocent man may surely speak his heart.

An innocent man may surely speak his heart.

Your Honor, why do you hate me?

Why wish me so much evil? I lie here trying to get my mind clear from the drugs and the stiffness and the awful memory of my trial and I think of you, your hatred of me, kept so hidden. But why? Why? When I first walked into your courtroom I believed what the plaque said on the wall—JUSTICE IS THE GUARANTEE OF LIBERTY—and I was prepared to love you and work for your conversion (as I am dedicated to the conversion of men like yourself), but not violently and not through hate. Never would I have consented to your imprisonment . . . for any crime at all, anything at all, but especially not for your private beliefs. And yet you must have hated me so much that your hatred overcame your natural instinct toward justice. Why is this? Until the very end, until your charge to the jury, my attorney and I and many others truly believed that even though the jury might be against me, Your Honor was impartial, unbiased, and sympathetic, and would rule on my innocence or guilt (for I suppose I was "guilty" of a legal lapse, if not a conscious crime—and my admission of this point should not have been used so repeatedly against me by both the Prosecution and Your Honor) of the crime I was charged with in the indictment, and not on any personal philosophy of mine or on my soul, though I am still confused about why anything I say or do or my entire personality should be assumed to be "in violation of all community standards of decency."

Why?

In conclusion, I submit also to Your Honor that the publicity surrounding the case all along (to which I inadvertently contributed, believing always the good will of the various reporters and interviewers who approached me) made a fair trial impossible. If a suit can be initiated for an after-the-fact crime, I would like to sue a local newspaper for its editorial entitled "A Victory for Decency" and I would like to bring an injunction against the press and the communications media to prevent any further such libels, in that an appeal, if and when I am granted an appeal, will be influenced also negatively. All this, I submit, represents a conspiracy to thwart my receiving justice, on the part of people I have never met, and it is all in tragic excess of any charges originally brought against me in the indictment, which I hereby restate for Your Honor's information:

> The Grand Jury of the County of Wayne, Michigan, by this Indictment accuses Meredith Dawe of the crime of violation of Public Health Law with respect to Narcotic Drugs, a Felony, committed as follows:
>
> The Defendant, on or about the 5th day of December, 1970, in the City of Detroit, County of Wayne and State of Michigan, unlawfully and in violation of Public Health Law, had in his possession and under his control one quarter of an ounce of a preparation, compound, mixture, and substance containing cannabis.

Must I be destroyed because of ¼ ounce of marijuana . . . ?

Very sincerely yours,
Meredith Dawe

August 18, 1972

Your Honor:

In the event that you might misread and misinterpret my letter of August 17 (yesterday), written under much distress here in the prison hospital (my writ will go into the humiliating detail of what all the prisoners are suffering here, in addition to their illnesses), I am writing another communication that Your Honor is respectfully requested to file for the record.

My previous letter ended with the question, *Must I be destroyed because of ¼ ounce of marijuana . . . ?* I request that this question be stricken from the record. I request most urgently that Your Honor not interpret that question to mean that I am accusing him of wanting to destroy (i.e., commit a crime) me or anyone. I have suffered many hours of anxiety since writing my letter of August 17, in which my emotions sometimes overcame my legal arguments, and I hope Your Honor will not see fit to instigate any suit against me for slander or (in the event my letter is somehow published) libel.

Please understand that it was not my intention to accuse Your Honor of acting with the premeditated intention of committing any illegal act or with any premeditation at all . . . in the sense of being pre-judiced (prejudicial) . . . or . . . meditational in any illegal sense of the word.

Sincerely,
Meredith Dawe

August 21, 1972

Your Honor:

Since having written to you last week (August 17 and August 18, to be exact) I have waited for your response patiently. But, receiving no letter from you, and in the event that such a letter was in fact sent to me and was not received (for the record I will state that *no letter was received* even if Your Honor's letter was sent by way of ordinary mail and not as a registered letter (which I would suggest for the protection of all concerned), I see fit to inform Your Honor that I am now preparing a brief that will petition for the appointment of an impartial observer (this petition will, of course, supersede the petition outlined in paragraph 4 of my letter of August 17, (paragraph beginning "My first petition . . .")) who is a non-native-born person of demonstrated intelligence, literacy, and human sympathy, but who is not conversant in any way with the English language. This observer will then function as referee, and his duty would be to carefully examine the lectures and public addresses and various interviews of mine, all the tapes, films, and transcripts used by the prosecution to argue its case against me (as an advocate of "anarchy through drugs"), this to be effected in two stages: 1) their original shape 2) the edited, distorted, abbreviated shape used by the Prosecution in order to poison the jurors' minds and bring about a verdict of Guilty. The foreign-born referee will then make a detailed report to Your Honor concerning the degree of editing, on a statistical basis entirely (since the referee would not know English, two very significant results would be achieved: 1) he could not be prejudiced against me 2) the court would be forced to assume the truly objective nature of his report.)

I will be awaiting your response and I suggest that for the protection of all concerned, this above-mentioned referee be appointed within one week of this notice sent to the Honorable Carl Couteau, Judge, District Court of Detroit, 21 August, 1972.

Sincerely,
Meredith Dawe

August 29, 1972

Your Honor:

I have uncovered new evidence that requires automatic reversal of the verdict against me, since it refutes the basic wording of the indictment originally handed down. I am basing my accusation on a statute of 1927 that states that such indictments must be filed within a certain amount of time of the offense allegedly committed. I believe that it is not demonstrable by any known scientific method that certain deeds have or have not occurred, since all witnesses and all alleged violators of civil and criminal laws have evolved since the historical time at which the "crime" allegedly took place, and in no way can their testimony be accepted as scientific evidence. If Your Honor doubts the validity of these statements, I will remind him that my original training was in the sciences, and that it is a matter of public record (or could very easily become a matter of public record, since my academic transcripts are on file at the following accredited universities: Harvard University (1962-1963); the University of Michigan (1963-1967); the University of Chicago (1967-1968); Stanford University (fall, 1968-approximately February, 1969) and that my training includes a wide variety of subjects in both the scientific and the humanistic fields, especially physics).

I submit to Your Honor that my findings entirely refute the Prosecution's arguments (further weakened by the Prosecution's failure to present a single scientist as a witness against me), my own attorney's procedure of defense, the jurors' probable deliberations and consequently their verdict, Your Honor's sentencing, and, in point of fact (canceling each of the above), the original indictment, which I am enclosing with this letter so that Your Honor can familiarize himself with it if he has forgotten certain key phrases.

Sincerely,
Meredith Dawe

(indictment enclosed)

September 8, 1972

Your Honor:

Your Honor will be pleased to be informed of my completion of the series of spinal operations performed by the following neurosurgeons: Dr. Monroe Baskin, Dr. Felix Quigley, and Dr. Raymond Doyle. If there is any conspiracy to render me impotent it will be medically evident upon examination by any physicians exclusive of the above, but note that I am not accusing said surgeons or the State of Michigan or (least of all) Your Honor of any conspiracy whatsoever.

The purpose of this communication (sent in a moral vacuum since I despair of its being answered) is also to inform Your Honor that, contrary perhaps to the tone of my earlier letters, I am considering the possibility of Your Honor's being innocent of any prejudicial hatred of me, which may inspire Your Honor to reply to some, if not all, of my letters. I am certain that a letter from a Detroit judge would be delivered to me here, quite immune from censorship (if Your Honor would indicate somehow that it is *not* to be opened by the prison authorities: he might simply write, in his own handwriting, such a request, signed with his initials, the envelope to be an official one with the return address clearly stating Your Honor's position and address) but, if such an act is actually committed, either party (correspondent or receiver) might then instigate suit against this invasion of privacy as well as a file for an injunction against its occurring again in the future so that, if this very document that I am now preparing, this very letter I am composing to you, is intercepted, and these very words are, in fact, studied by the prison censor, they might in themselves constitute prior warning (though I am somewhat shaky on the law concerning this point since the books available to me here stop at 1968).

The reason for my consideration of this alteration of blame (which did in fact never take the form of any accusation) is that, in the last several days, I have been hearing again the words of Assistant District Attorney Eliot Tyburn, sometimes as he sums up the case against me to the jury (in which he made cruel and unusual use of my own phrase, "lapse of legality," in order to poison the jurors' minds against me), but more often as he argued to Your Honor, at the sentencing of 5 June, 1972. That I am not interfering with Mr. Tyburn's privacy or autonomy in any way may be underscored by the fact that *I would rather hear* the plea made by my attorney, Mr. Morrissey, on that very same day (but, unfortunately, I can remember only snatches of Mr. Morrissey's argument . . . which was as close to being a human, passionate, loving speech as Mr. Morrissey could perhaps make, being himself a most limited and unloving man, though perhaps not incapable of *being loved* and, as a consequence, himself *loving,* were he able to re-create his soul to that extent; I remember only the phrases ". . . pure, self-determined . . . make kind of mistakes others . . . cowardly . . . we are frightened and demand revenge . . . he . . . they . . . he is not . . . he is . . . I plead for a . . . young man of . . . not a criminal . . . I plead for a suspended sentence . . .") but as if it were somehow part of the invisible tortures planned for me by the State, Mr. Morrissey's argument to you is continually outshouted and overcome by Mr. Tyburn's argument though, in fact, as I recall, neither man raised his voice. Therefore, helpless as I have been during the past several days (unless time has lapsed longer than I know, and the date is actually not 8 Sept., 1972, but some other date, unimaginable to me) I have continually heard Mr. Tyburn's voice, but not willfully or intentionally, and, inadvertently hearing this voice (of a private individual *but* in his role as public prosecutor), I have come to the conclusion that this powerful, deathly, terrifying voice may have had the effect, on the morning of 5 June, 1972, of influencing

Your Honor unduly, in his sentencing of me; and that this reconsideration would seriously recast the entire event, absolving Your Honor entirely of blame. I know the words so well now that I may include them here without the slightest fear of misquotation (though this is *not* an official document, but simply a personal letter to you, between two parties who share a mutual concern over the tragedies of injustice sometimes committed by well-meaning people). Study this speech carefully, Your Honor, and see whether it does not attempt to influence the listener (you), and to sway him against any human act of mercy:

> I ask on behalf of the People of this County that the defendant Meredith Dawe's sentence be one of the maximum imprisonment under the law of the State of Michigan . . . and in support of that request I would like to state, if it please the court, that the defendant has not, prior to the trial, during the period of the trial, and since the trial, suggested in public or in private that he has felt any remorse for his criminal act, that he does not totally countenance in others the wholesale repetitions of that act (and others contrary to the legal and moral code), and that, by his unique influence as a local public figure (whose talent for publicity may indeed transform him into a national public figure if he remains free) . . . he has in effect encouraged among young people the use of narcotics. He has shown no remorse at all. He has shown no remorse at all . . . no remorse at all . . . no remorse. . . .

Now, Your Honor, leaving aside for the moment the mind-shattering riddle of how I can show remorse if *I am innocent*, let us consider this: You, Judge Carl Couteau, had perhaps formed a certain sympathy with me during the course of the trial, such sympathy being, of course, not demonstrated by any facial signs or, certainly, uttered words directed toward either my attorney or me, and, perhaps inclined to believe me innocent, accepted the jurors' verdict as a commonplace miscarriage of justice perpetrated by frightened and angry citizens to whom the notion of "love" must be obscene (especially as underscored and exaggerated by prosecution witnesses who lied, under oath, about observing me in various postures and behaviors offensive to community standards—though it is debatable, in my mind, as to whether a "community" exists at all, being the legal definition of a political entity, or rather *not* being, so far as I know, any legal definition of anything, but simply a poetic expression of an indefinable mood), but intended, quite autonomously, to rectify this verdict by a wise, humane, and very generous atonement (i.e., a suspended sentence); such intention then being savagely mutilated by Mr. Tyburn's words, and totally obliterated, due to the confusion of the moment and the fact (which Mr. Morrissey informed me of, and I have no reason to suspect that he would lie on this issue) that the most important words to be said to the judge at the time of sentencing are *those of the Prosecution*, it seems to me likely that Judge Couteau, either overwhelmed by the Prosecution's demands or for reasons of his/your own not listening closely to Mr. Morrissey's plea, was influenced.

Therefore, I ask you, Your Honor, to re-examine your mind before the day of sentencing, to re-experience the vicious argument against me, and to inform me as soon as possible whether, in fact, this argument did sway you. I hope I will hear from you at your earliest convenience, since it is possible (indeed, probable) that the words of Mr. Tyburn are such a din in my head *because* they are meant to inform me of your actual innocence. This would mean so much to me. . . .

They have said that the operations are concluded, and yet certain humiliating and very painful examinations continue (involving surgical needles at least 12″ in length that I would not look at, to lessen my terror, but that I feel I must see in order to note any possible prior staining, rusting, or evidence of filth) at all hours of the day and night, often when I am deep in meditation, so far from the externalities of my body that my body is defenseless. It is becoming clear that the original operations were not successful, and that more operations are being planned, though the Director denies this, no doubt in order to protect the surgeons responsible for these errors from charges of malpractice, such charges not contemplated *at present* because the information I would require concerning medical malpractice suits is mysteriously missing from the book it should be in (one-third of the book's pages have been torn out) and, yesterday, the book itself was not where I hid it, but vanished. If it turns out, as I think it might, that Your Honor did feel this prior sympathy to me, you might also be moved enough by my sufferings here to make a quick telephone call (it would probably have to be in person—I doubt that your secretary's voice would be sufficient) to forbid any further mutilation of my body, especially when I am not sufficiently conscious to defend it.

Thank you very much.

Sincerely,
Meredith Dawe

Morning–Unnumbered Day

Your Honor:

Is it possible that a well-intentioned action of your own has resulted in an evil? I refer to the request made to you in a direct communication sent some days ago (my records state 8 Sept., 1972, but it is possible that one of the prison officials has altered the notation, imitating my handwriting)—that you simply telephone the Director of the hospital here and state your preference that I, Meredith Dawe, not be subjected to any further medical actions (whether "for reasons of health" or for reasons of torture (unstated)). Assuming that, at last, you were moved and disturbed by my helplessness (I am confined in a kind of circular bed, a device that must be rotated every two hours in order to allow for (according to the torturers) maximum circulation and utilization of nerves and the expenditure of muscles that would otherwise atrophy and, most significantly, for distribution of weight-pressure on the damaged vertebrae; as Your Honor might well imagine, my condition has deteriorated seriously), and perhaps influenced by petitions from citizens of Michigan, or, if such petitions do not exist, the possibility of such petitions when the *Autobiography of Meredith Dawe* is made public, and the well-intentioned voters and taxpayers of the State realize what a miscarriage of justice has been perpetrated in their name (I cringed every time Mr. Tyburn uttered the words "The People of the State of Michigan" as if the People, and not Mr. Tyburn himself (and the police) wanted my destruction), such miscarriage made more pathetic by the senseless and unprovoked beating I suffered prior to the trial and subsequent to the issuing of the indictment, by a man whose name I will not mention here, in the company of other like-minded individuals who, acting murderously in order to defend, as they stated, the United States against a "traitor" (choosing to isolate my pronouncements on the war in Vietnam, as if I did not clearly state, in all my lectures, that the present war is but one symptom of the total rottenness, decay, despoilment, vandalization, and doom of the Empire represented by the United States of America and that, of course, all young men are morally bound to oppose it and to refuse induction) . . . assuming this, that your crisis of conscience did result in a telephone call, it may well have been resented by the medical staff here, especially the Director (a long-faced, bony, slow-speaking man, obviously an enemy of the Body, though he imagines himself a skillful physician), in that, and I speak cautiously here, and wish that I retained more of my Latin so that I could switch into a language that Your Honor might read that would be protected from the eyes of prison officials, spies, and other tax-supported creatures of the State, one professional man might be angered that another professional man would see fit to interfere with his actions. In other words, may a man of the Law, however legally sound his actions are, have the slightest influence whatsoever over a man of Medicine? It occurred to me, Your Honor, almost as soon as I mailed that perhaps fateful letter, that I had made a blunder and that the very effectiveness of my arguments to you (urging you to intercede here in my behalf) would work against me. . . . The scalpel of the surgeon is perhaps more deadly than the sword of Justice.

Your Honor, the next morning they started on me again.

Your Honor, there is a paradox operating here: if you feel pain, you are dehumanized. If they do not allow you to feel pain (by way of drugs—medically sanctioned nonpleasure drugs), you are dehumanized because you are not in control of yourself. Doped-up, drowsy, slow-moving and slow-thinking, a spiritual and physical cripple . . . all this results from that beating, in which my entirely nonpolitical lecture ("Light and Heavy Love,") was interrupted by men somehow sworn to destroy me, but against whom I had no ill-wishes (refusing, as Your Honor must know, to press charges against them). If you telephoned the hospital and spoke to the Director, perhaps you antagonized him (secretly—he would not have hinted anything to you) and the result was, contrary to Your Honor's wishes, further neurological torture of me. I do not know.

Might I request that you undo the damage by another telephone call? Based upon the perhaps erroneous (but probably valid) assumption that you *did* call to forbid them their tortures, might you now call to say you have experienced a change of heart, and that further spinal examinations and even operations are permissible? This may have the anxiously awaited effect of their reversing their procedure, and allowing me to return to my cell, my reading, and my preparation of the lengthy writ (now my main reason for existing). . . . Your Honor, my very soul is in your trust.

Sincerely,
Meredith Dawe

Morning—Unnumbered Day

Your Honor:

I realize that you are not my father, since my father does physically exist (though he has not communicated with me since 1968, at which time he ordered me out of his home under threat of police violence) but, in my dreams, it has become clear that you are designated as my spiritual father. I am not your son and yet I am willing to be your son, if you will have me. Why must there be only formal relationships, based entirely upon biology tempered by law (only "legitimate" heirs recognized)? What is the Law, that it renders us into totally separate beings?

When you asked me, staring down at me from your bench, if there was any reason why sentence should not be imposed at that time, I am sure you understood my staring back at you mutely and then my smiling at you, my need to communicate spiritually with you though my attorney had told me I should answer "No" and nothing more. I based my appeal on human sympathy and not on the sterile logic of the Law (needle-sterile logic of the Law), and also on the fact that human contact of souls is sacred *whether it is loving or destructive* and that I, loving, might well absorb your un-loving.

I dream of you often, and I wish myself into your dreams, so that you will understand our relationship. Nothing is accidental in the universe—this is one of my Laws of Physics—except the entire universe itself, which is Pure Accident, pure divinity. So it cannot be an accident that I think of you so constantly.

Sincerely,
Meredith Dawe

Winter morning XXX yr.

Your Honor:

I request a reversal of all prior communications sent to you, and in their place file this single brief:

My failure in my single experience with the Law derives solely from the fact that I attempted to absorb into myself the hatreds of a great body of spectators (not simply those crowded into the courtroom, but the entire world) and that this did, in fact, distract me from Your Honor and his importance in that courtroom. This might in itself constitute an illegal action or a sin.

I request forgiveness for the above-mentioned error.

Being that there seemed to be, at that time, a physical essence to Your Honor, I was perhaps doubly distracted, by the evidence of 1) my senses 2) yours. The senses are something that must be overcome. In my former life I often utilized a saying from Confucius: *The way out is via the door. Why is it that no one will use this method?* To achieve the door one must obliterate his senses and, at the time of my trial, I had failed to do so. This may well constitute the sin Your Honor noted in me.

However, there being no verifiable physical essence to Your Honor (except through the senses), it is evident that my love for you is transcendent and sacred in itself, immune to any object. To have termed you my "father" is surely a gross blasphemy for which I beg forgiveness, noting, however, that I was at a crude stage in my development at that time. You will have patience with me.

Am I sullying you just by this communication? Is your name perhaps too holy to be uttered?

In my past life I sometimes gave a lecture in which I utilized the expression, "*Nécessité fait loi,*" which in my profanity I interpreted as "Necessity knows no law." I tried to influence my audiences accordingly, not knowing of my own ignorance. Now I have come to see that "*Nécessité fait loi*" does in literal fact mean that Necessity Makes Law and that, conversely, Law Makes Necessity.

Law Makes Necessity.

And so in your Law, or in you, as the highest emblem of the Law, I have the possibility of being fulfilled. A necessity unit in the accidental universe is, in itself, *necessary* (i.e., loved). Therefore I am partly and, I hope, will be someday totally fulfilled in your judgment and annihilated in my own profane being. I will say good-by to you.

In one of the sacred books of the Buddha there is a parable of the necessity of this fulfilment (i.e., annihilation), but to my shame I did not understand it at the time, though I imagined I did. Now it is constantly with me, in your words and with your (visible) face:

The Zen Master holds a stick over the pupil's head and says to him fiercely, "If you say this stick is real, I will strike you with it. If you say this stick is not real, I will strike you with it. If you say nothing, I will strike you with it."

—Meredith Dawe

MARVIN HOWE

1 A face leaped out of the prismatic lights, the sleek fake-silver obelisks and pyramids and urns and sexless hooded profiles. Smoke seemed to give way to that face, opening a pathway for his vision.

He stared.

In the slightly soiled pocket of his Chinese-red silk shirt was a list of expenses one of his clients had handed him angrily, expenses that ran to over $50,000. These had been presented to the client the day before by a certain private investigator in St. Louis who had, himself, been presented with the expenses by another St. Louis party, or parties, names unknown to either Marvin's client or to Marvin, who had arranged for the accidental death of a certain St. Louis businessman by a fall of some twelve floors. The client was contesting the investigator's good faith because the expenses were far higher than the estimate—one item was particularly outrageous, $145 for breakfasts alone at the Hotel van Dusen—and some of the handwritten entries were illegible. Marvin was to confer with all of the parties in the morning, separately, and tonight he felt a little sick.

He interrupted the man beside him, who was telling a joke: "Is that Sadoff over in the corner? I'd like to meet him."

"What? Sadoff?" the man said in amazement. "Why do you want to meet that bastard?" He had a gritty, good-natured voice. He was not really a friend of Marvin's—Marvin had no friends—but the two men had known each other for so long that they considered themselves friends. "That third-class pimp?—I can oblige you, sure, he's a client of mine, but is there any special reason?" The man craned his head around and looked across the room; then he laughed and said, "Why yes, I see, yes, I see a special reason. In fact, I see two."

So he led Marvin across the noisy room and, as they drew near the table in the corner, Marvin saw how the girl's gaze seemed to rest upon him, or upon that diminishing space between him and her, in a kind of sacred, silent nothingness across which Marvin moved, like a man in a dream, a man entering a dream.

Marvin was introduced to everyone.

Very honored. Honored.

2 The Venetian blinds were shut and the stylish green-denim drapes drawn to keep out the afternoon sunshine; so high in the air, on the twentieth floor of this building, Marvin's windows seemed to look out into the sun itself, directly into the sun, on days when Detroit was not overcast.

He sat with a glass of bourbon and a bottle of bourbon before him on the desk blotter. Off to one side, on a small aluminum typing table (he sometimes did his own typing when he wanted his letters to be confidential) was another bottle, not yet opened, and the gun he kept in his office—a Luger automatic, with an 8-shot magazine, a gun he thought quite handsome and kept well-oiled, though he had never used it. At home he had several other hand-guns—another Luger automatic; an ordinary police revolver; a Walther .38 automatic, a fairly rare gun with an 8-round magazine . . . he had permits for each of these guns, but he did not have a permit to carry them on his person, so it was necessary to keep a gun in various parts of the house and in this office; he would never carry a concealed weapon.

He clicked on the machine:

I came to be sweet to you. . . . Because you're going to be a father . . . because you're moving away from me . . . I want to start saying good-by to you . . . I want to love you. . . .

And then the other voice, abrupt, surprised:

Oh, do you? Is that–is that the idea? And nothing else?

He listened for a while and then pushed the *Stop* button. He selected another tape out of the pile before him, placed it in the machine, sipped at the bourbon, and heard the man's voice again:

You love me . . . ? You do love me . . . ? You aren't pretending to love me?

He heard the woman reply, *No.*

Not pretending?

No.

He was listening, relistening. After weeks of weighing the evidence, he had given himself a full day and a night to come to a decision. He had told his secretaries to stay home; he had told his wife he was out of town, in New York. It was necessary to restrain himself, to go slowly, slowly . . . he must not make an impulsive decision. It was necessary to go very slowly.

He pushed the *Fast-Forward* button and released it and listened, again to that man's voice, which he was able to hear now without flinching:

. . . can't bear it. . . . I'm like a man who believes in God . . . I'm nobody, I'm Morrissey and I'll never be a judge. . . . All I have is a conviction . . . that the Law is permanent and will save us. . . . I mean that: it will save us. . . . *Extra ecclesia nulla salus.* . . . Do you understand . . . ?

Marvin listened for a while. He sorted through a handful of photographs, let them fall, listened again to the tape . . . removed it and put on another, which he experimented with until he found the words he wanted to hear . . . skimming over his wife's voice, which turned into a comic, squawking, staccato series of sounds, and over much of the man's words, stopping at:

. . . allowed to become gods. . . . on the understanding that they would eventually have their hearts cut out . . . agreed to be gods, and then . . . agreed to have their hearts cut out. . . . I wonder if the godliness is worth it? . . . What comes at the end, the public ceremony . . . ?

Some hours later, Marvin pawed through the tapes and played again:

. . . the Law is permanent and will save us. . . . *Extra ecclesia nulla salus.* . . . Do you understand?

Early the next morning, around five o'clock, after thirty-nine hours of this, Marvin came to his decision. He went to the window, opened the drapes and the blinds groggily, and told himself that this would be unalterable: he would never alter his decision. Once made, it would not be unmade. Shaky, not wanting to look at his hands for fear he might actually see they were trembling, he stared out at the invisible sky and told himself that it was obvious: he had to make no arguments personally, since his wife's lover had made every possible argument. Everything was there. Every plea, every self-incriminating remark, every acknowledgment of misery, shame, guilt. . . .

Though Marvin did not have the legal right to get rid of Morrissey, he had the moral right; Morrissey himself knew this. He knew he was guilty and must be punished. In a way, he yearned for punishment. Marvin could detect it in his voice. But they both knew that Marvin had no legal right to do anything, not to Morrissey's body, which had engineered so much crime . . . and they both knew that the legality of any human action was infinitely more important than its morality.

So Marvin stopped listening to the evidence. Though he did not terminate the investigation, he chose never again to torture himself with it.

It was the only possible decision.

3 The big house smelled of cold, of damp, of the ocean. Marvin sat in the room he was using as his study here, a boxlike, handsome, but rather chilly room on the inland side of the house; he had been working for a long time, for so many hours that he could not even guess whether it was very early morning or a dreary, fog-heavy day, another of the disappointing days they had had this summer in Maine.

He heard her walking somewhere—upstairs, at the rear of the house—and his head jerked up, he tried to fix her in his imagination: a woman approaching one of the windows by the ocean, a woman staring out at the ocean, at that infinite unknowable space.

He had brought her here to recover. He had presented her with this house—one of his many houses, one he hadn't even visited before—and with the ocean. But in her there was that same infinite, unknowable space, not an emptiness but a mysterious substance that could not be controlled.

In a while, in a few hours or in another day, he would go to get her: would ask her to sit with him. By then the bottles of bourbon would have been removed from the room, the large yellow notepads with his scribbling hidden in the desk drawers, all the physical evidence of the terrible labor he had undertaken gone, hidden, destroyed. He would have memorized his argument and he would begin it gently, very gently, so that she would have no reason to be afraid.

I want to talk to you, Elena, he would say, *but I don't want to frighten you.*

I don't ever want to frighten you.

JACK MORRISSEY

1 June 5.

At the sentencing, Jack heard his voice with astonishing clarity, through a small angry blizzard of particles, scraps and bits of his own brain that seemed to be fighting him, yet his voice continued its calm progression and became only a little emotional, just at the right time, as if he had lived through this many times before. . . . *Jack Morrissey surfacing, surviving, in control of himself though not of anything else.* His own client stood there, dazed and disheveled and half-smiling, like an animal still stunned by the blow of a hammer, awaiting death, yet not really awaiting it because the thought is too immense. Dawe had tried to fire him, had spoken out in court several times politely and then wildly and then politely again, but Jack was still with him, yes, he stood now and spoke up toward the intelligent, youthfully middle-aged face of the judge, arguing for mercy. His opponent, a young man named Tyburn, an Assistant District Attorney who was going to rise steadily after this case, listened to Jack as if listening to an old friend, his eyes fixed on the table before him, his head almost nodding, imperceptibly nodding; yes, he knew all that, he knew it and rejected it, he knew he had won. But Jack kept talking. He had never argued more eloquently. If he was going down, if he was defeated, he owed it to his own vanity to seem to be the only man in the room who didn't know this.

His voice was precise and slightly on edge; he imagined vast numbers of people listening to him, among them Elena, and he felt a bitter, dizzy triumph in even the certainty of his defeat, as he had felt at the certainty of that other defeat. . . .

He was saying: ". . . young people like Meredith Dawe have enraged their elders, people of decorum and propertied lives, because they are free . . . to be pure, to be self-determined, to make the kind of mistakes others are too cowardly to risk. Because of their freedom they put to shame those of us who are not free . . . and so we fight back because we are frightened and demand revenge. But revenge for what? I think we are beyond wanting revenge, acting out of our own fears and jealousies. . . . And I believe that the court has realized during the session of this trial the essential faith of the defendant in our system of law, regardless of his occasional remarks—his firm, implicit faith that the law will deal with moral and humanistic problems, that it will call attention to our human predicament, so painful to all of us in the last decade. . . . Mr. Dawe is a young man of exceptional integrity and honesty, and his commitment to society should be obvious to the court. He is not a criminal and must not be treated as such. I plead for a suspended sentence. . . ."

Afterward, Dawe stumbled against Jack and clutched his arm and said vaguely, wildly, staring at Jack: "What did he say? What? I didn't hear all the words. . . ."

2 One day he was going through his pockets, emptying them of scraps of paper and stiff unspeakable Kleenex and coins and bits of debris, when he came across a much-crumpled note the size of a theater ticket: *Pay W. 2/15.* And it went through him

like a shot: a reminder of that room, that rented room, a reminder of *her.*

He threw everything away and washed his hands afterward.

3 *The Self-Starting Self-Stopping Word Machine.*

When he slept, the Machine slept, but only slyly. Really it continued, humming by itself, a perpetual motion machine of words and images, so that if he lay in one position he always woke up in another. The measure of his exhaustion and the sourness of his breath indicated how far he had traveled during the night and how little he had accomplished. *That is life, Morrissey,* he told himself. But he didn't believe it, he usually disbelieved the terse ironic little statements he made to himself; he was a poor liar.

But the Machine really clicked into operation as soon as he woke. Its night-time activity was turbulent enough, but its daytime activity was unstoppable. He knew he was locked for the rest of his life inside a machine of words, the Words becoming Flesh (i.e., Morrissey, a human substance). But Words were his business, his profit-making business, and he had to respect them . . . had to know how to market some, to stifle others, to turn others into harmless laughs or shrieks no one could hear at a distance of a few feet.

He sat at his desk thinking, doodling, trying to work, trying to read, trying to think and not to think, sometimes terrified of what the Word Machine would bring him that day, sometimes hopeful the Machine would bring him good news. For instance, one day in June, after the sentencing of Mered Dawe, and after the post-sentencing outrage, and after the post-outrage depression, the Machine had clicked out this message quite unexpectedly: *You did well.*

But later that afternoon, as Jack reached for and somehow overturned a cup of tepid coffee, the Machine inquired: *Did you believe that?—that you did well?*

No reply.

"I plead for a suspended sentence," Jack had said. Jack's Machine had said. And a better-bred Machine, looking down dispassionately upon him, had clicked out its own message: ". . . a period of no more than ten and no less than eight years. . . ."

It was a confrontation of Machines, a gathering of Machines. Aimed, set into motion, programmed, functioning more or less perfectly—except for Dawe, who was not plugged in, but who did not count—and if one Machine was defeated, another triumphed, so that the balance of the universe was always maintained. It was impossible, within the Law, not to achieve justice: if someone lost, someone else won. Sometimes the scales were evenly balanced and no one lost, no one won; that was disappointing but it happened sometimes, with Machines of the same approximate complexity.

Another day, out in the street, when Jack was hurrying through a sudden rainstorm and walked right into a girl who looked nothing like Elena, in fact a dark-haired girl much too tall for him, he had spun away suddenly stricken with lust for her, for Elena, and his soul shriveled and twisted itself and writhed in agony; and the Word Machine delivered this unexpected gift to him: *No, don't regret it, You did well.*

So he walked along, dazed, in the rain, his coat unbuttoned and his steamy skin exposed to the stares of passers-by, trying to adjust to the news that he had done well, he had done the right thing, *the right thing,* though the Machine refused to click out such words: *the right thing, the only thing, the only sane sensible thing, the necessary thing, the thing we all applaud.*

Was it true?

He half-doubted the Machine. He waited for a sly nasty joke, a clever question slipped in sideways while he was turning his mind to something else. But the Machine had mercy on him. The Machine viewed his lust for her, or for any woman, with pity, embarrassment, occasional alarm . . . obviously, Morrissey in a pathological state, not the true Morrissey. It consoled him, when he couldn't sleep at night, by rerunning old arguments against her, all the reasonable, obvious arguments he had invented back then, in his former life, to cure himself of her . . . such as, *Who can afford her?* Or: *What about other prowling men, other thieves?* Or, best of all: *Who is she?*

He slept, or did not sleep, beside a woman he knew very well, who was his natural and legal wife, exactly the woman for him. The Word Machine never made any declarations about Rachel; it seemed not to know she existed.

4 Very late one night, Rachel was saying to him: ". . . don't you love him at least? . . . feel any responsibility for him at least?"

"Of course," Jack said. He answered quickly, but guiltily. He was in the habit of answering his wife's questions quickly, even when he sometimes did not hear them. It held off another question.

"I don't see what that has to do with it . . . with whatever we're talking about," Jack said. But his advantage faded, because he was sitting with his head in his hands, the solid despair of his head cupped in his hands, and this was not a posture for victory.

"Doesn't it? Doesn't it?" Rachel asked.

Jack glanced up, squinting. He remembered where he was now: they had come out into the kitchen to sit at the table, both unable to sleep, miserable with the humid summer night. Rachel had lit a cigarette and tossed the package down, a dare, or perhaps a loving gesture, and Jack had acted quickly before his Machine could say: *Don't you—* And now he was smoking again, raw-throated again, relieved at having succumbed at last because he was not heroic and it was sensible of him to admit it. *Morrissey, you failure.* What upset him was the fact that smoking again, lighting that cigarette, seemed to mean nothing at all; it turned out to be just another gesture, another way of getting through a few minutes of the night. And did Rachel pity him, or did she love him, or did she despise him for being so weak?

She was saying: "I wish you would examine yourself, Jack, I wish you'd go deeply into yourself . . . without lying about anything. Ever since the Dawe business you've lost something, you've become a different person. . . . Why do you look so disbelieving? And now you want to quit the only kind of work you know how to do, the kind of work you're good at; you want to turn your back on people who need help. I don't understand you."

"I haven't quit. I'm not going to quit."

"You want to, though, don't you? You want to move somewhere where we won't know anyone, where we'd have to begin all over again . . . you want to uproot us . . . and I don't understand why. Mered Dawe is just one person, one case. Nothing like that ever happened to you before and it won't happen again. It shouldn't be so important to you, to make you want to quit and leave the country."

"It isn't," Jack said sharply.

"Then what is?"

He did not look at her: his Rachel, a woman of shrewd traps.

She went on slowly, as if trying to be patient with him, pulling another cigarette out of the package: "So you failed. So he's in jail. I liked him, of course, but his appeal was always too broad, he couldn't concentrate on one thing—like the War—he was politically naïve, ineffective. So what? He made it clear that he wanted to sever connections with us and with the defense committee—so—let him go, forget about him. Stop wallowing in your own failure. Everyone says—"

"I don't care what everyone says," Jack interrupted.

"You don't care about anything," Rachel said. That's what is poisoning you and you have no right to it, it's immoral. . . . Would you like me to leave? Would you? And take Robert? So you can work yourself through this, whatever it is, this poisonous selfishness of yours?" She tried to smile angrily. "The Resnacks would be happy to have me stay with them. And it would be good for Robert, to show him another kind of life—a communal life—and I know you'd like me to leave—"

"That isn't true."

"If you were alone maybe you could force yourself to think: about the direction your life is going in, about what you want to do, about why you wanted to adopt that boy if you can't be a real father to him."

Jack stared at her. "You must know you're exaggerating. I don't understand you."

He was challenging her to say: *I will make you understand me, then.* But she drew back, not daring this. For a while neither spoke. Jack's gaze moved reluctantly and irregularly around the kitchen with its old-fashioned sink and refrigerator, its too-yellow walls, a mock fearful gaiety out of place in this apartment. The former tenants had left plaster-of-Paris plaques up on the walls: one decorated with the stylized figure of a bird in flight, another with an orange-and-yellow splotch that might have been meant to represent the sun. Jack didn't know. These things depressed him, the constant evidence of other lives in rooms he now rented, always the pressure of other people crowding him, boxing him in. It crossed his mind that he would live out his life in rented rooms, too gaudily painted for his taste, or soiled, somehow run-down, blotched, never rooms that represented his own personality . . . just as he manufactured words, daily and hourly, that somehow did not represent him.

He was married to a woman, seated here with a woman, and he must look at her closely and listen to her closely, and respect her. Because she was very unhappy. And she could not explain it, could not quite explain why . . . though now she was coming very close to it, now she was actually saying: ". . . because you're never here. You're never here with us."

"Rachel, what the hell . . . ? I've been overloaded with work. You know that. This is just temporary. . . ."

"I mean you're *never here,*" she said viciously. "We promised . . . we vowed . . . to make our marriage strong, stable, to give him a real family, after the other families failed him. . . . But you don't cooperate with me! You're always away, your mind is away, you don't listen to me, you're never here with me, with us—"

You never love me, she was saying.

No reply.

No excuse.

Jack sucked smoke into his raw, dry throat. That did him good. It seemed to clear his brain a little so that he could hear his wife's unvoiced pleas: *I want to know, I dread to know . . . I want to leave you but I can't leave . . . do you want me? do you want me to leave?* They had been married a long time. Inside their long, comradely marriage was a short, brutal hallucination of a marriage, Jack's and Elena's, which seemed to have contaminated the permanent marriage.

No excuse.

"Even when you sit here with me like this, a few inches from me, pretending to listen . . . even at these times you're not with me," Rachel said.

"Oh Christ—"

Are you thinking of her? Right now? But Rachel did not ask this question. Jack pitied her suddenly. He took her hands in his, tried to soothe her. It was very late, very warm. Their apartment never seemed to get aired out, but was always overhung with smoke or cooking odors or the day's stale heat. Jack tried to talk to her, listening with a kind of detached amazement at the gentleness of his voice—it was almost a lover's voice. He was not saying: *Go to Seattle, then. Leave me.* He was not saying: *We are both lying, we're both criminals.* Instead he was saying: ". . . what good would it do to live out there with them? You and Robert? We don't really know what sort of activities they're into now, there's a very good chance the police are harassing them . . . and what would that do to Robert? How would that help him? Rachel, I think this is the problem: it's very hard for us to be parents. It's a strain we didn't anticipate, this constant closeness . . . especially for you, being his mother, acting as his mother and feeling that intimacy, that constant intimacy with him. He's a wonderful child and we both love him. But love isn't easy. I don't think it comes naturally to us, to either one of us. . . . I've got to help you more."

Rachel laughed nervously, surprised.

In the past, she would say with her bright, maddening enthusiasm: *Now we'll know what it is, at last, to be parents—to live for someone beside ourselves—* And Jack had agreed. He had believed it, in a way. He had wanted a child very much; he wanted that child. But at the same time he had known Rachel was exaggerating this, it was confused in her mind with something else: with the salvation of their marriage, with her personal salvation. She had said so often: *Now we can live for someone beside ourselves!* To live, to continue to live, to find a purpose for living—this seemed a challenge to her.

As if one of her closest friends, a woman named Estelle, hadn't killed herself in spite of having three young children. . . .

Don't think about that, Jack instructed himself.

Don't think.

Eventually they went into the child's room, carrying their separate confusions into the darkness of their son's world, as they had in the past: sentimental parents, adults a little too old to be the parents of a child this age, unskilled, inexperienced, clumsy people. But hopeful. Sincere. Coming in here to stand by his bed was a kind of vow they were each making . . . or perhaps it was a vow Jack was making, while Rachel watched him shrewdly, ironically, waiting for him to give himself away. Eventually she would win. But tonight they stared at the boy, who slept inside a bed with railings, a small, prim, pure, beautiful child. Jack stared at him. Rachel whispered, "Don't wake him. . . ."

Here, Jack had no thoughts at all. No need for thoughts. He felt only love and the simplicity of love. How could he not love this child? Robert was three years old, curious and shy and silent, with an air of always waiting, waiting. Like all of us, Jack thought, he was waiting to be loved.

"I love him. I love you," Jack told his wife. It was another vow of his. "You shouldn't exaggerate us; are we that important?"

5 One day, downtown, a black woman came up to Jack on the sidewalk and said, "Hello, Mr. Morrissey, how're you today?" She looked cheerful, almost attractive, her hair very finely frizzy so that it seemed to float darkly and vaporously around her head. She was a hefty woman but she wore a red halter-top dress with a short skirt. Jack had seen her coming, had noticed the animated expression, and had wondered if he should look away—this neighborhood was famous for prostitutes—but she looked too cheerful to be a prostitute, and her manner was friendly. He couldn't remember who she was. Evidently he had helped her some time ago and she was still grateful, so she talked boisterously while he smiled and nodded and tried to remember her.

She said: ". . . now you read all about the big trouble, huh? . . . all them kidnapings back and forth? Well, it was my brother, the one that got turned up in Toledo, you know, where he was that famous case of two people who looked alike, remember? But he was not the one they wanted. So now I won't burden you with a lot of crazy stuff," she laughed shrilly, "but just to show you how it's changed on the street since then—*my brother is working for Parks an' Recreations!*"

She laughed and shook her head. Jack guessed there was something wildly amusing here, so he laughed politely.

Then the woman sobered and said, touching his arm: "One sad thing in my life, Mr. Morrissey, my little boy got taken away—that has the burned-out stomach—you know—that they all tried to blame me for, when it was Herman's fault, that I had to be out all day working— Yes, he got taken away, was placed somewhere, in custody or something, where they give him some special medicine or something—I don't know—I thought maybe I'd get you to help me, some court order or injunction or something to forbid them; then what the hell, I lost my spirit, was downhearted for a long time and gave up the struggle—so—anyway—"

She sighed.

Jack remembered her now. Her husband had tried to kill her several times.

He said cautiously: "Is your husband still around?"

She stared at him as if he had asked an incredible question. "Why, Mr. Morrissey, didn't you read?—all them shootin's? Around the time them men got kidnaped back an' forth, you know, you must of seen in the paper that he was shot . . . they killed twelve or fifteen, however you want to count it, depending on how you want to count it," she said. Jack nodded slowly: the woman was referring to a heroin-dealers' war that had taken place some months ago, the second in recent years, but he had not paid close attention to it. It sometimes astonished him, how much local activity had gone on without registering on his consciousness. . . . Was that good or bad, to be insulated? Loving Elena had disrupted the Machine, had used up too much of the voltage. Now, back to normal, he should have had more energy but in a way he had less: flying to California seemed the act of another man, a much younger man; now, even the thought of taking a bus across town demoralized him. . . . The woman said good-by and thanked him again and walked away, having regained her good spirits.

For some reason she set his mind going, set the Word Machine into operation. He needed good news, encouraging news. He needed an optimistic hypothesis; a way of maintaining his family, the structure of his family, which was a very small family—only one child—but somehow weighty. *I love him, I love you:* that was true. But he needed something more.

The Word Machine came up with this hypothesis:

In a former life, Jack had loved and married a woman who had given birth to a child, his child (who was Robert); and the woman (who was Elena) had died or somehow disappeared. Had died, that was best. Was dead. . . . Yes, permanently dead, dead for the remainder of the narrative. But the child, Robert, was alive. And the father, Jack himself, was certainly alive . . . he would be alive in order to be the father, if not the husband, not much of a husband . . . Jack Morrissey would be alive in order to fulfill all obligations, contractual or otherwise, and to pay the bills, because he was a responsible adult and because. . . .

The Machine clicked off and would not operate any more. But he liked what it had given him: it would do. It was an excellent hypothesis. It would get him through the remainder of the narrative.

Maybe, he thought, he could be proud of himself again . . . ?

6 Rachel turned over the stiff, 5″ by 10″ invitation printed on expensive stationery, and read again the personal note on the back. She said, frowning: "I don't think you should, Jack. Why? Why bother? These people aren't our people . . . tell them to go to hell. I doubt that Dawe would even sanction this."

Jack had noted the address: 778 Fairway Drive.

But he did not show his alarm. Instead, he waited for a while, letting his wife talk . . . she disliked the way the Dawe case had been taken up by people, not people she knew, the way it had been publicized and made fashionable by people who had either ignored the efforts of the original, small, much-maligned defense committee, or had despised them, hadn't given any money at all when it was really needed. "This is just someone's excuse for a party, this fund-raising," Rachel said irritably. "I don't think you should go. They'll all fuss over you, they'll give you their versions of what went wrong, and what the hell do you care? Dawe fired you. He's finished with you and you're finished with him professionally."

"I'm never finished with anyone professionally," Jack said.

"You should sue him for your fee, the little bastard," Rachel said. "He likes being a martyr! I don't think it's legitimate, his freaking out up there . . . I don't trust him . . . he had too much of an eye for publicity, he was too damned photogenic. . . . Now these people, these fashionable people want to take up his cause. . . . All this makes me sick."

Jack took the invitation from her and read it again. That address: 778 Fairway Drive. Yes, it was the same address; exactly the same. The same house. "I think I'll go," Jack said slowly. It was strange, how his life was turning into a kind of narrative, with surprising reversals and recognitions and coincidences. He scorned melodrama, he scorned people who exaggerated themselves. And yet. . . . Yet this was the same address. It would be the same house.

Rachel said, surprised: "But Jack, they'll just paw over you . . . you'll be a conversation piece for their party. . . . Anyway, you have other clients who need you, what do you care about Dawe? Let someone else worry about getting him an appeal. He's told everyone how he feels about you. . . ."

"Oh hell, I don't care who likes me and who dislikes me," Jack said. He smiled oddly, still studying the invitation. Now a man named Steiner lived in that house—no longer Stehlin—but the name was rather like Stehlin—another coincidence. How Jack despised drama, melodrama, exaggeration! He said, "I took on Dawe's case without either liking or disliking him; I'm not in this business for emotional rewards. I think I'll go. Let them look me over if they want to, it's fine with me."

"But these people— I hate them, I know exactly who they are," Rachel said; "they make a fuss over someone like Mered Dawe now that it's too late—anyway there are dozens of cases like his, right here in Michigan, people sent up for ten, fifteen years on contrived charges—why is Dawe suddenly so important? One day we see a full-page ad in the paper with a lot of signatures, the next day this invitation comes in the mail— When our committee needed help, when you needed help, nobody gave a damn," she said bitterly.

Jack laughed. "That's life," he said.

They both went to the party, arriving late, so that Jack had to park half a mile away. There were no sidewalks on this private road, and by the time he and Rachel walked to the house, past dozens of enormous, expensive automobiles, they were both irritable.

They walked right in, since the door was open.

A black man, a butler, asked Jack what he wanted to drink and he said, "Anything," and looked around at all the people.

It was the old Stehlin house, now owned by another couple—the man as successful as Stehlin—and now, inside it, Jack wondered why he did not feel more emotion. It was like coming home, in a way. And he had received an engraved invitation, with a personal note . . . he, Jack Morrissey, Jack the son of Joseph, *Jack himself* . . . he had been invited here, legitimately, he was a legitimate guest in this house. He looked over the crowd of strangers without having bothered to take off his sunglasses. The only emotion he felt was a slight half-painful half-pleasurable tinge, since he saw that he was the only man in the room who was wearing a white shirt.

Rachel, in a shirt and slacks, defiant and plain and even more out of place than Jack himself, looked around, unsmiling, at the horde of people. "Do you see anyone you know?" she asked Jack.

A woman detached herself from a group nearby and approached them. She stared at Jack, smiling slowly as if uncertain, or delaying her recognition of him. "You're . . . ? You're Jack Morrissey, aren't you?" she said. Then she introduced herself, she shook hands with both Jack and Rachel, and leaned close to Jack to tell him in a serious, angry murmur that she admired him very much, she was very bitter about the Dawe case and the miscarriage of justice and the old-time Detroiters who were fossilized, dying, dead, but who still had so much power—that clique to which Judge Couteau belonged— She was a woman of no age Jack could determine: maybe forty, maybe fifty. She had a hot, meaty odor, an air of ferocity that was like Rachel's, but more confident. While she spoke to Jack and Rachel, Jack sipped his drink and ate cashews from a silver bowl he had noticed on a table nearby, not bothering to show much interest in the woman's conversation.

Morrissey at the Stehlin house, years later: very calmly eating cashews from a silver bowl. He was a legitimate guest, he had been invited. He was eating handsful of expensive nuts.

He noticed other people chewing nuts nervously; he noticed nuts on the floor, ground into a black fur rug. The conversation of the woman with the bright, militant, ferocious manner began to tire him, so he edged away, leaving her with Rachel.

Then a man came up to him—Morton Steiner himself—evidently very pleased to meet Jack. He looked surprised. He shook hands. "I didn't think you would come," he said. Rachel hadn't bothered to accept the invitation, she had tried to talk him out of coming up until the last minute. Steiner led Jack to a group of people, who were all pleased to meet him and flashed eager, knowing, sympathetic smiles. *Morrissey of local fame,* like his father. Jack managed to smile and to shake hands with everyone, though all this business of shaking hands, of smiling and appearing so warmly pleased, was new to him; these people were very different from his own friends. He answered their inquiries shortly, bluntly, and felt a curious sense of pride in the way his manner jarred with theirs—he liked to be in control, even to make a few minutes awkward for other people. He liked to be in control of sinking-down events as well as triumphant events. Why not?

An attorney named Cox, a tax lawyer who had wealthy clients and who was wealthy himself, and who would never have bothered with Jack Morrissey a few months ago, now introduced himself and even put his hand on Jack's shoulder. While several people listened closely, he reviewed the Dawe case in a rapid murmur, pointing out how Jack had done the right thing here, the wrong thing there, a questionable thing here, but. . . . Jack hardly bothered to listen, he was so used to this by now. But it was something of a surprise, here in this enormous living room, with these strangers around him, to discover that he was well-liked. Strangers liked him. Even some of his own friends liked him, now that he had failed. Cox, with a dark, handsome, flushed face, was angrily recounting the principal events of the trial, which he had attended; he informed Jack of exactly the remark by Couteau that had tipped him, Cox, off to what would happen, and he wondered if Jack had noticed it . . . ? Jack said no, not really, he couldn't take credit for being so prophetic. Cox continued and seemed to be growing more outraged. His listeners agreed. Their anger was dramatic and genuine, as if they were all friends of Dawe's, or friends of Jack's, or old, hateful enemies of Couteau and the Detroit Establishment. Jack did not bother to reply to them. In defeat, now, he was liked but he would not be likable. He had preferred the old Morrissey, unliked and unlikable, his own man.

"As soon as you let him take the stand, you were finished," Cox said. "It might have worked out with another defendant—but Dawe was just too crazy, too innocent. I guess you haven't had much experience, Mr. Morrissey, with innocent people . . . ?"

Everyone laughed except Jack. He did not laugh. What Cox said was true, in fact it was brilliantly true, but he made no response. Cox went on hurriedly: "No, no, it may have been a tactical error, as it turned out, but it was morally perfect, a moral triumph. No one could have kept the reins on him, and that's the point, maybe . . . that he was so innocent, so genuine, the whole courtroom procedure was made to seem artificial. Morally, you did nothing wrong. Maybe you knew how it would turn out . . . ?"

"No," Jack said. "My errors are all innocent."

A small, black-haired woman pushed into the circle. She said, taking hold of Jack's wrist and giving it a tug of sympathy, and yet of impatience: "You shouldn't have been so restrained! It isn't possible for anyone to get a fair trial in this country today—the courtrooms are just a mockery—you shouldn't have played their dirty little game with them, Mr. Morrissey—"

"Now Hilda," Cox said, alarmed, "you know that isn't—"

"Oh hell," the woman said fiercely. She stared up at Jack and he saw with alarm that she was very beautiful. She had a heart-shaped, girlish, perfect face, a widow's peak, gleaming black hair. . . . She leaned close to Jack as if cutting out the others and whispered, "What do they know? These people *don't know anything.*"

"Hilda is basically right," someone else said, "but if you believe it you're a nihilist . . . and the kids today, Hilda, the kids and the blacks today, you know they don't need nihilism, they need faith. What about that? Mr. Morrissey, isn't that right?"

Jack shrugged his shoulders. He thought it was extraordinary, that this small woman, someone's wife, should lean right up against him in public and all but embrace him. She said: "What that courtroom needed was some excitement! A few well-planted bombs; *I'm serious,* I'm deadly serious . . . yes, of course, people need faith, but let's be realistic about this. When the law itself is a mockery, you're forced to mock it. Isn't that true, Jack? Now that you look back upon it, now that you can see what a rotten deal your client got, what do you think?"

"That's my business," Jack said rudely.

"Yes, of course it's his business," another woman said at once. "Hilda, what on earth are you doing? For all you know, you might be asking him something illegal, or something . . . the trial has to be appealed . . . aren't there certain things that put a person in contempt of court? I mean, certain personal questions . . . ?"

"There are too many stifling, rotten, inhuman rules in our society," Hilda cried.

Jack looked over her head at the crowded room. These people were all so handsome, and so handsomely dressed. *What is real, and what is a hallucination?* he wondered mildly. The woman he had loved was dead, declared dead, but he outlived her. She had been beautiful, but there were other beautiful women—in fact he could see several without even turning his head—and the woman who stood beside him, arguing, so hot-voiced, so fierce, was as intimate with him as any woman had ever been, really. He believed he could have picked her up under his arm, and carried her off. . . . She squeezed his wrist and said she thought it was damned good of him to come here today, to put in an appearance with this bunch of phonies.

Jack glanced down at her, alarmed. He saw the glitter of jewels or perhaps of her fierce eyes; he was a little confused. He wanted to tell her *Thank you, you're very beautiful, yes, but I tried one of you once and it almost killed me. . . .*

Jack escaped her. He found himself in a hallway. More people were standing out here, holding drinks; there were odd works of art on the walls, canvases that seemed to be dripping, wire structures, a three-dimensional thing that looked like the front page of a newspaper . . . the headline said *30,000 Killed by Tidal Wave.* Jack finished his drink. He happened to see his host coming toward him, leading a young woman in a red pants suit, the front slashed down to the waist and fastened together by silver spikes. Jack pretended not to see them and turned sharply and walked back into the kitchen.

He pushed his way through the swinging louver doors. Out here, activity also, though more domestic and coordinated—a black maid was just taking a baking tray out of an oven, another black woman was placing pastries on a plate, picking them up and setting them down briskly because they were hot. They both stared at Jack in alarm. He must have looked dangerous.

The black bartender hurried up to Jack. He said: "Would you like another drink, sir?"

"Sure," Jack said, handing him the empty glass.

He made his way around the women, squeezing past, and wandered over into the breakfast area. It was an extremely handsome, modern room, decorated with golds and browns and greens. The table was round, quite large, a wicker basket heaped with fruit in its center, and a wrought-iron chandelier over it, in a style meant to be Colonial American and yet modern at the same time. But the most striking thing about the room was the enormous glass window, which looked out upon the lovely green lawn and then the golf course. . . . Jack stared. It would have been difficult for anyone to judge, seeing this, where he was: in the city or in the country . . . in the present or in the past. . . .

Someone handed Jack his drink. He accepted it, not glancing around.

There it was, the big plate-glass window. And outside, the evergreens his father had trampled . . . but the evergreens had survived, in fact they looked very healthy; they had survived Jack's father as well as his victim, Stehlin. They would probably survive Jack too. Jack sipped at his drink, contemplating the glass pane and the misty lawn outside and the wide, remote expanse of the golf course. That day had been a winter day, however, not a summer evening; the lighting would have been completely different.

Steiner was saying: ". . . really appreciate you and your wife coming here, I know how busy you are. . . ."

Jack finished the drink.

"Everyone is pledging very generously for Mered's appeal," Steiner said, as if this were news Jack was anxious to hear. "I think this is going to have a happy ending—in spite of Couteau and the newspapers and the rest of them—I think we're going to save this country—"

"Do you," Jack said. He inspected the floor near the window. Smooth dark-brown tile, highly polished. It looked good. Jack remembered suddenly someone's testimony: *he was at the window pressed against the window with his face pressed flat against the window we were terrified. . . .*

"Is something wrong?" Steiner asked.

He half-closed his eyes and seemed to see him there—a man in an overcoat, his face pressed against the plate glass. He would have been carrying the pistol in his right hand, but not yet aimed. Then he had aimed it. Jack wondered where Stehlin had been standing—maybe where he himself was standing. Then he had stumbled backward and had fallen. He had died here.

"—something wrong, Mr. Morrissey?"

He noticed people watching him—the kitchen help, the Steiners, one of the guests from the party.

"There was a murder right here once," Jack said. "Did you know that?"

"A what?" Steiner asked.

"A murder," Jack said. "Didn't they tell you that when they sold you this house?"

"What? I'm afraid I don't—" Steiner said. But he spoke rather guiltily, as if he did know, but was ashamed. He tried to laugh and made a gesture as if to draw Jack toward him, back toward the party. "There's someone who is very anxious to meet you—"

"There was once a man killed here, about where I'm standing," Jack said conversationally. "He was shot several times. He died. There must have been a lot of blood . . . though there's no sign of it now . . . or maybe this new floor was put in to disguise the bloodstains. They might have made a stain the size of a man." Jack stared down at his feet and even stepped aside, as if he believed he were standing on something. Mrs. Steiner laughed nervously and said something about a friend of hers anxious to meet Jack, who had to leave to catch an airplane in ten minutes . . . and wouldn't Jack like to . . . ? Jack glanced up at her and saw her for the first time: a pretty, frail, frightened woman, about the size of Mrs. Stehlin, wearing a violet pants suit and several strands of pearls. "Bring the party in here," Jack said. "Your guests would be amazed to learn that someone died here; it would be a conversation piece. That doesn't happen in every kitchen along Fairway Drive, does it? Your guests would be delighted, especially the women."

"That isn't funny," Steiner said angrily.

"No," said Jack. "But women are like that."

Rachel came up to him and took his arm.

"Jack, Jack . . . ," she said miserably. He gave in to her, surrendering, knowing it was pointless to resist; anyway, he had begun to feel a little sick. She led him out through the kitchen, out along the jammed corridor, through the packs of people, such good, intelligent, eager, sympathetic people!—and a few, recognizing him, seemed about to say something but hadn't time, so they smiled sympathetically to let him know that *they knew, they understood, they were very sympathetic.* The black-haired little beauty sighted him, waved at him, was shaping his name or another terse monosyllable with her pretty lips, but Jack didn't hear and kept on walking, and then he was outside, safe, and Rachel was muttering: "Damn you, what are you doing to me?—to both of us? Oh damn you, damn you. . . ."

Another half-mile walk, back to the Morrisseys' rusted Pontiac. It was now early evening. Rachel was saying: "You've lost other cases and you didn't disintegrate. Why are you doing this? You want to fall apart, to destroy yourself . . . it's a way of destroying me. . . ."

"No," Jack said.

At the car he sat, his head in his hands. Rachel slid in behind the driver's seat. She was half-sobbing with frustration; she jammed the keys into the ignition. "You never used to drink like that. It goes to your head, you can't handle it. Oh damn you. I'm taking Robert and I'm going away . . . that's what you want, isn't it?"

Jack saw again the smooth tile floor of the kitchen: very clean and polished. If anyone had died there, the bloodstains were certainly not visible any longer. Perhaps they had formed a large stain the size and shape of a man. It would have been a dark shape, something one might topple into. Or out of: springing out of, being born. It occurred to him that he had been born there, on the floor of that kitchen.

Rachel was saying: ". . . you want to destroy us both, our life together . . . but what about Robert? . . . what about . . . ?"

"Excuse me," Jack said politely. He opened the car door and leaned out to vomit—something sour and unrecognizable, except for a few gritty salty remnants, tasting of expensive nuts. Then he wiped his mouth and closed the door again. "I'm fine now," he said. "I can answer all your questions now."

Rachel wept angrily.

7 Jack watched his son approach the sofa . . . watched him pick up Jack's glasses, a pair of reading glasses he had just bought . . . he watched as the child tried to put them on, bringing them with both hands up to his face. A small, frail-chested child, serious as if experimenting with something deadly. Jack watched him. He smiled at the boy's sightless gaze, the black-rimmed glasses too large for his face. Yes, he was experimenting.

"Can you see anything?" Jack asked.

Robert snatched the glasses off and dropped them back on the sofa. Somehow the gesture was not playful. "Couldn't see nothing," Robert said.

Jack was absurdly hurt.

8 She telephoned him one morning.

He had so forgotten her, forgotten the threat of her, that he asked her quite innocently to repeat herself—he couldn't hear—what was the name?

She told him. "I wanted to talk to you . . . ," she said apologetically.

Jack was so stunned he could not reply.

"Jack . . . ? I wanted just to talk to you . . . to ask. . . ."

Wildly his eye leaped to the calendar tacked on the wall above his desk—his first impulse was to check the date, to get facts settled—it was September 5. Then he heard himself saying, "Elena, no. No." His voice was adequate, though he was sitting hunched now, his body rigid; he no longer saw anything at all.

Elena said: "Could I come to visit you? And Mered Dawe also . . . sometime . . . ? Could you take me to visit him?"

"I'm not his attorney any longer."

"Could I visit him?"

"He's too sick, he's in a psychiatric ward," Jack said shakily. "No, you can't see him. And Elena, I can't talk to you, I'm going to hang up. Don't do this to me."

"I've been thinking of you . . . I've wanted to talk to you for a long time," she was saying faintly. He wondered where she was: she seemed at a great distance. "Jack . . . ? I only wanted. . . ."

"No, please. Stop."

"I know you've adopted the child—haven't you?—and I know—I know what you said—and I understand—I don't mean that I would—"

"Yes, you do. That's just what you mean, otherwise why did you call? I'm hanging up."

She was silent, as if acquiescing. He felt a terrible rush of emotion for her, a purity of feeling that was almost impersonal.

"Jack . . . ?" she said.

Then he did hang up.

He left the office building and walked several blocks, to a bar on the other side of Woodward Avenue, far enough away so no one would know him. He felt sick. He thought wildly that he must telephone her back: he had wanted to say—he had wanted—

The bar was fairly crowded, though it was not yet noon. Jack thought with surprise how good this was, this atmosphere of dim, shabby people, men who would not recognize him or anything in him, whites and blacks, who didn't bother noticing anyone's color or anything at all. . . . He took his place at one end of the bar; there was just room for him, for one man. He ordered a glass of beer. He ran both hands through his hair and tried to think—

His heart was pounding inside his body as if he were in the presence of an adversary. He must defend himself, must fight. It was necessary to fight—otherwise why the tension that now charged his body? He remembered the anticipation of her, his waiting for her in the room or, earlier, in a hotel room—the tension in him, the misery of it, which was shameful. He had known himself to be a giant, malevolent thing, ready to rush into the visible world, attracted by the odor of blood and flesh, ready to do any violence in order to discharge itself. Waiting for Elena, he had imagined her, dreaded her, summoned her up and dismissed her and demanded her back again countless times, but he had not loved her, really, until she actually appeared and he had been able to subdue her, to sink himself in her. And he had been racked with pleasure as if with torture, a sensation that went beyond his ability to register; it was not human. It was degrading.

Elena, no. He had said those words to her just now, and very sanely. And again: *No.*

He had hung up.

He had performed an act of perfect sanity and he was pleased with himself. It was not necessary to live, but if you live you must do certain necessary things—Jack knew that. His eyes stung even now with the memory of his old lust, but he forced himself to drink beer, beer in the morning, *Jack Morrissey in a bar at eleven-thirty in the morning,* another of the surprising but necessary things he was discovering he must do. Why not? He was in perfect control of himself. He was calming down; his body realized now that it might not have to fight.

A television set above the bar was turned on, though no one watched. The program seemed to be some kind of documentary on the subject of underwater warfare . . . Jack stared at the dim sharklike missiles and rockets and could make no sense of them. He thought: *I couldn't telephone her anyway, I don't know where they live now.*

The next time his telephone rang, it would not be Elena.

Still, he felt a little sick. He didn't really like to drink, had never been able to drink much, but it helped keep down his terror. He had a panicky flash of a knife being brought down into his chest, so that the heart could be exposed and seized and yanked out. . . . He closed his eyes, wondering if men really did die like that, wondering if it was true that men had had their hearts cut out, that the hearts had been held aloft so the cheering crowds could see them. . . . *Those things don't happen,* someone had told him. And yet, what if it had really happened? Even to a single human being, just once in history? Just once?

He felt that old, horrible edginess, a white-hot racing of his brain that accompanied his desire for Elena, fear that something would go wrong: she would not come to him, she would not love him, or his body would fail him and he would not love her. And then, what a death! All he had to pit against his terror was a woman's body, and it was not a human desire, it was oversized and mad, it could not be endured. He wasn't going to endure it again. . . . He glanced around at the other men, who were solitary, like himself, not really aware of one another. He had always wanted to be an ordinary, honest man. He had always chased after people, wanting to help them, bullying them, in a way envying them, as if learning about other lives could somehow make his own more endurable. Did it work? His criminals, his rapists, his would-be murderers, his innocent ordinary clients—did they help him? He had begun to realize that studying life doesn't make your own more endurable, only more inevitable: like dissecting corpses in a pathology laboratory. It wasn't a way out of death but a way into it.

The Word Machine addressed Elena directly and allowed Jack to overhear: *Did I love you?—did you know me well enough to love me?*

That night he helped Rachel bathe Robert, and he stared with love at the boy—that small body, the bones so delicate and yet so beautiful beneath the flesh! The child fascinated him. Sometimes he helped Rachel put Robert to bed, as if he were participating in a ritual with her, but assisting her and acquiescing to her authority; she was the woman here, the child's mother, and he, the father, must be subordinate. He liked this feeling, this unbalance of power between them; it was so easy of him to acquiesce and it seemed to please his wife. . . .

Robert was usually quiet, especially at the end of the day, and often in Jack's presence. He seemed not to trust Jack, not entirely. At times he glanced up at Jack as if, in entering a room, in coming very ordinarily through a doorway, Jack had taken on for a terrible moment the shape of another man, another father—and he had to work hard to exorcise that other shape, he had to smile and be very gentle, very gentle. But tonight the child seemed happier than usual. He was chattering about something and from time to time he glanced up at Jack almost covertly, his dark shy eyes the color of Jack's—in coloring they were a good match, they looked like father and son, which had pleased the adoption agency but which had always seemed to Jack a trivial point, almost an insult to him; now it seemed to him a wonderful coincidence. Robert was talking on and on, breathlessly, excitedly, a vague rambling speech about an animal he had seen, maybe on television, or maybe someone in the building owned it—a dog, a cat?—and couldn't he have one; or maybe, as Jack listened and tried to concentrate, maybe it was a toy of some kind, something dug up in the back yard, but it was dirty, why was it dirty?—could they wash it?— Robert's bright, keen, breathless voice teetered on the edge of great joy, it was almost feverish, and Jack noticed how calmly and even sweetly Rachel had learned to reply to him, never saying yes, not yes, never saying no, but *maybe, maybe,* they would see about it, if he was good, *if . . . if. . . .*

She seemed to be changing at such moments. She seemed to be almost a mother now.

Jack thought of how life runs in patterns, of how we come up only with combinations of familiar things, words, gestures we've learned in the past and must relearn and use again. The uses of love, for instance. He had had to give up Elena because the Machine, with its sanity and its rigorous morality, had been unable to control her.

So: he was a man fleeing from a telephone call, a man in a bar on a weekday morning, and now a man helping his wife to bathe a child and to put him to bed.

The Machine passed judgment on all this: *You did well.*

9 But three days later, the doorbell rang and Jack let the newspaper fall and looked toward the door, knowing—

He got slowly to his feet, because the doorbell had rung and it must be answered. Rachel was in another room, in the kitchen . . . the little boy was playing with the television set, which had just broken down that day, pressing his face against the zigzagging lines, the smeared screen. Jack went to the door and hesitated only an instant before he opened it.

It was Elena.

But his shock was somehow worse because he had expected her. She stood there, looking at him, she was saying in exactly the voice he knew so well: "Jack . . . ? I'm sorry, I . . . I didn't want. . . ."

"No," he said at once. "I can't see you."

He was very shocked, almost trembling. No. Not this. He had a confused impression of her hair, which looked different than he remembered—worn loose now, the ends turning up—a starkness about her, as if she were a stranger thrust suddenly toward him, pushed at him, and terrified of what she might see in his face. She whispered: ". . . only for a minute? . . . could you . . . ?"

From the kitchen Rachel called: "Is that Leonard, honey?"

"No, not Leonard," Jack said.

He felt he must guard himself against Elena, he must not even look at her. "I can't talk," he said abruptly. "I'm sorry."

"If I could . . . I could wait for you outside, on the sidewalk," she said. "And then if . . . if you. . . ." He saw that her eyes were stark, urgent, almost blind-looking. Helplessly he stared at her, he could not move . . . and, as if giving him permission to turn aside, to shut the door, Elena began backing away. It was incredible, to see her there in that dreary, ordinary hallway he had been seeing and not seeing for years; Jack felt he would never recover from the ugly shock of it.

"Why, why—?" he whispered. "Why did you do this?"

He shut the door. When Rachel came out to him he was standing there with his forehead pressed against it.

"What's wrong? Who was it?" Rachel said sharply.

Jack said nothing.

"Did something happen? Is it trouble? Who . . . ?"

Jack turned away from her and walked somewhere . . . toward

the rear of the apartment . . . he found himself in the boy's room, formerly his own study, a small room with a single window that looked out into the back yard. He listened to his wife's slow footsteps in the hall . . . ah, she was slowed down, baffled, his brave wife!

It was a joke, really. He knew he had boxed himself into a joke; yet he could not make himself smile, not just now. That would take time.

Rachel stood in the doorway, looking at him. Jack seemed to be staring out the window and down into the back yard, a mess of broken cement and wild, ragged weeds and small trees. After a while Rachel said softly, wonderingly: "Is it . . . ? A woman . . . ?"

"Yes," said Jack.

The television set blared in the front room; Robert turned the volume sharply up, and then down, and Jack waited helplessly, angrily, for him to turn it up again. Of course, Robert had to play with the television set at this moment, of course it would drive Jack insane. A chorus of people in the living room were shrieking with laughter about something: of course. The screams sounded mainly female. Damn them all, all women, Jack thought viciously.

"It's someone you don't want to talk to . . . ?" Rachel whispered.

"That's right," said Jack.

She hesitated. Then she walked away . . . and Jack turned to see, yes, she had left; might this be the end? Maybe Rachel would forget all about it and go back to the kitchen and. . . .

The television set was turned down. She must have turned it down; then she turned it off. Good. Thank God. Jack bumped his head softly against the windowpane, trying to think. The back yard here looked dangerous, so much broken concrete. What was wrong? Why so much debris? Jack realized that his wife must be at the front of the apartment now, looking out. She must be looking out. And she would see Elena there, on the sidewalk, a stranger. A young woman. Two stories down, on the sidewalk, waiting. . . . But maybe, Jack thought, this was not the case: maybe Elena had walked away and everything was over. And then the Morrisseys would simply have supper, the three of them would sit down to an ordinary meal, on an ordinary Friday evening. . . .

Or . . . ?

Rachel returned. He heard her footsteps in the hallway, he heard her voice gaining strength: "She's waiting for you, did you know that? She's waiting for you. . . ." She was half-running with this news. Now, Jack thought, it was going to happen. He flinched when he saw her—her bitter, triumphant smile. She said mockingly, "You look very nervous, you look almost sick! Why are you so afraid?—it's just a woman who wants to talk to you! Why should you be afraid of her?"

"I told her to leave. I told her I couldn't talk," Jack said.

"Yes, but why? Why? I want to know that," Rachel said.

"You already know, so shut up."

"What is she, Jack, a shot in the belly?" Rachel laughed. "That she should affect you like this? I thought you were so strong, so stable, so much more stable than your neurotic wife—? Is she like a shot in the belly?—in the groin? So this is what frightens you so, a woman? Why don't you want to talk to her?"

"I'm not going down there," Jack said.

"Why not?"

"I'm not. So shut up."

"You really look sick," Rachel said mockingly. "Obviously you didn't expect her. How long have you two been out of contact? Do you think I don't know about her, Jack, you think I didn't feel her with you, the three of us in bed together? You look so guilty, just like a criminal! Oh, you're so sick, so white, so guilty! Are you going down there to talk to her?"

"No."

"Are you? Because if you do, you're not coming back."

"I'm not going down," Jack said angrily.

"Too bad I'm home, isn't it? Bad luck for you! Too bad I didn't go to Seattle, you could invite her up here, she could move right in with you," Rachel said. "She looks too good for this place, frankly, but if she wants you she must not be too good herself—she must not mind—"

"Shut up," Jack said.

He thought: *I'm going to kill one of them.*

Rachel approached him. Her face was livid, almost triumphant. He feared she would touch him, would actually put her hands on him, and this would drive him mad. She was saying words but he could not hear, could not interpret, because the expression of her face was so terrible. And behind her, in the doorway, Robert stood watching—his arms strangely limp at his sides, showing little surprise, little curiosity, as if this were a natural scene: a woman said to be his mother screaming at a man said to be his father, official mother and official father, two murderous adults.

"Stop, please!" Jack said, clutching at his hair. "Rachel, Robert is—"

But she interrupted him, she did not hear him. She said viciously, happily: "Go down and talk with her, why are you so terrified? Go down, go to hell, don't come back—why should you come back?—do you think I like being fucked while you think of her, when you're able to make your imagination work that well?—which isn't often, is it?—is it? But maybe you should talk to her, just to rejuvenate yourself? To give you a shot, give your manhood a shot? To last for a few months, to help with our strained marital relations?"

"Rachel, there's no point to this, to what you're saying," Jack said. "You're just trying to hurt yourself. I'm not going to help you. You want to ruin everything; all right, fine, but I'm not going to help you because I don't want to see her and I'm not going to see her. So shut up. Get away from me."

"You're not going down to her? You don't love her?"

"I'm not going down there, so shut up."

"You don't love her?"

"No."

"No, you don't? You don't?"

"No. I said no."

"Then why do you look so sick?—so terrified?"

"I am terrified, all right!" Jack shouted. "I'm terrified of her!"

"What?—Why?"

"Because with her I touched bottom—I almost killed her and myself—because at one time in my life nothing mattered except her, and I don't want to go through that again—"

"You almost killed her and yourself? When? When was this?"

"Never mind—get away."

Rachel hesitated. She stared at Jack with that triumphant certainty she did not want to relinquish; it was almost an odor about her, overheated and fierce. Yet she hesitated—as if she realized how their marriage was just words, a matter of words—and yet she could not resist undoing all the words, in her low, charged, mocking voice: "You're terrified of her, but not of me? Why aren't you afraid of me, just a little, why not of me? Aren't I your neurotic wife, your unstable wife? Aren't you afraid I might do something to myself, haven't you been afraid of that for a long time, that I might do something?—and now to Robert too, to him too? Tell the truth, Jack, aren't you afraid of that? Why don't you ever tell the truth any more?"

Jack pushed her away. "Don't threaten me. There's no need to threaten me," he said calmly.

"You never used to lie but now you lie constantly, you yourself are a lie," Rachel cried. "You won't even tell the truth now, will you? About her, about me, what you want or what you're afraid of—will you?—or are you such a coward you don't even know? Is that it? Is that it?"

Jack turned away. He was still at the window, he found himself pressing his forehead against it . . . calmly and yet powerfully against the glass . . . trying not to hear what that woman was saying behind him, trying not to see anything, to think anything. He pressed himself into it and seemed to go blank, neutral, as the thin but ungiving pane of glass itself.

ELENA

1 A garden of weeds, fixed by boundaries that were almost straight lines, almost human barriers—a ridge of sand and tufted grass, another ridge of stunted trees, and, on the far side, the road. Elena walked down into it as if into a garden. Burdocks caught at her slacks. There were thistles everywhere, moist spiky green weeds, low-lying bushes with very small yellow flowers. Side by side with the fresh weeds were last year's dead things, dried-out husks and remnants of pods, brittle spiky balls that clung to her clothing.

Over the ridge was the ocean. She would begin to see it in a minute. She was walking slowly, out of breath from the climb, matching her steps to footprints in the sand; the footprints must have been made by a child a few days ago.

At the top of the ridge she happened to turn and seemed to see someone back at the road, several hundred yards away.

She looked quickly away and slid down the incline to the beach. It was May, very cool, and the wind whipped her hair back wetly from her face. She thrust her hands into the pockets of her heavy, baggy sweater. She walked along the edge of the ocean, sinking a little in the sand; her shoes were already wet. She thought: *There's no one watching me.* She had to walk fast because of the wind, which was so relentless, it seemed to urge her forward, to thrust her forward. She thought: *Or maybe it was only a fence post.* . . . But she was not very disturbed.

In the hard-packed sand at her feet there were small hills, miniature mountains of pebbles and shells and seaweed that had the appearance of being still alive, aggressive as snakes. So many shells, bubble-like husks, out of which the meat had rotted ages ago. . . . Small gasps beneath her feet, small exploding sucking breaths. It was as if things were somehow caught beneath the surface of the sand, struggling for breath. Elena stared down at the sand, wondering. The ocean was so loud that she forgot everything else. . . .

A strong wet breeze, curling currents of air, like separate, angry, conflicting channels of air—her hair whipping toward the land, blown back toward land, the right side of her face almost numb from the constant wind and spray. The wide, colorless, rocky beach was deserted. Elena paused to look up and down the beach, flinching from the spray, and saw only a few mounds of debris, two or three large pieces of driftwood. She was alone.

She took a few steps out into the water, so that the foamy surface ran up past her shoes, at first shocking her, it was so cold, and then becoming neutral, almost warm. Numb. She felt very good now. The currents of air swirled and whistled about her. In the sky were sea gulls diving toward the water, one of them struggling viciously as if with a wave . . . then it fought loose and rose with something caught in its mouth. The quick, deft, skillful beating of wings . . . everything strong, loud, blinding. Elena felt a tug of excitement. She didn't know why. She walked faster. The world at the land's edge, here, this rough edge of the continent, was so loud and confused and yet uncomplicated that she felt she might disappear into it safely, as contained and skillful and beautiful as the sea gulls. *No one is watching me,* she thought, *there's no danger anywhere.* She did not even know what she meant by this: all of her life leading up to this moment, all the footprints behind her, the decades of footprints . . . ?

On the sand before her a vague shadow moved along, not clearly defined because the sun was partly obscured by clouds. It moved along quickly, yet it had the unclear unsteady appearance of something only partly imagined, partly in control. Elena's head was filled with the noises of the surf and the birds' cries. An ugly, sharp-faced bird darted near her. It alighted on the swaying branch of a nearby tree and shared the clearing with Elena, watching her. They stared at each other curiously, without fear. "What do you want, what are you looking at?" Elena said. She paused, shivering. She felt raw, exposed, very much alive; her hair had come down in damp, jagged coils. Where her skin was exposed the pores were puckered against the cold. For a while she stood there, listening to the discordant noises around her, everything out of rhythm, not needing any common rhythm. The gull remained, watching her.

Everything was still, inside the motion of the wind and water. It was strangely silent, inside, and unhuman, very consoling. At the back of Elena's mind was the conviction, new to her, that no one could touch her, no one was even watching her.

2 The sun rose all morning from the east, rising slowly, transforming the sky every morning, moving slowly upward, upward. Elena had never really noticed the passage of the sun in the sky before. Now she was aware of it, sometimes watching it in fascination, in silence. She felt at times she was aiding that mysterious passage, somehow absorbed into it. When she was alone and had nothing human to think of, no other human consciousness to deal with, she felt in her body a cool, detached sympathy with the sky and the sun, the coldness of this part of the world, its elemental privacy. It was not human, yet it was not threatening. There was nothing really to see except the rough, half-formed clouds and the changing waves, no colors except shades of gray, yet she thought it was beautiful: her body seemed to move in its jarring, unpredictable rhythms, it seemed to open itself secretly, in a kind of sympathy. But if her husband was at home she lost this sensation entirely; she had to think of him, reply to his questions,

she had to present herself constantly to him . . . like a person in a room walled with mirrors, unable to escape the image of himself, under the partly terrible, partly magnificent spell of his own existence.

On the day Elena had been told she would be discharged from the hospital shortly, Marvin, pleased with her recovery, grateful for everything, had spread a map of the United States across the bed and asked her what she would like: where would she like to live, how would she like to live? And, after a long while, after fifteen or twenty minutes of serious thought, Elena had pointed to the Maine seacoast. She had never been there, she said. She wanted to live there.

And Marvin had smiled and said that was fine, that was excellent. That could be very easily arranged. In fact, he owned some property north of Deer Isle. . . .

The house was immense, with three fireplaces. Its clapboards and shingles were a uniform, weathered gray, its shutters a slightly darker gray: not a handsome house, but sturdy and private, isolated from the blacktop road by an expanse of fenced-off sandy scrubland, well posted with *Warning* and *No Trespassing* signs. Inside, the house was immediately recognizable—except for one or two rooms upstairs, which were spartan and drafty, it was like any of the houses Elena knew as a visitor, or like Marvin's Grosse Pointe house, outfitted in an expensive professional style, the main room long and visually striking, almost overwhelming, with its windows facing the ocean and its roughly upholstered furniture in whites and reds, the wood floors stark, rubbed to a high, almost painful pitch of gleaming beauty, covered here and there with coconut-colored deep-piled rugs. . . . A look of impenetrable textures, wooden armrests and low-lying tables and chests and indefinable objects, perhaps functional, perhaps only artistic: yet there was something very social and crowded about the room, its chairs and settees arranged in several conversational circles, prepared for noisy evenings, excited evenings. Rings made by glasses were visible here and there on the tables and even on the floor by the gigantic fireplace. The lamps were all complicated and festive, they swung down into position or were arranged on elaborate poles, painted a dead white or a very bright red, or were the size of small trees, driftwood branches studded with pale globes that gave off light very cleverly.

Elena liked the upstairs rooms, one of which had a bare, unfinished floor and a jumble of furnishings, boxes, crates, stacks of old mildewed books, even aged dusty firewood; rugs rolled up and tied with twine; odd cupboards and trunks filled with junk, many children's toys and books. When Marvin was gone and it was too cold outside for a walk, Elena sat up here, on one of the stained old sofas, and leafed through books or old magazines, or searched through one of the boxes, as if looking for a sign. . . . Sometimes she stared out the window, doing nothing at all, and time passed quickly; she felt the vibrations made by the wind, the irregular cold drafts of air that came through the walls; her mind seemed to dissolve out into the high, buffeting air and the daily rains, not womanly now, not even human. . . .

The first week they had lived here, at the end of April, she had wanted to ask her husband a certain question about this house. She had prepared, nervously and anxiously, a question that might not offend him . . . and she felt she must ask it, she must know. *Did it take place here—the murder?* Because of course there had been a murder, somewhere. Marvin had "inherited" houses all over the country and behind each house was a murder, or an "accident" temporarily identified as "murder." Elena felt she must know whether someone had died here. But as the days passed she thought of how well she was living here herself, of how easy it was to live here, especially when she was alone; and so she had decided not to ask.

And he would never tell her, unasked.

Because she had put her fingertip on the coast of Maine, he had brought her here. And now he kept asking, every few days: *Are you happy here, so far away from everything? Are you forgetting?* Elena replied: *Yes, I'm happy here. I'm forgetting.*

3 The weather changed very slowly, sluggishly. In a way, Elena had forgotten what May and June should mean: it was still cold here, it rained every morning and sometimes all day. But she liked the abrasive monotony of the wind, the sound of rain blown against the windows, the inhospitable look of the ocean. When the days began to warm and the wind died down noticeably, she walked out along the beach, but felt almost a resentment against summer . . . an ordinary, human season, predictable. She be-

lieved the summer universe would fill up slowly and humidly, thickening to its farthest boundaries, yet unable to discharge itself, and that this would madden her. . . .

Alone, she was safe. But with her husband she felt the tension between them, a constant awareness, a watchfulness. The corners of her eyes sometimes contracted involuntarily when he spoke to her; she hesitated, she did not want to turn to look at him, and yet of course she must look at him . . . she was very polite, exquisitely polite . . . even in her illness she had been polite, apologizing for the spells of stupor and tears and depression. It should not have been an effort for her to reassure him: *Yes, I'm happy here. Yes, I'm forgetting.* But somehow it was difficult. And when he leaned over her, drawing his lips along the long, endlessly long, maddeningly long expanse of her skin, her bare skin, she could not bear to lie there and yet she must lie there, waiting.

Something had happened to her: she could no longer go into sleep, into peace. She could no longer shut her mind off from him.

So she could not withdraw from him, from the moist familiar terror of his touch, his touching of her, his nearness. His infinite nearness, the nearness of his soul! She could not get free of him. She could not shut herself off from him. Everything was open, raw, ready. Her brain ached with consciousness, raw as the ocean, the slap of the waves, the screaming of the birds—nothing that could be imagined or controlled.

She told him: "I don't know what's wrong with me."

And he stroked her, soothed her. He was patient as a bridegroom. He forgave her and, in his gentleness, tried to make her forgive herself. His face seemed bruised, aging, the face of a very generous man. "I understand," he said, to console her.

But no, she thought, no: he didn't understand.

Her body was made up of thousands of taut, tense, inflamed nerves exposed to the air, to her husband's scrutiny, his harmless but terrifying touch. He loved her. She loved him also, but her body closed itself against him, tightly and stubbornly. Always it closed itself, gone tight and dry and angry, almost cunning. She then began to think, in flashes of panic: *This will kill me.* She made herself embrace him, she held him tightly, she tried to annihilate her mind and she failed, jarred to an increasing sensitivity, a bewilderment, her eyes open and staring straight into nothing, into her own future. *This will kill me . . . he will kill me. . . .*

He slept, out of her sight. Lying beside her heavily, out of her sight. She listened to his breathing. Up and down her body were inches of aroused, angered skin. She had rejected him and she would reject him again; helplessly she gazed down upon her body, knowing she could not withdraw from it, not even to sleep. She couldn't relax even after he fell asleep. She couldn't even remember how she had been able to relax in the past.

She was awake.

She realized that everything is awake, the universe is awake; that it cannot be escaped.

On the surface of her body she was dry, tight, sullen, fierce, the pores of her skin aroused openly, publicly, as if she were out in the wind; inside, she felt a thickened pulsation, a dull angry throbbing, a muscular anger. Nothing could discharge it. She hated it, this tension, because it was a demand and she had no answer for it, nothing. She couldn't cry. Even her face was warm and dry and closed. She was destroying her husband but she couldn't cry.

One day he said: "You seem feverish, Elena. Are you sick?"

"No. I don't know. I don't know," she said.

She loved this man as a presence in her life: her husband. She was obligated to him, spiritually she belonged to him, and yet physically she was continually surprised, almost repulsed, by him, by even his most innocent gestures, the way he often touched her—as a way of talking, part of his conversation. The tension rose in her at once, she felt how dangerously close she was to drawing back from him in disgust. *What have we to do with each other? What is this . . . ?*

Marriage? A husband?

She loved him for his patience, for the infinite busyness and complexity of his life, which she could not understand; she loved him for his existence, the fact of his existence. When the telephone rang and he answered it . . . that seemed a kind of miracle, an event in the impersonal drowsing life of the house that Elena could never have created herself. Yet it was difficult for her to take an interest in it. Several times a week he flew to New York, sometimes only for an afternoon, conferring with associates or clients or with his own tax lawyers—he had won his case before the Tax Court, but a few days later Internal Revenue laid claims to some portions of his 1970 income, and the case involved such a confusion of definitions of certain words and phrases, that his principal tax lawyers had had to hire a five-man team specializing in one area of tax law. He was making an effort, he told her, to keep his work away from home down to a minimum; he wanted to be with her, to help her through this difficult period in her life.

But he did have to go away often, and as soon as he left she would walk out along the beach or down the road into town, alone, grateful for the way her hair blew messily in the wind, careless of mud, of thistles and burdocks that caught onto her clothing. Sometimes, even when she was in the house and she heard the telephone start to ring, she would think calmly: *I don't have to answer that.*

She inhabited her body, every part of it. Alert, aroused, conscious and thinking, always thinking. . . . On his worst nights, when he came upstairs drunk, when he demanded that she lie facing him so that he could sleep, she obeyed him, and yet her mind ran wild with short, sharp cries like spears, like birds' beaks, *I don't love him, I don't love anyone, I don't want to love anyone. . . .*

Once or twice he even wept in her arms. She comforted him without asking what was wrong, though she was frightened, unable to cry herself. She thought it was an event, a meaningful event, for a woman to hold a weeping man in her arms, to have the power to soothe him into sleep . . . and she must value it, she must force herself to value it. But as soon as he slept, she would disengage herself. She would get out of bed and watch him, standing a few feet from the bed. He was a middle-aged man, almost ugly, almost handsome, somehow in her keeping. She was responsible for him. She instructed herself: *You are responsible for him.*

He sometimes asked her: "Would you like to move somewhere else? To New York City, for instance?—where you'd see other people?"

No, Elena thought at once, almost shuddering. But she replied calmly: "Not right now. Not yet."

"You don't mind being so isolated, Elena? Being alone so much?"

"No."

As the summer passed, he brought this question up less and less. He had come to like this way of life—Elena secluded, hidden, safe from all other people. From all other men. At times she believed she could see a peculiar satisfied glow in his face, as if he had at last solved a vexing problem.

. . . In July she was leafing through a national newsmagazine and she happened to see the name *Mered Dawe.* It sprang up at her. She read of how he had been found guilty back in Detroit, given a maximum sentence, and evidently denied bail. . . . But the "Dawe case" took up only a brief paragraph in a lengthy article concerned with the inequities of justice in the United States, the need for reform of the countless drug laws. Indeed, it was only the "Dawe case" and not "Mered Dawe" that interested the author of the article. Elena read and reread the paragraph, trying to force it to expand, to tell her something about Mered, about how he was?—how he felt?

She sat for a while in a kind of trance, staring at the page. Where was Mered in all this, what had happened to the person "Mered Dawe"? They had solved the problem of Mered Dawe, his "case": he had been handed down a maximum sentence. He was now in prison; he was *put away.* He was *solved.* In the end they hoped they might figure everyone out and solve them, "solve" them like puzzles. Some would be put away, some would be allowed to remain at large. All would be *solved.*

Yet a thought edged into Elena's brain, quick and unsuspected as that stroke of terrible pleasure Jack had given her: *she* would not be solved.

She thought of Mered's embrace, the calm intimacy of his arms, his face, his presence. He might have united them all—himself and Jack united in her, in her body, as Jack and her husband were united despite their hates—she could not understand him except with a part of herself that was not expressible in words, but she knew he was her truest lover, as he was Jack's truest lover also, had Jack been more than simply "Jack"!—but Mered had come too soon, and Elena herself had not been worthy of him, sunk as she was in love with another man. That *love* had been too much for her to overcome then. And so she had not been worthy of Mered. She had not really known him, only sensed him; she had been in *love* all that time.

4 In late August, walking back one day from town, Elena noticed a car parked at the edge of the road. Marvin was spending several days in New York; she was alone. Her hair was tied at the back of her head in a long careless coil, her legs were bare, she wore dirty scuffed heelless straw shoes . . . she was very tan by this time, her legs strong from all the walking, the calves tightly muscular.

She saw the car parked off the road, near a long tapering sand dune. It had not been there on her walk to town. It was an unfamiliar car, a stranger's battered rat-colored car. And suddenly, so powerfully that she felt almost faint, she thought: *Now it will happen.*

For some reason she transferred the small bag of groceries she was carrying from her right arm to her left.

Then she continued walking along the edge of the road, watching the car. After a while she could make out two men sitting in it. She walked at the same pace, not quickening her steps. She was going to pass right by the car. Though she walked calmly, her heartbeat raced, her head flooded with mysterious shouts she could not understand: *Now they are, who is this . . . ? when did . . . ? it will happen, it was. . . .* Two young men were sitting in the car; she saw them turn their heads almost at the same time, noticing her, and then giving her their fullest attention. They were in their early twenties, perhaps. They watched her. As she came closer she could make out their faces clearly, the faces of strangers, and yet their expressions were not strange to her—the look of surprise giving way to awe giving way to a peculiar heavy disapproval, a confusion that showed itself plainly in the tense line of their mouths.

So she walked toward them. She felt no fear, only an intense heady excitement.

And she felt their excitement also: in the very tightness, the intensity of their faces. She seemed to be feeling their heartbeats, their beating calculating minds. *Now. Now.* It was necessary for her to pass within a few feet of their car. One of the young men lowered a beer can from his mouth slowly. His tanned elbow jutted out of the opened window and he stared, he stared bluntly at her, his lips tightly pursed. Elena felt almost a kind of ecstasy. She seemed to see herself in his eyes, in his head. A woman in a dress, alone, barelegged, alone . . . walking alone. . . .